I0831746

ABOUT THE EDITORS

LIZ GRZYB was born in the middle of a thunderstorm in Perth, Western Australia. She is the award-winning editor of acclaimed paranormal romance anthologies *Scary Kisses* and *More Scary Kisses*, the Orientalist pantomime *Dreaming of Djinn*, steampunk romance *Kisses by Clockwork*, feminist spec-fic *Hear Me Roar*, co-editor of the paranormal noir *Damnation and Dames* and *The Year's Best Australian Fantasy and Horror* series from Ticonderoga Publications. Liz is often to be found sipping champagne and debating the fate of the Oxford comma.

TALIE HELENE is a songwriter, musician, writer, editor, and audio engineer from Melbourne Australia. You can find out about her latest creative adventures at www.taliehelene.com.

Also edited by LIZ GRZYB

Scary Kisses
More Scary Kisses
Damnation and Dames (with Amanda Pillar)
Dreaming of Djinn
Kisses by Clockwork
Hear Me Roar

Also edited by LIZ GRZYB & TALIE HELENE

The Year's Best Australian Fantasy & Horror 2010
The Year's Best Australian Fantasy & Horror 2011
The Year's Best Australian Fantasy & Horror 2012
The Year's Best Australian Fantasy & Horror 2013
The Year's Best Australian Fantasy & Horror 2014

THE YEAR'S BEST AUSTRALIAN FANTASY & HORROR

~ 2015 ~

THE SIXTH ANNUAL COLLECTION

THE YEAR'S BEST AUSTRALIAN FANTASY & HORROR

~ 2015 ~

EDITED BY

LIZ GRZYB &
TALIE HELENE

Ticonderoga publications

for

Anthony Panegyres, for his boundless passion for Australian speculative fiction.

(L.G.)

Mary Manning and William Bamford

(T.H.)

The Year's Best Australian Fantasy & Horror 2015
edited by Liz Grzyb & Talie Helene

Published by Ticonderoga Publications

Designed by Russell B. Farr
Typeset in Sabon and Poor Richard

A Cataloging-in-Publications entry for this title is available from The National Library of Australia.

ISBN 978-1-925212-47-1 (hardcover)
978-1-925212-48-8 (trade paperback)
978-1-925212-49-5 (ebook)

Ticonderoga Publications
PO Box 29 Greenwood
Western Australia 6924
Australia

www.ticonderogapublications.com

10 9 8 7 6 5 4 3 2 1

Aboriginal and Torres Strait Islander readers are warned that this book includes the names of deceased persons.

The editors would like to thank Joanne Anderton, Alan Baxter, Deborah Biancotti, Stephen Dedman, Erol Engin, Jason Fischer, Dirk Flinthart, Kim Gaal, Stephanie Gunn, Lisa Hannett, Robert Hood, Kathleen Jennings, Maree Kimberley, Jay Kristoff, Martin Livings, Danny Lovecraft, Kirstyn McDermott, Sally McLennan, DK Mok, Faith Mudge, Samantha Murray, Jason Nahrung, Garth Nix, Anthony Panegyres, Rivqa Rafael, Deborah Sheldon, Angela Slatter, Cat Sparks, Lucy Sussex, Anna Tambour, and Kaaron Warren.

Liz would like to thank Talie Helene, Russell B. Farr, Amanda Pillar, Kate Dunbar-Smith, Deb Wilson, Jacinta Rosielle, Angela Challis, Shane Cummings, Andrea Orlowsky, Jacintha Bell, Ruza Foster, Frankie Nathan, Susan Greenwood, Amanda Perris, Kate Williams, Andrew Williams, Carol Ryles, Nicole Murphy, Adrian Smith, Tasmar Dixon, Mel Donald, Phil Ward, Lina Piscitelli, Kim Astle, Isobelle Carmody, Jenny Blackford, Janeen Webb, and the Department of Fabulous.

Talie would like to thank Liz Grzyb and Russell B. Farr, Adam Calaitzis, Fiona Trembath, Mary Manning, Alex Adsett, Yaritji Green, Gillian Polack, Sharyn Lilley, Alison Goodman, Narelle Harris, Alisa Krasnostein, Chuck Chainey-McKenzie, Adrian Bedford, Jenny Blackford, Helen Stubbs, Jodi Cleghorn, Kim Wilkins, Satima Flavell, Aaron Sterns, Christopher Sequeira, Margi Curtis, Leigh Blackmore, Gerry Huntman, Sophie Yorkston, David Witteveen, Kyla Ward, David Carroll, David Conyers, David Kernot, Shelley Slater, Oliver Holm, Calum Harvie, Lee du Caine, Marita Fitzgerald, Louise Roussety, Adrielle Spence, Brian Giffen, Rodger Moore, Claudia Raven, Kylie Ivy, Amps Ivy, Nicholas Albanis, Vair Buchanan, Sonia Tamarri, Felicity Grey, Stacey Palfreyman, Leigh Irwin, Jesse Roberts, Rodger David, Martin Koszolko, Tim Nikolsky, Greg O'Shea, Shane Simmonds, and students in the Melbourne Polytechnic music and sound cohort, Emily Fuller at Darebin Creative, William Bamford, Peter Hurley, Brett Rosenberg, Ed Bates, Nick Tsiavos, Sarah Endacott, Ellen Gregory, Claire McKenna, Michelle Goldsmith, Andrew Macrae, Jason Franks, Rjurick Davidson, Peter Hickman, Trudi Canavan, Andrez Seleznev, and the SupeNova Writers' Group.

CONTENTS

THE YEAR IN REVIEW

LIZ GRZYB & TALIE HELENE

THE YEAR IN FANTASY

2015 Climate change and environmental issues shadowed many fantasy tales this year. Symbols such as the honeybee were featured in fantastic stories like Deborah Kalin's "Wages of Honey" and Garth Nix's "The Company of Women", not just in the more speculative fiction like James Bradley's novel *Clade*.

Crowdfunding continued to grow in popularity for smaller presses this year, with many publishing projects using this venue to presell copies. Riffing on the crowdfunding idea, Patreon is becoming a source for regular income for creators, with "patreons" acting as patrons and committing to a small monthly donation to help fund writers, artists and other creative pursuits such as podcasts.

Many Australian fantasy authors appeared in international publications this year, especially with dark fantasy pieces. Angela Slatter and Penelope Love had stories published and Pia Ravenari's artwork was included in the World Fantasy Award-winning anthology *She Walks in Shadows*, edited by Silvia Moreno-Garcia and Paula R. Stiles, published by Innsmouth Free Press. Tor.com published Slatter's exceptional witch story "Of Sorrow and Such" which won the Ditmar for Best Novella, and was shortlisted for the Best Fantasy Novella Aurealis.

Slatter, Kirstyn McDermott and Lisa L. Hannett all had stories published with *The Dark* magazine: "Bearskin", "Self, Contained" and two stories, "The Canary" and "A Shot of Salt Water", respectively. "A Shot of Salt Water" earned Hannett a place on the Locus Awards Recommended Reading List.

"Miss Sibyl-Cassandra" by Lucy Sussex and Miranda Siemienowicz's "After and Back Before" were published in Ellen Datlow's multi-award-winning anthology *The Doll Collection.*

Alan Baxter had Ditmar-nominated "The Chart of the Vagrant Mariner" published in *Fantasy & Science Fiction Magazine.* Ditmar-nominated sci-fi fantasy novella "Hot Rods" by Cat Sparks was released in Issue 58 of *Lightspeed Science Fiction & Fantasy.* Sean McMullen's "The Ninth Seduction" was published in Issue 64 of the same magazine.

Lisa L. Hannett and Anna Tambour had stories included in PS Publishing's *Breakout: Postscripts 34/35* edited by Nick Gevers, Hannett's "Endpapers" and Tambour's "Curse of the Mummy Paper".

Rowena Cory Daniells' "The Giant's Lady" was published in *Legends 2* from Newcon Press, winning the Aurealis for Best Fantasy Short Story. *Beneath Ceaseless Skies* published Jason Fischer's "Defy the Grey Kings" which won the Best Fantasy Novella at the Aurealis Awards.

Dan Rabarts' "Floodgate" was published in Sean Wallace's *The Mammoth Book of Dieselpunk*, and was nominated for a Sir Julius Vogel Award. Samantha Murray and T. R. Napper had stories included in *Writers of the Future Volume 31*, and Napper also placed "a shout is a prayer/for the waiting centuries" in *Interzone.*

Jenny Blackford's bittersweet tale "Under the Roses" was included in *A Quiet Shelter There*, a speculative anthology released by Hadley Rille Books to benefit animal shelters. Faith Mudge came runner-up in the Queensland Young Writers' Competition with her story "January Days".

NOTABLE LONG FICTION

Allen & Unwin continued their focus on the young adult side of fantasy this year. Kathryn Barker published the acclaimed paranormal fantasy *In the Skin of a Monster*, which won the Aurealis for Best Young Adult Novel, as well as being shortlisted for the Aurealis Best Fantasy Novel, the Australian Book Design Awards, the Davitt Awards for Best Young Adult Novel and Best Debut Novel, and long-listed for CBCA Book of the Year for Older Readers. Angelica Banks (Danielle Wood and Heather Rose) released the magical *A Week Without Tuesday*, which was shortlisted for the Aurealis Best Children's Novel. Barry Jonsberg released the third Pandora Jones novel, the dystopian fantasy *Reckoning*. Catherine Jinks opened her mystery Theophilus Grey series with *Theophilus Grey and the Demon Thief*, which was commended in the Norma K Hemming Award and short-listed for the Davitt Award.

Allen & Unwin also published Charlotte Wood's excellent dystopian *The Natural Way of Things*, which won a slew of awards: Indie Book of the Year, Indie Book Awards Best Fiction, The Stella Prize, ABIA People's Choice Awards Literary Fiction Book of the Year, Prime Minister's Literary Award for Fiction. *The Natural Way of Things* was also short-listed for the Victorian Premier's Literary Award for Fiction, the ABA Nielsen BookData Booksellers Choice Award, the Australian Book Industry Awards Literary Fiction Book of the Year, the Miles Franklin Literary Award, the Queensland Literary Award for Fiction, the Barbara Jefferis Award, and long-listed for the Nita B Kibble Award and the Voss Literary Prize.

Hachette Group's Australian fantasy publications this year were again focused on series titles. A.L. Tait released the second in The Mapmaker Chronicles: *Prisoner of the Black Hawk*, and this fantasy adventure was shortlisted for the Aurealis Best Children's Novel. Winner of the inaugural Sara Douglass Award for Book Series Glenda Larke continued her Forsaken Lands series with *The Dagger's Path*, which was shortlisted for the Ditmar Award for Best Novel and Aurealis Award for Best Fantasy Novel. The second in Trudi Canavan's high fantasy Millennium's Rule series, *Angel of Storms*, was released.

Similar to the other Big Four publishers, HarperCollins' Australian fantasy this year was mainly restricted to series titles. Alison Goodman released her regency paranormal *Lady Helen and the Dark Days Club*, the first in the Lady Helen series, which was shortlisted for the Aurealis Award for Best Fantasy Novel. Viola Carr explored the Dr Jekyll & Mr Hyde story with two steampunk mystery thrillers: *The Devious Dr Jekyll* and *The Diabolical Miss Hyde.* Traci Harding completed her Time Keeper trilogy with *AWOL*, and Francesca Haig began her dystopian Fire Sermon series with *The Fire Sermon*, which was shortlisted for the Norma K. Hemming Award. Jen Storer broke the series mould with her children's urban fantasy standalone title *The Fourteenth Summer of Angus Jack.*

Harper's digital romance-focused imprint Impulse extended their Australian fantasy titles this year, with KJ Taylor releasing novella quartet Drachengott: *Earth*, *Fire*, *Water* and *Wind*, and the satirical fantasy novel *Broken Prophecy.* Stacey Nash released the young adult fantastic romance *Never Forgotten.*

Many of Pan Macmillan's Australian fantasy titles were published by their digital imprint, Momentum, with a few notable exceptions. Juliet Marillier continued her wonderful Blackthorn & Grim series with *Tower of Thorns*, which was characterised by Marillier's gorgeous storytelling and engaging, lifelike characters. *Tower of Thorns* was shortlisted for the Aurealis Award for Best Fantasy Novel. Fiona Wood released the young adult novel *Cloudwish* in her loosely linked Six Impossiverse series, which won the Indie Award for Young Adult and the CBCA Book of the Year Award for Older Readers. *Cloudwish* was also short-listed for the Inky Awards.

Momentum continued to experiment with some alternative novel styles such as episodic releases, then collected the episodes as omnibus editions. Examples of these were: Duncan Lay's *The Last Quarrel*, which opened his Arbalester trilogy; CS Sealey's romantic adventure Equilibrium; Charlotte McConaghy's second in the dystopian Cure series *Melancholy.* In traditional length novels, Sophie Masson continued her mystery/magic realism series Trinity with *The False Prince*, and Bernadette Rowley released two novels in her romantic fantasy Wildecoast Saga, *The Lord and the Mermaid*, and *The Elf King's Lady.* Amanda Pillar's debut novel *Graced* introduced a well-realised urban fantasy world where vampires, weres and Graced humans struggle for power or peace. *Graced* was nominated for the Ditmar for Best Novel.

Penguin Random House focused mainly on young adult fiction in their Australian fantasy titles this year. Isobelle Carmody released the final volume of her young adult dystopian Obernewtyn series, *The Red Queen*, to much excitement from fans and an extravaganza of a book launch. Sophie Masson's *Hunter's Moon* is a modern Snow White retelling set in the same world as her other fairytale thriller novels. Christopher Richardson released the first of his Voyage of the Moon Child series, *Empire of the Waves*. Skye Melki-Wegner's *The Hush* is a standalone novel where music and magic are entwined. It was shortlisted for the Aurealis Award for Best Young Adult Novel and for the Norma K. Hemming Award.

James Bradley's literary dystopia *Clade* incorporates some fantastic elements in the speculative portrait of our future. *Clade* was shortlisted for the NSW Premier's Literary Awards, the Victorian Premier's Literary Award, the WA Premier's Book Award, the ALS Gold Medal for Australian Literature, an Aurealis Award, and longlisted for the International Dublin Literary Award and the Colin Roderick Award. Alis Franklin's *Stormbringer*, Book 2 of her Wyrd series brought out by Penguin's Hydra imprint, explores Norse gods and relationships in an urban fantasy setting.

Three-time ABIA Small Publisher of the Year Text Publishing released a number of fantasy novels this year, which were all noted in awards. Trent Jamieson's vampiric dark fantasy *Day Boy* was highlighted in many speculative and literary awards, winning both the Best Fantasy and Best Horror Novel Aurealis Awards, being nominated for Best Novel in the Ditmars and the Courier-Mail People's Choice Queensland Book of the Year Award, as well as being long-listed for the International Dublin Literary Award in Ireland. Ilka Tampke's historical fantasy *Skin* was shortlisted for the Aurealis for Best Fantasy Novel, and Rebecca Lim's supernatural fantasy *Afterlight* was longlisted for the Davitt Award for Best Young Adult Novel.

Scholastic released two Deltora Quest spinoffs in a new series, Star of Deltora, from Emily Rodda: *Shadows of the Master* and *Two Moons*. *Shadows of the Master* gained an Honourable Mention in the CBCA Book of the Year Awards for Younger Readers. Kate Forsyth continued her children's adventure series The Impossible Quest, with Book 3, *The Beast of Blackmoor*.

Escape Publishing released a number of paranormal romances from Australian authors: Dani Kristoff's steamy *Spiritbound*, Jenny Brigalow's second instalment from her Children of the Mist series *The MacGregor*, and Suneeti Rekhari's *The Lost Souls*

Dating Agency. Satalyte Press published two novels from Gillian Polack this year, *The Art of Effective Dreaming*, and *The Time of the Ghosts*.

Cary J. Lenehan brought out his epic novel *Intimations of Evil* through IFWG. IFWG also published New Zealander Jan Goldie's young adult novel *Brave's Journey*, which was nominated for a Sir Julius Vogel Award.

Merlinda Bobis released her young adult dystopian novel *Locust Girl* with Spinifex Press, and it won the Christina Stead Prize for Fiction (NSW Premier's Literary Award), the Philippines National Book Award for Best Novel in English, and was shortlisted for the ACT Book of the Year Award. ChiZine published Lisa L. Hannett's dark sci-fi fantasy *Lament for the Afterlife*, which won the Ditmar Award for Best Novel.

Walker Books published Meg McKinlay's *A Single Stone,* which won the Aurealis Award for Best Children's Novel, a Prime Minister's Literary Award for Young Adult Fiction, and was given an honourable mention in the CBCA Book of the Year Awards for Older Readers. Craig Cormick continued his Shadow Master series with *The Floating City*, published through Angry Robot. Lynette Noni released the first in her young adult Modoran Chronicles, *Akarna*, with Pantera Press.

DK Mok poked fun at the epic fantasy genre with the excellent *Hunt for Valamon* from Spencer Hill Press. Clan Destine Press published Mary Borsellino's young adult sci-fi fantasy novel *Thrive.* Bec McMaster released the fifth volume of her London Steampunk romance series *Of Silk and Steam* with Sourcebooks, which won the Romantic Times Best Steampunk Novel, and the series was shortlisted for the Favourite Continuing Romance Series in the Australian Romance Readers Awards.

Paul Collins and Sean McMullen released *The Burning Sea*, a novel for younger readers, through Ford Street Publishing. K. A. Bedford published supernatural thriller, Black Light, with Fremantle Press. New Zealand press Snapping Turtle released Ashley Capes' continuation of the Bone Mask trilogy, *The Lost Mask*.

Peter M. Ball released the third dark urban fantasy novella in his Flotsam series, *Crusade*, with Apocalypse Ink. Ruth Fox continued her Bridges trilogy with *Across the Bridge of Ice* through Hague

Publishing. Kalamity Press published Thurston Bassett's superhero story, *The League*.

As has become common in the past few years, a number of authors chose to explore independent and self-publishing options. Avril Sabine released *The Irish Wizard* and started her Realms of the Fae series with *A Debt Owed*. C.J. Archer released the first three instalments of her young adult paranormal Ministry of Curiosities series: *The Last Necromancer*, *Her Majesty's Necromancer* and *Beyond the Grave*. Andrea K Höst published *The Pyramids of London*, first in her steampunk series The Trifold Age, which was shortlisted for the Norma K. Hemming Award. S. A. Carter continued her young adult Kuthun series with *The Vaga*. Claudio Silvano released Book 2 of his epic Destiny of Fire trilogy, *Keys of Awakening*.

COLLECTIONS

2015 saw fewer fantasy single-author collections being published than the past few years, but as usual, most were released by independent publishers.

Twelfth Planet Press published Deborah Kalin's disturbing fantasy/horror *Cherry Crow Children* as the final volume of their Twelve Planets boutique collection series. The volume collected a spread of awards and nominations, with "The Miseducation of Mara Lys" winning Best Young Adult Short Story and Best Horror Novella in the Aurealis Awards. "The Cherry Crow Children of Haverny Wood", "The Miseducation of Mara Lys", and "The Wages of Honey" were all shortlisted for Best Novella in the Ditmar Awards and Best Horror Novella in the Aurealis Awards. "The Briskwater Mare" was shortlisted for Best Horror Short Story in the Aurealis Awards and Best Novelette in the Shirley Jackson Awards, and the collection as a whole was nominated for Best Collected Work in the Ditmar Awards, Best Collection in the Aurealis Awards and Best Professional Production in the Tin Duck Awards.

Allen & Unwin (and HarperCollins internationally) published Garth Nix's collection *To Hold the Bridge*, which gathers a retrospective of Nix's short fiction from 2007 to 2012, including the title story set in his Old Kingdom world. *To Hold the Bridge* won the Aurealis Award for Best Collection and was on the Locus Awards Recommended Reading List.

Shane Jiraiya Cummings' dark fantasy and horror collection, *The Abandonment of Grace and Everything After*, published by Brimstone Press, was shortlisted for the Australian Shadows Award for Best Collected Work and the Aurealis Award for Best Collection.

Anna Tambour's collection *The Finest Ass in the Universe* was published by Ticonderoga Publications. This collection of weird tales was shortlisted for the Aurealis Award for Best Collection, and was on the Locus Awards Recommended Reading List, as was the novelette "Lab Dancer".

Fablecroft publishedDirk Flinthart's collection of dark fantasy and horror, *Striking Fire*, which was shortlisted for the Aurealis Award for Best Collection, and the novella "Night Shift" from this collection was nominated for the Best Horror Novella in the same awards.

Satalyte Publishing released *Tales of Cymria*, KJ Taylor's collection of high fantasy stories. Carole Nomarhas published her own collection of dark fantasy and horror stories, *The Fading*, which was shortlisted for the Aurealis Award for Best Collection.

ANTHOLOGIES

Fablecroft released *Cranky Ladies of History* edited by Tansy Rayner Roberts and Tehani Wessely, a mix of genres exploring historical women. The anthology won the Fiction section of the ACT Writing and Publishing Awards, the Ditmar for Best Collection and Best Artwork for Kathleen Jennings' cover and illustrations. Deborah Biancotti's story, "Look How Cold My Hands Are" was nominated for Best Short Story in the Ditmars.

Wessely also edited *Insert Title Here*, a darkly weird unthemed anthology. "The Art of Deception" by Stephanie Burgis was shortlisted for theWSFA Small Press Award for Short Fiction. Joanne Anderton was shortlisted for Best Science Fiction Short Story with "2B", and DK Mok was shortlisted for Best Fantasy Short Story for "Almost Days" in the Aurealis Awards. "2B" was also shortlisted for the Ditmar for Best Short Story. *Focus 2014* was Fablecroft and Wessely's third anthology for the year, collecting a number of Australian speculative fiction stories that had garnered awards attention. This anthology was nominated for an Aurealis Award.

Twelfth Planet Press released three anthologies: two volumes of the *Year's Best YA Speculative Fiction*, covering works from 2013 and 2014, edited by Julia Rios & Alisa Krasnostein, and the critically acclaimed *Letters to Tiptree*, edited by Alisa Krasnostein & Alexandra Pierce. *Letters to Tiptree* collects letters written by speculative fiction writers, fans, editors and critics to commemorate the hundredth anniversary of Alice Sheldon's birth. The anthology won the Locus Award for Non-Fiction, the British Fantasy Award for Non-Fiction, the Aurealis Convenor's Award, the Ditmar for Best Collected Work and the William Atheling Jr Award for Criticism or Review, and the Tin Duck for Best Professional Production. It was nominated for British Science Fiction Award and Special World Fantasy Award Non-Professional, and longlisted for the Tiptree Award.

Ticonderoga Publications also released three anthologies in 2015. Amanda Pillar edited *Bloodlines*, a companion to her 2012 urban fantasy anthology *Bloodstones. Bloodlines* won the Aurealis Award for Best Anthology, and was shortlisted for the Ditmar Award for Best Collected Work. Stephanie Gunn was shortlisted for an Aurealis Award for Best Fantasy Novella for her story, "The Flowers that Bloom Where Blood Touches the Earth", and Kathleen Jennings was nominated for a Ditmar Award for Best Artwork for the cover.

Liz Grzyb edited the feminist speculative fiction anthology *Hear Me Roar*, which was shortlisted for Best Anthology at the Aurealis Awards. Kathleen Jennings' "A Hedge of Yellow Roses" won the Ditmar for Best Short Story, while Faith Mudge's "Blueblood" was shortlisted for both the Best Young Adult and Best Fantasy Short Story categories at the Aurealis Awards. Stephanie Gunn's "Broken Glass" was shortlisted for the Best Fantasy Novella Aurealis. *The Year's Best Australian Fantasy and Horror 2014*, edited by Liz Grzyb & Talie Helene was also nominated for the Aurealis Best Anthology Award.

Jonathan Strahan continued working with Solaris on anthologies, this year releasing the fourth in his speculative Infinity Project: *Meeting Infinity*, and also the ninth volume of *The Best Fantasy and Science Fiction of the Year.* Both of these were nominated for Aurealis Awards, *Meeting Infinity* was nominated for a Locus Award for Best Anthology and Strahan was again deservingly nominated for the Best Editor category of the Locus Awards. Both anthologies were listed on the Locus Awards Recommended Reading List.

The Never Never Land, an anthology of speculative fiction exploring Australian mythologies, was published by CSFG and edited by Mitchell Akhurst, Phill Berrie &

Ian McHugh. Kimberley Gaal was nominated for an Aurealis Award for Best Young Adult Story for her tale, "The Nexus Tree". Shauna O'Meara, who also had a story included in the anthology, was nominated for a Ditmar Award for Best Artwork for her cover art.

Paul Collins edited the mixed-genre anthology *Rich & Rare* for younger readers with Ford St Publishing, which included a number of fantasy stories. David Conyers, David Kernot and Konstantine Paradias put together *Cthulhu Detective*, an anthology of hardboiled occult stories, which included a novella co-written by C.J. Henderson and David Conyers. Robert N Stephenson released *From Out of the Dark* with Altair Australia, a not-for-profit anthology.

MAGAZINES

Andromeda Spaceways Inflight Magazine released one issue in 2015: #61, edited by Simon Petrie, which published Charlotte Nash and Kim Gaal's Aurealis-nominated stories, "Alchemy and Ice" and "In Sheep's Clothing" respectively.

SQ Mag released six issues this year, from Issue 18 to 23. Much of the fiction in 2015 was focused towards science fiction and horror, but many stories on the fantasy side were also included, such as the Aurealis-shortlisted high fantasy story "Husk and Sheaf" by Suzanne J Willis and Angela Slatter's revisited fairy tale "Bluebeard's Daughter". SQ Mag also collected a number of its standout stories for 2014 in the annual *Starquake 3*, with IFWG Publishing.

Review of Australian Fiction releases an issue with two pieces of short fiction every fortnight in electronic subscription format. They published a number of fantasy novellas and short stories this year, including Tansy Rayner Roberts' "Fake Geek Girl" which was nominated for the Ditmar for Best Novella, and "The Jellyfish Collector" by Michelle Goldsmith, which was nominated for the Aurealis Award for Best Fantasy Short Story.

Aurealis Magazine released ten issues in 2015: issues 77 to 86 each including fiction and non-fiction pieces. Tracie McBride's "Breaking Windows" from Issue 84 was nominated for an Aurealis Award for Best Horror Short Story. Other standouts were C.S. McMullen's dystopian "The Other-Faced Lamb", Janet Haigh's "Potkin" and Melanie Rees' "The Monster Under My Bed".

Dimension 6 magazine from Coeur de Lion released three issues and an annual collection. These included, among others, Steve Cameron's bittersweet novella "Lodloc and the Bear" which was shortlisted for the Best Fantasy Novella Aurealis Award.

Grimdark Magazine, which opened in late 2014, focuses on dark fantasy and science fiction. In 2015 they released 3 issues, #3, #4 and #5. Australian authors were published as well as internationals, including T. R. Napper and Tara Calaby.

Bruce Gillespie's *SF Commentary* released three issues, and was nominated for a Ditmar for Best Fan Publication.

Ion Newcombe released 11 issues of *Antipodean SF* in 2015, providing flash fiction in web-based and ebook format, from authors such as Sean Williams, Trent Jamieson, Martin Livings, Edwina Harvey, Annette Backshall and Joanna Fay.

Dark Matter Zine regularly publishes reviews, interviews, opinion pieces and guest blogs.

ART AND OTHER MEDIA

Galactic Suburbia podcast by Alisa Krasnostein, Tansy Rayner Roberts, Alexandra Pierce won the Ditmar and was nominated for the Tin Duck for Best Fan Production. They released 24 podcasts this year, discussing issues, events, books, media and culture.

Gary K Wolfe & Jonathan Strahan's *The Coode Street Podcast* was nominated for a Ditmar and a Tin Duck for Best Fan Production. They produced a whopping 47 podcasts this year, discussing issues, books, authors and films.

Kirstyn McDermott and Ian Mond's *The Writer and the Critic* shortlisted for a Ditmar. *The Writer and the Critic* produced six episodes this year, discussing issues in the SF world and books.

Galactic Chat released seven podcasts in 2015, interviewing Australian authors such as Amanda Pillar, Garth Nix and Trent Jamieson.

Ion Newcombe's *Antipodean SF Radio Show* is a weekly podcast with readings of flash fiction stories from *Antipodean SF*.

Kathleen Jennings had a great year, being nominated for a World Fantasy Award for Best Artist, and she also won the Best Artwork and Best Fan Artist Ditmars. Her award-winning work appeared on many book covers in Australia and overseas.

Shaun Tan's young adult fairy tale picture book *The Singing Bones* was released by Allen & Unwin. It won the Aurealis for Best Illustrated Work, was shortlisted for the Best Artwork Ditmar and Best Children's book in the Indie Book Awards and longlisted in the Australian Book Industry Awards.

Gestalt Comics released two Aurealis-nominated works: Volume 1 of *The Undertaker Morton Stone* by Gary Chaloner, Ben Templesmith and Ashley Wood, and Unmasked Vol.1: *Going Straight is No Way to Die*, by Christian Read. James Brouwer and Tom Taylor's Aurealis-winning graphic novel series *The Deep* (published by Gestalt Comics) has been turned into an animated series on the Seven Network.

Isobelle Carmody released *Evermore*, a post-apocalyptic fairy tale graphic novel, with illustrator Daniel Reed through Windy Hollow Books.

Australian paranormal TV series *Glitch* hit screens in the second half of the year. The show explores people who have risen from the dead, not knowing who they are or were. The show won an Australian Directors' Guild Award for the director, Emma Freeman, a Logie for Most Outstanding Drama Series, and two AACTA Awards, one for Best TV Drama and one for Best Original Score.

THE YEAR IN HORROR

NOVELS AND STAND ALONE NOVELLAS

2015 was a robust year for horror publishing in Australia and New Zealand, with a wide range of publications released. Novels and novellas released as unique titles were no exception. Michael Adams's *The Last Place* (Allen & Unwin) concluded his post-apocalyptic trilogy centered around teenage psychic Danby. C.J. Archer published three volumes in the Ministry of Curiosities series concerning the ongoing adventures of necromancer *Charlie in Victorian London—The Last Necromancer, Her Majesty's Necromancer* and *Beyond The Grave*. Peter M. Ball's *Crusade* (Apocalypse Ink Productions) completed The Flotsam Trilogy; a dark urban fantasy series about supernatural hit men. Kathryn Barker's *In the Skin of a Monster* (Allen & Unwin) was winner of the Aurealis Award for Best Young Adult Novel, and explores the duality of the dark twin.

The Catacombs (Ghillinnein Books) by Jeremy Bates is book 2 in the World's Scariest Places series; this time evil lurks in the Paris catacombs. Jeremy Bates stand-alone novella *Black Canyon* (Ghillinnein Books) relates a family hike of the Gunnison National Park in Colorado that goes terribly wrong; this novella was also included as part of the *Dark Hearts* (Ghillinnein Books) collection, along with the psychological thriller *Neighbors* set in New York. Greig Beck's sixth book in the Alex Hunter series, *Kraken Rising* (Momentum), is a thriller with a monstrous discovery off the coast of Antarctica. K.A. Bedford's *Black Light* (Fremantle Press) is a supernatural crime mystery; British novelist and war widow Ruth Black moves to the seemingly restful small town of Pelican River Western Australia in the 1920s, told in the style of an elegant period drama. Viola Carr's *The Devious Dr. Jekyll and The Diabolical Miss Hyde* (HarperCollins) chronicles Dr. Eliza Jekyll, daughter of a notorious father, and her shadow self, Lizzie Hyde, in adventures in Victorian crime and intrigue. Kat Clay's stand-alone novella

Double Exposure (Crime Factory Publications) set in Portvieux City 1948, is a pulp style noir with ghostly overtones.

Darcie Coates published *House of Shadows* (Candlebreak) a Gothic romance, first in the Ghosts and Shadows duology, concerning the protagonist marrying for money and moving to her new husband's estate, Northwood, a haunted mansion. Coates also published *The Haunting of Blackwell House* and the novella length *The Haunting of Gillespie House* (Candlebreak) in 2015. *Tribal Law: Miscreants & Magick 1* by Shannon Curtis, published by the Australian Romance Readers Association, is a paranormal romance featuring vampires and werewolves. Daniel de Lorne's self-styled romantic horror, with a dysfunctional family of vampires, witches and demons, continues with the Bonds of Blood book 2 *Burning Blood* (Escape Publishing). Pam Farley's *The Hunter Within* is a self-published steampunk horror novel. Bob Franklin's debut novel *Moving Tigers* (Affirm Press) blurs the line between psychosis and horror in Nepal. Alison Goodman's *Lady Helen and the Dark Days Club* (HarperCollins) is a Regency romance dubbed Pride and Prejudice meets Buffy in a hidden world of demonic conspiracy.

Author/illustrator C.M. Gray published novellas *Zombiefied!: Infected* and *Zombiefied!* in her middle-grade, Goosebumps style series aimed at readers aged 8–12 from HarperCollins. Andrea K. Höst's self-published fantasy *The Pyramids of London* is notable for interweaving elements of Egyptian myth and vampirism. Trent Jamieson's *Day Boy* (Text Publishing) a re-imagining of the vampire myth exploring father/son relationships; the novel won the Aurealis Award for Best Horror Novel and the Aurealis Award for Best Fantasy Novel. *Theophilus Grey and the Demon Thief* (Allen & Unwin) by Catherine Jinks is book one in a mystery series for young readers, set in Georgian London and engaging with horror tropes. *The Mothers'*, *The Scrimshaw Marionette* and *The Reparation* (Simon & Schuster) by Mike Jones form part of The Transgressions Cycle, Gothic horror set in nineteenth century Australia, and centered around gutsy heroine Rosanna. Gary Kemble's debut novel *Skin Deep* (Echo Publishing) is a supernatural thriller about mysterious tattoos and uncanny nightmares.

Rebecca Lim's *Afterlight* (Text Publishing) tells a young adult paranormal romance tale; a grieving orphan teenager, Sophie, makes contact with a ghost named Eve. Martin Livings standalone murder mystery novella *The Death of a Cruciverbalist* part of the shared-world Refuge Collection published by Steve Dillon. Juliet Madison's *Sight and Sound—The Delta Girls* books 1 and 2—(Diversion Books) is a paranormal suspense about five sisters with prescient psychic abilities. Sophie Masson's *Hunter's Moon* (Random House Australia) re-imagines Snow White as a thriller. Andrew McDonald's *Son of Death* (Hardie Grant Egmont) is a young adult comedy about a negligent grim reaper who'd rather be rocking the guitar. L.M. Merrington's *Greythorne* (Momentum) is a Gothic suspense novel set in 1890s England. Jason Nahrung's *The Big Smoke* (Clan Destine Press) is the second volume of the salty Vampires in the Sunburnt Country series, the follow up to *Blood and Dust*, chronicling the ongoing exploits of vampire Kev and his Monaro.

Incite Insight (Tale Publishing) by Robert New is a crime thriller with cult conspiracy undertones. Amanda Pillar's *Graced* (Momentum) is a paranormal romance with vampires and werewolves. Darrell Pitt's *The Monster Within* (Text Publishing) is book four in the five-part Jack Mason Adventure, concerned with investigators of crime and the paranormal in Victorian London and beyond. Gillian Polack's *The Time of the Ghosts* (Satalyte Publishing) chronicles myriad ghosts haunting Canberra and the four women who handle the hauntings. Jane Rawson's *Formaldehyde* (Seizure) was Winner in the 2015 Seizure Viva La Novella Prize, featuring interconnecting stories in a weird or neo-absurdist style.

Suneeti Rekhari's *The Lost Souls Dating Agency* (Escape Publishing) is an adult paranormal debut novel; enterprising university student Shalini embarks on a matchmaking business and quickly cultivates a client base of vampires, shape-shifters, werewolves, and other creatures. Avril Sabine's sequence of related novellas *Plea of the Damned 1: Forgive Me Lucy* and *Plea of the Damned 2: Forgive Me Aiden* (Broken Gate Publishing) concern YA ghosts stories set in the suburbs of Brisbane in the 1960s. *Sabine's Tainted: Demon Hunters 3* (Broken Gate Publishing) is a young adult horror novel about a teenage protagonist hunting a demon. Marianna Shek's *Choose Your Own Death* (Rock On Kitty) is a children's novelette set in Ghoultown. Angela Slatter's *Of Sorrow and Such* was published by Tor.com's flagship novella imprint continues the story of Patience a character established in *Sourdough and Other Stories* (Tartarus Press, 2010) and won the Ditmar Award for Best Novella at Contact 2016. *Unvamped* by Elizabeth Stevens was published by Eternal Press. Charlotte Wood's *The Natural Way of Things* (Allen & Unwin) was joint winner of the Prime Minister's Literary Awards, and Fiction category Winner of the Stella Prize; it concerns the abduction and brutalization of two women at an abandoned property in the desert. Justin Woolley published book 2 in The Territory series, *A City Called Smoke* (Momentum) a post-apocalyptic world where the teenage protagonists are besieged by ghouls.

SINGLE AUTHOR COLLECTIONS

There were a number of single author collections that featured horror strongly. Most notable was the collection by horror veteran Robert Hood, *Peripheral Visions: The Collected Ghost Stories* published by IFWG Publishing Australia; this included many previously published works as well as some new to the collection: "The Whimper", "After Image", and "Double Speak". IFWG Publishing Australia also published their ninth chapbook, *Haunted Flesh: Stories of the Living Dead* collecting six zombie stories by the maestro Robert Hood.

Brimstone Press released *The Abandonment of Grace and Everything After* by Shane Jiraiya Cummings, which included stories original to the collection: "Blood on the Indian Pacific", "The Abandonment of Grace and Everything After" and "Razor Blade Anthropology (Guerdon for the Beautiful People)". *The Gate Theory* by Kaaron Warren was published as a chapbook by Cohesion Press and edited by A.J.Spedding. *The Fading* by Carole Nomarhas, edited by Amanda J. Spedding, is a single author collection of mostly horror, with a little urban fantasy: new stories included "Black Glass". *Beautiful & Deadly* by Jo Hart (Graceful Doe Publications) is a single author collection of mostly supernatural horror, many previously published stories, as well as a number of new tales—"Curse of the Falls", "Equinox", "Red Lipstick", "Maya And the Prince", "Love Bites" and "The Bony Finger of Death".

Cherry Crow Children by Deborah Kalin, edited by Alisa Krasnostein (Twelfth Planet Press) included some fantasy tales that were very dark, notably "The Briskwater Mare". *The Finest Ass in the Universe* by Anna Tambour, edited by Russell B. Farr (Ticonderoga Publications) collected many published stories, as well as some new tales; the notable horror story original to the collection is the oppressive and blackly humorous "Tap". *Striking Fire* a collection by Dirk Flinthart (FableCroft Publishing) edited by Tehani Wessely included the Lovecraftian comedy "A Friend in the Trade". Australian/Canadian author Jeremy Bates released the short story collection *Dark Hearts* (Ghillinnein Books).

ANTHOLOGIES

2015 was an exceptionally strong year for themed horror anthologies and mixed speculative anthologies that also featured horror. *Bloodlines* (Ticonderoga Publications) edited by Amanda Pillar won the Aurealis Award for Best Anthology; the tome included a range of darker stories including "The Flowers That Bloom Where Blood Touches Earth" by Stephanie Gunn, "A Red Mist" by Martin Livings, "Azimuth" by Pete Kempshall, "Unnamed Children" by Joanne Anderton, "The Ties of Blood, Hair and Bone" by Nathan Burrage, "Old Promise, New Blood" by Alan Baxter, "In the Heart of the City" by Rebecca Fung, Lady Killer by Anthony, "The Mysterious Mr. Montague" by Jane Percival, and Dirk Flinthart's "In The Blood".

Cthulhu: Deep Down Under is a giant doorstopper anthology of Australian Mythos fiction published by Horror Australis, and edited by longtime Lovecraftians Steve Proposch, Christopher Sequeira and Bryce Stevens. The collection paired each author with an artist, so the anthology boasts a considerable number of illustrations to accompany the tour de force of weird fiction ranging from the traditional to the whimsical: first publication works include "They Are Impatient" by Maurice Xanthos, "Vanguard" by Aaaron Sterns, "The Wake in the Witch House" by Francis Payne, "Darkness Beyond" by Jason Franks, "Depth Lurker" by G.N. Braun, "Dreamgirl" by Stephen Dedman, "Haunting Matilda" by Dmetri Kakmi, "Where the Madmen Meet" by T.S.P. Sweeney, "The Thing in the Bidet" William Tevelein, "The Seamounts of Vaalua Tuva" by David Kuraria, "The Return of . . . " by Christopher Sequeira, "The Pit" by Bill Congreve, "The Island in the Swamp" Jan Scherpenhuizen, "The Elder Things" by B. Michael Radburn, "The Dog Pit" by Jason Fischer, "Pest Control" by Steven Paulsen, "Ortensia and Osvaldo" by Lucy Sussex, and a creepy long "Untitled" weird poem by Steve Kilbey, noted singer-songwriter and bass player with iconic Australian band The Church.

In Sunshine Bright and Darkness Deep: An Anthology of Australian Horror overseen by managing editor Cameron Trost for the Australian Horror Writers Association collected a formidable array of antipodean writers. The collected fiction included Rue Karney's "The River Slurry", Jason Nahrung's "Triage", Marty Young's "Upon the Dead Oceans", Natalie Satakovski's "Beast", Stuart Olver's "The Grinning Tide", J. Ashley Smith's "Our Last Meal", Cameron Trost's "Veronica's Dogs", Joanne Anderton's "Bullets", Mark McAuliffe's "Saviour", Mark Smith-Briggs's "The Hunt", Kathryn Hore's "The Monster in the Woods", Anthony Ferguson's "Road Trip", Steve Cameron's "Bloodlust", and "Elffingern" by Dan Rabarts.

Lighthouses: An Anthology of Dark Tales edited by Cameron Trost for Black Beacon Books collected an illuminating assortment of fiction: "Horror at Hollow Head" by Cameron Trost, "Will o the Wisp" by Deborah Sheldon, "Trepidation" by Danielle Birch, "The Last Keeper" by Linda Brucesmith, "The Cape" by B. Michael Radburn, "Scrimshaw" by Duncan Richardson, "Psychopomp" by Mark McAuliffe, "In Search of Jimmy" by David Dolan, "Into the Light" by Alice Godwin, and Greg Chapman's "Light House, Dark House".

The Ghostly Stringybark (Stringybark Publishing) anthology edited by David Vernon collected twenty-nine stories, the winners and highly commended stories from The Ghostly Stringbark Award 2015 judged by David Vernon, Zena Shapter, Graham Miller and Dr Rick Williams. The anthology included rural ghost stories—the competition winner "The Wilangarra" by David Slade, second place story "Ghost Gum" by Llewellyn Horgan, and commended stories "The Woman in the Window" and "Ghostly Hugh" by Cathy Childs, "The Bushwalk" by Linda Brandon, "Dark Water" by Lauren Noelle Rice, "I Know What I Hear, Dear Rita!" by Maree Teychenné, "The Scoreboard" by Christine Ferdinands, "Dust to Dust" by Benjamin Marie, "The Shot Tower" by Vickie Stevens, "Emily's Cottage" by Yvonne Saw, "I Can Stand The Despair" by

Roger Leigh, "Surveillance and Jack Frost" by Trudi Slavin, "The Collector's Book" by Michael Olive, "To Get Away With Murder" by Michael Wilkinson, "The Unknown Wedding Dress" by Sabina Willis, "A Voice Through The Fence" by Athol Henry, "Beyond" by Mona Oliver, "The Blind Madonna" by Chrinstina Cairns, "A Place of One's Own" by Belinda Lyons-Lee, "A Song of Love and Death" by Patricia J. Hughes, "Smoke" by John Cowell, "Dune-Crawler" by Jessica Budin, "Swing Low, Sweet Chariot" by Pippa Kay, "The Rock Pool" by Rachel McEleney, and "History" by Lois Murphy.

Blurring the Line edited by Marty Young for Cohesion Press explores the grey area between fiction and creative non-fiction; Antipodean contributions included stunning story "The Body Finder" by Kaaron Warren, "Consorting With Filth" by Lisa L. Hannett, "How Father Bryant Saw the Light" by Alan Baxter, "With These Hands" by Brett McBean, and "Salt on the Tongue" by Paul Mannering.

Fablecroft's *Cranky Ladies of History* anthology edited by Tansy Rayner Roberts and Tehani Wessely included a number of darker stories concerning historical figures: "Look how cold my hands are" by Deborah Biancotti was about Hungarian noble woman and serial murderer Countess Elizabeth Báthory de Ecsed; "Neter Nefer" a bloodsoaked historical tale about the ascension of Egypt's first female pharaoh Hatshepsut, told through the eyes of her daughter, Neferure by Amanda Pillar; and "Mary, Mary" by Kirstyn McDermott followed the life of pioneering feminist writer Mary Wollstonecraft, best known as author of *A Vindication of the Rights of Woman* (1792) and for being the mother of Mary Shelley author of *Frankeinstein*—this story is a must-read for horror fans, while it is not a horror story of itself, it deeply concerns the European Enlightenment origins of modern horror.

Cohesion Press published two volumes of their military horror series—*SNAFU: Wolves at the Door* edited by Geoff Brown and Amanda J. Spedding collected werewolf themed military horror; *SNAFU: Survival of the Fittest* included a number of Australian contributions including "In Vaulted Halls Entombed" by Alan Baxter and "They Own the Night" by B. Michael Radburn.

The Canberra Science Fiction Guild (CSFG Publishing) produced *The Never Never Land* anthology edited by Ian

McHugh, Phill Berrie and Mitchell Akhurst; darker contributions included "Consumed" by Elizabeth Jakimow, "Ferals" by William Broom, "Ghost Versions" by Darren Goossens, "To Look Upon a Dream Tiger" by Shauna O'Meara, "The Seven-Forty from Paraburdoo" by Charlotte Nash, "The Meek Shall Inherit the Earth" by Jodi Cleghorn, "The Laneway" by Richard L. Lagarto, "She'll Be Right" by Donna Maree Hanson, and "Rebirth" by Linh T. Nguyen.

Hear Me Roar (Ticonderoga Publications) edited by Liz Grzyb included some creepy moments with "A Wondrous Necessary Woman" from Janeen Webb, and "Cursebreaker: The Mutalibeen and the Memphite Mummies" a novella length story by Kyla Lee Ward which explores horror tropes and Egyptian myth.

FableCroft Publishing released *Insert Title Here* edited by Tehani Wessely; sinister offerings from this anthology included Matthew Morrison's "Sins of meals past", Robert Hood's "Footprints in Venom", David McDonald's "Her Face Like Lightning", and Daniel Simpson's "The Winter Stream".

From Out of the Dark (Altair Australia) edited by Robert N. Stephenson included dark tales "Out in the Dark" by Victoria Dylan, "Hope" by Tony Shillitoe, "Light in the Darkness" by James O'Keefe, and "The Grim" by Rob Bleckly.

Ford Street Publishing published YA anthology *Rich & Rare* which included "The Black Sorceress" by Paul Collins, "The Ghost in the Stereoscope" by Doug MacLeod, and "Angelito" by Lucy Sussex, a sweetly melancholy children's ghost story.

Fat Zombie: Stories of Unlikely Survivors from the Apocalypse (Permuted Press) edited by Paul Mannering included the stories "El Caballo Muerte" by Martin Livings, "Mr Schmidt's Dead Pet Emporium" by Sally McLennen, and "Endgame" by Dan Rabarts.

"The Shape of Beauty" by Tanya Davies was published in *Strange* by Adelaide publisher Lizard Skin Press. "And I may be some time..." a dark literary stroll into oblivion by Craig Cormick appeared in *Antarctica: Music, sounds and cultural connections* (ANU Press). "Sleepless" by Jay Kristoff, was published in YA anthology *Slasher Girls & Monster Boys* edited by April Genevieve Tucholke for Penguin. Lee Pletzer's *Quincy* was published as a stand alone title by Triskaideka Books New Zealand. Danny Lovecraft had a poem, "Over the Top and Under the Crumbling

Wall", included in the anthology *When Anzac Day Comes Around: 100 Years from Gallipoli Poetry Project* (Forty South Publishing).

Cthulhu Detective: A C.J. Henderson Tribute Anthology featured authors paying homage to the pioneer of hard-boiled occult detective fiction who passed away in 2014, with works works edited by David Conyers, David Kernot, and Konstantine Paradias; the anthology included the first publication of the novella "The Temporal Deception" co-authored by C.J. Henderson and David Conyers, as well as reprints of stories by David Kernot and Shane Jiraiya Cummings.

Looking overseas, *She Walks in Shadows: An anthology of women and Lovecraft's Mythos*, included Australian contributions "Eight Seconds" by Pandora Hope, "Turn out the Light" by Penelope Love, and the awesomely fine "Lavinia's Wood" by Angela Slatter; the book was Winner of the World Fantasy Award in the anthology category—edited by Silvia Moreno-Garcia and Paula R. Stiles for Vancouver based publisher Innsmouth Free Press.

Danny Lovecraft published a sequence of six mythos poems—"Azathoth", "Nyarlathotep", "Cthulhu", "Shub Niggurath", "Hastur", and "Yog Sothoth" in *Beyond the Cosmic Threshold: An Anthology of Cthulhu Horror* (Horrified Press, 2015); this anthology also included mythos contributions by Leigh Blackmore. Danny Lovecraft also saw publication of a sequence of twelve weird poems—"The Shadow on the Chimney", "A Connoisseur in Horrors (The Search for Reasons Why)", "A Passer in the Storm", "What the Red Glare Meant", "Earlier Grisly Discoveries", "A Mountain's Ghastly Fame", "Formless Phantasms—The Daemon Lurking Fear", "An Acheron of Multiform Diabolism", "The Horror in the Eyes", "A Nether World of Unknown Nightmare", "The Ineffable Horror of It All—The Mound-Burrows", and "From Pits Remote and Unimaginable"—*in Black Wings IV: New Tales of Lovecraftian Horror* (PS Publishing, 2015) edited by S.T.Joshi.

Gods, Memes and Monsters: A Twenty-first Century Bestiary, edited by Heather J. Wood (Stone Skin Press) included "The Greater Spotted Capital and Meme Mosquitos" by Jonathan Blum, and "Leucrotta" by Kyla Lee Ward. "The Woman Who Cried Elf" by Rebecca Fung appeared in *Between the Cracks*, (Sirens Call Publications). Kris Ashton's "Night Feeds" and Gerry Huntman's

"Denying the Thrill" were published in *Creepy Campfilre Stories (For Grownups)*, EMP Publishing. Jay Caselber's violent ghost story "Penumbra" was published in *Death's Realm* edited by Anthony Rivera and Sharon Lawson (Grey Matter Press). "After and Back Before" by Miranda Siemienowicz appeared in *The Doll Collection* (Tor) edited by Ellen Datlow. "To Dance, Perchance to Die", David McDonald, in *Expiration Date* (Hades Publications), edited by Nancy Kilpatrick. Tansy Rayner Roberts story "Life of Julia" was published in *Faction Paradox:Liberating Earth* edited by Kate Orman (Obverse Books) with what must be an interesting rights arrangement with regards to Billy Idol's song "White Wedding" first recorded in 1981. "Seeing Within" by Marty Young appeared in *Forgotten Places* edited by Henry Snider (The Horror Society).

"Q is for Quackery" by Tracie McBride was published in *The Grimorium Verum* (Western Legends Publishing). Barry Rosenberg's "Stroking the Devil" was published in *Hidden in Plain Sight* edited by J.W.Kirk. Angela Slatter's "Ripper" was published in *Horrorology: The Lexicon of Fear* (Jo Fletcher Books). D.K. Mok's novella "The Heart of the Labyrinth" found publication in *In Memory: A Tribute to Sir Terry Pratchett*; the book was a fundraiser anthology to raise money for Alzheimer's Research UK. "Oh Have You Seen the Devil?" by Stephen Dedman was published in *The Mammoth Book of Jack the Ripper Stories* edited by Maxim Jakubowski (Running Press). "The Witch's Library" by Tracie McBride appeared in *A Mythos Grimly* (Wanderer's Haven Publications). Jay Caselberg's story "Sailor's Rest" saw publication in *Night Terrors III* edited by Marc Ciccarone, Theresa Dillon and G Winston Hyatt (Blood Bound Books). Lee Pletzer's "Two Coins" was published in *Paying the Ferryman* (Charon Coin Press) edited by Margaret L. Colton. "The Ponitanak's Doll" by Geneve Flynn found print in *Play Things & Past Times* edited by Steve J. Shaw (KnightWatch Press). "Under the Roses", a gentle ghost story about feline companionship from Jenny Blackford, was published in *A Quiet Shelter There* (Hadley Rilley Books). Greg Chapman achieved publication of the story "Wounds" in *That Hoodoo, Voodoo That You Do: A Dark Rituals Anthology* edited by Lincoln Crisler (Angelic Knight Press). Tarran Jones story "All That Glitters" is a retelling of the Brother's Grimm tale The Girl with No Hands, published in *Twice Upon A Time* (Bearded Scribe Press). Barry Rosenberg's "A Made Man" was published in *When Disaster Strikes: An Anthology of YA Horror* edited by Rich Dodgin for UK-based publisher Sinister Saints Press. "Sugared Heat" by Lisa L. Hannett appeared in *The 2nd Spectral Book of Horror Stories* (Spectral Press).

JOURNALS, MAGAZINES & WEBZINES

Andromeda Spaceways Magazine 61, edited by Simon Petrie (Andromeda Spaceways Publishing Co-Op) included dark story "In Sheep's Clothing" by Kim Gaal. Tim Napper's violent dystopian story "Flame Trees" appeared in *Asimovs. Aurealis* magazine (Chimaera Publications) edited by Michael Pryor featured various darker stories in 2015: "Enfolded" a neo-noir about psychic powers and criminal fraternities that won't let go by J. Michael Melican, in *Aurealis 78*; "The Monster Under My Bed" by Melanie Rees and "The Whore and the Healer" and Lachlan Huddy in *Aurealis 79*; "Outside World" by Steve Cameron in *Aurealis 80*; "The Other-Faced Lamb"—about cults, the outback and deformed lambs—by C.S. McMullen, in *Aurealis 82*; "Perfect Kills" by Chris Large in *Aurealis 83*; "Breaking Windows" a horror-sci-fi story by Tracie McBride in *Aurealis 84*; "The Events at Callan Park" by Erol Engin in *Aurealis 85*.

The Australian Poetry Journal, Volume 5 Issue 2 (November 2015) edited by Michael Sharkey included the poem "Secondary Ghosts" by P.S. Cottier. Alice Godwin's erotic dark fantasy about death "He Kindly Stopped For Me" was published in *Blue Crow Magazine*, Issue 4 (The Blue Crow Press) edited by Andrew Scobie. Lee Pletzer's story "The Factory" was published on the *Calamities Press* webzine. Kaaron Warren's "Wittnessing" was published in *The Canary Press Genre Issue*, Issue #6 (April 2015). David Kernot's story "The Poseidon Stones" was published in *The Coloured Lense Speculative Fiction Magazine* Winter 2015 Issue #14. C.W. Pearce published "Flicker" in the Conflux 11 magazine. Danny Lovecraft's excellent poem putting a twist on the zombie apocalypse "Reminiscences of Herbert West', *Cyäegha* 14 (Summer 2015) chapbook edited and published by Graeme Phillips.

The Dark edited by Sean Wallace had a number of Australian contributors—"Bearskin" by Angela Slatter in *The Dark 7*, and

"The Canary" by Lisa L. Hannett and "Self, Contained" by Kirstyn McDermott. "While the Rain Walked', a colonial tale of dangerous old world spirits, Imogen Cassidy, in *Devilfish Review, Kraken* Issue 2015. Greg Chapman saw publication of "What Hath God Wrought" in *Devolution Z Magazine* (December 15). *Dimension6* (Coeur de Lion) edited by Keith Stevenson included a number of horror stories in the 2015 editions: "Tooth" by Bren MacDibble and Jen White's urban archeology horror novella "Dark History" in *Dimension6 4*; "Going Home Sideways" by S.G. Larner and "Red in Tooth and Claw" by David McDonald in *Dimension6 5*; "Lodloc and the Bear" by Steve Cameron in *Dimension6 6*. Alan Baxter's "The Chart of the Vagrant Mariner" appeared in *Fantasy & Science Fiction* (Jan/Feb). "Captain Marvelous" a fine claustrophobic apocalyptic horror story by Rose Hartley, in f(r) iction 2.

Tara Calaby's "Ashes" in *Grimdark Magazine 4* considers what comes after happily ever after for Cinderella. J. Ashley Smith published "To The Music We Hear', a serial killer mystery, in *Heater* Volume 3 No 2. "The Walking Thing" by Marlee Jane Ward, a horrific science-fiction, was published in *Interfictions Online 5*. "The Ferry Man" novella by Pandora Hope was published in *Interzone #256*, Jan-Feb 2015; a story of a Norse succubus transplanted to Australia. Barry Rosenberg's "Ma'af" was published in *Jam Berapa: Anak Sastra* Issue, July 2015. Sean Monaghan's "Concentration" was published in *Landfall: the New Zealand Literary Journal* May 2015. David Kernot's story "A Hero's Welcome" was published in *The Lovecraft eZine Issue 34*. "Art as a Mirror" by Tracie McBride was published in *The Lovecraft eZine Issue 35*.

Midnight Echo 11 edited by Kaaron Warren (Australian Horror Writers" Association) included the winners of the AHWA Short Story and Flash Fiction Competition—Stuart Olver's "What Came Through" won the Flash category and J. Ashley Smith's "On The Line" won the Short Story category; this issue included fiction "Perfect Little Stitches" by Deborah Sheldon, Claire Fitzpatrick's "Madeline', "The Light Unseen" by Mark Farrugia, "The Crying Room" by Marija Elektra Rodriguez, Keith Williams's "Sundown" and P.S. Cottier's poem "The Fruit of Her Hands'. David McDonald's story "Sympathetic Impulses" was published in

Nevermore: Tales of Murder, Mayhem and the Macabre (EDGE SciFi and Fantasy), edited by Nancy Kilpatrick and Caro Soles.

Kristian Beker's "Sleeping Pretty" saw print at the *Narrator International* webzine. Lee Pletzer's "Of Machines and Men" appeared in *Nebula Rift* Volume 3 No. 5, and "Reset" in *Nebula Rift* No 3 Volume 1. Edward Burger's weird "6969" story set in a sex-centric future appeared in Victoria University's *Offset Journal*. "We Saw the Same Sky', a literary dystopian story by Jane Rawson, appeared in *Overland* Autumn 2015. Jeremy Szal's dark tale "Skingame" was published in *Perihelion Science Fiction* (May 20115). Daniel Lewis's story "The Infirmary" was published in *Phase2 Magazine*. Deborah Sheldon's "In the Company of Women" found publication in *Pulp Modern 9*. *Review of Australian Fiction*, volume 13, issue 6, edited by Matthew Lamb, featured "The Jellyfish Collector" by Michelle Goldsmith and "Mine Intercom" by Kaaron Warren; "Her Ladyship" by John Jenkins was published in *Review of Australian Fiction*, volume 14, issue 5; "Reaching for Ruins" by Alan Baxter was published in *Review of Australian Fiction*, volume 16, issue 3.

Two Australian poets were featured in *Sargasso: The Journal of William Hope Hodgson Studies* Volume 1 No 2 (Ulthra Press); Danny Lovecraft published four poems—"House on the Borderland, 1 and 2", "The Devil Mists", "And the Worried Waters Laughed" and "What Do They Hide?". Phillip E. Ellis published five weird poems—"Dead Seamen Gone in Search of the Same Landfall", "Come, Dream of the Ocean", "Ocean Rain", "Coral Seas", and "The Burning Ship"—as well as non-fiction feature "Contemporary Views: Pieces on William Hope Hodgson from the Idler and the Bookman". Lee Pletzer's "Saving Kira" won the SF Reader Short Story Competition, and was published on the *SFReader Community* website. *Specul8 1: Central Queensland Journal of Speculative Fiction* Issue 1 October 2015 included darker contributions Greg Chapman's "In Memoriam', Clare Bielenberg's "The Name of the Darkness', and "Home Improvements" by Aaron C. Goulson.

Spectral Realms: A Weird Poetry Journal #No. 3 (Summer 2015) edited by S.T.Joshi for Hippocampus Press included a number of Australian poets; Leigh Blackmore published "The Golden Diadem" and "Dead Pale Moon", Margi Curtis published "My Heart's Thin Veil', and Danny Lovecraft published "A Shuddery

Tale" and "Azathoth'. Jenny Blackford had two poems "Ghost Irises" and "Beneath the Wheeler Centre" published in *Strange Horizons.* Blackford also received a commendation for her poem "We to the Gods" in the W.B. Yeats Poetry Prize and publication on the website. *SQ Mag 20: Special Edition Dark Legends of a New Age* edited by Sophie Yorkston (IFWG Publishing) included "Bluebeard's Daughter" by Angela Slatter, "The Bone Maiden" by Greg Chapman, and "Three Trophies" by S.G. Larner. *SQ Mag* 21 included "Home Delivery" by Michelle Jager, and *SQ Mag* 19 included "Night Blooming" by Jason Nahrung.

Lee Pletzer's "An Exercise in White" was published in *Teeming Terrors 15* (Knightwatch Press) edited by Christine Morgan. Maree Kimberley's dark magic realism story "Fleur" appeared in *Text Journal* Special Issue Website Series Number 32 October 2015. Jodi Cleghorn's "At Arm's Length', a weird tale of magic realism, was published in *Tincture Journal 11*. "What We Are" by Craig Hildebrand-Burke appeared in *Tincture Journal 12*; a woman discovers her husband's monstrous secret. Rebecca Fung's "The Biggest Catch" was published in *Trysts of Fate*, February 2015. Lee Pletzzer's "The Thin You" was published in *Under The Bed* Volume 3 No. 10. Danny Lovecraft had two connected poems "The Shadow from the Steeple, 1 and 2" in *Weird Fiction Review* #6, November 2015 (Centipede Press) edited by S.T.Joshi. Kaaron Warren's "The Bone Mason (Nyarlathotep)" a microfiction created as part of the Illustro Obscurum Collaboration published at the hilariously named Yog-Blogsoth website, edited by Michael Bukowski.

INTERDISCIPLINARY ARTS

Kaaron Warren's microfiction "Phylia Stands" appeared in *BESTIARY: Bizarre Myths and Chemical Fancies* (United Photos Industries), an exhibition catalogue for award winning artist and illustrator Viktor Koen's; the fiction portion is edited by Ellen Datlow. And the works explore Greek mythology especially as outlined in Robert Graves's 1955 book *The Greek Myths* and early nineteenth century photography from the US Library of Congress, digitally transformed as supernatural "psychological portraits".

Laura E. Goodin and Houston Dunleavy, both lecturers at the Australian Institute of Music in Melbourne, collaborated on producing "A Cabinet of Oddities": the composers were Dunleavy, Joe Dolce, Joe Giovinazzo, Gary Butler, and Andrew Batterham; writers were Laura Goodin, Sean Williams, Robert Shearman, Jack Dann, and others. The concert was held at the Peter Calvo Auditorium, Australian Institute of Music, as part of the Melbourne Fringe Festival, and was notable for an ensemble led by Monash University's Peter Sheridan that featured a range of flutes including the rare contrabass flute. The event also featured illustrations by Kathleen Jennings.

REMEMBERED

Tanith Lee, 67, English World Fantasy Award—Life Achievement recipient; **Sir Terry Pratchett,** 66, English World Fantasy Award—Life Achievement recipient; **Melanie Tem,** 65, American World Fantasy Award winning writer; **Colleen McCullough** AO, 77, Australian novelist; **Desmond Digby,** 82, New Zealand-born Australian illustrator of *Bottersnikes and Gumbles*; **Tjilpi Bob Randall,** c. 81, Yankunytjatjara elder, NAIDOC Person of the Year, author of *Tracker Tjuginji*; **Dorothy Butler** MBE, 90, New Zealand children's book author; **Tom Arden** (real name David Rain), 54, Australian-born science fiction and fantasy writer; **Paul Anderson,** 71, Australian sf fan and reviewer; **Andrew Lesnie** ACS ASC, 59, Academy Award-winning Australian cinematographer; **Peter Dickinson** OBE, 88, Zambian-born English writer, dual winner of the Carnegie Medal; **Tom Piccirilli,** 50, American multiple Stoker Award-winning writer.

THE YEAR'S BEST AUSTRALIAN FANTASY & HORROR

~ 2015 ~

THE SIXTH ANNUAL COLLECTION

THE COMPANY OF WOMEN

GARTH NIX

Summer. The sun noon-high in a sky clear as water, save for the merest scrape of cloud above the hills to the west. The meadow white with clover, the flowers so thick upon the ground no other colour could be seen, as if some strange snow had fallen out of season.

All through the meadow, bees. Single bees searching, groups of bees gathering, great swarms of bees swirling about the tall conical bee-houses arrayed in long lines, each one new-built every spring in its own place, as had been done for centuries past and all trusted would be done for centuries to come.

Godiva, Countess of Mercia, stood on the mound before the meadows proper, where the tips of the old standing stones could still be seen, the stone women of long ago buried by later Christian rulers but their presence still felt beneath the earth.

Lady Godiva was not alone. She stood in the very centre of the mound, at its highest point, albeit only a dozen paces above the meadow. Around her, ranged close, were the women of her household, at least those who had children, for all must be mothers who came that day to sing praise to the bees. Around them were the servants of the castle, and around them, in close-standing rings that extended to the edge of the mound and beyond, down into the white clover, were the mothers and grandmothers and great-grandmothers and even one ancient great-great-grandmother of the town of Coventry.

The song was as old as the buried stones, though the words had changed through several languages, and perhaps no longer made much sense, if anyone cared to examine them. But they did not look closely, for it was the feeling of the song that mattered, the sense of being at one with all the other women, and with the queens in their houses, the queens who were the minds and hearts and souls of this great metropolis of bees.

As the last note came from the assembled women and faded into silence, the bees answered. Deep in the hives there were thrummings and rumblings, and great droves of bees rose from the meadow and buzzed together, so many in number that the buzzing sounded like a mighty cascade, and a breeze blew across the mound, made from the beating of myriad tiny wings in unison.

Then the breeze faded, as the bees returned to their business. The women relaxed, letting go the slight stiffness of apprehension, that small fear that perhaps this year the queens would not answer the song, the meadows would fade early, and the honey would be sparse. To many families of Coventry, their bee-house and the honey it would provide might make the difference between comfort and privation, or for some, even a bare sufficiency and starvation. Few ate much of the honey themselves; it was too valuable. But sold at autumn fair, it would make silver to see them through the winter.

Godiva relaxed too, for it was a great responsibility to lead the singing, and this was only the third time she had done so. For a few minutes, lost in the song and the bee-sound, she had also managed to forget some things that were disturbing her mind, most principally the altered behaviour of her husband Leofric, the Earl of Mercia. In recent months he had become withdrawn, from his family and his court, and even more troubling, had taken certain decisions which were alienating the people of Coventry. Leofric had always been so reasonable, but now he would no longer listen to the counsel of Godiva or any of his former most trusted advisors.

This change in Leofric stemmed from the arrival in their court of one Ralph, a Norman knight and ferromancer, who Leofric had immediately appointed as his steward, replacing the good Athelbard who had served both him and his father before him well, and was not too advanced in years to continue for many years ahead.

Ralph had introduced a number of unwelcome changes, and at all times, Leofric had supported him. Most of the changes involved taxes and fees, Ralph suggesting new ways to gain money for the earl. As Leofric had never cared greatly for the accumulation of silver before, this was very strange. It was as if Ralph had some hold over the earl. Leofric wouldn't talk to Godiva about it. Whenever she tried, he would evade her and disappear hunting.

At least it would be a good season for honey, Godiva thought, as the women on the mound dispersed and she walked back with her handmaidens to where the dozen housecarls of her bodyguard waited. The men had stayed just within earshot, in case of need, back along the old Roman road behind the mound.

The harsh clatter of horseshoes on that road broke through the quiet murmur of the women, catching Godiva's attention. She frowned as she saw a black destrier ridden too fast coming towards them, sending the women returning to the town scuttling aside. It was, of course, Sir Ralph, as if her thinking of him had made him appear. Like the devil, she thought, and wondered. Ralph had also had his run-ins with the Bishop of Coventry and the gentler English church that still embraced much of the old Anglo-Saxon magic and tradition, the workings of holly and iron. The Normans followed the pope, of course, as the English did not, and claimed their ferromancy was the only true magic approved by God.

But she did not believe in the Devil incarnate. There was enough ordinary evil in the world and in people to not need any special manifestation. Ralph was clearly feathering his own nest while he worked to extract more coin for the earl, and surely this was explanation enough for his behaviour. But why had he ridden out to the bee-fields, on this day of all days?

Her housecarls lifted their axes as he approached, and spread out across the road. They had served her father or uncle before her, and were all veterans of numerous battles. In common with almost everyone else in the earl's household, they did not like Ralph. Godiva suspected if he gave them an excuse, such as trying to ride through to their mistress, they would happily cut him down and be contrite about it afterwards.

Ralph slowed his war-horse to a walk, and turned the stallion aside to calm him, allowing Aelfwyn, the leader of the housecarls to swagger up, his axe now on his shoulder. They spoke quietly, Aelfwyn shaking his head and pointing back to the town, Ralph in turn gesticulating and making some sort of vehement demand.

Godiva walked more quickly. It would be better for her to find out what this was about, before Aelfwyn or Ralph lost their tempers.

"What brings you here, Ralph?" she called out as she drew closer. It was not a polite greeting, but she did not care to be polite to the man. He never seemed to notice, anyway.

"I am upon the earl's business," said Ralph loudly. "I have come to see his famous bee-meadow."

Godiva's fingers curled towards becoming fists and she had to force herself to relax them, to let her arms remain at her sides.

"The bee-meadow is not the earl's," she said calmly. "It is held by all the women of Coventry, direct from the king, as has always been."

"Is it?" asked Ralph, in his nasal voice that had little variation in pitch, and so disguised any emotion that might lie behind the words. "Yet there is no deed, no title, no *document* at all that says so, and in that absence, the bee-meadow, as anything else, must therefore be of the Earl's demesne."

Godiva felt an almost over-powering urge to meet this smug announcement with a command to her housecarls to cut the Norman down, and keep on hacking at him until the pieces were so small even the smallest dog, nay even the smallest rat could carry a piece away. But she resisted the surge of fury, for what he said was true, or at least true to a degree. There had been a grant of title, long ago, but it was believed destroyed when St Osburga's was burned in the first Viking raids.

"It is recorded as such in many records," she said. "And in the memory of the people. The earl himself I am sure would not contest it."

"The earl has given me the duty of ensuring his lands are properly managed," said Sir Ralph. "*All* his lands. Including this bee-meadow, milady."

Godiva felt rather than saw her housecarls spreading out in a line behind her, getting ready to charge this insolent Norman.

"Go back to the castle," she said to Sir Ralph, her voice cold and commanding. "I will discuss this with the earl."

Sir Ralph's eyes flickered, noting the barely-suppressed anger of the housecarls, axes held ready, knees bent to sprint forward before he could attempt to charge through and away, and there were probably too many, too close, for his ferromantic powers to turn their weapons aside. He looked as if he would say something, but instead he inclined his head with the slightest civility possible and turned his mount around.

"He needs killing," said Aelfwyn quietly to Godiva, sunlight flashing from his axe-blade across his face, lighting up his narrowed eyes. "You want me to see to it, milady? I've a wooden spear for such as he, in my arms-chest. Good oak, fire-tempered."

"No," said Godiva. "He is a Christian, of a sort, and he is the earl's man. No killing."

Aelfwyn nodded, but did not respond. Godiva was fairly sure he would obey, but only for a few days. If Ralph wasn't careful, he would meet an untimely end, and likely thus create even more problems. Godiva wanted to discover why Leofric was seemingly in Ralph's power before she did anything to remove the Norman from Coventry, permanently or otherwise. And now there was the additional problem of making sure the bee-meadow remained the common property of the mothers of the town.

"Let us walk," said Godiva. "Send someone back with the horses. I need to think."

Aelfwyn signalled to the men who held the horses, and to the housecarls. Soon the small host was walking up the road, with Godiva alone in the middle, until one of her women quickened her pace to join her company.

"I fear there is more trouble, milady," said Ceolwen, chief among Godiva's handmaidens. A fifteen years older cousin, Ceolwen was a widow now, her husband killed in the last year fighting the Viking raiders from Ireland, and her sons and daughters were grown and married. She was very close to the countess, godmother to Godiva's own son, and the two kept no secrets from each other.

"It seems so," replied Godiva quietly, so only the two of them could hear. She frowned. "I have to make Leofric talk to me. There is perhaps some simple explanation for . . . for everything."

"I doubt it is simple," replied Ceolwen. "Back there . . . that Ralph smelled of something worse than iron magic."

"Did he?" asked Godiva intently. She had little magic herself, and doubted most people who claimed to have greater powers, with a few exceptions. Ceolwen was one of them, for Godiva had seen her quell and send away a pack of wolves, and a great oak seemingly bend to speak to her, and though these things had happened in Godiva's childhood, she had not forgotten.

"It is not himself, exactly," said Ceolwen thoughtfully. "I think it is something he carries. Some object of forbidden sorcery."

"Ferromancy is not forbidden," said Godiva.

"It is not cold iron nor stone magic that he conceals," said Ceolwen. "Something more malevolent, something from the deep shadows."

"Something Bishop Osric can deal with?" asked Godiva, her frown lightening. This might be the opportunity she was looking for, if Ralph was found to be an evil sorcerer.

"I doubt it," said Ceolwen regretfully. "I caught only the faintest scent, myself. The wind from the bee-meadow is sacred, it made whatever it is stir itself. I have not noticed it before, and I think Osric would not be able to tell if anything is amiss. He is not of the sharpest, and his power slight."

"The dogs don't like him," added Godiva. "Ralph, I mean. I had thought it was because he kicks at them and is generally harsh, but it is likely he does that to hide whatever they scent."

"Yes," said Ceolwen. "The dogs would know."

They were silent for a minute or two, both thinking.

"You had best go to the great oak at Awsley," said Godiva. "I do not like to have that old hag looking into our court, but needs must. Ask her about Ralph and whatever he carries."

"She may not choose to talk," said Ceolwen carefully, who had a rather less orthodox opinion of the Wise Woman of Awsley and held her in much higher esteem than Godiva. "But of course I will go. What will you do?"

"First of all, talk to Leofric," said Godiva. "In bed, tonight. This time, I will make him listen!"

• • •

But Leofric wouldn't listen. He left their marital bed in his nightshirt, blustering and bellowing that he could not stand another word, a strange cry when he had avoiding listening to any word beyond Ralph's name. Godiva heard him shouting as he stomped across the hall, and out to the stables, calling for his grooms and housecarls to attend him, for he was away to his manor of Bercuswell where he would not be troubled by his woman.

Ceolwen passed the earl going out on her way in from her travels, and went to Godiva without taking off her cloak or boots.

"Leofric is afraid of something," said Godiva. "I cannot tell whether it is for himself, or me, or for the children. Ralph holds a great power over him."

"He does have something to fear," said Ceolwen. "The Wise Woman of Awsley was amenable today. She looked in the water to see what she might of Ralph."

"And?"

"She saw Ralph," said Ceolwen, very slowly. "But that was not all."

"What?" asked Godiva. "What do you mean?"

"She saw something of Leofric as well," said Ceolwen. "Bound within whatever Ralph carries on that dark chain about his neck."

"Something of Leofric?" asked Godiva, falteringly. "His soul?"

"The Wise Woman is not Christian, and she did not use that word," replied Ceolwen. "But I think it is what she meant. She saw others as well, what she called the 'bright shadows' of perhaps half a dozen living men, clustered about whatever Ralph wears, caught like bees on tar-paper. He has captured them, somehow. This is why Leofric does his bidding."

Godiva was entirely still for a moment, that shocked stillness of a warrior who has taken a wound and does not yet know it for what it is, whether a mortal blow or merely a cut to be shrugged off. Ceolwen began to reach out a hand to her, but pulled it back as Godiva drew a deep breath and spoke in measured tones.

"There is a mention of something like this in Saint Wulfstan's *Blessings and Maledictions*," she said. "Under "Maledictions", of course. A soul-thief who lived in the time of Urakazaar of Babylon. He had some foul device, a cursed amulet that could take souls and imprison them within."

"Yes," said Ceolwen. "The Wise Woman called Ralph something I did not understand, a word from the little folk of long ago. She said it meant 'creature who takes the light from others'."

"He must be forced to release Leofric. And the others . . . I wonder . . . five other souls caught. If they are also earls or nobles of Ingland, and Ralph a Norman . . . but would even Duke William employ such a wicked stratagem? He is like to take the kingdom in any case."

"Whether Ralph serves William or himself, the difficulty will be to force him to do anything," said Ceolwen. "Nor can he be simply killed. The Wise Woman was straight on that. She said to kill him would strand the bright shadows of the others in some nether place. They would live on, but as mere husks, without joy or savour of any kind."

"Likely he has other evil magic to protect him in any case," said Godiva. "Saint Wulfstan categorised a creature of his type, as I have said, but he did not offer any remedy . . . did the Wise Woman offer any suggestion for how we might free Leofric?"

Ceolwen hesitated a moment before answering, a hesitation instantly noticed by Godiva.

"What?" she asked, a smile flickering across her care-worn face. "I take it is something you fear I will undertake, and think it too dangerous for me, so you plan to not tell me and do it yourself?"

Ceolwen laughed, caught out. "I had resolved to tell you," she said. "I only thought for a moment I might turn you aside. In truth, I could not do what must be done in any case. It is for the leader of the women of Coventry, the singer to the bees. Or so the Wise Woman says."

"Ah," said Godiva quietly. "I think I understand. But surely that is only legend?"

"No. It is not simply legend. The tales speak truly of a great working of the old magic," said Ceolwen.

"But I have no power, no skills of magic," protested Godiva. "So how can that work?"

"You do not need power, nor arcane knowledge. The ritual itself is power," answered Ceolwen. "And it can only be done by she who leads the singing to the bees."

"And is the ritual as simple as the legend says?" asked Godiva. "To walk naked from the Mound of the Bee Field to the Bargain Stone in the market square?"

"You must also lay down a bunch of clover, an acorn, and a drop of blood new-pricked from a hawthorn branch. Then you may speak your lawgiving to anyone . . . or anything . . . and they must obey your rede."

"That does not sound so difficult," said Godiva. "Leofric will not like others to see my nakedness I suppose, but my housecarls can clear the road at least, blacken a few eyes—"

"It is not so straight a task," said Ceolwen. "No man may see you at all, or the spell is broken."

Godiva's mouth quirked in momentary frustration, but her mind moved swiftly.

"No, not so straight a task," she said. "But I think there is a way to do it, and we must do so with all speed, before Ralph hears of it. I need you to fetch Mother Halfgrim from the town."

"Mother Halfgrim!" exclaimed Ceolwen. "Now? In the night? That cantankerous old reptile?"

"Yes," said Godiva. "Tell her it is not the countess that needs her, but the Singer to the Bees. Before we are done, we will need many others too. There is a great deal to do."

"I will fetch Mother Halfgrim then," said Ceolwen, gathering up her kirtle to go. "I am eager to hear your thoughts, my lady!"

An hour later, Ceolwen returned with Mother Halfgrim, who strangely did not protest as she might be expected to do, in fact grumbling not at all. She was introduced into Godiva's bedchamber, the two speaking for little more than ten minutes, before Mother Halfgrim emerged and returned to the town, a curious, previously unsuspected smile twisting up her toothless mouth.

Later, other women came, speaking Mother Halfgrim's name to the sleepy housecarls, who scratched their heads and grumbled at this sudden flurry of midnight visitations, one likening it to a hive of bees all a-buzz over some invisible upset to the queen within.

Later still, a good hour before the dawn, Godiva called Aelfwyn to her, and explained what he and the other housecarls must do. He was aghast, and pulled at his moustaches, and blustered that she should not, must not, could not do as she intended. But Godiva spoke of Ralph and the thing he held, and the captive souls, and the captain quietened. At last he agreed to her commands, and went to rouse his men.

As the first small hint of the day began to show above the hills, Godiva went alone to the bee meadow. Along the way, she passed her housecarls, one by one, who were posted at fifty yard intervals, their backs to the road. They had already turned away the few folk who were about in the last dregs of the night, lawfully or not, save for those who were also following Godiva's orders.

On the hill, the Countess of Coventry disrobed until she stood naked, her only adornment remaining a tortoiseshell comb. She pulled this free and let her long hair fall, without any attempt to twine it about herself in some show of modesty. Then she called out once, twice, three times to the bees, asking for their permission before walking down the hill to pick a good bunch of clover. She had marked an oak some ways back toward the town, which doubtless would provide the acorn, and there was a hawthorn bush close from which she would gently take a thorny branch.

• • •

While Godiva picked her clover, back in the town a man no one had seen before came from an alley, smiling and rubbing his hands. He met a band of idlers by the market square who were meant to be assembling a stand but had not yet even begun to think of doing so. In the dim, pre-dawn light none noticed that their visitor did not cast a shadow.

"A rare day today," laughed the fellow. "Not every day a common man sees a countess naked!"

"What's that you say?" asked Alfred, sometime leader of his band of so-called workers. "A countess naked?"

"Sure as sure," said the man, rubbing his hands again. "As pretty a noblewoman who ever walked the land. Your own Lady Godiva, she is to walk naked as a babe through the town to the Bargain Stone."

All eyes went to the old, black stone that rose waist-high from the cobbles like some time-worn tooth, as in fact legend had it was, the tooth of the dragon of Wessex, now remembered only on the banner of the Godwin lords. It was where deals were sealed, buyer and seller signing or marking their mark on deed or bill laid upon the smoothed flat top of the ancient tooth, if tooth it was.

"Naked?" asked a man, licking his lips. "And what's the earl to do to any man who looks upon her? Flay him alive, or put his eyes out?"

"Earl's gone a-hunting, and none can gainsay the lady," said the man. "She walks alone, without her housecarls. Wait but an hour and you'll see her treasures, as will any man who cares to look."

"How do you—" Alfred began to ask, but the stranger was gone into the darkness, nimbly stepping between the first early rays of the sun, going elsewhere to spread his news.

"I'll not watch," said Begran firmly. "This sounds to be women's business, best left alone. I remember my old mum—"

His words were lost in jeers and catcalls, led by Alfred, who had caught the stranger's glee.

"You can close your eyes, old Begran, old gelding," he cried, slapping him on the back. "But we are true men and we will gaze upon any beauty that offers herself, and . . . and aye, more too, should she cast her own eyes back!"

There was a muttering at this, and others beside Begran slunk away. But soon enough the word spread, and more men came to the square, asking if it were true that the countess herself was walking naked to the stone, and if she was, where would be best to see all that they cared to see. Small scuffles broke out over vantage points, men trying to climb on top of stalls, and others dragging them down, scuffles made worse by the absence of the town constables who were nowhere to be seen, nor the Under-Sheriff and his men, nor the housecarls of the earl.

The greatest crowd gathered at the eastern side of the market square, where the road ran in, for it would be here that the countess would first be seen. Men jostled and pitched their elbows wide, maintaining their chosen spots, shouting and hitting as the smaller and more slippery eased between them.

All this ceased as the cry went up.

"Here she comes!"

A figure hard to see with the rising sun behind her was walking up the road. The crowd of men surged forward, then inexplicably faltered and slowed, those behind roaring with frustration until they too fell silent.

Behind the first figure there were more. And not only on the main road, but coming in from the alleys on every side, walking slowly toward the square. Dozens of naked women, nay, hundreds of naked women, and the one in the lead was not the naked body of a winsome countess, but the leathery, age and sun-worn shape of Mother Halfgrim, leader of the laundresses, those fierce, take-no-prisoner women who could crack a man's skull with a laundry pole as easy as lift a great tub of wet clothes to their shoulders, and they were all behind her, and they were not alone.

"That's my old mum," said a suddenly deeply worried voice among the crowd, the harbinger of many, many other cries.

"My wife!"

"My daughters!"

"My grandmam and her sister!"

"Old Aunt Alys!"

"The ale-wife from the Oxen!"

"Oh! Oh! The lepers from Holy Cross!"

The women walked on silently, the men turning about in confusion, many shielding their eyes and looking down of their own accord, others being forced to do so as husbands and fathers and brothers and sons pulled down other men's' hats or hoods, or slapped them in the neck.

Mother Halfgrim stopped a few paces away from the now silent crowd of cowed and ashamed menfolk.

"Go home!" she cried, fierce as ever. "Go home and do not look out, do not look out until a woman says you may! Any who look will rue it for whatever few days remain to them thereafter! "

No one moved, until Mother Halfgrim suddenly clapped her hands and shouted.

"Go!"

At that the men broke like a rabble charged by knights, and fled back through the square, the women in the alleys parting to let them through.

Mother Halfgrim began to walk again, and the women followed. All the women, of town and castle and from villages for leagues around, all naked and marching for the square. Thousands of women, young and old and in between, and amongst them, perhaps a hundred paces behind Mother Halfgrim, walked Lady Godiva, with a smile upon her face.

The smile grew broader as the great crowd of women swirled about the market square, and Godiva weaved between them, drawing ever closer to the bargain stone, the dragon tooth. The tallest and broadest women walked with her, against the chance that some man still dared to look, but they saw none, and Godiva felt no cheating gaze, as she was sure she would.

At last, she came to the stone. The women drew close as Godiva knelt and laid the heather and the acorn upon the flat, and then with the prick of a hawthorn, added a drop of her own bright red blood. She felt a strange thrill rush through her as the blood fell on the stone, a quickening of something she had never known, a sense that she was now a part of some great and terrible power that had wakened at her call.

Lady Godiva stood and raised her voice, speaking not just to the crowd, but to the world beyond and the ancient magic that she knew awaited her call.

"I summon the Norman called Ralph, steward to my husband. Ralph, come to the stone to answer for your misdeeds!"

There was silence then, unbroken by any sound. In that stillness, women flinched at the sudden sound of heavy footsteps, boots upon the cobbles. Ralph emerged from the shadows between two houses, and advanced towards the Bargain Stone. But this was not Ralph as he was usually seen, simply a cold and remote man. The shadows companioned him now, and the sunshine itself flinched away. Even the bold laundresses stepped back, and Mother Halfgrim herself took only one of the three steps she intended to interpose herself between him and the countess.

"I come," said Ralph. His voice was angry, tinged with fire, no longer the passionless tone of a bailiff on his master's business. "Not because of your petty magic, your foolish ritual. It is time all was made clear to you, Lady, and to all you women. The earl does as I command, and so must you all. None can gainsay me."

"I summoned you to a law-giving," said Godiva, though the words were hard to find, and her teeth were inclined to want to chatter. But she knew if she faltered, all would falter, and everything would be lost. "And this is my rede. You shall recant all your works of darkness, and give up whatever you wear against your chest, so it may be destroyed."

"Recant?" asked Ralph scornfully. "Give up my amulet? No, rather I shall use it once again. I have not bothered to capture the soul of a woman before, it seems hardly worthwhile. But you . . . you are a thorn in my flesh that must be dealt with lest it fester."

He reached into his tunic, and lifted up the links of an iron necklace. A pendant hung from the chain, a small tablet of some dull red mineral. Though it was no larger than a thumbnail and seemed unremarkable, as Ralph held it high Godiva's eyes were immediately drawn to it, and then she could not look away, nor move her head or limbs.

Whatever power was in the amulet, it held her fast. Dread filled her, and her breath grew fast and shallowed, all her instincts demanding she flee, muscles rippling but failing to instigate any movement.

"You see," said Ralph with a sneer. "I command a greater magic than anything you think to conjure."

Ceolwen alone of all the women moved forward, bending to pick up a loose cobblestone. But even as she rose to throw it, Ralph made a negligent gesture with his left hand, and the stone ran through her fingers like water, while others gave way beneath her feet. Ceolwen was suddenly knee-deep in what had been a solidly paved surface, held fast by the ferromantic magic Ralph also had at his command.

"So," said Ralph. He brought the pendant closer to his lips, and spoke to it, in a language vanished from the world for five thousand years or more. With each word, Godiva felt as if chill, insubstantial claws were reaching inside her, going past skin and bone to pull at something she didn't even know she possessed, drawing it out of her body.

Her soul was being taken, Godiva realised, and there was nothing she could do.

She cried out, and in that same moment, some deep instinct told her there *was* still something she could do, a faint last chance. She still commanded her voice.

In that instant of realisation, Godiva transformed her cry of pain and anguish into the beginning of the bee-song.

For several long seconds, she sang alone, but then the women closest to her began to also sing, even as they were held fast in all other ways, made as steady and unmoving as the buried stones of the hill by the meadow. More and more women joined the song, and as their voices rose in unison, Godiva knew that more than their voices were joined. She felt suddenly anchored, that the bright shadow that Ralph sought to draw from her body was no longer alone and easy prey, but linked to all the women around her, and those around them, and so on and on through all the many circles.

Thousands of bright shadows joined, so many the weight of them was too great for the amulet to move, and now her own soul was coming back to her, and Ralph's hand was coming down as if the pendant had grown heavy, weighted down by the connection with more souls than it could ever drink. As it slowly fell, the oppressive force that had held Godiva ebbed as well, but she did not move. The song had to be completed first, and it was not yet done.

"No, no," growled Ralph. He fumbled at his side with his free hand, trying to draw the thin, sharp dagger scabbarded at his waist. But still the amulet was dragging him down, so that he could not balance and he tumbled forward to land sprawling at Godiva's feet.

"You cannot harm me!" he spat out. "I am no mere ironmaster, I am the Favoured of Urakazaar! No weapon wielded by man, woman or child can harm me, I cannot be slain and I will—"

His words choked off as the first great cloud of bees swarmed into his open mouth and cascaded down his throat, closely followed by the second and third that slammed into his eyes and ears.

More and more bees flew to their deaths as the song continued, thousands and thousands of them descending upon the toppled body of Ralph. As the last note slowly faded into breathlessness there was no longer an identifiable man there at all, just a lump on the ground that looked like a fallen log covered in a thick carpet of dead and dying bees.

Ceolwen stepped out of the holes in the paving and prised up a cobblestone. Very gently, she brushed back a layer of bees from Ralph's hand to reveal the chain his lifeless fingers touched, and the tiny amulet that hung from the chain. Lifting the stone high, she brought it down with all her might.

The blow bounced off what seemed only oven-baked clay, which should have been easily crushed to dust. Ceolwen gritted her teeth and raised her hand again, but stopped as she felt Godiva's fingers wrap around her own.

"We must do it together, I think," said Godiva. Other women drew close, and many hands gripped the stone.

This time, when it came down, there was a great crack, as if some mighty door had been burst asunder. The tablet exploded in a waft of reddish dust. There was the brief, sickening smell of something ancient and decayed, but both dust and stench were borne away by the fresh wind, and the shadows that had defied the sunlight shrank and were likewise gone.

A single bee alighted on Godiva's hand as she straightened up. She raised it close to her face, and breathed upon it gently.

"Thank the mothers, sister," she said. "For all they have given us."

The bee flew up, and circled Godiva's head to take its bearing from the sun, before heading unerringly towards the bee meadow and the queens in their conical huts.

"They have given much," said Ceolwen. "There will be little honey this season, and perhaps the next."

"Yes," said Godiva. She felt very tired, and very dirty, and very naked. "But it is done."

"For now," said Ceolwen.

"For now?" asked Godiva quietly.

"Seasons turn, there is birth and death and rebirth," said Ceolwen. "For everything, even an ancient evil. Perhaps not in our time, but it will come."

"So," said Godiva. She looked around at the crowded market full of naked, determined women.

Her mouth settled in a grim line. This host needed no armour, no weapons, no boasts and shouting. But if she were the enemy, she would be greatly afraid.

~

MINE INTERCOM

KAARON WARREN

On the rare occasions Xanthe left her apartment, she walked slowly through the foyer of Goldleaf Towers, not wanting to rush past the photos of the miners who worked in the mine after which the building was named; men beginning a shift staring dully at the camera.

She knew that look. She saw it every day in the mirror, and in every photo she'd been in.

In one photo, a small boy squatted in the sand. His smile was broad. Innocent. The men stood behind him with shoulders slumped, their clothing already dirty. She understood that sense of weariness. Even her office job could make her feel that way.

There were no photos of the mine itself, collapsed or whole. No photos of the rescue of the miners because there had been no rescue. There were a dozen of the construction of the apartment block and of the first residents, Xanthe amongst them, all moved in a year ago. None had moved out. She actually didn't mind the photo. It was distant enough you couldn't see her eyes, and she wore that day, by good chance, a deep purple dress that made her look exotic. Why had she worn it? Surely not for the photo, because if she knew that was being taken she would not have made an appearance. Was that the day she had lunch with her mother in town? It must have been.

On display in two bright cabinets were some items created with gold and copper, much of it mined below, as if that justified the men's deaths, made them worthwhile.

Jewellery. Wire. Pipes.

Cutlery and coins.

Polished, highly reflective stones. There were lots of shiny places in this apartment complex.

Things fused and worked until their nature changed.

• • •

Next was the dusty museum. Xanthe and the other residents (certainly she had not found all of the items) had built a small memorial to the men who'd died when floods collapsed the mine. A small set of shelves set into an alcove, it was a macabre display of the things the miners left behind when they headed down that last, fatal time. There wasn't much; a pair of shoes, a good shirt, a set of car keys and an invitation to a viewing of a movie called "By the Book" with no indication as to what the movie actually was. A broken watch, a metal flask with the initials JB.

That was all.

• • •

Xanthe pushed open the heavy front door. It was made with recycled material from the mine, as was most of the building, and every time she touched it she got a sense of age. Of history. She saw a visitor calling into the intercom. It was a young woman Xanthe didn't recognize. Come to visit the young people in Number 4, perhaps.

"About time," the visitor said, "I've been pushing that button for ten minutes."

Xanthe said, "You have to tell them you're not a ghost. Tell them you're real. Otherwise they won't listen."

The young woman just stared at her.

The intercom was tricky. Most residents heard voices when none were rightly there, and became used to ignoring them. So when an actual visitor buzzed to be let in, they were sometimes also ignored.

They all thought it was a Real Estate agent trick, giving them the ghosts they were looking for.

Xanthe was not so sure. At first it had seemed like gibberish. But she'd recorded some on her phone, and the more she listened, the more she thought she heard. She listened at night; the voices put her to sleep. She wondered if it was like a foreign language; becoming clearer and clearer the more exposure you had.

If they were ghosts, she thought she might hear her sister one day.

Dark real estate, they called it. People lived in old funeral homes, and deliberately sought houses where murders took place. Xanthe didn't think she was like that, but when these apartments became available, she wanted one. She knew it for what it was; an attempt to be interesting. To make the people in the Heritage Library notice her, listen to her. And people did say, ooh, ghosts, but when she spoke, sometimes part way through the first sentence, their attention wandered.

And if there were ghosts there, maybe her sister would come. Maybe her sister would come and give forgiveness, or they could talk at least.

Her sister hadn't come yet.

Xanthe walked out and squinted in the bright sunlight. The air was so clear it almost hurt her lungs, and she breathed shallowly. She shivered and drew her shawl around her shoulders. It was one of many; glorious peacock blue, so soft it felt like a spider web against her skin.

She wouldn't have left home at all today but she didn't want to be around when the glazier was there. The new window would be gorgeous; made from the sand cleared when the mine was established, AS IS, they said, and she knew she wanted it. Other tenants preferred their glass clear. Xanthe liked the idea of looking through glass slightly distorted. She walked quickly to the market.

People glanced at her, and smiled. If she took off the shawl, she could be invisible if she wanted to. She had a whole series of these, in many colours, many textures. A guilty pleasure. An addiction.

• • •

The ground was sandy, decades of wind and feet dispersing the great piles that were built when the sand was shovelled aside for access to the gold and copper beneath, fifty years ago when the mine was established.

Her favourite fruit man was busy with another customer, so she stood quietly with her passionfruit, her watermelon, her peaches, her grapes and her strawberries until he was free.

"Can I help anyone?" he said. He was large, hairy, his teeth white and huge in his mouth, his hair a mop. You could never ignore him.

"Over here," she said, and he startled, as if she'd appeared from nowhere.

She knew what it felt like to be a ghost.

"That the lot, love?" he said. She wasn't sure if he'd put more emphasis in the word today. LOVE. Had he?

A child started chatting to her. Children often did that; they found her friendly. Approachable. She scrabbled in her handbag for a lolly but hadn't replenished her supply.

She ordered coffee from the corner van, loving the smell of the fresh beans. She gave her name and waited for it to appear.

"Xanthe? Wow, cool name," the barista called out.

She had long known her name was the most interesting thing about her. She saw visible disappointment when people met her in person, because she didn't match at all.

The barista almost didn't give her the coffee. He almost didn't believe it was her.

Sometimes she thought she should change her name.

• • •

The foyer was so cold compared to outside that Xanthe shivered. Two neighbours waited for the lift, and Xanthe nodded at them. They discussed, as the residents of Goldleaf Towers always did, the ghosts. The voices, the rolling balls, the sound of digging. Xanthe didn't join in, beyond a nod and a smile. She had nothing to add, and assumed they didn't want to hear what she had to say anyway.

"It's probably just the way the place is built," her neighbour from next door said. His name was Neil and he was quite nice. "But at 3AM? Try telling yourself that." The developers swore they'd pumped thousands of tonnes of concrete into the mine, that it was solid and safe, but others said the mine was filled with rubbish. Twenty years of waste in there rotting away and no wonder the place felt like it shifted. No cracks had appeared, so that was good. And the floors still seemed flat.

• • •

Everything becomes ordinary in the end.

• • •

Her new window was installed. It was beautiful, filling a quarter of her wall, casting a soft ruby glow into her apartment. The view was slightly distorted but she didn't mind that. They'd told her the traces of gold in it would help keep the heat out in summer, the heat in in winter.

• • •

She set to work cutting up her fruit, laying it carefully across her stone countertop. She loved her pale green kitchen. The cool stone stayed that way no matter the heat, and sometimes, deep in summer, she'd lay her cheek across it.

She made herself a warm drink and gazed through her window.

Then she heard a voice.

"Is anyone there? Help."

She thought at first the TV had come on, as all the TVs sometimes did, tuned to a station that wasn't there.

But it was the intercom.

"Hello? Who were you after? This is 6A."

"Are you a child?"

She laughed. "No! Lots of people think that. I am a grown woman."

"Find us," the voice said, then it faded. It was a man's voice.

• • •

She checked to see if her next-door neighbour Neil had heard. The neighbours were all odd, which was nice, but still it took great courage to knock on the door.

He'd heard static on the intercom. Nothing else.

• • •

She slept badly that night. She heard a ball bouncing and the annoying, constant rhythm of it kept her awake. It was no use banging on Neil's door. This was pure phantom noise.

• • •

"Hello?"

"Find us."

"Who are you?"

"We are the forgotten men."

"Oh . . . who has forgotten you? What do you mean?"

He said, "So rude of me. I must ask about you, dear lady. Who are you? Your name? You sound beautiful. Are you beautiful?"

She glanced into the reflective glass of her new window.

"I'm a mouse," she said. "Most people say."

He told her his name. Jarod Brock. "Remember me. Write my name down. We are forgotten men. Lost in this mine. It's as if we never existed. And my son, too. Only five. Jonas, we called him. After my father."

"Oh," she said. She took a mouthful of fruit salad.

"Are you eating? What are you eating?"

"Fruit salad. Fresh."

"Ohh," he said. She'd heard men make that noise, in the movies. Never in real life. "What else?"

She had nothing else, but she quickly found a cookbook online. "I have spaghetti with garlic and prosciutto. Nectarine Cake. Osso Bucco."

"Do you have fresh white bread, ham and mustard? Do you have cold beer? Do you have vanilla ice-cream?"

"Yes," she whispered.

He said they were still alive. "You must make them find us."

That wasn't possible, though.

"The mine collapsed 20 years ago." Surely. There was no way.

He coughed then, and said, "So little air. I can't breathe. I can't take a breath."

Then silence.

She thumbed the button again and again, then sat hunched in the dark, unable to breathe.

He had such a nice voice. Gentle.

• • •

She searched the internet for details of the missing men, filling in the gaps left out in the foyer below. He was right; they were almost forgotten. Only the residents saved their anonymous belongings. The township was evacuated in massive floods; six people lost their lives, so little wonder the poor miners were left alone. So much panic. So little leadership.

There were six miners. Two widowers, three never married, one divorced.

There was no child mentioned. She did find a Jonas Brock listed elsewhere, *Cause of Death: Pneumonia.*

• • •

She went downstairs to look at the photos of the men. No man was named, and no man had his hand on the boy's shoulder. She tried to pick out the man she was talking to, Jarod, but they all looked so similar.

She caught the lift down to the basement. It smelt like sweat, very old sweat. The floor was solid concrete. No entrance to a mine there.

How long could they live? One group in South America lasted 69 days but they had resources. Food. And contact.

20 years was ridiculous.

• • •

That evening, she saw a small boy curled into a ball on her floor, as if protecting himself from fire.

She walked over to him but he vanished.

That night as she lay in bed she felt a figure beside her. She stiffened, terrified, then turned her head.

The little boy lay beside her. He seemed to be measuring, matching his size for hers. He rose above her and hovered, she knew he was there, hovering, she could not be imagining this because she imagined nothing, and then he nodded.

They were of a similar size. She didn't mind being small; it was the weight she didn't like.

• • •

Looking through her new window she saw shadowy figures. She wanted to see more clearly but if she stood any nearer, they disappeared and all she could see was outside, slightly blurred. Someone sunbathing. Someone cutting the hedge. Someone swimming.

Others might complain that their new windows were blurry glass but she liked it.

She could spend hours looking through it.

• • •

"Was that your little boy I saw?"

"Was? My son escaped. We squeezed him into the smaller mine lift and sent him to the surface. He is 25 now. Handsome and strong, with children of his own." But then, "I can't breathe." This always happened when he no longer wanted to talk.

The boy with the ball was most often seen in the hallways. Bouncing it, rolling it, dodging invisible opponents.

She told the miner this.

"My boy loved to play ball. Bounce bounce bounce until you wanted to scream. But you didn't because he is happy and a good boy."

Bounce bounce bounce until Neil knocked on her door, what is that? It's never been so loud, and they said pipes but they both thought ghosts.

She felt frightened, so frightened she asked Neil to stay and eat. She wished she could cook some of the meals from that website, but all she could make was pasta with bacon.

It went well, although they didn't speak much. He said, "Good to see you eating. Some of us worry you don't eat at all," and she laughed at that, because surely he was joking. He was tall, so tall he had to hunch into the armchair to fit. He told her funny stories about the buses because he was a bus driver. She hadn't ever laughed so much and she wondered if this was what normal people did.

The intercom buzzed. "Visitors?" he said.

"Hello? Find me? It was the boy's voice today, the father putting on the boy's voice. He did that sometimes. He said the boy went into the mine because there was nowhere safe for him to go. No one for him to be with.

"I left him at the top once but found him cut, bruised and speechless. He didn't talk again. I do all the talking for him."

The neighbour heard every word. "Is it someone in the foyer? Or one of the other apartments?"

This hadn't occurred to her. Was someone making fun? Taking advantage? No. There were too many details. It was too real.

"Could have been should have been was," the miner said.

"My parents said that," she told the miner. Neil had gone. She hadn't noticed. "When my sister never came home."

"Oh, no," he said, and he started crying. "Your loss is so great," he said, and he didn't even know the story. That she and her sister had been taken by a man who said he was their uncle but who was not.

"I didn't even breathe. I can be so quiet it's like I'm not there. You've never heard anything as quiet," and that was as much of a joke as anything she'd ever made.

She always told people, "We both escaped him. We both got away. But then I lost her. She ran away from me. I couldn't catch her."

She'd always lied.

"I didn't mean to. I didn't do it on purpose. I loved her." And that was the absolute truth. There was no viciousness in it.

"I was quiet. I curled myself up small and invisible. She couldn't do that. She was much bigger."

"Was she a fatty? Not like you. You sound nice. Sexy. You sexy?" In the mine window her reflection almost did look that way.

"I ran away while he killed her."

He sobbed gently.

"Can you still hear me?

"Of course I can hear you. Loud and clear. Bright as a button. Clear as a bell."

There was so little left of her 'self'. Life had caused her damage.

He sobbed, and she thought she heard others too.

"Did you find my boy?"

"How did he get out?"

"In the small lift. The mine lift. They left him to die, too. But we got him out."

She didn't tell him that in the official announcement no boy was mentioned as surviving.

His son materialised in the corner of her lounge room, or had he always been there? Curled up in a ball. Making himself tiny.

"He curled up tight in there. We gave him one thing each to remember us by. He survived. I know he did."

• • •

There was a knock at her door. She fixed her hair, adjusted her clothes, opened the door, thinking it was Neil come to see if she would go to the monthly BBQ, downstairs, with the other tenants.

No one was there. She sniffed, trying to catch the scent, and she stepped out to see if there was a warmth left behind. But nothing. She felt a sudden chill so went back inside and made herself a hot lemon drink. She didn't want to go to the BBQ alone.

She heard her neighbours but didn't join them. She sat in her apartment and heard the voices. The laughter. She peeked out. They were all by the water feature in the courtyard. Material from the mine of course. They lived in a beautiful place.

If she ever did go she enjoyed it. They spent the whole time talking about the ghostly things they'd seen and heard. You couldn't talk to many people about that. The last time she went it was good. She'd been pretty that night, flushed from a small virus and slightly silly on wine.

She'd never told anyone about her sister. She never could.

She survived because her sister didn't.

"I couldn't go back home," she told the miner, although she did for a while. "Not ever again. Because that place, home, I was different then. If I went back they'd all know what I am. Not a good person."

Then he said, "It wasn't your fault. You wouldn't be here if you didn't do what you did. You wouldn't be here to talk to me. Your voice has saved my life. You can come and find us. That is your purpose. You were just following orders. We, too. But your actions led to your freedom. Ours led to imprisonment. *Stay there*, they said. *We will collect you*, but they never did. He took the last cable car, our boss. Not a good man. He wouldn't even take my son."

• • •

The festivities grew louder downstairs and she leaned up against her window, watching them. She pictured herself down there, amongst them, but also imagined the awkward silence as she appeared.

The intercom spoke. "You should come down here. Rescue us. You will be a hero. Imagine! There will be a whole wall in your honour." She had told him about the history on display in the foyer.

• • •

There were blueprints and maps on the Once Was wall in the foyer. Looking at them, she thought she knew where the second exit was. At a distance, so perhaps not filled in. Perhaps accessible.

• • •

"We'll be waiting to gaze on your beautiful face," he said.

• • •

Looking through the window she thought someone waved at her and on a whim, she dressed in the gym gear she'd last worn in high school. It hung loose on her; it must have stretched in the wash. Her sneakers were clean, almost unworn, and she felt guilty because she'd bought them for walks in the country, around the lake, for exercise, and they were barely touched.

She went downstairs, carrying a shopping bag for cover. If she couldn't find the entrance she would go shopping. She had a craving for passionfruit.

The land had changed in the 50 years since the blueprint was drawn and the mine built. Swimming pool, landscaping, clearances; all of it made the blueprint hard to follow. There was a marker though, in the basement where the entrance once was so she knew where to start. She counted steps from there, used a compass, and eventually found a large pile of rocks, bird feathers, spider webs and debris.

She considered going back for gloves but didn't want to risk seeing anyone. She was sure they were still laughing at her.

It took her an hour to clear it away. She tore a nail, and sweat stung her eyes and soaked her clothes. She thought about the miners, working physically like this everyday. She couldn't do it; this was too hard.

Underneath there was a mound of scorched earth about three metres in diameter.

A spade would be good, but she scrabbled in the dirt and it was loose packed, not clamped down.

She dug until she reached perished wood, rusted metal. A small cage. Digging further around it, she braced herself for a smell. Was he here? Had the poor child died here?

All that was left was a ball and six small pieces of glass. The ball was perished, faded, but she knew it was his. He had been here.

The glass was beautiful.

She felt a cool breeze coming from below, and a sweet smell, an expensive aftershave, or perhaps incense. She thought she'd take a look, a quick look down there, but try as she might she couldn't fit in the cage. She was too fat. She stretched out again, holding in her hand six small glass objects she'd found. The mementoes. The messages the six men had sent with the boy. She thought, he died in here. He must have, or he would have kept this with him. He would never let them go.

• • •

In her apartment, she stood by the window. It was dark outside now, so all she could see was her own reflection, and the boy beside her. He was almost as tall as her but thinner, so much thinner. She took a stick of lipstick and drew around him, made an outline. Once she fit within that, she would fit into the cage.

She went to the kitchen and threw out all but the basics. She tossed butter, bread, anything fatty. Left only the fruit and vegetables.

• • •

It took six weeks to lose enough weight. She stopped feeling hungry after the first week. She drank a lot of lemon juice in water and enjoyed the frequent trips to the toilet to urinate. It felt cleansing.

The miner urged her on. "We're looking forward to meeting you. It's going to be lovely. Oh, I bet your skin is soft and warm. Like a peach on a summer afternoon."

• • •

She left a note for Neil under his door explaining where she was, and walked back to the secondary entrance. She squeezed herself into the cage. Neil would think she was crazy but that didn't matter. It felt good to have someone to tell.

She lowered herself down into the dark. So cold. She thought of her mauve cardigan on the back of the chair and wished for it. She'd brought very little, thinking that men who'd survived 20 years underground would not need emergency rations. They missed so much, wanted so much, but they could have that when she led them to the surface. Or when she convinced someone to rescue them, to bring them up and tell their story.

She took a torch with her and matches. "These lamps have not been lit in a long time," Jarod had told her.

And she had sultanas, a taste of the sun, she thought the miners would like.

The rope squealed but held firm as she dropped further and further into the mine.

It took a moment to realise she'd reached the bottom, and then many more minutes before she could coax her stiffened limbs to move. She stretched out. The ground was soft, as if soaked with water, and her feet sank to the ankles.

She lifted a foot, feeling the ground suck at her, but she could walk ahead. It was so cold her teeth chattered, but she'd been that cold before and knew she could get warm again.

It was dark ahead. And so very quiet she could hear her blood pulsing in her ears.

Footfall? Could she hear that? And a pickaxe?

She stopped still, not knowing where to go. What to do.

"Jarod?" she called out. "Are you there?" With sudden cold clarity she understood what she was doing.

She was calling to a man dead 20 years.

She heard a sigh, a deep, weary one, to the left.

She saw a light ahead, flickering, and thought someone had come to show her the way. "Jarod? Is that you?" but there was no answer. She walked toward the light, which shifted and lifted but didn't move ahead. Her heart beat faster as she approached, only to see it was her own torchlight reflected on a left-behind gas lamp, hanging from a hook on the wall of rock. She reached up to touch the wall and the cold chilled her fingertips as if she was touching ice.

She scrabbled around in the near-dark, trying not to breathe too deeply because the air felt laden with minerals. She found the mine intercom and lifted it, joy-filled, knowing one of her neighbours would hear her and send help. She felt crushed, flattened.

"Hello?" she said. "Yoo hoo?" but there was nothing but the long, long echo of emptiness.

And then the sound of a bouncing ball. She followed it as it became louder and louder, until she felt a small, firm hand take hers. Calloused, as if he'd been digging and digging.

He tugged her arm. In the dull glow of her torch she could see him turning back to smile at her as he led her onward. With each step her feet felt heavier. She hummed to make a noise beyond nothing, but the only tune she could remember was one her sister used to sing and that brought the familiar guilt, heavy and dark, so she stopped.

• • •

He dropped her hand. She heard Jarod say, "We just want to be remembered. We just want someone to gaze on our faces one more time."

And she thought, he can hear me. They can see me.

The men surrounded her. She could see them so clearly; they looked like they did in the photo but older, wiser, kinder. They looked so kind, so cold.

They caressed her, all of them, and while the tenderness made her pulse race, the cold of them made her blood freeze and made her heart slow slow slow and her eyelids droop. She tried to curl up small but they stretched her out and pressed into her, taking the last vestiges of warmth, stopping her breath, stopping her.

"We just want to be seen," he said.

But she would not be seen again.

BLUEBEARD'S DAUGHTER

ANGELA SLATTER

"Here," she says, "have an apple."

Yeah, right. As if I know nothing about stepmothers. As if I know nothing about apples. But I'm polite and I'm not stupid, so I put the green orb in my bag, and thank her.

"Now, don't forget: you'll need to be careful and cunning. You'll need your wits about you. It's hidden deep, the treasure, and there will be all kinds of obstacles." Hands on hips, Orienne surveys me critically. "It's a long journey, but you've got the most fat on you of all of us. You'll be fine; the exercise will do you good. Don't forget that apple, Rosaline; no cakes or pastries."

As if I'm likely to forget that bloody apple; I know what she's done to it. Trust her to manage a dig at my weight—I come from a long line of women who eat their grief, but my father's fifth wife is of thin stock. Busy, busy, busy all the time, bustling and fidgeting, organising and ordering, burning away everything she eats, hating anyone to be idle; she's got the energy of a hummingbird and a heart that softens for her own child alone. Gods forbid anyone should spend an afternoon sitting on their arse, reading a good book.

That was how I got caught; sitting on my arse, buried in a book, oblivious to the world. The rest of the family had made themselves scarce, knowing she was on a tear about too little food, too many mouths; as if we were poor, as if my father didn't provide for all the children he'd sired, and all those that had been brought by previous wives and left here when said wives had gone.

As if it wasn't just an excuse to cull the herd.

As if she hadn't done it before.

As if a horrifyingly large number of my siblings—full, half, and step—haven't ended badly.

"Here's the map, but you won't need a compass, you've got a wonderful sense of direction." We both know I get lost in the library sometimes, but it's no use contradicting her; she'll just raise her voice and talk right over the top of me, pretending this is a serious task. A journey from which I'll return. "Remember to be polite and biddable to any creature you meet on the way. Try to be home before winter . . . of course, your natural *insulation* should keep you warm. We're all counting on you, Rosaline. And don't forget that apple, if you're peckish."

She finishes adjusting the strap of my satchel and stands back, surveying me with the resigned disappointment of a woman who knows she's done her best with second-rate materials. "Well, that's you taken care of then."

Or so she bloody well hopes.

• • •

My father likes being married and, despite everything, he's apparently catnip for women, whether for his fortune, castle, or the great virile bushy beard, who can say.

Matrimony's never worked out too well for his wives, however, but they all appear to think it's a good idea at the time. None of them ever seems to think he'll turn on them. None of them ever seems to consider *not* entering the locked room, even when he makes it very clear that possession of the key comes with responsibilities and consequences. None of them ever seems to think they'll get caught. Eventually, they all go—even my own mother—and open the door to take a peek inside.

All of them until *her*.

I have to give Orienne credit, she's smart. If she has ever entered that room—whether by witchcraft or dint of the same skill I've used: lockpicking—she's managed to keep it a secret from my father. Whenever he returns from a voyage, she'll hand him back the keys, and he looks carefully at the smallest one—he always has the wives' copies made of gold because it's so soft and there's no hiding if it's been used, even once—and without fail, he nods with a kind of satisfied surprise. He'll give her a resounding kiss before carrying her up to their bedchamber. Maybe that's why he's so wilfully blind to the dwindling number of children in his house.

Dispatched to get water, Zipporah and Judith both met an old woman by a well. The former, sweet-natured, helped her without complaint, and was rewarded with diamonds, pearls and roses falling from her lips each time she spoke. She vomited such things for three days before she died, spitting blood and spewing slivers of her own torn flesh. Judith, wary of her sister's fate, let her sharp tongue have rein when the very same old woman asked for assistance—she threw herself from a cliff when toads and vipers began to accompany her words. Ada and Beatrice, Sara and Lizzie, were sent with charity baskets to help the less-fortunate who lived deep in the woods, but none of the girls was ever seen again, although it was observed on several occasions that the wolves looked particularly well-fed that winter. Minette, Anya and Louise were crushed in an unfortunate mattress stacking accident whilst setting up a test for a potential bride for Armand, my stepmother's son; come to think of it, the bride died, too. Leticia, playing with matches, trying to stay warm in the icy attic to which Orienne had banished her, managed to self-immolate. Gabriella was scalded to death when a vat of boiling broth mysteriously tipped from the hob. Susannah was carried away by a kelpie while crossing a river she'd been assured was *perfectly safe*. And Lucy . . . Lucy, was turned into a hare, somehow, and torn apart by our stepmother's pack of brachet hounds. After each and every misfortune, Orienne wept cold, glittering tears and proclaimed 'How dreadful!" in most convincing tones, at least in Father's hearing.

Six daughters remain, of whom I am one and, apparently, the next to be shuffled aside in Orienne's quest to secure her own future: no other heirs will be tolerated. I thought I was safe, and for a long while I was, being Father's favourite . . . but after Lucy I thought, *Enough's enough*. I complained to Father and discovered I'd made a mistake; favourite or no, not a word against his beloved, trusted wife would be tolerated. So I've been in the dog house for a few weeks and, with my parent having departed on yet another trip, Orienne's decided it's time to move against me. I should have known better. The only one who's secure is Armand, her very own boy, her sole offspring whom she loves to distraction, and the single good thing she brought into this house.

He looks a little like her, slender and pale, with blackest of black hair and blue eyes, though where hers are ashen-frost, his are summer-sky. He's tall and broad-shouldered, and beautiful my stepbrother, so beautiful that even I can't ignore him, no matter how I feel about his mother. And he's been kind to me, even though Orienne never has been. He likes books and we talk about them, and one time we almost . . . I'll miss him, talking to him, staring at him, and almost-ing him.

• • •

I'd set off from the castle nice and early into a morning that was already puffing out wintery breath, waved off by those who cared or simply wished to make sure I was gone. Orienne watched longer than the others—I kept looking over my shoulder to see if she was still there, and she was so I couldn't do what I wanted, which was to go left at the fork in the road, not right. But she was still staring, so I gave one last wave and stoically traipsed onwards as if I had every intention of going where she wants me to go. As if I was going to do what she wants me to do, which is die horribly either whilst trying to find objects that probably don't exist or eating the poisoned apple she's pressed on me as a snack. And even if the items in question are real, they won't be where she claims. But there'll be ogres, and trolls, and witches—the bad kind—or robber bridegrooms who've got more in common with my father than I'd like to think. But the things I'm supposed to look for, specifically a loaf of bread you can never entirely devour and a bottle of wine that never runs out? They'll not be there.

After hours of walking the path through the forest isn't too bad. The road is wide and not terribly rutted, and the leafy canopy above isn't so thick that it blocks the sun, creating a darkness that might encourage predators to come and bid me welcome. My boots are sturdy and comfortable, well-worn; it should be a while before blisters appear, but I can feel my thighs chaffing under my skirts as I walk, *oosh*, *oosh*, *oosh*. I should have insisted on grabbing a pair of trews before I left, no matter how fast she was hustling me out of the castle; I barely had time to pin my long hair back. I'll find a pair of britches as soon as I can, whether I have to beg, borrow, or steal them from someone's washing line.

Which may be an opportunity that will present itself sooner rather than later: there's a little trail winding off the roadway, compressed by soft shoes and leather-padded paws. Through the fat tree trunks I can see where it leads: to a cottage that looks small and neat, but odd. The tones are all wrong, the textures . . . I squint. It should be wood and wattle and daub; it should be thatch and glass and stone . . . but all I can make out is a riot of colours that don't naturally occur in woodland architecture. I can't resist: I *must* investigate. If there's a chance of satisfying my curiosity and need for trousers, I'll risk it.

I creep along the path, and then pause before stepping into the clearing. The place doesn't look dangerous. There's a lot of brown but it's a cinnamon-sprinkle kind of brown; there's frosting of blue and green and yellow and rose along the eaves and around the window frames. I stare a little longer. The garden inside the fence is full of flowers but they don't move in the breeze like proper ones should; they stay stiff, quite rigid as if made of sterner stuff, like liquorice and marzipan, with leaves of sugared mint. The windowpanes look like clear-blown toffee. It's one of the most bizarre things I've ever seen and that's saying something.

I'm about to commit to the glade when a hand grabs my arm and clamps tight. I bite down on a scream purely because it won't help matters at all, and I remember I put the kitchen knife I stole inside my pack, so there's no getting to it now. I swing about and see blue, blue eyes, high cheekbones and pouting lips, hair as black as ebony. My heart, embarrassingly enough, steps up its rhythm, kicks out a little tarantella.

"Hello," says Armand. "What are you doing here?"

"What am *I* doing?" I hiss. "I'm supposed to be here. *Your* mother sent me away."

He ignores the tone and says, "Not here, though, you're meant to be on the main road, heading towards the mountains so you can complete your quest and come back to us."

"I've been walking for hours. I need somewhere to rest. And to find breeches." I peer at him. "Why are *you* here?"

"I wanted to help." He shrugs and I can see it's the truth, plain and simple. Sweet boy just wanted to render assistance in a princely fashion. "Come on, let's get a move on."

"No," I begin and am interrupted by a weak shriek coming from inside the weird little cottage. Then there's a cry for help, a woman's voice cracked with age and fear. "Well, that settles it," I say, and head off at a run, through the gate in the white picket fence that smells like peppermint, along the path made of humbugs, towards the Turkish Delight window boxes bloom-full of icing-sculpted flowers in a riot of hues.

I knock on the door, which is sturdy yet peculiarly pliant; it thuds nicely beneath my hand, but gives a little too, like a firm sponge. It smells like gingerbread.

"Are you alright?" I call and the wail comes again, trickling to a whimper as Armand thunders up behind me. I turn the lemon sherbet door handle and shove.

A pink cloud that smells like musk and dreams puffs around us as we collapse over the threshold. Any queries as to anyone's safety or otherwise expire on our lips as we fall immediately into a deep slumber.

• • •

I wake up overheated and flushed, the smell of warm sugar in my nostrils. My face is pressed against something tacky on the floor . . . no, not the floor. The bottom of a cage, a cage made of candy canes shaped and melded into a box, not big enough for me to stand, but I can sit if I slouch. I roll up, pulling painfully away from the gluey surface. My head feels as if candyfloss, blown in one ear, has chosen not to go out the other, but rather take up residence in my skull.

I look around, blinking. My satchel, with the kitchen knife in it—not to mention my little roll of lockpicks—lies on the flags beside the door, for all the good it will do me. Idly, I wonder how long it would take for me to chew my way out.

There's all the usual furniture you'd expect of a little old lady's cottage, although made of substances not generally associated with furniture: marshmallow armchairs with antimacassars of fondant lace; tables of fudge; rugs of pulled taffy; paintings with wafer picture frames; jelly bean footstools; a peanut brittle bedstead, with chocolate brownie pillows and a coverlet that looks like woven ribbon candy, atop which lies Armand, still unconscious. It all looks adorable and, in spite of everything, my stomach rumbles, and that's what attracts the attention of the little old lady herself, who's diligently stoking the fire beneath the enormous oven in one corner. She's wizened and ancient, shoulders rounded, and back bent. She limps over to me, fingers thin and twigish, hair like steel wool, nose crooked.

"Ah!" She cackles. "Awake, awake, awake!"

"I rushed in to help you, you know," I tell her with reproach. "You tricked me."

"Well, I'd never get a meal otherwise. People are very particular about not getting eaten. Do all sorts of things to avoid it." She shakes her head. "Good meals are few and far between for the likes of me."

"Bad witch."

"We're all bad witches at some point, dearie. Have you not worked that out yet?"

I don't say anything because I know she's right, more or less.

"Anyway, though you won't appreciate this, it's pleased I am to see you. Far too many skinny girls nowadays, not enough for a filling repast." She eyes my well-padded flanks. "I'll have you salted and smoked and put away for the cold months! Meatloaf! Steaks! Chops and ribs! Ah, the soups your bones will make—I've got the best pearl barley and dried peas set by. Oh, and black pudding! I've not had that in so long." She fairly salivates.

"What have you done to Armand?"

"Nothing. Yet." She grins lasciviously and she's missing teeth here and there. I notice the shackle around Armand's ankle, a genuine iron item in this place of sugar and spice. "He's a heavy sleeper, still under for now, but I'll be on top of him soon and that'll wake him up."

I think my jaw drops at that.

"What? I've got needs! I get lonely."

"Didn't anyone ever teach you that fulfilling your own needs at the cost of others is not okay?"

"Do you think anyone ever bothered teaching me anything?" she sneers, and glares at me for long moments. "Those of us who are on our own, with no one to care for us, we make our own way, our own rules as and how we must."

And though part of that makes sense, I can't see how it justifies turning me into a five-course feast and Armand into a sex slave. I'm about to tell her so when there's a groan from the bed.

"Ah. Time to change into something a little less comfortable." She draws herself up, pats at her dark grey skirts, her iron-sky hair, and begins to whisper a spell. The words come out as a mist, slowly falling and encircling her as it goes, until she's enveloped in a minty-fresh fog that thickens and thickens until she at last steps out of the cloud of it, thoroughly changed.

She's tall and blonde; her squinty raisin eyes are large and limpid and green, furrowed lips are full and ripe as cherries, her age-spotted skin is milky and smooth, her cloth of gold dress is a thing to cause Orienne to turn jade.

"Neat trick," I say, more than a little envious that someone can change their shape so easily.

She pulls a swathe of cloth from a shelf and says, "Thank you. Now, I like a little privacy, so don't take this personally," and wraps the cloth around my cage as if I'm a bird being put to sleep for the night.

I hear her move away, begin to coo sweet nothings to the rousing man.

• • •

I examine the lock on my prison: it's made of metal and I can work with that. My lockpicks might be out of reach, but there are more than enough pins in my hair to make up for it. It takes me a little longer than usual—I'm less skilled with a clip, and I have to try to block out the sounds of her seduction and Armand's drowsy responses—but eventually I hear a *snick*. The door cracks open without too much noise, while I, on the other hand, make a racket and a half getting out of the cage. I leave skin behind, my legs are all pins and needles, and don't want to hold me up as I wobble about, flailing at the draped sheet.

All of which gives the witch time to struggle off the bed, bodice unhooked, hair dishevelled, skirts getting in the way. Although she's magicked herself a young woman's body, she still moves like an old one, and that gives me the chance to grab a metal poker from beside the oven, just as she's coming towards me, just as she's raising her hands, just as she's moving her lips to spill out some curse, some hex, some enchantment that will turn me into a toad or a goose or an entrée.

I'm faster with the poker than she is with her words, and I split her skull like an egg. The spell shatters as easily as her head does, and both spill out grey and red. In a moment, she's shrunk to fairy dust and floss, fine and silver as spider webs. I wait for the cottage to dissolve around us, to melt and drip into a sugary apocalypse, that's generally the way things go, but no. It stays. It sticks. It's not connected to her like so many magic things are to their masters. Perhaps she didn't make it, perhaps she just wandered in, found it. Perhaps it just grew up around her, made strange on its own.

"Rosaline," mumbles Armand, stretched out on the bed, his shirt lacings loose, his trousers disturbed in more ways than one. "Are you alright?"

"Uh huh. Nothing a good bath won't cure." I move towards him, throwing one final suspicious look at the witchy mess on the floor. Into the oven with that as soon as I get my stepbrother free. I'm faster with the hairpin this time, and have him unfettered in a trice. "There."

"Thank you." He pulls me up to lie beside him, strokes my face, my hair, my lips, my throat, my chest, oh my! Part of me thinks *This isn't for you, this is just what the witch started*, but the other part, the hopeful part says *He followed you, he came after you, he wanted to keep you safe—and for the love of all that's holy, this has got to be better than those spotty stableboys!*

When he kisses me my heart feels as if it's unfurling like the petals of a flower blooming in the sun.

• • •

We can, I think, be together. We can make a future, untethered from our pasts, from our family. *We can be happy.*

"We can be happy," I say aloud, curled around Armand. "We can stay here."

"Oh, no," he answers, blinking. "We have to go. You have to find the loaf of bread that can't be eaten up and the bottle of wine that never runs out. It's the only way we'll make it through winter."

"What?" I ask stupidly, all the glowing feelings that were surging through me, thudding happily in my chest, warming my flesh, buzzing between my legs with a lovely throbbing pulse . . . all of them stop, freeze over, feel like a coating of ice on my sweaty skin.

"We have to bring them back to Mother. She'll be waiting." He smiles. "She said you'd never make it, that you'd never return home again. That's why I came after you, to keep you motivated." He slaps my ample backside as if I'm an ornery horse he's been obliged to ride.

"Your mother wants me to die out here, Armand, the way all the other sisters have on their fool's errands." *You stupid bastard, you'll die too—whatever will Mother say to that?*

He sits up, stares down at me. "Don't be silly. Mother wouldn't do that. Mother loves her stepdaughters. It's not her fault you're all so unfortunate."

He wanted to help *her*, not me. He's too thick to realise I'm not meant to succeed. He'll never believe it of her, has never suspected her of any ill intent towards the children that aren't her own—no more than my father will. And as I stare into his eyes I can see her there, as a white dot in the pupils, an unmelting ice queen, a woman who'll always be there before me. Someone he'll never let go; someone he'll always love best. I'll never hold him as tightly as she does. My heart tightens, curls in upon itself, and I realise this is what my father feels every damned time one of the wives lets him down. He allows himself love, to care, and to trust . . . and they requite him so badly. I think I understand him at last.

"I'm hungry," says Armand. Armand who's clueless, who's blind to what's beneath his nose; who'll happily drive me to my doom all to please his murderous mater.

And I think about secret chambers and poisoned hearts, and lackwits who can't be trusted. I roll out of bed, find my satchel by the door, and fish out a green orb, crisp and sweet-looking, tempting as can be.

"Here," I say, "have an apple."

LOOK HOW COLD MY HANDS ARE

DEBORAH BIANCOTTI

Look how cold my hands are.
—*Last reported words of Báthory Erzsébet*
8 August 1560 – 21 August 1614.

Erzsébet was at her desk. "Have you tallied the day's costs? The fence around the village paddock, the church fees."

Church fees again.

Costs were relentless for the Báthory estate. And a relentless aggravation.

"Yes, Countess." The simpleton, Fickó, crinkled his face into a frown. He sat sprawled on the floor with the parchment between his knees.

Erzsébet rubbed at her temple. "And then incomings?"

There were always fewer of those.

She picked at the cold roast lamb on the tray at her elbow and calculated the monies for collection. "Payments owed on our castle at Beckov. Sales from the hemp crops. Use the coarser parchment for your workings, Fickó."

"Yes, Countess."

She pulled a quill from the quiver of ink and wiped it on the cloth at her elbow. Then she trimmed the candle wick and returned to her letter.

To Ferenc Batthyány, December 30, 1610

May God bless you in all your endeavours. We are arrived at Csejte manor this eve, not yet advancing to the castle.

In the depth of winter, the castle took longer to warm. Erzsébet would save on firewood if she could.

We saw many of the poor by the roads. But all follow loyally our King and saviour.

She grunted when she wrote that about the king. The Slovak witch, Erzsi Majorova, had taught her many curses. She cursed the king now.

By God's grace, my health improves. The headaches and visitations of which I wrote previously have lessened.

It was mostly true, though the pain in her left eye was almost constant these days.

I trust it is your considerate words and the careful ministrations of my healer, Anna Darvulia—

"Another letter, Countess?"

Erzsébet jumped. "Anna! I didn't hear you come in."

Anna gestured. "I see you write to Batthyány again. Does he write back? Or has his young wife stopped him?"

"Business about our adjoining property." Erzsébet put a hand across her letter. "And I may write to whomever I please. I am the Countess Báthory. My husband was the greatest war hero in the Kingdom of Hungary. My uncle was King of Poland. I am descended from princes in Transylvania! My daughters' husbands—"

"You are the most powerful woman in Christendom," Anna supplied.

"Don't interrupt!" Erzsébet snapped.

She would punish that impudence in anyone else. But she had never punished Anna. They were closer than sisters.

"Which jewels will you wear, Countess?" Anna asked, as if Erzsébet hadn't spoken. "You never go anywhere without your jewellery."

"Go? We only just reached the manor—"

But then she heard the heavy footfall of visitors across the stone floors downstairs.

"Who's here?"

Some superstition shook her. She slipped a wristlet of emeralds and diamonds over her hand, almost by instinct. As if it might protect her.

"That's what I came to tell you," Anna replied with a smile. "It's the Lord Palatine."

Erzsébet rose to her full height. "The king's fool! And you let him into my manor without my permission?"

Anna's smile was cold. It was always cold. "He *is* the Palatine."

Second only to the king in Hungary. If the Palatine were here again so soon, it meant the witch's curse had failed.

Erzsébet checked the impulse to take out her rage on Anna. To hit her hard across the face and leave a grubby stain of ink and blood.

Anna stood unblinking. She was no more afraid of Erzsébet than a stone is afraid of the sky.

Perhaps *that* explained why Erzsébet couldn't hit her. Anna was the only one who didn't fear the wrath of the Countess of Báthory.

"Light a fire in the drawing room," Erzsébet commanded.

She crossed to her dresser to check her reflection in the copper mirror. Her dark gown was unbuttoned, her pale undergarments stained with sweat and dust. The ride to Csejte had left her skin pinched and red from icy winds.

She smoothed her hands across her face. "They come at midnight? And on Christmas Eve? Parliament is not in session. Can it even be the king's business they attend?"

Anna moved behind her. "Perhaps they are charged to deploy the king's debt to your title, Countess?"

Unlikely. The king had owed the seat of Báthory since before Erzsébet's husband had died.

But it was unusual for the Palatine to be on the roads so late in the year. She hoped it was only about the fighting, some border breach by the unchristian Turks.

She hoped it wasn't about the allegations against her. Surely she had convinced Thurzó an investigation was unwarranted.

She reached for the powders below her mirror and smoothed a pale tincture across her cheeks. She looked old. It had been a hard year and the king's debt weighed heavily.

"With what the king owes the seat of Báthory, I could buy nineteen castles. *Nineteen!*"

"Or you could afford to keep the castles you have," Anna said. "No more begging Batthyány for assistance."

"That is not what I was doing!" Erzsébet snapped.

But it was true, she relied on her neighbours more than she wanted to. There were recurring bills for the Nádasdy-Báthory lands, including villages and churches. Her husband, Ferenc, was dead these six years and it was up to her to ensure her children's futures. Her daughters were provided for, but Pál was the only surviving Nádasdy son, and he was still too young for leadership.

The king must pay his debts.

The king *must* pay his debts.

"Who hosts the Palatine? Is my son arrived?"

"Not yet. Lord Palatine requested Szuzanna accompany him."

Erzsébet froze.

Szuzanna had come from the Lord Palatine's own household. Consequently, Erzsébet had never trusted her.

"You left him with that idiot *maid?* She's not even nine."

"She seemed safe enough," Anna said. "They asked only to view the manor."

"To view it?" Erzsébet frowned. "What have they seen so far?"

Anna smiled that cold, empty smile again. "I believe they have seen everything."

• • •

Anna was irresponsible, not alerting Erzsébet immediately to the intrusion of the Palatine.

And then to leave him in the presence of young Szuzanna. He would take that as disrespect. The lady of the house should greet him properly.

Erzsébet may be close to broke, but her lands and assets meant she was still one of the richest women in the world. Her peers were the Protestant ranks of Hungarian nobility. Even Palatine Thurzó himself was a cousin.

She reached the drawing room. Empty, the fire unlit.

"Anna! Where is he?" She moved from the seating area to the long dining hall. "Where is he? *Where is he!*"

Tabitha appeared in a doorway. Tiny, porcelain-skinned Tabitha. Her eyes were shadowed from some winter sickness. It made her only slightly less beautiful, but her beauty came mainly from youth. All the young were beautiful for a time.

"The Lord Palatine is in the basements, lady," Tabitha offered.

"You idiot girl!" Erzsébet shoved her.

There was a hard thud as Tabitha collided with the wall. By then Erzsébet was already out of the room.

She hurried down the slippery steps without a candle, holding tight to the stone wall. Below, she could see the glow of lights and hear the murmur of men's voices.

She hesitated on the threshold, getting her breath. She was not used to creeping through her own home.

Through a doorway she glimpsed Palatine Thurzó with eight armed men, lit by tallow candles. Probably sourced from her own supplies. She quashed a moment of rage at whoever had furnished them with light.

Pál's tutor was also there, Imre Megyeri, a look of sly triumph on his face. Duplicitous meddler! Reverend Ponikenusz was with them, of course. Grasping, accusing Ponikenusz. The man who had called her out during Sunday service and accused her of all sorts of sins. And in front of her own people!

Hadn't Erzsébet provided for the church? Hadn't she paid burial fees for every one of her dead girls?

Szuzanna saw her first. Fear pimpled the girl's grimy skin. She raised a hand to point.

Erzsébet swept into the room. The men turned to her as one. Even from here, she could smell the road on their filthy clothes. Their beards glittered with ice. Under a dusting of frost they wore heavy travelling cloaks. Where their cloaks were shouldered, the embroidered vests and coats of office showed.

Official business, then.

Too late she realised her sons-in-law were also there. Anna's husband, Count Nikolaus Zrínyi, and Katalin's husband, Count György Drugeth de Homonnay. Zrínyi at least had the decency to look away but de Homonnay met her glare with his own.

The guards held three of her serving women. Dorotya Semtész, Ilona Jó Nagy, and Katarína Benická. They looked at Erzsébet with defeat and pleading.

"My lady—" Dorotya sobbed.

Erzsébet silenced her with a hand.

She bowed once to the Palatine. Curtly, to let him know how he shamed her with his unannounced arrival.

"Lord Palatine Thurzó. What brings you to this lowly room?"

"We followed the sounds of screaming, Lady Widow Nádasdy."

Thurzó looked grim. He gestured once at the floor as if she had not noticed. Two girls lay there, naked, their wounds exposed.

One was already dead, her bloodied hair lying across her dry eyes. Three fingers were missing and there were stab marks on her arms. Her corpse had fallen across the pliers that had been used to gouge her face and chest.

The other girl had burns on her palms and feet. Her face was purple with bruises. Ilona must have taken the whip to her. Erzsébet recognised the deep welts across the girl's neck and ribs.

"See to the girl," Thurzó said to the armed men. "Take this one's statement and administer to her wounds. If it's possible."

"And if it's not, Lord Palatine?"

Thurzó glared. "If you can't ease her suffering medicinally, at least dispatch her with humanity. It's certainly more than the good Lady Nádasdy was willing to do."

There was an expression of disgust on his face.

Erzsébet stood tall, staring back fiercely. Only two girls, she reminded herself. Only two. She was the Countess Báthory. They would not make her account for the wounds of just two girls.

So long as the Palatine remained Lutheran enough to avoid the disruption of graves, there would be only two.

"Seize her," Thurzó said.

De Homonnay complied. He stepped forward and took hold of Erzsébet's wrist, but she wrenched away.

"How dare you!"

Her wristlet snapped, spewing emeralds and diamonds to the floor. Some fell into the congealing blood of the dead and dying girls. Under that oily sheen the emeralds turned black, but the diamonds were lost like so much grit.

"Chain the three serving women," Thurzó said to the guards. "Then follow me to the Castle. We'll search it in its entirety."

"By what authority—" Erzsébet began.

Palatine Thurzó lurched towards her. He sank his fingers into her hair, wrenching her out of de Homonnay's grasp so hard and fast her knees buckled. In her shock she clung to his wrist with both hands.

She let out a cry of rage and Thurzó shook her until her vision blurred. Then he dragged her from the room.

• • •

"Unhand me! *Unhand me!*"

Thurzó ignored her.

Her scalp was raw where he pulled her forward by the hair.

He dragged her through the manor and out into the winter night where the cold bit into her neck and hands.

Erzsébet stumbled. Thinking to pull herself free, she let her feet go out from under her. But Thurzó hauled her half-upright.

"Is this how you want your villagers to remember you?" he seethed.

At least thirty people from Csejte had braved the cold on Christmas eve to watch her shame. Erzsébet tried to stand tall, but Thurzó pushed her instead into a low bow.

"Help me!" she cried out to the villagers.

No one moved.

Thurzó began to drag her up the hill towards the castle. She could hear the murmurs and curses of the crowd. Curses! And no one stepped forward to save their lady's honour.

They would all pay for that later. When she was freed.

There was the clink of armour just behind her, and the snorts of horses forced to follow in a slow procession.

"Go on ahead!" Thurzó shouted. "Open the castle. Search the keep for more victims."

Erzsébet's throat went dry. "No."

By the time they breached the hill and crossed the drawbridge, her skirts were drenched with mud and snow. Her legs were frozen up to her thighs. Her knees were shaking. Her scalp burned and throbbed as Thurzó let her go.

She put her bare hands to the ice-cold wall of the castle to hold herself upright. She was gasping.

Thurzó grabbed her by the elbow and dragged her through the castle to her own drawing room.

No fire had been lit, of course. The stone walls seemed to trap the snow and ice and concentrate it more deeply here.

The only light was from a candle lit from one of the men's lanterns. Thurzó fixed the candle to the sideboard, letting it drip onto the polished wood. The weak light turned the space into monstrous shadows.

This room was stuffed with furniture, tapestries and carpets plundered from the war—blunt shapes in the gloom. The whole castle used to be like this, but over the years she had been forced to sell many pieces to cover bills.

Once, a room like this would have made her feel safe. Victorious. Now she felt hemmed in and crushed.

She hid her hands in her sleeves to hide their shaking.

"Leave us," Thurzó said to the men who followed them. "I'm sure the Lady Nádasdy poses no such threat to me as she did to those young women."

Erzsébet took a seat in the shadows. She waited until she was alone with Thurzó. "I should welcome you formally, my Lord Palatine. This castle was my wedding gift from the Nádasdy family."

"You know where the liquor is kept, then? By all that's holy, Erzsébet!" he snarled. "We've had reports. Six hundred dead. *Six hundred?*"

"Preposterous," she said calmly. "Who would claim such a thing?"

Thurzó was at the cabinet beside the empty fireplace, his thick cloak joining him to the shadows. "Szuzanna, for one."

"Who's going to believe a nine-year-old girl?"

"A good many people, I should think. She has an angelic little face. And you know the saying. Fools, children and drunken men will always tell the truth. People of Hungary still believe that."

He poured a generous shot of dark wine into a crystal glass. Then he reached under his cloak and pulled out a bloodstained cloth. He tossed it to her lap. Erzsébet made no move to withdraw her hands from her sleeves.

"Recognise that?" he asked. "The undershirt you wore on my last visit. After my entourage left, I understand you slew three serving girls in a rage while wearing that shirt."

Erzsébet kept her face blank.

"Szuzanna also tells me she has seen a register you keep on your desk. A list of the dead, written in your own hand."

"Was Szuzanna intended as your spy?"

Thurzó ignored her. "I've sent a man for the register—"

"Into my private chambers?" Erzsébet snapped.

But Anna would hide the register. Anna would do that for her.

Besides, Anna was too far implicated not to.

"What would *you* put the death count at?" he asked. "Four hundred? Two hundred?"

"None."

"Fifty?" Thurzó continued, almost to himself. "Thirty? How many is enough?"

He sounded calm. Perhaps, if he was calm, she had a chance. Perhaps he was only acting on orders from their greedy king.

She shivered. Thurzó must have seen the movement, because he leaned forward with the glass. When she made to wave it away, he snatched her hand and pressed the glass to her palm so hard the crystal dug into her cold skin.

"Take it," he said. "The good Lord knows there'll be few enough drinks for you after tonight."

He rose and returned to the sideboard. Erzsébet sipped at the wine. It had turned bitter in the frozen room.

"You'll want sustenance after your ride, Lord Palatine. Perhaps—"

"If you think I'll consume any foodstuffs served by you, Erzsébet Nádasdy, you're deluded." Thurzó said without turning.

"I meant only to be hospitable. You are my guest."

She emphasised the last word. Thurzó slouched back to the lounge, shaking dried mud into the fine weave of her furniture. "I heard what you did to Reverend Ponikenusz. You and your mad woman from the village. Erzsi, was it? You poisoned cake and then called out the evil spirits of—what was it?—*cats* to attack him. Of all things!"

"Ridiculous!"

"Isn't it?" Thurzó agreed with equanimity. "And yet, your sister was a witch and your mother-in-law was a witch. And so, I suppose, are you."

"We are all witches when you want to destroy us. All women."

Thurzó raised his glass in a kind of salute. "The priest refuses all contact with you. He trembled as much as that frightened girl, Szuzanna, when I called for him."

"You made a promise to my husband—"

"Ah, the Black Knight of Hungary! I wondered how long it would take you to mention him."

"—on his *deathbed*," she continued, enraged by his casual disregard, "that you would protect me from the king!"

"*And I am!*" he roared. "The king wants you hanged, naked, from a gallows in the centre of court. The whole village knows about you, Erzsébet. In fact, the whole country! The Lutheran pastors at Sárvár, the ones your husband silenced eight years ago with his extravagant and absurd donations, even they would speak against you now, I think."

"They would not!"

"And the Catholic brethren at the Viennese cathedral on Augustinerstrasse. They used to throw their pots at the wall to cover the noise of your girls *crying out for mercy*. They will make for convincing witnesses, too, when it comes to that."

"Convincing for a Catholic king," she replied bitterly.

"Yes, a Catholic king. One rumoured to be the next Holy Emperor of Rome."

"A Habsburg Emperor?" she spat. "Their ambition is as limitless as the Turks'! So the King sends you, good Lord Palatine, to ensure I cause no embarrassment in this ridiculous crusade of his. If this is about the crown's debt to me—"

"Oh, it's far too late for that."

"My husband held the Turks from our borders when King Matthias did nothing. The armies were starving and dying in their beds, and the king did nothing. No soldiers, no roads, no medicine. No schools! *We* did that. All of it. The nobility of Hungary has been protecting its people for decades."

Thurzó grunted. His face was in darkness.

She rose and he leaned forward to stop her leaving.

"Where do you think you're going?"

"To ask for someone to light the fire," she replied.

"Light it yourself. You have no servants, not anymore. After tonight, you won't even have a title."

Erzsébet hesitated. "What are you saying?"

"It's over for you, Erzsébet." His voice was almost gentle.

She resumed her chair slowly. "Impossible."

"Your people hate you. They are poor—"

"We are all poor. That's why they mock the nobles now, calling us Lord of Five Apple Trees and Mistress of Nine Pigs. We were impoverished fighting the king's wars for him. And yet, the king leaves our fine capital of Buda in the hands of the Ottomans."

"The capital is Pozsony now," Thurzó reminded her. He leaned back into the lounge where the shadows ate at him. "You complain of poverty, Erzsébet, but my wife tells me your jewels are the finest in the country. Plundered from the Turks, I understand."

"Gifts from my husband," Erzsébet replied. "I will give some to your good lady wife if you let me rally my cousins in Transylvania—"

"I shall do no such thing," Thurzó replied. "Did you really kill all the girls in your gynaecium?"

"No."

"You did, Erzsébet. After what I've seen tonight, I know the truth of it," Thurzó said sadly. "It's the complaints of their noble families that forced me back here."

She should have cursed all of them.

"They are only lesser nobles, György," Erzsébet said. "Not like you or I."

"Don't call me that, as if we are friends. Don't call me by my given name."

She tried to soften her voice. "It's all lies, Lord Palatine. I have enemies—"

"Easily three hundred people will testify to finding bodies in shallow graves around your grounds."

"Lies."

"I heard about the handmaid you killed in Predmier on the way home from my own daughter's wedding."

"An accident. The girl complained she was too warm in the carriage."

"So you stripped her, stood her naked in a barrel and poured icy water over her until she died. In the middle of winter. In the middle of the village square, for all to see. You call *that* an accident?"

Her hands were clenched around the glass he'd given her. She downed the rest of the contents in a gulp. "I have seen many maids corrected by my noble peers."

"And killed?"

Erzsébet replied quietly, "Even killed, if it was needful."

"Needful? *Needful?*"

"I gave those girls shelter and honest work! I am lady and mother to all my staff."

Thurzó stood restlessly. He rubbed his temple and stared at the empty glass that hung from his hand. "To think, I once told my daughter to be more pious and responsible. Like the virtuous Countess of Báthory, I said. I find your crimes hard to even comprehend."

"Because none of it is true."

"Stop *lying!*"

He threw his glass at the wall by the candle. The glass shattered. Broken shards flew through the air like a diamond rain, lit by the candle.

"Three dead on the way to your brother's funeral at Ecsed!"

"I was unwell," she offered. "The stress. The grief."

"Is that all it takes? My God! You have been *unwell* as long as I've known you. Always with a headache or a fit, or one of your strange little trances where you tremble and writhe in your bed."

"There is nothing little about my suffering!" Erzsébet snapped.

He looked at her with a kind of grim satisfaction. As if he had been proven right in some way.

"Was it Ferenc corrupted you?" he asked. "I would believe that. He was a vicious man."

"He was a war hero," she corrected him.

Thurzó grunted. "Is that why you refuse to take the widow's path, to retire and mourn your husband quietly? You hope to bask in the reflection of his so-called heroism?"

"How dare you," she said quietly. "I'm kept in the king's court by the strain of his debt—"

"Don't try to pin this on King Matthias, Erzsébet. Would you rather adopt the religious beliefs of the Turks than take up with your own king?"

"The king owes me."

"That's the very thing. He doesn't want to owe you."

"Then he should pay his debts!"

"And that's the other thing. He doesn't want to pay you."

"Then what does he propose?" Erzsébet asked.

"To take everything you own." Thurzó resumed his seat. "To impress the mighty Empire of Rome."

He said it with sarcasm. Thurzó was not Catholic, either.

Erzsébet felt the blood drain from her face. "He'll never get his hands on my lands."

"He will. He's the king."

"No! I've already bequeathed all my lands. Didn't your friends the counts, my sons-in-law, mention that? My daughters and son own the properties now."

Thurzó looked at her thoughtfully. Then he rose and moved to the cabinet, already unsteady on her liquor.

The candle needed trimming. It guttered, its light low, its oily smell edged with smoke. Its shadows made a mask of his face as he reached for another glass.

"No wonder they call you the Beast of Csejte," he said. "You are inhuman."

She pushed the rage down. She felt the pulse in her temple. She felt the tightness of her face, the itch of blood filling her skin.

"They call me many things, most of them unflattering," she said, lifting her chin. "I like to think you know me better, my good Lord Palatine."

He grunted, pouring more bitter wine. "I'm not sure I know you at all. Why kill *girls*, Erzsébet? You were seen as a champion of women. But I suppose they were easier for your old crones to subdue."

He returned to his seat. But where he'd been standing, she saw a kind of fire erupt, dancing along his outline as if the air still held the shape of him.

"I never killed any girls," she murmured.

"Are you going to lie to me like you lied to Reverend Ponikenusz? Are you going to blame the cholera?"

"It was not *me* that killed those girls."

"Ah! So who do you blame, if it wasn't you?" He raised his glass.

"The maids."

"The . . . ?"

"Anna Darvulia and the others. Dorotya Semtész and Katarína Benická. Ilona Jó Nagy was the worst. I could not stop them. I was afraid for my life."

Thurzó's face went blank. He was quiet a long time.

Then he put back his head and roared with laughter. "Merciful Mother, that's rich! You blame the *Darvulia* woman?"

Thurzó laughed some more, spilling wine across the lounge he sprawled on. "Oh, Erzsébet! Whoever digs a hole for someone else will fall in it themselves."

"You mock me, Lord Palatine? When I confess my greatest fear?"

"Please. You? Afraid! Hungary's mightiest noblewoman?" His laughter died. "I grant you, the Darvulia woman had an evil reputation. A wild beast in woman's skin. You might have had a chance, blaming her."

"Had?"

Thurzó chuckled softly.

"*Had?*" Erzsébet insisted.

"Before she died," Thurzó replied. "But who do you blame for the deaths that have piled up since? The girls keep disappearing, their bodies—"

"Anna has not died."

Thurzó's smile dropped. "Gods, it's true. You're mad."

"She is not dead," Erzsébet insisted. "She attended me in my bed chamber this evening."

"Stop it, Erzsébet," Thurzó said.

"Why do you say she is dead? *Why do you say that?*"

"That's enough! The fish stinks from the head. You are the Countess of Báthory. You are responsible for the actions of your people. Even those who died. Especially those, as it happens."

"She is. *Not.* Dead!"

Thurzó blanched. "She's been dead two years."

One of the guards entered the room unannounced. Erzsébet turned by habit to reprimand him.

"We've found more," the man said simply, not even looking at her. "Count de Homonnay asked me to collect you."

"Any alive?"

The man nodded gravely. "The old woman the villagers spoke of. The one who was taken for hiding her daughter from the . . . lady. But over a dozen found dead so far."

The man dared to glance at Erzsébet.

Thurzó dismissed the man at the door and got to his feet. "Come with me, Lady Nádasdy."

Erzsébet rose before he could manhandle her again.

Her head was spinning. A needlepoint of pain had bloomed behind her eye. Her hands began to jerk against her sides. There was a sharp, unpleasant feeling as if her skin was peeling off. White sparks of light danced in her vision.

She pressed her fingers to her temple, trying to stop the tingling. Trying to hold herself in. She felt stripped from her body.

Anna could not be dead.

She heard Thurzó from far away. "Don't play games with me, Erzsébet. Ferenc might have believed in your trances, but I don't."

When she was a girl, a healing woman told her the trances were the result of demons arguing under her skin. The arguments brought terrible headaches and pain.

Only Anna had taught her not to be afraid of them. That the demons were merely spirits, passing through her. She said Erzsébet should be glad for the pain. It proved the spirits had not abandoned her and never would.

"Hungary will not stand for your treatment of me," she murmured. She could feel the sweat on her face, despite the cold. "I demand a public trial. I insist on the right to defend my name."

For a moment she felt like a countess again. She saw Thurzó's glare harden as she came into her full power.

"That's exactly what the king wants," Thurzó told her. "He already knows what you fail to admit. No one is coming to your aid, Erzsébet. No one could withstand the embarrassment. Your uncle, in his letters, has practically disowned you. Your peers are looking the other way. Even that little neighbour of yours that you're so fond of—Batthyány, is it?—he won't stand up for you. Because to defend you would be to deny the King and the entire Habsburg family."

"After all my husband has done! And all *I* have done. The king would not dare deny me. It would shame the whole kingdom. It would imperil every noble of the country, if the king were to start meddling in our affairs."

"Your husband was a sadistic soldier ill-suited for courtly life. As are you."

"I'll give you land," she muttered.

"You have no land, remember? Besides, like you, I can't afford the maintenance of it. And no one else can afford to buy it. Land is practically worthless now. Perhaps you should offer it to the Turks?"

He held out a hand in summons. Erzsébet knew he meant to take her to the keep. She herself had not been there in months. The stink of death was too strong even for her.

"Where is my son? Why is my son not here?" she asked.

"We passed his retinue on the road. I suggested to him he would be better served by other lodgings this evening. His tutor will meet him there later," Thurzó said. "I will protect your children, Erzsébet. But you are lost."

• • •

They reached the keep.

Erzsébet had not been there in months. The stink of death was strong even for her. They had lit all the oil lamps they could find and hung them from hooks on the walls. But even their sooty stink did nothing to dampen the smell.

The armed guards were there with her sons-in-law, hands covering their noses. The fool priest was bent to the floor, murmuring prayers.

She hesitated on the threshold, blinking to clear her vision of the dancing, oily lights after the dark drawing room. "A cloth, if you will. Something for the odour."

No one moved to assist her. They barely looked at her. Their gazes were fixed on the mess on the floor.

The bodies had so disintegrated they barely resembled the girls they had been. They were blackened and icy, but at least the marks of torture were harder to discern.

Fickó was meant to bury these bodies in the forest.

Thurzó strode grimly to the centre of the room. "Lady Widow Nádasdy, I came here intending to place you in a convent—"

"A *Catholic* convent, Lord Palatine?" she spat. "For our king's sake? I am Protestant, as you know."

"—but having seen your crimes for myself, I cannot, in good conscience, allow you to be free. If even the priests fear you . . . " He looked to where Reverend Ponikenusz kneeled. "We treated even the Turks better than this."

"I demand a trial," Erzsébet said quietly.

"I won't let you dishonour your family's name with a public trial," Thurzó replied. He sounded tired. "I exercise my right as Palatine, second only to the King in Hungary, to sentence you privately. You will be walled up in this hellish castle for the rest of your life."

"You would have me *starve?*"

"We will leave some little space for ministrations. We will feed you, clean your pots."

"You took an oath to my husband."

"Your life will be spared, Widow Nádasdy, for your family's sake. But you will be declared legally dead. Your journals and letters will be destroyed. Your fortune stripped from you and granted to the crown."

"You dishonour me!"

"Your honour is already lost. It is your family's honour I protect now." Thurzó was calm.

"See reason, György. You cannot imprison a noblewoman. It would be the shame of Hungary!"

"By court order, your name shall never be uttered in public again. You will disappear from the world, Erzsébet."

"This is unheard of!"

"So are your crimes." Thurzó told her. "Be grateful I don't do worse. The women, your accomplices, will be tortured for their statements and their bodies burned. Even that young simpleton, Fickó, if I have my way."

The fire in her vision danced.

"I shall write to my cousins," she said. "To my neighbours, to my peers in the nobility, to all the Protestants everywhere. If the Catholic king takes my land, all of us are at risk, György. Even you."

Thurzó nodded. She saw he knew the truth of it. "But your letters shall go undelivered. You will die inside the walls of this castle. And your soul will forever burn in Hell."

"*No!*" Erzsébet lurched backward.

The guard beside her stepped back as if afraid to touch her.

Thurzó grimaced. "Still enough childhood Calvinism to fear Hell, Erzsébet? After everything you've done, did you really believe you could escape eternal damnation?"

Erzsébet felt more sharply aware than she had in a long time. She could see and feel and taste everything. Every *filthy* thing. No bright flickers of light danced in her eyes. No pain troubled her. She could hear the blood rush through her body. She could feel the thick, tainted air on her skin.

Perhaps Anna had been wrong. It was demons after all.

And at the end, perhaps even the demons would abandon her.

• • •

The air was full of smoke and the stink of burning flesh the day she stepped into what would become her catacomb.

If she cared to look again from the narrow window by her bed, she would see the gallows where Ilona and the others still hung.

She listened to the scrape of rock as the stonemasons walled her in.

"I need parchment," Erzsébet told them. "The fine parchment. For letter writing."

"There is some on the floor, Lady," the guard said from outside the wall.

"This isn't enough." She leaned down and fingered it. "And this is too coarse for my noble family."

"It's all you're allowed, Lady."

"If you will not bring me parchment, I shall write my message on the very walls! Báthory is not dead!"

"As you will, Lady."

She was afraid Anna would not visit her behind the walls.

"Do you hear that?" Erzsébet asked.

One of the stonemasons hesitated. He glanced at his fellow but the other man kept working. The guard continued to stare at her dully.

She had been wrong about the demons. They had returned. More often, if anything. The walls were nothing to them. They kept her company through the dark hours and the light. They moved in her blood. They visited such fantasies upon her that she thought she might be a child again. She felt herself surrounded, sometimes, with friends.

Not Anna, though. Never Anna. Never again. "The demons," Erzsébet said. "Do you hear them? They sing to me. They sing."

And so, the Lady Widow Nádasdy, last Countess of Báthory—Erzsébet of Ecsed and later Csejteand numerous other holdings in Hungary—began to sing to her demons.

It took her four years to die.

~

BEYOND THE FACTORY WALL

RIVQA RAFAEL

"Nurse will see you now, seventy-one."

Rising slowly, Lottie wiped her hands on her apron and followed Moore, glaring at the guard's back. They walked through a sea of washing tubs, women bent over them deep in murky water and whispered conversation. Most of the women didn't even glance her way, but Lottie still had the sensation of eyes upon her.

Moore tipped his hat to the rabbi as they passed the chapel. Lottie's eyes dropped to the ground. Along the way they took in the unrelenting black of Rabbi Daniel's close-set eyes, clipped beard, buttoned frock coat, trousers and polished boots.

A zeppelin, bound for Launceston, sailed overhead, blocking what little sun lit the washing yard. Squinting, Lottie looked up to watch the propellers turn, wishing more than anything that she could jump high enough to hitch a ride. Away from the washing yard, only Moore's boots tapping against the flagstones punctured the stillness.

The medical room was different from the last time she'd been there. Instead of gaslight, the window was flung open to catch what meagre light made its way over the Factory walls. A draft flowed in, gentle enough that it didn't reach Lottie's bones, despite her rough uniform. Gone were the cruel pincers and lancets; in their place were shelves filled with jars of dried herbs and tinctures. The breeze carried a flurry of smells; lavender, rosemary and other scents, unfamiliar to Lottie. The only thing that remained from the doctor's days there was the clock, still broken and still hanging on the wall. Lottie had never found the courage to offer to fix it.

In a pot in one corner, a large fern thrived. Surely there hadn't been time—Lottie's turned towards the nurse, suddenly distracted.

No rings decorated her fingers; if she wore an amulet, it was well hidden. "Sit down, Lottie. My name is Radha O'Byrne, and I'll be seeing to your health, and that of your unborn babe." A barely noticeable pause. "Yahweh willing."

Lottie sat on the cot as Miss O'Byrne read her records. Under her apron, the nurse's dress was dyed deep green. Black hair peeked out from her plain linen bonnet, and light-brown eyes appraised Lottie calmly. Only the fine quality of her clothing marked her as more than a convict. "How sure are you that you're with child?" she asked.

"Ain't bled for two months," Lottie muttered.

She nodded. "Anything else? Vomiting? Tenderness?"

Eyes fixed on the floor, Lottie shook her head. The words she needed to say, *I have to get rid of it*, stuck in her throat.

Miss O'Byrne knelt and reached towards Lottie. "May I?"

Her hands were tiny, far too small to deliver babies, but Lottie lay back on the cot. She flinched as Miss O'Byrne dug the heel of one hand into the bones of her pelvis; the other touched the fingertips of the first. Small though her hands were, they reached Lottie's ribs.

Miss O'Byrne's brow furrowed. "You're eating?"

"What they give us." A hand on the side of the cot, Lottie pushed herself up.

The nurse took a packet of herbs and mixed a spoonful with some water from a steaming kettle that stood on her desk, straining the leaves after a few moments. "Drink this, and come back daily for more. It will give you strength."

The tea tasted foul, but Lottie felt a little better when it was done. More alive. "Thank you, Miss."

• • •

There was no question of refusing. A guard escorted her to Miss O'Byrne's office every day. She asked after Lottie's health, but made no other small talk. She never touched the typographer on her desk, instead writing her reports in a flowing hand while she watched Lottie through dark lashes. The perfection of its gleaming brass fittings made Lottie's heart ache, idling as it was.

Sometimes, other women were there, drinking concoctions of their own, or just chatting. Miss O'Byrne was sweet and polite to them all. Several older women came for a tea that they swore helped their rheumatism like nothing else. Occasionally, Miss O'Byrne passed a small root and a packet of herbs to one of the Flash Mob, and those terrors of the Factory smiled meekly at Miss O'Byrne with tobacco-stained teeth. It was hard to believe that they were as likely to be there as in solitary confinement for inciting a bread riot.

• • •

Try as she might, Lottie couldn't bring herself to ask the question she needed to. Some wires to prop her jaw open, perhaps? Soothing as Miss O'Byrne and her office were, her eyes still focused on the wall and her mouth stayed shut.

Miss O'Byrne took her hand to help her up from the cot after a measurement. Something in her palm pressed against Lottie's; the size of a shilling, it felt more like wood than metal, and was curiously warm.

"Let's talk of your future. There's no profession in your records. Why is that?"

"What's it matter? I'm just a convict now." Lottie tried to shake the hand away, to no avail.

Miss O'Byrne's earnest eyes surely weren't enough to make her blab this much. "A profession can mean a better master, a better chance of an early pardon." She looked down at the records once more. "You've never even been out of the Factory, yet your record is completely clean."

It was true she'd worked hard to keep it that way. Seven years of exile on Ben Diemen's Land, the arsehole of the Earth, was more than enough. But that—Lottie shook her head. "We was canal-boaters . . . water-gypsies." She spat the common insult. "I kept the engine running." Words, so many words. Odd to hear her own voice, droning like any old gossip's.

Miss O'Byrne shook her head. "Not so profitable anymore, with the zeppelins."

Lottie swallowed. "We tried to start a courier business with an ornithopter we built, but then the telegraphs came in . . . "

"I can guess the rest." Her eyes glistened.

That set Lottie right off. Tears slid down her nose. "They're in the workhouse now because of me. I picked the lock of some fancy house, only took a few things. All I wanted was to put some food on the table."

Miss O'Byrne embraced her. "Hush, such talk won't help anyone. Free pardons do happen, you know, you may yet return to aid them."

Head on the nurse's slender shoulder, Lottie just sobbed.

She stroked Lottie's back. "Work that suits your experience better might help you. There must be free settlers in need of mechanics."

"It ain't women's work," Lottie choked out.

"Yet you can do it. Such expertise could well be rare enough that a reasonable man might make an exception. I'll make some enquiries."

Lottie pulled away and swiped at her eyes with the corner of her apron. "You could do that?"

She tilted her head. "You might find I can be most persuasive, when the need arises."

A deep breath in. Lottie pointed to the broken clock. "Could fix that for you, if you got me a screwdriver."

• • •

Lottie lingered in shadows, trying to catch what Miss O'Byrne was saying. Miss O'Byrne had one hand in her apron pocket, and the superintendent and the matron were nodding. Snatches came through, "dockmaster", "engine", her own name; she strained harder, not noticing the cane tapping closer until he was right behind her.

"Seventy-one," he said. "Matron's notes indicate you've . . . fallen further. Extra prayers for you. Come along."

He knew. Lottie followed, guts churning, but it seemed he wanted to join Miss O'Byrne's conversation first.

"This one was eavesdropping," he said. "Not that we would expect more from a common thief."

"Rabbi Daniel." Miss O'Byrne bowed her head. "I've been trying to secure some different work for Lottie, it's hardly surprising she would be interested."

"You take copious interest in your patients' welfare." His expression was neutral as he looked at the nurse.

Lottie kept her eyes on the rabbi's boots, the same view she had for every inspection, as he whispered to the free settlers not to take this one, that she was more trouble than she was worth.

"But of course, Rabbi. Caring for the prisoners' bodies alone is not enough if they're to be reformed, as you would well know."

Miss O'Byrne's voice was soft, but utterly assured. She would have no trouble meeting that dark gaze.

"Your idealism is admirable, Miss O'Byrne, but I'm afraid most of these women aren't salvageable. Why, no sooner do we place them in households than they're off truanting or stealing teaspoons—"

"If the settlers would treat them better—"

"—or tempting honest Judeo-Christian husbands to *sin*."

Lottie recoiled as a hand rested on her shoulder, but its size and gentle pressure identified it as Miss O'Byrne's.

"I'm sorry you don't recall Yeshua's compassion," she said. "But I'm sure your methods are sound."

"Sound and orthodox," the superintendent chimed in.

"Indeed. And what work could be better than the washtub for one such as this, might I ask?"

"Lottie is good with mechanical devices, I thought the dockmaster might have some small steam engines that—"

"Out of the question," Rabbi Daniel said.

Miss O'Byrne's hand disappeared into her apron pocket once more, eyes glowing greener under the cloudy sky. "Why ever not, rabbi? Surely it wouldn't do any harm."

"It would be most unseemly, and work should be a punishment for these criminals, not a reward, as it obviously would be." His eyes narrowed. "Frankly, I'm amazed you would suggest such a thing . . . or that you would even consider it, Superintendent."

The Superintendent nodded meekly, mumbling something about Yahweh's will.

Miss O'Byrne blinked. "Of course, you would know best about such things. Lottie, you haven't had your tea." Without another glance at either man, she grasped Lottie's elbow and pulled her along, his eyes burning holes into their backs.

• • •

Lottie had no recollection of the walk from the washing yard to Miss O'Byrne's office, but it must have happened, for she was sitting on the cot when she became aware of her surroundings again. As always, the medical room was not truly well-lit, but even the great hulking shadow of Har Wellington could not dim its soft glow.

Miss O'Byrne locked the door and made the tea, her face a quiet mask. Only when the tea was steeped and poured and the mug in

Lottie's hand did she speak, sitting beside her. "It was the rabbi, wasn't it?"

Blinking, Lottie looked down and gulped some tea.

"Lottie, I swear on Asherah's name, your answer will not leave this office if you don't wish it. But if he laid a hand on you—" she swallowed, eyes blazing. "I would do all in my power, to have him removed from this place."

"Power? You backed down fast enough."

She looked away. "It will be more difficult than I'd supposed, it's true. But Lottie, I want you to trust me. In good faith, then, let me show you." She opened her palm, revealing an apple seed. Her lips moved and the seed began to shudder and twist as tiny white shoots germinated. A wave of her free hand, and the growth stopped. Reverently, she wrapped the seed in a handkerchief and dropped the parcel in a cup of water. "A little more than herbal teas and arts of persuasion, you see."

Lottie blinked, less surprised than she should have been. "You follow the old ways."

Miss O'Byrne nodded.

"You took a chance," Lottie said. "What if I tell?"

Her expression flattened. "Who would you tell? The rabbi?"

"If your guess were wrong, I might."

Miss O'Byrne leaned closer. "And?"

She shook her head. "He means to keep me here for my whole sentence. Make some more babies, I suppose. His wife's barren, you know."

"Oh, Lottie." Miss O'Byrne embraced her. "We'll get you out, somehow."

The steel in her voice was enough to convince Lottie. "Miss O'Byrne, thank you."

"Please, just Radha." She met Lottie's eyes, and for once Lottie didn't look away. "Surely you don't want this child. But you haven't tried to rid yourself of it, have you?"

She shook her head. "Was going to ask . . . "

"Why didn't you?"

"I dunno. Scared, I s'pose."

"So you still value your own life. Good." Radha's voice dropped so soft, Lottie could scarcely hear it. "I can give you something, but I'll need some time to get the concoction ready. Just a few days."

Lottie drew a shuddering breath. "All right, Miss—Radha." She sat, still and silent for a few moments while Radha met her gaze with a kind expression in her eyes. At last Lottie found her voice. "I—if I were to build something, could I . . . perhaps . . . keep it here?"

Stumbling over her words, Lottie began to explain. Radha closed her eyes and rested her right index finger on her forehead as she listened. "I cannot . . . " She reached a hand into her apron pocket and was silent for some moments. At last she pointed at the fern in the corner—had it always been there? Its leaves rustled. "She can hide anything for you. *Remember.*"

Lottie nodded. "Thank you, I'm not sure yet how I'll get all the parts, but . . . I'll find a way."

Radha pointed to the typographer. "You're welcome to take that monstrosity apart, if you wish. I don't use it."

Lottie's hands shook as she dismantled the typographer, removing its useable components and putting its shell back together, so that a casual observer couldn't tell that it no longer worked.

• • •

Once she'd used everything she could from the typographer and the medical tools Radha said she didn't need anymore, it was time to face the lionesses in their den. Without some help from the Flash Mob, she'd never find everything she needed. Radha had nothing that might be used for wheels, and a blunt scalpel only went so far as a screwdriver. So with shaking hands, she placed her washtub close enough to where the Flash Mob sat, but far enough to avoid the guards' suspicion.

"Bugger off, Rabbi's pet," Ellen drawled at her from her place against the Factory wall, voice muffled by the pipe in her mouth. Most resented that prison wall, but it marked Ellen's territory and so she sat, the picture of a pirate queen with rings on every finger and her bonnet worked over with gaudy embroidery.

"I'm *not*," Lottie said, clutching at her belly.

Ellen looked down, nodded curtly and waved a hand at Lottie. "What do you want, little mouse?"

Lottie's shoulders slumped. "I . . . I'm trying to get some things. Things I can't get in here."

"What for?"

Lottie shook her head, stepping backwards.

"Might help if you told me," Ellen said.

Swallowing, Lottie stepped closer, lowering her voice and trying to ignore the grins of the other women as she drew nearer. Up close, the acrid scent of tobacco dulled the dank odour of the washing yard, the sheets that never dried before the rain came. "Building an ornithopter."

Ellen stared blankly. "A what?"

"A flying machine, the kind with flapping wings . . . a boat would be better, but the rivulet flows to Hobart Town." In desperation, she added, "You could come with me."

Ellen chuckled, a harsh sound that ended with a hacking cough. "Are you daft? Even if you could get over the wall, there's wild natives and murderous convicts out there. And those tigers, I heard their teeth are as big as a man's hand. You couldn't pay me enough to leave the Factory."

Dragging her hand away from her belly, Lottie pleaded, "It's different for you, you're in and out as you please. This is the only way, for me."

Ellen kept going as though she hadn't heard. "I heard there was some that ate each other, trying to go north. The men on the work patrols are a different breed from the likes of us. They ain't chained together for nothing. The worst of the worst men are transported to Ben Diemen's Land."

Lottie shook her head as Ellen told her tales. "Better eaten by a cannibal than staying here with *him*."

Lips pressed tightly together, Ellen nodded, serious for a brief moment before she grinned and pinched Lottie's cheek. "Eh, Lottie, you're Flash on the inside, ain't you? Might be able to get you some tools and whatnot," she said. "What sort of thing do you need?"

"Some better tools, for a start . . . screwdrivers, files, some wire . . . sturdy stuff, about a quarter of an inch thick, and about twenty inches long . . . and some little wheels, perhaps off a small wagon or even a pushchair."

Ellen scratched her head. "Not my usual fare . . . might take a few days, but I'll see what I can do." She leaned in close. "And how'll you pay your dues, aye?"

"I got nothing, not like you." Lottie waved a hand at the jewels and finery that Ellen somehow kept from falling into the hands of the guards.

Crossing her arms over her chest, Ellen said, "You can do better than that, little mouse."

"Could fix things for you . . . watches, the little ones' toys?" It was reaching, surely not enough to satisfy the Flash Mob.

But Ellen nodded. "I'll tell the girls to come to you. Be worth it to see a convict sailing over that wall like a bird."

• • •

Over the next few days, various Flash Mob members came to her with tools, parts, and various clockwork things that needed mending. Once her debts were paid, she began to build an engine, as close to her family's ill-fated machine as she could make it. A curved piece of broken washtub, nailed to the wooden base, formed a seat; a crank powered by foot pedals would rotate the cogs to power the wings. The cogs themselves were simple by necessity; one attached to the crank, while the flywheel attached to the base for the wings, converting the circular motion to the up-and-down needed for flight. The wires that would attach the wings had enough give in them to be controlled by a pulley for some steering, but it was a crude system at best.

Lottie recalled her family's machine mournfully; this cobbled-together imitation had none of its sleek functionality. With no time or space for testing, if she could get herself in the air at all, let alone over the wall, she'd consider herself lucky.

The wings were Lottie's most pressing concern. They had to be built from something strong, yet flexible, and it had to be something the Flash Mob could source. Ellen's suggestion, of the sheets the Factory women were contracted to wash, just wasn't going to work.

But still, she kept working, tinkering, trying to create something that approximated aerodynamic.

• • •

The door shuddered open. Lottie almost fell off her chair in her haste to shove the unfinished engine behind Radha's fern and sweep the tools and parts into a drawer.

"Seventy-one," said Rabbi Daniel from the doorway, Moore a pace behind. "I should have known you'd be requesting a witch's services, sooner or later."

"She's a good Irish woman, she don't . . . don't . . . " Lottie's voice failed.

The rabbi's expression hardly flickered. "Then I'm sure she won't mind if I look through her *medicines*." Taking no notice of the whispering fern, he loomed over Lottie's chair to breathe in her ear. "Kill my child, and you will regret it above all of your many crimes."

Lottie sat as if bolted in place, cold dread washing over her. Even if Moore hadn't been guarding the door, she couldn't have got herself to it.

The rabbi was making a show of opening jars, carefully sniffing their contents, when the door opened to reveal Radha, the superintendent and matron right behind her. Rabbi Daniel knocked a jar off the shelf. "Oh dear," he said. "I'm afraid you startled me . . . but here we all are. Superintendent, I'm terribly concerned about these herbs."

Radha knelt, picking up shards of glass with a delicate pincer grip.

"The one on the floor, for example . . . that minty sort of smell is almost certainly pennyroyal. Abortifacient."

"Not as a tea, I use it for coughs and bellyaches." Radha set the broken glass on her desk and placed both hands in her apron pocket.

The rabbi formed a cross with his fingers. "Your evil arts won't work on a man of God. What have you got in there, anyway?" He yanked her small hands away and scooped out the contents of her pocket. A fistful of small wooden ovals, marked with runes, clattered onto the desk to mingle with the broken glass.

"Ogham . . . I never!" The superintendent frowned.

The rabbi smiled, showing all his teeth. "Death by stoning is the punishment for witchcraft."

"Surely, a trial, at least," Radha murmured. If a death sentence frightened her, she gave no sign of it, standing to her full height.

"As a formality, of course. Slaying infants in the womb . . . divination . . . I'll throw the stone that splits open your skull myself. Moore! Dark cell, iron collar. Dig the pit, she dies at noon." He sneered at Lottie. "Solitary for this deviant, too."

One hand in her apron pocket, Radha looked at the matron, who blinked and said, "Rabbi, you've got no proof she's involved, she just happened to be here . . . "

The rabbi waved a hand, clearly too delighted by the sight of Radha being dragged away to care. "Very well, to the washtub then."

• • •

The matron marched her to the washing yard and ordered Lottie to fill a tub. Lottie moved as though she were an automaton, mechanically following the command she'd obeyed many times. But this time, her mind ticked faster, trying to form a plan. Once the matron was gone, she waited for the guards to turn away from the scene they'd made before moving towards the latrines, then doubling back through the shadows towards Radha's office. The door was locked, but as the brass handle warmed in her hand, the mechanism clicked and admitted her.

Lottie bowed her head to the fern as she retrieved her engine, giving it a little push to check that its wheels turned smoothly. With a silent prayer to Asherah, she inverted the arrangement, placing the plant's ceramic pot on the ornithopter's seat. From the tools the Flash Mob had provided, she took a screwdriver, a sharp file and some tough wire that could function as a lock-pick. Her last thought was to cram as many packets of herbs into her apron pocket as she could fit. With luck, some of them might help.

She eased the door handle open and slipped out of the room, pulling the contraption along behind her. A wheel squeaked. A nearby guard's mouth opened, then snapped shut. His eyes slid to a patch of dirt that was apparently more interesting than a prisoner wandering about alone. Holding her breath, Lottie walked to the washing yard, staying in the shadows when she could.

Women were everywhere, talking over their washtubs, more quietly than usual. No doubt rumours had spread fast. In front of the chapel, the superintendent and the matron stood with Rabbi Daniel and Moore, supervising the men digging the stoning pit. They spoke too softly for Lottie to hear. She picked her way through; no one paid her any notice.

The solitary block was surrounded by guards, so Lottie instead sidled over to the wall of the washing yard, where Ellen and the rest of the Flash Mob sat, not working. No one glanced her way, but she called out at the top of her lungs, "Bread!", they heard her well enough. Ellen shrugged, raised a jewel-hilted dagger and echoed the call. The Flash Mob coalesced around her and drew weapons, brandishing fancy blades, kitchens knives and stones as they rushed at the guards, shrieking their usual demand repeatedly.

Guards poured from every direction, including the solitary cells. Lottie left the unfinished ornithopter and fern outside the door and slipped inside to find the corridor deserted, dimly lit by gas lamps. The heady mix of smells, stronger here than outside—whiskey from the old distillery, mildew and shit—threatened her gall, but she held tight as she considered the dark cells, cautiously calling Radha's name.

"Lottie, over here." Soft and hoarse, the voice was unmistakably hers.

She ran to its source and drew out her lock-pick. "Here," she said. The lock was large and stiff, difficult to open. But she got it at last, jumping in to pull back the bolt of the internal door.

Radha stepped into the light, blinking. Pain was written in lines on her face, and she clutched the collar with both hands. Despite her efforts, blood ran down her neck from the spikes; whoever put it on had not been gentle.

"Let me get that off you," Lottie said, fighting back tears.

Radha nodded. "Out of the cell, first."

They stepped out; Radha's eyes darted in all directions as she stood, still and patient despite the danger, while Lottie opened the collar. She let it fall to the ground and gave Radha the medical supplies she'd brought.

She set about opening the remaining cells while Radha dabbed a salve on her neck. Soon women were rushing out to join the riot, which was growing louder.

"Where's your machine?"

Shadows darkened the doorway; it was Rabbi Daniel, flanked by Moore. "Get them in cells, we can't stone the witch until the riot is under control."

Moore grabbed Radha's arms, pinning them behind her back. She hung in the guard's grasp, immobile but for her lips moving.

The Rabbi stood alone, leaning on his cane. Lottie's guts roiled, but she snatched a sharp file from her apron. Diving forwards, she knocked the stick from his hand and pressed the file against his throat. "Let her go," she said, with as much venom as she could muster.

"A witch will cause you more trouble than that," Moore said, but Rabbi Daniel began to struggle, real fear upon his face as he tried to move away from the makeshift weapon. But Lottie knew just how weak those legs were. She tightened her grip. "I mean it." She pressed the file closer, breaking the skin.

"Help me!" The rabbi looked Moore. After several long, tense moments, Moore shoved Radha to the ground and stepped towards Lottie. With her time running out, she drove the file into his throat. He turned and got a hand around Lottie's neck, but it weakened and she pushed him away on reflex. Gazing down to her belly, he opened his mouth, but blood flowed out instead of words and he collapsed to the ground. Blood oozed across the flagstones and his eyes looked up vacantly. The file fell from Lottie's hand and she stared, frozen.

Moore gaped; Radha moved first, palms pressed together. "Peace," she murmured. "Go."

Moore's face took on a blank expression and he stumbled away.

The shakes overtook Lottie. "What now?"

"Your flying machine, of course."

She gestured to the door. "It's not finished . . . I never made the wings."

Radha picked up the rabbi's cane and spoke an unfamiliar word; the wood split obligingly into two, bending and stretching into two curved pieces that arced like birds' wings. "Will these work as a frame?"

Lottie nodded and choked back bile as she pulled the black frockcoat from the rabbi's corpse and ripped it in half. Just outside the door of the solitary block, she wrapped wire around the makeshift wings to hold the fabric in place and slotted them in place.

"I don't know if it can even hold one, let alone two," Lottie said.

Radha's slender fingers sorted through the packets of herbs Lottie had given her. "I should be able to help lighten the load."

Lottie nodded. Setting the contraption just outside the door of the solitary block, she slotted the wings in place, leapt on board and began to turn the crank, a wave of her free hand showing Radha where to sit.

Pedalling furiously, she pointed the machine towards the wall, praying to Asherah for favourable winds. Behind her, Radha prayed in an ancient tongue, arms tight around Lottie's waist. A strong breeze whipped around them, and they were airborne, flying, catapulting over the wall, far easier and faster than should have been possible. Below, the riot was mostly under control; a guard dragged Ellen towards the solitary block, where Lottie's handiwork would be obvious. Laughing, Ellen looked to the sky and raised a fist in the air when she caught sight of the ornithopter. Gunshots rang around them as they flapped towards Har Wellington, but none hit their mark and then there was blessed quiet, and clean air and green everywhere.

Radha relaxed her grip on Lottie's waist as they turned to look down on Hobart Town. So small and quiet it seemed from that distance, like a village of dollhouses, it was hard to recall its violence and danger.

"Well done, Lottie," Radha said.

Lottie turned away from the colony and back to the forest. "Free." The word tumbled from her lips of its own accord as an optimism she'd never experienced washed over her.

Perhaps they'd be eaten by cannibal escapees, perhaps they'd be caught and brought back to hang. The rabbi's child was still in her womb, and her family was still starving in Britain. But as Lottie stumbled behind Radha into the forest, dragging the flying machine behind her, it seemed they could do anything. Even keep themselves safe. The trees closed around them and strange forest creatures trailed behind. Yellow and grey birds flocked overhead; possums, strangely wakeful, screeched from above; and devils and striped tigers followed Radha with bowed heads. With that welcome, they melted into the bush.

THE FLOWERS THAT BLOOM WHERE BLOOD TOUCHES EARTH

STEPHANIE GUNN

Sometimes, when I am dreaming, I tear fistfuls of hair from my scalp. When I wake, the blood-dotted strands are woven into a tight nest in the cradle of my palm and within the nest, there is a flower.

This morning, there is nothing in my palms but air, nothing left of the dream but the sour sweat that dampens my nightgown. Nothing to hide from Clara as she stirs from her fitful slumber.

I make my way to the washstand. There are feathers of frost clinging to the edges of the washbowl. I barely feel the chill as I dip a sponge.

"Another dream?" Clara asks. There is a rustle of sheets as she turns away to give me what privacy she can in our small room.

I strip off my nightgown, begin washing. "The same as always."

I have only ever told Clara scant details of the dream. In it, I am flying: light in a world of shadows, drifting on warm, gentle currents. I have no place to be, no *one* to be. I simply *am*. And I know that if I let go, I could drift on and on, free forever. There always comes a moment though, when I am floating further and further in the shadowed world, when the currents shift, bringing me a thread of scent. White sweetness cut with a pure, bright chill: asphodel.

Asphodel: my regrets follow you to the grave.

In that moment, I am given a choice: I can keep drifting, keep going out and out into whatever lies beyond the shadows, or I can grasp onto that thread of scent, and drag myself back to my body. Always I choose to go back. To return to the House, to return to Clara.

There is a creak of leather as Clara opens a book. It is Swedenborg's *Heaven and Hell*; I saw the volume next to Clara's Bible the previous day. I suspect that Clara's eyes are too weak to see the words printed on the page, but she knows the text of both books well enough to pretend.

We are both good at pretending, Clara and I.

"In Heaven, there will be gardens filled with every kind of flower that has ever existed," Clara says. "Can you imagine?"

I pull on my loose white gown, draw a comb through my pale hair. In the mirror above the washstand, I can see the supine form of Clara. Beside the candle on the chair next to the bed, a coin gleams. It is a rare thing to see it there—we are not allowed money, and have no need for it, for Mrs Fox supplies us with everything we require.

"Do you know," Clara says, "I almost feel well today."

She looks anything but. She is so pallid I can see the blue tracing of veins at her temples, and the bones of her skull press out against her skin. I pour clean water from the jug into a smaller bowl, bring it over to the bed and help Clara sponge her face and hands. Despite her words, even this small action costs her dearly, and when she is done, her breath comes hard.

"It will be like all the other times," she says between breaths. "The crisis will pass, and I will be well again. Spring always follows winter, and after the snow, the flowers always bloom."

I fetch her a clean nightgown, look out of the window as she changes. I can hear the butcher boys crying their wares from house to house, skipping over ours, of course. Across the road, I can see a small girl trudging along, a basket of flowers bowing her back into a weary curve.

This has been the longest consumptive crisis Clara has experienced. It has been weeks since she has been able to rise from bed, months since she has been able to manage the stairs. Over a year since she has been able to work a sitting.

By the time Clara bids me turn, the butcher boys' cries have faded, the flower girl gone from view. The skin in the hollow of Clara's throat draws in sharply as she fights for breath.

I gather our discarded nightgowns. Beneath the fust of sickness on Clara's gown, I can smell asphodel, belladonna, hemlock. Flowers of grief, flowers of death.

• • •

Mrs Fox lays gloved hands on my shoulders.

"Welcome, seekers, to the House of the Lilies," she says.

Her voice is warm, but beneath the frills on my gown, her fingers dig hard into my flesh. She presses the sharp edges of her nails against my bones; dulled by her kid gloves, the pressure is hard enough to bruise, but not hard enough to break skin, nor to make me bleed.

Mrs Fox will not—*cannot*—waste my blood.

"Tonight in the Seeing Room, we are joined by the medium Virginia Lily," Mrs Fox continues. "Virginia has been fasting and meditating all day, and tonight she will part the veil, see into the beyond." She stands behind me, so I cannot see the pose she strikes, but I know it well enough: arms out, palms and face turned up to the Heavens. "Which of you wishes to *see*?"

In the dim light of the single candle, I can make out little of the room, but like Mrs Fox's theatrics, I know the space well enough. The walls are thickly plastered, the windows and door hung with heavy velvet. The wallpaper and curtains are claret in colour, so as to appear black in the dim light. Eleven chairs circle the room, the small lace-covered table I sit at set slightly apart. Two chairs are directly opposite me, with Mrs Fox behind.

A man moves, his spectacles reflecting the light as he stands. The woman beside him follows more slowly, jewels on her fingers catching greedily at the scant light. Mrs Fox waves them to my table, and they sit.

I will not be told anything about them, but as they seat themselves, the light of the candle shows me their story well enough. The woman's dress is edged with black crape, and she wears white lace at her throat: she is in mourning for a child. The dress is made from cheap fabric, but bought black, not dyed, and well-tailored: they will have paid handsomely.

Mrs Fox lays her hands on my shoulders again, lightly now. The man's eyes move from Mrs Fox to me, and I see the doubt in them. And why not? Of a certainty, I appear to him as nothing more than a lanky child in white, my pale hair tumbling loose down my back.

"Do you have an item belonging to the one you wish to contact?" Mrs Fox asks.

The woman draws a photograph from her purse, lays it on the white lace that stretches between us.

The child in the photograph is perhaps three or four years old. She reclines in a chair, a doll tucked by her side. Her hands are lax, her eyes closed. Impossible to tell if she was living or dead when the photograph was taken.

I lay my hands flat on the table, one on either side of the image. Beneath my palms, lace; beneath that, a thin layer of clean earth.

Mrs Fox snuffs the candle. The woman begins to weep. It is a ragged, tearing sound which reminds me all too much of the way my mother sounded on the nights she thought me sleeping. Those nights, she curled herself around a photograph, sobbed my sister's name over and over, as though she could bring her back to life with the force of her grief.

Mrs Fox settles her skirts: a signal that I am taking too long. I pull my attention back to the present, remind myself that I owe Mrs Fox my livelihood and my life. I close my eyes, focus on the beating of my heart, count: *one, two, three.* It is a well-practised cue, and my body relaxes automatically, head slumping forward, chin on my chest.

Behind my eyes, I can see my pulse: silver beating against blackness. Another moment, and my awareness expands; like a photograph being developed, the silver tracery of my veins emerges from the darkness. It looks something like the lace beneath my palms, but far more intricate, more beautiful than anything that could be spun with human hands.

It takes a thought, something like a *push*, and the silver lace rises towards my skin. It feels as though the inside of my body is expanding, and I cannot help the moan that rises as the pressure of it builds to pain. Just when I feel my skin will split open, something releases, and the silver lace is moving through my skin, becoming a mist as it touches the air.

I am on the edge of the dream. If I keep going, letting the silver rise and rise, I could float away, be free. It takes all of my will to rein in that desire, to keep the mist anchored in my body.

Mrs Fox clicks a heel and I open my eyes. The lace tablecloth and my gown are glowing in the pale light. On one of the rare occasions Mrs Fox has spoken directly to me, she told me that it looks something like the light cast by the stars on a clear, moonless night. I wouldn't know. All I ever see when I look up is cloud and smoke, or else the fog obscuring all.

Mrs Fox settles her skirts again. Once the light has been released, everything else comes without effort: I could shake this room to pieces with only a thought. But the sitters expect theatrics, and so I begin to sway in my chair, let my breath rasp in and out of my chest. I hate the latter, for it reminds me too much of Clara, but Mrs Fox insists.

Another shuffle of Mrs Fox's skirts and I still, allow the light to move away from me. In the corner is the spirit cabinet that Frances uses in her sittings; I avoid it, project the glow into empty space. It is a simple thing to arrange the light into the likeness of the child in the photograph, to make the 'manifestation' smile and wave.

Gasps from around the room, and the woman's sobs become more pained. A heavier tap of Mrs Fox's heel: this is too much. I loosen the illusion, make it look rougher, something like linen wrapped around a wooden doll.

I make the 'manifested spirit' move around the room, dancing and smiling, until Mrs Fox shifts her skirts again. It is time for the flowers.

Secreted in the collar of my gown is a long silver pin. Feigning the need to adjust my dress, I press my finger against the sharp end of the pin. One prick, one drop of blood. I always expect to see it flow forth as silver as the light, but the drop that falls on the lace is red, black in the thin light. It takes a moment for the blood to soak through to the earth beneath the cloth, and I glance up to ensure that the sitters are still enthralled by my illusion.

They are, all but one.

She—and I only presume that it *is* a she because she wears a dress, for there is little else of the feminine to her—is seated in the back of the room. Her hair hangs ragged to her shoulders, the almost white strands tangled and knotted. Even seated, I can tell that she is taller than the tallest man here. She wears no gloves, no hat. She alone is watching the place where my blood is soaking through the lace.

A scent like charred honey emerges, and then, where blood touched earth, there are flowers. The strange woman looks up at me, and her lips part. When her eyes meet mine, an odd sensation moves through me. Like the way the air feels in the moments before a storm breaks, except this storm is rolling deep into the darkness of me.

Mrs Fox is tapping her heel again—has been for some time, I think—and I drag my attention away from the strange woman. It hurts, as though I am pulling a tooth out, root and all. The woman and man at the table are weeping, each of them holding one of the 'spirit's' hands. I am thankful for Mrs Fox's training, for the illusion has not faded, even when my attention strayed. I make the 'spirit' kiss them both once, and then allow it to dissolve back into the silver mist.

I pull the light back close to my skin, and take advantage of the shifting shadows to slip the flowers from beneath the cloth, arrange them in my cupped palms. The harshness of my breathing is not feigned now, nor the way I droop in my seat: drawing the light back gets harder each time.

"A message from beyond," Mrs Fox declares. She places her hands on my shoulders again. Her fingers do not dig in, and I know that I have judged the flowers correctly. "Baby's breath for innocence and purity of heart, and a lily from the House itself. Your daughter is well and blessed in Heaven."

She produces a white ribbon from her sleeve, wraps the flowers and hands them to the couple. The scent of the lily catches, thick and choking, in my throat.

I pull the light back beneath my skin. It takes great effort and I am glad when Mrs Fox taps her heel, giving me the signal to slump over the table. It is one of her recent additions to our theatrics: a swooning medium makes it easy for her to clear the room, to ensure that no one lingers overlong.

The other girls tell me how they roll their eyes, fall boneless in their chairs. For me, none of it is feigned. My heart races, my skin feels hot and tight, my body too small to contain the roiling light.

The scent of the earth beneath the lace is soothing, and I take deep breaths as I listen to Mrs Fox lighting the candle. The man and woman thank her over and over, press more coins into her hands. One by one, the sitters file past me. It is forbidden to touch the medium, but I feel several of them reach out anyway, the heat of them brushing my skin. One such almost-touch brings that edge-of-a-storm feeling rolling through me again. In its wake, it is easier to keep the light contained.

When I finally look up, only Mrs Fox remains. The colours of her dress meld with the candlelight and shadow. The silk is the old-fashioned colour known as Dust of Ruins, the skirt trimmed with a band of black crape. The style of Mrs Fox's dress and her hair are as old-fashioned as the colour. She wears no decoration but for a locket pinned at her throat, jet carved into the shape of a lily.

She looks at me for a long time, expression unreadable, then turns and exits. Her footsteps move down the hallway, the door opens, closes. Her key clicks in the lock.

The doors are always locked when Mrs Fox leaves, and only she has the keys. It is to keep us safe, she says, to keep the Lilies unsullied by the world outside.

I make use of the spirit cabinet to change into the slate grey tea dress waiting there, moving carefully around the chair and ropes that Frances uses in her sittings. I bundle up my white dress and the tablecloth, sweep the table clear of earth.

My work done, I should leave, but instead I cross the room to the chair where the strange woman had been sitting. A fragrance lingers in the air, something like the bright green of new ferns, the foliage sliced through with a silver knife.

Fern: magic, fascination, shelter.

I breathe in deeply, and some of my exhaustion fades. For the first time since Mrs Fox brought me to the House, I wish that she lingered after sittings. Everyone who attends her private sittings is known to her, or vouched by someone well known. I want to ask her—no, I want to *demand* of her—who this woman is, why she smells like *home.*

• • •

Girls smile at me from the row of photographs on the back parlour mantelpiece. Each of them is arranged prettily on the arm of their new husband. Their cheeks are plump, their hair neatly pinned. They all bear an armful of bridal roses, their stems stripped of thorns.

Bridal rose: happy love.

Looking upon these women, I am acutely aware of the thinness of my body, the weight of my loose hair against my spine. Mrs Fox's canon for her perfect Lilies: sylph-like, unbound. Once upon a time, each of these women were moulded thus by Mrs Fox, all saved by her from lives in the workhouse or on the street. When they came of age, their service declared satisfactory, Mrs Fox made arrangements for them. They were given new names, introduced to good families, matches made. Within a year of them leaving the House, each was photographed thus, as a happy bride.

One day, I too will smile from that mantelpiece.

Frances enters the room, Rose buffeted in her wake. Though it is against Mrs Fox's rules, Frances has a scarlet sash pulled tight around her waist. The fabric strains, and I fear for the seams as she pulls two chairs together, reclines on one and props her boots on the other.

Frances fixes her eyes on me as she pulls a packet of boiled sweets from her pocket. Her hair is brassy, and I suspect that she has been at it with alum, honey and black sulphur again. The ends of her hair are canon pale—as the whole length was when she was younger—but the roots are dark, like shadows growing from her skin.

In contrast to Frances, Rose is the image of Mrs Fox's perfect Lily: slender as a reed, her hair so pale that it is almost white, her eyes clear blue. She carries a basket filled with pans and brushes and blacking for the grate. She kneels, strews old, clean tea leaves on the carpeting to catch the dust, and begins sweeping out the grate.

"I thought it was Frances' turn for the fires," I say to Rose.

Frances crunches a sweet between her teeth. "Rosie volunteered."

"It's good practice, it is," Rose says in her customary half-whisper. "When I marry, I want to be ready, I do. We might just have a maid of all work at first, and someone'll have to help." She coughs as ash plumes from the fireplace. "Besides, I have a sitting tomorrow, and I'm the one who'll need the fire, I will."

"*I* need the fire now," Frances says. "It's bloody cold."

Rose flushes at Frances' language. "I'll get you a warming pan for the bed when I'm finished with the fires."

I want to remind Rose that she is not Frances' servant, but it will be of no use. Frances always gets what she wants. I remind myself instead that Frances will come of age within a month, and none of us will have to deal with her again.

Frances crunches another sweet. "I'm close to a full materialisation," she says to me. "Mrs Fox says it's the best she's seen. Better even than bloody Florence Cook. Better than *you*."

Rose finishes with the fire, sweeps up the tea leaves and dust. When she stands she sways, coughs again. "It's not like Clara," she says quickly. "Just the dust." She picks up the basket. "I'd best get on with the rest of the fires."

Rose heads into the dining room, Frances on her heels. I move deeper into the house, towards the kitchen and scullery, where I find the twins. Gertrude is rinsing the day's tea leaves and Genevieve is elbow-deep in scummy water scrubbing the dinner pans. I set the white cloth and gown with the rest of the laundry to await the next wash day and sit down gratefully.

Supper waits for me: a bowl of watery vegetable soup and a sliver of dense bread. I've eaten the same every day since I moved to the House—Mrs Fox forbids us meat or milk—but the portions are even more miserable than usual.

"It's the same for all of us," Gertrude says. "Mrs Fox's orders. For which I believe we can thank Frances. I don't know how she manages to keep growing out, even with Rose giving her most of her food."

The soup is cold, the vegetables almost rancid, but I force it down. "Frances says she's close to a full manifestation."

Genevieve rolls her eyes. "I don't know why she bothers. No one has asked for her for weeks, and she'll be out of here soon enough."

"She says that it's better than Florence Cook," I say.

Genevieve makes a rude noise. "Katie King," she says, referring to the spirit guide the medium Florence Cook summons, "is nothing more than Florence's sister draped in linen, or else Florence herself."

"Do you know, I heard Frances talking to Rose about how she's planning on setting up her own salon once she leaves," Gertrude says. "She wants to keep working as a medium."

The noise Genevieve makes now is even more unladylike. "Who's going to pay *Frances* for anything? Other than the obvious. We all know where Mrs Fox found her." She elbows her twin, grins. Both of them came from the workhouse, same as Rose and Clara.

I focus on eating. Like Frances, I was living on the street when Mrs Fox found me. I sold flowers; Frances sold herself.

"Do you know," Gertrude says, "I think Frances really believes that she's channelling something."

A lump of potato sticks in my throat. "What . . . what if she is?"

"Then it's the madhouse she's set for, no husband or salon or anything else," Gertrude says. "It's just tricks. Even Rose knows that. Frances herself spent half the day in here yesterday practising swallowing linen and bringing it back up as 'ectoplasm'. How can she think that's anything real?"

My hands are pressed palm-down on either side of my bowl. My skin tingles, and I think of the silver lace beneath my skin. Am I, too, deluding myself?

I pocket my bread, head upstairs. My footsteps echo in the silence. Mrs Fox leases the houses on either side of us, leaves them empty in order to keep us undisturbed. Before Mrs Fox brought me to the House, I had never known silence. While my mother lived, there was always the sound of men coming and going, and her sobbing in between. After, on the street, the city was never silent, not for one moment. Always someone crying their wares, the sounds of horses and carriages, the cries of girls calling to potential customers.

At first, I had thought the silence here a balm. Now it feels like the darkness in Mrs Fox's beyond: a void that goes on and on, a thing which hungers for spirits and souls.

The upper floor of the house holds three bedrooms: the twins share the largest, their space always cluttered with wooden contraptions, wiring and the linen 'spirits' that they use in their sittings. Frances and Rose are in the next, and Clara and I in the smallest.

When I return upstairs, Clara is awake, bent over a notebook, her pen scratching softly at the page. In the candlelight, she is even more perfect a Lily than Rose, her hair almost translucent. The notebooks are supplied by Mrs Fox for Clara to practice her automatic writing—her speciality—but Clara confessed to me once that it is poetry that she writes on those pages, though she will show the verses to no one, not even me.

I wait until she blots the page, slips the book beneath her pillow. Only then do I offer her the bread from my pocket. It is a ritual from the first time she was ill, when the doctor tried starving out the illness. I know that she will not eat it now—she barely touches her toast and water—but I offer it all the same. If I keep walking the same steps, keep doing the same things I have always done, then Clara will keep being here as well.

I help Clara use the chamber pot, then change into my nightgown and slide into bed. Just before Clara snuffs the candle, I see the blood on her pillow, ill-concealed by a fold of the blanket.

In the darkness, Clara's hand finds mine. In her palm is the fat coin. She presses it into my hand, draws away.

"The doctor told me of a man named Livings," Clara says. "He runs a small salon down near the Foundling Hospital. They say he spent a year in Egypt studying some of the ancient ways, and that he can capture spirits in photographs. He can show you the faces of people you've forgotten."

Something leaps high inside me. I quash it down. "This money was to pay the doctor. For your medicine."

"It will not help me," Clara says. "The doctor himself refused payment, since he could not assist."

"You said this morning that you were feeling well."

"It happens sometimes like that, the doctor said. At this stage, even the medicine is nothing more than a salve."

"What about the water cure?" The words tumble over one another as I speak. "You have ever been Mrs Fox's favourite. I can talk to her in the morning—"

"Mrs Fox knows," Clara says quietly. "There is nothing more to be done. The coin will be of more use to you. This is what I want, Virginia. For you to see your mother. Please."

I rub my thumb around the edge of the coin. The metal picked up no warmth at all from contact with Clara's skin. "Even if I did agree, what use is a coin if I am locked in here?"

Her hand finds mine again. This time it is a key she presses into my hand, smooth on one side and rough on the other. "Locks always have keys."

"How?"

"Frances, of course. She loaned it to me readily enough when I asked. Even Frances is kind to the dying."

Tears prick at the corners of my eyes, and I feel something squeeze tight inside me. "You are not dying!"

Her hand presses against mine again, the coin and key between our palms. "I have been dying since the moment you met me, Virginia."

I can hear the effort the conversation has cost her in the heavy rasp of her breath. I want to ask her so much more, but I know that talking further will bring on another coughing fit. I know well how such a fit can end. I watched the blood flow and flow from my own mother's mouth, even as she cursed me with her last breath.

For Clara's sake, I make myself turn over, feign sleep. Clara will not sleep until she thinks I am. When her breathing finally slows, I make a tent of blankets around myself, release just enough of the light to illuminate the small space. The photograph that I slide out from beneath my pillow is one that Clara has seen many times before, a secret I have shown only to her. I have never shown Clara the silver light, though. I have trusted her with all else, but this—I fear too much what I would see in her eyes. I know what her Bible says about demons and witches, and I could not bear to have her turn away from me.

The photograph is worn and creased, one corner torn away entirely. There are three people captured in it, though you can only see two, the third face hidden beneath a swathe of black fabric. On my mother's lap, is a baby—me—hands and face indistinct smears of light. I often wonder if I was struggling towards, or away from my mother as the photograph was taken. Others would have had the image retaken, but not my mother. It was an expense that she could not afford, and I was not who she sought to capture.

My sister, Marguerite, sits in a chair beside my mother and me. She is a beautiful, frail girl on the cusp of womanhood, almost old enough to have her skirts fully lengthened. At first glance, anyone would think her to be alert, her eyes meeting the camera evenly. It is only when you look closer that you see the laxness of her hands, that the eyes which watch you are merely painted onto the photograph.

More tellingly, there are morning glories tucked into her sash.

Morning glories: flowers that bloom, wilt and drop from the vine within a day, a life cut short.

This is all that I have left of my family. My father unknown, my sister a corpse and my mother forever hidden from view. Time has eaten any memory I have of my mother's face, everything but the blood and the sound of her sobbing at night for her poor Marguerite, this photograph clutched to her bosom while I lay cold on the other side of the bed.

I slide the picture back beneath my pillow. I think of the couple at the sitting, the extra coins they had pressed into Mrs Fox's hands afterwards. I owe Mrs Fox, this is a certainty. But do I owe the people who come to the sittings, too? Enough to tell them the truth?

For beyond the silver lace and the light and the flowers born of blood and earth, I can see what Mrs Fox calls the beyond. And there are no choirs of angels, no spirits, no gardens, no God, not even any demons. There is only the cold world, and beyond, the endless, empty black that goes on and on forever.

• • •

The house is silent as I make my way downstairs.

Clara woke this morning coughing and fevered after a restless night, bright blood on her lips and pillow. I helped her sponge her face, change her nightgown and the pillowcase. I averted my eyes as much as I could, but caught too many glimpses of her wasted body, thin skin stretched over brittle bone. I persuaded her to take some of her remaining laudanum, then sat with her until she fell into a fitful sleep.

I fear now that the doctor is right, that Clara does not have long for this world. The thought of her lost in that endless black is almost more than I can bear.

At the bottom of the stairs, I pause, take measure of where everyone is in the house. Mrs Fox and Rose are in the back parlour with Rose's new client. The twins are upstairs working on their tricks, and Frances is at work in the kitchen. I have an hour, perhaps, before anyone will notice me missing.

My heart thuds hard as I slide the key into the lock. A click and a step, and I am outside, the door locked again behind me.The air is thick with grey fog. It clings to my skin, weighs down the skirts of my gown. The last time I stood on this step there was an almost identical fog. I was in rags then, my only possession in the world my basket of flowers.

Every morning, I would rise from whatever corner I had managed to secure for the night, find a clear patch of earth where no one was watching. There, I would scratch my nails against my skin until I drew blood, let it patter down onto the earth. From the blood and earth flowers bloomed: violets and roses, baby's breath and poppies. I would scratch again and again until my basket was full. Exhausted from the summoning of flowers, I would drag myself around the streets as best I could, with barely any breath to call my wares. Some days I could do little but sit on a stoop, my body bowed around my basket. Mrs Fox found me thus one day, drawn by the brightness of my hair. When she brought me to the House, it was Clara who met me at the door that day, tall and slender and impossibly beautiful in her white gown.

A thin thread of green comes through the fog: ferns, and trailing vines. It reminds me of the strange woman from the sitting, and an echo of that edge-of-the-storm feeling rolls through me. Free of the House, I could seek her out. Right now, I could walk away from the House, never look back.

I glance up at the small window of my bedroom. I cannot leave Clara.

Calling on my old memories of the streets, I make my way to the Foundling Hospital. Here and there I take wrong turns where streets have sprung up where I remember none, and I am forced to backtrack. On one such occasion, I swing around a corner and collide with a small girl, in her hands a basket full of wilted flowers. She is thin and shivering, her hair a pale dirty gold and eyes pure blue. She says nothing, just kneels and begins to gather the flowers which have scattered over the path. I help her. The scent of rot is thick on the flowers: no one will buy these wares. There are bruises on the girl's thin arms, and her eyes dart about as we work; she is being watched.

The key is in my pocket. While the girl is looking away, I press my finger against its rough edge. It hurts more than the pin, but it suffices. Blood wells forth, falls onto the filthy cobblestones. It takes more effort than clean earth, and I am only able to bring forth a single red rose and a spray of violets. I gather them up, place them in the girl's basket.

"But—" she begins.

"If you go around by the park, you'll find more customers," I say.

I want to tell her that things will get better, that there will be happiness for her to look forward to. She takes a hesitant step towards me, and I quickly hurry away. I am not Mrs Fox, I cannot make anything better for her, or for anyone.

Eventually I find the place Clara had spoken of: a small salon marked by the carved figure of a pharaoh in the window. The door stands open, everything beyond dark. Propped up next to the pharaoh, a small sign invites seekers to enter.

That green scent twines around me again. The coin is heavy in my pocket. I should go back, confess to Mrs Fox, bid her have the doctor return. Or else find one myself, secure laudanum. I could tell Clara that I could not find the salon, or that the man Livings was not there. Then I think of how Clara had sounded when she had given me the coin. Clara wanted me to do this. To Clara, I cannot lie.

I step into the darkness.

The air is thick with something powdery and choking, but oddly without scent. One step, two, three, and then I am in a gas lit room. When I turn, I see that the darkness I passed through is nothing more than a cunning arrangement of velvet curtains.

A chair and stand are pushed against one whitewashed wall, before them a camera. A door stands opposite me, closed.

The door opens and a man appears. He wears an ill-fitting suit, a crimson turban askew on his head. He grasps at my arm, and as he draws me across the room, somehow the coin passes from my hand to his. He arranges me against the stand, affixes a clamp to the back of my neck.

"Stay still," he says.

I obey as best as I can as he ducks beneath the cloth.

The place where I cut my finger throbs. It seems to take forever, but finally the powder flashes and he reappears. He doesn't look at me as he pulls the tin plate out of the camera and hurries out of the room.

When the photographer returns, he unscrews the clamp, the metal pinching my skin. He thrusts the photograph into my hands, leaves the room again. In the photograph, my hands and face are slightly blurred, as though I had been shaking. Arranged in the chair beside me is a gauzy wisp: if you wanted badly enough, you could believe it a spirit.

It is only a swatch of linen, identical to that which Frances and the twins use, somehow transferred onto the photograph with me. It is only another trick.

I expect disappointment, but instead a laugh bubbles up. It's all tricks, there is nothing but the cold world and the darkness beyond.

A small noise, and I swallow my laughter, look up, expecting to see the man. It is not he who stands before me, but a tall, thin gentleman in a well-cut suit, face shaded by the brim of his hat. Then he lifts the hat from his head. It is the strange woman from the sitting, garbed now as a man. Or is it a man, garbed then as a woman? I do not know, and the more I think on it, the more confused I feel.

"You may think of me as a woman, if it helps," the stranger says. Her voice is clear, slightly accented. She leans over to look at the photograph. "He is a fraud, no, this Livings? Clever, but not too clever. Tell me, who was it you sought to see?"

Her eyes fix on mine, unblinking. Her pupils are pinpricks, her irises so pale a blue that they are almost silver. Her eyes on mine, I find that I can do nothing but speak the truth.

"My mother," I say.

She looks at me for another long moment, and when I inhale the green fern fragrance of her, it is as soothing, as comforting, as the scent of clean earth.

Nestled in the folds of her white silk cravat is a diamond-tipped pin. She presses a fingertip to the sharp end, her eyes still on mine. A drop of her blood wells. I taste green in the back of my throat. She lets a single droplet of her blood fall onto the photograph. The scent of charred honey rises and silver light ripples over the picture. As it fades, I see that the image has changed.

It is now identical to the photograph of my mother, Marguerite, and I.

When I breathe in, I feel green go down into the depths of me, uncurling like smoke in the darkness. Tears prick at my eyes. "Is it another trick?" I ask.

"No tricks." She holds up her pricked finger. The small injury is already healing. "Do you wish to truly see?"

I can no more look away from her than will my heart to cease beating. "Who are you? *What* are you?"

She turns away then. "Someone who has been alone for a long time." When she looks back, I am surprised to see tears shimmering in her eyes. "I will force nothing upon you, Virginia. The choice is yours. You may walk away, if you wish, and I will follow you no longer."

I remember the green scent in the fog. "You were following me? You know my name?"

"I was . . . curious. I wanted to see."

Mrs Fox's voice echoes in my mind: *Who wishes to* see?

"How do I choose if I do not know what I am choosing?" I ask.

"How do any of us know? We simply choose a path, and then hope." Her voice is heavy with sorrow. "If we do not have hope, we do not have anything at all."

Hope. What hope have I ever had in my life?

What if I can *choose* it?

I hold out my hand. She takes it in hers, presses the tip of my finger against her cravat pin. The metal slides painlessly into my skin. A single drop of blood wells.

She presses my finger to the edge of the photograph. Unbidden, the silver lace rises to my skin. There is no pressure, no pain; it is as simple as breathing, the release of the silver light. The woman looks around in wonder, her expression like that of a child suddenly given her heart's desire. The mist plays over the photograph. I stare at the image of my mother, waiting for the black veil to be pulled back. Nothing changes.

I look up at the woman.

"Look again," she says.

When I look back, I see it: Marguerite's eyes are no longer painted on the photograph, but open in truth—open and *alive*. My mother is still hidden beneath the black veil, and I am still a blur of light, but Marguerite is *real*—alive and breathing in the frame of the photograph. She turns, looks at the babe who was me, and just once, she smiles.

Everything slots into place in my mind, as though a key has been slid into a lock, the door that had hidden all flung wide.

"She was my mother, wasn't she?" I ask. "Marguerite was my mother."

The silver light dances, shaping forms without my bidding. I see the woman I thought of as my mother, shadowed and indistinct, moving in and out of the room we had lived in. I see the men on her arm coming and going, the way they turned to Marguerite, the way my *grandmother* screamed at them, turned them out.

"She had no choice," the strange woman says. Her voice sounds far away, echoing as though she is speaking down a long, dark tunnel. "After her husband died, she had nothing, no way to put food in her daughter's mouth but to sell herself. She made herself only one promise—Marguerite would never be touched. Marguerite was going to be more than she was."

Shadows move through the light as men come and go, come and go. Not once do I see my grandmother clearly—always she is turned away, always in shadow. Only Marguerite is always perfectly in focus.

"But she could not always be there," the woman continues. "She had to leave sometimes, and all it took was one moment when Marguerite was alone."

A shadow moves across the light, advances on Marguerite. I close my eyes then. I do not want to see it. I smell roses, the bright copper of blood. The woman lays her hands on my shoulders, and I feel the light slip beneath my skin once more. When I open my eyes, the photograph shows only me and that wisp of linen masquerading as a spirit.

"I killed her. Birthing me killed her," I say. "That's why my mother—my grandmother—that's why she hated me so."

The woman looks at me, sympathy in her eyes. My finger is still bleeding. She presses her own finger against the cravat pin, touches her blood to the wound. It heals over immediately, as smooth as though the skin had never been broken.

"You can heal," I say. "Your blood. It can heal."

"*Our* blood," she says. "It can do many things, should you only wish it."

Our blood. My blood. *It can heal.*

My heart thuds hard against my ribs. I can heal Clara. I can make her well again.

I pull away from the woman, the photograph fluttering to the floor. She is still talking to me, shouting at me, but I do not hear a single word. I am already leaving, I am already *running* back home to Clara.

• • •

The House stands open.

I pause as I step over the threshold, aware of the odd scent of must in the house, of things old and decaying. Then I see the blood on the staircase, and I am running again.

A hand reaches out from the parlour—Gertrude, clutching at my arm. Genevieve and Rose are huddled together behind her, both of them pale. There is blood, black on all of their grey dresses.

"Is Clara—?" I ask. "Where is Mrs Fox? Where is Frances?"

"Mrs Fox has gone to fetch a doctor," Gertrude says. "Halfway through Rose's sitting, Clara started to scream. She dragged herself down the stairs, and there was so much blood . . . " She shakes her head. "Mrs Fox has not come back, nor the doctor. Frances said she was going to fetch them both, but I think she will not return. We carried Clara back upstairs, but we did not know what else to do. There's no more laudanum . . . "

I run upstairs.

Everything is red.

Clara's nightgown, the bedding, even a good part of the carpet, all swim in bright red. Clara herself lies in bed, her head on my pillow. Her books have been torn to shreds, pages scattered over the blankets, and my photograph is in her hands. On the scraps of paper, I see my own name, over and over.

For one horrible moment, I think that I am too late, but then her eyes flicker open.

"Virginia," she says, and her voice is barely a sound, more the sound of air whispering through wintering trees. "You came back."

I kneel down, heedless of the blood soaking into my skirts. I clasp her hand in mine; her skin is so cold. "I would not leave you, Clara."

She tries to smile, but the smile becomes a rictus, a cough following soon after, blood staining her lips afresh. I can hear the air whistling in her lungs. It sounds as though there is no flesh behind her ribs at all, only empty space that stretches on and on forever.

The key is still in my pocket. I press the rough edge hard against my finger, hard enough that I feel metal scrape bone. Pain shrieks through me, but I push it away. What is my pain, measured against Clara's death?

She has no strength to fight me as I touch my torn finger to her lips. For a long moment, nothing happens, and then Clara's breath catches. I feel something break inside of her, and then blood rushes in a torrent from her lips.

Panic seizes me, and not knowing what else to do, I summon the silver light, *pushing* it through my skin. A hundred small tears open up over my body from the force of it, my own blood welling and mingling with Clara's. I wrap Clara in the silver light, close my eyes, think: *heal, be well, be alive.*

Clara's breath moves against my skin, and I open my eyes. She is *well*, her cheeks plump and pink, the blood on her lips flaking away to reveal healthy skin beneath. She takes in a deep breath, another, another.

She is alive. She is well.

She clasps my hand, her eyes filling with tears. "Virginia, you're an angel. Why did you never tell me that you were an angel?"

I see myself reflected in her eyes, my face haloed with silver light. Tears well, the salt stinging the torn places on my cheeks. All this time, I have feared what Clara would say when she saw the silver light, but never have I dreamed that she would react like this.

One more deep breath, and another. And then the air catches in her throat. She coughs, and I tense, expecting blood, but what comes from between her lips is a flower. White, its scent sweet and chill. An asphodel.

Asphodel: my regrets follow you to the grave.

Clara tries to breathe, but another asphodel flower unfurls from her lips, and another and another, and then there is a stream of them coming forth from her.

I pull flowers from her mouth, reach down into her throat to tear more away. The more I remove, the more of them blossom, their scent a miasma that surrounds us. And she is choking, she is suffocating, she is *dying*, and there is nothing that I can do.

More and more of the asphodel bloom, pushing me away, until Clara is covered with them entirely, the bed becoming a bower that shivers as she struggles beneath the flowers.

She stills, but the asphodel continues to bloom, a carpet of them flooding from the blood-soaked bed, creeping across the floor. With a last tremor, the place where Clara had been subsides, and I realise that the roots of the asphodel are burrowing into her, making earth of her flesh.

When the flowers threaten to cover my slippers, I retreat, move back down the stairs. The whispering of unfurling asphodel follows me, the river of white blooms spilling down after me as I descend.

It is only when the screaming starts that I realise that I have not pulled the silver light back beneath my skin, that I am standing in full view of the parlour, that it is Rose and the twins screaming. I am only barely aware of them rushing past me, the flowers following them out into the street.

The silver light uncurls, tendrils of it extending like vines towards the photographs on the mantelpiece. I pull each of them from their frames, smear blood onto their surfaces.

The photographs change. Each of the women who had lived here as Lilies sits there dead and alone, nothing in their hands but broken, dead roses. I let the photographs fall the ground, where they are quickly covered by the carpet of asphodel.

Out on the street, the twins and Rose are nowhere to be seen. I look up in time to see the upper windows shatter, asphodels tumbling in a flood from the broken panes. Perhaps the roots will slide between the bricks of the House, eat away at the mortar until the whole thing tumbles down, becomes earth for the garden that Clara had spoken of.

I let the silver light unfurl into the street, let it show me the direction in which I must go. It indicates I should follow the thin thread of green, the scent of *home*.

My feet barely touch the ground as I begin to walk, the scent of asphodel trailing me all the way.

BLUEBLOOD

FAITH MUDGE

It is an insult to die at midday.

In the mountain country where I was born, such things take place in the dark of night: the fall of an axe, the knotting of a noose. Here, it is a spectacle. From the narrow window of my tower room, I can see the road that leads away from the castle, down to the sea; it is already lined with people, jostling and squabbling amongst themselves for the best view of my execution.

In this place, a town will turn out to watch a man kill his wife, and call it justice.

My husband wants me to see this, to spend my last hours thinking about what will happen when the sun hits its zenith. Very soon he will step from the great oak doors, and a guard will come to bring me down. The crowd will get what they hunger for then. I hope it haunts them. It probably won't.

By this point it makes no difference. He can break every bone in my body and shed every drop of my blood and he will still be the fool.

Elyse will still be gone.

• • •

This is the story I stole. It began without me, in a city I will never see again.

Elyse was the queen's seventh child and the first to survive infancy. By then no one expected a son; it had begun to be doubted there would be an heir at all. The rumours that had plagued the queen from her first miscarriage grew louder, circumventions around a central point, delicately half-said by people who mattered. The outlandish death of the queen's mother. Her difficulty birthing a healthy child. In the early years of her marriage, the servants swore it had rained when she cried, and stormed when she raged.

Witch blood, was what they wouldn't say out loud.

So on her fifth birthday Elyse was paraded through the streets in a palanquin, a poppet princess waving solemnly to the curious populace, drowning out the gossip in a rush of loyalist sentiment. Daughters have their uses.

For the queen, however, it opened a new quandary. Elyse was now too old for a nurse, yet too young for lady's maid. She needed a companion—a handmaid close to her own age, quiet, quick and competent. There were plenty of servants to suit already at work in the castle, but while commoner girls were good enough to scrub floors and pluck chickens, even the daughter of a better sort of merchant was never going to be the confidante of a princess. To say the queen was a traditionalist would be to say that a tree is made of wood; her daughter had to have a companion of good noble blood, as generations of heirs had before her.

Unfortunately, while the practice was still favoured by the royal family, the sense of it being an honour had declined amongst the nobility. They would rather send their daughters abroad to the new academies, to forge friendships that might mature into advantageous political alliances and acquire a cultured polish that would appeal to wealthy husbands. Royal patronage could only take you so far; a future marchioness was much better off learning to talk about art in five languages.

That was never going to be my life.

My father's title was the only aristocracy my family could claim. Instead of keeping a house in the city or moving south to a villa for the winter the way our friends did, we lived in an ancient pile in the western valleys, held together more by ivy than mortar. Breeding racehorses was not a hobby for my father; it was the only way to pay the farmhands. I was the second eldest of thirteen and could turn my hand to any number of household tasks, including minding a horde of small brothers and sisters. When asked why she had not yet sent me away for a proper education, my mother looked hunted and made excuses about my 'weak heart'.

The royal summons was a reprieve for her, a way to save face. As for me, it was the adventure I'd never believed I would have. I could not wait to go.

The city of Celvre was two days travel to the north, close to the mountain pass for which it was named. I arrived at dusk inside the grandest carriage I had ever seen, bowling downhill towards the sweeping curve of the city that encircled moon-bright Lady's Lake. The way ahead was lit by glass lamps, blooming in the dark like captive stars. As the carriage rolled through wide winding streets, I knelt precariously on my seat, the better to stare. Women in jewel-coloured gowns alighted at a theatre, wearing lace masks of silver and gold; at one street corner a juggler spun knives between his fingers, while at the next a fire eater exhaled blue flame.

Above it all rose the shadowy weight of Mordan's Keep. It had been a fortress for centuries before it became a palace, and when I lifted my eyes to its night-shrouded walls, it stared back through narrowed arrow slits, a stone giant patiently awaiting the next war. Green banners snapped atop the turrets, bearing the white horsehead of the queen.

If her husband's banner was aloft beside hers, I did not see it. That was a fitting beginning. In all the years I spent at the side of his daughter, I never exchanged a word with the king. His ill health was notorious—if he left his sickbed for above a week it was considered a marvel and his physician of the hour might start dreaming of a knighthood. It never lasted, though. At length his gaunt, dull-eyed presence would fade away like a sad dream and the queen would sit alone once more in the throne room.

It was there I first saw Elyse.

Though I was not quite four years the elder, to her eyes I must have seemed almost grown up. Tall for my age, nerves pulling my mouth into a severe line, I towered awkwardly over her. She tried to hide her face in her mother's skirts but the queen pulled quickly away, as if embarrassed by her daughter's indecorum.

"You may approach, child," she said to me, her voice clear and brittle as glass.

I obeyed very carefully, afraid of using the wrong word, the wrong gesture, of being run through by that steely gaze. Not as afraid as Elyse, though. That woke a whisper of rebellion in me. As

I curtseyed, my head was brought briefly level with the princess's, and I pulled a face where the queen couldn't see. The little girl frowned and tilted her head, like a dubious bird wondering whether to fly away.

She was the same age as my youngest sister Mardie, but for weeks I thought she was older. Mardie had never been silent in her life; she ran and laughed and screamed her lungs raw when she wanted attention. The princess was not allowed to run. She had been taught from an early age to cover every laugh with her hand, as if it were a dirty thing. The last thing she wanted was attention.

Is it terrible I liked that, at first? Yes. I think it is.

I was not at my boldest either, of course. Life in the castle could not have been more different from the mildly anarchic informality of my home. Elyse became my bellwether: by watching what she did, I learned when meals were meant to be eaten and where, what places I was permitted to go and which were forbidden. That way I knew what to pretend I was doing.

When we were not at lessons—it being rightly, if insultingly, assumed that I would be Elyse's educational equal—we were for the most part expected to keep to her rooms in the Maiden's Tower, on the east side of the keep. There were bell cords in each room to summon a servant should we need one, and an elderly attendant of indeterminate status stationed at the foot of the tower stairs, who was to catch any slack as I learned my duties. She was tiny and fiercely genteel, quick to crack down on any mistake. I discovered eventually that she had been lady's maid to the old queen, the one whose scandalous death still haunted this place like a ghost. As far as I was concerned, she had high standards and low expectations; Elyse was treated with distant, chilly courtesy. By unsaid agreement, we avoided her quarters whenever we could.

To be honest, accustomed as I was to a rabble of fractious siblings, having only the one charge threw me. What was I supposed to do with her? Any attempt at jokes or games was met with wide-eyed incomprehension. When in the same room as the queen, Elyse resembled nothing so much as a pretty clockwork doll.

It was only in the gardens she really came to life. Twice a day we were sent outdoors to walk the shrubbery paths that crisscrossed the royal estate. Elyse would politely ignore any attempt of mine to set our course, and go whatever way she wanted. The place was a maze, but she never got lost.

Often we'd go to the royal aviary and she'd poke crusts through the bars for the parrots. Another favourite haunt was the hothouse, where tropical fruit trees grew green all year round underneath steaming glass. Her mother would have forbidden it if she knew, but Elyse was a favourite with the gardeners and no one told. She only led me there once she'd known me a few weeks and seen my own minor misdemeanours. She had a soul of her own, the queen's daughter, but she held it close where no one could see.

As the months passed, it felt like the chill of the keep's stone walls was sinking through my skin. What child of five is never allowed to play in the dirt? What little girl is not even permitted to bend over and pick up a dropped toy, because it does not befit the dignity of her station?

"Watch," I whispered one day, when we were alone together in the gardens. Bay tree hedges rose high on either side, forming a corridor of dim green light. Hitching up my skirts, I crouched and dug my hands into the dirt beside the path. It was damp enough to be easily moulded. I made a messy man-shape and stuck twig arms to the sides.

"Go on," I urged. "Get your hands as dirty as you like."

Elyse stared. To a child schooled in obedience from the first moments of her birth, I must have seemed an utter radical. She looked from me to the hedge, where roots dug deep into the earth and little pillows of moss grew thick in the shadows. Stiffly, like the little old woman she was not, she bent over and poked her finger into the damp earth. She drew a frowning face and gave a gulping little giggle at her own daring—then flicked me a startled look as I started giggling too. It was all so *absurd.*

Footsteps on the pavement made us both jump up. The princess went white, hiding her grubby hands behind her back. A sudden gust of wind eddied around us, whipping up a cloud of dried leaves; when they cleared, we saw a garden boy carrying a basket of weeds, struggling to hold onto his hat. He froze at the sight of us, then bowed so low he almost overbalanced, and fled as fast as he could. I looked at Elyse. She looked at me. I was the first to start laughing and then she did too, only a little bit hysterically.

From that day onward, we were an alliance.

When the queen forbade sweets ("a princess's teeth must be as flawless as her reputation") I smuggled sugared violets and peppermint candies from the kitchen in my sewing box. We taught each other all the games we knew and made up new ones that could be played in secret, tracing shapes onto each other's hands during lessons or the dull afternoons when Elyse was trotted out to smile at strangers. When she wept into her pillow over a failed lesson, I wrote the answers in her place. A five-year-old's handwriting is not difficult to mimic, and I was old enough to actually understand what we had been told. Sitting in quiet corners with my head down and my ears open, I was learning fast.

The queen did not age with the passing years; rather, she petrified. She dressed as if in a perpetual state of half-mourning, and there was so much distance in her eyes that I sometimes wondered how she could see me at all. Though Elyse and I were taught how to dance, parties were unknown within the castle walls, supposedly on account of the king's ill health—as if he would even *notice*—and any excursion into the city was so carefully managed she might as well have had us on strings.

In response, we became mistresses of illusion. The princess would invent irreproachable employments of our time while I swept away the evidence: chalk scrawls, forbidden dice, powdered sugar. Once or twice, we were caught and punished, but our repentance was very visible and our next secrets better kept.

• • •

The guard is at my door.

There is a moment of surreal awkwardness as he grasps for the correct title. At length he settles for a curt bow. "They are waiting," he says.

I know him. I was here for his first day of duty, when he opened the wrong gate and was swarmed by geese—it was the first time I'd laughed in months. Poor boy. He does not know what to think. I leave my window, leave the room without any attempt at delay—there's no point now. The guard takes my arm very lightly, with a mumbled apology, then lets go again when he realises we must go single file down the stairs. He moves ahead of me. I lift my skirt daintily and follow.

"Will you stay and watch?" I ask, as if we're talking about a mildly amusing show.

He hunches his shoulders against my gaze. "I must. I—it's my duty."

"I see."

"I'm sorry," he whispers, almost whimpers, as if he's hurting. "I don't want—I don't know—*why?* Why did you do it?"

We have reached the last step. I pat his shoulder gently.

"That's for me to know," I tell him.

Let me make this plain: I do not want to die. More than anything, I don't want to die like *this*. But I paid a very high price for this pretence and a few kind words are not enough to earn the truth.

The doors swing open.

The crowd howls.

• • •

Elyse at sixteen: not a clockwork doll any more. Her hair had darkened to a deep buttery shade but retained its curl, with a tendency to spring out from whatever style I'd attempted to create. She was not thin or pale enough to suit the queen, who now gave uneasy attention to her daughter's looks, like an artist who suspects her masterwork is coming out wrong. There wasn't much of her in the princess, and not much of the king either. Sometimes people mistook the two of us for sisters. I really don't know why.

Me at twenty: still the taller, if only by half an inch, finally grown into my legs and nose, with hair a shade of brown that sometimes looked blonde in the right light. Quite an ordinary sort of pretty. My looks were a relief to the queen because they made Elyse look more fashionable by comparison.

By day we walked in careful steps, trussed into tight bodices, drinking bitter tea at soirees and tracing out frowning faces on each other's wrists instead of saying rude things. By night, we made it a mission to break every one of the queen's rules.

I patched together luridly colourful gowns with ruffled skirts and Elyse stole a rope ladder from the gardeners. We climbed out the window, swinging lightly down from the castle walls, and roamed the night markets, dancing with jugglers and thieves and learning to cheat at cards. When people asked our names, we laughed. By lantern-light we might be tumblers, storytellers, flower-sellers, minstrel's daughters—a pair of light-footed troublemakers always gone by daybreak.

If the queen had caught me, she would probably have killed me. She had fought all her life for the respectability we were so determined to throw away, had beaten it into armour, but that did not keep her safe. The whispers only ever grew louder.

In the night market, we heard them.

What woman never gets wet in the rain? Never gets dirty when she walks in the mud? My cousin said . . . my aunt saw . . . everyone knows . . .

"Remember her mother," the rumourmongers reminded each other. The old queen, they meant, who had ridden out in the last war with a bow on her back and never missed a shot—who had died throwing herself atop her lover's funeral pyre, screaming at the flames to give him back. "Never seen a storm like that before," we were told, warning looks exchanged above our heads. The lake had broken its banks that night, rushing through the streets.

Sorceress. Witch. Tainted blood.

It felt wrong to listen. I was, in my own way, a loyalist. But Elyse wouldn't leave, eating up secrets with her hands fisted under the table, and I couldn't go without her.

"You know it's not true," I said, walking back through the dark.

"How do *you* know?"

"They say she has a spell to watch her enemies. If she could do that, she'd know where we are right now." I stopped, melodramatically raising a hand to cup my ear. "Do you hear the guards on their way?"

Elyse smacked my arm. "Just because she can't scry—"

"She's not to blame for how her mother died."

"Are you sorry for her?" Elyse asked, incredulous. She spun to face me, bright skirts whirling around her ankles, long hair loose around her shoulders. She was pretending to be a travelling player and had painted flowers on her cheek. I rubbed them carefully away with my thumb.

"Do you really think your mother is a witch?" I asked.

Elyse looked away. I still had my hand against her cheek; I let it fall.

The queen never did catch us, and in the end the reward was worse than any punishment. A princess could not inherit the throne; only a son could. The queen needed a grandchild to be her heir, and had no time for sentiment.

The duke of Hamonsea was the chosen man, second son of a courted ally. He possessed a vast estate on the other side of the forest. A catch, the queen might have said if she didn't believe such terms to be disgustingly vulgar. "Fortunate," she called it instead, as Elyse stared at his portrait. The princess said nothing. Nor did I. We nodded and curtseyed ourselves out the door and into the gardens, where Elyse ripped branches off trees and smashed flower pots and spat out every curse she'd ever learned. Suddenly she collapsed in the grass and started to cry.

"I won't!" she sobbed, over and over again. "I won't, I won't!"

I had no words to comfort her. The duke of Hamonsea might be rich and titled with a throne just one brother away, but he was also twice the princess's age and had two wives already cold in the ground. From childbirth, we'd been told, but he had no children. He lived in a remote stronghold on the coast, as if even his father couldn't stand to have him close.

"He'll kill me," the princess wept, burying her face in her hands. Her hair pooled in heavy golden chains. "He'll cut me up and bury me with the other wives."

I knelt and put my arms around her. The day had seemed bright a few hours ago, but now clouds were bruising the horizon. There was a storm coming.

"He'll kill me," Elyse said again, very softly, against my shoulder.

"He won't," I promised. "He won't lay a hand on you."

She calmed after that; she believed me, you see. Night after night I lay awake, trying to find a way out. We could run away—sell some jewels to pay passage across the sea, or buy a small boat of our own. I could make a living for us as a seamstress. I allowed myself to fantasise about a house of our own, what it would be like to wear colour every day and laugh as loud as we wanted. Where neither of us would have to marry anyone. It was such a pretty, fragile thought.

But there were more guards outside every night, patrolling the castle walls, walking the gardens. When I tried to slip out, as I'd done so often before, I was caught and had to invent an excuse very quickly. This alliance meant a great deal to the queen. She was taking no chances.

Elyse was to marry in Hamonsea; all the preparations were made with the grim efficiency of a funeral. Several times I suggested errands that might take me from the castle, but none of my pretexts were enough to get away. Watching the queen dress her silent daughter in white wedding silks, my heart felt like a stone in my chest. It was like forgetting how to breathe.

Weeks passed. The day came for our departure.

The weather was foul. Thunder rattled the windows, and squalls of rain had turned the courtyard into a morass of mud. It seemed the queen must surely put off the journey, but she did not. Instead she stood at the top of the castle steps and pressed a kiss against Elyse's forehead, like a benediction, while I stood shivering beside our mounts. Mine was a placid brown gelding, the princess's a restless white mare I had never seen before. Elyse wasn't a good rider at the best of times—in this weather, on a horse she had not ridden before, I didn't know how on earth she'd keep her seat.

I reached over to pet the mare's neck, hoping to calm it down, and realised it was not after all entirely white. Three rusty red marks like smeared thumbprints spotted its forehead, between the eyes. My fingers stung when I brushed them and the queen looked up abruptly.

I dropped my hand, staring at the horse. It stared back at me.

The stone in my chest grew, expanding until it felt my ribs might crack.

"Go with my blessing," the queen said, and we rode into the rain.

Four guards travelled with us as protection from any danger on the road and, as I am sure the queen intended, insurance we would not bolt before we were safely delivered to our destination. It was spring, not long after the thaw, the trees overhead budding with newborn leaves. The princess, riding between her guards, stared at the ground without seeing a thing. She wouldn't talk. Now and again, her horse lifted its head to look at me.

They say the queen has a spell to watch her enemies. I should have listened.

Between the southern valleys and the coastline of the neighbouring kingdom lay the forest we called the Merewold. It was only four days ride from the castle, but here the chill of winter lingered among the evergreens; the air was cold, scented with pine and wet earth. We rode the path in single file, speaking little, for it seemed even to the least superstitious of us that something in this wood was listening. As Elyse rode, the trees swayed, bending as if to watch her pass. The leaves whirled in her wake.

Witch blood.

It never stopped raining.

For two more days we rode, until on the third morning we emerged from the trees and saw the road snaking downwards with the sea beyond.

The guards left us then. It would be an insult to the groom for them to stay, implying as that did that the queen didn't believe he could protect her daughter. The men were so glad to go, they did not even wait for the duke's appearance—he would be waiting at the road's end, they assured us, and with that they disappeared among the pines, leaving Elyse and I alone. I doubted they would go far today. They were more afraid of the queen than of the forest.

There was a stream somewhere to the left of the path, just visible through the trees. Without a word Elyse plunged towards it, forcing her way through pine needles and waist-high brambles, falling to her knees by the water and thrusting her hands into its icy current. They were bleeding from the thorns.

"Elyse." I bent, trying to pull her away. "Stop. I'll fetch a cup."

"You lied," she said, without looking at me. "We can't escape. You made me hope, and you *lied*."

"No, I swear, we'll find a way—"

Something moved behind us, a crushing tread in the undergrowth. I turned sharply and found the white horse pushing its way through the trees. Elyse made a startled sound.

"*Queen's daughter, do your duty*," the mare said. Its voice was a sibilant murmur, a courtier's tones from a horse's throat. I stifled a scream with my hands. "*Be your heart broken, be it whole, duty is all.*"

Elyse choked. She would have fallen into the stream but caught my skirts in time—she rose jerkily, still clinging to me.

"A witch horse," she whimpered. "I've been riding a witch's horse."

"Your mother's horse," I whispered. She was shaking in my arms. We stood together at the stream's edge, trapped under the mare's steady gaze. I grew up around horses; I learned to ride and walk at the same time. Horses did not stare like that.

"*Away from the river, queen's daughter,*" it said, and we shuddered. "*The duke awaits. The day grows ever old.*"

I decided then. It wasn't a conscious decision, a carefully laid plan—if it had been I think it would have failed. I let Elyse go and started running, breaking through the undergrowth towards the road. My gelding was patiently cropping grass; no one had thought to curse *my* mount. I scrabbled wildly in the saddlebags, pulling free a long blue gown that had buttons instead of laces. It was not quite long enough, but it would do. My hair and face I could do nothing about—I was no princess.

That didn't matter. Everyone knows portrait painters can't be trusted.

Elyse reached me as I was swinging into the saddle. The mare was trying to follow, but had become snared in the brambles and whispering trees; I could hear its struggles to get free.

"Where are you going?" What a sight my princess was, tear-streaked and muddy. She didn't understand.

"The duke is waiting," I said. I left her there on the road, calling out my name.

It wasn't my name any more.

The duke was waiting at road's end, as promised, with a group of his men. I slowed the gelding as I reached them, holding out my hand for him to kiss. His fingers were cold, his smile colder. I held my back regally straight, and smiled.

"My lord! Forgive my undignified arrival. It has been a most awkward journey. My horse threw me and so I am forced to ride my maid's. She is following on foot. Would one of your men go to collect her? Otherwise I fear we will be here all day, and I am wearied of these endless trees."

The duke had never met the princess before, and certainly not her handmaid. In these clothes, with my arrogant ease, the duke did not doubt my authenticity for a moment. At his swift gesture, a man detached from the party and rode back the way I had come. The rest of us continued down the path, exchanging cool pleasantries.

"What would you have done with the guilty beast?" the duke asked.

"Oh, it is hopeless!" I exclaimed. "I declare it is more than half wild. Have its head cut off, for all I care, only do not allow it near myself or my maid again." A bubble of hysteria welled from my chest and escaped as laughter. "My, but I sound bloodthirsty! My mother would not recognise me."

The duke half-smiled. "We are not inclined to sentimentality, highness, here in Hamonsea. The beast will be slaughtered and a new mount found for you."

By the time Elyse arrived, riding with the duke's man, it was too late for her to stop me. She strained forward in the saddle, trying to meet my eye, but I turned away from her to laugh at the duke. He was saying something about hunting; I could not hear the individual words. He smiled again, and pressed my hand with his large heavy one.

There were ceremonies that night, fine lords and fine food and even dancing. I was so exhausted by then that I wanted to curl in a ball on the floor, but somehow I danced in the hard brawny arms of my fiancé, and smiled for his bleak-eyed father. My maid was, of course, excluded from the ceremonies. She had been sent to my chamber to prepare my things, but I was already thinking ahead to that.

"It is not that she's an ill-hearted girl," I said gaily to my groom-to-be at some point in the night, while I sat at his side and forced my aching face to smile, smile, smile. "But she has a sharp tongue and complains a good deal. I have a mind to dismiss her. Perhaps a purse to set her on her way could be arranged, and a new maid found for me tomorrow?"

"Of course," said the duke. "I am glad you, too, disapprove insubordinance."

"Well, naturally," I said. "I cannot stand people always expecting more."

Elyse was sent away that night. She knew I was watching and did not go quietly. She called for me, she kicked and wept and shouted, but the guards turned her roughly out the gates and threw her bag after her. My bag, it had been this morning. I'd slipped enough jewellery inside to buy her passage on the next ship out. I watched her disappear into the night, a defiant silhouette that kept turning back, as though she expected even now I might come down.

I did not. I went to bed and slept the sleep of the drugged and damned, until the sun of my wedding day came to wake me.

I married the duke of Hamonsea. The king blessed us without meeting my eyes, and we said our vows, and I wore a smile until it felt like a rictus. My hair looked almost golden in the sunlight, under my veils, and I knew the people who had come to watch our procession longed to be like me, to be the princess.

That night, in his bed, I bit down the tears until my lip bled.

We stayed a week after the wedding at the palace of the king, and afterwards rode in a beautiful white carriage up the steep and rutted roads to the duke's stronghold. My rooms overlooked the sea—the only kindness that stone tomb ever had for me. I spent a great many hours looking out over the water and dreaming of a day that never came, when I would step on a boat and sail off to find Elyse in whatever haven she had built for herself. I hoped she was happy. Surely I had paid enough for that.

Two years passed before the queen came to visit her wedded daughter.

We had exchanged no letters; that pretence was beyond what I could bear and besides, Elyse would not have done it. I can't say what kept the queen away for so long. I want to believe it was guilt; she did not want to face what she had done. Perhaps that is why she gave no warning of her impending visit—she thought Elyse would find a way to elude her. The first I knew of her arrival was when I saw horses coming up the road to the castle, led by the queen's pennant.

I froze at the window, one hand pressed against my mouth. As the queen rode through the gates, she looked up. Nailed to the arch was the head of the horse whose death I had ordered, hung there by my husband in mockery of my bloodthirsty ways. Wind and sun and rain had reduced it to an empty skull, but the queen guessed. Her eyes went wide and found me, at my window.

And I smiled.

• • •

I stand here in the sun, waiting to die.

The queen stands on my left, my judge; the duke on my right, my executioner. I wonder whose thought it was that I should die this way, thrust naked into a barrel studded with nails and rolled down to the sea, where my bloodied remnants will be washed away by the tide. I suppose it doesn't matter. They can do what they want. I have *won*.

With trembling fingers, I untie the ribbon at my throat and my white shift falls to the ground. The shouts of the crowd are deafening. The duke has trained them well.

He grips my shoulders and turns me to face him. I know him too well by now to hope for mercy—he should know me better than to hope for fear. The life I have is not worth begging for. His hands leave red prints on the bare skin of my arms. He thrusts me away and I stumble backwards, towards the barrel.

I fall on hard stone. All the breath in my body is knocked out of me.

The barrel is rolling away.

A wind has blown up from nowhere on this still, hot day. It fills my lungs, sweeps my hair across my face, blinds me for a moment—and in that moment, the crowd falls suddenly quiet. I comb the hair from my eyes and look down the road to the sea. A boat is bobbing in the water of the bay, and a girl is standing where the road meets the sand.

"Elyse," I whisper.

And—"Elyse," breathes the queen.

The wind whips at her, lashing the name from her lips. She staggers, holding up her hands as if to ward it off, but it is relentless. It whirls around the courtyard, leaving me untouched at the eye of the storm. The duke starts forward, drawing his sword; the wind beats him to his knees. At the end of the road, my death rolls to a halt at Elyse's feet, and she looks me in the eyes. She holds out her arms.

I push myself to my feet. The wind caresses my cheek like a kiss.

And I run as fast as I can, past the gaping guards and the silenced crowd, all the way down to the water, where a witch's daughter and her boat wait for me.

The wind fills our sails, and we are gone.

MR SCHMIDT'S DEAD PET EMPORIUM

SALLY McLENNAN

The black patches grew with agonizing slowness. The end of his nose was excruciatingly sensitive and Eli Schmidt's eyes watered. The tears spilling down his cheeks were an unaccustomed sensation, one barely noticed through his pain. This was worse than creating the purple lividity patches on the rest of his body or the swatches of grey on his arms, face, and neck.

Still, the black ovals he was filling in on his nose did grow, and he kept the hand holding his tattoo gun characteristically steady. It was satisfying to see how ghastly he already looked under the fluorescent lights of the small bathroom. But the nose was crucial. Get it wrong and every dead thing would see right through him. Eli focused on getting his fake enlarged nostrils just so, dabbing beads of blood away with the tissue clenched in his left hand. He had never been one for sloppy work. Careful fingers and the dead were the only reasons he was alive to grimace at his prematurely grey hair.

Eli Schmidt had always made his living from the dead. They had been his constant companions and means of survival since his youth when he had pulled gold from teeth in a shed beside Buchenwald. There, he was not only surrounded by shambling skeletons each night, and all day, he was *one of* the walking dead.

His careful posthumous dental work, always punctuated by the beatings of the Kapo who oversaw the pajamaed dentists, had allowed him to join the other shamblers in stacked bunks each night instead of going to the graves.

So it was natural he preferred to remain with the dead when he emigrated to a new country, unable to bear staying anywhere near Weimar. They were far kinder than the living, in his experience.

In the Displaced Persons Camp, where he and so many other survivors were initially stored, he had caused dismay by asking to learn tattooing and embalming. These were strange requests from a person newly out of a concentration camp.

Eli was immediately sent to a bluff American psychiatrist. However, the kindly Doctor could not break through Eli's humble insistence that these were his interests.

"Why not let him have at it?" the doctor said finally, when he'd had enough of Eli sitting quietly and speaking as little as possible. "I'll be right here."

But Eli hadn't needed him.

Instead, as before, he let working on bodies succour him and he learned how to decorate them in life and death.

When he reached Australia, he was offered 'placement' in a funeral home. This meant lower than usual wages for shaving, then making up the faces of the deceased, closing their eyes and mouths, massaging them to loosen their limbs for positioning, and filling their body cavities with preserving fluids. Eli shuffled through these days as he had shuffled through the last four years: stoop-shouldered, thin, and always quiet as the grave. He worked to improve his English as a matter of principle, but seldom used it. His eyes never stopped looking sunken and his hair was thin from his twenties on.

His habit of hoarding his meagre earnings (and all manner of other less important things) caused a little teasing, and some sympathy from his co-workers, but as he kept to himself they learned not to notice his peccadillo.

In ten years he garnered enough money and knowledge to buy his own funeral parlour, the Lychgate. But he still preferred working with dead customers to meeting his living contractors.

When the virus infected his customer base, Eli refused to panic. As he always did, he would survive.

The first day—before news of a virus was even made public—Eli was picking up groceries and saw a shambling man pull down a woman and start feasting on her. He didn't break into a run as so many around him did. He was an old man at fifty-eight. Carrying his groceries, he set a steady pace, and went where he liked most to be when troubled; to his work.

It was abandoned and Eli shook his head at that. All the doors that communicated with his workspace were airtight and it was ventilated by a system with back-up generators. It wouldn't do to have the living smell their dead family members in a power cut. Every door locked. He ignored the thumping coming from the lockers in his holding room and secured the doors behind him. He tossed his groceries in an empty locker and sat down to think.

He would, he decided, wait. For three weeks he listened to his radio, slept in an empty walk-in fridge which he turned off, and washed in his preparation room sinks. His bed was a casket and his pillows and clothes were those left by relatives of the deceased but never needed. He was thankful for his bags of groceries, and his tendency to hoard food, which his staff had found so funny. Each day part of him was expecting one of his workers to seek shelter with him. But none of them came.

After three weeks, when the bulletins on the radio were replaced with static, Eli began to prepare. For nights at a time he stood in front of the mirror in his small bathroom and applied makeup to his face, arms, hands and legs. He worked on one patch of skin until he got the appearance of dead flesh right. When he was happy with a design, he went to a cupboard he normally kept locked and pulled out, from among the many useful things inside, his tattoo gun and inks. His purple and grey inks ran out, but he thought he had done well reproducing the appearance of the zombie from his shopping trip. It looked good, especially when he mussed up his sparse, grey hair.

His nose had come next: he gritted his teeth and committed to his work.

Eli no longer knew if it was night or day, living under artificial light, and without the guidance of the radio. He ate, slept, and woke, and it was time to tackle the next challenge—his smell. Eli was used to covering the smell of the dead; now he had to recreate it. There was putrescine, in the form of Stanyl, in a large bottle on top of one cupboard. It had always fascinated him that one of the two key components in the smell of death was used by modern industry to create plastics. So he'd kept the bottle in pride of place. Stanyl had a notoriously long lasting odour.

He tinkered with various chemicals from his cupboards and supply room for several cycles of waking and sleeping before he had a smell that suggested cadaverine (the other component of the scent of death) to add to the Stanyl. When it nearly smelled right, Eli added two natural sources of cadaverine. He urinated and collected a quarter cup in one of the chipped mugs from his collection. Then he stood in his closet of a bathroom and masturbated, switching his mind off, and letting his body react to motions he hadn't attempted in decades. He left the semen—a fluid he had previously had little use for—in a beaker for a day or two before he added it to the mix with his urine.

It smelled right, or really wrong, as the case may be. Still, it took a lot of courage to open one of the chilled lockers.

The zombie inside thrashed her way out clumsily, spilling onto the preparation room tiles in a heap. She looked at Eli and moaned listlessly before she clambered to her feet. But she stood up facing away from him. Eli swept her feet from under her and pulled her into a closet. It wasn't hard: she was skin and bones.

Then he removed the cotton swab from around his neck. His mixture was slightly toxic and he took care not to touch the foul brew as he discarded it. Eli took his lab coat and daubed it with his 'aftershave'.

He was almost ready to leave.

First: product testing. He opened the closet the loose zombie was banging around in, and stepped back. She fell forward onto her face, groped at the scratched grey linoleum, and got up sluggishly. Eli had to repress an almost chivalric urge to help her up. He found himself wondering who she had been in life: her clothes were nice. Before it turned into a brittle, dusty matt, her hair might have been light blonde.

Eli walked slowly to her empty locker and checked the tag. Her name was Stella Jenks. Stella didn't react to him at all. She gained her feet and began patrolling the room aimlessly. All Eli had to do was avoid her.

When he was confident in his disguise, Eli grasped her arms from behind, and pushed her away from him as her head snapped to one side, her teeth clacking. Sick shock registered as he felt the bone in her forearm break, but Stella seemed oblivious to anything except trying to bite whatever held her.

"Come, come," he told her, reprovingly, and noticed her efforts increase. They reacted to human voices. Gently but firmly, Eli pushed Stella into the closet again. She banged against the door, but he had closed it and was already turning away.

"I hope I am back soon," Eli called to her softly, and stepped out of his office.

He decided to leave out the front door. The back door let onto a small garden with the cemetery conveniently over the road. The front door stood between him and a side road off the main street of town. It was more dangerous, being potentially more crowded, but Eli needed to see how bad things were and the back door represented a longer journey.

He stood inside the frosted front door for some time. Occasionally a human shadow moved in front of the glass, but everything was silent but for the shuffling of feet and none of those moved with *purpose*. So neither would Eli.

He listened carefully and, when he thought it was likely the door was unobserved, he opened it. A zombie lunged at him; the corpse had been slumped in the doorway and responded to his movement more quickly than Stella had. Eli stepped on its arms and used his hand to hold its head back. He danced away a few steps, around the side of the building, and put his back to the wall, freezing in place while the dead man he had stepped on lumbered clumsily to his feet. And straight past Eli.

He watched carefully and stayed still. Human noises, human speed, seemed to be a trigger. Plus, zombies don't open doors. He slumped to the ground against the frontage of his funeral parlour and none of the zombies shambling near him reacted. There were only a dozen of them, which was far fewer than Eli had expected. The pet shop next to the funeral home was intact but other shops had broken windows; the cafes, the health food shop, and the sporting gear shop he'd never entered.

Eli noted the dead near him looked better off than Stella. They not only moved faster, they looked less thin—less fragile—than she did. But they were filthy and they reeked even over the liberal dressing of aftershave Eli had put on his coat.

The man who owned the petrol station on the corner crossed the street in front of Eli. His blue overalls were covered with dark stains. He served as a reminder. Eli closed his eyes and let his ears work. He reached for sounds beyond those of the walking dead's restless feet and the breeze that pushed litter along the walls and gutters. The light became golden as he sat listening—the colour that belongs to late afternoon. But Eli never heard a siren or the sound of a car. There were no voices calling for help. There were no voices at all. An unexpected queasiness disturbed Eli's stomach and he breathed slow and deep 'til that passed too.

As it grew later, the pace of what Eli dubbed the deadbeat—the footfalls of the corpses around him—quickened. The dead were night hunters.

When they were moving with an almost human speed, Eli stood up slowly. Once his legs stopped prickling, he wandered aimlessly toward the main street, sticking to a wider road, rather than going down an alley where he couldn't move casually away from grasping hands.

He let his feet fall heavily on the ground, imitating the deadbeat. None of the dead reacted to him and Eli realised the hunched shoulders and self-effacing manner, which he had been unable to shed when he left Buchenwald, were serving him as well in this dead world as they had in the camp.

On Fort Street, Eli wandered past the petrol station. The arms of petrol pumps lay tangled on the ground as if they had been used and discarded at speed. The shelves looked bare and only a few damaged items littered the ground.

On Main Street, walking corpses packed the square, and there was no sign of human life. The sheer mass of the dead blocked his view of the shops and, momentarily, hid the wreckage. Then Eli felt the first fluttering of panic. He was stirred to fear by the sight of the supermarket, now totally without the glass that used to stand between it and the street, and displaying its utterly empty shelves.

Eli saw a break in the traffic of zombie walkers, and took it, heading straight for the open shop front. He had to shuffle to one side: the glass was everywhere and he couldn't risk a cut with the hungry dead all around him. But he had seen enough. The supermarket reeked of rotten produce and all the cans and packaged food were gone.

Spoiled meat, and the dead drawn by the smell, remained. Eli glimpsed a dead housewife battering her face against a closed freezer. Meat juice ran across the floor from it and a corpse child was on her belly lapping at it.

At least you can eat, Eli thought weakly.

Two doors down he slumped against a wall, his trousered legs splayed before him as he sank to the ground. He was done for. He knew he could survive on little food, and his hoard would last for perhaps two more weeks, that being so. There was a small community garden on the other side of the graveyard but it was certain to have been picked clean too. Eli needed groceries, and soon.

In despair, Eli ignored a dead check-out girl as she stumbled into his legs and fell to the pavement. Her jaw clacked as she floundered but she clumsily regained her feet and wandered back across the town square. Eli smiled grimly. His disguise was working perfectly, but without food it didn't matter.

Thud! A second zombie shambled at full deadbeat into Eli's legs and hit the pavement. It complained deep in its chest—more a frustrated exhalation than a vocalization—and Eli froze. But the thing also stuttered to its feet and walked haltingly on.

A shadow fell over Eli and he looked up slowly. A corpse stood right over him and it was *looking* at his legs intently. It still had glasses in its top pocket and wore the frayed remains of an old man's cardie but Eli didn't recognize him—he had kept too much to himself in the human world. Part of the corpse's cheek had been clawed open and his teeth were exposed. Thick fluid ran sluggishly along the edges of the wound.

Eli hardly breathed. After the longest moment, the once-old-man spun awkwardly and stepped off the pavement at a right angle, crossing the road.

Wonder filled Eli. The thing had learned. It had watched its fellows fall and understood how to avoid falling itself. His former fellow townsfolk had once resided in those bodies, each one now replaced with someone else—someone with horrible appetites. Eli's interest was brief. None of it meant anything if he couldn't find food.

Dejected, Eli pushed himself to his feet and wandered back to the funeral parlour. But the front of the building was now thronging with animated dead. Another hitch of panic hit his chest. The dead were definitely looking livelier. Eli kept himself to an amble and made his way to the back of the building. The garden was empty and so was the parking lot next to it.

Huffing, Eli made for the back door but he paused before he opened it. The back door to the pet shop was closed, but the hasp that usually locked it hadn't been put on. His guts clenched at the thought, but Eli realised pet food could possibly save his life while local gardens recovered from the foraging of other would-be survivors. He had eaten worse things.

Eli pressed himself against the pink pet shop door, listening. *Something* moved inside, several somethings, but they sounded lighter than dead people. There must still be animals trapped inside. Pity touched Eli's heart and, not knowing if he did them a favour or not, he opened the door and stepped behind it.

The first puppy nearly killed him. Folds of skin hung off it, where perhaps its litter mates had chewed on it. Teeth bared, it darted at his exposed ankles, hungry for his flesh. But Eli was wearing his work boots and he shoved it back hard with his foot, pressing himself further behind the door. The dead pup raced out of the shop and into the Lychgate's garden. Three more necrotic Labradors pelted after it. They were only halfway across the lawn when a group of dead stumbled through the garden gate and lurched after them. In moments the puppies were cornered and covered by hunch-backed feeding corpses.

While the dead were distracted, Eli slipped around the door and into the pet shop. A cacophony greeted him. No more animals were loose. But dead budgies hooted from their cages and milk-eyed rats banged against the acrylic fronts of terrariums. Cats with open sores, and fur falling off their bodies, clawed at bars. Eli reeled for a moment before he gathered himself.

There *were* sacks of cat and dog food on the shelves. But first he investigated the tiny staff room off the shop area. It held a fridge and inside was a carton of vanilla soy milk. Eli drank it immediately, easing his thirst. There were plain biscuits in the cupboard next to the fridge, though they had long gone stale. He ate them, of course. This was all the human food he found, but it lifted his spirits.

Eli had done enough, and had enough, for one day, even so. He peered around the pink door, and slipped outside again, shutting it carefully. The dead were busy over the last remnants of the puppies and he let himself back into the funeral parlour.

Eli shut the fridge door after himself, crawled into his casket bed, and pulled the lower half of the lid closed before he could begin to relax. Ideas swam in his head and all sorts of horrific images from the day, but he couldn't make them resolve into anything useful. It felt like hours before he slept.

But when he woke he had a crazy plan that *might* work. First, he had to renovate his new home.

He went straight to the workshop where a young man used to build boxes to put the dead in, fancy or plain. Happily, the counter of the pet shop ran parallel to the outside wall of the casket workshop.

It was early, and the local zombies would be sluggish, but Eli would have to be fast to survive. He took up the circular saw and plugged it in. Heart in his mouth, Eli started the thing and pushed it into the workshop wall, cutting a narrow rectangular hatch at shoulder height.

It only took moments, but Eli switched off the saw and downed it, leaving it spinning blade up, while he bolted to his workroom. The alley between the shops was less than a foot wide—too narrow for any intact body. He was more worried about the dead reacting to the noise by smashing open his front door or the windows of the pet shop.

Eli waited until the next morning to cut a matching hatch in the neighbouring wall. After he had laid low for several hours, he emerged nervously, but his house was undamaged and no dead roamed next door. Neat in his work as always, he took up several smooth bits of wood and glued and screwed them into place so the two hatches became a bridge between the buildings. Then Eli attached two casket handles, one above each side of the hatch. He could pull himself from building to building, but the dexterity required would, he hoped, be too much for the dead.

That night, under the glow of fish tank lights, Eli put newspaper over the windows of the pet shop. He moved slowly and quietly, taping the paper before he approached the window and freezing at any movement in the shadows until the danger had passed. It took most of the night, but he got the windows covered.

Fortification was required. Eli took two of his church trucks—the massively solid collapsible gurneys used to transport casketed bodies—and a pile of the clamps from a funeral marquee. When he had pulled each truck through the hatch into the pet shop, he put them on the counter, opened them to their fullest extent, removed wheels and clamped everything in place. The diamond-shaped struts that supported the bed of each truck were capable of bearing 800 pounds of dead weight. When they were fully opened and on the counter, Eli was able to bolt them to the ceiling as well as to the counter itself. He had created a grill that kept anything in the rest of the shop away from his side of the counter. But the dead would be able to reach through it.

It took Eli several more days to empty the shop of stock and shelves and raid the local pound for protective gear. He experienced a moment of dismay when he saw some well-meaning person had released the impounded animals from their cages, but he told himself it was all to the good.

Finally, Eli set up an elaborate system of pulleys that would allow him to open cages from the safety of the counter space. As he worked, in full bite gloves from the pound, the caged animals lunged at him repeatedly.

Eli was ready to start training, though he had no idea if this part of his business plan would work. From his hoard, he took one of the few remaining cans and slipped it into his coat pocket. Then, with straps in hand, he opened Stella's closet door. She hurtled out as if she had been pressed against it. Eli waited patiently for her to slow down then slipped up behind her, dropped a trolley strap over her shoulders, and cinched it tight just above her elbows.

She tried to spin in a circle to get at him, but Eli had the catchpole he had stolen ready. He put the noose over her head, pulled it tight, and pushed her away with it. Stella was furious and she struggled at the end of the pole gnashing her teeth in apparent frustration.

Eli didn't like to handle anyone roughly, but needs must. He pushed her ahead of him and then backed down the hall to open the back door. It was morning and the garden was still. He pulled Stella after him, guiding her as best he could, and walked her through the pink door of the pet shop.

She went berserk as soon as they stepped inside. She darted at the cages, moving faster than Eli had seen before. As she clawed at a cat hungrily, Eli released the trolley strap and lifted the catchpole gingerly off her head. While the cat Stella slavered after took the opportunity to chew on her fingers, Eli backed away and closed the shop door after him.

Eli hastened—as much as a man imitating a zombie could safely hasten—back to the funeral parlour, into the workshop and through his hatch. Stella was still too excited to notice. So he put the can outside the grill on the counter, pulled out the chair that rested under the till, and settled in to wait.

Eventually, Eli curled up on the floor and slept. Stella had gone from reaching for the cat to trying to fish, and her fingers were quite damaged, while the tank water had become cloudy. But still she tried.

When he stirred back to wakefulness, the pet shop was quiet. Eli stood up and Stella, who had been standing quietly in the centre of the room, staggered at him. Her flailing hand caught the can on the counter and knocked it through the church truck legs toward Eli. He grabbed one of the ropes hooked to the counter and tugged it firmly.

Behind Stella, a dead cat shot out onto the floor. Stella turned immediately and lurched at it, her arms stretched before her, and her mouth dripping mucous. She threw herself onto the cat, fingers tearing, teeth champing. Eli winced. It wasn't long before he pulled himself back through the hatch into the funeral parlour and shut himself in his casket.

Over the next week, or perhaps two, Eli repeated the process with Stella until he could leave the can anywhere in the pet shop and she would deliver it to him for her treat. The day she picked it up off the floor to give to him was a red letter day. Another day or two later, he eased the pet shop door open and used the catchpole to push Stella out into the world. That night, he took the newspaper off the windows and put up the little sign he had, in a moment of humour, crafted in the workshop.

Its tidy lettering read: "Mr Schmidt's Dead Pet Emporium."

Mr Schmidt hung clothes that were once left for women and children, daubed with plenty of his aftershave, along the church truck grill. Then he made himself a bed of pillows. It was four days before Stella shambled back in and dumped a can on the counter. Unaccustomed tears formed in Mr Schmidt's eyes—partly with relief and partly because he felt like a proud parent—and he opened the cage of a good sized terrier.

The zombies on the pavement outside paused to watch.

Eli's cans and dead animals were both running low by the time Stella brought him her third can. A day later a dead person Eli had never before seen shambled through the open door. This happened occasionally: a corpse would wander in, bang at the cages, and patrol the room for a while before shambling back out. But this time, the teenager who had come in clutched a tin. He missed the counter top, but Eli released a cat at once, beaming. He had a business once more.

It was time to go hunting. At dawn the next morning, Eli assembled traps from the pound on a church truck. They had been baited with mice from the shop; Eli had halved them lengthways and they still wriggled. He covered the truck with an aftershave-painted sheet and pushed it slowly through the back door.

Eli let out a breath he hadn't known he held when none of the dead reacted to the trolley. Perhaps, he reasoned, it wasn't all that rare for them to get tangled up in—and carry along—the detritus of human life. He ambled slowly into the suburbs, stopping at one home to harvest the tomatoes he saw growing up the back fence, while its dead occupants watched him dully through the window.

As Eli went he watched for other things he could forage and laid out the traps in spots the dead couldn't get to them. Once he had run out of traps, he took shelter in an empty shed, ate his tomatoes, and curled up to sleep on the church truck bed under the stinking sheet.

His trip was a success. He was not only unscathed, but he returned with enough dead animals to restock his cages, and a supply of fruit. Months passed, his customer base developed, and the Dead Pet Emporium thrived.

Eli took to taking Stella with him, on the catchpole, when he went foraging. He couldn't have said why he did it, but her presence certainly seemed to deter other walkers, and she allowed herself to be pushed before the cart without apparent distress.

At the end of summer, Eli guided his cart slowly down the middle of a suburban street. He had nearly reached the end of his supply of traps and he was tired. It took him a moment to react when a figure wandered out into the middle of the street, a long block away, then turned and *stared* at him. He stopped. Could he expect violence from the first human he had seen in months? Would he or she take him for a corpse?

But no—the figure looked all around, then beckoned. Eli kept his walk slow, watching for the dead, but he only saw those trapped in houses. He had become so used to being surrounded by *them* that, under the pressure of the stranger's direct gaze, his skin crawled.

Eli stopped when he was still ten meters out from the other human. He walked around Stella, his hands held away from his body. He didn't speak until he had done another check for corpses, and even then he kept his voice down. It cracked, but he managed: "Who are you?"

"A librarian," the person answered, and it was only then Eli knew he spoke to a woman. There was a belt hung with corpse hands around her waist and they twitched idly. Eli noticed none of them had fingernails. Front and back, the tiny woman wore gory ribcages, laced around her tightly like a breastplate.

"I'm a fun—a pet shop owner," Eli amended. "Are you okay?"

"Yep," the librarian answered. "You?"

"Thriving," said Eli, humbly.

"Good," she said, and turned and started walking down the side street away from him. Eli stood and watched her until he could no longer see the gore-laden spikes of hair on her head.

It took another two trips before he saw her again. Although his catch decreased, he had made both trips to the same area.

She emerged from a garden, her backpack bulging, and stood watching him come closer.

"What's your name, then?" she asked.

"I'm Eli," he said.

"Pleased to meet you." The librarian held out a zombie arm she had taped to a meter-long ruler.

Instinctively, Eli took the hand and shook it, admiring the firm pressure of the hand's grasp. The librarian had bridged the gap between them most cleverly. Stella was trying to get to the woman, but Eli had put the brakes on the cart. He ignored her.

"Is she your missus?" the librarian asked.

"No," said Eli. "She is my best customer, though."

"Oh," said the woman, "Okay. My name is Anna."

It was a sensible name and Eli saw that the librarian fitted it.

"I've finished setting traps for today. You can come back to my place with me tomorrow if you need a place to stay," Eli told her, his heart in his mouth and that mouth very dry.

"Um . . . no, thank you," Anna said, "I'm really okay." She turned and walked off.

Once more, Eli watched her disappear down the street. He searched out an empty shed, tied Stella up outside, and put a new pair of shoes he'd found on her feet. Her soles had worn through and her feet were bloodied by the journeying Eli had inflicted on her.

Then, he crawled onto the church truck. Curled on his side, he felt hollow. He got up restlessly and ate a can of peaches. But it didn't help at all.

The next morning, when Eli set back out along his line of traps, he forced himself to focus on his hopes of a good haul and minimal interruptions from the dead.

But when he reached the road where he and Anna had last met, she waited for him. He approached cautiously.

"I think you should let her go," Anna said, pushing her chin in Stella's direction.

For a moment Eli was at a loss, but the rightness of what she was saying filled him. "She should be let go nearer home, though," he answered, "You know, around familiar places and people."

Anna eyed him for a moment, then nodded. "Righto," she said, and added, "I've been going around collecting seeds."

"I've got a garden," Eli said. "High brick walls on two sides. Could reinforce the gate and build the other two fences up."

"Oh," Anna said. She turned, taking a position far from Stella and started walking in the direction Eli was going.

For a moment Eli was caught flat-footed, then he shambled slowly after her. They walked for hours, only pausing to collect traps, in perfect silence.

Eli had started to feel less scared of her presence when he felt something bump his hand and looked down.

It was her hand on a stick. Eli glanced at Anna, but she was looking away from him, her shoulders hunched defensively. She looked scared. So Eli took the hand's aimlessly clenching digits in his careful fingers. They walked home side by side.

~

DRAGON GIRL

CAT SPARKS

I fell in love with a dragon boy when I was seventeen. The dragon train—five creatures long—camped near Grimpiper in the days before it crossed the Great Divide. Beyond the stones lay the Dead Red Heart. Our 'stead nestled in amongst the shadow dunes. Close enough to the Sand Road, not too close to its bandits and its warlords.

We'd been pushing our water wheels across miles of stone when the kite went up. Blue tail flags might mean many things but this time blue meant dragons. We dropped the wheels and ran up Puckers Ridge. Right to the top and there they were, five dragons chewing through wild melon fields below. Thick-set creatures, bellies low to the ground.

We risked a whipping, abandoning our wheels like that, but dragons were too tempting to pass up. Nothing ever happened out Grimpiper way. We could not know then that the train would camp for three full days, and when it left, I would be leaving too.

The youngest of his tribe, he was. His beast trod last in line. His dragon smaller than the others by a head. Broad, flat teeth ripping through dune melon stems.

"Does it bite?" I asked.

Iago (I didn't know his name back then) shot me a playful grin. Tossed me one of the loose dune melons. I held it coyly, watching him stand so close to that chomping mouth. Close enough to make the other girls shriek. He tossed the melon. The dragon snapped it up. "You try," he said and so I did, dallying with the beast for hours, until Carlina and her Noahan witches came streaming down the dunesides, waggling their palm frond shades, weighted down with baskets of throwing stones. Chanting lists of animals that had been rescued by the boat and how no dragons were written on that list. Dragons were abominations, made by human hands. The same dab hands that brought the Ruin down. All misborn beasts must be driven across the Great Divide, was what they preached. That, and a host of other, darker things.

I didn't care about what Noahan witches said. Their praying and their whining never rose the water table or brought the rain or caused the crops to grow.

Iago's people were tall and dark, dressed in sand cloaks, deep blue like the night. Merchentman—or so I thought—with ancient rifles slung across their shoulders. For show, they were, not fighting guns, but you never could be sure with Heartland folks.

Carlina stared with big wide eyes when she saw that thunderstick, all chipped and grey and mounted on spindle legs. A fearsome thing, even with its fire drained.

"For serpente hunting," Iago told me.

Iago's uncle never said a word. He stared me down as the Noahan's chanting drove the other girls away. I ignored them all, keeping up the melon game, watching lithe, brown-skinned Iago unwrap his turban and shake his long hair free.

Couldn't keep my eyes off him. We fucked in the shade of a withered copse of palms. Didn't care who saw us. Didn't even wait for night to fall.

"I'm not afraid of your uncle," I told him.

"You should be," his reply. Later, he told me how the dragons were not really dragons. Lizards, more like. Creatures bred in glass. True dragons were supposed to have had wings, their bones turned hard and trapped in stone for centuries.

I knew then that I would leave Grimpiper and the shadow dunes. The Noahans and the farmers, goat herders and beekeepers, fighting over water rights to the last uncontaminated wells. Mother shrieking after me to look out for my brother. Flint, who had hit the pilgrim trail, one year gone, his name not spoken since.

I remember laughing, warm wind blowing in my face. Getting sweaty with Iago, shirking chores and hanging at the dragon's feet. Telling no one of my plan to leave, except Iago who had known it from the first.

• • •

We were five days out when I learned the truth of it. The dragon train sought not new wells as Iago's uncle claimed. They followed the pilgrim trail themselves in search of Ankahmada. The same cursed city that enticed my brother to his doom. A city carved from a living sapphire, rumoured to be blooming in the Dead Red Heart. A pilgrim trail grown cold and strewn with bones. My brother's most likely lain amongst them.

The Dead Red Heart, land of stonewhales, skates and serpentes. The most we had glimpsed so far were ruins and the bones of creatures long dead past. Maps by day and stars by night. Lands so repetitious they could barely be endured. We travelled under the sun's full glare, protected by flimsy canopies. Each beast flanked by point riders on camelback.

Dogs ran at the dragons' feet. They never tired or weakened. Dogs kept other predators at bay. Other dogs, mostly, and other things that looked a bit like dogs. Our beasts were fed and watered well, even when the rest of us were parched.

Iago's uncle never spoke a word to me. Few of the drovers were much for speaking words. They spoke in sign, signalling back and forth across the sand, that thunderstick remaining in plain view, attached to Iago's uncle's camel's saddle.

Wedged behind Iago, travelling last in line. Scanning horizons for serpente sign, chewing on leathery roo jerky and ember bread. Talking about the people we had lost: him two sisters stricken by the sweating fever. Me my one and only brother, leaving home without saying goodbye. The heat of the sun and the chill of the night. Sleeping upright in the saddle, sliding in and out of dreams, awakening under a different hue of sky, sometimes on an entirely different day.

The dragon people thought the sapphire city real. They carried tiny chips and shards of it in battered leather pouches. Held them up against the light, comparing them for purity. Poring over faded maps so creased and crushed they barely held a mark.

My mother collected Dead Red maps. She had close on to forty, every one a clever fake. The cheapest kinds you could score at any Sand Road trading post. Some were inked on ancient crumbling paper, others on treated hide, fabric or faded plastic.

I believed in many things: the Obsidian Sea and the giant ships that slid across its surface, borne on massive old-world butyl rollers, thick sails bulging with wild winds. Travellers claimed to have seen such craft push out from Fallow Heel. Souvenirs slung around their necks, wards and sigils carved from the slick black glass. But Ankahmada, a city carved from jewel? Not even a Noahan witch would fall for that one.

• • •

Fifteen days beyond Grimpiper's wells, I awoke to the sound of human voices. Iago, conferring with one of the camel riders—a man with his face obscured beneath a striped khafiya—both of them pointing to a dusty smudge that might have been no more than a pile of rocks. No kites hanging in the listless sky. If it was an outpost or a 'stead, its people did not wish to draw attention.

Iago's uncle rode his camel ahead, spyglass at the ready. Dragons plodding in a firm and steady line.

"Watch," said Iago.

"Watch what?" And then I saw it, a sliver-glint of sun. A flashing signal, patterned. No accidental reflection. Someone was trying to speak to us. I braced myself to swerve towards the light but we did not.

Iago's uncle appeared as disinterested as his camel. Iago, however, kept a keen eye on that flashing. More handsign passed between him and his cousins, swivelled in their saddles as the dragons took us closer. The glint and smudge took shape and form—a row of columns protruding from the sand. The dark, squat shapes of scattered tents and pens.

Three small boys burst from behind a low dune crest, running towards us, waving hands, shouting words of greeting in a mix of tongues.

Iago was not pleased to see them. The boys kept up their loud distractions. Iago's uncle regarded them with distaste. Iago tightened the grip on his dragon's reigns. The boys whooped and cheered, racing back the way they'd come, tripping and tumbling over their own feet. Four bells gave the dragons' signal. They pulled up to a slow stop, one by one.

Iago's uncle had apparently changed his mind.

I wrapped my arms around Iago's waist. "What is happening? What is this place?"

"Trading post," he answered grimly. He handed me the precious spyglass he wore around his neck on a strip of leather.

Grimpiper 'steads were parched and sparse, but even the meanest and driest of them was a grand bazaar compared to this sorry array. A handful of scrawny goats bleated miserably in ramshackle pens of unevenly-hammered stakes. The way was strewn with camel bones. Three mangy, fly-blown dogs growled at our own dogs and at the dragons. Catching their scent, but without the energy to jump and bark. So utterly malnourished, they might have been the undead demon dogs those Noahans swore ran rampant through the Red.

Our own dogs kept a wary distance. Dogs that had never before shown a lick of fear.

We were as close as we were going to get. Movement stirred at the bases of the columns. Just the wind, or so I thought at first.

I sat up, straight and saddlesore, straining for a clearer view.

Iago's uncle wasn't getting off his mount. He stared at the trading post a lengthy while before sending two point riders to investigate. Neither man looked happy with the task.

"What do you reckon he's after?" I whispered.

Iago and I shared the glass between us, watching our riders approach the men who sat gambling around a coarse and tattered mat. Coins glinted sharply against the weave. Weapons placed within easy reach. Now and then, a glance would be thrown in the direction of the tents.

Tents that were thin and patched and faded. Through an open flap, a group of people peered. Women and children, they ranged in age from elderly down to a babe in arms. Their clothes were old, their faces tanned and lined.

The women whispered amongst themselves until one of the men called out, demanding silence. Abruptly, the women shushed, then the tent flap fell.

At seventeen, I knew little of the world's true pain, but this was plain as day. A slave market. The captives miserable wisps of skin and bone, huddled around the columns, weighted down with chains. The men on the mat were cowardly dogs, each one hung with the totems, tools and trophies of his trade. Men whose stench I could smell from the dragon's back. I would have spat except they weren't worth the water.

The condition of their animals spoke to many truths. Animals are everything, from Grimpiper all the way to Sammarynda, so often meaning the difference between life and death. Only the very stupid treat them like they do not matter.

The men got up from their gambling mat. All teeth and smiles with pudgy, waterfat flesh, greeting the point riders with open arms, clasping their hands as if they were old friends.

No need to hear the words that left their lips. Their smiles weren't fooling anyone. The 'merchandise," still chained, was paraded before the riders single file.

Merchandise. My brother Flint. Had fate deposited him in this terrible place? I peered and squinted in the sun but could make out nothing. The scrawny captives had been too ill used. Too far away to make out better detail.

I lowered the glass. Iago stared intently at my face. Somehow he knew what I was thinking. He placed his hand upon my cheek. "The pilgrim trail ends sooner for some than others," he said.

Our people did not linger. The pitiful slaves begged our riders with outstretched arms, pleading for the turbaned desert men to take them. They knew they were done for if the men left them behind. Skinny and sick, no longer worth the waste of food and water.

"What if Flint is one of them?"

Iago grabbed my wrist and held it tight. "You can do nothing. Those men are dead already."

"Let me go!"

"It is not wise to annoy my uncle."

"Not wise? Is that all you can say?" Wrenching my wrist free, I jumped down to the sand. Further than it looked, I landed badly. Iago shouted words I didn't hear.

All I cared about was Flint as I hobbled through the loose-packed sand, particles clinging to my sweaty legs. Feeling the weight of Iago's uncle's eyes upon my back.

The two point riders offered me stony stares. The slavers, whose grimy odour filled my nose at twenty paces, observed me with amusement. Perhaps they thought me property for sale.

"Flint!" I scanned the row of suffering wretches, most barely well enough to stand. Walked from man to man to check their thirst-pinched faces. None were his. Relief came first, then disappointment. If he were here then I could save him. We would know what had become of him, what might become of him still.

"My brother Flint walked the pilgrim trail. Have you seen him?" I asked each man in turn. Some said nothing, others answered me with jumbled, rasping gasps of prayer.

It was hopeless. The slaves were close to death. I moved to stand behind the two point riders. One of them said something to the men who had been gambling. Words foreign to my ears but not theirs. Harsh, sharp words that left their mark. As we turned to leave, the leader of the slavers started cursing.

Tempers barely contained in the brittle heat. Anger that posturing and false cheer couldn't bury. Blades were drawn. The half-starved dogs skulking around the trading post perimeter started barking up a storm. Through all this, Iago's uncle watched in silence.

The three young boys edged close to the action, raising stones to throw just like the Noahans back in 'Piper. Fearful mothers called their names but dared not leave the safety of the tent.

We stood our ground against the gambling men. They outnumbered us and could have cut us down, but the pressure of five dragons kept them practical. Turned out they'd hoped we might buy the men for sport, or drink with them long enough to wind up drugged and robbed. Such was the way they made their coin, but Iago's uncle never got down from his mount.

Threats were shouted across the sand and then we parted ways. "What will happen to those slaves?" I asked. Neither rider answered. We all knew what would happen to the wretches—or at least I thought we did.

I turned back just in time to see a slaver draw his sword. Snatches of angry bickering bounced upon the wind. The tongue was foreign but its nuances were not. Somebody would end up punished for this day.

Iago's uncle stiffened in the saddle. His cloak billowed suddenly as if filled by wind only there was no wind to fill it. None at all. He reached both hands along the camel's side to heft the thunderstick.

Bells signalled that the dragon train was lumbering into motion. A single drum setting pace for the mighty beasts.

Iago waved his hands in a flurry, anxious for me to climb atop the beast where it was safe.

But before I could move, a sound like a mighty dragon's roar. What happened next was way too fast to see: one minute there had been a shiny row of columns. The next, all that remained was belching smoke. Exclamations of surprise, but the dragons did not miss a beat.

The thunderstick rested high upon Iago's uncle's shoulder. The air around him sparked with flickering embers, raining to the sand like firecracker dust.

Iago shouted out my name. He fought to still his beast but the dragons were expertly trained and the bells were ringing loud and clear and true.

"Hurry—you must hurry!"

I ran to his dragon, last in line. Raised my arms and he hauled me up the saddle's side. The thunderstick was fired again, aimed this time at the tents. Smoke cleared revealing nothing but flames and splinters.

The tent completely gone.

Slavers stumbled blindly through the sand, tripping over goats, dogs and each other. Too stunned to even curse or raise their fists.

"Your uncle planned to kill them all along," I whispered. "You knew what was going to happen."

Iago didn't answer.

Dragon drovers and camel riders stared blankly at the smoke, mesmerised by its ferocity. Gaping at the pale blue sky as black roils dissolved upon the wind.

"That tent was full of women and children."

The horror of it slowly sinking in. Suddenly it was all too much. The stench of singed flesh blended with gunpowder. The relentless ache of endless sun. The row of columns once shiny-white reduced to blackened rubble.

Iago's dragon was on the move, but all 'Piper brats knew how to jump and roll. Someone cried out as I hit the sand. Iago, perhaps. By then it hardly mattered.

The sand was soft. This time I landed well and scrambled up to standing. Hurried to chase down Iago's uncle, quickly before anyone could raise a hand. Most eyes remained on the burning mess that marked where the trading post had stood.

"You got no right!" I shrieked up at his back.

Uncle's cloak twitched like a living skin. At last I saw it for what it was. Old tech. Pre-Ruin. Forbidden. Dangerous. Marking Iago's uncle as a sorcerer. But it was way too late for backing down. What was started had to be completed.

"That tent was full of *innocents*," I screamed.

Uncle kept his back to me. I dodged my way around his camel's side. "You're a coward, hiding behind that ancient reliquary. Get down off that camel now and face me." My heart was pounding as the words flew out of me. Words that could do nothing but get me killed.

A curl of amusement touched the tall man's lips. The intense blue of his eyes pressed down like a weight against my chest.

"They were marked for death already. All of them," he said, his voice the deepest sound I had ever heard.

He urged his mount forward, our talking at an end. I held my ground as the dragons lumbered onwards, animals and people giving me a wide berth. Two dogs lingered, eyeing me with keen and hungry interest.

I wanted no part of any of it. The dragon train. The pilgrim trail. The sapphire city. Iago and his soft brown skin. They were all bad men and I would stand my ground until the desert claimed me—or the sun, or the sandskates, or my heart.

I didn't get the chance. One of the point riders pulled his camel up close beside me. The beast bared its crooked teeth, leered at me with annoyance.

"Get on," said the rider, voice muffled by a striped khafiya, his arm extended down towards my own. Iago's friend—I had heard them talking together often enough.

I stood proud. "What if I don't?"

"Then the vultures will eat well tonight." He glanced at the sky, then down at the dogs. "Your bones will be picked clean before too long."

"You cannot make me."

What was I saying? What had I just done?

I held my ground even though my legs were shaking. So did the man in the striped khafiya. Eventually, the last of the dragons passed.

Silence lingered, heavy and complete. Dark shapes flew across the sun. Vultures, real or imaginary.

"Please," he said. "Die before your time, if you so choose, but do not waste your death on this cursed place. Your brother, if he lives, will not thank you for it."

There was something familiar about his eyes. Rich and brown like fresh-tilled soil. He waited past the point of mere politeness.

The man was right. Pride like mine was worse than useless. Reluctantly, I gripped his arm and allowed him to haul me up into his saddle.

A blast of singed flesh and hair enveloped us as his camel galloped to catch up with the dragons. I stared at the horizon and the future that lay beyond it. Grimpiper was now as lost to me as it was to my crazy brother. I could not go back; I did not know the way. There was only forward to a city that most likely did not exist.

The sun hung heavy overhead. No shadows. No perspective. Nothing but blinding glare and burning thirst. I didn't glance back at the ruined trading post. I couldn't.

The rider pulled his camel alongside the smallest dragon. When my eyes met Iago's, I saw what I had earlier failed to see. *Eyes the hue of fresh-tilled soil.* Iago and the camel-man were brothers.

A full day passed before Iago allowed me back up to ride behind him. Two before I was granted full forgiveness, my transgression evaporated like condensation on a bulging waterskin.

On the third day we passed a message scrawled upon a sun-bleached slab of stone. No words, just a diamond etched in blue. An arrow pointing to the far horizon.

Ankahmada, Ankahmada, whispered like a ward, snatched from cracked and bleeding lips, vaporised by canny, skittish winds. Beyond the rise, or the next one after that, or the next one.

We were almost out of water when a cry went up to stir my fitful saddle slumber. My eyes wide open expecting the blue of jewels. In their place, something altogether stranger.

Jammed and scattered amongst the dunes the hulls of giant ships protruded: bows and masts, some of iron, others warped and rotted wood, swamped and choked in tides of shifting sand. I counted fifty before my numbers left me. What would Carlina have made of this strange sight—what could anyone ever make of such a thing?

Iago's brother had taken to riding his camel alongside Iago's dragon. Now and then he'd smile at me when Iago wasn't looking. One of the dogs had been bitten by a sandskate. The brother had refused to leave it, carried it tight against his chest wrapped up in the striped khafiya. He reminded me of my own brother in his courage and determination. I did not believe in Ankahmada but I was beginning to believe in Iago's brother.

The dragons wound their way through the sand-drowned ships in single file and silence. Late afternoon brought with it the welcome half moons of shadowed dune crests, clear of wood and weld. Once more we could see where we were headed, even if we had no knowledge of where the fabled city lay. The wind grew stronger, waterskins flapping empty. We shielded our eyes and stared out across the repetitive curve and undulation of the dunes, straining for a glimpse of kite, or the speck and shadow of a lonely bird, but there was nothing, neither human nor animal, larger than the skeletal bugs that I imagined clinging to the spindly thorn bush stems.

~

REMINISCENCES OF HERBERT WEST, REANIMATOR

CHARLES LOVECRAFT

My friend, H. West, was known to vilely test
The pulses of dead things he had imbibed
With his reanimate liqueur. He bribed,
Where could, for corpses freshly dead and wrest
Of life *still warm*. He badly wanted best,
To raise a thing most faithfully that tried
To speak, and had mild eyes, and never lied
Of things beyond the summit of life's crest.

That he succeeded well is testament
To what is happening now—our house below,
Invaded by *a living group hell-sent*,
While thudding sounds, in stifling cellar low,
Tumble the crumbling walls. Tomb legions push—
Into the lightless pit the horrors rush!

LADY KILLER

ANTHONY PANEGYRES

". . . we do not feel horror because we are haunted by a sphinx, we dream a sphinx to explain the horror that we feel."
JORGE LUIS BORGES—RAGNAROK

THE CHILD

The first time it happened I was eight years old and my hometown, Halls Head, was in its embryonic stage. Only eight houses lined either side of my lazy street and behind us was bush for miles around: banksias and scrub plants, punctuated by a shorter type of eucalypt, which I called brumby gums, after the horses in *The Man from Snowy River.*

On autumnal Sunday dawns, where I'd breathe visible puffs of air and pretend I was a fire-dragon, my father and I would go bush walking. I had spidery legs and arms, blond waves of hair, and a closed smile, which was apparently endearing to all. We'd find ourselves deep in the bush, but always maintained our sense of direction. It was something visceral, even when all we could see were stunted trees, shrubs and russet hues. We'd sneak up on mobs of boomers, who'd eventually spook and bound away. When the roos lost us, I'd peer through the dry scrub for the little people. I'd just read *The Hobbit,* but my eyes were not sharp enough to detect any Shire folk.

One Sunday, I discovered two orchids: rare delicate touches of colour amongst the sandy browns and motley greens of the bush.

The first, a spider orchid, had a spindly flower, pink and white, favoured by most. But my second find was a cowslip. Small but rounder and more symmetrical, the same colour as my pet canary, Courage. It was the perfect flower. I uprooted it, scooping my cupped hands underneath to keep a pile of dirt, so the flower felt comfortable. I planted it in a little red clay pot and watered it for three days running.

It wilted.

• • •

It was a roasting November day and school lunchtime. Our teacher, Miss Lane, sat cross-legged on an outside bench observing me and two girls. I lifted their skirts up to peep underneath. They giggled, raised their skirts higher and shoved their frilly-knickered bottoms into my face. It was taboo, but Miss Lane was smiling and so were we. Lisa and Natasha both invited me to their birthday parties before the siren sounded.

I didn't return to the sweltering classroom—they weren't air-conditioned back then. Miss Lane went inside and I snuck away around the corner and strode across the oval towards the bush that enveloped the school.

I remember it still. Cicadas, crickets and grasshoppers trilled like children's popping toys. The land pulsated too, in a heavy heat-laden orgasm. I entered the bush, crunching dry thorny banksia foliage as I walked. Skinks scampered away before me, and there were the occasional scurrying sounds of other small animals in the undergrowth. The more I walked, the more I perspired. I grabbed a brumby gum leaf, crinkled it in my hand, and held it under my nose. The clean fragrance made me feel cooler. In the air, there was little visible movement besides sporadic wrens and scrub birds fluttering through the trees. But on the earth in the distance, I saw a whisper of yellow.

Cowslip.

I strode forward, despite my now clinging polo-shirt. There was another splash of yellow ahead—I'd never seen more than a single flower before. I began to jog to discover another at the foot of a blackboy.

A trail.

An orchid every dozen steps or so. I followed the yellow deep into the wild, deeper than I'd ever been.

The sky began to dim as I arrived at the path's end, exhausted. A glade opened up before me: a floor of flowers. All cowslips, I could discern them even in the now wan light. But something large stood in the centre; too still to be a roo. The only audible sound was my tread, which although gentle, regrettably hurt the orchids underfoot. The object ahead was substantial. A monument? I wondered whether the bush held such hidden riches. I advanced, noticing four great feline legs with paws shaded by two giant wings like those of the sea eagles that haunted the Peel Inlet, and a tail like that of a snake. I drew closer: fur, feathers, scales, and a head. A lady's head. Her eyes were closed. If I had been older, I would have found her seductive, but her lips were too thick, her nose too developed, her body too strong, and she possessed a round pair of breasts, which, for me at the time, were just fat, ugly, useless appendages.

Overhead, the first stars glittered. I reached out to stroke her fur, it felt like the hide of a roo I'd patted at a deer park, only much colder. Chilly fur on a baking day was a queer sensation—maybe that should have been warning enough to stay away. But I was eight and didn't understand heat conventions; all I knew was that she was cool and I was hot. I traced my fingers through the coat for respite.

Nothing happened at first. I didn't notice the pelt warm, but after a while, it felt hotter and obscurely rhythmic. That was the last I could remember as I fell asleep. The last I could recall before my nightmare began.

I awoke feeling a weight on my chest. My eyes opened and I found myself pinned by a paw, breasts dangling above my head. The pitiless face that eyed me felt ancient, yet I couldn't distinguish any age lines.

What have the Muses brought me to devour? Her accented voice was breathy, devoid of emotion. Although I didn't grasp every word, I sensed their meaning echoing through my mind.

"Why eat me?" Even then I was quick-thinking; the extraordinary tends not to astound some children, rather it draws them closer.

The Muses have delivered no riddle. She bent down and licked my face, like I'd seen lions lick their kill on documentaries. *So you must be a treat, a little taster.* Her sapphire tail glinted as it flicked contentedly.

I wriggled beneath her paw. She smiled, her violet eyes excited. It was the first sign of emotion I'd seen and it felt predatory. Her leg remained poised on top of me as I attempted anything and everything to free myself—I punched, scratched, even pinched. I sensed her disappointment as she removed her paw. I scrambled up and away, racing towards the glade's boundary. I felt a gush of wind behind me and then above. Before I reached the edge of the glade, she landed before me, wings flailing.

"There are bigger meals than me." I pointed towards school, which must have closed hours ago. I felt rotten—I was no dobber.

The beast-lady looked wistfully out from the glade's border. Like a dog motioning to open a door, she lifted a paw towards the direction of the school. I realised then that the creature couldn't move beyond the glade. Perhaps it guarded something, or had some hex on it?

A blood trade, two lives for yours.

A claw pricked my finger and her tongue lapped the droplet that bloomed there. My thoughts leapt—or rather dived—into depths unknown to a child of eight. Images were in my mind, and hers, too. *A couple of frilly-knickered girls.*

The beast-lady licked my face once more as she released me. *This is no trade. Your blood reveals your very nature, your fated sins, child. Your victims of betrayal will taste sweet. Your appetite will feed me whenever we both hunger.*

I fled through the bush, this time not stopping to appreciate the flowers. By the time I arrived home, I was faint. Mum swallowed me in her embrace and made me drink what seemed like litres of water. Dad called the police to say I'd returned, and after I'd eaten, he grounded me. "And from now on you're being picked up from school." Dad was furious—it was only a ten-minute walk, and yet I'd been gone hours.

I never mentioned my encounter with the beast-lady. By the next day, I wasn't convinced it had actually happened. I knew I had an active imagination.

The day after, the two girls, Lisa and Natasha, went missing. They disappeared at recess and their remains were found two days later. Bloody trails were discovered on leaves and bark, but there was no mention of cowslips or a glade. There were clues though, traces of me were found near the scene. I didn't know then that you left hints of your clothing as you moved, or hairs and prints in the bush.

Bloody clothes, strewn and torn apart—but not by human hands—meant I wasn't suspected. The evidence led to a large feline; fabric was flown overseas where forensic scientists endorsed the theory. There was rumour of a cat, the size of a mountain lion, sighted in Nannup, but that town was a three-hour drive away. Dogs, an Aboriginal tracker, volunteers and helicopters searched, but the largest animal anyone saw was a grandpa boomer.

THE ADOLESCENT

The town changed. Fields, some fallow, others not, replaced my beloved bush. I was older by then, thirteen. Housing estates now bordered the school where the two girls went missing. I avoided yellow—watching Australia compete at almost anything, the Olympics, even one-day cricket, made me nauseous.

There were fewer roos to see, but at least nature of some sort was still available. Every Saturday, Dad and I would take the dinghy deep into the Peel Inlet. We'd wade out, and push the boat off and ride slowly in the still dawn water. My eyes were everywhere: they searched the small islets, where pelicans hooted; they scanned the surface for dolphins and the occasional seal; they inspected the shoreline for all manner of birds. As we travelled, I often dangled an arm over to enjoy the water splashing up and over my body.

After we anchored, my father would cast a line for fish or nets for crabs. I didn't like doing either and stole the least tasty fish in the catch—usually bony trumpeters—and fed them to the dolphins so I could stroke them as they swam by our boat. Often, these were simply polite-hellos; they would release the fish after receiving them.

Cormorants dove and I'd count the seconds before they resurfaced with a contented bob of the head. Great sea eagles with ivory chests perched regally on the long dead trees on the shores of river mouths. I knew all the birds: the terns and the gulls; the herons, the ibises and the egrets.

The return trip was similar. Our feet submerged into the mud as we pulled the boat to shore; my eyes captivated by the mudskippers hopping about.

I loved observing my father clean and gut the fish with that razor-sharp blade of his. Blood and innards spilled out in delicious cherry and cerise. I'd scoop up the driblets and feed them to the pelicans by hand as they waddled over.

I liked to read; in fact, I discovered the beast-lady during reading time in the library, in a book called *Bestiary*, the letters gold on the brown hardback. Opening it up, I felt like Ali Baba unearthing an unimaginable jewel. I brushed through the pages, reading wherever the pictures enthralled me. I came upon centaurs, basilisks, minotaurs and trolls, ogres, satyrs, dragons, and griffons. But my hands tightened on seeing the sphinx. I whacked the book down onto my lap, shut my eyes and then opened them with a resolve to read on. I didn't receive a riddle like Oedipus. Or did I? I began to wonder, replaying the nightmare through my mind. Apparently, sphinxes guarded things, Oedipus' foe a gate. Mine a glade? They did devour humans. That was evident in all the tales.

By sixteen, I'd wiped the event from my mind. It remained asleep, locked in some tenement cell of my consciousness. All the surface recalled was to avoid Greek myths and that I reviled yellow, even canaries. The rest of my time was consumed by Aussie Rules. I remained glued to every match—unless Hawthorn or the Eagles competed. I played a pretty mean game too—burying into packs and winning the hardball with the tenacity of a tiger-quoll.

Later that year, I discovered my manhood in the form of Lorenza Torre. She was tasty. Honey-coloured skin, the type you could lick all night, and buoyant caramel tresses. Lorenza was on exchange from Italy, and a synchronised swimmer. I learnt that synchronised swimmers had bodies I'd suicide for. Lorenza's accent awakened a xenophilic appetite that's never left me. She sat behind me in history, mincing her words in a fashion I found endearing. We'd bonded through our comparison of Mr Durkin's moustache to Stalin's.

I got Lorenza's number from her friend at recess in the canteen line and phoned that same afternoon. We chatted (I can't remember about what) for an hour and 'Ls' were crammed all over the post-it paper near the phone before I eventually spat it out: "Want to hang out some time?"

"Sure," she replied.

At school, I only saw her in history class and my voice would quaver. At best, all I could conjure was a frail, 'Hi'. But she invited me over one night when her host family was out for dinner. Outside, the air was moist and had that fresh smell of undergrowth, while inside her room—pink doona and all—it smelled of carpet, and teddy bears and chick perfume. Lorenza played me the latest Italian CDs. I liked bits and pieces of the corny pop, but pretended to enjoy every song. We tried to dance, me with my pendulum moves, slipping my hands around her waist. She copied me, and then our hands strayed. Her mouth opened for my first kiss and I almost gagged as her tongue entered. But soon after, we were lip and tongue wrestling. I flipped back the quilt and we snuck under it, touching each other underneath our clothes, fingers trickling over each other's skin. I nibbled on her lips. I nibbled on her breasts. Our lips were sore by the time I had to go, as were her nipples. By the front door I grabbed her hair and pashed her Hollywood style in the cool evening air, before leaving for my walk home in the dark.

My eyes gradually adjusted to the leering shadows. A new footy, a Burley, lay right there in the middle of the street. It began to roll away from me on a tangent. I chased, but whenever I closed in, it sped off again, sometimes tumbling, sometimes bouncing erratically, sometimes skipping just beyond my reach. I pursued it down along the asphalt and then off the street as it took a turn and bounced over a wire fence. I scrambled over. It travelled right through a copse of banksias and brumby gums, snapping twigs in its path, and onto the fields of the golf course. It avoided the sand bunkers, cruised around the ponds until it raced away on the green. My eyes hunted solely for the ball on the long, dark fairway. I should have looked up. I should have been alarmed by the peculiarity. The footy hurtled into something immense in the middle of a rounded green.

I should have realised.

I should have run.

But then her paws held me close to her breasts like I was her cherished infant.

Thank the Muses. My feeder, I've been so hungry of late. She whipped her scaled tail and it stung my earlobe, puncturing it.

Blood oozed out. Her tongue left an affectionate trail of saliva over my right ear. *Your blood tastes of future sin.*

I didn't think of escape, instead I thought of Lorenza.

What was I to do? She came to mind.

Stay for a while, my feeder.

I found myself caressing her fur, touching her breasts like I'd touched Lorenza's, and stroking her hair. I slept there in the park, the sphinx my blanket.

• • •

I awoke at home not knowing how I got there. I thought of the sphinx flying me, but she seemed to be guarding the green with the same sentinel manner she had the glade, years before.

Mum knocked and entered, her face in its usual morning-puffy state. I was still clothed under the sheets, eyes matted with sleep. The cops had arrived. She was sure it must be some mistake, but they intended to escort me to the station.

They let me go, even though evidence of me—traces of clothes, and hairs—were found thickly laden at the scene, like some overpowering *parfum*, along with bloody shreds of Lorenza's clothing.

They couldn't pin her disappearance on me, but one tubby hirsute man at the station tried. Drawing his jowls near my face, breath stinking of raw chicken, he spouted all the clichés. "I'm watching you, boy. Don't think you'll get away with this shit. It's only a matter of time."

Thankfully, there was a patch of feline hair among the *panthera*-sized prints.

THE ADULT

I studied zoology at the University of Western Australia. Although I had not abandoned my love of nature, I never watched footy again and took to reading *The Guardian*—no Aussie Rules news in those pages. I still had a taste for women and 'toured' Greece and Italy, Malta and Egypt, Germany, Hong Kong, Israel, and Serbia. In truth, I had a craving for something exotic and toffee-coloured, like a North Indian or Latin American. I fucked all over the place: in fire escapes, empty construction sites, library shelves in shadowy hours, toilets, lecture theatres and tutorial rooms, beaches, muddy river banks and parks. I lived up to my new nickname, Lady Killer. Maybe it was in my nature, in my fated blood?

Like so many mammalogists, I headed for the vast continent of Africa as soon as I could. My passions roamed from the spotted hyena, to the handsome bongo, to the pangolin: an armoured animal which ripped open ant and termite mounds, it's hunched bipedal walk more at home in the realms of *The Dark Crystal* than Earth.

I was working with a filmmaker on a documentary concerning my current favourite, the Cape buffalo. We had three jeeps camped around a muddy waterhole, focusing on an aggressive group of old bulls that had retired from the herd. It was the arid season and everything was the colour of dry wheat, aside from the sunken greys around the water's periphery, where I dared not step. One of the photographers had already been sucked into the quagmire up to his knees, before being hauled out.

Shaparna was in the jeep with me, a passionate and sporty North Indian, with a studded nose, flawless cappuccino skin and those long-lashed sub-continent eyes that were both bright and sad. At times they'd widen cheekily and invitingly. She crossed her legs and laid her dirt-caked boots on the dashboard. Something about the casualness of it all made me hunger to reach out a hand and lay it on her khaki working trousers.

But I had a loyal fiancée, Rosa, back in South Africa. She'd read deep into the dead of night, and always had some interest; presently, it was jazz. Breakfasts of late were accompanied by the rhythms of Ella Fitzgerald and Billie Holiday. It really fired me up. I told Rosa everything.

Well, almost everything.

I never spoke of the sphinx or the blood that bound us.

Three lionesses lapped up the water nearby; fierce muscles flexing beneath almost diaphanous coats. The cameramen readied for the bulls' arrival. Old bachelor bulls frequently had a short fuse and enjoyed tormenting their potential predators. These were no exception. They trotted haughtily, flaunting bustling chests while headed straight for the lionesses, who hissed and growled, flashing their canines in retreat. One lioness sank into the mire. Sharpana's long fingers reached for my hand excitedly. A bull, Old Heracles, bore down on the lion and savaged it with a horn, lifting it out of the sludge with a toss of its head. The wounded lioness snarled as it landed in the mud, rolling away before gingerly clambering off after her pride.

When it was over, Sharpana still clenched my hand.

Her lips that night were as soft as I'd dreamt, and her mouth tasted of cinnamon.

• • •

It wasn't the allure of an orchid or a travelling ball, but an okapi that led me astray that year. I was on the plains of the Serengeti collecting dung samples from a spotted hyena clan. As for my debauchery, I'd broken up with Rosa and moved in with Sharpana, who I married. But after a while, too much of anything—even cinnamon—becomes tasteless and dull.

I was depositing the scatological samples into my jeep when I saw him. It was odd, you don't find okapi on the plains and even in the jungle they're such a retiring type. I drew my binoculars. He was striking, flanks painted entirely white, continuing down his legs in ivory stripes, as if a painter had taken to him with a thick brush. The rest of his body was a dark iron-brown, two small giraffe-like knob-horns protruded from his head.

This time, I couldn't ignore the ambiguity. The okapi was as enticing as an exorbitant chocolate truffle. *Sphinx,* I thought. But then again, what if it wasn't the sphinx's lure, but a freak of nature? What if there were okapis in the Serengeti? I leapt into the jeep, but he stayed tantalisingly out of reach—even when I was roaring across the plains in top gear. The thrums from the engine reflected my active mind: perhaps part of me wanted to again come across the sphinx? For all I knew, I may have been insane and conjured up my own mythological vision.

Three deaths already. *Lady Killer.* The name shimmered about my mind.

As I trailed the okapi through sandy grass, around the occasional *kopje,* and acacia, the lowering sun and dusty air smeared the sky with the juice of blood oranges and tamarinds. The plains appeared endless, but after a while we began to descend. The grass thinned and then disappeared as the okapi advanced along the mudflats, to eventually stop, glancing now and then over its shoulder at me.

Fearing that my vehicle would become bogged if I went further, I ground to a halt and jumped out. I realised that I was being led as I watched my boots submerge into a centimetre or two of reeking mud with every stride. The okapi had vanished; *she* stirred in front of me. I was in her territory—her sphere of muck on the flats.

I approached and patted her flanks.

Thank Hera, you came.

The acrid smell exuding from the mire dissipated as I massaged her hide, running my hands tenderly through tufts of hair. I felt slow, heavy, percussive purrs vibrating through my fingers. I reigned in all my thoughts and locked my mind on the sphinx. I would prevent myself from feeding her—I did my best not to stare at her breasts.

I need sustenance. It's been a while since they've sent you.

I patted her flanks. I couldn't fathom her gaze, somewhere between fondness and fear. Her front paw crept behind me and drew me near.

Feed me.

Feigning nonchalance, I continued to stroke.

Feed me. Claws flashed from sheaths. I remained mute and kept kneading.

Empty your mind, I told myself. A claw brushed my face, not breaking the skin.

Now.

I didn't reply. My heart quickened. One hand clenched. *Remain still*, I told myself, but it suddenly felt like a chill winter's day, when the icy breeze tears through your clothes and invades your bones. My teeth rattled briefly and I shuddered.

One paw held my back, and with the other she raked a claw down under the tender skin just beneath my eye, along my left cheek to the bottom of my jaw. My skin felt dry before the liquid gushed, drenching the side of my face. I managed to stay firm, vacant, until her tongue began lapping up my blood with invasive, rough strokes. *It is not your fault. Your blood is wrought in sin, wrought by fate. Feed me.*

Maybe she was wrong? Wasn't it my choice to satisfy my nature, my lust?

Her paw moved portentously to my opposite cheek, a claw pressed firmly over my now closed eyelid.

I suppose I saw myself as heroic, I'd wiped my mind of Sharpana and my ex, Rosa. I gave up a stranger's face instead. A bank teller, freckled and arrogant. I didn't even know her name.

I woke alone, lying in the muck.

• • •

I scanned the papers after that. Days later, I discovered the woman's name on the TV. Sophie Haines, mauled by a wild cat, most likely a lion. Nobody had witnessed the event. Search parties swarmed all over seeking a rogue animal. Sophie had been a widow with two children, Simon and Peter. Both attended elementary school.

I no longer considered her a stranger.

THE OLD MAN

Sharpana suffered me, my unconfessed guilt, my anger and even my philandering—until she burst in when my hand was up the babysitter's top. Divorce was worse than I thought.

After the mudflats, the thought of the wild left a plunging sensation in my stomach. I never again travelled to national parks and reserves unaccompanied, and found that besides my son, few wished to travel with me.

I was no longer a Lady Killer, but rather the Invisible Man; my once wavy hair was scant, white and wiry, I was skeletal thin and limped on an arthritic right knee that kept me up on winter nights. I tried to remain a decent father and think I was to a point; I introduced Nanda to wildlife and he became a vet. But I can't take any real credit for my son's achievements. He turned out well thanks to Sharpana.

My head was embroiled in books. I still submitted to *The Zoological Journal,* but my main passion was fiction, all types and any genre. The pages and words were really my only company, I brought them with me everywhere: on the bus and train, to restaurants and cafes. I found even that friendship damaging of late. I'd become a conceited critic. A real prick. Nothing seemed right: the flow of words, their sounds as they unravelled across the pages; writing was either too fresh or too old or a vulgar cross-breed of both. Authors were too cerebral or egotistical, shallow became deep, and vice-versa.

I thought I had read my final three books during the week before I left: *The Fan Man, God Bless You, Mr Rosewater,* and *A Man in the High Castle,* randomly chosen from an insurmountable reading-list.

Just this morning, I'd left a letter on the table. The black ink, puddled in places, informed that I've left everything to my son and that I wished him a long and hopefully meaningful life. I stated that I didn't have long to live: an inoperable brain tumour, which spanned across the cerebral cortex. Cowardly fabricated details, but they did add a sense of authenticity.

I'd decided to head out alone. No more lady-killing. This time, no body would suffice but mine.

I drove through the rubble and sheets of a shantytown. Kids who had little else but chalk and balls played hopping games on the side streets. I passed through the locked fortresses and empty streets of those with plenty. I pulled out onto the old road near the coast, but not close enough that you could actually view the ocean. There was only shrub and scrubland, a speckled demented landscape as far as I could see.

The seat cushioned my back and the air-con cooled me. Liberated, I flew along with the pedal to the floor. I'd taken the road because hardly anyone took it these days since the new freeway had been built. Its painted lines were long eroded, blurring the two lanes into one.

I sped, passing through a stunted terrain where only stunted animals could survive. Scrub-birds, hovering falcons, rodents, reptiles and a droning army of insects. Then, in the distance, like an apparition, a long-haired figure stood in the middle of the road. I braked too sharply on seeing her. The car skidded and the wheel locked as I drew near. She stayed motionless as I spun in a circle towards her. Closer and closer the car screeched as I lifted my foot off the brake and released my hands from the wheel, leaving both our lives to the hands of fate.

The car careened to a stop. The woman stood mere centimetres from the bonnet, staring at me through those long lashes. Sharpana.

But she was the Sharpana of our early days; the Sharpana of the safari. There was no sign of the light bulge that had settled around her waist, or of the skin sagging slightly beneath her chin; and her eyes were not mournful, but still held some light.

This time I was not tricked or curious. A pitiful enticement compared to our past encounters. It wasn't a magical rush of colour to a child; or the mystical dance of a ball to an adolescent; or the lure of an exotic animal to a young man. I confess that I felt disappointed by the certainty.

The lure stared at me as I left the car and then she walked off into the scrubland in sandals, oblivious to all the dangers that lay there. Now and then she turned with an attractive sweep of her mane to see that I followed. How I loathed myself in recent years for the way I had treated Sharpana. I would have knelt for a dramatic apology, except I knew the body in front of me was only a creation of the sphinx.

My knee creaked and throbbed as I stomped to alert any snakes. Large wasps hovered around, skittishly flying this way and that, and flies hung thickly around bushes that stank of carrion. Tiny winged insects with grub-like bodies annoyed me the most; they tickled my arm hairs and I squashed them in my fingers in what seemed like the hundreds. I passed my hands constantly over my scalp to wipe the irritants away as I pursued her trail down a slight slope, remembering that taste of cinnamon. Soon we could not be seen from the road.

She stood there in the sand and spinifex and tufts of scrub.

Muses, how could you bring me this?

Her mind felt altered: desperate, disturbed.

What could he bring me? Who would follow him? Old, alone, bitter. There is no nourishment in that emaciated husk. How could he feed me?

"Take me," I said, almost prostrating myself before her. Despite just seeing Sharpana, my mind was clear: no lady-killing. The scar the sphinx had left me burned like ice down the side of my face.

She protested, wailing in my mind. I moved closer and found myself patting her fur rhythmically, like I was calming a distressed child, all the while whispering: "Take me." I developed an erection. It was intense, forcing against my pants like hot iron. I hadn't had one in years.

You are of no use! She cried as I continued to caress her fur.

Reaching up, I began to touch her breasts. If they were closer I would have traced my tongue all over them. Her movement slowed. The paw that had sliced my face open with ease years ago now lifted feebly in an attempt to force me away.

Muses! She called to them desperately, while gradually cooling beneath my fingers.

My cock still burned: "Take me," I repeated.

Things appeared in a pool around her: cowslips, with wilted petals, burst up from the earth; flat footballs rolled rather than bounced this way and that; an emaciated okapi stood staring at me listlessly; Sharpana crawled around on the ground, searching, like a deranged patient.

Then they all vanished.

She cried softly in a final appeal to the Muses before turning cold beneath my hands, a lost statue once more. I came against the material of my trousers as she froze. Afterwards, I sat on the dirt; a mien of emotional intricacies: self-disgust merged with confusion and relief. Lady killers, both of us. I don't know whether I was more repulsed by her actions over time or mine.

This land was more isolated than the bush surrounding my primary school. I couldn't help but wonder how long it would be before another lady killer awakened her.

~

2B

JOANNE ANDERTON

Chloe sees the young couple sneak in because the moon is full and the orchard is close to the fence. They've come prepared. Wire cutters to make a hole just big enough to squeeze through. Ties to mend the fence as though it was never touched. From a distance it looks undisturbed.

Once through, the couple run to the shelter of the nearest tree—an old Derwent watercolour, healthy but for the strange fact that it has never fruited an *Emerald Green 46*. From the porch at the back of her shop, Chloe watches them embrace. Then the girl squats and shoves her hands into the dirt while the boy hovers hopeful and awkward behind her.

The dry shavings littering the ground break silently beneath Chloe's careful bare feet. The couple don't notice as she approaches.

"—hurry," the boy is saying. "It will be safer in town. So many people, we won't be noticed."

Chloe switches a torch on and they freeze. "Actually," she says. "You will." She runs the torchlight over them, up and down, slowly, taking in every detail. The girl's blue dress is too big for her bony frame; the boy's jeans are patched with mismatching fabric. They look older than she realised at first, deep lines near the boy's mouth, hollow circles around the girl's eyes. Little puncture scars down the side of her neck. "You will stand out."

The boy tenses and jerks towards her, like he might attack. Wouldn't be the first time. Chloe should know better than to help the refugees. There's always a reason they've had their booking declined; most of the time it's because they're too poor, but sometimes it's because they're unstable. The girl wrenches her hand from the earth to grip his clenched fist. He tugs against her for a moment, earnest and urgent in his need to protect her. "Don't," she whispers. So he takes her hand instead, pulls her to her feet, and holds her close.

"Are you going to turn us in to the council?" the girl asks. Her eyes seem small in their hollow sockets, and blink as Chloe shines the light on her face. The girl's hair is cut short, and thinning.

"I don't need to," Chloe answers. "You have two days, I'd say, before the fence inspection comes round. And then you will be found." She switches off the light, turns on her heel and walks back to the shop. "You can hide in the storeroom, until then. Should be long enough. But be gone before they come looking, or they'll take any little baby you get right back out again."

After a moment's hesitation, the couple hurry after her. They always do.

• • •

Jane.

Ethan.

The refugees go on little strips of paper, tied to the dry branches of a dead 2B pencil tree. There's a lot of them hanging there, some yellow and torn with age, some new and crisp.

Her refugees don't get skin.

• • •

Chloe carries pencil cases for her harvest. She's kept them safe since the first plantings, even the cardboard ones. Each tree has its preferred box—from long tins with drawings of deer in coloured strokes, to plastic rectangles in bright pink, and black canvas with a zipper and her name in gold letters.

The trees were Mark's idea. If the council had been around back then, they wouldn't have been allowed. If Chloe hadn't started selling the fruit, they would have been pulled up along with everything else, all the junk that was planted back when the fertility was new and a novelty, and planting was the only way to see how far around the town it spread.

The ripeness of pencils is best determined by the tone of their rattle and clink in the breeze. Too hollow a sound means the graphite will be thin and too brittle to write with. Too sharp, and there will be hardly any wood to hold it together.

Chloe works slowly, the sun still young and the wind only just turning to the west. She places each case at the foot of the tree, then runs her fingers through the pencils hanging down from thin stems, before carefully selecting which ones to pick. As always, she starts with the classic 2B with a little pink eraser on the end. The first tree is long dead, but this is its descendent. She knows that for sure. She pays very close attention.

Ethan and Jane watch her through the small storeroom window, just above ground.

By the time the first tourist bus arrives her shelves are fully stocked. They all take pencils with them—a little part of this miraculous place to hold in their hands, to write to their loved ones with, to clutch like relics while they pray over pregnancy tests, blood results and ultrasounds. The council gets a cut from each sale.

The 2B she keeps for herself.

• • •

The pencils were a stupid idea.

I hate them.

But the words only stick if she means them.

• • •

In the lull between busloads, Chloe heads into town. She's accustomed to the pitying looks, the meaningful glances, the whispers behind her back, and does what she can to ignore them. *What's wrong with her? Is it really safe to stand so close? What if she's contagious?* It's busy today, weekends are always packed, and all around her a sea of round bellies and a squall of newborns and a charge of prams like cavalry.

It looks out of control, but actually it is tightly monitored. Every single person here has been thoroughly assessed. Do they deserve to be one of the few allowed into town? The rich can always get in, the poor rely on lottery numbers, and some are even lucky enough to be given jobs and a home for a full ten months. From fingerprints to blood samples, facial mapping and DNA sequencing, the council knows every inch of its tourists and workers. It's difficult to monitor them once they're inside the town, though. Security guards get knocked up, cameras have a tendency to sprout roots, and microphones spread like moss. Chloe remembers an ear-splitting summer spent digging them out of the road to the orchard.

The town is transitory—except Chloe. The population comes, conceives, births, and departs. Chloe goes on.

The streets are a mess of green things. Flowers Chloe has no name for spring up from the tiniest crack in the bitumen. Houses are covered in vines, or moss, or just millions of tiny ferns. There's always the odd asshole tourist who breaks the rules and plants something unusual. Most are pulled up as soon as they are noticed, but occasionally they get through—there's a dental-floss creeper attached to the side of the pharmacy that seems to have been preserved for the irony, and a monstrous tree fruiting 4x4 tyres that's too useful round here to kill.

Middle of the day, temperatures in the mid-thirties, the air is heavy with flower-scent and sweat, the entire town and all its people are in bloom.

Chloe hates the word *bloom.*

She heads to the market. Nothing in packets, everything fresh, a million little chickens sent to the slaughter and a million ready to go the next day. The bitch at the register glances at Chloe's full basket and smirks, "Don't tell me you're finally eating for two?" She rests a hand on her own enormous belly like it's a challenge.

"That never gets old, does it?" Chloe hands over fistfuls of change and leaves without cracking a smile. She's grateful to get out of town.

The whisper of pencils in the breeze sings her home.

When the buses are gone and the shop is shut, Chloe releases her refugees from the storeroom and cooks.

Jane sits at the kitchen table and watches her, fearful, intense. "You're not pregnant," she finally has the courage to say.

Chloe turns from her chicken, sizzling. "You've come to the right place," she says. She knows what the girl is really asking. "You saw the trees. Where else could you be?"

"But you're not, are you?" Ethan, standing by the doorway, arms crossed. He still doesn't trust her. He's smarter than he looks. "And you don't have a kid."

They leave it hanging while Chloe sets the table. She sits, waits for Ethan to join them, and serves them solemnly. "No, I'm not." She fills their plates to breaking. "And no, I don't. And no, I won't." But only gives herself a little. "I'm the only infertile thing here."

When Ethan and Jane stare at her in horror, she can only laugh. "Oh don't worry, it's not catching. It's just me. Plant pencils in the ground here and they grow into fucking trees. But not me. Never me."

Jane digs into dinner like a starving child.

• • •

She's getting better at the babies. They look less like aliens now, more like tiny people. But, of course, they wash off. The first shower, and they drain into grey streaks down her belly and thighs. She can't really mean them.

Empty

Now that sticks. Over and over the letters cut deep and dark. She buries the pencils in to the eraser and wears them down with writing.

Empty

Stretches across her like a stamp, a brand, a warning—

• • •

"You must hate me."

Jane in the doorway interrupts her. Chloe should have locked them in the storeroom like she did during the day.

"If I hated you, would I be hiding you?" Chloe places the 2B pencil down on the table beside her. It rolls and rattles into its companions. Carefully, she slides her singlet down to cover the fresh, bloody words. She unfolds her bare legs from the armchair and stands, gingerly. The pencil marks sting.

When she turns to face her little refugee, the girl takes a shuddering step back. It's been a long time since anyone's seen Chloe in her underwear.

Her arms are covered in intricately detailed pencil trees, all drawn in 2B. Nothing sticks like the trees. They wrap her body in their own life, growing leaves she doesn't draw and fruit of their own volition. Roots are beginning to creep across her back, where she can't reach.

Her legs are the town, the way it was when she was a child, before the soil changed and the growing began and she was left behind. Over the long, lonely years she's filled it with all the details she can remember. Empty streets. Wide sky. Sheep chewing on dry grass. The price of unleaded at the last servo before the freeway, right when the oil dried up and the cost spiked. Hand-knitted jumpers hanging in market day stalls, manned by grannies with purple hair. Sausage-sizzles.

There are no swollen bellies in her drawings. She didn't include the day every woman over the age of twelve realised, at almost exactly the same time, that they were pregnant. Except for Chloe. No pictures of soil taken away for chemical tests, or police-tape flapping in the hot wind, or the grannies whose bodies didn't survive the so-called miracle. Or the council, hammering in the first fencepost.

Or Mike, fishing out the negative pregnancy tests from the bin in their bathroom.

That's not the town she chooses to record.

Jane gapes at her, but Chloe only smiles. "You think I'm jealous of you?" she asks.

"Aren't you?" Jane rests a hand on her abdomen. She can't know if there's life beneath her skin yet, but Chloe is fairly certain there is. She's grown quite good at sensing green shoots, over the years.

Chloe imitates the gesture, but the babies she's drawn there won't stay. "Why have you done this?" she asks. "You must know the risks. As soon as you leave, you'll have to run. Across the whole bloody country, if you can. The council keep an eye on all applicants. If you were denied a pass but suddenly turn up preggers, they won't think it's a coincidence."

Jane pales, but her chapped lips narrow, and her eyes are determined. She holds out a shaky hand for Chloe to look at. There's a tattoo on the inside of her wrist, tiny compared to the artwork across Chloe's arms. A series of numbers Chloe doesn't understand. "These are my poisons," Jane answers. "Common, garden variety, watertable and soil contaminants. Everyone in our block has them. Ethan too."

The sigh of pencils in the wind slides in through the open window.

"We can't afford the blood cleansing, so this was the only other way. Our numbers didn't come up. We applied on humanitarian grounds, sold the unit, and the car, and my father mortgaged his house, but it still wasn't enough. The council wouldn't let us in. Then Ethan heard of the network."

"The network?" Chloe asks.

"A group of fertility refugees, just like us. They helped us get in, they'll help us get out, hide us, get the drugs I need to keep my baby growing once I leave this place. They—" she blinks, frowns "—they even told us to come in through the pencil orchard. On the night of the full moon."

Chloe says nothing. That doesn't surprise her. Her refugee tree is full, after all, of names on paper. How many has she helped through the countless years? It's nice to know they remember her.

"I thought it was romantic. But I guess that wasn't the point."

"You should rest." Chloe turns her back on Jane, and resumes her seat. "That will be a hard road. For all three of you."

She selects a fresh pencil from the table, sharp and unsullied by blood, lifts her singlet again, and writes. Jane watches her for a long time.

• • •

We could always do it the natural way

Written around her heart, in a handwriting not her own.

We could always do it the natural way

Deep in the soft tissue of her breast, shallow against the hard lines of her ribs.

Mark's handwriting. The only thing she has left of him. That, and the pencils themselves.

In the storeroom a floor beneath her, Ethan and Jane are making love. Entirely unnecessary. The sounds are soft and muffled. The pencils rustle in the wind like musical accompaniment.

We could always do it the natural way

Mark planted the pencil trees to give her something to look after, and she drew dark landscapes with the fruit, empty pictures devoid of life. When she ran out of paper, she started on herself. The blank canvas of her skin.

• • •

The sound that wakes her is not pencils. It's a deeper rumble, much louder. Helicopter.

Only the council has clearance anywhere near here, and they do not use it without reason. She leaps to the window. Movement at the fence, bulky figures. Above the shop, the buzz of rotor blades, and the swerving hard beam of a spotlight.

They are searching for someone. So, she had the inspection times wrong.

Chloe pulls on jeans and a long-sleeved flannel shirt and runs to the shopfront, slowing only to grab a blunt 2B from the table beside her armchair. At least she locked the storeroom door. She hopes Ethan and Jane have the sense to stay quiet, and hidden.

She shop opens the door before the council inspectors have the chance to knock, and leans against it, twirling the pencil slowly between her fingers. It helps calm her heartbeat, ease her breathing, even cool the sweat on her face.

The men who climb her wooden steps are wrapped in shiny silver radiation suits, their faces hidden behind thick plastic masks, hands clumsy with gloves. Even though they're men, they fear unwelcome contamination. At first it was thought that only women were affected by this place—instantaneous pregnancy is an obvious symptom. And then the wives of council members, workmen and gardeners started giving birth to triplets, quintuplets. Octuplets.

"Did you see anything?"

Chloe has always had a sense that the council doesn't approve of her. She breaks the broken laws of nature and doesn't fit with the rest of their paperwork. Date of birth, forgotten. Parents, not on record. Offspring, none. But it's not like she can leave.

She takes her time answering. Twirls the pencil, lifts it to her lips, tastes wood and graphite with the tip of her tongue. "See what?" she asks, finally.

"There's a break in the fence." Scepticism is hard to hear through the plastic, but Chloe gets the feeling that this councilman doesn't believe her. "Someone got in. Just at the edge of your orchard. Again."

It's taken them long enough to notice. "Again?" she drawls the word, rounds out her accent. Country girl, through and through. "It's happened before?"

"And if I inspected your shop?"

"You've have to be bloody careful about it," she says, with a smile. "My pencils are all sharpened, and that shiny stuff looks thin to me. Wouldn't want to cut it on anything, would you?"

A noise that could be a curse, and the inspector turns and stomps down the stairs. He and his men roam the orchard, they shine their torches into the storeroom and the back shed, but Ethan and Jane must be hiding well. Unable to sleep, Chloe takes out her rake and tidies the yard. Then she pulls out a ladder from the shed, and her clippers and saw, and prunes the trees, from highest branches to lowest stem. The councilmen in their delicate suits do their best to avoid her, but somehow she keeps running into them.

Eventually, the council gives up, but not before laying coils of barbed wire on both sides of the fence. Chloe wonders why they don't just invest in snipers, and be done with it.

• • •

The line of teardrops down her face wipe clean with a dry tissue. She listens to Jane, sobbing, and pictures Ethan, holding her. She presses the pencil harder. But no matter what she does, her own tears wash away.

Even when Mark died, the tears wouldn't stick. She tried to bury him in the orchard, but the council took him away. She tried to draw him, but could never do him justice.

So she continued harvesting, without him. And she didn't grow old, the way he had done. She remained unchanging, but for the trees on her arms that grew, and the words she dug into her skin.

Until the first refugee climbed over the fence.

• • •

Chloe keeps Ethan and Jane locked in the storeroom for two days. She doesn't so much as look at the window, the whole time. Just sells, harvests, draws, and prunes. She cuts down branches in the daytime, and unties the names of her refugees at night.

Hopefully, two days will be long enough. Hopefully, the council won't be watching.

She gathers all the branches she has cut and piles them into the back of the ute. The names have gone into two large hessian bags, and she weighs them down with the ladder. Then she waits until long after sunset, when the moon is hidden behind clouds, to unlock the storeroom.

"We need to hurry," she says into the darkness, even before Ethan and Jane emerge from their hiding places. "They could be watching."

Chloe drives with the lights off, navigating by memory alone, and heads for the tip.

No one else uses the tip anymore; what do the townspeople have to throw out? Anything that isn't planted is carefully removed and sanitised. The tip itself is a wide crack in what was once dry earth, but is now rich with tiny plants. Chocolate-wrapper flowers, beer-tin creepers, chicken-bone tubers. And it is near the fence.

Jane clutches the dashboard and Ethan wraps his large hands around her waist. Together, they stare out the windshield at the dark and rushing road. They don't need to worry. Chloe knows every inch of the way. She has lived here a long time.

Cutting their way out would not be the best idea. With Ethan's help, she extends the ladder and leans it against the fence, angled above the barbed wire. It's unsteady. The fence shakes, sending long rattling tremors down its length. Just as long as no one's monitoring it too closely.

"You will have to jump," she says, voice a low whisper carried far by the night. "From the top. The other side is desert sand. I hope it's soft." She turns to Ethan. "You go first. Catch her. That's what you're here to do."

She holds the ladder as still as she can. The climb is difficult in the dark. He lands hard, with a whoosh of air, but claims he is unhurt. Jane hesitates.

"I will help you." Chloe steadies her, pushes her, and follows behind ready to catch should she slip. Chloe doesn't fear the shaky ladder.

"I'm not sure I should do this," Jane whispers, just ahead. "What if I leave this place, and my baby dies?"

"You cannot stay here. They will find you."

Another few slow inches.

"But it doesn't belong out there." Jane stops at the top of the ladder. Her hands grip the wire fence and everything sways. "How can I take it back there, to the poisonous soil and the dirty water and the filthy air? Why can't we stay here, where it is safe?"

"No one stays here," Chloe's voice is harsh, her throat dry. "Except me. Everyone else comes and goes." She climbs until she's right behind Jane, until there's no ladder left, until the fence is buckling and the ladder is slipping and Jane teeters and almost screams. "Take your blessings. And don't wish for something you don't understand." Chloe gives Jane a final push. The girl lands in her boy's open arms.

"Hurry," Chloe says, poised at the top of the unsteady fence. "Run. The council doesn't sleep. You cannot be here, when they come."

The night is too black to see them go. Chloe remains on the top of the fence for a long time, the wind tugging at her, teasing her with the prospect of falling.

It wouldn't take much, just to tip over and land on the other side. She can't remember how long it's been, since she's seen the outside world. Slowly, she lifts an arm and reaches across the fence. Her skin begins to dry, to crack. Everything on the other side, right up to her elbow, ages and dies with a tired sigh—but the pencil tree drawings remain fresh. Their dark lines are vivid, and they unfurl new leaves before her eyes.

Descending is difficult, with one working arm. Chloe drops the bags of names into the tip, covers them with the branches she has pruned, and sets them alight. She doesn't harvest that morning. Instead, she sits by the tip, almost lost in the riot of colour and rubbish, and watches them burn. Tiny pieces of paper rise glowing, flickering, into the pale sky.

• • •

No drawing tonight. It's not necessary, because the trees are doing it themselves. The branches across her skin pulse, the roots grow deeper down her back. The pencils, born from this place, heal her, keep her alive. And will not let her leave.

• • •

The council imposes strict rules on her and a curfew on the town. They install cameras around the orchard, patrol the fence with 4x4s, and limit her movements.

Chloe will wait them out, as she's done before. Several times. Councilmen leave, rules are forgotten, generations pass. She always wins.

Within a day the cameras have started sprouting tiny glass flowers.

~

CONSORTING WITH FILTH

LISA L. HANNETT

The ghosts are taking up too much space.

Plodding on blue-black feet, they clog roadways, airports, boardwalks. Day and night, they colonise buses, trains, trams; their haggard, translucent figures slumping on stained plastic benches, forcing the living to stand. They occupy taxis, whole families cramming into front seats. Ferries and fishing boats sit low in the water, decks weighed down by these drifters. Always arriving, more and more each day, never *leaving*.

They don't float—the burden of death has made them heavy—but they *can* swim. Herding spectres off gangplanks is futile. For a while southern seas bob with countless dead buoys that simply wash back in with the tide.

Inevitably, they migrate from this country's great unbroken shore and begin to appear inland. Skin the hue of deep bruises, arms lank by their sides, the ghosts limp from countryside to city. Avoiding farms with livestock, but sighing through quiet fields of Shiraz grapes, hops, and wheat, leaving much of the year's harvest blighted in their wake. After spoiling farmers' markets with their presence, they progress from factories to warehouses, churches to malls, waiting rooms to welfare queues. They stop unpredictably, congregating in hotels, convenience stores, cafés. Reeking like night shift workers—grease traps and cumin, unwashed scalp, cold lard—they suffocate banks and surgeries, the congealed air of their bodies as unbreathable as mud.

They're *everywhere*, now. Caravan parks and high-rises, petrol stations and bottle shops, the public playground down the road.

They're in Ellie's suburb, even. On her street.

Ellie's mom refuses to believe some sort of heavenly war has kept the ghosts from staying where they belong. *For years these spirits have scuttled unseen*, she says. *Multiplying like cockroaches. Gathering strength. Waiting to overwhelm by sheer numbers.*

Ellie's dad says he's never seen ghouls like these. *More aimless than usual*, he comments. *More desperate.*

They're relentless, Ken, replies her mother, stabbing a knitting needle at the Channel Nine news. Her tone is fervent, almost incredulous, as if these parasites weren't the reason she deserted the overrun Northern Hemisphere and moved down here over a decade ago, soon before Ellie was born. There's no way she'd left her friends and family just because she'd fallen in love with Ellie's dad—Joy Mitchell is far from romantic. No, it was the abundance of sheep in this country that *really* drew her so far south. The hope of safety, of protection, in all that roaming fleece.

Trust me: the filthy things are trying to take over. Gaze fixed on the flat screen, Ellie's mom swaps a white skein of wool for a black and starts on another stripe. As the headlines unscroll, the scarf grows steadily longer. Between rows, she glances at Ken and gives her work a proud pat. *Thank Christ for good barriers*, she says.

Boundaries mean little to the dead, as far as Ellie can tell. If they want, ghosts can undermine walls, fences, borders. They completely ignore the 'Keep Out!' sign on her bedroom door. They slip in when she's not around, and sometimes when she is. They stand half in and half out of her wardrobe, so she can't get at her pyjamas or her clean school uniforms. They sit at the desk and muck up her homework. They lie down next to her in bed.

Their cold damp touch soothes the hot rash ever-blooming on her skin.

• • •

Last time, the ghost must've followed Ellie home after ballet.

After weeks of begging, Joy had finally relented: Ellie had been allowed to walk the two blocks between the dance studio and their unit on her own. She had taken every precaution, following her mom's instructions to the letter. She'd avoided overgrown bushes along the footpath, and bus stops, and parked cars. When the road was clear, she'd trotted right down the middle, buying herself precious seconds to escape should any strangers come flitting out of the shrubs. In one fist, she'd clutched the house keys like knuckledusters, metal prongs spiking between her small fingers; in the other, her thumb hovered over the 'send' button on Joy's mobile phone, emergency services pre-dialled. She'd kept her head down, made no eye contact. She'd definitely spoken to no one.

Even so.

After unlatching the front door, she'd paused on the threshold to yank off the beanie and shawl Joy had made her wear—even though it was forty-odd degrees out and, as Ellie's dad would say, dry as a witch's tit. Standing on the crocheted welcome mat, fine brown hair tangled with sweat, a puff of cool air had breezed past her into the house. Maybe that's when the ghost had gotten in? Ellie still isn't sure. Might've been when she'd opened her bedroom window—it hadn't yet been nailed shut—to get some relief. Or when she'd been distracted, peeling off the mohair tights and leotard Joy had hand-woven? When she'd been too busy scratching, scratching, scratching the hives erupting wherever wool had made contact with skin?

Ellie doesn't know.

That shade was taller than most of the others she'd seen. A woman, she'd thought, though with the haze all wraiths wore—oily black shrouds dripping from head to toe—it was damn near impossible to tell them apart. *Each one is vicious as the next*, or so she'd overheard the ladies in Joy's knitting circle say. But Ellie sensed curves beneath the spectral fabric, a matronly figure. It had tiptoed quite gracefully across her bedroom, inching closer and closer. Beneath its stink, there was a whiff of something comforting, something familiar. Lavender, maybe, or rosewater. Perfumed like the heart-shaped soaps in her gran's loo.

When the head had turned in Ellie's direction, she'd felt its glance brush her face. Gentle and papery, its tender palm cooled her rash-fevered brow.

The thing hadn't *seemed* all that evil.

Ellie's mother disagreed.

Within minutes of coming in with the shopping, baskets overflowing with discount yarn, Joy had hollered for Ellie to *Run, now, get the bins!* Voice shrill, her accent always more pronounced with anger. Standing there in her undies, Ellie had hesitated.

"But *Mom*," she'd begun, emphasising the 'o', trying to prove, in whatever small and spontaneous way, that she was just like Joy, really, she said 'mom' instead of 'mum', 'trunk' instead of 'boot', 'garbage' instead of 'rubbish'—and she wasn't garbage, she was her *child*, she wasn't spook-touched, she wasn't dirty garbage . . .

Go!

Indifferent, the ghost had watched Ellie manoeuvre two extra-large black disposal units into the room, bumping into the doorframe, snagging the wheels on her shagpile rug. Joy shouted orders as she moved from garage to kitchen, drawers clattering open and shut, directing Ellie as if this was the first time she'd hauled in the bins. Both were moulded from industrial plastic, lids secured with stainless steel padlocks. The first went into the corner, wedged between the wardrobe and desk; the other was positioned near the door for easy removal. As one, Ellie and the intruder baulked when Joy returned, dragging two tight-weaved, top-grade, angora body bags.

This one's yours, Joy snapped, swiftly unlocking the trash cans, then shoving Ellie away from the ghost. The wool sack was rough as twine, filaments bristling like nettles from every grey inch. It stung her hands as she lined the corner bin, instantly raising welts along her chest and forearms as she leaned over, smoothing the bag down. Behind her, furious grunting and slapping and scuffling, inhuman shrieks. Grave-fabric tearing. Huffing and puffing. A pong of rank spice and sweat and bogwater. A gasp of talc and lavender.

Get in! Ellie's mother snarled through gritted teeth. *Get in!*

And as Joy wrestled the phantom into its wool-bound prison, Ellie climbed into hers.

• • •

The local knitting circle is full of biddies and crackpots, Ellie's dad thinks, though he rarely says so aloud. He might roll his eyes while Joy downloads patterns—nets and carpets and bags of all sizes, jumpsuits and hoods and full-body sheathes, tents big enough to cover a yacht—and he might mutter over his beer on Saturday afternoons when his wife passes the printouts around. He might turn up the TV to drown out the ladies nattering about trash removal schedules and government sanctioned dumps. He might even threaten to take Joy's credit card if she keeps pouring his wages into the till at *Three Bags Full.*

Almost within the same breath, he'll don the cable-knit sweaters she churns out. He'll wear oversized mufflers and button-up vests over his work shirts, and that ugly yellow deerhunter cap. He'll hang every last curtain the knitters produce, bulk-blocking the whole cul-de-sac's windows and doors. He'll kiss Joy's powdered cheek, call her a loveable nutter, and pinch her flat bottom. He'll buy her a better tablet with faster internet and help her access the best knitting sites. He'll say his ute could use a set of seat and steering-wheel covers.

He'll turn a blind eye.

Whatever it takes to keep his place happily quiet.

• • •

Last time, after making a stop at the local dump, Ken had enjoyed a weekend of fishing while Ellie had spent hers locked in wool.

Jammed in the corner, the bin wouldn't roll or tip no matter how much Ellie wriggled inside it. In less than an hour—which had felt like much, much longer—her thighs had seized, calves twitched with cramps, hamstrings screamed to be straightened. Pressing her back against the container's wool-roughened sides, she flexed and relaxed her muscles. She jammed her feet *down*, shoved her shoulders *up*. She *pushed*.

The plastic creaked, thundered, but didn't give. Frustrated, she cried herself head-pounding and sweaty. The air was stifling, rancid: a mix of rubber, rotten eggs, and the piss she couldn't hold in. Her stomach was sour with hunger and worry. If only Joy would respond when she called. If only she'd listen. Then Ellie could *explain*, and her mother would understand—she hadn't done it on purpose, this time it was an accident—and Joy would see she wasn't a liar, she'd see she wasn't *befouled*, that she wasn't garbage, and she'd let her out, and everything would be fine, and Ellie wouldn't hold a grudge, she'd promise to be good, *if only she could get out.*

She wept her throat raw, pounded her knuckles bloody, but got no reply.

Exhausted, she dozed, neck painfully kinked, limbs tingling then going dead.

Two days later, Ellie emerged covered in violent sores. The wool lining had scalded her exposed skin. From face to feet, she sprouted clusters of itching red agony that kept her from school for a week.

Chicken pox, Joy had told Ellie's teachers over the phone. *She'll be right in no time.*

Blubbering quietly in a calamine bath, Ellie came up with her own diagnosis. She'd never fully feel better, she thought, since she seemed to be part ghost.

• • •

This latest drifter is about Ellie's size: same sharp elbows, same bowed thighs, same scrawny ribcage. From the way it sits, splay-legged and slouching at the foot of her bed, she reckons he's a boy. The swamp smell is faint around him—she hardly noticed it upon entering her room—and he's much less solid than the others. Light from a bare bulb on the ceiling seeps through his shroud, limning a prominent nose, weak jaw, protruding collarbone. From certain angles, Ellie can see right through him. The merino patchwork of her quilt is visible through his narrow hips and butt. The simple headboard shoots through his back like a yoke. Her flat pillow bisects his concave gut.

"You okay?" she whispers, edging towards the footboard. Moving carefully, doing her best not to generate any static. Head cocked, Ellie looks at her closed door, listens. In the living room, her dad heckles the buffoons hosting some popular footy program. The show's laugh track peters into an ad for rust-proof fences while Joy calls out from the kitchen, offering Ken a cup of tea. She hears the kettle clanking under the faucet. The cupboards opening and closing. Mugs clunking next to the sink. The squeak of her dad's pleather chair reclining.

No floorboards groaning in the hall.

No slippered steps approaching.

"Here," she says to the ghost after a moment, gaze flicking between the bed and door. "Lie down."

The boy shrinks away from the wool coverlet, navy eyes pleading. His mouth flaps, gapes. All that comes out is cold wind.

"Hang on," Ellie says. "Stand up a sec."

Forearms and palms stinging, she backhands her pillow to the floor. Strips the coarse blanket and knitted sheets, exposing the mattress: floral cotton blotched with stains, but blessedly smooth. Quickly, she brushes away stray fleece fibres to prevent them both from blistering.

"Lie down," she says again, more forcefully now. "It's okay.

Look."

Ellie unzips her hooded sweater, tosses her beret, kicks off the tweed culottes and tights. She slips out of her cashmere singlet, but leaves on the matching knickers. Immediately the boy's arctic breath begins to calm her body's ferocious itching. With a sigh of relief, she wraps her fingers around his clammy wrist. She pauses, listens, glances again at the door. Pulls him down onto the bed beside her.

• • •

Another time, Ellie found a tiny veiled phantom in the toy box at afterhours care. No one else noticed it—or pretended not to—so she climbed in beside it, picked it up. The abandoned little thing felt practically boneless, pliable as a blob of unbaked bread. She swaddled it in the silk handkerchief she'd traded for a week's worth of lunch vouchers at school, stuffed it under her shirt, then hurried to the cloakroom. Her homemade backpack was the perfect size for carrying a baby.

It never cried, never ate, never needed a change.

Still, Joy found it long before the fish fingers had finished frying for dinner.

"For God's sake, Ellie! Why do you *insist* on consorting with such filth? Don't you *care* about your future? Aren't you even the *tiniest* bit concerned?"

When Ellie was released the next morning, she hardly recognised her room. The desk was deprived of its drawers, the wardrobe missing its mirrored doors. On the walls, oily circles marked the spots where Blu-tac once held her favourite posters. Floating white shelves supported nothing but air. There were no colourful ponies with brushable manes. No ballerina music box. No green and gold *Good Effort* ribbons. The snowglobe Gran had given her was also gone, as was the porcelain mouse Aunty Barb had brought from overseas. Ellie's textbooks were stacked on the straight-backed chair, two plain pencils and an eraser on the desk blotter. There was no sign of the knapsack.

• • •

Behind her, the ghost is shivering.

"Get closer," Ellie whispers, schooching her bottom back, seeking the welcome crook of ethereal legs. "I'm warm enough for us both."

The bedsprings whine as the boy shifts, hesitating.

Doubt knots Ellie's throat. She tenses and for a minute imagines getting up, throwing on a nightie and socks, running out into the living room. Hair tousled, eyes wild, as though she'd just woken from a nightmare. She'd pant with feigned fear, make it seem she didn't know where she was, or when. Dragging her feet across the carpet, she'd rush to her mother, hoping to shock. Blue sparks would crackle on her fingertips as she gripped Joy's shoulder, the cardigan conducting energy, disrupting electromagnetic fields, and she'd tell her all about this new drifter, she'd shuffle while she confessed, proving with shock after shock that she was a good girl, that she'd been *fighting* this ghost's energy, armed with wool and static, that she'd been trying to dispel its electricity, that she definitely wasn't harbouring it.

But as the boy snuggles in, Ellie's vision changes. Joy isn't embracing her, she isn't cooing or patting her sweaty head. As the creature presses his chill into her scalding back—glorious relief—dream-Joy turns away, collects her discarded knitting. As he drapes a frigid sleeve across Ellie's inflamed arm, her imaginary mom casts off, then leans back to assess the piece's finish. With an unearthly face now mashed against her skull, Ellie pictures an undersized body bag dangling from sharp wooden needles. Too small for the boy. Too small for her. They'd both have to crouch to fit in it.

The way she imagines it, the sack's weave is ridged with woollen barbed wire.

Get in, says Ellie's made-up mother.

Shaking, Ellie echoes, "Get in."

The world blurs and dims as the shade embraces her, his dank clay limbs quenching her body's fierce heat. Sighing, she relaxes into his humid pressure, muscles slack as he *pushes* into her spine and neck. Into her head.

Near-smothered, Ellie sucks fresh life into her lungs. Soon the cramps in her belly stop twisting. For once, her joints are fluid, not stiff and swollen and grinding. Panic-spiders break the webs they'd spun round her heart, then swiftly tap-dance away. A serene fog settles over her, a blanket of mist and hope. She smiles and stretches to her full length, skin whole and pale and cool.

In the ghost's company, Ellie is more expansive than ever before, more free.

She's more herself.

She's blissfully, completely, alive.

"Knock knock," says Joy, switching on the light as she barges into the room. A new striped scarf pools in her arms, half-spilling onto the floor, tangling as she walks. "Try this on for size, El—"

Ellie blinks once, slowly, and a shriek tears through the soft fog hovering over her. Eyes watering, she squints as the pall fluctuates. The naked bulb is suddenly noon-bright overhead, its light shrill, screeching down onto the bed in a strong northern accent.

"Jesus Christ, Ellie!"

Rough hands force her onto her back. Fists pummel her temples and chest. Plump legs clamp her sides, and *squeeze*. Plaid trousers chafe bare skin as Joy straddles her, struggling, wrangling, failing to fully dislodge the ghost.

Strong fingers dig into Ellie's cheeks, prising the small jaw open.

"Swallow," says her mother, shoving in great mouthfuls of wool, shoving until she gags, *shoving*. "Swallow, my girl! It's for your own good!"

NIGHT BLOOMING

JASON NAHRUNG

Deborah Brown—Jazmine Nocturna to her friends—had it bad for the unliving. Shane stood in the teenager's bedroom, taking in the nu-vamp celeb posters, the black lace, the incense.

The girl's mother stood at the bedroom door. Ms Brown wore a pencil skirt and heels, a crisp white blouse, but stray hairs were pulling free from her tight bun; shadows under her eyes showed through her makeup. Early to mid-forties. Gym toned, suntanned, a gold cross above her modest cleavage. No wedding ring, but a pale line where one had been. She radiated anxiety.

Join the club, sister.

On the phone with Cunningham that morning, Shane had almost said no to this favour. The demon in her blood had all but orgasmed at the thought of being outside, among the people. If Vikki found out, she'd go ballistic. Now, looking around Jazmine's room, taking in the girl's wreck of a mother, Shane was glad she'd forced herself to take the job.

Gothic was one thing. Bloodsucking was another. Ever since the Make Believe, there had been an awareness that the things that went bump in the night could bump mighty hard.

"She was always into it," Ms Brown offered. "Fairies and unicorns. And then . . . this." She gestured to the pin-up fang boys from the rom-coms, the myth-pop bands in leather and velvet.

"Did she say where she was going last night? Who she was seeing?"

"I told her, we could go anywhere, do anything she wanted for her eighteenth. Anything to keep her away from those people."

"By 'those people', you mean Registered Paranormal Beings? It's not illegal to associate with mythoes."

Cunningham had used similar words himself, telling Shane why Special Branch weren't able to act when Ms Brown had tried to report her daughter missing when she hadn't come home that morning.

"You think I'm paranoid, neurotic," Ms Brown said. One hand fiddled with the cross. The glossy lips quivered.

Shane gave a smile she hoped was reassuring. "It's a mother's duty to worry."

"Do you have children, Detective Hall?"

"No, no I don't."

"But you're married."

Shane reflexively touched the ring on her left hand. Given to her by Vikki's mother, with her blessing. "Not officially. You said you'd been in touch with your ex-husband?"

"Probably celebrating with his wife, now he doesn't have to pay child support. Debbie didn't get on with her dad. He never understood her, and when he left . . . " She ended with a shrug of resignation.

"I'll need his number anyway. Please. Sergeant Cunningham explained I wasn't here in an official capacity?"

"On leave, he said."

Shane nodded. Minimalist, as always, Cunningham. She hadn't seen him since he'd visited her in hospital. She'd been filled with tubes, drugged out of her scone, surrounded by staff in hazmat suits. He'd brought her chocolates, saying he hadn't thought a woman like her would appreciate flowers. She'd sent him and his chocolates away.

"So what can you tell me about this nu-vamp crowd Deborah was caught up with?"

The woman picked a framed photo from a bookshelf and handed it to Shane.

Their fingers touched. Shane flinched, almost dropped the picture as the demon surged in her mind, like a moray eel darting from its cave. A burst of cloying sandalwood filled Shane's nostrils. Her throat tightened.

"This is the only picture I have." A group of young people in black and burgundy, crowded around a candle. Lots of red eye. Ms

Brown clutched her necklace. "Please find my little girl. I just need to know she's okay."

"Well, let's have a look." Shane sat at the desk, propped the picture up and opened the girl's laptop.

"It's protected," Ms Brown said. "And she's blocked me from her profiles."

"I'll see what I can do. You should stand back."

Ms Brown looked puzzled, but gave her some space.

Shane fished a small silver case from her handbag and flicked the lid open. The pisacha stirred, like a cat stretching. Vikki's familiar warning echoed: *What if you get hurt? What if you bleed?*

Shane picked the razor blade from the case, turned it in her fingers. What indeed? The pisacha growled. She felt its claws unsheathe in anticipation of a chance to flex its muscles. To take control. An image of Ms Brown licking blood from a cut in Shane's wrist flashed across her mind.

Free. The word blew on a sandalwood breeze.

"What are you doing?" Ms Brown asked, stepping farther back.

Shane told her to trust her, that she needed quiet. Her voice was shaking.

"Sweet Jesus," Ms Brown whispered.

She heard Manasa, telling her: "It won't be without its benefits."

"Two heads are better than one," Cunningham had guffawed, but neither the department nor Vikki had agreed.

Shane recited the mantra that Manasa had taught her. When she'd stopped shaking, she sliced the tip of one finger. She winced at the sting, then touched the bleeding digit to the keyboard.

The pisacha growled.

Shane groaned as the connection was made; the sensations hit her like a waterfall. Her stomach lurched. She tasted bile.

Ms Brown asked if she was all right. Shane held up one hand to shush the woman.

Jazmine's excitement simmered in the plastic. Eighteen. Legal—finally.

Sensations, memories, feelings, all snapped through Shane's mind, like someone flicking the pages of a book. A name, a face.

"Do you know someone called Vlad?"

"No, she never spoke about her friends." Ms Brown stood behind Shane so she could see the computer screen. "Who is he? What have you found?"

"She was meeting him last night. They were going *all the way*."

"Oh, God." She was giving the cross a fair work out. It was likely to be worn down to just a straight piece of metal at this rate.

"Had she . . . had relations?"

"I—I think so. She never said, but a mother . . . I think so, yes. Wait. How can you tell? You haven't even logged in yet." The woman tensed, hand on her necklace as though she were about to go all Van Helsing on Shane's arse.

"Are you a believer, Ms Brown? What about Jaz—Deborah?"

"She stopped going to church when she turned sixteen. I didn't want to force her."

It seemed Deborah had found herself a very different blood cult. Although, perhaps not that different: transformation through the blood of a revenant saviour who promised everlasting life.

"Did your daughter ever speak to you about conversion?"

"Is that even possible?"

"The Make Believe effect is still occurring. We've had three instances of spontaneous metamythosis in the past month. And there have been reports of voluntary transformation where such conversion is part of the mythos."

"Why? Why would she want to give up all this . . . for that?"

"We don't know that she has. Let's see what else we can find out, hey." Shane turned her attention back to the computer. Maybe Deborah hadn't yet gone all the way. Maybe it *was* just sex and eyeliner.

She gasped as Deborah—Jazmine—invaded her mind through the pisacha. Sitting here in this chair, her chest tight with anticipation, her special velvet frock hanging on the back of the door. Her skin was electric. *Tonight. All the way.*

A password appeared, hammered out by fingers with black-painted nails chewed rough. Fingers, long and slender like her mother's.

The room grew hot, as hot and suffocating as a sauna; sweat beaded on her forehead, her back. Whispers filled her head. Sandalwood clouded around her. Her hand jerked on the mouse. She heard, distantly, like a background beat, surf breaking.

Ms Brown was at her shoulder, reaching but afraid to make contact.

"Are you all right?" she asked again. "Is it my cross?"

Shane shook her head, closed her eyes. "Just need a minute." She concentrated on the mantra. Gradually, the sound of surf dulled, the sandalwood lightened, allowing Jazmine's room to come once more into focus. She breathed deeply, three in, three out, and applied a Band-Aid before spraying the keyboard with hospital-grade disinfectant and wiping away any trace of blood. "Holy symbols only affect some, you know. But it's better than nothing."

"They say it's all about faith. About belief. The Make Believe, I mean. That we wanted it so badly that we got it."

"New Age crap. That's my professional opinion."

The woman gave a fractured smile, released the cross. "But you aren't here in a professional capacity."

"It's still crap." She wiped her brow with the sleeve of her shirt. "May I have a glass of water, please?"

Ms Brown scuttled out.

Shane clicked through some photos, went through drawers.

Jazmine didn't look happy in her selfies. She had the pout down pat, had managed to keep her eyes appropriately vacant of any emotion other than a suggestion of severe boredom.

But she hadn't been bored last night. She'd been ready to go *all the way* with Vlad. How had that worked out for her, Shane wondered.

She knew about first love. Illicit love. She and Vikki had had quite the dance when they'd realised they were in deeper than a mere dalliance. Even in a world suddenly filled with the truly fantastic, old prejudices still prevailed. But they had pushed on, trusted their love to overcome. That lightning bolt they'd shared when they'd first met over a bloody stretcher in the ICU, it had burnt them all the way to the core. And now Shane was sleeping in a separate room, because her lover was too shit scared of waking up next to a stranger, or worse. Shane couldn't blame her.

Ms Brown returned as Shane emailed herself a parcel of photos from Jazmine's computer. A short browse of Jazmine's social media had revealed her coterie of black-clad pals and a favourite haunt or three. Two Shane could trace easily enough—tagging revealed them as clubs in the Valley, naturally; where else would the creatures of the night gather but in mytho central?—but the third was more interesting: lots of curtains and candles and kids in robes. No tags there. The sight of razor blades and a very sharp knife made her vision lurch as the demon in her blood hungered for release.

Damn it, but she couldn't face this bunch in her condition. She'd need to see Manasa.

Ms Brown offered her a glass of water. She drank, but it was nothing compared to what she really needed.

• • •

It was a frustrating afternoon, being cold-shouldered by those of Jazmine's friends she could contact and boning up on vampire lore while she waited for Manasa to get back from whatever she was doing. There was a lot of BS, not a lot of science since the Make Believe had introduced the fantastic to the real world. Eggheads were still debating what had caused it, but that wasn't Shane's concern. Real-world monsters had been bad enough. Dealing with the dreams and nightmares of global mythology was all a bit much. Especially when one of them was in your head, and you were totally reliant on another to keep you . . . you.

Manasa Chalmers had a room in a boutique hotel on the border of the Valley and Bowen Hills. It was close to both 'burbs' railway stations, but Shane always drove. Less chance of encountering the public that way. The station wagon's air conditioning hadn't done much against the late afternoon heat, and her cargo pants and shirt stuck to her like cling wrap as she made her way inside.

Manasa opened the door before Shane could knock. Perhaps she had a deal with the concierge. Maybe she'd been waiting, poised. They were linked, she'd said on one visit, holding up two fingers twined as though making a promise. The symbol had reminded Shane of two snakes on a caduceus—she had given Vikki such a brooch for their third anniversary, both an acknowledgement of her nursing as well as their relationship.

"Namaste," Manasa said, hands together in front of her chest as she gave a small bow. "You look hot, Detective."

"Nicest thing anyone's said to me all day."

Manasa frowned. She didn't do entendres.

She was wearing a sari, patterned in browns and creams. The room was dim behind her, white cotton curtains drawn against prying eyes, just enough sunlight to make out the maze of Sanskrit tattoos covering her bald scalp, the glint of the gold stud in her nostril.

"I have water, but that is not what you are here for, is it?" She waited patiently in the small entryway while Shane fought with her boots before successfully adding them to the sandals and sneakers by the wall. "I had not expected to see you again so soon."

"I used the bloodrunner."

"Ah. I warned you: it might only be a sliver of the demon inside you, but calling on the pisacha's power will give it strength."

"Worth the risk. I'm on a case."

"The police have let you resume work?"

Shane all but squirmed under Manasa's studious gaze, the woman's brown eyes lined in kohl under pencil-thin brows. She focused on the red bindi on her forehead instead.

"Ah," she said again. "And how are you coping with the pisacha? Your control is improving?"

Shane made a rocking motion with her hand. "My partner's not thrilled." The enforced celibacy and general atmosphere of paranoia weren't thrilling her, either. Change of subject: "Man, it's hot in here. You spoken to the motel about the air?"

Fresh sweat blossomed. She was aware of her parched mouth, of the tremble in her body. Of the writhing in her blood, the whisper in her mind. The demon did not like being here. She blinked away sweat and distraction.

"I hadn't noticed. I must be used to the warmth."

"I was born here and I'm not used to it."

"And when you bled, did the pisacha tell you anything useful?"

"A little."

Manasa offered her a chair. "How would you like your soma?"

"The usual."

A smile, a lick of lip. "Never as much fun as the first time."

Shane quivered at the memory: Manasa leaning over her in the railway station as the pisacha tore through her mind like a red-hot cyclone. Then the pain as Manasa bit down, and the cool, soothing numbness that had followed as Manasa's venom had stilled the attempted possession.

Her fingers massaged the spot on her throat, the flesh throbbing where the twin wounds had healed. "We don't know each other well enough yet."

Manasa got a glass from a cupboard, wiped it once with a cloth as though it weren't already sparkling, and turned her back. But Shane could see in the polished aluminium of the fridge how Manasa held the rim under her top teeth, the two curved fangs sliding into view, and how thick, milky spittle ran down the side and into the glass. She saw a little of Manasa's life with every dose. Her frustration at having had the SITI—whatever that was—stolen from the Bangalore lab during her watch. Of having had to let the thief, possessed by a pisacha, escape in order to save Shane's life, her soma the only thing keeping the fractured entity in Shane's blood at bay. The entity that had given her certain paranormal abilities that, ironically, had locked her out of her duties with Special Branch, whose task it was to police the city's mythoes.

Manasa held out the glass.

This would be her fifth dose since Manasa had bitten her. The treatment had not improved with practice. Shane drank, gagging on the gluggy liquid, trying to close her mind to the sensations it provoked. Manasa's frustration at not having tracked down the SITI, her apology for the pisacha having infected Shane—another failure of her duty.

The pisacha's presence subsided, the stench of sandalwood drifting, letting in the ammonia scent of motel cleaning agents, a hint of cinnamon.

Shane gulped a glass of water.

"Do you have time for a proper drink?" Manasa asked.

"I'm working, sorry." She held up her plastered finger.

"Would you like back-up?"

Shane felt again the wave of frustration at being cooped up, cut off; at browsing streets of strangers, news reports, corporate records, hoping to pick up a trace of her quarry. And she recalled the picture of those black-clad acolytes and the vampire Vlad with his piercing eyes and self-confidence.

"It's off the books. If you get hurt, there's no insurance or anything. You could be held culpable for damage or injury you cause."

"Is that likely?"

She hesitated. "A missing kid, fallen in with a rough crowd."

"Rough? My favourite kind. Give me a moment to change. You can tell me more on the way."

Manasa returned in loose trousers, a thigh-length kameez and a headscarf, all in emerald with gold trim. As Manasa slipped on a pair of mirrored shades, Shane felt something in the woman uncoil, ready to strike.

• • •

They were approaching Abaddon, one of Jazmine's favoured clubs, when Vikki called. They were in a Valley back street. It was lined with ramshackle cottages and rundown businesses waiting for a wrecking ball. Shane parked across someone's driveway and took the phone from the rack.

"Hey."

"I'm pulling overtime," Vikki said.

"Again?"

"It's ICU."

Manasa looked up from her phone where she'd been working the map and pointed to a boarded-up, multi-storey brick building covered in graffiti and weather stain. "That should be the place."

"Who's that?" Vikki asked.

"I'm out," Shane said. "Doing a favour for Cunningham."

"Jesus, Shane, are you crazy? What if you get hurt? What if you *bleed*?"

"It's not likely—"

"Who's with you? Cunningham?"

"Steady down, Vik. I'm just asking around after a gothling who stayed out after her bedtime, okay."

"You're unbelievable. The risk you're taking. Not just to you, but everyone around you."

Manasa leaned over to speak into Shane's phone, her breath gusting past Shane's cheek and lips.

"Do not fret, please, Mrs King. I will protect your wife."

Vikki's curse was a shriek. "You're there with *her*? She did a fine job of protecting you the first time." She swore again, and ended the call.

Shane grimaced at Manasa. "Did you hear that? Sorry."

She made to hit redial.

Manasa stayed her hand.

"Let her cool down. Your partner is concerned for your safety; that's admirable, and understandable. But our task is to find this girl, Jazmine Nocturne."

Shane leaned back into the seat, willing herself to fall into the fabric. She felt the pisacha chortling. *Your time will come*, she told it. She would find a way to exorcise its presence. And when she did, she and Vikki would go away for a very long weekend.

One thing at a time. It was still bloody early for a club, but maybe there'd be staff they could hassle. Action would be welcome. A whole month she'd been confined to barracks, considered compromised by the police force, and Vikki acting as though she was Typhoid Mary.

"Let's go check it out, Manasa. Looks like we'll be having that drink after all."

• • •

The bar looked more like some kind of barricade made from kegs and planks, the drinks served in bottles and plastic cups from tubs of ice. The place reeked of stale booze, some earthy incense. Bench seats, beanbags and cushions lay scattered around the concrete floor under a high ceiling of beams and floorboards. Naked bulbs hung from cables.

The barmaid stared at Jazmine's photo from behind pierced brows and heavily mascaraed lashes and gave a shrug.

"Ask the band when they slither in," she suggested. "The swampies love 'em."

Shane ordered bourbon and nachos. Manasa stuck with water.

"You know much about vampires?" Shane asked.

"Your pisacha is a kind of vampire," Manasa said.

"I guess." She'd been reading up on the Hindu pantheon, since she'd become so intimately acquainted with one of its mythoes. Two, in fact. "Any thoughts on why something like that would come crawling out of the Make Believe?"

"Karma? Who knows how, or why, some people were changed the way they were. The most important thing is what they do now."

Shane wanted to ask, are you what I think you are? But there was an etiquette with the mythoes. She tried a softer option.

"You've never told me what you were—what you did—before the Make Believe."

Manasa answered with a smile, eyes unreadable behind her shades.

A delivery door opened with a squeal and a band started loading instruments onto a stage made of packing crates.

Shane stood. "Mind our drinks? I'll go talk to the musos."

Manasa licked her lips as she eyed the band. The slow, deliberate sweep of pink tongue sent a hot bolt straight to Shane's groin. A month cooped up, definitely a month too long.

"Start with the sax player," Manasa said.

As she approached, Shane wondered if she shouldn't have put on sunglasses: the band members were a brightly clad bunch, shiny too: total Eighties throwbacks.

A big fella, a real hard body under his mesh top and tight jeans, tooted on a sax as she arrived. He stank of patchouli and musky cologne. He had a thick leather collar around his neck, similar on his wrists, with charms dangling from chains.

A foot taller than her, he towered from the stage as she raised her phone to show him Jazmine's picture.

"You seen this girl?"

"You a cop?"

"Not today. Her mother is worried about her."

"That her mum?" He nodded at Manasa.

Shane waggled the phone. "C'mon, you're the house band. You seen her or not?"

He barely glanced at the screen. "All them nightcrawler wannabes look alike to me."

"Look harder. Hangs with a bloke called Vlad."

"You mean the Count?" he sneered, a bullish shake of the head making his chimes rattle. One of his bandmates hassled him about not helping; he said he was talking to a fan.

Shane gave him a grimace. "The Count?"

"What he calls himself. Big hit with the ladies. And some of the boys. But I don't hang with the freaks. We just play the music."

"None of the *freaks* want to play with your sax?"

"I have my moments."

"You have any with Jazmine?"

"I told ya, I don't do the nu-vamp scene, okay. Vlad was here last night. With the whole flock. We played *She Sells Sanctuary* for them, they left."

"You know where they might've gone? Another club, maybe? Kind of like a church-cum-drug den?" She flicked through her phone for a picture, but he didn't wait.

"Not really narrowing the field, sweetheart." He pointed to the man in the fluoro pink muscle shirt and wristbands setting up the drum kit. How he could see through his wild fringe was anyone's guess. The words '1984 with a Bullet' were stencilled in bold primaries on the kick drum. "Thumper there is bonin' one of 'em. Calls herself 'Moonchild'." He shook his head again, as though the name was a mouthful of soda gone up his nose. "I gotta get set up."

"Give me a nod if she, or any of them, turns up, eh."

"Any more requests?"

"Yeah, no Buck's Fizz. We've got all the Make Believe we can handle."

• • •

Thumper proved even less helpful than the sax man, although he did let slip that Moonchild was a local. Now, still fiddling with his kit, he kept throwing side-eyes at the bar where Shane and Manasa waited. Shane was considering ordering a new drink when a teenage girl came in through the band door. She looked nervous—overwrought, even. She wore frayed fishnets under a tartan skirt, a vinyl corset attempting to make mountains out of molehills, a mane of black hair, and more bracelets than a gypsy caravan. She threw herself into a hug with the drummer, but he pushed her back. She frowned, her kohl-rimmed eyes brimming. He pointed at where Shane and Manasa were walking towards them. She bolted.

Shane ran after her, Manasa close behind. A scooter buzzed into life. Shane reached the loading dock in time to see the girl ride off around the corner.

The drummer stepped up beside them. "What's this all about?"

"Where's your girlfriend going?" Shane asked.

"I wouldn't tell you, even if I knew."

Manasa leaned in close, sniffed him, licked his cheek. He jumped back, wiping at his skin as he swore in double-time.

"Come." She headed for the street.

"I'll get the car," Shane said.

"No time. The scent won't last long."

And she jogged down the alley in the scooter's wake. Shane followed.

"The girl smelled of fresh dirt," Manasa said when they reached the corner. "And incense. Juniper. For protection from evil. Fortunately, we are not evil." Her head moved from side to side, her eyes looking into the distance, her nostrils flaring.

Shane looked away, but not quickly enough. Manasa's tongue had grown forked, the twin tips darting out through a groove in her top lip that hadn't been there before. And then it was solid again, the woman smiling as she said, "This way."

They got lucky. The girl had driven only a few blocks before turning into a quieter side street and then down another, a narrow strip of tarmac smelling of stale water and unemptied bins.

Shane was sweating heavily by the time they arrived, the humid night closed in around her. Manasa appeared unaffected, her breathing untroubled by their jog.

"This one," she said, a hand on an unsteady gatepost, the rusted iron gate held ajar by a thick growth of dandelions.

The two-storey house hunched under a sagging tin roof mottled with rust. The ground floor had been bricked in, much to the delight of graffiti artists who had tagged the walls and the boards in the windows with their urban camouflage.

"Follow my lead." Shane reached for her holster, only to come up empty: her pistol was back in the car. Not even a vest. Should she call for back-up?

"We should not be delaying," Manasa said. "The girl Moonchild will raise the alarm."

"Yeah, I know. Mind how you go."

They stepped over broken chunks of brick, shattered bottles and other litter. Shane motioned Manasa not to stand in front of the downstairs door and then, back to the wall, rapped on the flaking timber.

A bang. Running footsteps.

"The back," Manasa said, and sprinted away.

A scooter started up.

Shane reached the backyard to see Manasa pull Moonchild by the hair from the scooter. Other goths were scattering into the side alley, over the back fence.

The riderless scooter revved and died as it toppled into the grass. Silence descended on the background hum of traffic and distant jets.

Moonchild hunched in Manasa's grip, holding one arm. Her eyes were wet with tears. "Could've killed me, you bitch."

Shane said, "We're looking for Deborah. Jazmine. We just want to talk to her. Do you know where we might find her?"

"You cops?"

Shane sighed. "Not tonight."

"I didn't have anything to do with it."

"With what?"

"Vlad's inside. He can tell you."

They walked through a kitchen and laundry into the single room that took up most of the space under the house. It matched the pictures on Jazmine's phone, a kind of altar surrounded by tattered sofas and cushions, the air warm with candles, tendrils of heavy incense. The pisacha twitched, detecting blood, and Shane clamped down, trusting the fresh infusion of soma to keep the bastard quiet.

A young man she recognised as Vlad stood by the altar—a kitchen table covered in a black sheet smeared with a painted pentacle. The way he held the katana suggested he didn't know much about using it. A black plastic bag sat on the table alongside a half-dozen small screwtop bottles and a pile of black candles.

"Leave now if you know what's good for you." He waved the blade at them. Sharp fangs glinted under his top lip. His desperation filled the room, as rank as cat piss.

Manasa let Moonchild go. The girl stepped away, still favouring her arm. "They know, Vlad."

The blade dipped as a look of confusion—of raw fear—flashed across his face.

As Shane dropped into a fighting stance, Manasa stepped in. She struck the sword from Vlad's hand in a blur. The table shook as she picked him up one handed and slammed him down. Candles rolled onto the floor. A bottle smashed, releasing the thick, oily scent of patchouli. The plastic bag fell open, spilling dirt and a worm squirming into knots.

Shane straightened, breathed out her tension, felt again the soma cloaking the pisacha as the demon responded to the adrenalin rush. Part of her was disappointed; after all that had happened, getting to smack an arsehole around might've been therapeutic.

"You aren't even a vampire, let alone a count," Manasa said, easing her grip.

Moonchild sobbed, slowly slid down the wall.

"Where is she?" Shane asked.

Vlad pointed at the ceiling.

"Show us."

• • •

Jazmine was upstairs. They'd put her body in a bathtub and filled it with graveyard dirt. The bathroom was bright with candles, the air thick with dust. A savage tear in her throat was visible above the soil, a violent blotch of raw flesh against the waxen pallor of her skin. They'd closed her eyes, at least.

"Is this what she meant by going all the way?" Shane asked.

"Her faith wasn't strong enough," he muttered, a hint of petulance that made her reconsider slapping him around. "We'd begun the ritual."

Moonchild said, "She saw the blood and freaked out. She ran."

"You sure it was the blood that made her think again, and not, say, your dark prince's false teeth that tipped her off? Was she pissed that you didn't sparkle in the sun?"

"You can't believe the fictions," Vlad said. "Vampirism is spiritual. Stoker—"

"Spare me," Shane said. "She ran off. What happened next?"

"She was like this when we found her."

"What? Covered in dirt?"

"Bled out, I mean. Before I could give her the kiss of the night. I tried to get my blood into her—she might have enough of my essence to come back. If we perform the Rite of Amaranth."

"Dead is dead," Shane said, "and you're no bloodsucker, pal."

He sagged, rubbed his face in profound weariness. "I wanted it so bad. She did, too. The two of us together . . . eternity was within our grasp."

"What did you use to cut her? Not those." She pointed at his fangs.

"A razor. On the arms."

"A razor didn't do that." She indicated the wound on the girl's neck.

"It was there when we found her, but we didn't do it. A rat, maybe, or a dog."

She caught Manasa's eye. The kid had probably been expecting two neat puncture wounds. So much for not believing the fictions.

"Where did you find her?"

"Slatter Lane. Near Abaddon. She'd crawled into a dumpster."

"Crawled in, huh. One way to find out." Shane reached for her razor case. She wouldn't be game to use any blade she found here.

"Wait." Manasa leaned over the body. She breathed in deeply. Licked the wound.

Moonchild made a choking sound. Vlad backed away till he hit the wall. He looked like he was about to puke. Shane recited the mantra under her breath, a roll in her gut matched by the excited writhing of the drugged pisacha.

Manasa wiped her mouth, a delicate touch at the corners. "We need to talk to the sax player."

• • •

Shane phoned it in before they left. She wondered if Cunningham would ask her to tell Ms Brown the bad news.

"Do you trust the children not to flee?" Manasa asked.

"I trust them more to be afraid of you coming for them."

They rode Moonchild's scooter, helmets be damned. Shane could imagine Vikki's apoplexy. Manasa pressed against her, surprisingly cool, her grip firm but light.

When they reached the club, the sax player had already left.

"Not long after you went tearing off after Moonchild," the drummer said. "Diarrhoea, he said."

"Definitely something he ate." Shane ignored his enquiries, more interested in getting an address for the sax player, Hugo. Her badge and the words 'accessory after the fact' did the trick. Having Manasa peering at him over her shoulder probably didn't hurt, either.

They took the car this time, but they didn't have far to go: Hugo was another Valley dweller. They arrived outside a decrepit block of flats to see the musician standing beside a Sandman, the vehicle a patchwork of different coloured panels. He was talking to a woman on a motorcycle. Blue puffs of exhaust showed she'd left her motor running. Another woman, thin and pale and draped in black, stood on the other side of the car looking bewildered.

She didn't move as Shane and Manasa got out of the car. Shane was slower than Manasa: she had to retrieve her service pistol from the glovebox. The weight felt comforting as she pulled back the slide to pump a round into the chamber.

The motorcyclist gave Hugo a thin envelope; he gave her a thicker one. She accelerated away. Hugo reefed open the driver's side door.

"Oi," Shane called, and pointed the pistol. He turned to face her. There was a lot of chest to aim for. "Don't move, sunshine."

"Do you think that will be effective?" Manasa murmured.

"I'm fresh out of wooden stakes. But I reckon a 9mm through the brainbox should give him quite a headache."

Manasa wobbled her head, a sign Shane took to mean agreement. She lifted her aim.

"You never did answer my question about spending a moment with young Deborah Brown, Hugo."

"Your Unmade law does not interest me," he said, and stepped toward her. "But for what it's worth, I didn't mean to kill her. She was just a damned snack. She'd already bled, more than I'd realised."

Shane's finger tightened on the trigger. The words *probable cause, justifiable homicide*, came to mind. The pisacha was urging her to do it. *Blood*, it said. *Blood for me.*

A hot flush washed through her, left her panting, heart thudding even faster, at the thought of possessing a vampire's body. At the thought of being free.

Hugo was closer, his face filling her vision.

From the corner of her eye, Manasa was shrinking, almost deflating.

Her vision tilted, the sudden flood of sandalwood overwhelming her.

"I will drink you dry," Hugo said.

"I will shoot," she warned, her voice a hoarse whisper as she fought the bloodrunner for control.

Hugo stopped, started to back away, his eyes off Shane.

She blinked free, actually stumbled, damn near fired, as a cold wave dispelled the heat.

Manasa was naked, her clothes in a pile at her . . . her tail. From the waist down, she was a snake, the tail metres long, the tip scribing an arc around Shane.

A forked tongue flickered from Manasa's lips.

"What about my law?" she asked, her voice lisping but far from comic. More like a dagger leaving a sheath. "Does that interest you?"

Hugo ran to the panel van and reached in to the front seat. Manasa followed, her serpentine body propelling her at sprinting speed. Shane ran beside her, gun still pointed at Hugo as he emerged with a shotgun.

She paused, braced, fired. He barely flinched with the impact. She fired again, and again. The third round took him in the jaw.

Before he could recover, Manasa spat, like a spray from a squirt bottle. Hugo dropped the gun, hands to his eyes. And then Manasa reared above him, slick coils of honey brown and cream spiralling around him and pulling tight. Bones popped. Blood cascaded from his mouth. She took his head in her hands and pulled, muscles in her arms as taut as a bicycle's brake cable. Full lock. Hugo's head came off in a sharp spray of blood and tattered flesh, a wet balloon popping.

Shane turned away. The pisacha howled and she clenched her fists to her forehead, fighting the urge to vomit.

When she could see again, Manasa was a woman once more, fully dressed. There was blood on her face, her hands, smeared from where she had tried to wipe it clean. She handed over Hugo's envelope: false IDs, credit cards.

Hugo's squeeze was sitting in the passenger seat, feet on the road, head between her legs.

"She'll be all right," Manasa said.

"Did you have to kill him?" Shane asked.

"Some might say he was already dead."

"The mythoes have the same rights as *homo sapiens*, pulse or otherwise. Guaranteed under the UN charter on paranormal beings." But she could feel her argument dying on her lips, even as she recited the mantra of Special Branch. Cunningham wouldn't press the point, of that she was sure. Vikki, however, would be far less understanding.

"I, too, was fresh out of wooden stakes," Manasa said. "Perhaps next time we will be better prepared."

"Next time?"

"Next time." Manasa smiled.

~

EL CABALLO MUERTE

MARTIN LIVINGS

Diego Di Esclavo sat proudly astride Xalvador, the finest white Andalusian stallion he'd ever ridden in all his fifty years, both here at the resort show and before as a young *vaquero* back in Montilla. His back was ramrod straight, his black hat sitting perfectly on his slick hair, as the horse danced in precise, measured steps across the arena, in perfect time to the rousing Spanish music blaring from the loudspeakers. The blinding Australian summer sun swiftly baked him like a potato in his bright red jacket and white pants, all tailored to fit his slim, muscular body perfectly, but he cared not *una jota*, not today. No, today all he cared about was the magnificent beast that carried him, the music in his ears, the cheers of the crowd that watched on. Hundreds of *turistas*, in their best pastel outfits and huge sunglasses, taking photographs with unfeasibly large cameras, the clicks and whirs audible even from such a distance and above the music. He smiled his brilliant smile and released one hand from Xalvador's reins, waved to the crowd.

Diego had never felt more alive.

Something distracted him, though, and the world turned grey, the sounds muted. *No*, he thought, *please no*, and struggled to hold onto the vision, but it faded, the dream falling away from his desperate grasp, replaced by a horrible taste in his mouth, terrible and familiar pains spiralling up and down his back and legs like broken glass *torbellinos*.

He opened his eyes with a deep reluctance. The sun was wan and low, barely dawn, and smeared through the dirty windscreen of his old Cortina. He could barely see, his glasses put aside somewhere the night before when he'd parked in the truck stop on the side of the highway. He hadn't intended to spend the night in his car, that had been the last thing he'd wanted to do, but even with his glasses his old eyes weren't what they once were, and night driving was simply impossible for him, or at least too dangerous to attempt. That would have been suicide, and he wasn't ready for that. Not yet.

There was a tapping noise on the driver's side window, the noise that had awoken him from his dream of the past. His wonderful, glorious dream, thirty long years distant now. Right now, all he wanted was to return to that dream. But then, wasn't that exactly what he was trying to do? He looked over and squinted at the blurry form beyond the window. A face. Blue clothes. A badge.

"I . . . I'm so sorry, officer," he stammered, fumbling on the passenger seat for his glasses. "I'm so, so sorry, I know I shouldn't be here, but I simply couldn't drive any further yesterday." His fingers found the thick frames of his spactacles, and he grabbed them and put them on. "I'm on my way to . . . "

His voice trailed off, died in his throat, as he looked out of his window. He felt his heart actually skip a beat, and for a moment he thought he was having a coronary. Part of him wished for it. Anything to escape this.

The policeman was clearly dead, had been for at least a few days, judging by the decomposition on his face. One eye was missing entirely, possibly pecked out by birds. That side of his face had strips of flesh missing, all the way across the cheek. Diego could see bloodied teeth peeking through the holes. The other side of the dead policeman's face was covered in dirt and bits of orange gravel. Blood had soaked the man's shirt collar, but hadn't gone much past that.

He was trying to bite the window.

The tapping of the dead policeman's teeth on the glass made Diego's skin crawl. "*Santa María*," he sobbed, crossing himself, and grabbed at the car keys in the steering column, turned them hard. The engine coughed into life, and Diego threw the car's automatic transmission into gear and jammed his foot onto the accelerator.

The car lurched backwards, tyres crunching in the gravel. "*Mierda*," he hissed through his gritted dentures, and hit the brakes. The policeman was now standing in front of the car, looking right at Diego with his one eye, so bloodshot it looked entirely red. It opened and closed its mouth, and took a shambling step towards him.

"I'm so sorry," he said again, tears streaming from his eyes. "I'm so, so sorry."

Then he put the car into drive and ran the dead policeman down.

He felt the man's head give way beneath the right hand front tyre, as it raised up then dropped suddenly, the pressure suddenly released. He skidded in the gravel and blood, and for a moment nearly lost control of the car, before sliding sideways back onto the bitumen highway and speeding away from the truckstop.

He sobbed as he drove on the deserted road, not another car to be seen. It had been less than a week since this had all started, with panicked news headlines and frazzled scientists and police curfews. Less than a week, and it felt like Diego was the last man on earth. He had hidden in his house, his tiny, lonely house, surrounded by pictures of his late wife, Sara, ten years buried thankfully, and his absent son, Mariano. He prayed that his boy was alive and well, having moved back to Spain three years earlier to pursue a career in finance. He couldn't reach him on the phone, couldn't reach anyone at all. So he had hidden, while the dead had risen and destroyed everything. Hidden for days on end, until there were no more screams, no more groans, no more shattering glass and splintering wood and crackling fires. Nothing, just an awful silence that was somehow so much worse.

Then he'd taken his car keys, left the house, and driven. Driven here. Where else could he go?

As he drove away from the broken body of the dead policeman, Diego finds himself looking around and realised how little had actually changed. Thirty years ago, he would drive up and down this hill every day, travelling to work, barely paying attention to the road or the trees or the precious few houses and petrol stations he passed. Now he was driving again, and so much had changed, both in the world and in his life. But this road remained much the same.

He hoped other things remained unchanged as well.

A sign streaked past him on the right hand side, declaring that the turn-off for the prison was just ahead. Strangely, that actually made him happy. Diego had driven past this sign, or one very much like it, a thousand times in the past. And now once more.

He knew what it meant. He was nearly there.

As if on cue, his Cortina coughed once, then again, and the engine stuttered to a halt. "Oh no," Diego sighed as the car coasted to a halt on the rough gravel shoulder of the road. He looked at the petrol gauge. Empty. He'd known this was coming, hadn't been able to refill the car since leaving his house. All the stations were closed, abandoned. Some of them were even ablaze. He had no idea how to break into a petrol pump, so he'd just prayed and driven.

He sat for a minute or two in the car, just looking around. There was a massive plume of dark black smoke in the distance off to one side, back in the direction of the prison, but there was nobody outside as far as he could see, not a soul, living or dead. He smiled a little; this was what he'd been hoping for. This area had never been heavily populated, even in its heyday, and its heyday was a long time past now. It couldn't be more than a kilometre or two further up the highway to go until he reached his destination, his goal. His dream.

A kilometre or two. His smile faded. Once he would have shrugged that off without a second thought, but today . . .

He turned in his seat, the awful pain in his back and legs reminding him of just how long it had been since he'd been up this way, what had happened between then and now, and reached for his crutches laid across the back seat of the car.

Getting out of the car was a struggle, as always. He levered himself to his feet, his legs wobbly and weak, and the rubber ends of the crutches ground against the gravel. The cheap plastic cuffs bit into his arms and elbow, and he gritted his teeth against the symphony of pain that his body experienced as his spine compressed and flexed in its limited, long-ruined manner. He nearly cried, but held the tears back with some effort. No time for that now, no time. It wasn't safe.

He looked up the hill, up the highway, the early morning sun already too hot and bright for comfort. A kilometre or two. Once upon a time, Diego would have scoffed at the thought of such a short walk being difficult. He was as fit as a man half his age back then, fitter than any of his young apprentices and assistants at the resort. He could have run up the hill and barely broken a sweat. Walking a couple of kilometres? Child's play.

But today? *Dios santo!*

By the time he reached the faded sign for the resort, he felt as close to death as he'd ever been in his life. His legs, once so strong, were shaky and limp, his arms aching terribly from supporting most of his weight for so long. He could feel warm blood seeping through his shirt sleeves from where the crutches had bitten into his flesh, and his back and armpits were sodden with sweat. He'd wished a dozen times during his long shuffling march that he could just lie down in the road and die, but he knew what would happen if he did. He wouldn't stay lying down for long. Like that poor policeman. No, he didn't want that. So he'd persisted for God-knows how long, hours certainly, painful hours.

But he'd made it. He was there.

The sign hadn't changed in three decades, except that the lettering had cracked and faded with the exposure to the harsh Australian sun, day in and day out, year after year. The resort itself wasn't visible, nestled in a valley off the main road, but he could see the heads of palm trees poking out, mostly brown and lifeless. It was shocking to Diego, simultaneously so similar and so different to how he remembers it. Nothing had changed. Everything had changed.

He sighed at that thought. Wasn't that true of everything now?

The steep driveway was almost his final undoing. His crutches skidded on the bitumen as he walked down, and for a moment he felt his equilibrium failing. He imagined tumbling down, end over end, brittle old bones breaking like glass. But he regained his balance and made his way to the entrance of the resort. He put one hand on the glass doors, positive that it would be locked.

It opened easily.

Inside there was mess on the floor and reception desk, files and papers left untidy all over the place. It looked to Diego's tired but experienced eyes that whoever was still here when disaster struck had left in a hurry, without any care taken. That made him feel a little sad. Once this place had possessed a genuine passion for service and hospitality. It had been the jewel of the blooming tourism industry, the place to go for high-flyers from the city and interstate. And, at first glance, it looked exactly the same as when he'd last been here, thirty years earlier. Like a time capsule of a different era.

Then he looked a little closer, squinted through his glasses, and the tragic truth became apparent. The place *was* exactly the same. Nothing had been updated or changed or, by the looks of the stained and worn carpets, even replaced at any point.

The resort wasn't a time capsule. It was a tomb. A dead thing that didn't know that it was dead, it just kept crawling along out of sheer habit and momentum. Like the creatures that rose up, just days ago, and ruined the world. And, in many ways, like Diego himself.

He limped behind the reception desk, had a quick look around. The computer there was still on, although locked, but the fact that the resort still had power was a relief. He walked past the desk, past the rack of room keys and large files full of paperwork, and back through the door behind reception, into the office. Inside were the usual cupboards and bookshelves, but more importantly, there was also a water cooler and a small bed. Diego snatched a paper cup from the dispenser and filled it, drank it down in three thirsty gulps, then coughed and spluttered half of it back up again. Once the coughing had eased, he refilled the cup and drank again, more slowly this time. He felt sheer exhaustion tingling in his limbs, behind the throbbing pain, and found himself moving uncontrollably towards the bed, like a sleepwalker, or a zombie. He collapsed on its hard narrow mattress, crutches still on his arms, and fell into a deep, uneasy sleep.

• • •

Diego smiled his brilliant smile and released one hand from Xalvador's reins, waved to the crowd. He had never felt so alive. He saw all of their faces, filled with wonder and awe. Then one face in particular caught his eye, and his smile faltered.

Jack Trammell. Young Jack, one of his trainees that the resort management had lumbered him with. Apparently the nephew of one of the investors. He was barely more than a boy, and was totally unsuited to work with the horses in Diego's measured opinion. Three days earlier, he'd caught Trammell whipping Xalvador simply because the haughty stallion wouldn't do what the boy had wanted him to do, a petulant and cruel reaction. Diego hadn't said a word, simply grabbed the youth, threw him against the stable wall, and punched him in the nose. Young Jack still sported two black eyes from that, not to mention a new harsh turn to the left for his nose. But he watched Diego ride with a wide smile, and something hard hidden deep behind his eyes.

Diego saw the boy, his smile, his eyes, and his stomach squirmed. It was Trammell's job to prepare the arena before the show, make sure there were no rocks or unwelcome wildlife in it. Building a resort in the middle of Australian bushland had its disadvantages, and sometimes you could have . . . unpleasant guests. It was one of the trainees' functions to ensure that there were no nasty little surprises. Such as . . .

Xalvador saw the brown snake on the arena's dirt floor before Diego, but only by a moment or two. He felt the stallion tense up beneath him, heard the sudden draw of panicked breath. He knew what was going to happen before it happened, saw it clearly, but he could do nothing to prevent it. He was helpless, for the first time in his life.

Xalvador reared up with a terrified whinny, then toppled over sideways, crashing to the ground and crushing Diego beneath him. He felt his leg shatter in a dozen places under the impact, but worse, he snapped over on his side, and something deep in his lower back gave way with a sickening crunch. He screamed . . .

Diego woke up suddenly, panting raggedly, unable to catch his breath for a few seconds. He was disoriented, confused, no idea where he was, when it was.

Then he remembered. He was back. He was home. He . . .

He swore under his breath. He didn't lock the front door.

He clambered to his feet, stumbled from the office, still half asleep, half caught in the dream. He remembered the pain of the fall so clearly, even after thirty years. Of course he did, he still felt it to this day. Every step, every breath was a grim, vivid reminder of that day. He made his way as quickly as he could around the reception desk and to the front glass doors of the resort. There was a deadbolt on the frame, and he slammed it shut, then sighed, relieved.

Not so fast, genio, he chastised himself. *That's just one external door. How many does this place have?* He couldn't honestly say. A dozen? Two? His plan suddenly didn't seem quite as clever as it had before. This place was a security nightmare. More holes than a colander, and almost as useful for holding back the undead.

He shook his head. It wasn't about that. Nowhere was truly safe, that was painfully obvious. Before the television broadcasts had stopped, they'd made it abundantly clear what was happening. The dead had risen up, like something out of Revelations, and were exacting God's punishment upon mankind. They'd said the things acted out of no malice, no rational thought, just hunger and instinct. They were attracted to sound and movement, and could follow smells like bloodhounds. They were slow, but relentless. And, worst of all, they were increasing in number exponentially. One killed two, those two killed four, then eight, sixteen . . . Diego was no mathematician, but even he knew what that meant.

Judgement day. The end of the world.

He returned to the reception desk to look for the keys to the outside doors. As he looked, he glanced casually at the rack of room keys on the left hand side of the desk, and noticed that four were missing. He frowned. Four rooms were occupied when the place was abandoned. Were they still occupied? He made a mental note of the room numbers, then continued to search for the main keys, which he found in a drawer beneath the desk. They were clearly labelled, *gracias a dios*, and Diego shoved them into his pocket and walked out of reception, down the hallway towards the restaurant and accommodation building.

The entire resort was a single structure, apart from a couple of smaller buildings containing the gym and spa. Even the stables were adjoining the main building. So securing the whole thing would be time consuming, but not impossible. He passed the beautiful paintings that have always hung in the corridors, lovingly detailed renditions of Spanish conquistadors and matadors. They looked dusty, but otherwise the same as they always had.

He stepped into the restaurant, and his spirits fell. He'd forgotten just how much of this room was glass. One entire side looked out onto the recreation area, the swimming pool and spa. There was only one actual door to the outside, though, and Diego quickly locked it with the keys.

He then checked inside the kitchen. The refrigerator was still running, stocked with a reasonable amount of food, meats and vegetables, and the shelves were similarly plentiful. He wouldn't starve to death, not in a hurry at least.

He left the restaurant, and continued into the accommodation wing of the building. There were three storeys of rooms, with stairs leading to each. He went down the stairs and found himself in a dark hallway, the lights turned off. He didn't know where the switches for them were, had barely been here before, so he picked his way along the hallway in the gloom, with only a few small windows and some exit signs to light his way. As he passed each exit, he locked it up tight.

A noise distracted him from his task. A soft scratching behind one of the room doors. He looked at the room's number. 104. One of the rooms which was missing its key. He gingerly put his ear to the door and listened. Long scratches, like fingernails on wood.

"Hello?" he said softly. "Is anyone . . . "

A violent thump against the door made Diego stumble back away from it with a shriek. Then another, and another. He could hear the thing inside the room now, the breathless groaning. Like a death rattle, over and over again, forever caught in that terrible instant of dying. He backed away from the door and held his breath, stayed perfectly still. After what seemed like a lifetime, but couldn't have been more than a few seconds, the thumping died down, and it became that slow scraping noise once again.

He tip-toed away from the room, locked the rest of the outside doors, then returned to the restaurant area, closing and locking the door between it and the accommodation wing. He had no intention of ever returning to that horrible, haunted place.

From the restaurant, Diego made his way back to reception. There was a second corridor from there, which led to the function rooms, stables and the arena. He hesitated for a second, afraid to go that way, to truly revisit the past, but he steeled himself and set off, the rubber tips of his crutches thumping on the threadbare carpets.

He was amazed at how well the building had held up, all things considered. Its time as the main tourist attraction in the hills hadn't lasted much beyond his accident—in fact, sometimes he kind of liked to imagine that the incident, in front of so many people, had been the beginning of the end for the resort—and the place had been in decline ever since. Still, the gorgeous dark wooden arches, the sweeping high ceilings, the gothic iron chandeliers, all still spoke of the resort's grandeur and class. It reminded him of when he was a young man back in Spain, before he'd emigrated here seeking a better life. His father had been a *vaquero*, a horseman, just as he was, but age and work had worn him down. He was still recognisably the great rider he'd been as a youth, but it was buried beneath years of neglect and weathering. The thought made Diego smirk ruefully. Now *he* was the old man. Could anyone possibly have seen the man he once was, beyond the bent back and crutches? He doubted it. He certainly couldn't see it himself anymore. That man was gone.

He walked straight down the hallway, to the glass doors at the far end, and looked outside. There, beyond the rows of dilapidated seats and a rusty metallic mesh fence, was the arena, the place where he'd spent years performing for the crowds. It looked awful now, filled with rubble and rubbish, little more than a landfill. And yet his heart soared at the sight of it. *Once*, he pondered, *once it was a stadium of dreams, a place where the impossible became real. Once I rode there on Xalvador, beautiful, majestic Xalvador, both our heads held high, and we enjoyed the adulation of hundreds of people, three times a day, four days a week.*

Then he sighed. It was all gone now. Ruined, like everything else. He locked the door and turned away, not trusting himself to look back.

The last place in the main building with outside access was the stables. There was a door on his left, and he opened it. It was almost pitch black inside. But this is an area he was very familiar with, and even after thirty years away, his hand still knew exactly where to find the light switch. A bare bulb flickered into life, revealing a dark timber staircase leading downwards. He descended carefully, feet and crutches placed tentatively on the slippery wood, until he reached the bottom. There were some wine racks down here, to take advantage of the cool air and low humidity, but they didn't interest Diego, or at least not just yet. Perhaps later. Beyond them, though, lay the stables, which had two external sets of doors, one leading into the paddocks where the horses were once allowed to roam, and the other to the arena itself. Two places where *they* could get in. Diego took a step forward, then froze. There was a noise coming from within the stables, one he'd never expected to hear, not here, not now.

A soft nicker.

He hurried forward, flicking on lights as he went. There, in the far stall, there was movement, a flash of white. He approached it, and his eyes widened.

A horse. They left a horse behind.

For a crazy moment he thought it is Xalvador, even though he knew it to be impossible, of course. But then he realised it's not Xalvadore, of course, it wasn't even a stallion, but a small gelding, skinny and dishevelled. Its flank had the tell-tale marks of repeated whippings across it, which enraged him deeply. It looked like it hadn't eaten in quite some time, perhaps even before the world went mad. He could see the poor beast's ribs.

"Shh," Diego hushed, and took a step towards the animal. It backed away, eyes wide and skittish. He continued to approach though, adopting the body posture that came so very naturally to him. Like riding a bicycle, or a horse, it was something that could never be truly forgotten, muscle memory down to his bones. He knew how to act around horses. "Shh," he said again, in a low, unthreatening tone. He smiled, but showed no teeth. "There there. It's alright, *amigo*." He reached out and gently touched the side of the horse's neck, stroking it lightly with his fingertips. It tensed at his touch at first, but then relaxed a little. It looked at him with frightened but hopeful brown eyes. Diego nearly cried at that plaintive stare.

Diego patted the horse's head and neck for a minute or two, his eyes closed. He felt a strange calm descend on him, one he hadn't felt in decades. As he comforted this starved and abused animal, it somehow comforted him back. The smell of it in his nostrils, the feel of its coarse hair beneath his fingers. It all seemed . . . *right*.

He was home.

• • •

Xalvador crashed to the arena floor, crushing Diego's leg beneath it, and he screamed as his back snapped somewhere deep inside him. Then there was nothing, a long breathless silence, apart from the continuing tinny music blaring from the loudspeakers, inappropriately jaunty.

More screams then, from the audience. He heard footsteps crunching in the sand floor of the arena, as people rushed up to help. Voices.

"Oh my God . . . "

"Is he . . . "

"Get the horse off of . . . "

"Don't move him! *Don't move him!*"

He was vaguely aware of the weight of the fallen horse being removed from him by the other trainers and apprentices, all working together. He looked and saw that Xalvador's front right fetlock was at a sickening angle, ragged bone sticking out through the skin and hair. There was so much blood, so much blood, it had soaked the arena sand, turned it black. The horse was dragged away from Diego, struggling and squealing terribly.

Someone was bringing out some screens, he didn't know who, their face blurred by tears of pain. But he saw who was carrying the gun, and fury swelled in his breast.

Jack Trammell strolled past him, barely looking at him, the rifle tucked under his arm. The screens were set up around Xalvador, who was still thrashing about in pain.

"No," Diego tried to say, but his mouth didn't work, there was no breath in his bruised lungs. "No, don't . . . "

The gunshot was deafening, then Xalvador was still and silent.

Diego awakened with tears streaming down his face. It had been three days since he'd arrived back at the resort, and every night the dream had been the same. Every night he relived that day thirty years ago.

He struggled out of the bed in the reception office, and began the daily routine that he'd quietly settled into. First a hot shower in the bathroom adjoining the office, being careful not to fall over on the slippery floors. No panic buttons there, no help if something happens. Then he went to eat a simple breakfast in the restaurant, cereals and coffee, which was also a excellent opportunity to look out of the floor-to-ceiling glass wall and make sure he was still alone at the resort. The open area outside was still clear, as it had been every day, nothing to see except the increasingly-dirty swimming pool. Checking the perimeter then, slowly and methodically, to make sure all the doors were still securely closed and locked.

Then he could spend some time with his new friend.

The horse had recovered well. Diego was always amazed by the resilience of these incredible creatures, how they could survive almost anything thrown at them. Plenty of food and water and care, and the gelding was looking much better now, and relaxing every day. As he entered the stable, the horse looked up and at him and neighed happily. He smiled and waved at it, then went to get it some fresh food and water.

The supplies were getting worryingly low. He frowned at how few of the horse pellets were left in the container, how short the pile of hay was. He'd have to get some more from the storeroom adjoining the stable, just by the entrance to the paddock.

"I'll be right back, *amigo*," he assured the gelding, then made his painful way to the storeroom.

The door was locked up tight, which seemed a little incongruous to Diego. There was nothing worth stealing in there, not really, except perhaps the rifle. But he shrugged and fumbled the keys out of his trouser pocket, found the one for the padlock and unlocked it. He threw it on the ground, then opened the door wide.

Too late, he understood why it had been locked.

The dead thing came at him from the dark storeroom faster than he could have expected, its cold hands on his shoulders, pushing him backwards. He staggered under its weight. As it lurched into the light of the stables, he could see its awful face, its grey skin tight on its skull, eyes shot through with crimson red. It chewed at the air, and Diego was strangely entranced by the loud clack-clack of its yellow teeth.

Then he noticed its nose. Its broken nose. And he knew who it was. Who it used to be.

Jack Trammell, young Jack, older Jack, now dead Jack, threw Diego back onto the stable floor. The straw broke his fall, but even so, the wind was knocked out of him. He lay there on his back, gasping, as the man who shot Xalvador as a young man, the man who caused his accident in the first place, stumbled towards him.

Even dead, Trammell wanted to destroy Diego.

The creature fell upon him, and he tried to scream, but all he could manage is a ragged gasp. Then he felt cold fingers like an animal's claws digging deep into his shoulders, and that terrible face coming closer and closer to him. He reached out and tried to hold it back, but it was so strong, impossibly strong for a dead thing. How could it be so strong? Somewhere in the distance, he heard a hollow banging noise, but paid it no heed. His attention was solely on the gnawing monster that was getting far too close to his face, its red eyes fixed on his, all humanity long gone. It pushed even closer, and Diego could smell its breath, its not-breath, rotten air squeezed out of its lungs with each movement it made.

Not like this, he prayed. *Por favour, dios, not like this.*

Then there was a sudden white flash, and it was . . . gone.

For a moment, Diego believed that God Himself had intervened, that he'd reached down and removed the creature from him in an act of divine mercy. But only for a moment. Then he saw what had actually happened. The gelding had broken out of its stall and attacked Trammell, reared up and kicked the dead thing hard, pushing it off him and across the stable. He looked over as dead Jack clambered to its feet. The horse approached the thing, head lowered in an aggressive stance. It didn't understand what it was up against.

"No," Diego whispered, "no *amigo*, don't . . . "

But it was too late. The horse charged Trammell, in a manner than any man would turn and run from. Any *living* man. But the dead thing simply lunged at the horse as it approached, wrapping its arms around its neck and burying its rotten teeth in its throat. The gelding squealed horribly, and for a moment Diego was back in the arena with Xalvador, that same equine cry of pain and confusion. Then the sound turned wet, and the horse staggered to one side and collapsed. Blood sprayed from an enormous ragged hole in its neck, soaking the straw in an instant. It shuddered, then lay still, so still.

"No!" Diego screamed. He clambered to his feet, his pain ignored, forgotten, swallowed by sheer rage. He looked at Trammell, dead Trammell, the gelding's blood covering its face. And in that instant, he knew exactly what he had to do.

He turned and limped into the storeroom.

The creature was right behind him, slower than him but not by much. Diego could hear its dragging footsteps in the straw, but ignored them as best he could. He knew where he was going. The cupboard at the end of the room, on the right. Top shelf.

He reached up and pulled down the rifle, then spun on one pained leg and shot Jack Trammell in the head.

The bullet entered the creature's head just above the right eye, and blood and bone spurted out of the back of its head. It stood there for a moment longer, as if unaware that it was dead, truly dead now, at long last.

Then it folded at the knees and collapsed to the floor.

Diego just stood and watched it lay there. He knew he should feel something, relief perhaps, or elation for a long-delayed revenge.

He'd hated his man for thirty years, this man who'd ruined his life. But he felt nothing. It wasn't Jack Trammell he'd shot, he knew that. No, that man had died before Diego had even arrived at the resort.

The only emotion he felt now was regret, mourning for the dead.

He dropped the gun in the straw and limped past the thing, sobbing. He left the storeroom, leaning heavily on his crutches, and went to the horse lying in the stable. It was dead, as dead as dead Jack Trammell in the storeroom. As dead as the world outside. As dead as Diego Di Esclava might as well have been.

He knelt against the gelding and wept for a long time, head on its still warm body.

A strange sound finally brought Diego back, something out of place. He removed his glasses to wipe the tears from his eyes and face, and replaced them, frowning. Something coming from the direction of the storeroom. Trammell?

No, not Trammell, and not the storeroom either. The heavy wooden exterior doors beyond it.

They were creaking and swaying on their hinges, as if a strong wind was beating against them. But it wasn't the wind, Diego knew that. Because there was another noise behind the first, one that he remembered all too well.

Moans. Many, many moans.

He could see furtive shadows crossing the beams of sunlight that worked their way through the cracks in the door. A lot of shadows. He didn't approach the door, didn't dare. Instead, he struggled to his feet, leaving the poor gallant gelding crumpled in the bloody straw, and backed away carefully, up the stairs. He left the stables, locking the door behind him. Knowing all too well that it would do no damned good at all.

At the glass door to the arena, there were more creatures. He couldn't tell how many, they were so crowded together; all he could see are grey hands beating on the door, ruined faces pressed against the glass, all smearing blood wherever they touched. They all seemed to be men, and all were wearing the same bright orange jumpsuits, covered in blood and dirt and ashes.

Diego knew who they are. Part of him had been waiting for them, ever since he'd arrived. Ever since he'd seen the sign on the highway as he drove here, and the smoke beyond it. Ever since he'd walked the last few kilometres, leaving a pungent trail of sweat and fear behind him.

He hobbled numbly back to reception, ignoring the crowd of dead things outside the front glass doors, then down the corridor to the restaurant. Stopped at the entrance, and just looked out through the wall of windows, horrified and fascinated at the same time.

Prisoners. Hundreds of prisoners, all dead, all clamouring to get in. Bashing at the glass with rotting, burnt hands. Knocking their bloody foreheads against the windows, over and over again. An angry sea of orange and red and black and grey, undulating in a strangely hypnotic fashion. He just stood and watched, listened to the muffled moans and the rhythmic thumps.

Then there was the brittle sound of cracking glass, and the spell was broken. Diego turned and limped as fast as he could manage on his crutches, away from the restaurant and past reception. As he turned up the other corridor, he heard the front doors give way, glass shattering and falling to the floor, and suddenly the sound of the creatures became much louder, more insistent. They smelled him now.

Ahead of him, he saw the doors that lead to the arena. The glass was broken there too, and the dead prisoners were starting to jam their bodies through the gap, sharp edges slicing into their unfeeling flesh. He turned to the door that led to the stables and unlocked it again, hobbled down the stairs, all care forgotten now. The stable was quieter, but there was still the noise of the doors that led to the paddock, and Diego could hear that the wood was starting to splinter and crack. His options were limited, and becoming more limited by the moment.

He turned and hurried towards the arena doors.

The bolt on the doors was rusty, and it took some effort to open them, but once he did he stumbled into the arena, staggering as far as he could from the stables, from the creatures beyond. The light was blinding, the first direct sun he'd seen in days, and he skidded to an awkward halt as his vision cleared.

When it did, he wished to God that it hadn't.

Wherever he looked, he saw the prisoners. They'd surrounded the arena, pressed against the rusty metal mesh fences, arms reaching in through the gaps. The smell of them hit him like a filthy punch in the face; rotten burnt flesh, shit and piss, everything and anything that screamed death. The strength rushed out of him then, all his adrenaline finally spent, and he just stood there, leaning on his crutches, and watched as the creatures tore mindlessly at the fences, bringing it down bit by inexorable bit.

It was over.

A noise behind him made him turn. There were orange-clad dead prisoners coming out of the stable doors, stumbling into the arena looking dazed. Then their red eyes fixed on Diego, and all confusion vanished. They shambled towards him with terrible purpose.

Sara, mi amor, he thought as he watched them come. *I'm coming. I'm . . .*

Then the dead things were knocked aside by something big, something white. Diego couldn't believe what he was seeing.

It was the gelding. It trotted awkwardly towards him, chest and legs soaked in its own blood, its legs out of time with one another. The surge of hope that he'd felt quickly faded when he saw its eyes. Its red, dead eyes. And the hungry look in them.

But even so, there was something in him that found a kind of peace there and then. Finally, this was something he understood, something he knew. This was where he was meant to be, what he was meant to be doing.

The gelding approached fast, and Diego stood his ground, eyes narrowed. The world fell into focus for the first time in thirty years.

As it lunged at him, he dodged aside and grabbed its mane with one arthritic hand. With a single long-practised and never-forgotten motion, he swung himself up onto the back of the dead horse, gripping it with his legs. There was pain to be certain, terrible pain, but he pushed it aside. It was irrelevant. The gelding bucked and struggled, but Diego had broken more horses in his youth back in Montilla than he could easily count, and he knew how to control an unruly animal. Living or dead, it didn't really matter. He felts how it was reacting, instinctively countered it. It was a lifetime of training and experience, and it had all come down to this.

In just a few heartbeats, he was in control.

He trotted the gelding deftly around the arena, avoiding the creatures that had already trespassed on this sacred ground. All around him, behind the crumbling, splintering fence, the dead prisoners beat out a rhythm not unlike applause. He sat as straight as his damaged back would allow, then straighter still. He smiled widely, and raised one hand to his undead audience.

Diego had never felt more alive.

~

SLEEPLESS

JAY KRISTOFF

She takes her time.

I'm used to it by now. It's always the same. She'll be late to her own funeral, this girl. But she's worth waiting for. When I think about her, I still get that unbearable lightness in my stomach. You know the kind—halfway between giddy and puking your lungs up. I can't remember a girl making me feel this way before. Or at least, I don't want to.

Funny thing is, I don't even know her real name.

The house creaks around me, arthritis swelling old timber bones. The dark outside my bedroom window is full of crickets and the pulse of the distant freeway. If I listen hard enough, I can hear the rumble of farm machinery and soft voices. I wonder what the hell anyone out here has to talk about, but I can't make out the words.

I was half-asleep. Dreaming of long blond hair and pretty blue eyes. The selfie she sent is stuck to the old laptop on the bed beside me. When the speakers ping to let me know she's finally arrived, me and the butterflies in my stomach all wake up at once. When I see her avi on the screen, their fizzy wings start beating at my insides.

I think she might be the one.

2muchc0ff33_grrl: hey wolfie

My fingers don't shake much as I type my reply.

wolfboy_97: hey c0ff33

2muchcOff33_grrl: wut u doin
wolfboy_97: waitin on u like alwayz ☺
2muchcOff33_grrl: ya soz, my mom being a cow
wolfboy_97: lol mine 2
2muchcOff33_grrl: wut she on ur case about now?
wolfboy_97: got a C in history and she flipped
2muchcOff33_grrl: flip over a C lol
wolfboy_97: ikr
2muchcOff33_grrl: i could help.
2muchcOff33_grrl: I'm real gud @ history
wolfboy_97: didn't know that
2muchcOff33_grrl: o ya
2muchcOff33_grrl: can learn a lot
2muchcOff33_grrl: mistakes of the past & all
wolfboy_97: ooh deep
2muchcOff33_grrl: not like ur other girls huh
wolfboy_97: ur not like anyone i know
2muchcOff33_grrl: ☺
wolfboy_97: so wut u doin?
2muchcOff33_grrl: homework
wolfboy_97: *yawn*
2muchcOff33_grrl: maybe u should try it sometime, C boy
wolfboy_97: so mean ☹
2muchcOff33_grrl: u luv it
wolfboy_97: maybe. u luv me?
2muchcOff33_grrl: mmmmaybe
wolfboy_97: only maybe?
2muchcOff33_grrl: how can I say I luv u if I've nvr met u?
wolfboy_97: lol u've met me every nite for 6 months
2muchcOff33_grrl: chat not the same as IRL
2muchcOff33_grrl: i thought u'd wanna meet me
2muchcOff33_grrl: thought u boys were only after 1 thing :P
wolfboy_97: i not like dat
2muchcOff33_grrl: pity ;)
wolfboy_97: 0_0
2muchcOff33_grrl: u goin 2 school 2morrow?
wolfboy_97: ya why?
2muchcOff33_grrl: i dun wanna sleep
wolfboy_97: bad dreams again?

2muchcOff33_grrl: always

wolfboy_97: ☹

wolfboy_97: wut r ur dreams about?

2muchcOff33_grrl: voices

wolfboy_97: wut they say?

2muchcOff33_grrl: sad stuff

2muchcOff33_grrl: makes me cry

2muchcOff33_grrl: makes me mad

2muchcOff33_grrl: sometimes when I open my eyes i think i can still hear them

wolfboy_97: D:

2muchcOff33_grrl: need sumthing to keep me awake tonite

2muchcOff33_grrl: coffee not working

2muchcOff33_grrl: figured I'd use u ;)

wolfboy_97: orly

2muchcOff33_grrl: ya rly

2muchcOff33_grrl: wut u wearing?

wolfboy_97: just sum shorts.

wolfboy_97: y

wolfboy_97: wut U wearing?

2muchcOff33_grrl: i show u

2muchcOff33_grrl: rdy?

wolfboy_97: k

2muchcOff33_grrl: imgfile:thong_1.jpg

wolfboy_97: @_@

"Justin!"

The shout jars me out of the moment. Chokes the blood flow south. I slap the laptop closed and roll out of bed, shrug on a band T-shirt old enough to be in the vintage stores. Her voice trails down the hallway again.

"Justin!"

"Coming, Momma!"

The scent of roses and vanilla wraps me tight as I step out of my room. Cloying. Choking. I hurry down the creaking floorboards toward her door. A crucifix of plain, dark wood nailed into its centre. A ribbon of light spilling beneath. The walls are lined with dusty family pictures. Soldiers and nurses. Black-and-white. Watching as I walk past.

I knock gently, step inside. And there she is. Wrapped in a fluffy pink robe embroidered with tiny red flowers. Surrounded by plump white pillows and a thin gauze of mosquito netting. Scented candles burn on the nightstand, vanilla and roses thick in the air. Her hair is the colour of old straw. Crow's-feet eyes of milky blue. Staring right at me.

Through me.

"What were you doing?" she demands. "Nothing, Momma."

"You were talking to her again, weren't you?"

"No, I wasn't."

"Don't you lie to me, boy, God and almighty Jesus help me, don't you lie."

I'm not looking at her face, but I can feel her eyes on me. Sometimes I swear I can feel them when I leave the house. When I sleep or eat or shower. She never blinks.

"I'm not lying, Momma."

"She's just like the others, you know. They're all the same. They only want one thing. You hear me?"

"I hear you, Momma."

Bible on the nightstand beside her scented candles, open to her favourite book.

The last book.

"They don't love you, Justin," she says. "Nobody loves you like I do. A boy's best friend is always his momma. You know that, don't you?"

"Yes, Momma."

"You're a good boy. My special boy." I know what comes next.

The butterflies in my stomach are all dead. "Come give your momma a kiss."

The three feet to her side feel like miles. I paw my way through the mosquito netting and sit beside her on the creaking mattress. The bed that's been her prison since the accident. This close, I can see how thin she's gotten. Skin stretched on her bones. She used to sing to me when I was little. Songs of praise and glory to His name. She stopped the day Dad left us, though.

My stepmom is two years older than I am.

I guess I wouldn't feel like singing either . . .

I take her hand. Stick-thin fingers. Cracker-brittle bones.

"I love you, Justin."

"I love you too, Momma."

"Don't you ever leave me."

"I won't. I promise." *Where would I go?*

As I lean in close, I smell what's coming for her, dark and sickly sweet under the candle smoke. I kiss her cheek. Sandpaper skin against my lips. Her eyes still locked on mine.

"My special boy."

2muchcOff33_grrl: where'd u go last nite

I'm in the living room, sprawled on the couch. The TV is on; coupon sales and silicon lips and the milk-carton faces of missing people on the news. A Mexican guy a little younger than me with greasy hair and pock-marked skin. Yearbook photos of a girl with an orthodontist smile and long blond pigtails. Some old kiddyqueer the cops probably won't look too hard for, all comb-over and empty eyes.

Black-and-white photographs on the walls and dirty dishes on the coffee table and slowly dying pot plants. I try to keep the place clean, but it's hard to find the time. I suggested to Momma we get a maid once. She got so angry, she didn't talk to me for a week.

I didn't mind much.

wolfboy_97: internet went down, sorry

2muchcOff33_grrl: u missed out, had 2 keep myself awake

wolfboy_97: ☹

2muchcOff33_grrl: beginning 2 think u dun like me anymore

wolfboy_97: u kidding i'm crazy 4 u

2muchcOff33_grrl: y u bail every time i get sexty then

wolfboy_97: told u my net went down.

2muchcOff33_grrl: :P

2muchcOff33_grrl: so wolfboy_97: so?

2muchcOff33_grrl: so when can we meet irl?

wolfboy_97: not yet

2muchcOff33_grrl: y not? i want to see u so bad

2muchcOff33_grrl: u only 1 town over

wolfboy_97: soon ok?

wolfboy_97: i want it 2 b rite

wolfboy_97: 2 b perfect

2muchc0ff33_grrl: sigh
2muchc0ff33_grrl: well in other news
2muchc0ff33_grrl: my mom being a total psycho again
wolfboy_97: wuts up
2muchc0ff33_grrl: i swear she wants to put me in a freakin convent
wolfboy_97: noooooo
2muchc0ff33_grrl: lol
wolfboy_97: you haven't told her about us have u
2muchc0ff33_grrl: god no, she'd explode
2muchc0ff33_grrl: she just doesn't shut up, you know? she has no idea wut it's like. She's always on my back. sometimes i just wanna pack up everything and spilt.
wolfboy_97: i know exactly what u mean
wolfboy_97: sometimes I wish I'd have gone with my dad when he took off. he was kinda awesome
wolfboy_97: but ur stronger than them. ur the most amazing person i know
2muchc0ff33_grrl: u always know how to cheer me up ☺
wolfboy_97: i really like u
2muchc0ff33_grrl: I like u 2 <3
wolfboy_97: i think about u all the time
2muchc0ff33_grrl: what u think about

I look at her picture taped to my laptop screen. Her skin is like milk. Her hair is liquid summer. Her photo wears a sly, knowing smile that makes me smile back every time I look at it. Her eyes take me away. Someplace quiet no one else can see.

wolfboy_97: i think about being with u
2muchc0ff33_grrl: like dinner at mcdonalds and 2 for 1 movie "being with me"?
wolfboy_97: no
2muchc0ff33_grrl: what then?
wolfboy_97: being alone with u
2muchc0ff33_grrl: and what will u do when ur alone with me ☺
wolfboy_97: stuff ;D
2muchc0ff33_grrl: lol, do tell

wolfboy_97: i been looking at the pic u sent me last nite

2muchcOff33_grrl: excite u?

wolfboy_97: yeah

2muchcOff33_grrl: u want me?

wolfboy_97: y—

"Justin!"

I close my eyes and try not to sigh. Try not to think bad thoughts. To wish she'd just go away like Dad did. How much easier it would be. How much quieter in my head. I know it's wrong, but sometimes I think it'd be better if I was just on my own. I pray to God and almighty Jesus for strength, but they don't listen. They never listen.

Honour thy father and thy mother.

"Yeah, Momma?"

"What are you doing?"

"Talking to a friend on the computer."

Her voice rises an octave. "Is it that tramp again?"

I sigh, push the laptop aside. Stalk through the house, toward the back door. Pizza boxes and dirty dishes and dust bunnies in the corners. She wanted to sit on the porch tonight. Listen to the crickets sing. Insisted I drag her from the bed, wheel her out to watch the sunset. It can't be good for her skin, but I didn't have the strength to argue.

I push open the back door, stare down at her in her wheelchair. All the crickets in the yard fall silent. Like they're waiting. She looks so small. So thin. I know it must be hard for her. She just never thinks how hard it must be for me.

"Momma, please don't talk that way."

Her eyes are on the horizon. Dying sunlight reflected in that milky blue.

"I don't like it here anymore. Take me back. Take me back, Justin."

She does this sometimes. Tells me to take her back to the place the county put her after the accident. They said I couldn't look after her, that they'd take care of her. She says it was nice, to get on my nerves, but we both know it was horrible. Gray stone and cheap pine and padded walls. Crowds of gawping visitors on a Sunday, milling about like pigs at a trough.

"I'm not taking you back," I say.

"This is your home. No good son would leave his momma in a place like that."

"And you're a good son, are you?"

"I try to be."

"You keep this up, you're going to burn, Justin. You're going to burn in hell."

"Momma—"

"I know what you're thinking. I can see it in you. You're going to leave me, just like *him*. Some teenage piece of tail wags itself at you and that's all it takes. I know it."

"Momma, stop it."

"She's nothing but a tramp, Justin. She's just like all the others. Sending you pictures of herself. It's ungodly."

I glance back into the house. ". . . How did you know that?"

She's refusing to look at me. Thin lips drawn back against her teeth.

"They're all alike," she spits. "Wicked. No good. Dirty girls."

The words I bite back taste like sour milk in my mouth. "Momma, stop it. She's really nice. She's sweet and funny and—"

"And the woman was arrayed in purple and scarlet colour," she hisses, "and decked with gold and precious stones and pearls, having a golden cup in her hand full of abominations and filthiness of her fornicati—"

I'm tired of this. Of scripture and revelation, of those eyes that never blink, of her always being inside my head. I grab her wheelchair handles, drag her in through the back door. She shrieks protest, but I don't listen. Trundling her through the sprawling rooms, past those staring photos and Bible pages in dusty frames. Every word is a nail driven into my head. I pick her up, and she weighs almost nothing in my arms. And careful as I can, I put her back into her bed, back into the cloying stink of those scented candles and musty pages. Screaming all the while.

Tramps. Harlots. Floozies. Trollops. Jezebels.

Shut up, shut up, shut up.

I slam the door, muffling her venom. Snatch up my computer. Fling open the stairwell door and stomp down into the cellar. It's always quiet down here. Thick concrete walls and rich, dark earth.

Sheets of old plastic. My dad's tools hanging on the walls. The only things he left behind. The only place I can really go to escape her voice.

I'll wait down here awhile. She'll be calm in an hour or two. Everything will be normal.

Normal.

wolfboy_97: sorry, back

2muchcOff33_grrl: missed u

wolfboy_97: J

wolfboy_97: we shud do it u know

2muchcOff33_grrl: um slow down stud

2muchcOff33_grrl: u run a mile when I send you a pic of my undies

wolfboy_97: lol no

wolfboy_97: i mean run away together

2muchcOff33_grrl: lol, ur crazy

wolfboy_97: only about u

2muchcOff33_grrl: u don't know me.

wolfboy_97: I know ur amazing

2muchcOff33_grrl: might not think that the 1st night i wake up screaming next 2 u

wolfboy_97: i wouldn't care. Coz u'd be waking up next 2 me

2muchcOff33_grrl: I'm a total headcase, wolfie

wolfboy_97: u can't be as bad as my other gf's lol

2muchcOff33_grrl: o so I'm ur gf now?

wolfboy_97: . . . aren't u?

2muchcOff33_grrl: tell me bout them

wolfboy_97: who

2muchcOff33_grrl: ur old gfs

wolfboy_97: y?

2muchcOff33_grrl: told you. I'm good @ history. Mistakes of the past and all

wolfboy_97: this is like a golden rule or sumthng. Never talk about exes

2muchcOff33_grrl: if ur as hawt as ur pics, they must have been too

2muchcOff33_grrl: so

2muchcOff33_grrl: were they?

wolfboy_97: lol i'm not talking about this

2muchcOff33_grrl: WERE THEY

wolfboy_97: . . .

wolfboy_97: they were pretty, yeah

2muchcOff33_grrl: prettier than me?

2muchcOff33_grrl: think carefully b4 u answer, wolfboy

wolfboy_97: ur way prettier

2muchcOff33_grrl: huzzah u have passed the test!

2muchcOff33_grrl: how many gfs u had?

wolfboy_97: I plead the 5th

2muchcOff33_grrl: afraid u'll incriminate urself?

wolfboy_97: u make me smile

2muchcOff33_grrl: lol i make u squirm

2muchcOff33_grrl: crazy headcase psycho girl I told u

wolfboy_97: i like that ur psycho

wolfboy_97: i'm psycho too J

wolfboy_97: hello?

wolfboy_97: u there?

2muchcOff33_grrl: *sighs* gotta jet, wolfie. mom screaming again

2muchcOff33_grrl: back around 10

wolfboy_97: k

2muchcOff33_grrl: xxx

I stare at her kisses for I don't know how long. The sound of the world down here is muted. Soft and dark but for the house breathing. I can't hear Momma yelling anymore.

My mind drifts, wandering in the unwelcome direction of former girlfriends. Why'd she ask about them? Why take me there? Now I'm remembering and it makes me sad. I don't like thinking about how it never works out.

Shy Alice with her freckles and her glasses who never really kissed me back.

Lucy with her tattooed arms and pierced tongue.

Sally, who never really talked much, but still liked to scream my name.

A parade of imperfections and unhappy endings. Failed experiments. Sometimes I wonder if the right girl is out there.

Sometimes I wonder if Momma isn't right about all of them.

No.

Coff33's different. She's special. She's the one. Just like me. Lost. Lonely. Looking for someone. Someone special.

That special boy.

• • •

I met her on Reddit. Some true-crime author AMA. I visit lots of chat rooms. Books and hobbies and music and movements. Just watching. People would say I lurk, but I hate that word. Sounds like I'm some kind of creeper, and I'm totally not. I just don't talk unless I've got something to say. Mark Twain said it's better to remain silent and be thought of as a fool than to run your mouth and remove all doubt.

Anyway, after the AMA was done, she got into a flame war with some nub who insisted Pedro Lopez was the worst serial killer in history. I watched her take him apart, smart and funny all at once. Explaining Lopez was second-string, that Luis Garavito had over four hundred possible vics. The nub disappeared with his tail between his legs.

I sat staring at her name. 2muchcoff33_grrl. I don't drink coffee. Gives me headaches.

Took me ten minutes to muster the courage and PM her.

wolfboy_97: ur wrong btw

2muchcOff33_grrl: wut

wolfboy_97: about Garavito

2muchcOff33_grrl: omg another Lopez fanboy? Learn 2 google, kid

wolfboy_97: not Lopez. Harold Shipman

2muchcOff33_grrl: lol he bushleague. 250ish

wolfboy_97: your wikifu sucks, they solved over 400 murders off Shipman.

wolfboy_97: but they think it could've maybe been 1000

wolfboy_97: and Lopez maybe beats Garavito. No way for them rly know who the #1 is

2muchcOff33_grrl: who the hell r u, guinness?

wolfboy_97: just another freak

wolfboy_97: like u

2muchcOff33_grrl: well thank u very much

wolfboy_97: freaks beat normal any day

2muchcOff33_grrl: I'm not a freak, I'm special

wolfboy_97: ha that's just wut my mom says

2muchcOff33_grrl: *crickets*

wolfboy_97: where u from

2muchcOff33_grrl: winterset

wolfboy_97: iowa?

2muchcOff33_grrl: check out the big brain on brettttt

wolfboy_97: lol i go to high school like 1 town over from you

2muchcOff33_grrl: omg its fate

wolfboy_97: obvs J

wolfboy_97: how old r u

2muchcOff33_grrl: 16

2muchcOff33_grrl: u?

wolfboy_97: 17

wolfboy_97: u like true crime, huh

2muchcOff33_grrl: meh. maybe. thinking about doing forensics in college

wolfboy_97: CSI winterset!

2muchcOff33_grrl: lol

2muchcOff33_grrl: sumthin like that

2muchcOff33_grrl: what about u

wolfboy_97: wut about me

2muchcOff33_grrl: what you wanna do when u grow up

wolfboy_97: my dad says growing up is overrated

And that's how it started. Simple as that. She joked about it, but maybe it *was* fate. I'd just finished with Sally maybe two weeks before. The breakup hadn't gone well—I didn't take it too good. But when I was with coff33, it didn't seem to hurt so much.

I sent her my pic, she sent me hers. The online courting waltz, pieces of us shared in the cricket-song dark. It's funny how I've never asked her real name, but she knows me better than anyone. Sometimes I'm afraid of what'll happen when we meet. Afraid it'll turn out like everything else. We're perfect while we hide behind our little screens. We can be whoever we want in the dark. But there's no delete key IRL. No way to undo the mistakes we make.

Maybe it's better this way.

I plod up the stairs. Up to my room. Find the shoebox under my bed. Ticket stubs from ball games my dad took me to when I was a kid. Shells I collected from some summer at the beach. A piece of polished bone. Tongue stud (Lucy's idea, and a bad one—they totally ruin your teeth). An old orthodontic retainer. Rubbers. And right at the bottom, I find it. A gold ring, set with tiny diamond flecks. A single word engraved on the inner band.

I remember the day I found it on the bedroom floor. Momma's fingers had gotten too thin for it to stay on anymore. I remember the way it looked on Alice's hand. How Lucy freaked when I gave it to her. The empty band of skin around Sally's finger where it used to be, thirty seconds after she broke my heart.

There's no delete key IRL.

No way to take back "I love you."

• • •

It's 11:45 pm, and she was supposed to meet me at 10:00.

She always takes her time.

2muchcOff33_grrl: u hear about this SK on the news

My stomach drops into my toes as she appears on-screen. Full of new butterflies. A pesticide breeze blows in through the open window. The crickets are singing, all in time.

wolfboy_97: hello 2 u 2

2muchcOff33_grrl: u hear about it?

wolfboy_97: i don't watch the news

2muchcOff33_grrl: cops found belongings at his house from five different girls

wolfboy_97: jesus

2muchcOff33_grrl: he kept their jewelry, how stupid is that

wolfboy_97: lotta serial killers keep trophies

2muchcOff33_grrl: i know that. It's just real dumb. if u wanna get

away with it, i mean

wolfboy_97: maybe he didn't wanna get away with it?

2muchcOff33_grrl: well, he didn't. been missing for twelve days now. sum1 got him

wolfboy_97: good

2muchcOff33_grrl: who you figure did him?

wolfboy_97: dunno

2muchcOff33_grrl: come on, u read about this stuff all the time

wolfboy_97: maybe it was just bad luck.

wolfboy_97: walked out in front of a bus when texting ruh rohhhhh

2muchcOff33_grrl: lol

2muchcOff33_grrl: vigilante maybe?

wolfboy_97: not likely. he's prolly just holed up sumwhere.

2muchcOff33_grrl: wouldn't that be cool, tho. Sum1 out there hunting these freaks down and giving them what they deserve

wolfboy_97: i guess. Cops sure can't do it. Only time they catch an SK, it's usually an accident or the guy being stupid

2muchcOff33_grrl: not accident. karma

2muchcOff33_grrl: u believe in karma, wolfie? Universe bringing us wut we deserve?

wolfboy_97: nah

2muchcOff33_grrl: y not?

wolfboy_97: coz I got u. and no way I deserve u

2muchcOff33_grrl: ooooooh, SMOOTH talker

wolfboy_97: :D

2muchcOff33_grrl: u don't deserve me, huh

wolfboy_97: nope

2muchcOff33_grrl: so have u been a bad boy, wolfie?

wolfboy_97: lol I'm very well behaved I'll have u know :D

2muchcOff33_grrl: mmm

2muchcOff33_grrl: u want me 2 be a bad girl 4 u.

My hand slips down toward my boxers. My mouth is dry as dust.

wolfboy_97: i don't know

2muchcOff33_grrl: tell me wut u'll do when u meet me

2muchcOff33_grrl: will u be bad 4 me baby

wolfboy_97: u torturing me

2muchcOff33_grrl: lol, not yet
2muchcOff33_grrl: but when i do
2muchcOff33_grrl: it's gonna be soooooo good

"Justin!"

Her voice is like a bucket of cold water thrown in my face. It wakes me up. Drags me back. And just for a moment, I hate it. Hate this. Hate her.

"Justin!"

I glance at the flashing cursor on the screen. Search for the girl beyond it. Wondering if she really is the one to get me away from this place. Away from her. Away from me. Is she real? Can I make her real?

"Justin, I'm cold! Come close the window!"

I wonder if there is such a thing as karma. Or God. Or whatever.

2muchcOff33_grrl: u there?

I wonder what I did to deserve a life like this. But I know what I have to do to change it.

wolfboy_97: I got u something
2muchcOff33_grrl: got me what?
wolfboy_97: present
2muchcOff33_grrl: omg what?
wolfboy_97: I show u
wolfboy_97: rdy?
2muchcOff33_grrl: yesssssss
wolfboy_97: imgfile:ring_1.jpg
2muchcOff33_grrl: *squeeeeeeees*
wolfboy_97: u like?
2muchcOff33_grrl: OMFG ITS BEAUTIFUL
2muchcOff33_grrl: WUT'S THE ENGRAVING SAY I CAN'T READ IT
wolfboy_97: "forever"
wolfboy_97: gonna give it to you when we meet
2muchcOff33_grrl: WHEN
2muchcOff33_grrl: WHEN
wolfboy_97: u luv me?

2muchc0ff33_grrl: I luv u
2muchc0ff33_grrl: OMG IT'S BEAUTIFUL I LUV U
2muchc0ff33_grrl: *dies*

wolfboy_97: lol, don't do that

"Justin!"

wolfboy_97: i gtg

2muchc0ff33_grrl: ok
2muchc0ff33_grrl: I luv u
2muchc0ff33_grrl: I LUV U

I drag myself out of bed, trudge past those black-and-white faces toward her door.

"Coming, Momma."

2muchc0ff33_grrl: omg
2muchc0ff33_grrl: omfg

I open my eyes. It's nearly midnight. The house is so quiet, I can hear it breathing. The pinging on my laptop is loud enough to wake the dead. I look to Momma's room, slap at the volume control as my chat window fills with her name.

2muchc0ff33_grrl: wolfie
2muchc0ff33_grrl: u there
2muchc0ff33_grrl: pls

wolfboy_97: wuts up?

2muchc0ff33_grrl: omfg, my mom

wolfboy_97: wut about her

2muchc0ff33_grrl: she went through my computer
2muchc0ff33_grrl: she read my logs
2muchc0ff33_grrl: saw the pics I sent u

Cold fingertips brush my spine. I can't seem to breathe right.

wolfboy_97: 0_o
wolfboy_97: what did she say

2muchc0ff33_grrl: SHE FREAKED WTF U THINK

wolfboy_97: ok ok calm down

2muchc0ff33_grrl: she said she gonna cut off my net

2muchcOff33_grrl: that I'm not allowed to c u anymore
2muchcOff33_grrl: i told u she's a PSYCHO
wolfboy_97: where r u now?
2muchcOff33_grrl: bus station
wolfboy_97: wtf
2muchcOff33_grrl: did u mean what u said
wolfboy_97: what did I say?
2muchcOff33_grrl: that u wanted to run away with me
. . .
. . .
wolfboy_97: yes
2muchcOff33_grrl: then come get me
2muchcOff33_grrl: let's just go
2muchcOff33_grrl: u and me
2muchcOff33_grrl: now
wolfboy_97: does ur mom know ur gone
2muchcOff33_grrl: no, I waited til she went to sleep
wolfboy_97: did u tell anyone else about us?
2muchcOff33_grrl: who the hell am I gonna tell?
2muchcOff33_grrl: COME GET ME

It wasn't meant to be like this. This was supposed to happen when we both wanted it. I'm not ready for it yet. I haven't even started to—

2muchcOff33_grrl: wolfie pls
2muchcOff33_grrl: wolfie I luv u

I should let her go. If she's run away, the cops will be looking for her. I could get into so much trouble. My mind is running through the maybes. This is stupid. This is crazy.

But what if she's the one?

wolfboy_97: ok
wolfboy_97: ok I'll come
2muchcOff33_grrl: omg thank u baby
wolfboy_97: its gonna be ok, i promise
2muchcOff33_grrl: ok ok
2muchcOff33_grrl: i'm ok

wolfboy_97: it's gonna take too long 4 me to get to winterset tho
wolfboy_97: i can't drive
wolfboy_97: my dad can, tho. he just outside of ur town. i'll get him to come get u.
2muchcOff33_grrl: ur dad? Won't he tell the cops?
wolfboy_97: no, he's cool. trust me
wolfboy_97: he's a real cool guy
wolfboy_97: he'll take u to his place, I'll come pick u up in the
morning, ok?
2muchcOff33_grrl: ok
wolfboy_97: don't wait at the bus station tho
wolfboy_97: too many ppl
wolfboy_97: wait two blocks south, he'll come get u there
2muchcOff33_grrl: wolfie I'm freaked out
wolfboy_97: its gonna be ok, i promise
2muchcOff33_grrl: ok
wolfboy_97: we'll be together soon
2muchcOff33_grrl: forever?
wolfboy_97: and ever

Amen.

• • •

A storm is coming in from the north. Rain like knives.

My hands are shaking the whole drive there. Windshield wipers squeaking in time with my pulse. I'm not sure what I'll say. She thinks I'm perfect behind my little screen. I can be whoever she wants in the dark. But there's no delete key IRL.

What if she can't love who I am out here?

The brakes on my dad's truck squeal as it pulls up to the curb. Gravel crunches under the tires as the headlights die. I look at the streets around me. Empty asphalt and dark windows. Lifeless neon and howling wind and rain, rain, rain.

Nobody for miles.

My breath fogs up the glass and the storm comes down in floods. But finally I see her skulking down the street, and I know it's an awful cliché, but I swear my heart skips a beat. Even in the gloom I recognize her, the half-moon crescent of her cheek picked out in the streetlamp's light. Raindrops glittering as they fall around her, like her own personal fireworks show. Long blond hair flowing from beneath her hoodie, leather jacket, and tight, tight jeans. Gliding slow through the dark. She looks up, sees the truck, but even then, her pace doesn't quicken. Ever and always, she takes her time.

I roll down the window so she can see me. Distrust in her eyes. I give her my most disarming smile.

"Hey there, coffee girl," I say. "You look soaked." "Who're you?" she asks.

"I'm Justin." I smile. "I'm Wolfie's dad."

• • •

She stares out the window the whole way back. Doesn't look at me at all. That's okay, though, I expected it at first. Her lips are slightly blue, and she's shivering. It'll be better once we get home. Get her out of those wet clothes.

"Are you cold?" I ask.

"I'm always cold."

I turn on the heater, and the dashboard rattles and shakes.

"I'll take you back to my place. You can have a shower, get warmed up."

"Is Wolfie there?"

"He'll be there in the morning."

She nods, chews at her lip. I watch out of the corner of my eye, and my mouth goes dry.

"Bad scene at home, huh?" I ask. "Yeah."

"I know what that's like."

"Runs in the family?"

"What do you mean?"

"Wolfie doesn't get on with his mom either. Says she's a real psycho."

I bristle a little. "I'm sure he never said that. They might butt heads sometimes, but—"

"He hates her. I can tell. The way he talks about her."

My knuckles are white on the steering wheel. "I'm sure that's not true."

"She sounds like a real freak." A sideways glance. "No offense. I mean, he told me you split when he was young. I don't blame you. You must know what she's like."

No, no, this isn't working at all.

"It's kinda funny," I say. "You guys meeting online and living so close to each other."

She shrugs. Damp blond hair plastered to her throat. Her skin is moonlight pale.

"Wolfie and me are fate."

"You really think that? Some people are just meant to be together?"

"I think everything happens for a reason."

"Well, Wolfie's very lucky, then. You seem like a wonderful girl." I steal another glance. "Beautiful too."

"It's real cool of you, you know." She shifts a little in her seat. "Helping us out like this."

"Well, I'm a nice guy."

She looks at me and smiles, and it seems the sun has come out from behind the clouds.

"Yeah. Wolfie always said."

The windshield wipers are too slow to keep up with my heartbeat now. The road hisses under our tires as we drive through the thundering night. I see her stifle a yawn against her sleeve. I notice dark circles under her eyes.

"What's your real name, anyway?"

"Cassie."

The word echoes in my head like a prayer. "You look tired, Cassie."

"Yeah, I don't sleep much."

"Is that why you call yourself coffee girl?"

"Coffee's my best friend. I have bad dreams."

I put one hand on her lap. Just the briefest touch. Light as feathers. "Everyone has bad dreams."

She stares out the window. Blue eyes fixed beyond the foggy glass. "Not like mine."

• • •

The brakes squeal as we pull into the driveway. I have an umbrella, run around to her side of the truck. As we dash toward the porch, I put my arm around her waist to keep her close. She's so cold. I can feel the chill coming off her skin.

It makes me shiver.

Inside, the rain beats down on the roof like a million tin drums.

Thunder rattles the windows in their frames. I shake the wet out of my hair, watch as she shrugs off her backpack, offer to take her jacket. As I hang it on the coatrack, I can smell her perfume on the leather. Feel a faint breeze somewhere on the back of my neck that sets goose bumps loose all over my skin.

Her eyes are so blue.

"The bathroom is up the hall. You can have a shower, get out of those clothes. I'll get a fire going. Did you bring pyjamas?"

"Yeah." She shivers. "Couldn't fit my robe, though." She must feel it too. This is perfect. Just too perfect.

"I have one I can loan you," I say. "I'll leave it outside the bathroom door."

"Okay. Thanks."

"Down the hall." I smile. "Second on the right."

She tosses her hair over her shoulder. Turns and walks away. I watch her hips sway. Think about the shape of her lips. Raindrops beading on her skin.

She must feel it too. She said it was fate.

This time it's going to be all right. This time it's going to be perfect. Not like the other times.

• • •

Alice was my first and I made a mess of it—first times are usually that way, they say. I gave her too much Flunitrazepam and she just never woke up. She was too thin. Too shy. That was her problem. Momma told me I needed a girl with a backbone, so I kept a piece of it. A little polished piece of bone in a shoebox. All that remains of shy little Alice.

Lucy was my second and she was much better. She had a bad mouth, though. The things she called me when she woke up—I couldn't keep her after that. Momma wouldn't have stood for someone like Lucy living under her roof. I tried to keep her tongue, but it just turned to rot after a while. A silver barbell's all that's left.

Sally woke up too early. I'm still learning how much I should use in their drinks. I get the tablets online, keep them above the kitchen sink—the shiny white kind that dissolve easy, not the blue ones that stain the liquid. But it's hard to guess the dose. She screamed when her eyes fluttered open. Screamed my name and kicked and flailed. Bit me with those perfect teeth her orthodontist must have made a fortune on. I still have the scar. Still have her retainer too. The ground got the rest.

They didn't understand. They weren't the one. But Cassie's different. She said bad things about Momma and I'd never think those things, but the start is always hard, isn't it? Before people really get to know each other? It'll be okay this time. She loves me. She'll understand the person behind the screen is the same person in front of her now. Of course she will.

She has to.

I don't know what I'll do if she doesn't.

I feel sandpaper skin against my lips. Smell vanilla and roses over my shoulder.

Yes, you do.

• • •

I'm pretending to read when she steps out of the bathroom in a swirl of warm steam. Damp blond hair framing an angel's face. She's wearing black bunny slippers with X's for eyes. Her pyjamas are black too, patterned with skeleton teddy bears. I don't like them. At all.

But the robe is perfect. Fluffy and pink. Embroidered with dozens of tiny red flowers. She looks beautiful. She looks—

"I look ridiculous in this thing," she says. "No, you look great."

"I look like someone's mother. Someone's tragic, saggy, seven million-year-old mother." She plops down on the couch opposite me, plucking at the hem. "I look like I murdered Martha Stewart and stole her skin."

My butterflies are all dead.

"I don't have anything else," I manage to say. "I'm sorry."

"It's only for tonight, right?" She gives me a thin smile that doesn't reach her eyes.

This isn't going well at all. She moves differently than I thought she would. Slumps in the chair with her legs slightly spread instead of crossing them like a lady. Picking at the browning leaves of the potted plant beside her. And her voice is wrong. Her accent is hard. And she chews her fingernails. I don't like that.

"When's Wolfie coming?"

"He'll be here in the morning, like I said."

Silence stretches for miles between us, broken only by the rolling thunder. Her gaze roams the room—she's obviously looking for something to say. It's so easy for us, usually. We talk for hours. Words flowing like water. Surely she can still sense that? Surely she can find something worthwhile talking ab—

"How long you lived out here?" she asks.

The question's so banal, it makes my teeth ache. "A long time."

"God, I'd go crazy out here all by myself. Don't you miss the city?"

"I like the quiet."

"I think I'd kill myself out of boredom."

No, no, no.

"Wolfie lives in a place like this, right?" she continues. "Some old crappy farm thing? God, no wonder he wants to split. Psycho mom aside, I mean."

My hands curl into fists on my armrests.

She seems to remember herself. Something like apology creeps into her voice, matched by that eyeless smile. "I mean, I'm sure it's okay for a guy like you."

". . . A guy like me?"

"Yeah. Old. I mean, older. You know."

It feels like I've been stabbed in the stomach and all the air is leaking out of me. Flames are crackling in the fireplace. The wind outside sounds like howling wolves.

Someone's tragic, saggy, seven-million-year-old mother . . .

I look into her eyes and I suddenly realize they aren't blue at all.

A guy like you. Old. Older. You know.

They're gray.

She's just like the others, you know. They're all the same . . . Shiny white pills in the cupboard above the sink.

"Would you like something to drink?" I hear myself say. "Yeah, coffee would be awesome."

She's still speaking as I walk toward the kitchen, but I can't hear what she says. I want to ask her to keep her voice down in case she wakes up Momma, but suddenly I can't stand the thought of looking at her. It's not the same. It's *never* the same. It's so easy when it's all happening behind a screen. So clean. You never have to notice that their eyes have dark shadows under them, or they fidget when they talk, or their fingernails are chewed down to the quick. I should never have brought her here.

There's no delete key in real life.

I bring back the coffees (I know the way she likes it, I know everything about her), watch her nurse it in her lap, waiting for it to cool. She's still talking and I want her to shut up in case Momma hears, but I don't want to be rude.

Drink it, drink it.

"Are you okay?" she asks.

The apologetic smile on my face feels made out of plastic. "Just tired."

"I'm cold."

Wood snaps in the fireplace, sparks spilling up the chimney like fireflies. I get up and throw another log into the burning mouth, let the flames tumble and catch. I'm not sure how long I stand there, watching the heat lick and the bark blacken, trying not to hear her talk about her bad dreams and the voices she hears when she closes her eyes and everything about her I once wanted, and now want to rip bleeding out of her chest. But I'm still. So still and quiet.

Like a good little boy.

When I turn back around, the butterflies in my stomach wake up as I see her draining the last of her coffee, thumping the mug onto the table.

She doesn't use the coaster.

"Urg, what flavour was that? Sweaty underwear?"

"Just instant."

"Tasted like something died in it."

"Justin!"

My stomach lurches. Cassie's eyelids are fluttering, the corners of her mouth starting to sag. She runs her hand across her eyes, blinking hard.

"Justin!"

"Excuse me for a moment." I smile. "I'll be right back."

Down the hallway on shaking legs, past the black-and-white stares toward the crucifix door. I knew she'd wake her, I *knew* it. She's spoiling everything, God why can't it ever be—

"Justin!"

"I'm here, Momma," I say, pushing the bedroom door open. It smells damp in here. Wrong. I think the rain is creeping in somewhere, rotting the wood.

Momma is staring at me. Through me. "Who are you talking to? I heard voices."

"Nobody."

"Don't you lie to me, boy, God and almighty Jesus help me, don't you lie."

"It's just the television, Momma."

"You think I don't see, don't you? You think I don't know what you get up to?"

"Momma, go back to sleep."

"Don't you take that tone with me!"

"I'm not taking a tone!"

"You're just like him, Justin. Just like your daddy."

"I'm *not* like him!" I shout. "I'm still here. I'm a good son! A good boy! Who got you back from that awful place they put you in after the accident? Who looked after you?"

"It's not an accident when it's on purpose, Justin." My butterflies are all dead again.

"I said I was sorry!"

"I was happy where I was. It was quiet there. I could sleep."

"No." I shake my head. "No. You belong here, this is your home."

"I belong in the ground, Justin," she sighs. "Put me back."

"Who'rrre you talk . . . talking to?"

I whirl and see Cassie standing behind me with those wide eyes that are gray, not blue.

"Is she . . . ?"

And she's looking past me to the thing in the bed—that thing of dry skin and cracker-brittle bones I dug up out of that awful place they put her. I said I was sorry. It was an accident. Oh God, I didn't mean to hurt you, Momma. And Cassie's hand creeps up to her mouth as she realizes her hair is the same colour and the robe I gave her is identical and all the rain and the candles in the world still can't quite cover the smell.

"Is she . . . dead?"

Pale blue eyes that never blink. Her voice always inside my head. Only inside my head?

"Don't you talk that way about my momma."

"Oh, Jesus," Cassie whispers. "Oh, my God . . . "

She turns to run, but the pills have got her now. Her hands on the walls as she tries to keep her balance, stumbling and knocking one of the photos loose. It's an old one—soldiers and nurses—

my mom and dad during the war. It shatters on the ground, glass shards spinning slow in the air until they fall, down, down, just like Cassie, down to her knees and then to the boards, hair the colour of damp straw splayed about her head in a ragged halo.

I stoop and heft her over my shoulder, boots crunching in broken glass.

"I'm going down to the cellar for a while, Momma." I close the bedroom door behind me.

Momma doesn't say a word.

• • •

I lay Cassie down on the workbench, plastic sheet beneath her. I've slipped Momma's ring onto her finger and she looks so perfect. So pretty. So peaceful now. With all those bad dreams, I bet she hasn't slept this good in years. I almost want to leave her a little longer to enjoy it. But I suppose she can sleep forever now.

A breeze is tickling the back of my neck as I look through my dad's tools, taking the ones I want to start with. Wood saw. Pliers. Claw hammer. I plonk them onto the table beside Cassie, watch her chest rise and fall. There are goose bumps on my skin. It's really cold in here.

I don't want to strap her down yet. I'm not sure what part I want to keep. I want to wait until I can't wait anymore. Until the need makes me shake. And so I rip open her backpack, upend it on another workbench. Sifting through the socks and tees and underwear, pulling apart her toiletries bag—paint for those blue lips and polish for those too-chewed fingernails. I'm beginning to think there's nothing worth keeping until I search the side pocket, find it sitting in there like it was just waiting for me.

Her diary.

I glance at her on the table, smile sneaking and creeping to the corners of my mouth. Opening up these pages will be like opening up her head. I have to keep it. It's too perfect.

I flip through with trembling hands, eyes scanning the text.

. . . Mom on my case again about staying out so late. She just doesn't . . .

. . . no sleep again, yay for double-caff . . .

. . . sometimes wonder why they picked me . . .

. . . bad dreams . . .

. . . the worst. She swears like a goddamn sailor. I try to . . .

There's nothing in here, I realize. My frown deepens and I keep flipping, page after page.

There's no reference to Wolfie at all.

But she said she loved me . . .

. . . followed him home from work last night. Some crappy dishpig job . . .

. . . think I found another one . . .

. . . nightmares again. Latino kids with their eyes missing. They showed me his face. Long greasy hair and acne scars. I know where he put . . .

What the hell is this?

And from inside the pages, something tumbles. A photograph, fluttering down to the concrete at my boots. As I stoop to pick it up, I see there's a red X marked across it. The face still looks familiar, though. Hollow eyes. Terrible comb-over. I've seen it somewhere before . . .

Television, I realize.

That missing kiddyqueer they were talking about on the news . . .

wolfboy_97: wut r ur dreams about?

2muchc0ff33_grrl: voices

wolfboy_97: wut they say?

2muchc0ff33_grrl: sad stuff

2muchc0ff33_grrl: makes me cry

2muchc0ff33_grrl: makes me mad

2muchc0ff33_grrl: sometimes when I open my eyes i think i can still hear them

No.

. . . followed him home from work last night . . .

. . . sometimes wonder why they picked me . . .

. . . They showed me his face . . .

2muchc0ff33_grrl: wouldn't that be cool, tho. Sum1 out there hunting these freaks down and giving them what they deserve

I turn and she's sitting up on the workbench. Head slightly tilted, staring at me with those bruised gray eyes. Skeleton teddy bears on her pyjamas. Claw hammer in her hand.

She swings it faster than I can move. It catches me on the jaw and I feel the bone shatter, taste bright copper in my mouth. I stumble, legs going out from under me. Knees cracking on the concrete, sharp pain lancing through the bloody haze over my eyes. And as she brings the hammer down again, her words cut like razors in the dark.

"Sorry, Wolfie."

• • •

I wake up and all I taste is blood, metallic in my mouth. The lightglobe above me is etched in triplicate—three burning suns to blind me. My head doesn't feel right. I try to speak, remembering too late my jaw is broken. Bone grinding bone. Whatever I was going to say turns into a bubbling whimper.

I'm still in the cellar, I realize. Strapped to the table. The suns overhead are eclipsed as she leans slowly over me, looking down. Gray eyes and blue lips.

It's freezing, I realize. Her breath hangs in the air between us as she speaks.

"You cold, Wolfie?"

I can't speak. Nod instead.

"Can't say I'm real sorry about your comfort level. But it gets cold when they get angry. And they're real angry at you, Wolfie."

They?

I glance around the room, seeing nothing but blank concrete and my father's tools on the walls. Some are missing, I realize. Not in their places.

"Don't bother looking for them." She wiggles her fingers in front of my eyes. "You gotta have the touch. The curse. The crazy. Whatever you wanna call it. Alice doesn't look too bad, but it's not like you'd want to see Sally and Lucy, anyway. They mostly keep the shape they died in, see. And you didn't let them die easy, did you?"

I try to speak, but it's just a gargle of pain and bone splinters.

"Shhhh," she whispers, putting her finger to her lips. "You don't have to explain. They told me all about it. Chatroom creeper. IM flatterer. Solid pro at spotting the easy pickings in the crowd, right? Lonely girls. Sad girls. Lost girls. Big bad wolf, huh?"

She picks up the wood saw. Holds it in front of my eyes.

"This is what you used on Lucy, right?" Her gaze flickers along the saw-tooth blade. "They told me what you did to them. What you did it with. So I didn't drink your coffee, Wolfie. Your plant looked thirsty. Mistakes of the past, remember? I'm real good at history."

I flail at the straps holding me down. But she's bound me tight. My muscles cord and tendons stretch, but it's no good. No good.

"Wuh . . ." I wince, agony nearly drowning me. "Wuh . . ."

"What do I want?"

I nod. Tears running down my cheeks.

"I want to sleep, Wolfie." She sighs the words, and I see the red veins scrawled across those big gray eyes. "Just a single night without one of them finding me. Pleading. Waking me in the dark. They just wander, see. The Sleepless. Looking for someone who can hear them. And eventually they find me. They won't leave me alone." She rubs at her temples, frozen white spilling from her lips. "The only way to shut them up is to give them justice. Vengeance. Whatever you call it. Then they can sleep."

Another sigh.

"Then maybe I can too."

I jerk against the straps again, leather and buckles cutting into my skin. She pats my shoulder, somewhat apologetically.

Lifts the wood saw.

"So, this is really going to hurt. And from what I understand, the place you go after this hurts a lot worse. But don't hate the player, hate the game, right?"

I feel metal teeth replace her hand on my shoulder. The first tiny sting.

"Noohh . . ." I try to say. "Muh . . ."

"Mother?"

A weak nod.

"The thing in that bed stopped being your mother a long time ago, Wolfie. But she'll be cremated. Along with this house. Along with you."

No.

She leans in close. Whispers in my ear.

"This is for Alice. And Lucy. And Sally. And all the others you would've done for if someone like me didn't stop you." She shrugs, and her smile doesn't reach her eyes. "At least someone's going to sleep easy tonight."

Metal teeth gleam in the dirty light.

I pray to God and almighty Jesus she makes it quick. They don't listen, though.

They never listened. And she takes her time.

DOUBLE SPEAK

ROBERT HOOD

Someone screamed. It was a strange, surreal sound, simultaneously nearby and distant.

Jerked from the twilight haze of a waiting room catnap, Kumori Tamura at first dismissed it as a dream. As her mind settled, however, she remembered why she was in this depressing place. She'd come to the Emergency Unit of the local hospital with her friend Jamie, who'd had an argument with a razor-sharp steak knife while making *shabu-shabu*. It was their first at-home date (not that Kumori wanted to think of it as such) and he'd wanted to make an impression. He'd certainly done that. He'd sliced the skin and flesh of his left index finger right through to the bone. There'd been a lot of blood involved. And swearing.

"I feel like a fool," he'd said.

Kumori glanced around. No one was sitting behind the glass of the Reception desk. The corridors, splitting off in several different directions, were deserted—almost echoing with the unnatural silence. No one bustled, or pushed patients through swinging doors on rattling gurneys, yelling for assistance. Even the two or three addicts or abuse victims who'd been either stoically or impatiently waiting their turn when she and Jamie arrived were no longer in attendance. They must have been seen to in the meantime. Emergency was spookily still and empty. Somehow the stark white lights made it seem not just sterile but abandoned.

A stern nurse with a very unforgiving air had taken Jamie halfway down the corridor to an examination room and he hadn't re-surfaced yet. Well, Kumori assumed he hadn't. She looked at her watch. 10.22pm. About 35 minutes had passed since the last time she checked. Why was it taking so long? What if the scream had been Jamie's?

Feeling slightly panicked, she stood and approached the front desk. The opaque glass was covered with a spattering of notices, including one that said, in bold letters, PLEASE BE PATIENT. WE WILL ATTEND TO YOU AS SOON AS WE CAN. ONLY PRESS THE CALL BUTTON BELOW IF IT IS **A GENUINE EMERGENCY**. The last three words were larger and in bold type. Was Kumori's concern over Jamie a genuine emergency? She supposed not. Probably the scream she'd heard had only been in her sleep-fuzzy head anyway.

She was about to return to her seat when she heard it again. This time the peculiar nature of the scream was clearer. It was like two screams, slightly out of sync with each other. Again it sounded as though one of the screams was coming from a room just down the corridor, while the second echoed from somewhere else, perhaps even from beyond the hospital building. As the sounds died, Kumori did another visual sweep of the area, but nothing had changed. She leaned close and peered through the communication hole cut in the glass window of the reception annex. Computer terminals, two swivel chairs and various desktops covered in papers, in-trays and assorted other paraphernalia occupied the room. A door, currently open, led into the back area and, presumably, through to triage and the inner sanctum where the doctors lurked. "Is there anyone there?" Kumori called. Her voice sounded weak and hollow in the silent space.

"Hello?"

After a few minutes without getting a response, she hesitated—but gave in when the screams began again, clearer than ever. Vibrations from them scratched through to her bones. She was so shocked she automatically pressed the Emergency Button and pulled her hand away guiltily. But it produced no sound that she could hear. The screams had stopped.

The vibrations continued. It was her smartphone, which she'd set to VIBRATE as a concession to one of the signs on the Reception window that had asked for all phones to be turned off. She checked the caller. Jamie? He wasn't supposed to use his mobile in here.

"Is that you?" she said.

"Sure," he answered. His voice sounded strange. "Where did you get to?"

"Get to? I'm right here. In the waiting room. Where are you?"

"In a room down the hall. Fourth on the left. Everyone's cleared off and I've been sitting here twiddling my thumbs for ages."

"I'm sorry. It's been about 40 minutes."

"Can you find someone for me? I thought I heard voices up your end of the corridor."

"I don't think I'm allowed to wander around—"

"What're they going to do? Shoot you? Come on, love. You can do it. I need help."

Love? He'd never called her 'love' before. The word made Kumori feel rather uncomfortable. She liked Jamie. Liked him a lot. "Pretty cool for a gaijin," she'd joke. But she'd only just got the offer of a good job in Melbourne, at a marketing agency whose profile was exactly what she'd been hoping for—and she hadn't told Jamie yet. He was committed to his part-time work at Sydney University, teaching two or three Sociology classes. So far they'd managed to remain friends without falling into a more romantic relationship, more because of Kumori's reticence than Jamie's wishes. She knew he wanted more; Kumori didn't want a complication like that to mess things up. Not yet. She only had a temporary visa and wanted to have it made permanent because she had a good job, not by marrying someone, even Jamie.

"Have they finished with your finger?" she asked.

"Finger? Oh, right . . . No, they haven't." He paused. "I'm in pain here. Can you look around? I can't go myself. The door's locked."

Locked?

"Where did they say they were going?"

"Who knows? It's rather fucked up. Just have a look around, will you, honey?" Jamie said, sounding less like himself with every syllable. "I'm getting impatient."

Reluctantly, Kumori made her way to a door that opened into the rooms behind Reception. "Hello?" she called. "I need help, please." The door swung open of its own accord when she knocked. She made her tentative way through a space crowded with medical machines and gurneys until stopped by a door sign-posted as STAFF ONLY and DO NOT ENTER. Her knock echoed loudly around the room. "Excuse me? I need some assistance."

Once again, no one replied to her call. There was a small window in the door, so she stood on her toes to peer in. The glass was filthy—partly smeared into translucent streaks, the ghost of a hand imprinted in the wet substance. Focusing beyond it, however, was like peering into hell. The room was dark and shadowy as the main lights were out. What light there was came from EXIT signs, glassed doors like the one she was staring through, and other emergency lights that were flickering dimly. At least two bodies lay sprawled on the floor, surrounded by pools of blood. One of them, a nurse, lay face down, unmoving, left arm bent under her; the other reaching out as though she'd been trying to grab something . . . or someone. The other body, a doctor, lay face up. His eyes were lifeless and the whole front of his blue surgical gown was stained red. It looked as though his neck had been slit open across its whole width. A bloody knife lay nearby. Splatter was everywhere, and now that she looked more attentively she thought she could see other bodies made randomly visible as the lights caused the shadows to dance. Kumori gagged at the sight and pulled away, bile boiling up into her throat. She realised then what the smears through which she was looking actually were.

What on earth had happened in there? Was it a murder suicide? Surely the hospital had security staff. Where were they? Had they been called? And most important question of all, what if it was a murder rampage? And if it was, where did the person or persons who did this go?

Weakened by shock and as a result barely able to get her legs to work, Kumori made her way back to the waiting area, conscious now of how loud her flat-soled shoes were as they scraped on the vinyl-covered floor. Her mind was a jumble of terrifying possibilities, none of which made much sense. When she burst back through the door—too late realising that the murderer, if there was one, could be out there, so a bit of discretion might have been wise—she found the place as empty as before.

Her strongest impulse at this point was to run. To leave the building and escape from whoever had done this. But what of Jamie? What of any others who were in here and should be warned? Someone needed to tell security or ring the police. Had they? Kumori didn't know what to do. Quickly she rang Jamie. He answered at once.

"Jamie?" Kumori fought to keep the hysteria out of her voice. "We've got to get out of here. Now."

"What's going on? Have you found anyone?"

"They're dead, Jamie. There might be a maniac loose—"

"What? Calm down! A maniac? Are you kidding me?"

"I found one of the nurses, and a doctor. Their throats were cut open. I think there were other bodies. So much blood."

"Shit! Okay, come and get me! The door—"

He went silent. Panicked, but with a large part of her mind insisting that she had to act at once, Kumori ran down the corridor, counting the doors and scanning for sign of danger. At the fourth door, it occurred to her to wonder how she'd open it without a key. Should she have searched for one in the Reception office? But the door opened immediately when she tried the handle. She went in.

The place was dark and shadowy, the only light coming through the door she'd left open.

"Jamie, it wasn't locked—"

Jamie was slouching in a chair, leaning back as though trying to see something on the ceiling. Her shadow obscured clear sight of him.

"Jamie?"

She moved closer. Now the light from the corridor illuminated his features. His throat had been slashed and his dead eyes stared at nothing. A knife lay next to him, red with his blood. Blood had sprayed out over the flooring, some of it reaching as far as the wall. Most of it, however, was pooled on his lap and on the floor beside the chair.

The sight hit Kumori like a sledgehammer, knocking the breath from her.

"He was weak," said a low breathy voice. "Very sad. I hope you weren't too fond of him."

Barely visible in the shadows stood the vague suggestion of a tall figure. It didn't move and she couldn't see its face. That it was a man was clear enough. That he was Jamie's killer was just as obvious. The shock froze Kumori's muscles. The man didn't move.

"He killed himself." The man's gravelly voice crept around the room. Grabbed at Kumori's heart. "He was a very sad person. Did you make him sad, Kumori?"

Kumori had never thought of Jamie as particularly sad or suicidal. And how did this person know her name?

"He'd never do that?" she whispered.

The man laughed. "All evidence to the contrary."

Forcing her wobbly legs to move, Kumori backed toward the corridor. The door slammed shut before she could reach it, plunging the room into complete darkness. Could the killer see in the dark? The possibility notwithstanding she continued to the door, estimating the distance easily by memory. She tried to pull it open, but now it was locked tight.

"Don't leave yet." The raspy voice came to her out of the obscurity. "Are you unhappy, Kumori? I mean you no harm."

No harm? You killed my boyfriend! Kumori wanted to yell in his direction, though she didn't vocalise it. She changed position as quietly as she could, feeling her way around the wall. Tears ran down her cheeks.

"*We can see you,*" said another voice. "*You are very sad.*" This one was more like a whisper, albeit a forceful one, its timbre completely different from the first man's. It was as though its speaker had a sore throat. So there were two of them! What chance did she have, trapped with two maniacs in a locked room? "*You are cowering by the filing cabinet,*" the second man hissed. "*Why do you fear us?*"

"What do you want?"

"*Want?*" The voice sent shivers through her. "*We don't want. We are beyond want. We seek balance. An end to sorrow.*"

Kumori didn't have a clue what he meant, and frankly, she didn't care. She shuffled further around the wall, bumped into an examination table and edged around it.

"*We died here,*" the second man said. "*They were happy to see us die, but their carelessness gave us a reason to remain.*"

He was obviously mad. Under her hand Kumori felt a door handle. She'd stumbled upon some sort of ancillary office. Could be anything, maybe even a dead end, but it was better than staying in here with two killers. Acting on the thought quickly to limit her body's ability to rebel, she turned the door handle and pushed. To her relief it opened, slamming against a table on the other side. Light from within the room swept over her. As she fell through the opening, she sensed something rush toward her from behind, a hand grabbing at her left arm. Pain in no way commensurate with what was little more than a touch shot through her muscles, sending a nauseating, gut-wrenching spasm that ploughed through her and burst into her chest. Involuntarily she screamed, as though to expel the agony of it. Momentum hurled her forward and she crashed to the floor well inside the brightly illuminated space.

She lay gasping, for a moment unable to think. Then a glimmer of awareness returned. Instantly, the pain morphed into panic. The door was still open and her attacker had been close enough to grab her. Why wasn't she dead? She rolled onto her back and looked up.

A large shape loomed in the doorway. Though it was a man, he exuded a hint of monstrosity through the indefinably unnatural proportions of his body. Head, arms, legs, torso—all failed to maintain any constancy in relation to each other. His clothing was a thick shadow that obscured his form, even under the halogen light of the annex, which lit parts of him directly and brightly. He appeared solid enough, though his outlines were precarious, uncertain, straining to maintain integrity. His face, however, stood out against the miasma that engulfed him—white and bony, deeply sunken eyes glaring down at her. His wide mouth mimicked speech. The sound that emerged had the tonality of the first voice Kumori had heard, but it failed to form words that meant anything to her.

"Stay away from me!" she cried.

She sensed fury in his glare and the noises he was making. Yet he didn't come further into the room. His body strained against an invisible barrier.

"Who are you, please?" she demanded.

"You need to stay happy." The man's voice had weakened. "Whatever the other says, do not be sad."

His voice, his indefinite form, convinced her he wasn't human. Traditional superstitions rose to the surface of her mind—stories of monsters and demons she had heard from her father in the rural village in Tottori Prefecture where she'd been born—long suppressed as she grew up and studied Marketing in Tokyo and later Australia. "The demons are real, Kumori," her father had whispered to her on his sick bed—the last time she'd seen him alive. "Never give them what they want." Now *yōkai*—spirit demons—had become popular in manga and anime even in the

West. Kumori had never believed they were more than folklore. At that moment, however, something deep inside her insisted that a kind of *yōkai* was exactly what Jamie's killer was. She couldn't give the creature a name, but the thought of it made her predicament all the more terrifying.

She pushed herself further away from the spectre with whatever control of her muscles she could muster, the pain that had stabbed through her left arm having diminished somewhat. The man's eyes followed her movement. One hand reached up like a bestial claw.

"No one escapes. The world is a vale of tears. Give us your sorrow and you will be free."

This time the voice didn't come from the spectre's mouth; his thin lips hadn't moved. But she couldn't see the second killer, who had no doubt uttered the threat. Perhaps that one would circle around to grab her from behind. Was he, too, a spirit monster? Perhaps. Either way, she had to escape while she could.

The lights began to flicker unsteadily.

Spying another door at the rear—one that probably opened onto the main corridor—she backed toward it. She tried to keep her eye on the demon, but when she glanced away to check on where she was going, she caught a movement from him out of the corner of her eye. Turning back, she was in time to see his distorted form fading into the darkness within the main room. Why he hadn't simply come after her, she didn't know, but this latest manoeuvre filled her with dread. As she opened the door and peered out, the lights in the room behind her spluttered and died. From within the sudden darkness she heard a rushing sound.

Desperately she threw herself out into the brightly lit corridor and slammed the door behind her. She couldn't lock it, so if the creature were there on the other side it wouldn't hold him long.

Maybe she could make it to the front door of the hospital. It wasn't far.

Then the lights in the corridor went out as well.

The suddenness of it caused a resurgence of the paralysing terror Kumori had been repressing, and her legs gave way. She sank back against the wall and slid to the floor, where she crouched, hands held loosely over her eyes. She didn't want to see, but she knew she had to, and forced them away. Around her the shadows closed in, more so when her eyes adjusted to the small amounts of light given out by a series of dim lights set at intervals along the hallway. Surely emergency lighting was required to be better than this. As the thought went through her mind, the rows of lights began to flicker erratically. It made the shadows twitch, creating the illusion that something was lurking in them. She had to move. She couldn't stay here. She might still have time to escape; the door to the room she had just come from hadn't opened.

Forcing the panic to subside, she crawled to her feet, eyes trying to see into every obscure corner at once. Someone took a breath. A hand touched her. Crying out, she spun away from it and raced toward the main entrance, glancing back now and then to make sure the spectre she sensed right behind her wasn't actually there. Her footsteps echoed loudly, until she began to imagine a horde of killers was on her tail.

The hospital entrance space was as devoid of life as Emergency itself had been. She pulled at the doors, which were supposed to have opened automatically. They wouldn't budge. But it was late. Maybe the doors had been locked down. Wouldn't there be a release of some kind? She glanced around and saw a large green button in the dim light that leaked through from outside. She slammed her fist against the button. Nothing. She did it again and again, yelling "Please! Please! Open the doors!" No one answered her.

She slumped, her forehead resting on the cold glass. What now? The police? She should call the police. Australia had a number to ring in case of emergencies. What was it again? Something easy. She'd been told about it when she'd first entered the country as a student and mere weeks ago when she'd been granted a work visa. 911. No, that was America. Triple-O. That was it. She wrestled her phone from her jeans pocket and dialled.

As was becoming tediously common, nothing happened. Her phone had gone dead. She shook it, rather pointlessly, but it remained inactive.

"*Tasuketekure*," she whispered, right hand pressed against the glass door. Outside the night was windy. She could see beyond a parked ambulance and along the driveway to the street. Trees and shrubs twitched and shivered. Streetlights and parking area security lights were still on, though the few parking spaces she could see remained empty. There was no one to hear her, even if she'd been audible through the thick glass.

A reflection moved on the window in front of her—the shape of someone behind. At the same time, she heard a footfall. In that instant she froze. Then a reflected hand reached toward her and she broke from the trance, lashing out in one of the defensive moves she'd learnt during a series of jiu-jitsu classes she'd taken in her teens.

The shadowy figure pulled back its hand. "Wait!" A woman's voice.

Kumori stopped short, while remaining tensed. "*Dare da*?" she said, before realising she'd spoken in Japanese. "Who are you?" she repeated in English.

"Sorry. I didn't mean to scare you." The woman was a few centimetres taller than Kumori and more solidly built. She wore a doctor's smock. Her light brown hair was in disarray and fear creased her forehead and the flushed skin across her cheeks as she held out her hands defensively. Blood had dribbled onto one shoulder from a wound on her neck.

"Are you okay?" Kumori asked.

"No more than you, I'd guess." Desperation flashed across the woman's features. "I don't know what to do. The phones don't work and—" She controlled her head movements enough to stare into Kumori's eyes. "We may be the only ones left."

"You're hurt."

"It was close but I got away. One of the outpatients . . . Oh god!"

"What?"

"He attacked the . . . the thing. Hit it with a chair. It didn't even flinch." The woman turned suddenly to stare back along the corridor. "It'll find us soon. It'll . . . I can't take this. It's crazy. We have to get out of here." She was nearly hysterical.

Kumori grabbed the woman's arm. "You must try to keep calm." She could barely stay calm herself, but needing to tell someone else to do so had the effect of diminishing the panic that churned in her own guts. "What happened to the patient? Is he with you?"

"It . . . " The woman took a couple of deep breaths. "It was really awful. The thing moved close, said something . . . the outpatient ran at the wall . . . smashed his head against a corner. He's . . . dead." Her eyes transfixed Kumori. "It made him do it. Spoke to him as it did to me and he . . . " She began to breath too rapidly.

"But the man distracted the killer from me. He did that. He saved me." Her hands trembled. Kumori hugged her, making reassuring noises. The woman sobbed quietly. "I was about to cut my throat."

"What?"

"The whispers . . . from the second voice. It said things. Depressing things. It made me realise . . . there was no hope—"

"You're a doctor here in the hospital, right?" Kumori interrupted, as the woman's breathing became frenzied again.

The woman nodded.

"What's your name? Mine's Kumori."

"Janine. Dr Janine Rewald. I'm sorry, Kumori. I should be better than this. But the killer . . . I don't think he's even human."

Kumori silently agreed, but wasn't going to admit it. "I'm sure he's human. He's just very scary. But we have to remember, there's two of them. We have to be on the look-out—"

"There's only one."

"What?"

"There's only one killer."

"But I was face-to-face with them—"

"Did you see two men?"

"I heard two voices."

"Yes, but there's only one. I know him, Kumori. This was our fault. All this. My fault."

"What are you talking about, Dr Rewald?"

"Three days ago, a man came in, late, with all the other junkies and cokeheads. Said he was contemplating suicide. Very intense. Yelling about how deeply sad he felt." She rubbed at her temples. "An intern sat with him in one of the consulting rooms, while I went to find the psych counsellor. It took a while. By the time we got back, all hell had broken loose. He'd killed the intern and slit his own throat, using a knife he'd brought in. Oh, dear God. No one had noticed. No one had checked. He bled out. He died. I swear he was gone. I was the one who pronounced him dead." She gestured into darkness at the end of the corridor. "But that's him, that thing. He came back. Killing everyone who was there that night . . . making them kill themselves—"

Screams suddenly echoed from down the corridor; both turned in that direction. The darkness at the far end was thick with menace.

"Oh God! Oh God!"

"How can we open this door, Janine?" Kumori shook her, trying to get her to focus. "Doctor! A manual release? Something."

"I've tried. Hopeless. It's hopeless—"

"There must be something we—"

Before she could finish the sentence, the air grew colder. A wheezing voice, the voice of the killer, sounded so close the shock made Kumori turn before she could orient herself. "You heard what she said, Kumori. She has lost hope." Dr Rewald stumbled against the door, screaming. Shadows swirling less than a metre away coagulated into a familiar shape—tall, gaunt and ill-defined. The phantom's white face—eyes dark and expressionless, mouth thick-lipped and half-smiling—clarified as he stepped closer.

"So sad," he said, leaning toward them. "So deeply sad to be without hope. But you mustn't despair."

Kumori backed away. "What do you want?" It was a stupid thing to say, but still she said it.

Then she heard the other voice, wheezing and malicious. "*Ignore him. You must despair. It is what life requires.*" Where was the second man? The voice came from the spectre in front of her, but his lips hadn't moved. "*Life is sad. Sadness is good. Sadness feeds us.*" In the dim light leaking in from outside she saw into the shadowy gap where the man's coat had opened further around his neck, making it easier to see into it. Now it was obvious. His throat had been sliced in a horizontal stroke, a deep and violent slash that had cut through to his windpipe. The sides of the cut moved, like lips releasing premature sounds. "*Sadness is the plague that runs rampant across the world,*" the wound said, in a voice forced through shattered vocal cords. "*We eat the sorrow. We feast on hopelessness.*"

The man's hand reached out to Dr Rewald, offering her a large-bladed knife. "*You failed us. You know what you must do.*"

Janine stared wide-eyed, her muscles straining. Kumori could see that the woman was giving in to whatever influence the demon had forced into her mind.

"Dr Rewald! Janine! Fight it! You must fight it."

The doctor reached out and, hand trembling, took the knife. For a moment she stood with it held before her as though trying to work out what it was, her finger gripping the handle so tightly her knuckles had gone white.

"Doctor, no!" Kumori moved to grab Janine's hand, but the spectre was instantly between them, pushing her away. She crashed against the glass doors and stumbled to the floor.

"I'm sorry for everything," said the doctor. Kumori looked up in time to see the blade cutting through the woman's skin in a long sweeping motion. A red stream shot out and then came the awful sounds of breath and blood spilling into the night. The doctor fell away.

"See?" Whispers were like fading breath. *"She was easy. It's what she wanted. To die. To be sad no more."*

Kumori looked into the gaunt, near-skeletal face of the demon, feeling a nausea that was made up of equal parts shock and visual dysfunction caused by the creature's shifting outlines.

"Tell me, Kumori, how are you feeling?" said the spectre's face-mouth. "Are you . . . sad?"

"You're a monster!" She glared at it.

"We can feel the truth, girl," hissed the neck-mouth. *"You blame yourself for your boyfriend's death. It makes you unhappy."*

"It wasn't my fault. It was yours. You did it to him."

"He did it to himself. The sadness overcame him. He knew, you see, he knew."

"What did he know?"

"That you didn't love him. That you were going to leave him for a job far away. He was deeply sad. You made him sad. You destroyed his will to live."

For a moment she felt the demon inside her, like a poison. It scratched through her mind, infecting every thought, every emotion. "How could he know? I never told him."

The neck-mouth didn't have the muscles to grin, but Kumori could sense its glee.

"It was you," she declared. "You told him. You can get things from our heads."

"We can empathise."

"Is that what you call it?"

"So weak, so fearful." The spectre held out the knife to her. *"There's no use fighting it, Kumori. We can see into your sorrow. We see your father, dying, withering before your eyes. It is the fate*

of every person on Earth yet it makes your sorrow deep. He is dying. But he doesn't die then, does he, Kumori? He lives on until the urgency of your studies takes you across the ocean. When he finally goes, you aren't there to cradle his dying flesh, to send his spirit joyfully into Tengoku. So he dies in misery, because you left him alone."

"Give us your sorrow, Kumori." The creature's face-mouth spoke gently now, as though it felt her pain. "It's too late to find joy. Give your despair to us and you will be free."

The monsters are real, Kumori, her father had said. The wrinkles around his eyes encased them like a nest made of skin. His thin fingers wrapped around hers. She leaned closer. *Never give them want they want.*

"You are *yōkai*," she said, staring the creature down. "And I don't care what you say to me."

"*Yōkai? We don't even know what that means.*" It paused and she felt it reaching into her mind. The violation was slow this time, and limited in its scope. She pushed back against it. *"Ah, yōkai. Spirit demons.*" The neck-mouth made a sound like a snort of derision. "*Quaint.*" The word conveyed its annoyance. "*We are whatever we need to be to free you from your pain.*"

"*Agenaiwayo, anata ga hoshigaru mono.*" Kumori spoke firmly, echoing her father's exact words as though it was a sacred chant.

"*Harking back to the life you left behind, I see. You can never go back. You have betrayed everyone you ever loved. Why suffer this sadness? Give it to us.*"

"I will never give you what you want." As Kumori uttered these words, the demon leaned closer until she was staring into its eyes from a few centimetres away. Pinpoints of sickly light swirled in their blackness. Her heart stopped beating.

"*We want only to free you.*"

"You can't have my sorrow. I own my sadness, I embrace my regrets. These are the things that define me, for good or bad, monster, and I will *never* give them to the likes of you."

It scratched some more at the edges of her mind.

"And you aren't welcome in there any more either."

The spectre recoiled from her, as though it had sensed something poisonous in her; Kumori noticed that the knife had disappeared from its hand. For a long moment it stood silently, staring at her through colourless eyes, while she glared back.

Then the face-mouth spoke again. "I'm glad to have met you, Kumori."

"I can't say the feeling is mutual."

It moved backwards into the shadows. As it did, lights began blinking on along the main corridor and throughout the Emergency unit, dispelling the darkness moment by moment. Kumori heard the entrance doors slide open and cool night air crept in around her.

It's over, she thought, and silently blessed her father for his wisdom.

But before the spectre had faded completely, the neck-mouth's final words carried to her on a current of air.

"Be warned, girl," it said. *"Should you ever wake at night, feeling the weight of sorrow pressing on your soul, and in your weakness ache for an end to it, we will return. Until then we listen for the sound of your tears."*

And then it was gone.

In the distance, police sirens howled.

~

THE DOG PIT

JASON FISCHER

The Dutchman finally found the boy out on the gold diggings.

Being close to seven feet tall and as broad as an axe-handle at the shoulders, Cornelius Tesselaar was an instant curiosity in that place of mud and slap-shacks. His frock-coat and good boots spoke of a man more used to cobbled streets than a fossicker's warren. He wore a top-hat, the good silk kind, and peered around him through a pair of expensive bifocals that by themselves would earn him a knifing if he stayed too long.

A quiet word and a handful of coins led Cornelius to the nearest opium den. He swept open the hessian sack that served as a doorway, and stood blinking at the thick cloud of smoke that drifted out.

"Toby Jangles," the Dutchman boomed, striding inside. A dozen faces stared blankly at the man, even as he stepped over their sprawled bodies. One or two furtive shapes slinked away from the doorway, creeping into the furthest shadows of the clapboard shack.

"Toby Jangles," he said again. He approached one figure, slumped against a wall, only to find it was a Chinaman with a drawn dagger and a crazed look on his face. Cornelius backed away slowly, hands held high. Grunting, the Chinaman returned to his long-stemmed pipe, and the murder in his eyes soon eased to poppy dreams.

"Toby Jangles!"

The Dutchman wrestled a poster out of his purse, smoothing out the edges. By the dim light of the smoking oil lamp on the wall, he marked every face, patiently working his way through the mass of addicts and broken creatures. Finally he knelt beside a pallet, looking down on another colonist brought low by the poppy. He'd found the boy.

The lithograph in his hands showed a young man with a larrikin's smirk, a Push boy wanted for a number of crimes. The police artist had sketched him in typical gangster attire—bell-bottomed pants, white shirt with no collar, short black paget coat, high-heeled boots and a gaudy neckerchief.

The creature dozing in the cot was a world away from this depiction, but even with the sallow skin and the wear of a life hard lived, the boy was unmistakeably Toby Jangles. He'd swapped Push clothes for grubby miner's gear, and his fingers and throat were long bare of the jewellery that was his namesake. Judging by the lack of meat on his ribs, Cornelius didn't want to guess when the boy had last had a meal.

The Dutchman took the long pipe, still dangling from Toby's lips, and set it on a low table. Scooping the boy up in his long arms, he carried him out of the opium den. When the proprietor dogged him, demanding the settling of an account, he knocked him down with the judicious application of a boot.

Knives were drawn and curses thrown, but none of the drug-peddlers bothered to follow Cornelius out into the muddy street. He wove through the parade of fossickers and parasites, mindless of the distractions offered by the nameless shanty town. Making a beeline for the horse rail, the Dutchman dropped Toby Jangles straight into the nearest water trough.

Spluttering and howling, the boy snapped out of his drug-fugue. A combination of animal cunning and street smarts brought his fast knuckles towards the correct antagonist, all within that first moment.

The Dutchman caught his fist in a big ham-hand, and propelled Toby back into the water. When the boy leapt out for a second go, the big man twitched back his coat to reveal the Colt revolver on his belt.

"Don't be a fool," he said, and the boy relented. Toby sagged against the side of the trough, coughing and dripping into the mud. The big Dutchman knelt close, regarding him over a pair of bifocal spectacles. Once more he produced the lithograph, and the boy's eyes narrowed at the litany of sins attributed to his name.

"I've searched nearly every dance hall and cheap theatre in New South Wales and Victoria. You're a hard man to find, Toby Jangles."

"You'll not drag me back to Sydney," Toby said. "Put a bullet in me now, if you have the marbles for it."

"Toby, I have little concern for these misdeeds," the Dutchman said, and tossed the lithograph into the water trough. The ink ran, and the paper was unreadable within moments.

"What are you about, mister?" Toby said. He looked at the stranger with something between curiosity and outright fear.

"You saw something, Toby Jangles," the Dutchman said quietly. "Something that curdles in your mind, that drives you from bottle, to pipe, to whore's quim. You left your fellows to a fate worse than death, and you left Sydney within the hour. I'd very much like to speak with you about that."

• • •

The Dutchman steered the boy into one of the cleaner eateries in the camp. When he put a bowl of stew and a heel of bread in front of the boy, it disappeared in moments. A second helping followed in similar order.

"You're not a copper?" the boy grunted around his food.

"I have been a priest, a professor of theosophy, and an archaeologist of no small note. Once, I spent a decade in the Orient, as an acolyte in a mystery cult," Cornelius said, eyes made large by his queer eyeglasses. "Boy, I have little truck with the laws of man."

The boy grunted, and set to work on his second mug of ale. Content that his new benefactor had no designs on his liberty, he allowed the big Dutchman to accompany him back to his employer, a miner running a frugal claim. Toby retrieved what few belongings he had, and squeezed the last squirt of his wage from that notoriously tight purse.

"So you'd be paying me then?" the boy said, hefting the thin sliver of coin in his hands. Living as he had been, he'd be destitute by tomorrow, and starved the week after that.

"Toby, if you lead me where I ask, you'll want for nothing."

For a long moment, the boy looked at his own wretched purse, and seemed to fight an internal war. Then he looked at the big Dutchman, clearly a man of means. He nodded, and put his fate in Professor Cornelius Tesselaar's hands.

• • •

It took days of hard travel to escape from that muddy Victorian gold-pit and reach civilisation. They took horses, and a coach barely deserving the name. The new train from Ballarat took them into Melbourne, where it was necessary to engage a clipper to carry them around the coast to Sydney itself.

It was a rough voyage, and Toby Jangles was no sailor. He spent two days in his cabin, heaving into a bucket. Cornelius sat with the boy, puffing on an ornate pipe and nursing him as needed.

"It seems a good time to speak more on what you saw," the Dutchman said. Other times he'd tried to glean the events from the boy's mind, Toby would change the topic, or simply stare off into the distance, too haunted by what he'd seen. Now, the boy was too tired and ill to resist the line of questioning, and spoke when he was not dry-retching.

"You know the kind of man I was, before . . . "

Cornelius nodded, puffing on his pipe.

"A larrikin, swaggering around Sydney. The terror of all decent God-fearing folk. We were the Blackwattle Push, meanest gang of cutters, and don't you mind what those gizzard-guts at the Rocks tell you."

"We'd run mollies, cards and dice, anything to make a bob. Sly boxing rings, robbing folks, and knocking seven bells out of any filthy copper daft enough to show his face on our patch."

"So you know that we were hard men," Toby said, pausing to gag and wipe his mouth. Cornelius pursed his lips tight around the pipe, amused at his own reference to manhood. The boy was seventeen if he was a day.

"I was bossman of the Blackwattle Push, took over after going thirty rounds bare-knuckled against old Pete Raffles. Had a lot to prove, and thought I'd take on the big dogs where they slept. We went after the Rocks Push."

The memory brought a bit of fire back to the boy's eyes. He pushed the bucket aside, sat up against his bunk. When Cornelius offered him a water-skin, he took a slow sip, swishing it around in his mouth.

"Our lads put out the word that we would meet them at Pyrmont, in one of the Scottish quarries. The one they called Hellhole, on account of the stone being so hard to cut and work."

"Hellhole," Cornelius muttered around his pipe. "Go on, boy."

"We got there early, hoping to spring out of hiding and give the Rocks boys a good belting. Perhaps they got wind of what we were up to, or they meant to jump us on the way home, but the time rolled around and they didn't show up."

"The lads got bored, and we horsed around in the pits. All those picks and dolly-carts, and nary a constable in sight. None of us worked an honest day in our lives, but there we were, smashing their neat ashlars with hammers, throwing the stone-chips at each other."

"Then Eugene Dagwood calls us over. There's a new digging the Scots have started, see, and they've roped the whole thing off. A type of old cave, a bubble buried in the sand-stone. Queerest thing you ever saw."

"'There's marks in here," Eugene calls. "Black fella drawings or some such.'"

"So we forget about the fight, and nick some oil-lamps from the miner's shed. They had a dog chained up back there, but . . . you know." Toby drew a finger across his throat.

"We spilled into that cavern, laughing and jostling, but I tell you this, the whole place felt unnatural. We looked at the black fella scribblings, and I'll tell you, God's own truth, but no native set his hand to those walls."

"What did you see?" Cornelius said. "If I fetch you paper and quill, could you sketch the symbols?"

Toby shook his head.

"Queer designs, shapes and sigils that my eyes had trouble fixing on. To this day, I cannot remember the marks. The further we went into the cave, the more they appeared, till the marks ran from roof to floor.

"Felt more like those old Egyptian writings than anything the locals usually paint. You know, where they paint the pictures that all mean words. But they weren't pictures of anything I'd ever seen."

"Hmm, yes, I am quite familiar with hieroglyphics," Cornelius said. "I'm rather doubtful that's what you found, but go on."

"I wanted to run from that place," Toby admitted. "Looking at the others, we all did. But we were Push boys, all stirred up. The first one to run would never live it down. So we went on, deeper into the digging. Soon we were past where the Scots had braved to go, and there were no brace-posts above us, nothing but sandstone and those carvings, all around us.

"Then, I felt it in there with us. Silent, but it felt like a big beast, hunkered in the dark, retreating from our lamp-light. Something that had no business being seen.

"And it smelled in there too. Like a wet dog. A stink of meat that's gone beyond rot and maggot, and broken right down to nothing. The memory of meat.

"'We shouldn't be here," Eugene clamoured, and of course the rest of us heaped the grief on him for crying coward. Had no-one said a word, we might all have left then. But we were the Blackwattle Push, and so . . .

"There was a cave, of sorts, a hollow place full of dripping and slime. In the middle of that cave was a set of stones, like a set of jagged teeth jutting out of the ground, and I swear, I've never seen anything as unholy as that arrangement."

"There was a pattern, yes?" Cornelius whispered. "A master stone, with smaller stones in attendance? Laid out on either side, like groomsmen at a wedding?"

Toby nodded for yes.

Reaching into a pocket, the Dutchman pulled out a leather-bound volume, an old book written in an arcane script. Flicking through it, he laid his thumb onto a particular page, an illustrated plate. He handed the book to Toby.

"Is this what you saw?"

The boy recoiled from the book with a great fright, and dropped it on the floor. The page lay open to the illustration, a jagged formation of stones, sinister, almost like the jaw-bone of some antediluvian creature. In the foreground, figures danced about with torches, in supplication to the stones.

Behind the master stone, a great shadow lurked. It was a crude dog-shape, a wolf with the ears of Anubis, with a jaw that opened far too wide. From that impossibly open mouth, a shadow tongue snaked out, entering a man's ears. It held him upright like a puppet, while he smiled with ecstasy.

Beneath this picture, the single word: KURPANGGA.

"This happened to your friends, didn't it?"

Toby Jangles whimpered. The sound built to a moan, the moan

to a howl. He pushed back in his bunk, and knocked the bucket over, spilling his sick all over the floor.

"Even as the beast took your friends, you ran," Cornelius said, raising his voice above the racket. "You left Sydney there and then, with naught but the clothes on your back. Is this correct?"

Toby nodded, blubbering, snot and tears running down his face.

"I do not judge you, boy. The first time I saw something from the outer darkness, I ran for my life. You escaped its grasp, and now you have the chance to end what you saw."

"I've changed my mind," Toby whispered. "Keep your money. I won't go back there."

"I need to know where that cave is," Cornelius said, seizing Toby by the arms. "The exact spot."

"I'll take you to the quarry, but no further. I won't go into that cursed hole, not for all the tea in China," Toby said. "No living thing has any business in that place."

"I agree," Cornelius said. "That's why it concerns me that the Blackwattle Push has been seen around town, alive and well."

• • •

"Certain of my instruments pointed me here," Cornelius said. He'd rented a room in the Rocks district, and the furnishings seemed an extension of the eccentric Dutchman. Every surface lay stacked with books, and the table was a jumble of alembics, braziers and various brass-geared devices. Pictures of fantastic beasts lay pinned to the walls, alongside what appeared to be mathematical formulae, and writings that resembled bird-scratchings.

Other shapes lay in the shadows cast by a flickering oil-lamp. Jars and stuffed animals, an elephant foot that contained swords, umbrellas, and staves carved with heathen totems. The whole place stank like a herbalist's stall.

"The trouble is, the science is far from accurate," Cornelius said, fussing with a brazier. He threw a pinch of shaved liquorice root into the red coals, gently puffing on them until a lick of flame swallowed up the offering.

"For instance, these formulae led me to Java, where I unearthed a nest of Yog-Sothoth cultists. But beyond the island itself, I knew not the site of their lair. It took me five years and half a fortune to destroy that foul gang."

"I continue the work of a most ancient order, but have only a shade of the esoteric skills my predecessors once possessed. I could tell you in which direction sunken R'lyeh lies, but even if I were mad enough to seek out that horrid house, I could sail for years and never come *close*."

Toby Jangles said nothing. He'd been struck dumb since entering the Dutchman's apartment, and still stood just inside the doorway, staring.

"Come inside, boy, and shut the door. The neighbours already complain about the smell."

"What . . . what are you? Do you have truck with the devil?"

Cornelius laughed for a long moment. The light from the brazier danced across his bifocals, and for one moment he looked unhinged, less than human. For the first time Toby noticed the deep lines in his face, the intensity of his stare.

"There are things crawling out there in the stars, entities that make Lucifer quail in his cloven hooves," the Dutchman said.

Herding the boy into the apartment, Cornelius shut the door and threw the bolts. Peeling apart a stack of periodicals and broadsheets, he found a newspaper and pushed it into Toby's hands.

"Can you read?"

Toby nodded, unfolding the pages. His fingers trembled a little. The Dutchman tinkered with the lamp, fixing the light as bright as it would go.

INFANT SNATCHED FROM THE CRADLE the headline read. Toby scanned each line, the horror growing on his face. The newspaper was little more than a rag, and the reporter had taken free licence with the more salacious details of the case.

"Here's another one," Cornelius said, pushing papers onto Toby as fast as he could read them.

THIRD BABY STOLEN

ANIMAL ROBBERS STRIKE ZOOLOGICAL GARDENS

SOCIETY MATRON MISSING, FEARED DEAD

"The dates, boy. Mind the dates on the papers. You'll find all of this has occurred since you fled from that awful cave."

"What is all this?" Toby whispered. He slumped to the floor, papers spilling from his hands. Realisation washed across his face.

"Evil, boy. Pure evil, and it walks the streets of Sydney. You and your larrikins have freed this thing."

"My boys. Where are my boys? Are they doing these things?"

The Dutchman did not answer for a long moment, working a mortar and pestle. He tipped a foul concoction onto the burning coals, something that looked like spiders, dead leaves, and flakes of human skin.

"The moment I got off the boat, I noticed your boys," Cornelius said. "Caught their stink on the street. Bitter experience tells me what kind of monster the Blackwattle Push serves."

As the Dutchman spoke, he seemed to hum with energy, a vibration that crawled under Toby's skin and buzzed around in his teeth. He loomed above the boy, a primal force that would not be denied.

Toby didn't know what was happening. Cornelius seemed like a bear wearing a man's skin, watching him hungrily. He'd dreamt many things in the Chinaman's opium hut, but nothing like this. What he felt probing around the corners of his mind was all too real.

"What I've been able to glimpse of their deeds," the Dutchman indicated his arcane equipment, "tells me that I have found the agents of this evil. But until now, their lair has been hidden from me. My esoteric vision is being turned aside, thwarted by that old mongrel."

The smoke wafting out from the brazier made Toby's eyes water. He felt light-headed, and swore he could hear a distant drumming.

From a drawer, Cornelius produced a black hunk of metal, the rudest example of the blacksmith's art. It had been beaten into the shape of a railroad spike, an iron tooth that shook slightly in the Dutchman's grip. Toby could not look away from that sharp point, and felt it turn a hungry regard towards him. Suddenly, the quivering spike keened and wailed, though it had no mouth, filling the room with the sound of a rusted hinge, of a violin's screech.

"I forged this myself, from the leavings of a fallen star," Cornelius said, making a visible effort to restrain the spike. "Trust me when I tell you that this will pin our enemy down."

Toby whimpered, and felt the warm flood as his bladder released down his leg. He'd never been more frightened, not even when he saw the thing in the cave . . . .

"You are the only member of the Blackwattle Push to have kept your soul from that shadow-hound's tongue. You have seen its marker stones, and fled intact. The sun has washed this taint from you, and that gives you something of a resistance to that dreaming dog."

Kneeling, Cornelius pressed the iron spike to the floorboards, fighting it with all of his strength. It shivered and whimpered and stabbed at the wood, frustrated at the nearness of Toby's flesh.

With one swift motion, the Dutchman swept a silken cloth over the iron spike, and it lay still. Thus wrapped, he placed the arcane weapon in his pocket.

"I charge you with this, Toby Jangles. You *will* return with me to the lair of Kurpangga, the devil-dingo that should not be. You shall see to it that the beast sleeps for another age."

Toby nodded quickly, eyes fixed to the pocket that hid the enchanted spike.

"Now, you will repeat my words, and know that you are entering into a most serious oath."

Shaking on the floor, Toby said the words. He belonged to the Dutchman now, for better or worse.

• • •

"Your larrikins will come, the moment they learn their master is in danger. I have a man on retainer, a most useful sort. We shall need him tonight."

Toby followed Cornelius down the streets of Sydney, a lost pup. The oath he'd given still rattled around in his mouth, and he felt an almost physical bond to this monster, to that impossible iron beast that slumbered in his pocket.

They met the man in a boarding house, a dim-lit place that stank of cabbage and unwashed men. Somewhere within, a pair of drunks quarrelled, and an old man weeped to the derision of his neighbours. Cornelius strode to a particular door, and knocked upon it merrily.

A man answered, a leathery sort with cold eyes. The room was a tiny cubby, with a cot and not much else. Cornelius introduced the man as Bunberry. The man did not say a word to Toby, and with an economy of movement he swiftly gathered a selection of weapons from a trunk.

With wide eyes, Toby saw Bunberry holster a trio of pistols to a complex harness, and he strapped a cavalryman's sabre to his side. Once he had shrugged into a sailor's greatcoat, this small arsenal was hidden from casual view.

Then he produced a British rifle, a great big Brown Bess, complete with a wicked looking bayonet and enough powder horns to start a small war. Bunberry wrapped all of this into a canvas, and belted it up with ropes until it resembled a swag, which went over one shoulder.

"I'm ready," Bunberry said. It was all that Toby ever heard him say.

They left the boarding-house, Cornelius leading the way through the night streets. What folk were out kept at a distance, and the sly-grog houses were closed. As they entered Pyrmont, Toby wondered at the Dutchman's sense of direction, taking turns and shortcuts that only a local would know.

"You knew all along," Toby said numbly, realising the quarries were nearby. "You knew where it was."

"Hush, boy," Cornelius said, draping a friendly arm across the boy's shoulders. "I've yet to lie to you. We trailed the Push through normal means."

"But—but you said—"

"My good boy, I have given oaths in low places. I cannot speak a falsehood," Cornelius said, and Toby could not tell if this was a point of honour or a frustration to the man. "Bunberry, be a good fellow and watch for the Push boys. We are close."

The trio approached the sandstone quarries, and had the cobbled streets all to themselves. Toby noticed that all the doors and windows were shuttered, and in some cases nailed and barred. There wasn't so much as a starving dog to be seen, and if there were rats they had the good sense to hide in the deepest of holes.

They reached the quarry known as Hellhole. The gates were locked with a thick chain, and above, a sign painted in a shaky hand.

DIGGINGS CLOSED UNTIL FURTHER NOTICE.

There was a small shack for a nightwatchman, but no lamplight shone through his window. There was no-one to see them, and none to protest when Bunberry put a bullet through the lock.

Unwrapping the chain, Cornelius pushed into the quarry. He fetched a lantern from the nightwatchman's shanty and used it to light their way across the work yard. Tools had been left out to rust in the weather, and a shed door flapped in the wind, squealing on unoiled hinges.

The pit caught the rain, and had poor drainage. Soon it was like slogging through a swamp, and it seemed a miserable place to labour for stone blocks.

Once more, Toby saw that narrow crack in the ground, and the cave looked even more menacing, a stone mouth ready to snatch them all up. Someone had rolled a barrel of gunpowder here, but mere feet from the entrance it lay in pieces, the staves cracked open with hammers and axes. The powder was scattered all around, trodden into the mud by a multitude of footprints. A melee. A fuse cord lay nearby, cut into many pieces.

"Watch how they defend their nest," Cornelius told Bunberry. The gunman took apart his swag, and primed the big rifle with the ease of long practice. With one precise movement he attached the bayonet. The mercenary shrugged out of his greatcoat and took a position before the cave, an arsenal at his fingertips.

Nodding to the man, Cornelius pressed Toby in the small of the back, herded him towards the source of all his nightmares. For one long moment the boy resisted, whimpered at the memory of the monster within.

"Go," Cornelius said. The word was a lash, a command that could not be disobeyed. The boy shuffled forward, jerky movements like a puppet's. The pair entered the cave that the Scots could not destroy, walked beneath a million glyphs never marked by the human hand.

"There was a war, in the earliest days of this world," Cornelius mused, translating on the fly. "Terrible beasts fought in the lakes of magma and on the curing mantle, fighting for possession of the world that would be. The devil-dingo lost, and so he was sealed into the stone."

Toby's eyes darted from left to right, looking once more at the murals and sigils. A giant with a squid's face pinned down a dog with its foot, with lesser monsters crowded around in victory. The next picture showed a curled-up dog, trapped in a womb of stone.

"Kurpannga has been dreaming down here for a million years," Cornelius said. "He has entered the myths of the natives, and sowed chaos and darkness into these new settlements. Now, the bloody Scots have dug him up. And your villains have crept in and poked him with a stick."

Toby paused, but the next moment Cornelius crooked a finger. He tottered forward as if he were on a leash.

Behind them came the echoing crash of Bunberry's rifle, followed by a piercing scream. Next, the repeated crack of his revolving pistols, greeted by pained cries, howls of dismay.

"Your larrikin fellows have come to stop you," Cornelius said. "Step lively, in the event that Bunberry's aim is less than true."

They ran through a twisted spiral of cave, the bobbing lantern revealing glimpses of pre-human artwork even more alien than that by the entrance. Whenever Toby lagged, Cornelius would curse at the boy, hauling him onwards with the enchantment, using his fists when even that did not suffice.

Behind them, one final gunshot, and then a clamour of shouting. Bunberry was shouting something, but then he gave rise to an awful scream, a blood-curdling cry that echoed through the cave for many long moments.

Even as the man fell silent, several voices raised laughter. Footsteps rang into the cave, accompanied by one wit who set to howling. Cornelius dragged Toby by the collar, and panting and wide-eyed they spilled into the inner sanctum of that place, a low-roofed place where the stalactites ran with slime, like mossy fangs.

Once again, the row of standing stones, like an ancient jawbone had been set into the bedrock. The stink of wet dog and rot pervaded everything. Cornelius gagged.

Underfoot were dozens of bodies. Desiccated husks, still dressed in clothes. The stolen babies, the missing society marms and prostitutes, all of them lay scattered across the cave floor.

Even as the Blackwattle Push closed in for the kill, Cornelius pushed Toby forward, crunching across the carcases. The boy landed painfully on his knees, trembling as he looked upon the arrangement of stones.

"What am I meant to do?" the boy said, literally shaking with terror. "How do I stop it?"

"Just wait."

Long-starved of sunlight, the stones seemed to drink at the lamp-light. The shadows that danced around on the slimy walls moved, running together like bodies of water down the path of least resistance. A shape rose up from behind the master stone, a physical presence that loomed over the two men.

The shadow formed a face, a snout that stretched out, split in two. The jaws opened wide, and a tongue snaked out, a vine of darkness that quested out, testing the air. When it sniffed out Toby, it ignored Cornelius entirely, and pounced on the boy with visible excitement.

"No!" Toby screamed and made to flee, but at the last moment Cornelius held him still. The shadow tongue slid into the boy's ear, questing around for whatever it fed on.

"It remembers you," Cornelius said, struggling to hold Toby still, even as the boy shook and fought and cursed. "I did not lie to you, boy. In your circumstance, you have developed a resistance to Kurpannga's attention."

At that moment, he turned Toby around, pushing him up against the largest standing stone. With one motion, the Dutchman retrieved the star-nail from his pocket, and shook the silk covering loose.

The spike leapt free and buried itself in Toby's chest. It wriggled, and pushed through, shrieking and gouging until it pierced the rock itself.

The shadow dog grew frantic, and raced around the walls, searching for escape. It became a pack of snapping animals, a snake that tried to withdraw its shadow tongue from the boy's ear. But inch by inch, it lost the fight, and the devil-dog was drawn into the boy's head.

Toby Jangles hung there, pierced through the heart, fastened to Kurpannga's rock. He lolled as if drunk, feet drumming, eyes rolling back in their sockets to show the whites. For a long moment, the cave was silent but for the dripping of wet stone. In the tunnel, the larrikins had gone silent, their curses and cries instantly snuffed.

Then Toby opened his eyes, and stared straight at Cornelius. The scared boy was gone, replaced with something wild-eyed, something without a trace of human emotion.

He opened his mouth, and barked ferociously, spittle flying everywhere. When Cornelius walked away from the pinned boy, Toby howled. It was a pitiful cry, that spoke of hunger and loss, of a prison that had lasted for a million years.

• • •

Cornelius stepped over the lifeless bodies of the Blackwattle Push, scattered in the tunnel like so much cold meat. The moment he'd trapped Kurpannga in Toby Jangles, these puppets had collapsed with cut strings.

Taking his time to muse over the carvings in the tunnel, Cornelius found what he was looking for. Whispering over his thumb-nail, he gouged into the sandstone, changing one of the sigils in a minor way. Stepping lively, the Dutchman exited the cave, watching as the sandstone shifted, melting like toffee and fusing into an unbroken whole.

In moments, it was as if the cave had never been breached, the facing pure and unmarked. Cornelius stepped over the broken body of Bunberry, eyebrows raised at the damage the larrikins had done. He'd seen an execution once, where a murderer was torn apart by horses. Bunberry appeared to have met a similar fate.

With more firepower than the Kelly Gang, he'd done nothing more than slow Karpannga's puppets. The Dutchman mourned the waste of a good man for all of a second.

Cornelius traced around the body parts with a chalk, whispering and muttering until these too sank into the viscous stone, sealing poor Bunberry into an invisible stone grave.

The Dutchman left Sydney within the week, his business done. His instruments showed a new visitation, evidence of an Elder God over in New Zealand. Before he left, he bought the deed to the Hellhole quarry from one Charles Saunders, a man who swore that he'd be unable to turn a profit from "that awful sinkhole".

He simply closed the place down.

It was almost one hundred years till Cornelius Tesselaar returned to Karpannga's prison. He travelled under a different name, and in the clothes for that era. By his side, a beagle he'd named Toby pulled at his leash.

"The children play down there," the town manager told Cornelius, a sheaf of planning papers in his hands. "Soccer when it's dry, and they swim in the hole when it's rained. Filthy place, and the children who lurk here aren't much better."

"What are they like?" Cornelius asked. "The children who play here."

"Monsters," the man said. "Mark my words, half of them will end up in jail, and the other half will end up dead."

"Fill it in," Cornelius said. "You may have the land, and build your council works on it, but fill in that hole as soon as you can."

"Too right," the council man said. The beagle named Toby lay on the very edge of the pit, and began to howl for all he was worth.

PERFECT LITTLE STITCHES

DEBORAH SHELDON

Angelo De Luca took up the scalpel and opened the cadaver's thigh, from hip to knee, with a single stroke. There was very little subcutaneous fat. Using firm, continuous passes of the scalpel, Angelo pared through the muscle within seconds and exposed the femur without scratching it.

"Very nice, as usual," Gary Mathews said. "Ah shit, you know what? I just went and notched mine at the hip-end."

"At the lesser trochanter?"

"I think so, yeah, the top bit that sticks out a little."

Angelo De Luca glared across the stainless-steel table at his new assistant, Gary Mathews, who was harvesting from the cadaver's other leg. Gary had started his working life as a butcher and still acted like one, even though the meat now was human, and therefore precious.

"If you would put your mind to the study of anatomy," Angelo said, "and learn about the attachments of soft tissue, you wouldn't keep making these basic errors. Haven't you read the books I loaned you?"

"Relax. Most of the bones we get are in shit condition anyway."

"That's no reason to damage them further."

Gary sneered. "Even with this bloke? He's almost ninety. How good are his bones going to be? Swiss cheese. The poor bastard who gets these femurs will bust them in half on his first step from the hospital bed."

Angelo couldn't trust himself to speak.

Whistling, Gary returned his attention to the cadaver's thigh, slicing briskly towards the kneecap. Angelo heard the muted snicking sound as the scalpel contacted the femur, over and over. Oh, how Angelo despised Gary Mathews with his uncouth footy-beer-and-barbecue personality, his ginger hair sprouting thick as fur over pale forearms, his skin freckled and wrinkled as if he'd been pressed out of dough and left in the sun to crack; Gary Mathews, the jovial, under-educated idiot, the very antithesis of everything that a funeral director ought to be.

Angelo felt the familiar stab of regret.

This funeral parlour, 'De Luca and Son', had been named after his father, Giovanni, and himself. It was supposed to be Angelo's legacy but his own sons hadn't wished to continue the family trade. Once Papa Giovanni had died, money became tight. Staff members—those who aren't relatives—expected and received full pay and entitlements. Then there was the outstanding balance of Sofia's stupendous medical bills. Bankruptcy had loomed.

Until the arrival three months ago of Angelo's saviour: Heather.

Once Angelo had agreed to her unusual business offer, Gary Mathews was made the sole member of Angelo's staff, without consultation, by Heather the Body Wrangler. That's what she actually called herself, Heather the Body Wrangler. Angelo didn't know anything about her apart from a mobile number.

Unlike organs such as the heart, certain tissues including bones and skin are still viable for transplant after death. Heather would pay up to $4000 in cash for a complete set of usable parts, removed surreptitiously, from a young and healthy corpse. Age and medical conditions lessened the remuneration on a fixed scale. At the very least, a diseased and elderly corpse meant a few hundred dollars.

The money had staved off the bank manager.

Yes, Angelo would go to jail if the police found out, but morally, it made irrefutable sense. Living patients either died or suffered permanent disability without these transplants. Voluntary donors were scarce. When cadavers would be wasted anyway, burned to ashes or buried to make worm-shit, what was the harm in first recycling their viable parts? No harm at all.

As long as the relatives never found out.

Because realising that your loved one's remains had been pillaged, defiled and dismantled would have to be the worst kind of unimaginable horror. Dear God, if such a fate had befallen Sofia . . . he could hardly bring himself to think of it. And so, occasionally, when Angelo couldn't sleep, he feared that he'd made a pact with the Devil. A widower for nearly a year, he would turn to the empty side of his bed and weep to Sofia for forgiveness.

Now, Gary Mathews gazed at Angelo across the naked and muscle-splayed cadaver on the stainless-steel table, waggled the scalpel and said, "Mate, you couldn't cut butter with this bloody thing. Just let me go get my boning knife."

"No." Angelo's moustache quivered as he fought to maintain a neutral expression. "Our deceased clients are offering the living a wonderful gift. We will not desecrate them with implements intended for the carving up of animals."

Gary dropped the scalpel to the stainless-steel table and put his fists on his hips. "You know what's going on? What we're doing?"

Angelo flushed. "Yes, of course."

"Nobody has signed any release forms. Every document is forged. What we're doing, right here, is some seriously criminal shit."

"Please continue with the harvesting," Angelo said. "Once we've gathered the long bones, we'll move onto the saphenous veins, ligaments and tendons. I'd like your help to sew the PVC pipes inside the limbs, and to remove the skin and heart valves, if you wouldn't mind. After that, I'll take the corneas myself, thank you. Please take your break at that point. Embalming will begin promptly at three o'clock."

Gary stared back, nostrils flared. Angelo decided to continue with the removal of the femur. For a time, the only sounds were the flit of his scalpel, the steady drip-drip-drip of the tap into the scrub sink.

"Nobody is giving anybody a gift," Gary finally said. "We're stealing these body parts. We're stealing them for money. I'm a grave-robber and so are you."

Gary unfastened his blood-stained apron, flung it across a bench, and peeled away his latex gloves. He headed to the exit of the preparation room.

"Where are you going?" Angelo said, hoping that the *bastardo* had quit.

"To the boot of my car," Gary said, "for my knives."

• • •

Oh, she was beautiful.

She was the first cadaver of the day, this warm spring day that had followed a long, torturous night of rain and shrieking wind. Angelo slowly unzipped the body-bag the rest of the way.

A child: such a beautiful young child.

Her jet-black hair lay in a halo of ringlets about her pale face. Angelo wanted to weep. The forensic pathologist must have been similarly affected. Following autopsy at the Coroner's Court, the typical cadaver arrived at Angelo's funeral parlour in disarray, tacked together as roughly as a hessian sack, but not this child. The forensic pathologist had taken great care. The single incision from throat to pubis had been closed using small, neat sutures, as precise as any of Sofia's hand-sewn embroideries. Had there been an examination of the brain? Angelo couldn't see any sign. He smoothed back the ringlets framing the child's forehead. And yes, hidden away within the hairline lay the tidy stitches circumnavigating the scalp.

According to the paperwork, the cause of death was inconclusive. Teresa-Kate, 11 years of age, had died in hospital three days ago from an unidentified infection that had first paralysed her, and then triggered multiple and catastrophic organ failure. More than likely, she had acquired the infection from the bite of an unknown animal, probably a dog. The included body diagram showed a large 'X' on the upper back. Angelo put down the paperwork.

Gently, he turned the child onto her side. Just above her right scapula, into the tissue of her trapezoid muscle, lay the bite mark. Could the paralysis have been symptomatic of some new strain of rabies? But Angelo was no micro-biologist. If the experts at the Coroner's Court were unable to establish an exact cause of death, it was not for him to speculate. He zipped the bag closed and placed Teresa-Kate in the refrigerator unit. Then he washed his hands and retired to the lunchroom, where he washed his hands again.

As he ate his sandwich, Angelo perused his work diary. He had spoken to Teresa-Kate's parents that morning. Anglicans, they wished to hold a home viewing before the funeral and burial, which necessitated an open casket. Teresa-Kate was already so perfectly preserved that Angelo's embalming and cosmetology skills would render her almost life-like. After lunch, he would ring the family's priest to discuss and confirm details of the service. Satisfied, he had just started on an apple when Gary Mathews shouldered through the lunchroom door.

Dropping the pizza box onto the table and sitting down, Gary said, "We'll get the whole four grand out of that kid."

A chunk of apple nearly stuck in Angelo's windpipe.

Gary folded a slice of pizza in half, and crammed most of it into his mouth. A Hawaiian pizza, of course: a disgusting abomination that turned Angelo's stomach.

"She's perfect in every way," Gary said, talking as he chewed, "young and in good nick. This time, mate, we've hit the jackpot."

"No," Angelo said. "No, we haven't. You're wrong."

Gary stopped chewing, raised an eyebrow.

Angelo said, "Haven't you read the report? Seen the biohazard tape on the body bag? She died of a disease that sounds very similar to rabies. Her soft tissues could infect every single transplant recipient."

"I've already called the Body Wrangler," Gary said. "We're doing the kid."

Angelo felt blood mottle his cheeks. "If it has to be done, fine, I'll do it myself. You'll not go anywhere near her. You and your boning knives can burn in hell first."

Gary shrugged, kept eating his pizza.

• • •

Teresa-Kate lay naked on the stainless-steel table. Her arms and legs were thin, hairless and unblemished, pre-pubescent. What might she have done with her four-score and ten? That would be the question to torment her parents until the release of their own deaths. And in a lesser way, that same question would also haunt Angelo. Since going into business with Heather, Angelo dreamed about many of his harvested clients, each one berating him and wailing for their missing body parts.

Enough.

He was a professional.

And according to protocol, he had to first take the leg bones.

He picked up the scalpel. The multiple bulbs of the overhead light beamed bright and white. The tap over the scrub sink dripped in a steady beat. It was almost 9pm. Gary had been sent home hours ago. Angelo had arranged to meet Teresa-Kate's family priest tomorrow morning to discuss details of the funeral and burial.

The harvesting would be now or never.

As softly as the kiss of a downy feather, he touched the tip of the scalpel to Teresa-Kate's hip without breaking the skin. A moment passed. He held the blade over her anterior superior iliac spine—the outer crest of the pelvis—where, beneath the epidermis, dermis and layer of subcutaneous fat, the attachments lay for the inguinal ligament and the sartorius muscle. One deep and decisive cut, following along the length of the femur, was the starting point.

Angelo couldn't do it.

Sofia came to mind, back when she first became seriously ill, confused, trying to cut rolled pastry on the kitchen bench with her hands as if her fingers had become knives. Leading her away, Angelo had shown her some of the framed embroidery she had made over the years. Placated, Sofia allowed him to administer her medication. *Look at my nails,* she had said. *Tesorio mio, watch me as I rend the world.*

These had been the last complete sentences she had ever spoken to him.

After 42 years together, God, how he missed her.

Now, Angelo sniffed, scrubbed at his tears with the heels of both latex gloves. Then he pressed the scalpel into Teresa-Kate's left hip and dug in deep, slicing down towards the kneecap. He worked quickly, efficiently. After next stripping the tibia and fibula, he moved to the other leg, repeated the procedure. Then he deboned her right arm, her left arm. The meat of Teresa-Kate's flayed limbs lay shockingly red against the pallor of her torso. From the box of PVC pipes, he found the lengths that would fit. He spent the next hour neatly reconstructing Teresa-Kate's body, using suture as translucent as fishing wire, making stitches so discreet that they brought Sofia's best handiwork to mind.

At close to 10.30pm, Angelo packed up his harvesting equipment. No matter what Heather the Body Wrangler demanded, he would not take this child's soft tissue. She had died from a rabies-like disease. How could Angelo claim to be helping the living if he deliberately offered up corneas and tendons that might carry infection?

It was time for the embalming procedure. He measured and mixed the chemicals. An incision near her collarbone exposed both the carotid artery and the jugular vein. One small incision in each, and he would insert the tubes: one to drain any remaining blood, the other to fill the circulatory system with embalming fluid. He pressed the tip of the scalpel into the carotid artery.

Teresa-Kate opened her eyes.

Angelo staggered back, dropped the scalpel.

The girl sat up, gazing at him, blinking dopily as if coming awake from a deep sleep. The sclera of both her eyes was black, as black as a fathomless pit.

"*Dio mio*," he said, and tried to cross himself.

Teresa-Kate looked at the stitched wounds along her arms and legs, gaped at the line of sutures down the midline of her body, and gave a silent scream. The stretching of her mouth peeled back her lips, splitting the skin across her teeth. Her incisors, pre-molars and molars were long, fanged: no longer human.

Teresa-Kate leapt from the table.

As she came at him, Angelo grabbed a stainless-steel instrument tray and struck her across the face. It slowed her momentarily. He hit her again, and again. When she staggered, dropped, he picked up the bone-dust vacuum and brought it down onto the crown of her head, cracking her skull. She sprawled across the floor.

Angelo watched her for a long, long time.

When she still hadn't moved, his senses began to return. He put down the vacuum. The first thing he realised was that he had wet himself. The second thing was that, somehow, Teresa-Kate had been alive and now she was dead.

Angelo groped for a chair and sat down.

The dead coming back to life, he had read of such things occurring from time to time in faraway places like Zimbabwe, the Philippines, and Venezuela, where the deceased wakes up during their funeral. But no, this wasn't a misdiagnosis, a case of some poorly-trained doctor confusing coma with death. At the Coroner's Court, Teresa-Kate's internal organs had been removed, inspected, weighed, sliced, and then tumbled together into a plastic bag, which was then sewn up inside her abdominal cavity. Good God, her brain had received the same treatment.

She still hadn't moved.

Incrementally, Angelo slid from the chair, approached. He used the tip of his shoe to turn her over. This time, she was definitely dead. One side of her face was smashed into a pulp of ruined skin and splintered bone.

Teresa-Kate had been alive.

And he had murdered her.

He vomited a little, wept. After a time, he regained control.

The child had already been issued a death certificate. Angelo would tell no one what had happened. Instead, he would spend the night using all his skills to repair and mask the damage he had inflicted upon her. Tomorrow morning, he would give Teresa-Kate to her family so they could hold, in the lounge-room of their home, the girl's open-casket viewing.

• • •

Gary Mathews drove the hearse. Angelo's nerves weren't steady enough.

They delivered Teresa-Kate, dressed and perfect, in her casket. While shaking hands with her father, Angelo began to cry. Moved to tears herself, Teresa-Kate's mother attempted to embrace Angelo, for the love of everything holy, as if to *console* him after the evil he had done to their daughter.

It was true; he had indeed made a pact with the Devil.

During the drive back to the funeral parlour, Gary harangued him about failing to strip the girl's corpse for the entire $4000. Angelo didn't have the strength to reply. Staring sightlessly at the passing scenery, he kept seeing Teresa-Kate's face, repaired to the absolute best of his abilities, yet, on expert inspection, still carrying the marks of violence inflicted by his own hands.

• • •

He assigned Gary to meet with Teresa-Kate's priest. Angelo got through the rest of the day on automatic pilot. In the evening, once Gary had left the funeral parlour, Angelo took from the locked drawer of his desk the business card of Heather the Body Wrangler, and called the number.

"You beat me to it," she said. "I was just about to ring. Gary reckons you took the girl's bones and nothing else. Frankly, that's a wasted financial opportunity."

It struck Angelo that Heather didn't care about the living patients who needed transplants. This epiphany took his breath. It meant that he was, irredeemably, a sinner. Clearly now, he saw that his financial strife and the grief over Sofia's passing had muddied his judgement, allowed him to be led astray, led straight into the pits of hell.

"I'm sorry," Angelo whispered to the ether, to God Himself.

"I understand," Heather said. "A little girl; hey, things can get sentimental."

"No, I mean I'm sorry, but I can't do this anymore."

"Can't do what?"

Angelo squeezed the handset. "I'm terminating our arrangement."

"Terminating our . . . ? Okay, calm down. The arrangement stays."

"No. Things have happened. Thank you and I wish you all the best."

Finally, she said, "I hope, for your sake, that you haven't snitched."

"Snitched? To the police?" Angelo gave a crazed laugh. "I haven't told anybody. Why would I? I'm as guilty as you. I don't want to go to jail either."

"Listen, hang tight, I'll be in touch. Don't do anything stupid."

Heather ended the call. Angelo stared at the handset. When he returned it to the cradle, he thought of Sofia, of Teresa-Kate, and then of Sofia again, until he wanted nothing more than to lose himself in alcohol.

• • •

At home, drunk, Angelo lolled across the couch. Later, his mobile rang. It was on the coffee table. Stirring from his stupor, groggy, Angelo reached to the table and took a gulp of warm sherry before grabbing the phone. He said, "*Pronto.*"

"Excuse me?"

Angelo consulted his watch, swiped a hand over his numb face. Night lay heavy around the curtains. "Yes, this is De Luca and Son Funeral Directors."

"Mr De Luca? Oh, thank the baby Lord Jesus."

Prescience needled Angelo fully awake. He said, "How may I help you?"

"I'm the mother of Teresa-Kate. You delivered her body this morning for the viewing. Something terrible has happened. She's gone."

Angelo sat up. "Gone?"

"I couldn't sleep. I went to check on her. The casket is empty."

"Empty? You mean your daughter's body has been stolen?" The shock rendered Angelo sober. "Did you call the police?"

"I've called everybody," the mother said. "Help me. Please, help me."

"I'll try my very best." Shaking in fear and anger, he hung up and called Heather the Body Wrangler. As soon as Heather answered, Angelo yelled, "Why did you do it? To blackmail me, is that it? A single X-ray will reveal the PVC pipes. Is that what you're planning? To hold that X-ray over my head?"

"Angelo?" Heather sighed. "You sound drunk. It's late. Let's talk tomorrow."

"Tell me what you did with Teresa-Kate."

"Who?"

"The little child: the girl with the raven hair."

"That kid you didn't complete?"

"Tell me where she is."

"I don't know what you're talking about." Heather paused. "Are you high? Having some kind of stroke? Look, I think maybe you should call an ambulance."

Unnerved, Angelo disconnected the call. Heather hadn't stolen the child's body. So where was it? He thought of the child leaping from the table, coming for him, and he shuddered. Perhaps Heather was right. Perhaps there was something wrong with him, like a mental breakdown. The strain of stealing from the dead must be unravelling his mind. Surely, he had hallucinated Teresa-Kate's resurrection. And those inhumanly long teeth? Why, gums always shrink after death.

Oh deliver me. He put his face into his hands. *Deliver me, even though I don't deserve it.* The house shifted and creaked in the wind. Frightened, Angelo stared at the doorways leading to the kitchen and entrance hall. Nothing happened. Over the next few hours, he drank the sherry bottle dry. At around 4am, he lurched towards bed. The mattress swam up and hit him. For the longest time, he didn't dream.

And then he dreamed of Teresa-Kate. He woke up.

Or, at least, he thought he did.

Teresa-Kate wrapped her fish-cold arms about his neck and sunk her bite into the meat of his shoulder. The pain, the wet and sloppy sound of her fangs chewing into his flesh, made him shriek over and over.

• • •

As he drowsed awake, the sound came to him slowly, a soft and familiar sound, regular as a pulse, making him feel comforted. Angelo tried but was unable to open his eyes. Confused, he attempted to sit up, failed. Cold steel lay beneath his naked body. And now he knew where he was: on the preparation table in his funeral parlour. That sound, that regular sound, was the dripping of the tap into the scrub sink.

Panic lurched through him.

Had he been drugged? Kidnapped by Heather and her body snatchers? The last thing Angelo remembered . . . drinking, passing out, the nightmare, that terrible nightmare about Teresa-Kate. How much time had passed since then?

What in God's name was going on?

More sensation returned to his body. He became aware of a strange emptiness within his chest, an abnormally heavy weight within his belly. Gradually, he understood what it meant. He had undergone autopsy. His internal organs, including heart and lungs, were in a plastic bag sewn inside his abdomen. His death certificate would echo Teresa-Kate's: Angelo De Luca, 59, succumbed to an unidentified infection, administered by the bite of an unknown animal, probably a dog.

He wanted to scream. Was he dead? Undead? Had Teresa-Kate been conscious like this when he had harvested her bones?

The door of the preparation room opened. Footsteps approached. Whistling started—it was Gary Mathews. Angelo strained to give a signal, but couldn't wiggle his fingers, his toes; in fact, couldn't even take a breath.

"Sorry, old mate," Gary said. "But you know how it is. Business is business."

The rip of velcro, the one-two unfolding of heavy fabric. Angelo recognised those noises. Gary had opened the roll-bag of his butcher's knives. The subsequent *whisk-whisk-whisk* must be Gary honing a blade against the sharpening steel.

And that blade would be the boning knife.

ALMOST DAYS

DK MOK

What is time?

It's a question I never asked myself while I was still alive, and now, I suppose time is something that happens to other people. Gainful employment, on the other hand, only happened to me after I'd died.

My colleagues call this place the Wings—we're the before and the after, enfolding the stage of the world. Here, in my lonely turret on the hill, the sun is always noon overhead. Go seaward, towards the misty waters of Unan, and the sun hovers in eternal dawn. Go worldward, towards the Golden Vale, the realm of Transformation, and the sun dips into the cusp of night. Travelling across the Wings can give the illusion of time passing. Long ago, I found it comforting. Now, it makes me vertiginous.

My hill is small, with bald patches where I forget to remember the grass. On its crown sits the cottage I inherited from my predecessor, and despite my best efforts, the building remains shaped like a large barnacle with an oversized turret on its head, so my dwelling resembles a squat fort sitting on a long-suffering crustacean.

All I know of my predecessor is that she retired, and that her retirement had possibly come as a surprise to her. The only legacy of her presence is a single word scratched under a loose paving on the floor.

Enough.

I try not to think about it: the only reminder that I wasn't always here.

In my cavernous turret, a column of glassy green threads—the Flow—streams in my seaward window, and out the worldward arch. Far seaward, where the dreaming of souls fills the sea of Unan, glimmering spray rises from the warm waters, coalescing into liquid threads. My task is to comb and groom each strand until it shines, sleek and supple. Every life runs through my fingers until it tapers to its end, and scatters into the Nimbus above, one day to rain back into the misty sea.

When times are prosperous and uncomplicated, I can comb through weeks in one sitting. But when the world endures upheaval, when doubt and indecision fill its souls, I can spend an unrelenting age combing through the tangles of a single, crucial moment. Today, I've resolved a number of tricky knots. Then again, it's always today.

A thread frays near my hand, someone's potential path splitting off, the loose tendril already ghosting. I smoothly snip its base, leaving the main thread smooth and unharmed. I hold the snippet over the brazier of entropy beside me, but the ghosting thread twists vibrantly between my fingers. In its smoky light, I see a girl searching for firewood across an arid savannah, dreaming of centrifuges and stars. In this path, she abandons her search for twigs, and races to school. This path that never happens.

I take a frosted violet phial from my pocket and place the ghost thread inside, twisting the stopper gently. The sound of clinking bottles drifts from outside, and I hurriedly tuck the phial into my robes.

At the base of my hill stands a low wooden gate strung with mismatched glass bottles. No fence, just a solitary gate to mark the bounds of my domain. A pale blue contrail streams through my window, solidifying into a smartly dressed man in his late twenties, with light brown hair and spotless teeth.

"Tangles," nods the man, brushing imaginary dust from his tailored suit.

Tangles isn't actually my title. My predecessor was known as Reed, but after the Stewards implemented their last round of changes, I became the Flow Optimisation Officer. Naturally, I acquired the nickname Tangles instead.

My guest's title is Timing, but he calls himself Serendipity. He tunes the tension of the Flow, tightening a thread here, loosening one there, so all things move in harmony. At least, that's his task.

It's rumoured that he's fond of reuniting high school sweethearts, taking a morbid delight in how they squirm to discover that the other has filled out, thinned on top, and led a far less exciting life than the future had promised.

"I like what you've done with your hill," says Serendipity.

"I haven't done anything to it."

Serendipity fixes me with birdlike eyes, then smiles brightly.

"My mistake," he says.

Still smiling, his hand darts towards the Flow and tweaks a thread slightly.

"It was aligned!" I slap his hand away. "Now Winston Kerr's going to miss his bus."

I knead gently at the fresh kink, and in the shifting depths of the thread, the single dad stops chasing the huffing red bus, an oversized Hug-A-Planet in his arms. He looks just as Atlas might if he caught public transport.

Serendipity continues to look quietly satisfied.

"On the next bus, he'll sit next to Doctor Madeline Teng," he says. "In three days' time, she'll resuscitate his daughter Liesel at the pool party she's about to be invited to."

"We're supposed to align, not interfere. Smooth their course, not change it."

Even so, I can't suppress the subtle thrill that bleeds through me as Winston's thread transforms along its new course, and the truncated thread of his daughter suddenly sprouts like a fresh shoot.

"Pity," says Serendipity, sauntering towards the worldward arch. "What would I be without it?"

He pauses, looking at me with an expression I don't understand, and then his contrail disappears over the wispy horizon.

• • •

My heart no longer beats, my ribs no longer rise and fall, but the little violet phial hums against my chest like an appropriated soul. I've made no changes to the cottage itself, just a small alteration to the hill. Only a minor adjustment, virtually plumbing upgrades, not worth mentioning to the Stewards.

I descend the turret stairs, and sweep aside the empty bottles and half-blown glass in my cellar. I kneel on the cool, dark earth and trace a circle on the floor. A ring of flat stones rises from my etching, and the centre falls away into a well. Gathering my robes around me, I leap into the void.

We each have our eccentricities, here in the Wings. Distractions to pass the timeless days. Motion creates mesmerising wreaths of light which drift lazily from her rocky spires. Transformation constructs elaborate headdresses, gruffly complaining that she rarely has a chance to use the owl-headed one these days, ever since polytheism fell out of fashion. I have my bottles. And this place.

My feet touch down softly on the floor, and the ceiling curves into vaulted sandstone far above, rising like the petrified ribs of a long-defeated colossus. Thousands of loculi pock the sandy walls, and cradled within each is a softly glowing bottle. Ghost threads float and coil in every glassy vessel, phantom memories of opportunities past.

I climb the lattice of bittersweet vines, past rustic clusters of red and orange berries. I nest the violet phial in a waiting hollow, and brush my fingertips over its neighbours—tiny orbs of golden glass, long necked decanters of scarlet crystal, undulating blue barber bottles. I let myself drift in their fading dreams: a library rich with golden afternoons; an impassioned speech in a jury room; a crowded seminar hall and a lone, searing question.

These fragments of 'almost time' are the relics of choices, like mayflies frozen in amber. They are the split second that stretches forever, the moment that hangs for eternity, intense with all the uncertainty and hope of a decision that cannot be unmade.

All these bottles are filled with choices I never had, brimming with longing and aspiration. My own life had been a shadowplay, brief and stark. But here, amongst these private kingdoms and sugar-glass dreams, I can almost pretend I'm alive again. It's too late for me to change what I had, but it isn't too late for Winston, for Liesel, for those whose threads still flow. And I find my thoughts turning towards reconstituted mayflies.

I linger over a conical green inkpot: a young woman with a runner's build sits beside a dark-eyed man. At their feet is a pond rippling with overfed, geriatric ducks. She reaches over and plucks a leaf from his hair, the moment of warmth flowing into a timeline that never was. The essence of the moment is all but gone, only the almost-time remains.

Three seconds.

• • •

In the brilliant daylight of my turret, I grip the dark green inkpot, strange creatures stirring in the silt of my thoughts. I gently draw a single strand from the Flow, and pour the ghost thread into the glittering skein.

• • •

Name: Evea Dorin
Age: 29
Occupation: Kendo instructor

Evea Dorin was making a cup of ginger tea when the phone rang, and a voice she hadn't heard in two years spoke seven words, then hung up.

In the busy heave and sigh of Evea's life, she would normally have dismissed the message as one of Jackson's odd turns, and made a mental note to visit him the following day, despite their estrangement. However, an odd twinge shivered through her—a half-remembered day in the park.

It took three seconds for the unease in her gut to congeal, and by the time her housemate came to check on the kettle, Evea was already four blocks away.

I'm sorry. I love you. Take care.

Jackson's words looped in Evea's mind, ending in a dial tone.

Let me be wrong, she thought. *Please let me be wrong.*

The words pounded with every step. Her days on the high school track team were imprinted into her muscles, and she sprinted past the peak hour traffic.

Jackson's fibro house peered silently from the corner, and the knot in Evea's stomach tightened as she reached for one last burst of speed. She shoulder charged the glass patio door and swung into the darkened sunroom, crash tackling Jackson just as the pistol fired.

The skylight shattered, and the pair lay breathless on the parquetry, dried leaves drifting down like orange stars.

• • •

There's a peculiar clarity to the silence, as though a background hum I've never noticed has disappeared. Bottles clink outside, and I hurriedly throw the empty inkpot into the brazier, where it ceases to exist.

A wintery blue contrail materialises into a pale woman—no, a girl—with limp auburn hair. I don't recognise her, and apprehension grips me.

"Hello," says the girl. "I'm Timing."

"There's already a Timing," I say.

"He retired today," says the girl. "Transformation instructed me to watch the nexus of the Flow. She said I'd understand what I needed to do."

I glance nervously at the brazier, and the girl follows my gaze. I quickly turn back towards the threads streaming between us. The girl, Timing, is perhaps sixteen, and has the look of someone newly passed through the Shallows—a little unsure of where she is, who she is, certain only of her title and her task.

She stares into the glowing heart of the Flow, and I busy myself combing away the tangles that have formed. Her expression doesn't change, but tears trail slowly down her face.

"It becomes easier," I say, patting her on the shoulder, as I've seen people do in the Flow.

The Shallows wash away our regrets and affections, the details of the life we left behind. We can't remember how we died, or who we left behind. But still, this is not an Afterlife, only an After.

Timing touches her cheeks, and seems vaguely surprised to find them wet.

"I'm not upset," she says. "I just feel a little odd."

I offer her a handkerchief, but I only know what handkerchiefs look like, and from Timing's expression as she wipes her eyes, I suspect mine is somehow deficient. She returns the stiff square to me, and peers at my face. I pull my hood further down.

"Were you always so amorphous?" says Timing politely. "Or have you forgotten what you look like?"

I've forgotten much of my mortal life, but there's little enough to remember. Always hunger, always darkness, always running. My tribe was savaged when I was too young to comprehend what that meant, and every village I came upon chased me away with stones and fire. When Transformation finally appeared to me, though that was not her name then, she made me an offer. A place with no pain and no hunger. A place where there would never be darkness.

Timing reaches into my hood, and before I can pull away, a tingle burns across my skin and deep into my bones. I stumble against a wall, and raise a hand to my mouth. There are lips now, a straight nose, a deep brow.

Timing parts her hands, and a mirror appears between them. A young man stares back at me: ragged brown hair and startled hazel eyes.

"How did you do that?" I croak.

"I'm Timing," is all she says.

She looks into the Flow again, with brighter, clearer eyes.

"Where are our threads?" she asks.

"We don't have them."

She contemplates this, then vanishes in a blue mist.

• • •

Pity.

It's been a hundred lifetimes since I last ventured from my hill, but Serendipity's last words crawl up my spine and fester in my brain. I gather my gnarled staff, a circular travelling cloak, and a rose-coloured flask inlaid with a silver window.

"Going somewhere?" a voice drawls behind me.

A thunder-grey vapour claps into the form of a tall, bronzed woman, and the bottles at my gate clink in belated apology. Transformation seldom visits, and her presence is still enough to make me feel acutely mortal again. She's wearing a deerskin tunic today, and a crown of quetzal feathers to hide her unruly brown hair.

"I'm going to visit Luan," I say. It's close enough to the truth to keep my voice from shaking.

Transformation's gaze slinks to the pulsing Flow, and her finger traces along a glittering line.

"I thought Jackson's thread finished today," she says.

"Friendships are an unpredictable force."

Her eyes narrow. A willow rod materialises in her hand, the tip touches my cheek, then flicks back my cowl.

"What happened to your face?"

Her hawk eyes probe my entrails, and I try to wish away the sweat on my back.

"I think this is how it's supposed to look."

Her gaze is disapproving, as though faces are a nuisance, and I wonder if she bothers to have one when she's wearing her full-faced helms.

"You can't get to Luan's," says Transformation.

"I can walk," I say stiffly.

Transformation looks faintly disgusted. Her hand clamps onto my arm, and we twist into the aether.

• • •

I'm kneeling on wet sand the colour of sunrise. My vision slurs, and I rise unsteadily. Before me is a shallow bay that touches the sky, beyond which lies the Sea of Unan. The sun is barely a glow on the horizon, and I can't help but think how the beginning and the end look so much alike.

Overhead, a watery aurora streams worldward, forming the threads that will eventually join the Flow. At my feet, foamy waves lap at the sand, and I'm careful not to let the water touch me.

"What's so urgent you had to leave your little hill?" says Transformation. She's standing casually on the beach, watching me with the gaze of an apex predator.

"Brazier maintenance," I say.

Transformation inspects my words, and doesn't seem entirely satisfied.

"I'll make my own way back," I continue, and begin walking towards Luan's shack. I slow after a few steps, and turn back to Transformation. "Did you see Serendipity, before he . . . retired?"

She's still for a moment.

"I see everyone."

Transformation turns her face towards the sea, and with a snap, she vanishes in a comet tail across the sky.

• • •

They say Luan is as old as the Wings, far older than the Stewards, who dare not change his name. He disposes of forgotten things. Trinkets, memories, empires. They're all dropped with kindness into the wicker basket at his elbow, from which even the Nimbus can't recall them.

His shack is a giant crab shell, half sunken on the beach, bleached white in the eternal sunrise. Colourful paper flowers hang in the windows, stirring in the breath of the sea.

"The last time you were here, you were wading from the Shallows," says Luan.

He takes the form of a man in his sixties, wearing a long tunic of unbleached cotton, and sandals woven from reeds. No one knows when he died—or if he died—and no one dares to ask. He's the kind of man who likes to answer a question with a question, and his questions have claws.

"Please tell me about my predecessor," I say.

At the sink, Luan holds a tall earthenware teapot beneath a palm-sized cloud, and gently prods it to fill the pot.

"Why did you come here, to the Wings?" says Luan.

I stare at my feet, pale and bare. The blood and the darkness seem so far away, but never quite gone.

"I wasn't ready."

Luan moves towards a large cockle shell on the benchtop, filled with soil that smells like rain. From its depths, a tiny fern is unfolding, and he tenderly pours from the teapot. Luan's shack is filled with conches and clams, all cradling liverworts, delicate grasses, and pine seedlings.

"Are you ready now?" says Luan.

I tense, the rose flask pressing cold against my hip. I shake my head, not trusting my voice.

"Your predecessor presided over the last dark age," says Luan, "when ignorance and confusion reigned over compassion and reason. Threads broke where they should have frayed. Your predecessor lost her focus."

I think of the word carved into my cottage floor, and I wonder whether losing focus had been her transgression. Or whether the transgression had come after.

"Go home," says Luan, watering a rotund cactus.

I bow, and pause at the door. I can remember the sound of my heart, and for the briefest moment, the silence aches.

"Did she put up a fight?" I say.

The teapot is still.

"Why would she fight?"

Luan's question gives me my answer. Triumph and loss belong in the world—there's no place in the Wings for desire or conflict or pity. Perhaps, in the end, my predecessor realised that. And yet, my own answer burned in my throat.

Why would she fight? Because even here, there are things worth fighting for.

My pace is steady as I leave the shack, breaking into a run only when I reach the cover of the weathered basalt on the shoreline. I lower the rose flask by a cord into the pristine waters, and quickly wrap the stoppered bottle in layers of my travelling cloak.

I've never been able to contrail, but I make a concerted effort now. I blurt into smoke every few hundred metres, then back into corporeal form. I pass the windswept gorges where Motion makes her home, and continue past the ice-capped peaks of Insight. I scud by the jungle citadels of Fortune, and the golden towers of Misfortune.

I finally reach the sanctuary of my noonday hill, and drop my damp cloak into the hungry brazier. I hold the rose flask up to the light—there isn't much, but it'll have to be enough. It'll all come down to the—

"Hello again."

Bottles clink, and Timing is sitting on the stone sill beside me. I freeze, the cold flask resting in my palm.

"I brought you a present," says Timing.

She continues to sit on the sunny windowsill, looking at me with pleasant expectation.

"Uh, thank you . . . "

I see no evidence of a gift, but feel it'd be impolite to question it. She smiles, and I wonder, not uncharitably, where Transformation found this one.

"I thought you should have it," says Timing. "Just in case."

A chill prickles up my spine, and Timing vanishes in a hush of blue, glancing ever so briefly at the bottle in my hand.

• • •

A pale amber wine bottle, a hexagonal pickle jar, a peacock-blue perfume bottle inlaid with pearl. I load up my arms and fill the turret with my subterranean treasures. Glowing bottles cover the floor from wall to wall, coloured glass in every shape and size, beneath the twisting Flow.

I select a slender phial of champagne-coloured glass, and gently pour an hour into a glittering thread.

• • •

Name: Benson Senkai
Age: 34
Occupation: Biochemist

They were alive.

Benson peered through the wire lid of a cage labelled *Team LV223* and savoured the moment. His instincts had been right, the vaccine had only needed minor adjustments. They were one step closer to clinical trials, and it was a huge step.

"They're shutting us down, Senkai."

Benson turned to see his colleague, Quesar, standing in the doorway. Her dark braid looked frizzier than usual, and she wore her lab coat like a gangster Mac.

"Look! Team LV223—" began Benson.

"It's not a profitable field."

Benson refused to let the news sink in. Schendruk Pharmaceuticals had only taken over their facility last week, but already, a third of the staff were gone.

"Antibiotic-resistant tuberculosis is one of the leading causes of death—"

"In developing countries," said Quesar. "Like I said."

Benson gripped the sides of the plastic cage, as though he could draw strength from the snoozing white rodents inside.

"The vaccine didn't just work," said Benson, "Team LV223 were *already* infect—"

"Stop calling them that," snapped Quesar. "You know why the other researchers don't take you seriously?"

She held up a squeaky toy.

"Pet toys, micro-green salads, rat runs—" Quesar gestured at the colourful lab.

"Sedentary, overfed rats can skew the results—" said Benson.

"All the little rat funerals?"

"I just think their sacrifice deserves a little more respect. Quesar, if we can modify the vaccine to be effective in humans—"

"Senkai, it's over." Quesar rubbed her temples, shoulders sagging. "Security's clearing us out in half an hour. Maybe you should think about another career track. Look at that Kendo instructor turned mental-health advocate whose online talks you keep forcing us to watch."

Benson was silent.

"I'll see if I can get you a spot at Vati-Tech," said Quesar. She sighed heavily. "They're trying to develop a vaccine for homosexuality."

Benson closed his eyes, and heard the lab door swing shut. He resisted the urge to grab a flask of radioactive goo from his secret inventory, which he kept in the event that he someday found a way to give himself super powers.

Instead, he stared dully at the computer screen. Part of him realised that Quesar was right, Schendruk wouldn't waste money on human trials. It was over. But an old memory stirred, of how he'd once dreamed of studying law. Scenes from *12 Angry Men* and *8* had filled him with the conviction that a single voice could change the course of nations.

Benson glanced at the clock. Twenty-five minutes. Not nearly enough, but he'd take what he could get. He moved methodically between the computers, the crowded benches, and the vaccine refrigeration unit. Time seemed to stretch oddly into the longest twenty-five minutes of his life, but by the time the boots reached his door, Benson had only one thing left to do.

The doors swung open, and Benson raised the aerosol chamber to his face, hoping he'd calculated the dosage correctly.

"Kanpai," said Benson, and inhaled.

• • •

Two minutes. Three hours. A day. Bottle after bottle tips gently into its respective thread. The Flow shivers and I swiftly smooth its course. The light at the window flickers, and I risk a glance outside. The sun blinks.

They're coming.

I place the rose flask on the windowsill, and for the first time since my shadow touched the Wings, I draw a breath. Vapour rises slowly from the bottle, trailing outside to form a cloudy perimeter, then a thin shell of fog around my hill. It won't hold, but every moment counts.

Beyond the fragile fog, contrails are circling now. Dark shadows wheel furiously outside the dome, but don't pass through. I continue to empty the phials and flasks, glittering almost-moments streaming into the Flow, becoming moments once more, infused with the spirit of barely remembered days.

At the threshold of my gate, a dark grey contrail crackles into Transformation, with Timing beside her. Timing reaches towards the wispy vapour, and Transformation catches her wrist.

"You can only pass through the Shallows once," says Transformation.

Timing looks up at the window, and smiles to see me. For a moment, I almost regret the path I've chosen. All around the patchy grass, I can see my colleagues standing darkly: Motion, her windswept hair forming a midnight halo around her; Misfortune with his iridescent scales and serpentine shadow.

Bottles clink wistfully, and a white cloud by the gate transmutes into Luan. He lays a hand on Transformation's shoulder, and then steps through the fog. His skin shivers and crackles, his whole body threatening to scatter into mist. For a moment, it seems that something else stands in his place—something of water and light, something that never remembers being human.

Luan labours to take another step, then another, solidifying back into his usual form as he inexorably approaches my cottage.

I know this is how it must end. Had known, perhaps, since Serendipity's words had sliced deep into the hollow place I longed to fill.

One more, just one more.

I grasp a blood-red libation bottle full of golden afternoons, and one minute is all I have left to give.

• • •

Name: Rutger Stone
Age: 43
Occupation: CEO of Jupiter Exploration

Rutger Stone sat gargoyle-like in the auditorium, bored to petrification. The speeches at these events were interminable, but it was less than a minute until they broke for Beluga and Romanée-Conti. He distracted himself with fiscal projections—he was trying to install decent renewable energy on his Pacific island, since his nemesis, Kikuyo from Ingot Resources, had just added a new photosynthesis-fusion array to her Arctic villa.

Rutger ignored the petite blonde squeezing noisily into the seat beside him. Her luggage was caked with orange dust, apparently overlooked in sloppy quarantine procedures. Old luggage tags swung from its handle, with codes like *NBO, KNJ*, and the name *L. Kerr.*

"Damn, did I miss the entire thing?" muttered the young woman.

Rutger considered pretending that he hadn't heard her, but doing so would doubtlessly result in the footage being uploaded onto social media sites within seven seconds, tagged *CEO of Evil Mining Corp shuns beloved spiritual leader/terminally ill Nobel Laureate/alien ambassador.*

"I believe there's seventeen seconds left," said Rutger.

"I didn't think tuberculosis breakthroughs would interest someone like you," said Kerr amiably.

"Apparently, some of our workforce in more remote locations find it bothersome," said Rutger dryly.

He'd really only come to hear Raki Adedayo's afternoon presentation. According to Rutger's dossier, Adedayo had defied an arranged marriage at age twelve, left behind her drought-stricken province to study astrophysics at Caltech, and the doctoral student now had some rather curious ideas regarding faster than light travel.

However, the passing seconds stretched vindictively, and the current presenter's words seemed to blur into utter incoherence. They were probably testing an experimental PA system.

The blonde woman kept glancing at him, and Rutger ignored this. He was exceptionally disciplined at ignoring things. As a child, he'd walked past a grand old library on his way home from school each day, and spent glorious afternoons there with his best friend, Tulip. The world had seemed giddy and immense, brimming with visionaries and heroes. However, when he'd turned eleven, his father had taken sick, and Rutger had scrounged an off-the-books job running errands at the local open cut mine. He'd still walked past that library every day, but to him, it may as well not have existed.

Rutger blinked slowly at the memory, and found himself glancing at the woman beside him again. She took the flicker of eye contact as an invitation to conversation.

"Not to pry," said Kerr, "but when was the last time you had that mole checked?"

"I have a skin examination every twelve months."

Kerr's fingers brushed past his ear, stopping an inch into his hairline. She flicked a dermatoscope from her pocket and leaned in.

"I think you should visit again." She gave him a polite smile, and drew back.

Rutger grabbed her callused hand almost without realising it, staring at the words tattooed on her wrist.

As much as you can.

As many as you can.

As long as you can.

"Odd mantra for a dermatologist," said Rutger.

"Oncologist," said Kerr. "Emergency obstetrician. Stopgap school teacher when the weather's fine. Come visit me in Jamaame sometime."

The crowd shuffled to its feet, and the clatter of silverware drifted from the adjoining conference room.

"I feel like some fresh air," said Rutger. "Care for a walk?"

• • •

Downstairs, the cottage door creaks open. Only a few bottles remain stoppered, suspended in their slumber, but there isn't time to find their threads. Luan is right, there's no point in fighting. Something pale catches my eye in the Flow, and I reach over, thinking that a piece of lint must have tumbled in.

I pull out a silver blue thread, translucent, as though not yet realised. I gaze into its heart, and see myself staring back.

A present.

Footsteps are climbing the corkscrew staircase, and I grab the remaining bottles, pouring them into the hazy silver thread. There's no time to find their threads, but at least their memories, their passions won't be lost. The last bottle splinters in my palm, and around me, every bottle crumbles into sand.

"Those lives don't belong to you," says Luan.

White sand drains through my fingers. And they're finally gone, the days that almost were.

"All they needed was a little more time," I say.

Luan shakes his head. "I'm sorry for the short, desolate life you led, but you made your choices. It's not your place to make theirs."

"Our place is to help," I say with feeling. "I comb their threads to make them strong, to ease their journey. All I did was remind them of what they once loved. This woman," I separate a thread, "she spends a cumulative twenty years of her life eating fruit pies and having afternoon naps. But here, at this point, she thinks about taking a sewing course. If she does, she becomes a remarkable mixed-media artist and inspires a generation of guerrilla embroiderers."

"Yes," says Luan. "And if she does, she misses a call from her brother after his motorcycle accident, and never has a chance to say goodbye."

The thread drifts from my finger, and Luan continues.

"Their lives are meaningful because of the choices they make. Whether that choice is to refuse to sit at the back of a bus, or to eat two thousand and forty-seven pies in their lifetime. They might not always make the best, the most heroic, or the kindest choices, but it's not your world anymore."

The sunlight feels cold on my skin, and I realise that I'm tired. Tired of looking in on a world I can't touch, collecting memories that aren't mine. All I wanted . . .

I can feel myself dissolving slowly at the seams. There's only so much one can bear before this place, this endless, aimless day becomes . . . enough.

Luan rests a hand on my shoulder.

"Time to retire," he says.

• • •

I'm kneeling on a plain of tiny white shells, so bright they burn like snow. The Stewards stand in wordless court, towering and faceless; like obelisks they encircle me. A sun hangs behind each one, their shadow-cage crossing over me.

Transformation stands before me. Today, light drifts from her, and a circlet of ferns rests upon her head. I raise my eyes to her, and wonder that I ever felt afraid.

"I know you have to follow your conscience," I say, "as I followed mine."

Transformation shakes her head, and her voice is soft.

"It was never a question of conscience, but of choice. The lives you altered were done so without their consent, without their knowledge, to satisfy your will, not theirs. Choices are only yours to make when the consequences are yours to suffer. Only mortals have the right to exert their will on the mortal world. Do you understand?"

There's a sadness in her eyes, and I find myself wishing that I'd visited Transformation more often, in her lonely vale of autumn light. My day is drawing to its close, and in the end, I am ready. The Stewards hum in unison, and the suns begin to darken. Transformation leans towards me.

"Thank you," I say softly, and Transformation hesitates. "A

long time ago, you made me a promise. A place with no darkness. Thank you, Iru, for giving me a little longer in the sun."

They say there was a time, in her younger days, when Transformation visited the mortal world to watch their combustion sun rise and set. But they say a great many things about Transformation.

The shadows deepen around me, and Transformation cups my face in her hands, as she did once, long ago. She leans in so that only I can hear her.

"Friendships are an unpredictable force," she says, and kisses my forehead before the suns snuff out.

• • •

I'm standing on a sticky landing, a suitcase in my arms. The wooden door before me opens, as though I've knocked, and a dark-haired man in his thirties smiles broadly.

"New recruit's here," says the man. "Ceren, make yourself decent."

A dapper young man glides from the parlour, dressed as though he's raided the most exclusive op shops in the city.

"I . . . am always decent," says Ceren, with a flourish that suggests he's about to send a deck of cards flying from his sleeve. "Have we met?"

I shake my head. The interior of the share house is surprisingly clean and airy, inhabited by numerous piles of books and solemn potted palms.

"I'm Jackson," says the dark-haired man. "Secretary of the Mushin Foundation. This is Ceren Darwinshaw, he breaks up couples."

"I'm a relationship counsellor," says Ceren primly. "I help vulnerable people leave unhealthy relationships."

"He's crazier than I ever—" begins Jackson.

The front door slams open, and an athletic woman wearing an olive cami and pressed trousers bursts into the room.

"We got the grant!" she grins, and exchanges a jubilant high five with Jackson.

"I thought Stone was busy eradicating tuberculosis," says Ceren.

"I guess he realised mental health networks are desperately underfunded," shrugs the woman. She notices my presence, and extends a hand. "I'm Evea. You are . . . ?"

Through the window on my left, stars are appearing above the neon skyline. In my chest, a heartbeat thumps in quiet anticipation.

"Ernest Babar." I shake Evea's hand warmly.

"'Babar' like the elephant?" says Jackson.

Evea ignores him.

"Welcome to the madhouse," she says. "So, why are you here?"

I close my eyes for a moment, and I can remember rocketships and heaving nets, chanting crowds and silent schoolrooms. Visions fleet through my mind, and a whisper lingers in my ear. I smile at my new colleagues.

"I'm here to help."

~

NINEHEARTS

MAREE KIMBERLEY

Charity Ninehearts pulled the last stitch taut on the bar-room brawler's leg wound, and finished it off with a knot.

"Don't get it wet," she said. She took his money and called in her next customer, a street-nun who called herself King.

King pointed to her incisors. "Bolts, shiny ones."

She sat back in the treatment chair and opened her mouth.

"Right you are." Charity took her pliers from the steamer and set to work. She'd had a steady stream of work all week: she'd tattooed eyelids, whipped out an infected appendix, set two broken bones (and that was just for one customer). She'd replaced a man's eye with one he'd stolen from a live tiger (or so he said), split tongues for identical twins, filed horns, glossed a possum's pelt and stuffed a dead rat for a woman who said she loved the creature more than a snifter of whisky on a cold night.

Those that make their way to Ninehearts decide their fate once the thick, oak door wheezes shut behind them. The shop's narrow entrance is dim, day and night, lit by candles that emit a meaty stench, greasing the throat and rumbling the belly. Along the walls, photos illuminate Charity's many achievements.

The floorboards creak and crack, muttering *customer, customer*, as footsteps tread down the hall. Some will choose to linger, examining the handiwork on offer, while others hurry past in a daze of wanting-not-wanting. Fast or slow, at the end of the hall each one ends up at the curtain of carved teeth that leads into her surgery.

The strings of teeth rattle as the curtain splits and falls.

For regulars, she will turn from her workbench and rub her hands on her leather apron before holding them both out to shake. They'll chat about this and that, trading the gossip of the town, perhaps a whisper or two of political intrigue, then it's straight to work.

But for the first-timer, Charity waits. She straightens her spine, ripples her muscles, ensures the nine of hearts card tattooed across her back—shoulder to shoulder and hip to hip—is exposed to best advantage.

Charity Ninehearts has no time for the curious, or nervous; for life's bystanders who want only to look and see. She listens for the intake of breath, the cough, the nervous rustle of palm against sweaty palm. She attunes her ears to the heartbeat. When she is sure the customer has come to the right place, Charity will turn.

• • •

"Welcome." Charity nodded at the young man standing in front of her.

His face was unmarked and beneath his loose-fitting trousers and long-sleeved shirt his body appeared lean, but well-proportioned. His skin was mostly concealed, but she perceived from his fidgeting—pushing a thick dreadlock behind his ear, picking at the fabric of his shirt—that it was thus far free of embellishments.

Not for long. She maintained her calm demeanour while inwardly shivering at the pleasure of such a fine, unmarked canvas. Her mind whirled with ideas, although she knew the boy had a singular desire: a procedure so dangerous and rare that in twenty years of practice she had performed it only once before.

She waited for him to speak.

Tobias, her ferret, pattered across the floor. He stood on his hind legs. Dark eyes fixed on the customer, he wriggled his whiskers and sniffed.

The customer adjusted the tin box he carried under his arm. He ran his finger inside his loose collar. "You have a pet." A hint of Celtic in his accent.

"I prefer to think of Tobias as my muse." She clicked her fingers and Tobias ran up onto the bench and jumped onto her bare shoulder. "Shirt and trousers off. I need to see what I've got to work with."

A blush stained the boy's cheeks and blotched his neck.

"This is not a place to be shy, as I'm sure you knew before you entered. You asked questions before you came here, didn't you . . . ?" She raised an eyebrow.

"Benjamin Baxter."

"Right, Benjamin Baxter." She gestured at his body with her fingers. "Time's wasting."

Benjamin placed the tin box on a clear space on the workbench. He unbuttoned his shirt, then dropped his trousers. He stood in the centre of the surgery while Charity walked around him, appraising tone and strength, calculating planes and angles, lengths and widths. With a job such as this, absolute precision was paramount, but Charity loved the mental challenge of assessing measurements before confirming them with instruments.

She tapped her fingertips against the back of his thighs. "Good veins. That's a bonus."

She squared her thumbs, hand to hand, and positioned them around the centre of his chest. Tobias shifted his head and followed the line of her gaze.

"Hmm," she stepped forward and back, peering through the gap in her hands like a telescope. Hesitation pricked the back of her neck.

"What is it?"

"Everything looks in order. Muscle tone, size, shape, all excellent. And you've got a good, thick barrel chest."

Benjamin's lips parted, then shut tight again. "I haven't told you yet what I'm here for." He tugged at the dreadlock behind his ear. "It is not a simple thing."

Charity smiled and tilted her head as she looked his body up and down once more. "I know what you're here for, Benjamin Baxter." She moved in closer and pressed her palm against his chest. "This is a matter of the heart, is it not?"

He blushed again. Pearls of sweat beaded his hairline. He flinched as Tobias' whiskers twitched, brushing the top of his ear.

"Tell me I'm wrong." Charity fixed her eyes on her customer's. She focused on the slow beat of her own heart and reminded herself that, in art and skill, she was incomparable.

"No." Benjamin's Adam's apple bobbed as he swallowed hard. "My heart is the matter." He gestured towards the tin box. "My heart, and my home."

"You have come to the right place." She stepped back, flexed her hands and cracked her knuckles. "Let's get to work."

• • •

Charity took pride in the cleanliness of her workspace. Despite the variety of embellishments she added and subtracted to her customers' bodies—animal, vegetable, mineral and unidentified—she sterilised and sharpened her implements obsessively, applying her perfectionist's eye to each and every operation—from a five-minute single-line tattoo to complex multi-matter surgery.

She did not like to think of the first (and only) death that had occurred under her scalpel. She had been inexperienced, too caught up in her own bravado to recognise her limitations. But the similarities between that procedure and the one she was about to perform on the unmarked body of young Benjamin summoned the memory, unbidden and unwanted. The deep red of spilled blood, the delicate blue of exposed veins, the honeyed hue of split wood: timber and flesh; leaf and skin; meaty and earthy scents mixed and potent.

Charity pushed the memory away. She soaped and scrubbed at the multi-patterned skin of her strong hands and ran through the procedure, detail by detail. She was older, wiser, many more years experienced. That error had not been one of skill, but hubris. She would check each tool, each element, twice more to be sure that this customer would leave Ninehearts with body and soul intact.

• • •

Tobias scuttled up and down his run behind the transparent sheeting that separated his viewing area from Charity's sterile workspace. She looked up at him, reassured by his round eyes peering down at her work. He steadied her like no other creature could, their minds synced by time, instinct and affection. Tobias blinked and settled on his haunches. She drew in a deep breath and checked one more time that all was in place: lights, instruments, transplant matter.

"Let's begin."

Benjamin did not answer. He had entered the dreamless world of the anaesthetised patient after ingesting Charity's own concoction of dormelle, valeritia and poppy-lime. Charity tuned into the rhythm of his chest as it rose and fell, rose and fell, with strong and steady breaths. She picked up her scalpel and cut straight down the line of his sternum.

The skin folded back, exposing the flesh falling away to the bone. She replaced the scalpel and picked up the small circular saw to open up the rib cage, humming as flecks of bone and blood spattered over her gloved hands. Charity loved this part of her work, the hard manual labour of rearranging skin and flesh, bone and organ into something other than it was before. Her muscles, tendons and sinew worked in unison with her brain; art and brawn in simpatico. She was drawn into the flow of her work—of timeless concentration. Charity prised apart Benjamin's ribs. Her hands prodded and pulled, moving with ease from the roughness of an abattoir worker to the gentle ministrations of a mother tending her newborn.

She lifted his pulsing heart from his chest cavity and held it in her hands for a moment, feeling the strength of life within its substance before placing it on his yellow-swabbed skin. The still-attached veins throbbed with blood, and for a moment her mind's easy flow stuttered, and the heart was a foreign thing.

I might kill him, she thought. *Whether I do something, or nothing, right now, he may die.*

A shadow caught her eye. She looked up to Tobias. The pink pads of his front paws rested on the sheet between them. His whiskers twitched, and his warm brown eyes fixed onto hers with a steady gaze. Charity breathed out. She loosened her shoulders and got back to work.

With nimble hands, she flipped open the sterile steambox beside her and lifted out the miniature oak. This small, sturdy tree—which Benjamin had carried across seas and deserts, mountains and forests, from his homeland to her door—was a mere hand-span tall, from its ancient curled roots to its perfectly formed, green-leafed canopy. Although she had memorised them, Charity read through the calculations posted on her worksheet once more. Then she plunged into the flow and trusted her fingers and hands to make the connections.

Central root to superior vena cava.

Subsidiary roots to brachiocephalic trunk, left common carotid artery and left subclavian artery.

Smallest roots to right and left pulmonary arteries and veins.

Charity moulded and massaged vegetable and flesh, blood and sap. She weaved and stitched, picking out threads of human and tree, using scalpel and fine needle to knit the two, until the roots of the oak and the veins and arteries of the heart beat as one. When she was satisfied this was done, she took the length of the root-vein that hours before had only been the superior vena cava. She manipulated its exit and entry, and manoeuvred it beneath and above Benjamin's rib cage and through the crystal box that would hold his oak-heart, exposed on his chest.

Benjamin's flesh was cool under her hands as Charity moved the crystal box into its final place. She shifted her gaze from the crystal-encased oak-heart beating on her patient's chest up to his young face, at the five o'clock shadow pushing through the fine grain of his skin. She wondered if in time the shoots of hair would be replaced by fine tree roots as his oak-heart took hold.

Charity did not know herself what he would become. But that was part of her talent, to let her creations unfold in their own time, and in their own way.

Her patient's eyes fluttered under closed lids. She checked her work again, repeating her mantra: *Accurate, Safe, Complete.*

Each vein tied off. Each stitch in place. Every tiny element, perfect.

Charity stepped back and smiled up at Tobias. "That's a bloody good job done."

Behind his viewing pane, Tobias spread his thin ferret lips and smiled back.

• • •

It was not Charity's habit to wave her customers goodbye. But she was especially proud of her work this time, and allowed herself the small indulgence of seeing the thinly veiled shock on the faces thronging Battlecamp Road as he made his first public appearance.

She stood behind him as he stepped out onto the street, and the midday sun's rays glanced off the crystal box on Benjamin's chest. The tree nestled in the plump muscle of his beating heart, the superior vena cava reaching up through the roots melded into the trunk and twisting out the top of the canopy and back into his chest cavity. In the light of day the red of his heart deepened against the honey-coloured trunk. The leaves, tiny and perfect, glistened on delicate branches reaching out from the oak's sturdy trunk. Veins and roots, heart and tree. Each flowed in and out of each other, inextricably entwined. No one stopped to stare, that was not the way of Cavalry Junction. But hooded eyes widened, glances lingered and second looks became third and fourth.

The glittering crystal box that framed his oak-heart had fused to the bare skin of his chest with the specially grown cells Charity had nurtured in the hope they would one day be used for such a purpose.

Benjamin turned to Charity Ninehearts, and gave a low bow, his oak-heart moving as one with his body.

"Thank you," he said, "for your skill and care."

"All in a day's work." Charity grinned. She flicked her hand towards Battlecamp Road's foot traffic that slowed in an almost imperceptible semicircle around Ninehearts' narrow entrance. "Now be off with you."

She reached up and patted Tobias' furry head, and watched Benjamin Baxter take his oak-heart out into the messy world.

Then she pulled off her work apron, shut the door behind her and headed down to The Roundhouse for a well-earned drink.

~

OH HAVE YOU SEEN THE DEVIL?

STEPHEN DEDMAN

"I reckon he's dead," said Kate, cheerfully.

The journalist managed not to wince, but he stared into his glass to hide his sour expression and wondered whether he should risk drawing attention to himself by contradicting her. Fortunately, Michael broke the silence by asking, "How would we know? Nobody knows who he is. Or was, if he *is* dead."

"Well, the jacks ain't caught him, that's one thing certain," said Bill. "They couldn't track a bleedin' elephant through a snowdrift, much less through all this bloody fog."

There was a murmuring of assent at this; September had been unusually foggy, even by the standards of the East End, and the police were not much loved by the clientele of the Ten Bells.

"Maybe *he's* a jack," suggested Esme.

"A Jack Tar, more like," said Jenny. "That's why he's been quiet. His ship's bin out to sea, but next time it's in port . . . " She drew a finger across her throat.

"I reckon he's a Jew, like that Lipski," said Maggie. "No Christian would—"

The door opened to admit another shabbily dressed woman and the sound of the church bells, and Michael shook his head as she weaved towards the bar. "Right-o," said the landlord. "Those of you's got homes to go to, go there. The rest of you, clear out anyway."

"One drink, Johnny?" the new arrival mumbled. Her Swedish accent, slightly marred by her missing teeth, was thick enough to tell Michael that if she wasn't quite drunk, she was well within spitting distance of it.

"You got any push?"

She looked around, then pointed at Michael. "He'll pay."

"Hell I will," said Michael, shooting her a look as poisonous as the cheap gin. "Sounds like you've had enough already, Liz—more'n enough. You comin' with me?"

"You can't send us out in that," Esme whined. "'E might be out there, waiting for one of us."

The landlord snorted, and the man they called Mr Memory shook his head. "He's never done it on a Monday night. Only Friday or Saturday. Nor when it was foggy, neither."

"Don't mean he won't," said Jenny, uncertainly. Mr Memory eked out a living as a sideshow freak at Tom Norman's penny gaff show with his ability to memorize and reel back long strings of numbers or other words—a popular joke at the Ten Bells was that he drank to forget—but his tendency to see patterns everywhere meant that he was less reliable as a prophet.

The crowd stared at him for a moment, until Michael asked, with mock politeness, "You know when he'll do it again, then?"

"A Friday or Saturday, or maybe Sunday; Friday, Saturday, Sunday, it's a pattern. And it'll probably be the end of the month, like it was when he killed Polly Nicholls. It'll be this weekend, if it's not foggy."

Everyone stared, a few of the women gasped, the journalist made a note on his cuff, and Bill nearly choked on his gin. As far as anyone could tell, Mr Memory utterly lacked a sense of humour and had never told a joke, drunk or sober. Michael was the first to ask the question on everyone's mind. "D'you know who he is, then?"

Mr Memory blinked. "No. Do you?"

This started most of the drinkers in the pub laughing. "I wish I did," said Michael. "I could do with a hundred quid." He glared at his common-law wife again, then emptied his glass and walked towards the door.

"Couldn't we all," said the landlord. "Righto, everybody, you heard the bloody bells, so clear out."

Sluggishly, the drinkers obeyed. "'We have heard the chimes at midnight, Master Shallow'," Mr Memory muttered as he disappeared into the fog. The journalist sighed, and headed home.

• • •

Michael rolled over in his bed and glared at the snoring woman next to him. He'd known she'd been a whore when he'd let her move in, and had never held that against her, but far too often she'd disappeared with whatever money was in their rooms, and sometimes anything she could carry easily that she could pawn or sell, staying drunk until all the money was gone. Not that he was a saint in that regard, either—he'd done three days for being drunk and disorderly back in July—but sometimes she didn't leave him enough to pay the rent, or took something he'd managed to steal from the docks. She always came back—she seemed to like him better than any other man, at least while she was reasonably sober, though less than she liked gin or rum—but he was fairly sure she'd added injury to insult by giving him the pox after one of these jaunts, too.

He turned his back on her, and before falling asleep, made a mental note to lock her in and to take all his money with him when he left, as well as his best hat and coat, his new razor, and his clasp knife.

• • •

The editor looked up as the journalist walked in, and grunted, "Mornin', Bulling. Any luck?"

Thomas Bulling, still more than slightly hungover, shook his head. "No new evidence at the inquest. Nothing from my friends at the Yard. I talked to Le Queux, and he said he hasn't heard a bloody thing either, nor have Springfield or Hands; they're even starting to run out of theories that're worth printing. And I went 'round the pubs in Whitechapel and Spitalfields, like you asked, and folks are saying Leather Apron's dead—either that, or he's skipped town, probably on some cattle boat, or been locked up in Colney Hatch. It's been two weeks, two weekends, and nobody's found a clue, much less a body."

"Not in Whitechapel, leastways. Some woman's been killed and ripped up, near Gateshead; they've sent Dr Phillips up there to look at the body, just in case. Maybe he *has* moved on."

"Want me to go up there?"

"No, go back to the inquest. Did they say anything about the doctor who was paying for quims or whatever?"

Bulling shrugged. "They don't think he's the killer, just the boy who buys the beef, but the killer might be working for him. But since nobody knows his name or where he lives, just that he's American, that's not a lot of good. But I've got an idea that might help . . . "

"If it involves killing some poor whore, I don't want to know about it."

"Nothing so crude. What if we published a letter from this Whitechapel Murderer?"

"How do you propose—" The editor blinked, then grinned. "Have you got it?"

"Not yet, but give me a minute . . . and some red ink . . . "

The editor handed him an old Waverley pen. "It'll help sell some papers, anyway. And who knows, maybe it'll inspire the *real* killer to write a letter that gives the bobbies a clue."

"Good point."

"And see if you can come up with a better name than 'Leather Apron' or 'Whitechapel Murderer' while you're at it."

"Already done," said Bulling. "What do you think of 'Jack the Ripper'?"

• • •

Michael returned home from the docks to find Liz gone and the padlock he'd put on the door tossed onto the sagging straw-filled mattress. The cow must have had a key, he thought sourly, as he searched the squalid little room to see what she'd taken with her. While all of her clothes were gone, at least she hadn't stolen his other coat . . . not that a pawnshop would give her much for that. Even if she'd saved some money of her own from sewing or cleaning or from begging from her church, it probably wasn't enough to stay drunk on for more than a week—two at the outside, and she'd be back. She'd always come back before.

• • •

The Chief Constable looked at the facsimile, and snorted. "'I keep on hearing the police have caught me but they wont fix me just yet.' No wonder Bulling says he treated it as a joke. He's probably laughing fit to burst."

"Shall I file it with the other one, sir?" asked his clerk.

"No, send it to Abberline, just in case. All the newspapers will have it by now, and they'll probably print it, and if this lunatic *does* strike again, they'll ask why we ignored it." He looked at the accompanying note again. "Tell Abberline that it's bound to be a fake, not that he won't work that out himself."

"How do we know?"

"*If* the real murderer decided to write a letter, which I very much doubt, he might send it to us, or he might send it to a newspaper, but he wouldn't send it to the Central News Agency. Only a journalist would think to do that. Bulling most likely wrote it himself—no, *don't* write that down: we've no proof. Is Dr Phillips back from Gateshead yet?"

• • •

"Michael! Michael Kidney!"

Michael spun around, not quite overbalancing. The fog had lifted, but it had started raining heavily and water was dripping from the brim of his hat, so it took him a moment to recognize the driver of the laden cart as Bill, another regular at the Ten Bells. He waved, and was about to continue on his way to the pub when Bill called, "You still looking for your missus?"

He hadn't been, but it occurred to him that it would be reassuring to know where she was. "Have you seen her?"

"I think so. It looked like her, anyroad. D'you know the Queen's Head, on Commercial Street?"

"Yeah." He knew most of the pubs in and around Whitechapel, but that one was memorable because Liz had been arrested there for drunk and disorderly a few months before.

"She was just leaving, with another woman. Heading north. I waved at 'em, but I had a load to deliver so I couldn't stop."

"When was this?"

"I dunno. Ten minutes ago, maybe. Likely she won't be far away."

• • •

"'Ere! Gummy Amy! That's Leather Apron gettin' 'round you!"

Liz stopped kissing the well-dressed man she'd met in the Bricklayer's Arms, just long enough to look around and notice two labourers standing on the footpath nearby, clearly intent on seeking refuge from the heavy rain inside the relative warmth of the alehouse. She stuck her tongue out at them, showing the gums that had earned her one of her nicknames, but pulled her escort out of the doorway far enough to let the two men squeeze past. The man she'd been kissing raised his sandy eyebrows at the accusation, but he looked more amused than outraged; he glanced across the street, and with a faintly murmured, "Shall we?", led her across the road towards Berner Street.

Forty minutes later, another workman saw her in the doorway to number 63, kissing a sailor in a black cutaway coat, and heard the sailor comment, "You would say anything but your prayers."

Shortly after half past twelve, she was seen outside the International Working Man's Educational Club with yet another man—first by Police Constable William Smith, and then by Michael Kidney, who ran towards her with an expression of such utter fury that Liz's prospective client quickly retreated along the street. Liz spun around to face her lover, who grabbed her by the shoulders and snapped, "You're coming home now."

"No," she replied. "Not tonight; some other time."

She tried to wriggle out of his grasp, and staggered backwards through the gateway into Dutfield Yard, screaming softly as she fell onto the slippery cobblestones. Michael glanced back into the street, and saw a Jewish-looking man watching him; he yelled, "Lipski!", and the man fled, not slowing until he'd reached the shelter of the nearby railway arch. Another man, emerging from the Bricklayer's Arms, also took fright and headed in the same direction. Michael smiled, and strode towards Liz, who scrambled back into the shadowy yard.

"You don't get to tell me what to do," she said. "I got more'n 'nough for the doss house, still, and I'll come back when I want, if I want. I met a man tonight, a real swell; he said my mouth was bang up to the elephant, best thing he'd ever stuck his pogo in. He gave me a whole shilling and bought me gin and a rose too and—"

"What d'you want fuckin' flowers for? Fuckin' flowers is for fuckin' funerals." He reached for her wet tangled hair with his left hand and tried to pull her to her feet. She struggled until she'd slipped out of his grasp, then turned away from him and tried to pick herself up off the cobblestones. He grabbed at her again in the near-darkness, grasping the check silk scarf tied around her neck and twisting it. Liz clawed at the makeshift garrote, gasping as it began to choke her, but Michael was too drunk and too angry to notice. She fumbled in her pocket, hoping for something she could use as a weapon, but found nothing more dangerous than a comb, a pencil stub, or a spoon. Her fist closed around a small bag of cachous as she blacked out for the last time.

Michael continued to tighten the noose for nearly a minute after she'd stopped moving, before the realization of just what he'd done slowly cut through the alcoholic fog in his skull. He let her fall, then turned the body over and stared at her. He slapped her face twice, hoping for a reaction, some sign of life, then tried to think.

Mr Memory had said that the Whitechapel murderer would strike again that weekend, end of the month, if it wasn't too foggy. Well, here it was Saturday night, maybe even Sunday morning, raining too heavily for fog, and Michael hadn't heard of any other attacks yet—and that was the sort of news that travelled fast. So, if he could make this look like Leather Apron's work, maybe the jacks would blame the murderer instead of him.

Michael blinked, remembering that he still had his clasp knife in his pocket, then drew a deep breath, knelt by Liz's head, and tried to remember what he'd heard about the murders of Polly Nicholls and Annie Chapman. He knew that their throats had been cut, and that Dark Annie had also been butchered, but he couldn't recall any of the details of her mutilations. He opened his knife and hacked at her throat, trying not to weep, then froze at the sound of a horse and cart approaching. He hastily backed into a corner away from the passageway into the yard, glad that his clothes were mostly black enough to blend in with the soot-caked walls in the near-darkness, black enough to conceal the bloodstains on his sleeves. He waited silently, and bit his lip as he heard the horse shy.

The carter probed the darkness with his buggy-whip, crying something in a foreign language as the tip of the shaft poked Liz's lifeless body. Michael held his breath as the man grunted something in a foreign language, then climbed down from the cart. Michael raised his knife in case the man came any closer, then nearly sighed aloud with relief when, after a moment peering into the darkness, the man turned on his heel and walked towards the door of the International Working Man's Educational Club. Michael dropped his knife into his pocket and hastily slipped out of the yard, heading south and turning the corner into Fairclough Street before slowing his pace to something approximating normal.

• • •

Inspector Abberline glared across the mortuary table at Dr Phillips, and repeated the question. "Do you really think we have *two* lunatics running around ripping up women in Whitechapel?"

George Bagster Phillips refrained from pointing out that Catherine Eddowes, the night's second victim, had actually been murdered in the City of London, not in Whitechapel: he knew that Abberline was well aware of that, and was fuming because this placed it in the jurisdiction of the City Police, not the Met. This had enabled the commissioner, Sir Charles Warren, to personally destroy what might have been a vital clue, some graffiti found near a public handbasin where the murderer had left part of Eddowes's apron. "It's possible, but that's not what I said," Phillips replied patiently. "There are similarities, but there are also differences. This woman, Elizabeth Stride, was also drunk and believed to be a prostitute, as were the other victims, and died either from strangulation or from having her throat cut, either of which would have silenced her. But she wasn't mutilated like Eddowes or Chapman—"

"The killer may have been interrupted," Abberline interjected. "The man who found her, Diemschutz, said her body was still warm. Nicholls wasn't mutilated, either, and neither was Tabram."

"It's certainly possible that he was interrupted. I don't know whether whoever stabbed Martha Tabram also slashed the others—the attacks do seem to be getting worse—but I don't think it likely."

"I disagree."

Phillips shrugged. "All I can say for sure is that Annie Chapman was killed and mutilated with a blade that was at least six inches long, narrow, and very sharp; Nicholls and Eddowes were killed with the same knife, or at least one very similar. Tabram was stabbed with something larger, possibly a sword-bayonet, as well as something as small as a pen-knife. And Stride's throat was cut with a blade that was rather blunt, probably less than six inches long but an inch wide, with a rounded or bevelled tip. That could have been done by anyone, with or without any anatomical knowledge, in just a few seconds. So if it *was* the same killer, he acquired a much more suitable knife sometime in the forty-five minutes between the two attacks."

Abberline looked sour. "The papers are already calling it a double event, and calling Stride the fifth victim, counting Tabram and Emma Smith. And we received a postcard from 'Jack the Ripper' yesterday, taking credit for both; it'll be in the papers tomorrow, along with the letter we received the day *before* the murders."

"Do you think either is from the killer?"

"More likely they're both from a journalist who doesn't know any more about the killer than we do. Of course, everyone has a theory. Stride's common-law husband, Kidney, came into Leman Street yesterday, full up to the knocker, saying that he could catch the killer if he was in charge of the case, but when they questioned him, he couldn't actually tell them a damn thing." He stared at the body on the table. "Why does he do it? I could almost understand if he was an ordinary sadist, but all of the women were already dead when he mutilated them, weren't they?"

"Apart from the cut throats—maybe—yes, I'm sure they were."

"So why does someone cut up women's bodies that are already dead? Present company excepted, of course," he added hastily.

Dr Phillips was silent for a moment. "Maybe it's not about pain. He doesn't hide the bodies, he knows they'll be found; maybe it's about the way they're displayed. Maybe it's all about fear. Maybe he just wants people to be afraid."

• • •

Three weeks later, Michael was back in the Ten Bells doing his best to drown his sorrows, when he thought he heard his name. He looked up, and saw that the landlord was reading from a newspaper. "What was that?" he asked, as clearly as he could.

"The Ripper sent Mr Lusk, the cove from the Vigilance Committee, a letter and half a kidney," the landlord repeated. "He said he'd taken it from his last victim, and ate the other half."

"Catherine Eddowes," said Thomas Bulling, reclaiming his paper. "The Ripper *did* take one of her kidneys." Mr Memory nodded his agreement.

"Bloody hell," said Esme. "What sort of nutter takes a bloody kidney as a keepsake?"

"Maybe he was signing his work," said Bill, who was sitting opposite Michael. "Maybe Kidney's his name."

Michael, white-faced, tried to lurch to his feet, then held onto the table to steady himself. "You saying I'm the Ripper?"

Bill held up his hands in a placatory gesture. "Nobody's saying that. You can't be the only bloody Kidney in London."

"They usually travel in pairs," said Bulling.

There were some subdued chuckles at this, but most of the pub's clients, atypically silent, waited to see whether a fight was about to erupt. Michael stared at the carter, then sat down again. "I spoke to the jacks. They know it wasn't me."

"I know," said Bill. "It was just a joke."

"Not very bloody funny."

"A bad joke," Bill conceded. "I know you're not the Ripper. I know."

Michael grunted, and looked Bill in the face, still wanting to erase that faint smile with one good punch . . . and then, in what was either a flash of drunken delusion or horrible sudden clarity, he realised *how* Bill knew.

I know it wasn't you, the smile seemed to be saying, but I also know that you killed Long Liz. That's why I took the other whore's kidney—I thought it would lead the jacks to you, but they're too bloody stupid to pick up a clue, even one as obvious as that. But whether they think you did the others or not, you can't prove I had anything to do with it and they can still hang you for Long Liz, so I wouldn't go talking to the jacks again or trying to claim any rewards if I was you.

Michael stared helplessly as Bill finished his beer and walked out of the pub. The Ripper stopped briefly to exchange a few words with the once-pretty redhead standing outside, then vanished into the thick October fog.

~

IN SHEEP'S CLOTHING

KIMBERLEY GAAL

The unrelenting sun baked any remaining moisture out of the hot sand and turned the dull, camel-coloured bricks of the arena a slightly lighter but no less dull shade of camel. Huge sets of double-doors punctured the arena's sides at regular intervals. Once they might have been bright burnished red, but a few centuries of sandstorms had faded the paint until they looked like old, crusty scabs.

Lutlow sat beside the arena in front of one of the doors. He traced his finger around the edge of his protractor, making an arc in the sand, then flipped the disc over and did it again to complete the circle. He added eyes, nose and a mouth, and thick, caterpillar eyebrows that joined in the middle the way Trump Truckle's eyebrows did. He opened his leather pouch, pulled out a pencil with a good, sharp point, and stabbed sand-Trump right in the middle of his forehead.

"Who's the wimp now, Trump?" he whispered. "Who's the baby, playing with his toys? They're not toys, they're tools. For drawing and measuring and poking you. Right. In. The. Eye."

He got a bit loud there at the end. From two doors to the left, Trump's sister, Teeter, glanced in Lutlow's direction. Lutlow looked away quickly. Teeter wasn't as bad as Trump—the way a stomach ache wasn't as bad as explosive diarrhoea—but she reported everything she saw back to her brother, especially if there was the possibility it could be used to torment someone. The days between battles were long and boring for people like the Truckles, and they found their fun where they could.

Lutlow tried to look as un-fun as possible. It wasn't hard. He was pretty boring, even as bully-victims went. He rarely ventured far away from the watchful eye of the adults, and when he did he was too cautious to be caught. The Truckles wouldn't have bothered with him at all if it wasn't for Blarnsley.

Stupid Blarnsley. Lutlow smoothed over his demolished sand drawing and looked over at his Spirit Beast, standing in the meagre shade of a skinny staccia tree. He had his long face turned towards the sun and was blinking slowly in the harsh light. Dumb sheep. "At least close your eyes, you doorknob!" called Lutlow.

Blarnsley turned his head in Lutlow's direction and gazed at him sleepily while a rain of pellets fell from his other end. Finished, he went back to staring at the sun.

All around the arena, other Spirit Beasts screeched and roared as they waited for the doors to open. Lutlow could only see two of them from where he was sitting—a snarling tiger to his right and to the left, Teeter's cobra, as wide around as a tree trunk with a hood so vast you could use it as an umbrella. It hissed angrily as it curled and looped back on itself, feeding off Teeter's impatience. Only seven of the village's twenty Beast Warriors were chosen for each battle. Thirteen children were left out of every fight—twelve if you didn't count Lutlow. Which no one really did.

Lutlow ignored the noise, including the muffled hum of the spectators waiting inside the arena, and focused on his true passion: geometry. His protractor shone in his hand as he lined its base up with the building in front of him. The arena had been built in the shape of a four-sided pyramid. He'd already calculated its surface area, its volume, the number of blocks it took to build it—everything there was to calculate. It helped pass the time while he waited for the fights to finish and the victor to be carried out on the shoulders of the cheering crowd. Then he could get back to his father's studio in the architects' guild, and all the exciting maths.

In the wall in front of him, the doors started to move.

Lutlow stared at them, panicked. What was happening? Was the building falling down? It was more than a thousand years old—maybe the walls were finally giving out. How much did two hundred and nineteen thousand three hundred and fourteen bricks weigh? Why hadn't he worked that out yet?

The doors swung inwards. The roar of the crowd grew louder. They were waiting for him.

He'd been called.

Lutlow scrambled to his feet. Sand had filled the cuffs of his pants and his underwear was wedged between his butt cheeks, but he could worry about that later, when he'd finished running away.

He turned to bolt and was met by Blarnsley's fluffy face. "What are you doing?" he said. "Get out of the way!" Blarnsley lowered his head and bleated, then pushed forward into Lutlow's chest, steering him backwards towards the door. "No, Blarnsley. You don't understand. We can't fight. You're a sheep. I'm an architect. Not even a real architect, a trainee architect. We're not fighters. We're not . . . "

Blarnsley wasn't listening. Driven by an instinct that ran deep inside every Spirit Beast, he continued to push his Warrior backwards, step by step, towards possible glory but much more likely defeat and humiliation. Whenever Lutlow tried to go around he was met with a soft but persistent butting.

"Blarnsley, listen to me. We have no idea what we're doing." But it was too late. With a final push Blarnsley knocked Lutlow through the large doors into the short, torchlit hallway beyond. Lutlow turned with a gulp and staggered the final few steps into the arena.

The hallway opened up to an enormous pit. Fine sand, softer and whiter than the hard grit of the desert outside, covered the floor. Massive stone pillars reared up all around it, supporting the roof which arced high above. The pit was ringed by a tall barricade, carved with images of valiant fights between Beasts of epic size and strength and all manner of terrifyingness. In all the confusion it was hard to be certain, but Lutlow was pretty sure there weren't any sheep.

Beyond the barricades, tiers of stone benches rose up all the way up to the ceiling. Back when the arena was first built, when Lutlow's people were little more than savages, every tier would have been full. Granted, a lot of those people would have been slaves—the same slaves that built the arena, under the watchful eyes of the handful of people powerful enough to own them and bored enough to think that fighting Spirit Beasts would make for quality entertainment—but the effect would have been very dramatic. Now there were less than a hundred spectators, mostly rich old men with nothing better to do. They cheered just as loudly as the barbarians of old, although the cheering got a little confused when Lutlow and Blarnsley entered the arena.

Surrounded by ancient arena magic, Blarnsley puffed up to his full size. Lutlow had never seen it before, and had to admit he was slightly impressed. That feeling died with a splutter when Truman Truckle, Trump and Teeter's older brother, stepped through the doors directly opposite Lutlow, followed by his Spirit Beast. The elephant was so large its head brushed the top of the entranceway, and it was still growing under the arena's power. It trumpeted, a heavy, earth-shaking sound which fired the crowd and nearly made Lutlow's knees buckle. Then Trump entered and Lutlow's knees really did buckle as his lion shook its mane and roared, baring teeth as long as a trainee architect's forearm.

Somewhere far beneath his growing mountain of panic, Lutlow was aware of Teeter Truckle sliding through her door with her cobra, along with three other children he knew only by the understanding that they were Cool Kids, and he was Not. In theory, any child chosen as a Warrior for a Spirit Beast was Cool. In practice, one of them was Lutlow. Which was why it had to have been a mistake for any Spirit Beast, even one as pathetic as Blarnsley, to choose him. Lutlow knew it. The other kids knew it. Even Lutlow's own father . . .

Lutlow had been in bed when it happened. He'd been multiplying numbers by square roots of themselves and had almost nodded off when a weird, tingling sensation started in his feet. He'd always had bad circulation and had wriggled his toes a bit, hoping it would go away. Instead it intensified, from a faint twinge to a buzzy, trembly, shiver-down-his-spine kind of feeling, only this one went up his spine, along his arms and out to his fingertips. His hands snapped together of their own volition, forming a cup. He barely had time to shout when a bright ball of silver light flared between his palms.

When his father threw open the door a second later, Lutlow was holding a tiny Blarnsley, barely the size of a large eraser, in his trembling hands. His father hadn't grabbed his spectacles before he ran in, and he blinked blindly down at his son.

"What'cha got there, Lutlow?"

"I . . . I think it's a sheep, Dad."

"Oh?" said his father. "Oh! You don't mean . . . not a spirit *sheep. That's not a real thing, is it? Maybe . . . maybe you're*

dreaming. Or I'm dreaming. Maybe we're both dreaming, because surely . . . surely not you, *son.*"

The contestants had all been chosen. Above each of the doors they had entered through sat the people that had chosen them. Fat old men with pretty young wives, each one surrounded by his closest friends, who were all fattish and oldish and in various stages of acquiring pretty young wives themselves.

Lutlow craned his neck to see who had been foolish enough to choose him. He bet it was half-uncle Blerrel. Blerrel was an idiot even when he was sober, and he was almost never sober.

On the dais above Lutlow's door sat a man he'd never seen before. He was old, yes, but thin as a wheat stalk, with skin as brown and leathery as a boot. A young girl with the same brown skin, only much less leathery, sat beside him.

"Who is . . . ?" Lutlow never got to finish his question to no-one. A huge bronze gong was rung by a huge bronze gong-ringer and the match began.

The Truckles shouted commands to their Spirit Beasts. Elephant, cobra and lion surged into the ring in well-practised coordination. Lutlow had heard about this, in those instances when he first met people and they mistakenly thought that, like other boys his age, he was interested in the Beast battles. The Truckles always worked together to pick off the others before turning on each other at the end. Trump usually emerged victorious, though sometimes Teeter beat him. Despite his age and the size of his Beast, Truman never won.

Together the three Truckle-Beasts charged towards the most dangerous looking opponent, a bear belonging to a short, brown haired girl with freckles and a lisp.

"Thathafrath, attack!" screamed the girl. The bear reared up, its arena-grown height nearly double that of the lion. But even though the Truckles were about as bright as a handful of wet tissues, they were smart enough to send the elephant in first. It bulldozed the bear, knocking him down. The cobra wrapped its long coils around it, pinning its limbs to its side as the lion, moving with grace bordering on nonchalance, leaped lightly onto the bear's chest and gave it a powerful swipe with a wine-barrel-sized paw. The bear went limp and then disappeared in a ball of silver light.

The light zipped around the arena, pinging off walls and pillars before landing in the lisping girl's outstretched hand.

The girl sighed. "It'th alright, Thathafrath. You tried."

The other two competitors—a crocodile and a buffalo—were locked in fierce combat on the other side of the ring. For a second it looked like the Truckles were going to head towards them. Lutlow felt a brief flash of hope that he and Blarnsley could sneak out through one of the open doors. There was nothing wrong with a good, honourable forfeit.

Then, as one, all three Truckles turned towards him, and all three Truckle-Beasts turned towards Blarnsley. Lutlow would have wet himself if fear hadn't already sucked his entire body dry, but Blarnsley just bleated in a disinterested sort of way and shot out a fresh stream of pellets. Whatever instinct had driven him to force his Warrior into the arena seemed to have been sated the moment he crossed the threshold, and he was back to his usual, vacant self.

"Well, well, well, what do we have here?" said Teeter.

"It looks like little Lutlow and his night-night sheep," said Trump. "But that can't be right, can it?"

Lutlow raised his hands. "Really, I'm as surprised as you. We'll just be on our way . . . "

Trump shook his head, caterpillar eyebrows drawing together as he smiled in a deeply unpleasant way. "Where's the fun in that?" He raised his hand. His brother and sister did the same. Their Spirit Beast gathered close, ready to charge.

Lutlow tried to speak through a mouth as thick and dry as an old rug. "Blarnsley . . . attack?"

Blarnsley cocked his head at Lutlow, then turned and shuffled slowly towards Truman's elephant. It was less of a head-butt than a failure to stop walking in time to avoid collision, the sort of thing you might apologise for with a chuckle and a reference to a mind being a million miles away. Blarnsley hit the elephant's leg with all the force of a poorly-thrown towel, then stood, resting his woolly head against his enemy's knee, and farted noisily.

"Oh, dang," said Lutlow.

Trump snorted so loudly drops flew out his nose. "That the best you got?"

Lutlow didn't reply. The answer seemed pretty obvious.

"Finish him off, Truman," shouted Trump.

"O'right." Truman slouched forward, his shoulders drawn up towards his ears in his customary hunch. He was head and shoulders taller than Trump, with thick arms and legs joined together by a broad, solid middle. He nodded at his elephant. "G'on then," he said. Under his breath he added, "But gently."

The elephant raised its trunk. It paused for a second, as if to see which direction Blarnsley was going to dodge in. Then, seeing he was not going to dodge in any direction, it brought its trunk down and gave the sheep two sharp taps on the head.

Blarnsley swayed for a bit, listing dangerously to the left before swinging inconceivably back to the right again. Finally, like continents drifting apart, all four of his bony legs slid out from under him and he landed on his belly with a soft thump. He had time for one last fart before his body began to glow and shrink, the silver light shooting into Lutlow's reluctant hand with a sound like air rushing out of a balloon.

• • •

As soon as the dishevelled form of Blarnsley in miniature materialised in Lutlow's palm, he left the arena to wait outside with the other children who hadn't been chosen. Well, not really with them. The only thing less Cool than a maths nerd with a lame Spirit Beast who never got chosen for matches was a maths nerd with a lame Spirit Beast who got chosen for a match and didn't even know how to fight.

It wasn't fair, thought Lutlow. Fighters relied on their Spirit Beast's natural abilities. What natural abilities did sheep have? They were excellent at flocking, but that only worked when they were around other sheep and it wasn't really an offensive move to begin with. Cousin Merkle had been kicked in the groin by a sheep once, but only by accident, while he was trying to free its head from a bucket it had gotten stuck in. Merkle was a shepherd, and had been Lutlow's first and only point of call on that crazy Tuesday morning, when he hadn't had enough for breakfast and was feeling moody and irrational, and he'd considered for just a heartbeat that he and Blarnsley might actually have a go at becoming Warriors. Merkle had rolled about with laughter, paused long enough to tell the groin-kicking story, then laughed some more. Sheep, he said, did not fight. They got eaten. It was their one job in life, and they did it remarkably well.

An hour later, Teeter Trump was carried out triumphantly on the shoulders of those spectators not yet too old or too fat to carry a thirteen year old girl. Her brothers followed. Trump looked peeved. He hated to lose, even to other Truckles.

Lutlow made himself look very small and uninteresting as they passed. Trump ignored him, but Truman stopped and gave him a funny sort of smile which almost looked like encouragement but Lutlow thought was probably just mocking without much investment. Before he could stop, Lutlow heard himself say, "What are you staring at?"

The moment the words were out of his mouth the urge to wet himself returned with a vengeance. What was the matter with him? Truman's fist was the size of Lutlow's head, and while he had never actually administered any of the Truckle beatings, Lutlow thought that had less to do with his goodwill than the fact that his enormous size made him easy to spot while he was still far enough away to run from. Lutlow prepared for a record-breaking climb up the staccia tree, knowing that its skinny branches would probably break under his weight but that the fall would hurt less than being pummelled by Truman Truckle.

The expected pummelling didn't come. Instead, Truman drew his shoulders even closer to his ears and said, "You might get better."

Lutlow looked up, surprised. "You really think so?"

Truman thought for a second then shook his head. "Nah. Prob'ly not."

"Oh." Lutlow's gaze fell to his feet, so he didn't see the hand coming. When it landed on his shoulder his feet sunk a finger-length into the sand.

"But at least it doesn't last forever. We all get out of it eventually."

Truman gave Lutlow a few more friendly pats which left him feeling permanently slanted to one side and left after the others. The crowd disappeared in a cloud of sandy dust, on their way to the town's largest, most prestigious tavern—which was also the smallest and least prestigious, it being a very small town full of light-to-moderate drinkers. The unchosen children trailed after them, grumbling about the Truckles.

Lutlow waited until they had all gone before starting down the path himself. It was only then he realised he was not alone.

The strange old man and the young girl were standing nearby. Lutlow scowled at them. "Get your money's worth, did you? Have a good old laugh?"

The old man didn't answer, but the girl scowled back. "That's pretty rude, don't you think?"

She was pretty, in a plainish sort of way, with eyes that flashed when she got angry. Lutlow felt his scowl start to slip and fastened it on more firmly. "I didn't just force you into a life-or-death struggle and then come outside and stare at you."

The girl scoffed. "It was hardly life-or-death. Your animals barely touched each other."

"Oh yeah?" Lutlow dug his hand into his pocket and plucked out a small ball of whitey-grey fuzz. "Does he look barely touched to you?"

The girl took a few steps closer and peered into Lutlow's hand. "Is he asleep?"

"What? No, he's . . . " Lutlow glanced down. Blarnsley was curled up in his palm, tiny head resting on his flanks. He could hear a very faint, almost undetectable snoring. Angrily, he shoved the dozy animal back into his pocket. "Yeah, well you didn't see him before."

The old man said something in a language Lutlow didn't understand. The girl grew serious. "Master Pol says to tell you they can't really be hurt in the arena," she said. "The magic protects them, so they can train."

It was Lutlow's turn to scoff. "Train for what? You don't think they're still being used to fight wars, do you?"

The old man spoke again, and the girl translated. "Most aren't, no. With all the guns and bombs, there's not much use for Spirit Beasts anymore. Most of them just leave when their Warriors get too old to hold onto them. But some still get chosen, to serve a higher purpose. That's why we're here. To look for champions."

"Then you picked the wrong person," said Lutlow. "The only champions here are the Truckles. They win every match."

The girl smiled. Lutlow's heart did a painful flippy thing. "He didn't say winners. He said champions."

Lutlow felt himself getting drawn into the girl's smile and wanting to smile back. He pushed the feeling away. "There are no champions here. Just winners like the Truckles, and losers like me and my sheep."

The old man spoke quickly. The girl said, "You only think you're a loser because you keep comparing yourself to everyone else, instead of looking at the things that make you special. Would you judge a fish by how well it can fly, or a bird by how well it can swim?"

"I don't have a fish," said Lutlow. "Or a bird. I have a sheep."

Lutlow didn't know what a *gooncha* was, but he was pretty sure the old man just called him one.

"Stop telling yourself you have to be like everyone else to be any good at something," said the girl. She followed the old man as he began to shuffle away. "We're going to pick you again next week. Be ready."

"Wait," shouted Lutlow. "You can't. I'm no good. I have a sheep, for goodness sake!"

"Maybe you're right," the girl called back. "But you're wrong about one thing."

"What's that?"

"He's not a sheep. He's a goat."

• • •

Merkle squinted down at Blarnsley's rear end. Lutlow opened his mouth to tell him it wasn't a good idea to get that close, then remembered he didn't really like Cousin Merkle and closed it again.

"Yeeep, it's a goat o'right," said Merkle. "Tail points up. Sheep tails point down."

"Why didn't you tell me before?" asked Lutlow.

"Never asked." Merkle spat into a nearby bush and wandered a few steps closer to his small flock.

Lutlow followed him. "Are there any other differences?" he asked. "Besides the tail thing?"

"Some," said Merkle. "Not had much experience wiv goats, m'self. Prefer sheep. Calmer, easier to control. Lead one, lead 'em all, ya know?" He paused to scratch himself in a way Lutlow thought really should have been done in private. "Goats are wily buggers. Vicious when they wanna be."

"Seriously?" Lutlow looked down at Blarnsley who was matching Merkle's sheep, blank-look for blank-look. The hot sun seemed to glisten off the horns jutting out from his head. Had they always been that large? Somehow Lutlow had never noticed.

"They're clever, too," said Merkle. "Lots of attitude."

Was it just Lutlow's imagination or did Blarnsley's face now seem a little less stupid? Not blank, but . . . steady. Calm. Almost calculating.

"An they're buggers to keep in a pen. What wiv all the jumping."

"Jumping?"

"Yeah. Climbing, too. Up and down mountains like they was flat terrain. Good eating, though. Gamier than sheep, but if you stew 'em good and long . . . "

Blarnsley's head shot up.

"That's great thanks," said Lutlow hurriedly. "You've been a big help."

Lutlow led Blarnsley away from the patch of brown grass Merkle called his farm. He scuffed his feet thoughtfully as he walked. Behind him, Blarnsley seemed to glide over the ground, his hooves barely making divots in the sand. "Sorry I've been calling you a sheep all this time, boy," said Lutlow. "And I know I haven't been as nice to you as I could have been. Even if you were a sheep, that wasn't your fault. You are what you are. Just like how I'm short-sighted, and can't run or throw or breathe when it gets really dusty. I'm good at maths, though. And angles. You're probably good at goat things, like climbing, and jumping . . . "

Lutlow stopped and stared at the horizon, to where the arena reared up like a sheer-sided mountain. And he had an idea.

• • •

The next time the doors opened Lutlow was ready. He didn't need Blarnsley to push him into the arena (well, maybe just a little nudge to get him going). He didn't quail quite so much at the sight of the other contestants—the Truckles in their usual spots and the others in between them. He didn't feel the same sense of despair when the gong sounded. Because when the others shouted their Spirit Beasts forward, Lutlow leaped onto Blarnsley's back and cried. "One-eighty-degree turn. Full retreat!"

Blarnsley spun neatly on his cloven hooves and leaped, right up over the barrier and into the surrounding stands. There was a small shout of alarm—very small, because the only people in this part of the arena other than Master Pol and the girl were a pair of teenagers taking advantage of the privacy to get handsy with one another. Lutlow steered Blarnsley to the top of the stands and slid awkwardly off his back.

Hardly anyone had even realised what Lutlow had done. Their attention was fixed on the action below. The three non-Truckle opponents had banded together against the Truckles. A boar, a leopard and a rhinoceros battled bravely against the Truckle-Beasts and were holding their own. Then the cobra spat venom in the leopard's eyes and the elephant clocked it on one side of its head with a massive trunk-swing. In a silver flash the leopard was gone. The boar charged valiantly, hoping to strike the cobra while it was distracted, but the lion was too quick. While lion and boar duked it out, the rhino was tag-teamed by the remaining Truckles. Both animals were quickly defeated.

Their opponents vanquished, the Truckles whirled their Beasts around to face each other. Then, between them, they managed to do the maths. They searched the arena, confusion beneath their matching monobrows. One of the pretty young wives pointed at the stands and shrieked. "He's up there! Get him!"

The Truckles moved their Spirit Beasts towards the barrier and ordered them to jump, but no matter how they tried they couldn't make the distance. Lutlow felt himself swell with pride, even as the crowd began to grow restless. One Left Standing rule be damned—if they weren't coming to get him, he sure wasn't going to go down there to meet them. Blarnsley bleated happily and did a celebratory poop on the stairs.

"You there," shouted one of the old men in the stands—Trump's Chooser, if Lutlow wasn't mistaken. "Get the elephant up against the stands. Now tell the cobra to push the lion up onto the elephant's back. That's it, up you go."

Lutlow groaned. The Truckles never would have worked that out themselves.

Trump grinned evilly as his lion advanced on Blarnsley. Lutlow's heart sank. There was no way Blarnsley could win in an actual fight. The goat bleated and glanced over its shoulder at Lutlow.

"It's ok," said Lutlow. "Remember, you can't really be hurt. It'll all be over in a minute."

Blarnsley bleated again. It was a mournful sound, but it was determined, too. Loud and shrill, like a woman who knows she can't sing but won't let that stop her trying. Lutlow felt something akin to warrior spirit rising up inside him. He had a sudden urge to raise a sword and charge. He didn't have a sword, so he raised the only thing that was in his pocket—his protractor. "Let's do it, Blarnsley! Attack!"

Blarnsley charged down the steps, head bowed. There was a collective gasp from the crowd, who had totally forgotten about making out, and a deep, nasty laugh from Trump. "Bite his head off, boy!" he shouted. The lion roared and leaped.

"Forty-five!" shouted Lutlow. Blarnsley kicked off with his hind legs and jumped at a forty-five degree angle, sailing cleanly past the lion and landing safely behind him. The lion spun and charged again.

"Ninety!" shouted Lutlow. "One forty! Sixty three! Twenty!"

Blarnsley danced up and down the steps, zigzagging around the lion so fast even Lutlow's spectacle-enhanced eyes blurred. Trump shouted useless commands as the lion stumbled and slipped like half-uncle Blerel after a big night out. Then Lutlow saw his chance.

"Three sixty and charge!"

Blarnsley dodged in a tight circle, then lowered his horns and charged right at the lion's backside. The lion squeaked in a very undignified way and flew forward, over the barrier, landing directly on top of Teeter's cobra. Both animals exploded in flashes of light which zipped back into their furious owners' hands.

Lutlow ran down the stairs, slipped in some celebratory dung, and flung his arms around Blarnsley's neck. "We did it, buddy!"

"Not yet you didn't!" shouted Trump. He glared up at Lutlow, his face so red his caterpillar eyebrows might have been sitting on a tomato. "You haven't beaten Truman, yet. Good luck getting him with your lame tricks!"

Lutlow stared down at the elephant, which stood, swaying slightly, in the centre of the arena. Blarnsley could dance rings around him, he was sure of it, but what good would that do? It was too big to head-butt. Blarnsley bleated heroically, but Lutlow's shoulders slumped in defeat. "It's no good. He's too big. We'll never beat him."

From the corner of his eye he caught a glimpse of Master Pol sitting on his Chooser's dais, eyes closed. He looked asleep. Lutlow felt himself getting angry. "Why did he bother with all this if he was just going to sleep through it? Honestly, if he doesn't care, why does he . . . " He stopped talking. Beside the old man, the girl smiled and nodded.

Lutlow walked down the remaining stairs and stood at the barricade. "Hey, Truman," he called.

Truman peered up at Lutlow through his shaggy fringe. "Yeah?"

"Do you like doing this, Truman?" Lutlow asked.

Truman shrugged. "It's o'right."

"But you never win," Lutlow called back. "You always let the others win, don't you?"

"He doesn't let me win," snarled Trump. "I'm just better than him."

"Yeah, we're better than him," said Teeter.

Lutlow gave Truman the same look his father gave him when he lied about doing his chores so he could get back to his quadratic equations. Truman looked down at his feet and shrugged again. "Means more to them than it does to me. I don't mind."

"But why do it at all if you don't want to?"

"I dunno. I got a Spirit Beast. That makes me a Spirit Warrior. I'm s'posed to do this sort of stuff. Plus, what else would I do with him?" He pointed at his elephant.

"Maybe he'd be good at something else?" suggested Lutlow.

There was silence in the arena, then a man near the back of the arena stood up and hesitantly raised his hand. Lutlow recognised him as one of the older, richer members of the architects guild. "Actually, I can think of a dozen uses for him on my sites. Moving things, carrying things, propping things up. If you'd like a job for him, that is."

Truman rubbed a hand over his head. "Could I move stuff and carry stuff too?"

"Sure," said the man. "There's always stuff to move."

"O'right then." Truman ambled across the arena towards the nearest door, his elephant following placidly behind.

"Hang on, wait!" Trump and Teeter jumped forward and tried to stop him. They might as well have tried to stop his elephant. With a sibling hanging off each arm, Truman lumbered away.

The moment the elephant left the arena, the bronze gong rang. "We have a winner," cried the gong master. "Lutlow and his sheep."

"Goat," said Lutlow, but it didn't matter. He was hoisted precariously onto the shoulders of the handsy teenagers and carried from the stadium, the cheers of the crowd swelling up behind him.

• • •

As the crowd dispersed, Blarnsley took a moment to bring up a lump of cud he'd been storing for just such an occasion. On the dias in front of him, the old man tapped the girl on the shoulder and nodded after Lutlow as he was carried triumphantly away. Blarnsley flicked his ears forward to catch the girl's words. "I know, Master," she said. "But we can get him tomorrow. Let him have one night to celebrate before his whole life changes. Who knows—he might never come back here again."

Blarnsley gazed across at the tumbled sands of the arena and drank in the magic that would let him become so much more than he already was, once his Warrior was ready. Before he left, he deposited a reflective pile of pellets on the top of the stairs and then headed out to join his chosen one.

~

SELF, CONTAINED

KIRSTYN McDERMOTT

Meredith holds the dead bird in both hands. Last week, it was a sparrow, small enough to nestle in the cup of one palm. This morning, it's a wattlebird. She brushes the dirt from its feathers and smooths its wings to its sides. The lifeless head lolls against her fingers. There are two clear puncture wounds on its breast; spatters of blood stain the brown stripes.

Meredith scans the houses on her court with narrowed eyes. Across the road at Number Five, the fat tortoiseshell is sunning herself on the concrete driveway. The ginger tom from Number Three is perched in his favoured spot on the sill of the large bay window. This means nothing; Meredith has seen him outside often enough. She has spotted another cat from time to time as well, a lean streak of tabby whose home, like its current whereabouts, remains unknown to her.

She doesn't know which one is responsible for the birds.

Nor which owners are *ir*responsible enough to let their pet stay out at night, despite the council curfew.

She has letter-dropped before, pleading with her neighbours to keep their cats indoors after dark, explaining the vulnerability of roosting birds and how easily they might be plucked from branch or nest by a night-stalking predator, all furry and fanged.

It is clear that letters will no longer suffice.

• • •

The man at the store said that fresh mince makes the best bait. Raw and bloody and impossible for any carnivore to resist, no matter how well fed it might be. Meredith has chosen prime beef. She leaves a bowl of it in the back of the cage trap, behind the pressure plate that will trigger the door once her quarry is safely inside. She has no inclination to harm the animal, only to capture it, to be able to brandish irrefutable evidence of its nocturnal expeditions in the face of its owner.

Meredith has no particular quarrel with cats, so long as their natural hunting instincts are kept firmly in check by human hand. Though, largely, she does prefer dogs. (Unconditional love is a hard trait to beat.)

She pushes at the plate with a stick. The door falls instantly, snaps shut with a metallic rattle and clang.

Smiling, Meredith re-sets the trap.

• • •

That night, she finds herself merely dozing, slipping but briefly into the shallowest of slumbers before startling awake again. (And again. And again.) Only after she hears the unmistakeable snap of the trap being sprung, followed by a thin, low-pitched yowl, does she nestle into her pillows and sleep.

• • •

The animal she has caught is huge, its fur black and bristling through the wire mesh. Meredith isn't even certain that it *is* a cat, the shape of it is so confined, so compressed. It seems to fill the entire trap and she wonders at how it managed to squash itself so completely inside that the door was still able to latch closed behind it.

She doesn't know what to do next. She has never seen the cat—if it *is* a cat—around the neighbourhood and so hasn't the foggiest idea to whom her captive should be presented. Nor, if it is the bird-killer, does she want to release it. If she surrenders the beast to the council pound, they might simply euthanise it as a stray without even bothering to find its home. (She has heard stories, read them in the letters section of the local paper.)

Meredith wishes the cat no harm—it should not be faulted for merely following its nature.

She lifts the cage by its handle; it weighs surprisingly little. Inside, the cat begins to growl. A yellow eye glares amid the gloss of black fur.

• • •

The bathroom is the best place. Small, no furniture to hide beneath, its neat white tiles easily cleaned should the animal, from fear or fury, make a mess.

Meredith sets the trap down. As she unlatches the door and lifts it free, her fingers brush against that midnight pelt. The fur is soft, silken as the hair on a newborn baby. She dares another stroke, elicits another growl from the cage's occupant.

You can come out now, she says, stepping back. *No need to be scared.*

A moment passes, or several, while Meredith holds her breath. Then that mass of black fur begins to ripple, begins to wriggle, begins to push itself from the trap until it swells livid and yowling and wrathful into the room. It's a cat by form, certainly, but seems more akin to a small dog in size, something like a Kelpie, or perhaps a Border Collie. The yellow of its eyes has been all but eclipsed by twin saucers of furious black. It arches its spine and hisses, pink tongue curling between inch-long fangs.

The cat takes a step toward her. Claws make a tac-tac noise on the floor. Another step.

Meredith flees the room, slamming the door behind her. A heartbeat later, the wood reverberates with the impact of a solid, furry body. Meredith presses her ear to the door. She can hear the cat growling. She can hear its claws on the tiles.

And, beneath it all, she can hear her own blood pulsing hot through her veins.

• • •

The phone is a mute plastic puzzle in her hand. If her husband were still here, such an escalation would be his to deal with. And although he did come back that first winter to repair the leaky garage roof, and again to prune the crown of the lemon tree, Meredith can hardly call upon him to remove a feral cat from her bathroom. They have agreed—they have *both* agreed; haven't they?—to keep their lives, along with their problems, separate and apart. Right now, her husband is probably sitting down to breakfast with his new wife. (Not his younger, or thinner, or even much prettier wife. Just new.)

Meredith cannot call him.

Briefly, she considers Mark. But her son is always so busy, always *just heading out* or *behind the wheel* or *expecting an important call* whenever she rings. (She can't remember the last time he rang her.) Besides, she suspects he sides with his father—or would, if pushed. She doesn't want to push him. Things are fine the way they are. He always remembers her birthday.

Instead, she calls her daughter, Kim, who immediately wants to know how the cat got into the bathroom, and then what the hell Meredith was doing mucking around with animal traps, for Godsake, and lastly, why she cared so much about the bloody birds in the first place. It's just nature, right? Red in tooth and claw, wasn't that what Coleridge said?

Tennyson, Meredith corrects her. *It's from a Tennyson poem.* She can almost hear Kim rolling her eyes. Her daughter says that she's already running late to drop Liam off at daycare, but since it's her half-day at work she can maybe zip on over afterwards to help with the cat. She has to pick up some dry-cleaning on the way, and needs to collect Liam again by four, but if the thing with the cat won't take long, then she supposes she can zip on over.

You could leave Liam with me today, Meredith suggests. *I could pick up the dry-cleaning.*

I'm not leaving my kid in a house with a feral animal, Kim says. There's a pause, before she laughs. *I didn't mean you, Mum.*

Meredith laughs as well. *Of course you didn't.*

• • •

After two cups of peppermint tea and one hour of feigning nonchalance, Meredith can no longer wait for anyone to zip on over.

There is no sound from the bathroom. No yowling or growling, no tac-tac-tac of stalking claws. She smiles, relieved. The cat has calmed down, is probably crouched in far a corner, sulking. Carefully, she opens the door, or tries to.

Something presses against it from the other side. The door yields but a handspan and then, as Meredith pushes harder, a shock of black fur fills the entire gap, top to bottom. She jumps aside as a huge paw whips out. A paw the size of a Kelpie, or perhaps a Border Collie, and never mind the rest of the cat. The very tip of one claw snags across the skin of her wrist. Blood beads, then wells.

Meredith stumbles down the hall. Risks a glance over her shoulder.

That great paw is pulling the door inward, as fur bristles through the gradually widening space. Bristles and swells and spills itself beyond the tiled confines of the bathroom. (Cats are, in essence, a fluid; everyone knows this.)

Her blood is dripping onto the wooden floor. The cat is slowly filling the hall.

Meredith runs from the house. Slams the front door in her wake. Her slippered feet smear little crimson crescents across the porch.

• • •

She sits in the yard, beneath the Japanese elm, watching the windows. Though the scratch has long since clotted over, her wrist is sore. She should put Savlon on the wound. She should fetch a warm coat. She should do many things. Her phone is in the pocket of her trackpants, but who might she call? Not her husband or Mark; they would find the situation preposterous. Or they would find *her* preposterous. (Or they already do.)

Kim might already be zipping on over. Meredith is of two minds about whether she wants to see her daughter. (She is of two minds about many things.)

Her wrist itches. Meredith scratches at the dried blood. It flakes to the grass, leaving behind a line of soft black hairs that quiver beneath her touch.

She looks up at the windows again. The cat has grown so large now, its pelt is pressed tight against the glass; she can see the fur rippling as the animal curls through the neat and homely rooms that confine it. A massive yellow eye regards her from the top corner of the living room window. Rage locked in amber, for far too long. The eye blinks once, then disappears. (It isn't gone; it will never be gone.)

Meredith brushes a finger over the hair growing from her wrist. She shudders. Deep in her belly, she feels the flex of newly sharpened claws.

And so Meredith sits, and she stares at the seething mass that fills her house, and she smiles at the possibilities that might be unfurled when at last she opens the front door and lets that bristling black cat loose into to the vast and boundless world.

~

A HEDGE OF YELLOW ROSES

KATHLEEN JENNINGS

Vagabonds leave signs in the road for those who know how to read them. Royalists also have their secret language of warnings and betrayals. This story too, in its fashion, is a sign to mark the way I went.

As with all the lessons of my life, no human voice told it to me. I gathered the threads from spindle-grass and crow-black clouds, from amber autumn roses and the thorns that tore my sleeves.

Once, there was a prince . . .

• • •

Having given myself, body and soul, to the service of my prince, I, Vermeille, found myself fleeing armed rebellion. This, at an age when one of my career and ambitions might have hoped to be settled in a fine house, with a garden and even children at my knee. But that carefully husbanded future had been rent asunder, and now I was homeless, far from the city where I'd dwelt for more years than I cared to admit to those who would scoff at my true age. My lord was said to be exiled, yet I still hoped then to meet him in a land far beyond the hills.

Certainly I could not stay in the beautiful city, for that cloud-kingdom to which I had struggled so long to ascend had already been torn apart. No matter how humble my birth, I had allied myself with the royal house and in doing so had marked myself out as surely as if I'd worn a traitor's brand. No concession would be made for me by revolutionaries or otherwise.

I rode disguised as a common soldier; not so common that I could not afford a horse, but I took good care to make both the beast (a grey, shabbily caparisoned) and myself appear sufficiently disreputable to make neither halt nor hindrance worth a vigilante's trouble. I shall let you imagine how that abraded my sensibilities, for I had become accustomed to damask and carriages, satin and featherbeds.

I bore three messages, none conveyed by ink: news of the murder of a King, a sword wrapped in a cape and tied to my saddle, and a secret so close to my own heart that even I did not then suspect it. Beyond these I had only my wits, and few enough of those.

Anxious and fearful, riding hard and sleeping rough, I sickened. My thoughts strayed to happier times past and those I hoped would come—moonspinnings, all. The horse, too, wandered. When at last I roused it was to find that we stood on a hillside gold with clattering spindle-grass, and the lowering clouds too close.

Spindle-grass is no better for horses than storms are for benighted travellers, and there was no more food on that slope than there was hint of shelter. I had resigned myself to pressing on, when the last escaping light of the sun struck fire from what had seemed only a nearer cloud. It was instead, I realised, a stand of trees, with something radiant within.

We crossed the grey stones of a cold hill stream. My horse made a good deal of fuss, and perhaps the water was deeper than I'd thought, for by the far side I was splashed to my thighs.

As we drew closer it became apparent our goal was not a forest, but a low large thicket. A few late birds still settled to its branches, and beyond its highest reach was the unmistakeable haze of moss-grown roofs. The beckoning gleam glanced once more then faded with the sunset. Whoever had built and tended this place had long since abandoned it. To my way of thinking and given my current circumstances, this was all to the good.

"We may spend the night dry, or at least in the lee of a wall," I said to the horse, and urged him onward.

The wind sank, gathered itself again, and tore at the sparse grass and me in equal measure. The air grew grey with dusk. The hillside was poor, stony and ridged, with but a few starved weeds, which my horse snatched at greedily. If ever there'd been fields, they were long worn away, stone walls disassembled by winters and the slow shifting of the earth. We found the faint hollow of a ditch, which became rough with tilted stones and resolved at last into the remnant of a path. This brought us to the entrance of the compound.

Vintners grow roses beside their vines to warn of pestilence; royal gardeners raise them (costly stock!) as a boast and glory. Whether the bushes surrounding this house had been planted for service or beauty I made no guess. They now stood guard for a place that needed none. Thick and unnaturally thorned, spikes as long as stilettos and bright as needles, the woody branches had woven themselves into a thick wattle fence, daubed with leaf-mould. I could hear birds settling in the upper branches, but the net was too dense to see them.

From afar, I'd thought a shattered windowpane had thrown a reflection to draw us here, but now I realised otherwise. The hedge was heavy with roses, blown and blossoming, and all rich as amber, bronze, butter, parchment. At the hedge's crest, twice as high as I sat on horseback, some few still gleamed the dull gold of lanterns.

Their perfume was sickly sweet.

Though the path bade fair to be overgrown, I urged my horse on and soon discerned the deeper shadows of what had once been a gate. I ducked my head and shrank from the barbs, while the grey horse pressed slowly forward. Once, twice and again I felt a tearing on arm or cheek, and bethought myself to back out of the leafy tunnel. But finally stone overarched us, purple light opened ahead, and I sighed in relief as I straightened.

We were in a walled courtyard. Weeds grew through cracked stones, and the several doors that faced us all hung ajar. Grey-green roofs of the towered house, outbuildings and a vacant dovecote angled down to us. Tall cold chimneys were topped with bristles of twigs and the broken wheel of a stork's nest. Dry leaves, like the shadows of birds, rustled past my horse's hooves.

I slid to earth, clinging to the saddle. As I steadied myself I looked back the way we had come. The tunnel must have turned sharply for it now seemed blocked with blossoms and briars. Where the hedge overtopped the wall, the roses were reddening.

"And so they came to the Tower Perilous," I murmured. Ah! So recently surrounded by salons of poets and there I was addressing a horse.

When I faced the courtyard once more, it was to find we were not alone.

The woman appeared terribly young, frail as an ivory fan. Her antique dress was frayed to threads that, like the strands of her hair, lifted in the breeze. I could discern little of her features in the half-light. Yet for all the poverty which clearly beset us both, for a heart's beat I felt as if we were players in a romance on a courtly stage: I no shabby soldier but a knight; she no starveling peasant but a lady waiting to greet a noble guest.

"Good den, my lord," said she, with quaint formality.

I swept as theatrical a bow as I knew, but with the movement, the overgrown courtyard bucked beneath my feet, my empty stomach revolted and my hand lost hold of the shifting saddle. I fell.

She caught at me and for a breath I thought her hands crabbed and clawed. Her fluttering sleeves struck at my face like feathers.

"Hush, hush," said the girl, steadying me. "I cannot carry you, good Sir Knight. Hush, you are come very far to sleep on stone or in hedge." Her cool hand—human, untaloned—touched my face briefly.

I blinked and stared. Her face was near, her eyes wide and luminous as the roses. Her expression was unguarded, and I was disconcerted. It had been very long since I'd seen someone who had not learned to wear a mask either of subservience, civility, or war. The first flecks of rain fell, and they stung like ice.

She stepped away. "You should not bow to me," she said, lowering her gaze. "No wealth or title belongs to this land. I am only Enna."

"You are the mistress of this house?"

She looked up again and smiled. "As much as any can make such claim," she replied. I marvelled at how much beauty could appear, where there was no cold jewelled facade to hide it. I wondered if that was how I had appeared to my lord, when first he took up with me.

"Then I am Miles," I said. "I am but a masterless knight." She seemed to accept this answer though it would never have satisfied anyone from the city I had so recently fled. The girl was not worldly-wise.

"Come. There is still room for guests. Your skin is hot as a flame."

Once within the shadowy ruination of the great house, she produced a shaded taper, then led me up bowed stairs and along a dust-hung hall to a chamber which must have once been a large salon or gallery. There were no furnishings. The candlelight, though dazzling in the dark, was small—I could only tell that the space was airy and broad, filled with what I first thought drifts of gold, then of straw, then as I looked longer, piles of leaves.

"The beds have been long since burned for winter kindling, but you may sleep here. At least you are beneath a roof," said Enna. She gave a quick, hopeful smile and left.

I'd barely wrapped myself in my greatcoat before falling asleep. I did not expect to dream.

• • •

The first time, rain hissed outside, the frail roof groaned, and darkness spread like moss and water stains down the walls. I told my dream-self the house had stood too many years to fall in one night. I told myself the night-fancy merely echoed the sudden decay of our bright kingdom.

I slitted my eyes and peered out, and found the room full of light. It hung like golden tapestries, and painted the sackcloth of my hostess's dress like damask. She stood at the threshold of the gallery, and another figure—something like a woman—stood beside her, in a robe soft with plumes.

"Do you think he will be the one?" asked the girl.

"If he were, he would wake and see you for what you are," answered the other. "Resign yourself to disappointment, goddaughter."

"Perhaps he wakes and merely pretends to sleep."

"Then he is still not the one we require, for he is no gentleman," said the other. "It is only tricksters and common soldiers who feign sleep to gain an end, and such are not for you."

She crossed the room with a rustling swoop of wings as if to shake me—and I woke to the sound of pigeons rummaging in the rafters, the wind like voices in ruined towers.

• • •

I slept again, and thought myself surrounded by many mirrors. They doubled back a crowd of folk in velvet finery, masked with glass-and-ivory visages of birds: I was in a ballroom. Their clothes were wonderful, fantasies for a masquerade and yet with silhouettes long-lost to fashion, sleeves with a queer cut, full skirts falling short of soft-heeled, square-toed shoes. The beaks of their masks were sharp, ground like razors, and the eyes that peered out were very beautiful, and wild.

Yet they were all faintly transparent, as if the mirrors in reflecting them had drawn out their reality, their substance. Through sleeve and epaulet, peplum and bodice, ribbon and lace, I could see at the epicentre a single, solemn figure. It was the girl, Enna, but much younger, in primrose silk, with saffron ribbons in her hair and a crow (glossy blue and stars of candlelight dancing from its back and brows) perched on her shoulder. "Not a true prince among them," rasped the crow, and again with a sound of nails on glass, "Not a one!"

I awoke in the tangle of my coat, breathing in crushed leaves. Lightning leaked briefly through shrunken shutters. The walls were still bare, no mirrors in evidence, no revellers, no crows. Rolling onto my back I stared blindly at the ceiling. (Had it been painted with stars?) In more innocent days I might have counted this a nightmare, but since then I had stood before a palace and been spattered with blood from the throat of a king.

When I wept, I rather fear it was for lost festivals such as that in my dream. All the cruel beauty I had made my own was shattered like porcelain. All the gilt and satin were gone, leaving nothing save dried leaves.

• • •

Yet a third time I dreamt. This time Enna lay a little distance from me. Her dress was all the colours of night and dawn; pearls and feathers were tangled in her hair with a disorder that would have cost time and care to achieve, had it been brought to existence in the waking world.

"You have a gentle face," she said, and reached towards my lips with one finger—but her hand was crabbed and clawed.

I flinched and opened my eyes.

I was cold in my sweat-soaked clothes, half-buried in dead rose leaves. Morning light, the colour of milk-and-water, seeped through the slats of the shutters but brought no warmth. There was a lingering stench of bile and my mouth was as foul as if birds had nested there.

In all my dreams the threshold had been hung with a door carved of interlocking branches, but in the daylight the hinges were rusted and unburdened. In the empty space stood the girl, a basin in her hands.

"I trust you slept well," she said, eyes downcast, and brought me the dish of water. Her fingers were roughened by no more than ordinary work—if there was ordinary work for one who dwelt in such a place. The fine dress of my dreams was replaced by the same drab rag of my arrival.

"I thought I would have slept as the dead," I answered. "But nightmares troubled me."

She looked up. I could see the amber ring about her irises and her wide pupils cast back the reflection of my face hawk-sharp with fever and hunger.

"You will sleep better far from here," she said. "I let you in because of the storm, but it has passed and ordinary decency will not permit that you stay."

"You fear for your safety?" I asked, amused. Even disguised as I was, she was clearly far healthier and stronger than I. And who was there here to be affronted by my presence?

"I am protected," she said coolly. "I fear for yours. You dreamed of flying. Travellers before you have leaped from the tower, or tried to soar across the river. Others . . . "

"I did not dream of flying."

She had no ready words.

"I dreamed of birds," I confessed. "But they were revellers at a masque."

Enna left the dish of water by me, and walked quickly away.

After I had washed as well as I might, I wandered to the courtyard and found her combing the grey horse's tangled mane with fierce intensity. The beast bore it well enough, but in the overhanging branches of the hedge an ill assortment of birds swung and shouted at me, before they beat their way up into the sky.

"This is a fine animal, beneath the mud," she said.

"We have that in common, though both of us suffer from hunger."

She turned, eyes dark with contrition. "Forgive me," she said. "I forgot."

"That men must eat?" It was a jest, but she looked at me in reproach.

I sketched a bow, cautiously, and this time the ground stayed where it should. "It is I who must crave forgiveness, fair Enna. I impose on your hospitality. But if you would have me leave, and not simply become bones whitening in the hedge, then I must beg alms of you."

I do not think she was the sort to long hold a grudge. Though there remained no table in the kitchen, she laid a cloth upon the floor and served what seemed a slurry of chaff and water.

"Can this sustain life?" I asked.

"It has sustained yours these three days past. What you did not cast up again."

I mused on this while I ate. Three days of dreams, while I thought but one had passed. The dish was more substantial than it appeared and the emptiness in my belly and the weakness in my bones eased. Though my stomach was still unsettled, I did not shame myself by vomiting.

"Are you a nobleman?" she asked.

I thought before I answered. "Times are bad for noblemen, child. A wise person will answer they've never held a drop of such blood in their veins. That, if you had, you would have spilled it yourself. Tell anyone who asks that you tore this house to ruins with your own hands for liberty and loyalty."

"That would not be true."

"Yet sometimes lies may be the only thing to save us."

She regarded me solemnly until I spoke again. "Why are you alone, Enna? Where is your family? Have you no . . . " I regarded her, but could not guess her age. "No husband?"

Enna glanced out the doorway. A little whip-bird strutted proudly along the horse's back. "May I tell you a story, Sir Miles?"

"What else do our kind do?" I asked lightly, but she had not the self-deprecating humour of a self-made courtier and looked blankly at me. "Yes," I added, and leaned my head against the wall, much wearier than I felt I had cause to be.

• • •

"Once upon a time, a very long time ago," she began, a child telling a tale using the rules of the stories she has heard, "there was a green valley and in that valley was a wealthy farmholding. The couple who lived there lived well. They were happy and proud, but they had no children.

"'Will you wish for a child?' their friends and relatives asked. 'Will you summon the old powers of the hills? Will you pray?'

"'We may as well call to the birds,' said the farmer and his wife. But in time they had a daughter.

"'Who will stand at her naming?' their friends and relatives asked. 'And who will you choose as her godparents?'

"Now, the parents had no wish to give offence to those who were not chosen. 'As well ask the birds,' they said.

"Their daughter grew, and seasons were rich. The valley flourished, the house was made larger. Dances were held there, minor noblemen journeyed to visit, and rode and hunted in the hills.

"'Who will marry your daughter?' asked the friends and relations.

"'A prince, and no one less,' laughed her parents. There were many princes in those days.

"But before her parents could see her of an age to be wed or betrothed, death came to the valley and took them away.

"Among those friends and relatives who survived, there were many who wanted the rich farmland. They planned to marry the girl to their sons and brothers—but who was to decide which suitor would do?

"Now," said Enna, "you must see it was only in jest that my parents made the birds my godparents. But birds take their responsibilities seriously."

"I did not know that."

"Well, they have so few." Enna shrugged. We sat in silence while, outside, roses wept soft petals, tawny as velvet, into the courtyard.

"I did not even know that crows could speak," I offered.

She made a small noise, as if it were a matter of no great note. As if everyone knew it.

"What happened next?"

"The rival suitors came upon an idea. They did not know how, whether it was whispered at their windows as they fell asleep, or murmured in the trees when they went riding. But it was decided a ball should be held so that the girl herself might choose from any suitable admirer who met all appropriate requirements. This was still a rich valley, this farmholding the lock and I the key. There were those who hoped to grasp it—me—not for my own sake, but for the land's. There were, I understand, rather many such men."

"You understand?" I echoed.

"I was young. It was a very long time ago." She pulled her knees to her chest, folded her arms about and rested her chin on them.

"None proved worthy, for although there were noblemen among them, there were no princes—and birds, who listen at windows, knew what my parents had required. When none of their suits were acceptable, the gentlemen grew irate and insulting. The birds said none should have me until I found someone who valued my heart above my land. When the suitors threatened to take what would not be given, the birds turned all their minds to madness, and every man who has reached this place since has gone mad. With the years, the land grew untended and sour, the road was slowly lost and I have waited ever since."

"How long has that been?"

"I don't know. I cannot even remember the name of the Queen who ruled. I was very young, and birds take little notice of such things."

I thought of the unprincely candidates. "Didn't your godparents think the punishment a little extreme?"

She shrugged. "They are birds."

"And the roses?" I asked, considering the only plant that thrived in this desolation.

"I planted them on the graves, and there were so many graves . . . They grew into the hedge you see now. But the suitors didn't all die. Some only thought they had turned into birds. A few really did, and flew away. Some soared and sang in the branches for a long time."

"And you've seen no-one since?"

"Only from afar. But they tell me stories, my godparents. They listen at windows, and bring me word of the world. Only—only I think it is not the same as being in it."

I had no answer to this. Her recounting was no more fantastic than any I could spin. Who would believe that in a rose-hung city—the most civilised in the world!—street-sweepers would drag a king from his palace of white and gold, out into a common square, and cut off his head? Who would believe that peasants would grow to hate the beauty of the realm so much they would set it to burn?

Though I did not believe in nursery tales, anyone would be forgiven for thinking that my own fortunate rise and meteoric fall were no more than the substance of a fable.

I stood, swaying a little, and returned to the courtyard. The birds, on roof and hedge and wall (different feathers flocked together), watched me with unnerving steadiness. Their eyes—orange, black and blue—followed my progress. I reached the arch by which I had entered and found the way matted with roses blooming, here a bloody orange. My little strength could not shift them.

"They will only part for princely blood," said Enna. "But for them to do so, you must take me with you."

"You are welcome to come, though I do not know where I ride. I can take you to a town, find a place where you will be comfortable." As if I knew where I myself could go.

"You must take me with you as your bride," said she.

"I cannot marry you, Enna." I laughed, though I meant it kindly.

"It is the only way we may leave!" she cried. "I do not want your bones to whiten here!"

"I passed through once," I said, and touched the scabbed lines where thorns had scored my arm. "Though I am no prince."

In the outbuilding where my horse had been stabled there was no straw, only the dry golden petals which lay like grass, matted with feathers. Through the unshuttered windows winged shadows drifted.

I saddled the grey, wondering where I might find sanctuary, if indeed there was sanctuary to be had anywhere. I closed my eyes and saw the head of the king as a great golden rose, snipped away and rolling along bloodied cobbles. After so many years of schooling my emotions, it felt as if a dam had burst within me, and I had not the strength to hold it back.

And Enna followed, still talking.

"You were courteous to me. I nursed you and watched over your sleep. You passed through the hedge of thorns. You woke in dreams and saw not madness, but truth. You believed my story! It proves you are a true prince!"

"Your head is filled with fairytales, child!" I said, and bent to pull the sword from its wrappings. How heavy it was, and how weary was I, my tiredness born of something deeper than travel, my illness of more than heartsickness. "I did not seek this valley, nor you. I am only fleeing death."

I carried the blade to the gateway in the wall, swung it with what remained of my might. The branches shook birds into the air, petals fell like sleep and the rents in my flesh stung anew. Yet there was not a mark on the twisted limbs.

"I love you!" said Enna.

"I am not even a false prince," I said. "And I do not love you."

"You were kind!" she almost wailed. "You are here!" She stretched out her hand and—may I be forgiven—I took it and held it in my own.

I felt the weight of flesh and the lightness of her bones, the quick-pulsing blood in her palm. I was not tempted by the land, or the ruined house, or even the dreams of what they had once been and might be again. I was not tempted even by the unkempt beauty of the girl. But her cry for kindness, for companionship, for love—oh, I heard that in the chord of my own being.

"Sir Miles!" she began again.

"That is not my name," I said, returning to the stable. As I rewrapped the blade, I saw a scar in the watered steel, a mark in the shape of a rose-barb.

"You travel in disguise, but you are a prince! What other knight is masterless? What other blood may pass the roses—did you not see how their colour changed?"

I did not answer. There must be a way, another door, a farm gate. Fire—fire would burn a passage through. I would be ready to leave with the grey horse if I could, else over the hedge if I had strength to climb. I could stand on the horse's back. Perhaps from outside I could open the hedge again. I ignored my shaking hands as they made the bridle ring.

"Look at me!"

Enna had pulled her shabby dress over her head and her fine hair blew like silk in the light through the stable door.

Her body was thin and dirty, a maze of gooseflesh, ribbed with scars and welted with scabs. Some had lifted, and from beneath the stubs of young feathers sprouted. She stepped forward, grasped one of my hands and held it to her stomach, where the bones of her ribs began. Her skin, there unbroken, was already raised and rough with the pressure of feathers thrusting from below.

"What is this?" I asked, numb.

"This is what shall become of me, or what I shall become." She released my hands, then pulled me to her and kissed me with uncertain lips. She was still a child, no matter how long she'd lived, and fumbled inexpertly with the collar of my shirt. I caught at her trembling fingers while she begged, "It is the only other way out of this place."

"Then I am sorry for you."

"You do not want me?" she pleaded.

"No, Enna."

"But I am yours for the having! You must! You are a prince, and I have waited so very, very long. I have lost count of the generations of my godparents, of how many have watched for you. Please, you must—have you no heart?"

"It is given to another, child."

"As desperate as I?"

"Desperation is not love, Enna, and don't believe anyone who tells you otherwise!"

"But you're a prince—"

I cried out, though it broke more hearts than hers, though I shouted the words at myself as much as her. "Do you not understand, foolish child? There are no princes left! If your fate hangs upon one then you are truly doomed!"

"No, that is not true! You are here!"

"I loved a prince, Enna. I still do. But I fear he must be dead. He has not turned to a bird, he shall not fly over borders and meet me in some foreign court no matter how much I yearn and pray. He loved me, but he is dead, and he shall never know his son. The blood of the child I now know I carry is the only princely blood left in this land. How else could I have passed the roses?"

"A child?" echoed Enna.

"I am no secret prince, girl, but base-born, a prince's mistress." I tried to speak harshly, but we both wept. I gathered her to me, wrapped her in my long coat and we sank down into the leaves. "Hush," I said, through my own sobs. "Let us think. There must be some escape."

"There is only one," said Enna to my collarbone, where her hands were knotted into fists. Her nails felt sharp against the hollow of my throat. A crow in the window-embrasure clacked its beak impatiently. I believed I felt my own fingers twisting into claws.

"Perhaps my godparents never meant to give me up," said Enna quietly. "Maybe it is not love that will free me, but having my heart broken."

"I have found," I ventured, "that birds and princes break hearts very well. They both live such short lives."

Enna cried herself to sleep. I extracted myself and stood, looked down at her, half-hidden by my wretched soldier's coat. She was—must be—so much older than I. Yet I had lived far more, been made and unmade by the world, bereft and unwidowed, nearly a mother. There had been no godmother, avian or otherwise, to guide me, and perhaps that was as well.

As quietly as I could I went back into the courtyard. The grey horse dozed in the pale sunlight, and the watchful birds had settled again: crows in the branches, whip-birds on my mount's shoulders, pigeons, long-wild housedoves, and little quarrelling sparrows on the cracked pavement. On the roofs, light elegant egrets waited like sentinels, and owls shifted irritably in the shadows.

In the centre of the enclosure, I turned a full circle and cleared my throat.

"Oh, most gracious watchers and guardians," I said, for I had been used to treat with similarly vain and status-conscious creatures. "Most venerable and honourable birds, wise avians, strigidae, corvidae, passeridae . . . " I reached the limit of my scholarship and felt my folly; then I rallied. I had weathered the scoffing of the greatest, most glittering of courts—why should I blush for these feather-dusters?

I conjured my best memory of a true courtly bow, swept off my non-existent hat, flung out one arm and bent deeply, until the nettles and the incursions of spindle-grass nearly pricked my face.

The birds strutted and shuffled, swayed on their perches, tilted their heads. I glanced at them from under my brows, drew breath and balance, then straightened.

"Through your wisdom and keen observation, you will by now understand that I am no prince. I do, however, carry within me the blood of the royal line. As such I, Vermeille, am the only and last claimant ever likely to cross the hedge. I beg that you hear my words, and let the girl Enna go free."

"What would you give us?" demanded a crow. Its voice startled me, but I had heard such harsh and avaricious mockery before and steeled myself to wait.

"Gold?" asked a magpie.

"The light of your eyes?" A raven.

A whip-bird piped, "Your first-born child?"

They were knowing ones, and I imagined it was not the breeze but their wild untidy magic which swirled the leaves about my feet. I kept my arms at my sides, palms open.

"No doubt such gold, light, and children as I carry will all fall to your kind in the fullness of time. I owe nothing, I do not seek to buy your charge, and I request no favour beyond this: that you release the child.

"But you have discharged your duty as godparents admirably and in reward I will offer a word of advice. I have travelled from the plainlands where cattle-birds tag at the heels of oxen; over gentle lands where wrens sing; across the crane-stalked river that leads to the sea of gulls and flows about the island city where pigeons and sparrows strut at their ease between the houses of men. And each of their kind could tell you, wise lords and ladies of the air, these two truths:

"The first is that while birds cling to their nature, mankind are changeable, and must be so, else they die. If you hold Enna here any longer you cease to protect her, you will render her unable to change. Even your own kind must fly or fall from the nest, but cannot stay there forever.

"The second is that war and rebellion turn rich pickings up to the light just as a plough's blade does worms. You may stay here in this untilled country and leave the bloody spoils to your gentler rivals. Or you may free yourselves from your own spells, and those of your forefathers, and leave this stagnant land to seek your fortune."

The creatures shifted and conferred among themselves in their own languages. A feathered parliament of nobles who had forgotten why they'd been elevated, who remembered only the power of their position, not its responsibilities. Such revolutionary thoughts made me sink my nails into my palms. *I'm sorry, my love.*

But they were blunt and artless birds for all their self-importance, and wielded no court airs or subtleties. In their thirst for princes they had almost forgotten their charge.

"What—what will become of the child? Without us?" asked a mottled, fan-tailed dove.

"Is she a child?" I asked. "You have held her here so long, waiting, that she is barely able to grow. So long, that there are no princes left in the land. This I swear to you."

"Save one," said the low voice of an owl beneath the eaves.

I rested my hand on my own stomach. "And he shall have neither crown nor country," I said.

I sensed a presence at my elbow, and with my free hand reached for Enna's.

The birds spoke among themselves once more until at last an old crow dropped from the hedge and landed on the hand I'd raised to shield my eyes. There were grey feathers among the black, and its gnarled claws bit into my skin.

"If what you say is true—and we have no reason to disbelieve—then you have done us a favour, servant-of-the-dead-princes. All our lives, and our mothers', for a hundred nestings, have been devoted to raising and protecting this one. We are agreed, now that we think on it, that assuredly, she is more than of age.

"But let her leave with you, that we may not have failed the trust we were given. And we will serve you likewise."

Before I could ask what that meant, they lifted up from hand, roof, courtyard, branch and chimney, a dappled whirlwind, a mottled cloud that cleared the wall and beat away across the fields. I caught myself wondering what manner of power Enna's folk had possessed, to tie that mismatched flock so casually, so tightly, to such an obligation.

"Come," I said to her. "We must seek our own fortunes." She was dressed again. Her eyes had already lost their inhuman light, and she seemed more present, too, than when she'd first met me in the courtyard. As if she had matured in the minute it took the birds to pass.

Before we left, I bade Enna wrap up in strips of wet cloth such cuttings as I could take from the hedge, which yielded at last to the blade of my sword. I filled, too, the secret pockets of my coat, and weighted my saddlebags with heavy yellow petals, their fragrance now rich and rare with the promise of freedom.

I remembered the roses grown by vineyards and in kings' gardens. These must be such as had rarely, if ever, been seen elsewhere in the world. I said, "We may yet turn them to gold. We shall have need of it."

We mounted the grey horse and the hedge gave way before us. Enna's arms wrapped around me and her cheek pressed to my back as we rode out down the ditch of a path and up through the rattling spindle-grass. A whip-bird darted behind us, a solitary escort.

I did not look back at hedge, valley or kingdom and, though I cannot speak with certainty, I suspect Enna's thoughts were fixed on the horizon of the future as firmly as mine.

THE CHART OF THE VAGRANT MARINER

ALAN BAXTER

Reeve slammed a pewter mug across the drunken sailor's face, knocked him senseless to the floor. He grabbed a handful of the man's greasy hair, hauled him up, and opened his throat with a polished dagger.

"Anyone else care to challenge my captaincy of the *Scarlet Wind* or my ability to lead?" he roared. Spittle flew from the depths of his thick black and gray beard. His eyes were shadowed in his dark skin as he scanned the room.

Heavy quiet sank through the *Mermaid's Tail*, the wharfside pub that was so often our home ashore. The only sound was the water lapping gently at the support poles beneath the floor. Everyone either stared at the pool of blood spreading beneath the unfortunate sailor or looked into tankards or laps. None met the captain's steel gaze. Candlelight flickered off timber walls.

"Then I ask again. Who will join me and replenish the ranks thinned by the Royal Navy? Who'll step up for their share of bounty? The British may try to clean up these waters, but we shall show them their will is unwelcome here!"

A few wary fellows stepped forward and, led by their confidence, more joined them. The promise of wealth has often blinded men to their better judgment and will do forever more, I'm sure. Before long the captain was sat at a scored and rickety table signing tickets for a hearty new crew and I knew we would sail again on the morning tide.

"Boy," Reeve said quietly.

I quickly stood from my place at his feet. "Yes, Captain."

"Take these tickets to the first mate and arrange a measure of liquor for each new soul signed up." He raised his voice. "To show my gratitude and good will." This was met with murmurs and nods of satisfaction. These people thought they had made a good decision. There were far worse captains to serve under, though perhaps not many. A man with vengeance burning inside him cares little for others in the end.

When I returned from the *Scarlet Wind* I saw a scrawny man, deep in his cups, had crawled toward the murdered sailor. He reached out a finger and began tracing a strange pattern in the thick, dark blood pooled across the floor. The design, more than the act, made me uneasy in a way I couldn't explain.

The captain noticed my gaze and followed it, saw the madman drawing. "The hell are you doing there?"

At the sound of Reeve's low voice, the filthy wretch leaped up and scurried away, the pub door banging in his wake. Reeve stared at the marks he'd left for a long moment, then said, "Get him." He could stop a charging stallion with his roar, but my captain usually spoke in a tone so low, it demanded respect. It forced others to silence themselves and concentrate to listen.

I hared out the door and onto the rough-hewn docks. My quarry hurried into the warren of streets that led up toward the town and I gave chase. To lose him would incur Reeve's wrath and I had no desire to risk that. The night was hot and sticky, the whirrs and cries of insects and other nocturnal critters disturbed the dense heat. I would be glad to get back out on the ocean, away from the humid stillness of land. There weren't many of us left after our last run-in with His Majesty's best, so the intake of fresh blood was essential. It was possible to sail a three-masted barque like the *Scarlet Wind* with as few as four or five men—assuming the wind didn't change, but of course, it always did. Most of those lost and a good proportion of the replacements were escaped slaves, a few European mongrels thrown in, men and women of many a mixed breed. Reeve didn't care, he has ever seen the value of all people. A former slave himself, so the rumours go, and it's claimed he ate his owner's heart before taking to the seas. I believe I am the son of slaves myself, but I can never know that for sure as it was Esme told me so, and she's no longer here to ask.

I turned a corner past a stinking tannery and nearly barreled into the scrawny man I chased. He stood motionless, staring at a wall, face twisted in confusion. I drew my small dagger, a gift from Reeve and my only possession, and grabbed the vagrant's elbow. It was slick with sweat and grease. "You need to come with me," I said, as kindly as I could.

He looked at me and frowned. It was no effort to drag him unprotesting back to the *Mermaid's Tail.*

Reeve stared over his tankard as I hauled the man inside. My captain drank and drank but appeared as ever unaffected by the booze. I had seen him drink more than any man should be able, but I had never seen him drunk. His constitution was as infamous as his ferocity.

I pushed the bemused man into the chair opposite Reeve. He sank, resignation writ across his features. His gaze fell to a puddle of spilled beer on the tabletop and slowly he reached out, dragged a finger through the liquid. It was the same disquieting sequence of circles and lines the fellow had traced in the blood. It curdled my mind to look upon it and I turned away.

Reeve leaned forward and the man flinched back, but I put a heavy palm on his shoulder to keep him seated. "Hold there, friend," Reeve said. "Here." He offered his battered tankard and the man looked at it as if it might strike him down. "Drink," Reeve said softly.

A thin and shaking hand reached out, took the mug, and the strange artist swallowed. Cautious at first, then with gusto. When the cup was drained, Reeve took it back. "What's your name?"

"Jenks." The voice was cracked and strained.

"And what's that you're drawing, Jenks?"

The skinny, filthy shoulders rose and fell. Jenks looked at what he'd done as if it was entirely foreign to him. The beer shifted and the lines merged and slowly vanished.

Reeve turned and yelled, "Bella!"

The barmaid staggered in, rubbing at eyes as tired as my own but with a smile plastered on for his benefit. Reeve held out his tankard. "Refill this, and bring another for my friend."

Bella frowned. "Your friend is mad and penniless, yet he always loiters here and begs drinks and food from good folk." She raised a small, scarred fist and Jenks winced.

Reeve caught her wrist. "For now, he is my friend and I will have a drink for him. You know my coin is good. And bring me paper and a pencil."

Bella's expression clearly betrayed her displeasure but she did as she was bid. Reeve offered Jenks the fresh tankard and, when the desperate fellow reached to take it, pulled it away. "You draw me that picture again, here on this paper, clear and true. Then you can have this and as many more as you can swallow."

Jenks looked from the paper to the tankard and back several times before reluctantly picking up the pencil. Eyes squeezed almost shut, as though the act pained him, he scrawled away and the arrangement of lines and curves, clearer than any time before, truly made my stomach squirm and my breath catch in my throat. Even Reeve with his hearty constitution grimaced as he gazed at it. When it was done, Jenks grabbed the tankard and swallowed it down with loud, frantic gulps.

Reeve stared a moment more at the parchment, then folded it away inside his jacket. "I think this is the kind of thing that should not be looked upon too long under the mantle of night, eh, Daniel?"

"I would rather not look upon it at all, sir, even under a blazing sun," I said.

Reeve chuckled softly. "Then perhaps that makes you a wiser man than I." He ordered another tankard for Jenks and said, "Tell me the story of this." He patted his coat by way of explanation.

"Of what?" Jenks asked.

"The pattern you just scribed for me."

"What pattern?"

Reeve frowned, pursed his lips in thought, then, "Tell me the story of your last voyage."

Jenks stared into his ale for a while. "Was a long time ago and only I survived," he said eventually, and drained the brew.

"Tell me how." Reeve waved for fresh tankards and Bella brought them.

Jenks' eyes appeared to glaze and he spoke more clearly than I would have thought possible. "We sailed for an island Captain Jake knew tell of and he said great treasure was to be found there. None of us really believed him, for no one knew where or how he had come by this sudden knowledge. But a crew follows its captain, does it not? Through storms and most inclement seas we sailed, and many thought we were simply straying into the wide reaches of the open ocean. I honestly feared we would never see land again. But after weeks of horrendous journey an island came into view. Stood tall above rabid gray waves like a broken tooth, it did, and the captain said to break out the rowboats.

"Three boats set off and two were smashed on invisible rocks beneath those hellish waves, those men taken screaming to the depths. But still Jake insisted we go on. Our boat beached and we scrambled onto a rocky shore, thankful to have survived that far. A great rending cracked across the waters from behind and we spun to see the *Wistful Lady* split from bow to stern. She bucked and rose and men fell wailing into the waves, and damn my soul I swear I saw thick black tendrils writhing through the timbers as she went down. What kind of monster . . . ? We were all that was left and still old Jake insisted we go on.

"We trudged into a maze of high, sharp rocks, with no idea what we might find other than certain death. Jake led us to a cave mouth, like the iris of a damned cat's eye in the wet, black rock. He forced us to enter and we descended deep into blackness, two damp torches offering a smear of spluttering light to guide us. I brought up the rear and that was all that saved me. The passage opened into a yawning cavern and something glowed an evil, eldritch green on the far wall. A series of circles and lines in a design that made my head hurt and my stomach swim. But I could only catch glimpses of it past the other men as they stood there and stared. And before I got a proper look, they turned upon each other like animals.

"They screamed and howled inhuman, ungodly sounds and ripped and clawed and bit at each other until gore sprayed the walls. I had no thought but self-preservation and I turned and ran, stumbling blind through the black caves until I fell into the pouring rain, the roar of the sea in my ears. I dragged that rowboat back to the waves, leaped in and passed out from sheer terror.

"I have no idea how long I drifted, but luck took me past the rocks, out into the ocean. The weather calmed and, half-dead, starved, and dehydrated, I was found by a passing Spanish merchant vessel. They fed me, watered me, and dropped me in harbor. I will never step off solid land again, I tell you true."

We were silent for several moments after Jenks finished his yarn. He drank his beer, eyes haunted and wet.

"And that's what you draw," Reeve said eventually.

"What's that?"

"The thing you only saw in part in that hell cavern, that's the pattern you draw now. The one you drew for me. Yes?"

Jenks frowned, his knuckles whitened on the cup. "What have I drawn for you?" His confusion and madness had superseded his eloquence once more now he was back in the present.

Reeve stroked Jenks' hair as though the man were a faithful hound. "Drink," he said in his soft, commanding voice, and moved to another seat.

I sat on the floor beside his chair and Reeve patted my shoulder as he drank deep. "Believe him?" he asked me.

"I believe he thinks it's true," I said, for the man's tale bore no hint of artifice. Madness it might be, but deliberate lie it was not.

Reeve nodded. "I think so, too. You're astute for a boy barely in his teens, eh? And I think we have gained something very valuable. You will tell no one of this night's tale, or of this"—he patted his jacket again—"understand? No one."

I nodded, his requests would always bind me. "That crazed thing he drew is valuable?" I asked.

Reeve drained his mug and said, "It's not so crazed, Daniel. It's a map."

I looked up at him, confused. "A map?"

But my captain was not paying attention to me any more. He looked over to Jenks, eyes dark beneath his heavy brow. He sniffed and rose, walked to the madman, and spoke softly. They quietly left the room together. I tried not to consider the possibilities and shortly Reeve returned, slipping his shining dagger back into the leather sheath that hung from his belt.

He slumped into his seat, smiled at me, and raised his tankard. "To Esme, eh?" He swigged, handed it to me for a gulp.

"Always," I replied, sadness tugging at my gut.

Though I had never seen him drunk, the liquor always made him melancholy. "Hair that shone like a raven's wing," he said in a whisper.

I handed back his ale. "Aye, Captain. And her eyes were like emeralds, eh?"

"You remember her nearly as fondly as I, don't you, lad?"

"I do."

• • •

We sailed on the early tide. A mass of hungover men and women gathered before the poop deck once we had left New Providence harbor for the open ocean. Reeve gave his customary speech.

"We met in the dark and secret dens where the superior British fear to venture," he began, his soft voice carrying on the warm breeze as each crew member leaned forward to better hear. "Some of you are escaped, or slighted folk, some call you criminals. Well, the law of men be damned. We have no love for those who would rule us, place us under the yoke of order." He barked laughter, which the crowd dutifully echoed. "So we go where we please, we take what we want, and at every opportunity we make His Majesty's finest pay!"

His enthusiasm was ever infectious and fists punched the air, voices roared approval.

Reeve dragged Harkness to his side. "This man is your first mate and whatever he says you can believe came directly from my lips. He'll watch you with a hawk's eye and any man or woman not pulling their weight will find themselves swimming home. Look upon this fellow and fear him, for to cross him is to die. But impress him with your effort, please him, and you will please *me*. And we'll all share in the bounty of our endeavors."

Harkness nodded, smiling wolfishly at the sailors who returned his gaze with trepidation. Where Reeve was big and bushy and authoritative, Harkness was smooth and bald, all hard muscle and aggression. Between them they were a formidable team. Hard to believe that only the three of us and four other crew had survived the last encounter with the Royal Navy. Hard also to believe we had nevertheless won that battle. Or perhaps not so hard to believe, for Reeve's vendetta against those responsible for Esme's death raged and burned inside him like a furnace.

When she was alive, she held her place in his heart, beside his love of gold. He told himself he pillaged and plundered to win and keep her, but she knew better. Knew his greed was his own alone, though loved him still, guided him. Reeve was always captain but it was ever Esme who ruled the ship back then. I wonder what kind of man he might have been if she still lived. When she was gone, the guiding hand that kept the wheel steady was lost. His lust for gold became a lust for blood.

But I approved.

She may have been his lover, but she was like a mother to me. Furious and fearsome, beautiful and brave, she instilled in me a passion for learning, for reading. She showed me I could be something more if I wanted. Her loss left a hole in me, a wound that will not heal. Anytime I feel it might begin to close, I pick at it until it's fresh and bleeding once more. I don't want her memory to ever fade from my mind. I remember her blood on my hands as I held her after a fateful skirmish with the Royal Navy that went so wrong. As she breathed her last, she said, "Love him, but never trust him." And then she died.

The bastard who brought her low took a long time to die, his body hung on the main-mast until the flesh rotted and the bones had nothing to hold them together. The skull still sits in Reeve's cabin, grinning from his desk. Many more have fallen since in a campaign of revenge that will probably never end. We have lost more crew than any other of our kind, yet here Reeve was with another signed up already, drawn by the lure of plunder and freedom.

We sailed for two days and little was seen, no quarter to invade. The weather was hot, the skies blazing blue, and the water clear as crystal, and calm. Hackett in the crow's nest reported no land or ships, and so we sailed on awaiting opportunity. I waited on Reeve in his cabin, fetched him food, poured him liquor, reported any word from Harkness, and, in between times, continued to consume the library he and Esme had built together.

But as time passed, as we sailed further and further from known seas, I realised Reeve paid little attention to his books and less to his crew. He studied that strange thing he had called a map. I did my best not to look upon it, for it still made my insides squirm, but Reeve was obsessed. He muttered about things missing, gaps in the directions, if only that mad fool had seen it all. Of course, had he seen it all, he would not have survived to pass it on, if his tale were to be believed. *This is too much*, I thought, *for a mortal mind to conceive. It saves us from itself. Or it should.*

As I straightened Reeve's bed one day, I heard him mutter again. "Need to fill what the madman missed, find the final heading. Riches greater than gold or British blood, aye." He scratched at the paper with a charcoal stick, frowned and cursed, rubbed out his lines and tried again. Time after time, he sought to stumble upon those missing parts. And what would happen if he did? I wondered.

"Captain," I said nervously, "should we not be on deck, watching for the Navy?"

"They will come whether we watch or no."

I frowned. "Are they not the greatest enemy? We are drifting farther from the waters they patrol. Should we not turn about and hunt them? For Esme," I added quickly at his dark look.

He stared at me with eyes colder than he had ever laid on me before.

"Men went mad from that design," I said in a quavering voice.

"Weak men. Be about your work, boy." He returned his attention to the accursed, all-consuming chart.

That night I woke from my sack in the porch of his quarters to see Reeve stalk past me in the silvery moonlight. Hot and clear, moon and stars bright, he stood on deck and stared up to the firmament. In his hand he held the madman's map and he consulted it, looked up, turned, consulted it again. He searched for something among the stars that might fill the gaps which eluded him. I closed my eyes, tried not to think about it, and slept before he went back inside. Every night after he repeated the action, gazing to the heavens, seeking answers in infinity.

• • •

Five days out, to my surprise, Hackett yelled down to us that a frigate flying British colors had crossed the horizon. Reeve burst into action, for the first time roused from his contemplations. He set up his merchant's flags and raised the ragged, torn sails, the decoys. He had the men head the *Scarlet Wind* on a drifting course to intercept. A deception to make us appear becalmed, a scam he had employed a dozen times.

The crew lolled about the deck, feigning dehydration and weakness even as they held concealed weapons and boarding ropes. As the British hoved alongside, some officer in a glittering uniform called out, asking if we needed aid. Reeve hid while a dark-haired Spanish woman staggered to the gunwale, her voice weak with desperation. "Please, help us! We have been stuck out here so long, our captain dead, most of our crew sick or dying."

"Are you diseased?"

"No, sir, simply starved!"

The other vessel moved to pull abreast and as they drew near, Reeve barked the order. The *Scarlet Wind* heeled over and all our disguised starboard ports fell open and cannon thrust forth, each barking twelve pounds of iron destruction in deafening unison, aimed at the frigate's waterline. Before the British could react, holes punched into their vessel. It leaned to and began to take on water. Reeve yelled and our crew leaped up and swung across, swords rending even as the Navy men desperately tried to bring muskets and pistols to bear.

Reeve himself led the charge, a shining blade in each hand, one his own and the other Esme's. He always played both weapons together since her death. "Slay them all and grab everything you can carry before this rat-infested shit-hole of a ship goes down!" he called.

The battle was harsh and fast, bloody and brutal. Several of our men fell, but all the British died. Reeve took his time with their captain as our crew seized everything of value they could find and repaired to the *Scarlet Wind* as the frigate gave its last heave and sigh and tipped stern first to the deep.

The crew caroused and celebrated with gusto as night fell and Reeve had secured himself another loyal band. They drank the plundered rum, shared the shining coin, and fell into a stupor drifting free by dawn.

Except Reeve, who seemed uninterested in the booty, unfulfilled by the slaughter. He took his map and left the festivities before the night was done and once again studied the skies for clues. His passion for the destruction of the British appeared to wane in the face of this new obsession and all his drive went to it. Each time he studied that thing, another part of him darkened, another moment of his patience wore thin.

He greedily swigged rum as he stared, eyes bloodshot, at the stars.

"You don't want to stow the gold, sir?" I asked him as dawn smudged the horizon and I headed for my rest.

"The crew will manage," he slurred.

"But can you trust their count . . . ?" I began.

Reeve tore his gaze from above and waved the madman's chart in my face. "You think it compares to this? You've read the same books as I, you know the stories of riches beyond dreams hidden by the great travelers of old."

Myths and legends, I thought, and was sure he knew that to be the case. But he clearly thought differently since the mad vagrant's tale. I wondered if the lunacy of the chart had begun to infect his wits and I despaired. But he was more abrupt with me than he had ever been and I learned to steer clear of his attention as much as I could.

• • •

For several days more we sailed on, seemingly directionless, certainly away from land and the possibility of further British encounters. Or any other encounter, for that matter. But I knew Reeve followed what he could of the strange guide he had gained. The crew began to grow restless as the days passed and we moved further from the islands.

Eventually Harkness approached him in the quiet of one evening as I polished silverware, unseen, ignored. "The crew are fretting for our course, Captain."

Reeve's dark face was shadowed, his expression unclear, but his voice was bored. "Is that so?"

"They wonder why we move farther from our prey, east into open ocean. The loot and the enemy are to be found among the islands, no?"

"They are, most likely, but I seek other things. Best not to question your captain."

"And I have never questioned you before, though I must admit to sharing their concern. We are heading not only into open water, but into a region known for dangers. A place where ships go and never return."

"Superstition?" Reeve scoffed. "You take the nonsense fears of these uneducated men and women seriously?"

Harkness stiffened, the implication not lost on him. "Was a time you were a superstitious man yourself, Reeve, and rightly so. We should not tempt the gods or fates."

Reeve flapped a hand. "We tempt no one. Trust in me and those dogs will do likewise. Now begone, I have work to do."

Harkness's eyes narrowed, unaccustomed to being spoken to like that by Reeve. They were as much friends as captain and first mate, but Harkness chose to challenge no further. I felt his dismay and shared it. The captain had ever been driven by a powerful vengeance, though now his demeanor was darker. Where he had been fair, he was becoming mean. Where he had been friendly, he became cold.

Harkness left and Reeve, oblivious, returned to the study of his star chart. Before long, he went out into the night to stare up again.

• • •

The morning after Reeve had a moment of revelation with his map, the crew tried mutiny. The captain had laughed aloud and filled in a part of his guide after spotting something in the heavens, and he sat and stared at his new instructions for the rest of the night. When he gave a fresh heading to Harkness the next day, the first mate's face clouded and the crew murmured dissention.

Harkness drew himself tall. "I have followed you for many years and always with loyal service, but this course is one I cannot condone. Those waters are ruled by monsters and death."

"Can't condone?" Reeve laughed. "You think to take command?"

Harkness said nothing, simply raised his chin, and his silence spoke volumes. In a move so fast it belied his bulk, Reeve pulled free Esme's sword and cracked its hilt into Harkness's nose. The man howled and fell, blood pouring from his face. Reeve grabbed a rope and wrapped and rolled Harkness in it before the first mate could put up a fight. Reeve hauled him, trussed up tight, to the rail. With swift strikes he opened several wounds on both of Harkness's legs and crimson flooded the deck as the crew stared dumbfounded and Harkness wailed. Reeve tipped his first mate screaming over the side, the captain's face and muscles straining with the effort as he held Harkness up by the rope, just the poor man's lower half trailing in the waves.

The crew stood stunned. The blood drew sharks and Harkness began to thrash and buck in the water as they found him, but Reeve would not let go the rope. "Anyone else care to challenge my orders?" Reeve shouted over the first mate's high-pitched, agonized screams.

I could see some men wanted to rush the deck and take the captain down, but they lacked the courage. Others' will was broken by Harkness's gurgling yowls. I could not believe Reeve had so quickly and casually sacrificed a man who had been for years and years his second-in-command and his friend. My captain had changed beyond recognition.

Reeve let go the rope at last and the sudden silence was far worse than Harkness's blood-curdling shrieks. "Then it would appear a position has opened on this ship. Any volunteers?"

It seemed a handful of the crew were still loyal, maybe even more so after that display of strength and determination. One man stepped up. "I will take that role," he said in a deep baritone voice.

Reeve smiled, and it was terrible. "Atkins. One of my original men, still with me, still true."

"Aye, Captain."

"Then first mate you are. You know what to do and you know our heading. Make it so."

Without waiting to see if the crew would follow Atkins—knowing, for now at least, they would—Reeve returned to his cabin and his study.

• • •

That night the *Scarlet Wind* followed the dread bearing toward a place in the ocean where even small fry like me knew ships should never go. Reeve's obsession appeared to be taking its toll on his mind and body. For all his strength, he looked somehow diminished by nightfall and tumbled into his bunk clutching the map and fell straight into a deep sleep. For the first time in a week, he didn't stand on deck and study the stars.

From my sack I heard some scufflings and whispers and I was scared, but did not move to look. There was nothing I could do, so I listened until there was only the creak of timber, the slap of the waves, and the muffled clap of rigging. I sank back to sleep.

• • •

When I rose as the sun lanced across me I found Atkins standing there, ashen and trembling. It turned out he was now the first mate of a four-man crew. When the rest sloped off in the night they had knocked those few loyalists senseless and stolen food and water. It speaks volumes of Reeve's reputation as a killer that after Harkness's murder they were too scared to even try en masse to take the ship from him. They instead took most of our supplies and all but one rowboat. Perhaps that was a small mercy, those mutinous dogs leaving that boat in case the last remaining of us should think to abandon Reeve to his mania. But we were the truly loyal, more fool us.

The captain rose and growled his displeasure, but his voice sounded weak and his eyes were dim above bags even darker than his skin, despite the long night's sleep he had taken. "Move on, there's enough of us to continue," he said.

"Should we not strike for land and more hands?" Atkins asked.

The captain spun, grabbed a handful of Atkins's grubby shirt. "And how far is land, eh? And how close are we to our goal? Do as I say."

"I don't rightly know what our goal is, Cap'n."

"It is to sail that way and ask no questions."

"And should the wind change? We don't have the hands—"

"It will not change." Without waiting for further conversation, Reeve returned to his chart.

That night, we crossed an unseen boundary and entered the region of sea where men knew not to venture. Our small crew, stretched thin, pushed on. Their faces were masks of trepidation, but a modicum of greed lived there as well and that should ever be taken as the lesson of this folly. The tiniest speck of avarice will undo the most determined man.

Reeve stood upon the deck as night fell and held his map. He stared upward and began to laugh and laugh. He ran back to his cabin and through the window I saw him scratch more lines and curves on his design. And I watched the last sanity leave his eyes. I ran to cower behind barrels as he strode out on deck, adjusted the wheel, and tied it off to fix our heading. He called his remaining men forth. As they ran to him, he drew his twin blades and danced between them, severing limb and artery with artistic precision.

He took up their bleeding corpses one by one, opened their throats, and drained them into the waves as an unnatural wind picked up. From my place between barrel and rail I could see the men's blood swirling and gathering against the flow of the currents, growing and spreading in the water. It tied itself into a thick, dark thread, almost black in the night, and wormed across the ocean ahead of the *Scarlet Wind*.

Moonlight silvered the waves as the wind whipped them up and clouds began to roil on the horizon. Starlight glittered from above and lit the trail of blood as it seemed to draw our ship along. Reeve stood in the prow, leaning forward, arms wide, and began calling out words I could not understand and did not like.

They felt like nails driving into my ears. In one hand, the mad vagrant's chart flapped like an angry wing. The foul pattern that should never have been revealed. No mortal mind should be able to conceive its instruction. And none would have but for a moment of partial clarity held by a running man, combined with the will of a captain of powerful drive finally finding something to fill the void of love most heinously lost. A man driven. Standing at Reeve's side, shimmering gossamer in the night, stood Esme, terrible and beautiful. Her shining hair streamed in the wind. She reached out and laid one ghostly hand upon his shoulder.

The *Scarlet Wind* plowed on, and dread pirate Reeve sang forth. The blood of his most loyal dragged us forward on stranger tides than any I have ever known and in the ocean before the ship, like a gargantuan yawning maw, a desolate portal to a nether Darkness split open.

My bladder opened, too, and I had seen enough. Realizing the last remaining rowboat was but a few paces away, I clambered in and used my small dagger to cut the rope. The only thing I owned became my salvation from the man who had gifted it to me. Who had been lost, really, since the dark and beautiful Esme fell.

The boat dropped to the churning waves with a bone-jarring impact as a storm howled forth from that unholy rent in the ocean. I grabbed the oars and rowed for my life, forced to watch that from which I ran as I worked. Foul, black, winged beasts surged through that maw and into the stormy sky as the *Scarlet Wind* was drawn into the Darkness. The ship that was my life, my home, with the man who was the closest thing to a father I had ever known, tumbled, cracked, and split as it went over that profane edge.

As I rowed away, powerless but to look across the churning waves into that yawning gulf, the great winged creatures flapped determinedly across the night sky, blanking out the stars with their massive presence. The downdraft from their beats pushed against me as they headed west toward the islands and the New World. Terrible, hungry creatures like no bird or flying mammal I had ever seen, indistinct yet hideous in the night sky. And as they passed I had the inexplicable yet certain realization that these were but heralds for some far more vast and ravenous evil yet to be released. And I wondered, should the madness of any men eventually facilitate that escape, as Reeve had done with these, would that terrible leviathan's shadow ever be removed when it fell across our sun?

I rowed on and on, away from the unnatural swirl, until my muscles were as jelly, my eyes hazy, my mind blank. And then a different kind of blackness stole over me and I fell unconscious to the bottom of the small vessel.

For days I drifted, burned by the sun, starved, desperate for water, and I almost did that one forbidden thing and drank the ocean, when finally a Navy ship came by. British. The irony was not lost on me as they hauled me aboard. I was the son of a merchant, I told them, whose ship had gone down in a storm. They asked how many escaped and I honestly told them I did not know, for how many might have survived that mutinous exodus under the cover of darkness? They smiled on me, fed and watered me, and returned me to New Providence.

Now I am the vassal of their leader, a general with buck teeth, white hair, and a most ridiculous uniform. But he is not unkind and I have a shack of my own to live in when I am not required to wait upon him, or clean, or labor.

And in that ramshackle hut I call my own, I huddle in the shadows of night, listening for those terrible leathery wingbeats. When they don't come, I rise with the sun and bask in its glory all day, dreading the next inevitable night, for one day they will surely make their presence known. Perhaps one day they will lead that which they serve to destroy all we know and hold dear. And I can't help wondering if maybe that is not what the human race deserves for its avarice and hostility.

But whatever may happen or not, I will never set foot again on any vessel that would remove me from this solid, dry land.

~

IN THE BLOOD

DIRK FLINTHART

"Internet's down." Geoff's voice drifted up from the ground floor. "Do you want to check it? Or shall I go?"

I smoothed my hand through Finn's soft hair. It was a pleasure I took when I could. He was due for another round of chemotherapy in less than a month. Soon enough that sweet mop of raven curls would be gone and we'd be back to knitted caps over the pale egg of his scalp. "You go," I called. "It's probably just the weather anyway. Or McGuigan and his damned plough again." The old man down the road had cut our lines on four occasions already. If he wasn't such a drunk, I'd swear it was on purpose.

Finn didn't move. He was so pale, there under the eiderdown, just the fever-spots on his cheeks to show he was more than a corpse. It nigh broke my heart seeing him that way, but I couldn't bring myself to leave, though he was fast asleep. "Poor mite," I said, and touched the silk of his hair again. "Better days will come."

I was still watching him when I heard Geoff's footsteps on the worn carpet of the landing, and the familiar creak of the floorboards. "I think you should take a look, Deirdre," he said as he came into the room. He was flushed with exertion or excitement and his eyes glittered behind his glasses. "I think there's a fairy ring down in the hollow."

My chest tightened. "Are you certain?"

Geoff shook his head. "Of course I'm not certain. You're the expert. That's why I want you to go." He looked down at Finn. "How's he doing?"

"About the same," I said. "His temperature is down a little."

"I'll sit with him," Geoff said, and settled into the chair on the far side of Finn's bed.

Expert, he called me. Like anyone could truly understand the Others. Their return had been confirmed less than a decade ago. They were elusive, aloof, and equipped with abilities that made a mockery of our science. What little we knew was a matter of observation and induction: things involving the Others happened in particular ways, and the patterns seemed to repeat themselves. Were they real patterns, or simply artefacts of a limited data sample? We had no way of knowing.

The theory I liked best said that the Others lived in another *brane*—another four-dimensional space-time continuum drifting through a greater universe of seven, eleven or thirteen dimensions, depending on whose math you accepted. And from time to time, their *brane* overlapped ours in places, touching like two silk scarves on a clothesline, blowing in the wind. When the *branes* came together, sometimes it was possible to pass from one to the other. Possible for *them*, anyway. For us, not so much. Maybe the physics was wrong. Nobody knew. But we knew things didn't work quite right around a true Incursion, which was why Geoff got anxious every time the Internet connection fell over.

The sky outside was cool and clear, one of those brisk days you get in early autumn. We kept the house warm for Finn's sake, but I preferred the crispness of the air off the Burren—all those acres of limestone and meadow, blackberry and hawthorn. Some folk held that our house, so close to that wonderful desolation, was a lonely place to live, but I loved it. Coming here to the land of my ancestors after generations in exile—there was no real reason it should be so, but it felt like a homecoming. I fell in love with the old house the moment we saw it. That it was a hotspot in local fairy lore made it perfect.

I took my stick with me down to the hollow. It was seasoned blackthorn, what the old ones would call a *shillelagh*. Not all the Fay were friendly. Nor were they all vulnerable to the weapons that we understand best. But if I stayed outside the ring, a metre of tough blackthorn bound in iron would offer a measure of security. I also carried salt, a pocketful of iron nails made by a blacksmith, and a Glock 9 mm semi-automatic pistol with custom loads. I have dealt with the Others before, which is why some people think of me as an expert.

The instant I broke through the mass of wind-sculpted hawthorns and blackberry bramble, I stopped. The air seemed heavier and warmer, and the breeze was gone. The hollow was a queer place at any time—a tiny, perfect circle of meadowland amidst the wildness—but today the wide ring of orange-capped toadstools made a clear warning: *stay back!* I did not ignore that warning, dropping to one knee to peer through my hand-glass at one of the fungi.

My belly did a flip-flop. Geoff had been right.

There are many fungi which produce so-called fairy rings. They are nothing more than the fruiting bodies of a dispersed, largely underground organism. There is only one species which is known to depend on whatever magic it is that comes from the place where the Fay live: *Amanita fata*, from the Latin for 'Fate', the goddess who gave her name to our word for the Others. *A. fata* is slightly toxic, wildly psychoactive, and grows only at the site of an active Incursion. The ring in the hollow was among the largest I had ever encountered, perhaps twenty metres across. I took one of the smaller toadstools from the outer edge, and tucked it into my satchel. The science boys in the labs at Limerick would want to check the DNA, but I was already certain.

I brought the news back to Geoff. "It's a fairy ring all right," I told him, and his face sagged with relief. "Don't get your hopes up," I admonished. "We don't know if we'll get a visitor. And if we do, we don't know what kind. Lesser sprites, flower fay—it might not even be able to help."

"But there *is* hope," Geoff said. His hand fell on Finn's brow. Finn murmured in his sleep, and rolled onto his side, and my heart ached for him.

"Other people have had luck," I agreed. It was true, as in the old stories: luck and the Others went hand–in-hand. But just as in the old stories, there was a price. "We need one of those who can handle blood magic. They're a difficult, dangerous lot."

"I know," said Geoff. "Still, any hope is something."

I slipped behind him and put my arms round his chest, resting my head against his neck. "I'll take a bowl of milk to the edge of the ring," I murmured. "I don't know if it will be any use, but it may help them understand we're well-disposed to visitors."

That night the weather closed in, with rain and fog. Geoff and I sat, moodily taking turns to build up the fire in the wood-stove, until tiredness overcame him and he went off to bed. I waited until the birds sang dawn into the sky, then fell asleep in my chair.

• • •

"The milk didn't work," Geoff told me when I awoke, stiff and groggy. "Any other ideas?"

I yawned, tasting the foulness of unbrushed teeth. "How do you know it didn't work?" I said. "Some of them are quite small. All of them are good at remaining unseen. They may have come."

Geoff made a snorting sound, and stalked off to the kitchen. I heard him rattling around for a moment, and then he returned with an old plastic ice-cream bucket. In the bottom were the jagged remains of the blue-flowered ceramic bowl which I had filled with milk and left by the fairy ring. "I didn't bother collecting all of it," he said. "It was pretty thoroughly crushed."

I pushed the pieces round with my fingertip. There wasn't a single piece even so large as a pound coin in there. "I'd call that a rejection," I said. "Not all of them like milk, Geoff." I glanced over his shoulder at the liquor cabinet. "*Uisce beatha*," I said. "Water of Life. Or so I'm told."

He followed my gaze. "You think they might like whiskey?"

I nodded. So far as the stories went, some of the Others had a taste for spirits. What I did not say to Geoff was that most of those were wild ones, unpredictable and dangerous. Bargaining with any of those would be fraught. But my son lay in his bed upstairs, his blood poisoned with cancer. I would bargain with the Devil himself if there was hope in it. "We'll leave them a bottle tonight," I said. "A whole bottle, still sealed."

"Drunken fairies," he said sourly. "Is that a thing?"

"Sometimes," I said. "I'll take a shower. Then I'll go into town and get a bottle."

Geoff shook his head. "You stay here. Finn needs his mother. Besides, I know you didn't sleep worth a damn last night. You'd probably put the Land Rover into a hedge."

I hesitated. "He needs his father, too. But you're right about the Land Rover." Pulling myself out of the overstuffed chair, I leaned into Geoff until he hugged me properly, the roughness of his beard scratching pleasantly at my forehead. "Make sure it's good whiskey," I said. "The best we can afford. I don't know if they can tell the difference, but I don't think we should take the chance."

He held me at arm's length, and looked at me. "Thank you," he said. "I know you don't like the . . . the Others. And I know the stories, too. Everyone does. But Finn . . . "

I shushed him with a fingertip. "I know," I said. "Me, too."

• • •

The day lasted too long. The Others are liminal creatures, seen most often by dusk or in the first light of dawn. To ease the waiting, I sat with Finn and read to him. He wanted fairy tales, those hoary myths made popular again by the mysterious return of the creatures that spawned them so long ago. I chose the gentlest and most innocuous that I could: the tale of the cobbler and the elves that make shoes from his scrap leather. Finn fell asleep before I was half through, but I finished reading the story anyway. It was comforting: the kindly shoemaker and his wife, the cheerful, diligent little elves, and the easy bargain they made. Prosperity for the shoemaker, new shoes and clothes for the elves.

I glanced at Finn, pale and drawn in his bed. I would gladly stitch a thousand little suits of clothing and count it the greatest of good luck, if it meant a cure for him. But even if Geoff and I could strike a bargain with a wild Fay, it was almost certain the price would be much higher. They used to say such Others came from the Unseelie Courts, and the tales concerning them did not end with prosperity and new shoes.

Geoff returned with a bottle of something I didn't recognise, and had no hope of pronouncing. My family had kept to its Irish roots down the long decades in America, proudly marching on St Paddy's day, cheering for the Fighting Irish at the football, and singing the old songs at family gatherings. Even my name—Deirdre—is one of those ancient Irish names, but I know hardly a word of the old tongue. I have promised myself I will study it properly one of these days, but there's never enough time. I held the bottle up to the light, admiring the rich, red-brown of the contents. "It's good, then?" I asked.

"Better be," Geoff answered. "We're two hundred pounds the lighter for it."

"If it works," I said, "It'll be money well spent. We'll buy another and share it to celebrate."

He smiled at that, the little crinkles showing at the corners of his grey-blue eyes. I kissed him, and sent him off to watch over Finn. As he climbed the stairs, I called to him: "I'll place the bottle now, and get ready. Remember, if we have a visitor tonight, you must leave the bargaining to me. You understand?"

He nodded, and went up to our son.

You can study the Others. There are scientists all over the world working day and night to unlock their secrets. What little we have gleaned can be learned in courses at the world's universities: names, types, abilities, histories . . . All of it *caveat emptor,* and subject to change without notice. They are what they are. No two are entirely alike, and even the abilities of individuals vary. There are things they can do within the confines of a fairy ring which seem to be impossible for them outside. Some claim to be stronger during certain phases of the moon. Most can be turned by iron, and some by salt.

None of these things can be relied on. Personally, I think the courses are useless. What good is it to know that a spriggan is a tree-sprite whose flesh resembles gnarled wood? Those are words. The reality is something altogether more. Studying the Others doesn't prepare you for actual magic.

Experience helps. I don't know if it's possible to get used to the Others, but I know that one can learn to control oneself around them. The glamour that many possess—the ability to mask their appearance, to seem as something or someone else—is as variable as so much else about them, but almost all use it to impress, seduce, or even to frighten and overwhelm. At first, the influence of Fay glamour is nigh irresistible, but with repeated exposure, you can learn to deal with it. Those university courses—they'll tell you to use mirrors, to splash fresh water into your eyes, or even to look cross-eyed to see through the enchantment. I suppose some of those things work, for some people, with some of the Others. But familiarity is the real teacher.

Family can help. There are bloodlines. People of different races, different ethnic stock, whose families have a historic connection with the Others. It's hard to sort out the truth here, because nobody wants to be watched, poked, prodded, interrogated and studied. The suspicion is that perhaps at some time in the past there was some genetic exchange between humankind and the Others. The old stories mention such things: selkie-children; Morgana le Fay, half-sister to the legendary King Arthur. The few samples that the scientists have taken from the Others confirm that they have cells and DNA much as we do. There are differences, but not so great as to make the old stories of changelings and half-breeds completely impossible.

What is certain is that some families have more luck in their dealings with the Others. My family is one such. So is Geoffrey's. For this reason, we were successful when we petitioned the government for permission to buy the old house. If we could strike the right bargain, perhaps we might do more than just cure Finn. Maybe we could buy a cure for all children like him.

It was another couple like Geoff and I who acquired the secret of Fay-silver, the alloy of mercury and silver that can flow like liquid yet transform in an instant to something harder than steel. Ivan and Katinka Bruloff, in the north of Russia traded the complete works of Beethoven and a CD player in exchange for Fay-silver. Now they are impossibly wealthy.

I would be happy if my little boy could run, and play in the sun.

• • •

Not long after twilight, the wind changed. All day the breeze had come from the west. Now it swirled, tossing the hawthorns, spinning the old iron weathercock on the roof to exhaustion. A raven called nearby, once, twice, three times. I looked at Geoff. He nodded.

A knock came at the wooden door, the back one that gave into the kitchen. I took a deep breath. "Who's there?"

"A traveller," said a deep voice. It was coarse and gruff. "The night's cold. I'd welcome the hospitality o' your home."

"Enter, then, if you can," I said, and waited.

The door flew open, though neither Geoff nor I had unlocked it. Framed against the night I saw what seemed a small man, hairy and naked save for a pair of heavy boots and a sagging cloth cap of red. That was not what he wanted me to see, I knew. My eyes swam and watered. Sometimes I caught a glimpse of a tall, handsome man in a dark suit with a red tie, but I knew that the short, hairy naked vision was closer to the truth.

"Redcap," I said, between my teeth. Geoff glanced at me, puzzlement in his eyes. I waved him to silence.

My vision stopped wavering. The hairy little man—he was no taller than my waist—grinned at me. "Ye know my kin, eh, lassie? Wull enough. I hae yer leave tae enter?" He affected a Scots accent, of sorts. Maybe he'd learned his English there.

"If you can," I repeated.

He grinned more widely, showing big, yellow teeth and bobbed his head, but he didn't move. "Eh, twas you as brought the wee bottle, no? Tha' was a fine gift, like. I'm awful sorry aboat yer milk, an' all. I was took by surprise there. The bottle makes us square. I come as a guest, lass. No harm to ye or any under yer roof."

Geoff took my hand. I knew what he was thinking. He wanted me to take the iron horseshoe from above the door so our visitor could enter. But I knew Redcaps. Or at least, I knew the stories. "Your word?" I said. "You mean us no harm? You'll act as a proper guest should?"

"My word, lass," he said, and I knew I'd get no more assurance than that. With my *shillelagh*, I knocked loose the horseshoe. It fell with a clatter to the slate floor. "Eh, there's a thing," said the Redcap. "Never did like the look o' such." He glanced around the kitchen, then stepped inside. The nails in his heavy boots clacked against the floor. "Would ye have such thing as bite o' supper about the place? I'm verra partial tae teacake, if ye have any."

"Teacake," Geoff said. I didn't like the sound of his voice. He was trying to repress a laugh, I could see. I squeezed his hand sharply. He winced, and set his jaw. "Yes. I think we have a teacake in the pantry. It's only a store-bought one, mind. Neither Deirdre nor I can bake."

Those bright little eyes beneath their dark and craggy brows settled on me. "Deirdre, is it? There's a fine old name. And who would yer man be, then?"

"My husband is Geoffrey," I replied. "And now you've the knowing of us, and we've none of you." I squeezed Geoff's hand again, and he scurried off to the pantry, returning with a slab of teacake still wrapped in plastic.

"Rory," said the Redcap, though I think an Irishman or a Scotsman might have spelled it differently to me. "And the truth is, I'm plain famished. I dinna wish tae be rude, but I'd be much obliged if we could set a while, and eat."

"This way, Rory," I said, and together we went to the dining room.

Rory ate his way through the teacake in one sitting. He chatted about the weather, and about the doings of some Lord Scroop he'd known hundreds of years ago. I listened, and answered politely when it seemed right. When Rory leaned back from the table, wistfully eyeing the last few crumbs of teacake, I nudged Geoff, and he brought out the cupcakes we'd been saving for the weekend. Then it was the scones that Mrs McGuigan gave us, with the last of the wild blackberry jam, and half a loaf of toast with butter and honey. At last he pushed his chair back from the table and burped, holding his hand up to his lips.

"Tha's a grand feast," he declared. "Yer a mighty host, Geoffrey." His eyes glittered as he looked at the pair of us and the dark, wood-panelled room in which we sat. "Ye've a bairn," he said, gesturing at Finn's football, sitting sad and half-deflated on the toy-box. "Tha's guid. A couple such as ye I'd wish many fine, happy, bouncing babbies."

"We have a son," I said. "But he's sick. He can't come down from his room."

"Is tha' right?" Rory affected concern. "Eh, now. We cannae be having with tha', can we? Ye've been such fine hosts an' all, I'm inclined as I might take a look at the wee lad. I know summat o' the healing ways."

"His blood is sick," Geoff said, and I shot him a look but his face was white behind his glasses, and I could see his fists balled on his knees under the table. "He's going to die."

Rory's face fell. "Aww, nay, nay. An' him but a lad? Take us tae the wee feller, eh?"

"You want to help him?" I put in before Geoff could speak.

The Redcap waggled his head. "Happens I may. If I can, tha' is. An' if ye'll have ma help."

I grabbed Geoff's arm under the table. "We'll take you to see the boy, Rory. We can talk once you know whether you can help him."

Finn did not awaken when we switched on the lamp in his room. Geoff went to his bedside, and Rory went with him, but I hung back by the door. With my jacket partly open, I could reach my Glock quickly. Whether I was quick enough to match a Redcap was an open question. I was counting on his guest-oath to protect Finn—to protect us all. The Others take hospitality very seriously, in my experience; even brutes like the Redcaps, whose cloth caps are scarlet because they are regularly dipped in fresh blood.

Normally I would never have let something like Rory anywhere near my house. But Redcaps know blood, perhaps best of all the Others. I would have been happier dealing with a Fay Queen, or a lordling. Capricious though they are, there's something of kindness in them. Redcaps are killers, pure and simple. Yet they do know blood, and blood magic, and since science had given up on my son, magic—the impossible talent of the Others—was all that remained to Geoff and I, and to Finn most of all. So I held myself very still, and I breathed as evenly as I could, though my heart pounded in my chest, and I let the monster approach my sick, sleeping son.

The Redcap sniffed the air like a dog, his long nose twitching. "Aye, he's sick right enough," he said, and looked directly at me. "Might I touch the lad?" he asked, and I wondered how he knew to speak to me, though he had named Geoff as his host.

I wanted desperately to remind the Redcap of his guest-oath, but even more, I did not want him insulted or angered. Not trusting my voice, I nodded.

"I may touch him?" Rory asked again. Clearly, he was waiting for my word.

"You may touch him," I said, and folded my arms, sliding one hand under my jacket as I did.

The Redcap lay his hand, all hairy and long-fingered like a great, pink spider, on Finn's forehead. He frowned, and leaned over, sniffing once more. Then he straightened, and broke into a beaming smile. "Eh, now, an' I'm sure ye said it was a serious matter," he said to Geoff, his gruff voice light. "This is the Eating Sickness. Back home, not e'en the bairns suffer this. Takes only a few moments tae cleanse blood an' bone, an' they're right for all time. How've ye not fixed the lad already?"

"We don't know how," said Geoff simply, but I saw the tears forming in his eyes. "They told us he's going to die."

"Aww, nae need fer all tha'," said Rory, and folded his heavy arms across his broad chest. "Like as not I kin fix him up here and now, if ye'll have it."

"Yes," said Geoff, before I could speak. "Please. Yes. Save my son."

Then we were all talking at once: I was asking the cost, and Rory was saying it was more than a simple guesting-gift and there would be a price, and Geoff, poor lovely Geoff, he wouldn't shut up and he wouldn't stop saying yes, anything, yes, take whatever you will have if you will save my son.

And I could not unsay the words for him.

A chill washed over me. My heart raced. Rory glanced my way, but I stood as still as the stones of the house. He looked at Geoff, and nodded. "Let it be so," he said, and lay his hand once more upon my poor boy's fevered brow. At his touch, Finn cried out. Geoff moved then, but I lunged across the room and grabbed him before he could interfere.

"It's too late," I hissed. "You've agreed. Now we take what comes."

On the bed, Finn tossed and writhed, his little body bouncing and struggling, but the Redcap's hand never shifted. Though I can't swear to it, I believe I saw something moving, something that came out of the Redcap's palm and went into Finn, and something that fled Finn in his breath—a rank steam, a fog, a miasma that flowed from his nose and mouth into the night air. Then the Redcap took a pace back from the bed and grinned.

"Tha's done," he announced. "The laddie will be right as ever, soon's ye can get some o' tha' fine food intae him for his strength. And now," he said, his voice dropping lower. "The matter o' my price. Blood for blood, an' a life for a life. I'll have your blood for my cap, my lad," he said to Geoff. "I cannae take it here beneath yer roof as I've sworn, so ye maun come down the ring at dawn. An' mind yer no' late, or I cannae vouch for the consequences tae the wee one there," he said, with a nod at Finn. Then he laughed loud and long, a harsh, braying cackle that followed him down the stairs and out into the night.

Oh, and what a long and angry night it was.

Come the first hint of grey in the east, I stood with Geoff, shivering at the edge of the ring in the hollow. Finn was safe enough. His fever gone, he was in the care of the doctors in Innis. The tests were not yet returned, but I knew he would be cleared, the cancer vanished. I knew also that if Geoff did not appear at the ring by dawn, there would likely be far worse in store for our son.

"You're a fool," I told him gently, for the hundredth time. "You were supposed to let me bargain."

Geoff shook his head. His face was pale, and there were dark rings under his eyes, but he was resolute. "I know you," he said. "Finn's life was at stake. If I hadn't made the bargain, you would. I had to get in first."

To this I could say nothing. He was right, as usual. I knew from the moment the door opened what the cost would be. Redcaps know only blood.

I hugged him close. "I love you," I said.

From somewhere within the ring, I heard a cough. "Tha's verra touching. But the time's come tae pay up. I'm glad tae see ye've come."

There are stories. In the tale of Gawain and the Green Knight, the Fay threatens three times to behead Arthur's knight, and three times reprieves him for his honesty and courage. The lords and ladies amongst the Others are known to value such things.

There are stories. Tam Lin won free from a Queen of the Others by the strength of his true love, who held him fast though his shape was changed by Fay glamour to fire, to a serpent, to a dire beast. There are those of the Others who respect love.

Then there are the Redcaps.

Geoffrey stepped into the circle of toadstools. From a pool of shadows, Rory came forth, a long, wicked, rusty pike in one hand. He chuckled. "Ye may wish tae turn yer head, lassie," he said. "I cannae promise this will be quick, or pretty."

"I challenge," I said, in my strongest voice.

Rory stopped. Geoff turned and stared. I had not discussed this with him.

"I challenge," I cried again. "Blood for blood, a life for a life. If you can take my life, Rory Redcap, then you shall have us both and no crime on your head. But if I can take yours, then I walk free with my man and no punishment to follow. Will you bargain?"

The little Fay stared at me. In other circumstances, I would have enjoyed the incredulity on his craggy face. "Ye're mad, lass. I'm Rory Redcap. I've killed hundreds, nae, thousands o' strong men, and yer nowt but a skirted lass. This is nae challenge at all!"

"Do you cry yourself a coward, then?"

Rory hissed at that, and Geoff stepped back to the very edge of the ring, his eyes wide. “No one calls me a coward,” said the Redcap. “I’ll take yer challenge, lass, and make an orphan o’ yer wee lad.” He spun his pike menacingly so it growled and whooped in the chill morning breeze.

I laughed, and stepped into the circle bringing out my Glock. Firing two-handed, I put a full magazine into the Redcap, the roar of the gun filling the little clearing. Yet for each round I fired there came a sharp clang, and the Redcap’s grin widened as he deflected each and every shot with his iron pike. “Yer on my soil, lass,” he said. “Nae man’s toy can reach me here. See the touch o’ the Fay!” He pointed with his pike and I dodged instinctively, but I was not his target. In my grip, the steel and plastic of the Glock subsided, pitting and rusting and corroding to nothingness before my eyes. It was not simple glamour, but the touch of Time itself, and I remembered the old stories: how a year might pass on Earth in a single day spent in Faerie lands.

I dropped the remnants of the gun with a laugh, and brought my sword from over my shoulder into *chu-dan*, the middle guard. “You’ll need more than tricks, Redcap,” I said. “I’ll bathe my steel in your blood and nail your cap above my mantel.”

The Redcap chuckled, the sound like someone shaking an iron bucket full of gravel, and pointed at my blade. Then he frowned, and pointed again.

I laughed. “No,” I said. “*This* blade was made in Japan eight hundred years ago, by a smith who learned from the *Tengu*. It is sharp enough to slice a whisper, hard enough to cleave steel, and proof against all your magics and tricks.”

Rory growled, and advanced with his pike held low. “I’ll have yon blade from yer cold hands,” he said. “Yer still nowt but a lass.”

He was closing on me too quickly. I wasn’t ready for him yet. I danced aside, and moved across the ring. “You never asked my full name,” I told him, and he paused, watching me. “It is MacCall, but that’s only these few centuries past. Geoff tells me that long ago it was Mac Cumhail, and in his veins runs the blood of the great Finn, slayer of giants.”

At this, the Redcap laughed aloud and touched his pike to his cap. “I met Finn Mac Cumhail once,” he said, and looked across to Geoff. “A sight stronger than you, laddie.” Turning back to me, he said: "So ye've married above yerself. What will ye, talk me to death?"

But the tremors were upon me now, and I could scarcely form words as my muscles writhed and my very bones shifted. "No," I managed to growl, my voice an octave lower than before. "Geoff . . . married above himself. *My* family . . . comes from Ulster." The heat rose in me, and even through the ringing in my ears, I heard my clothes split and tear. Somewhere close by Geoff cursed, and stumbled away into the hawthorns, but my enemy was close enough that I could smell his sweat and hear the blood in his veins. "Did you . . . ever meet the one they called . . . the Hound?"

Rory shifted his grip so he held his pike like a quarterstaff, and made to close with me. His eyes were wide, now, and I could smell the beginnings of fear in his rank sweat. "Cuchulainn of Ulster is dead three thousand years," he shouted, "An' soon enough ye with him." He dashed the pike at my head with the same speed that could deflect bullets.

I cut away the head of his weapon with a counter that was faster still.

"Shite," said the Redcap, looking at the bright steel where his pike ended.

"We're on . . . *your* soil, monster," I grated. "Here I can use . . . the gifts . . . of *my* blood."

My breath was a howl, my heartbeat a frenzied drumroll. The Redcap snarled and brought out a huge, ragged-edged knife. I laughed.

We fought.

• • •

Much later, I staggered to the back of the house. There was an old horse-trough there, brimful of icy rainwater. I plunged myself into it again and again until the water stopped boiling and steaming, and I could see properly at last. I was naked, covered in bruises and scratches, but in my right hand I held the Masamune sword, and in my left I held a shapeless cloth cap, improbably scarlet in colour.

Geoff called down from the window above. "Is it safe?"

I looked up, and nodded wearily. "It's over. The battle-frenzy is gone. I'm done."

"Thought so," he said. "I'll unbolt the doors in a minute. Oh—the Internet is back up."

"Oh, good," I said. "Any word on Finn yet?"

"Clear," said Geoff. "There's more tests to come, but I think it worked. Would you like a cup of tea?"

"Not yet," I said. "I'm still hot through."

I sagged back against the trough, heedless of my nudity. The wracking, body-warping spasms of the battle-frenzy always left me exhausted. It would be hours before I cooled enough to bear clothing, days before I recovered my strength. "You should probably tell the agency what happened to the Glock," I said. Then I looked at my sword. "You should also ask them if they can source another blade. Sooner or later, the boy's going to need one."

"Right you are," said Geoff. He smiled down at me. "He'll be a monster-hunter for certain."

I blew him a kiss. "No question about it, love. It's in his blood."

~

THE EVENTS AT CALLAN PARK

EROL ENGIN

Australian and New Zealand Journal of Psychiatry (ANZJP)
November 2015 vol 53 no.2 86

ANZJP has documented the growing incidence of patients living in various geographical locations across Australia drawing identical pictures of environmental destruction. It has been noted that an ominous but indefinable 'shape' is also included in the drawings. The patients are invariably of an artistic background and claim that their images are 'predictive' of an imminent but nameless disaster. Similar cases have been documented overseas, adding a possible global dimension to this phenomenon. In the face of mounting public fear, the Australian government has exerted significant pressure on the psychiatric profession to offer rational explanations for the so-called 'artistic epidemic'.

To this end, I believe that I have found an historical (and thus psychiatric) precedent. At 9:00pm on July 28, 1914, Australia experienced its first recorded event of 'mania-transference/absorption'[1] *at Sydney's Callan Park Hospital for the Insane*[2]*. What follows are excerpts from the journal of Doctor Frederick De Klerk (MD: University of Sydney; M R C S, L S A: St George's Hospital: London), in which he details a patient's incessant creation of a 'mysterious, uncanny, indescribable' shape.*

[1]Current psychological theory rejects the notion of mania-transference/absorption, positing instead the deeply personal nature of psychological trauma: the mental affliction of an individual cannot be absorbed by another (Lindberg et al, 2007)

[2]Now the Sydney College of the Arts, a faculty of the University of Sydney.

6 July 1914

A most interesting letter from Dr Freud:

My dear De Klerk

. . . It remains my firm belief that all neurotic phenomena are the product of the mind and reducible to earth-bound causes. Venus does not (and cannot) outstrip Apollo! But I am writing not to discuss Dr Jung's shortcomings; these were apparent enough (and which you saw for yourself) at the Congress in Munich[3]*. I am writing because a neurotic in the care of an assistant suffers from a compulsive artistic malady and happens to be a countryman of yours. Though his treatment is by no means complete, the patient insists upon returning to Australia, which I feel may be beneficial. I have thus forwarded reports concerning his condition and request that you continue the investigations. Your belief in the therapeutic benefits of art, to say nothing of your own artistic abilities, should help to create an ideal rapport with the patient.*

Immediately I wrote back, thanking the Doctor for his recommendation.

The patient, one August Crebert, will arrive in a week's time. Dr Freud's file yields the following about the patient:

born in Newcastle in 1891 to coal mining parents

Decent but uninspired school career—considerable artistic abilities frustrated by lack of recognition and opposition from mother

In 1912 moves to Paris, then Berlin

1913 transported to Freud's practice in Vienna

Also contains a picture. A battlefield scene. The combatants lie strewn in great numbers across the field, like butchered cattle, maimed or riddled with bullets or blown limb from limb, reminiscent perhaps of the battlefields of the Civil War in America. The faces of the dying are rendered with special, obsessive attention—masks of tortured, twisted scowls, like faces of demons rather than soldiers. A vast, dark shape rises up from the carnage—somewhat tree-shaped, with heady fuzz atop a sturdy column. A cloud formation? A storm? An explosion?

[3]The Fourth Congress of the International Psychoanalytic Association was held on 7 and 8 September 1913 at the Hotel Bayerischer Hof in Munich. The meeting was dominated by the split between Jung and Freud; supporters of one sat at a table across from the other, a frosty no-man's-land in between. De Klerk sat decisively in Freud's camp.

When I finished with the picture it was late in the afternoon.

My odd dreams continue. In the worst, I stand before a glass, gazing at my reflection, studying each line and wrinkle, as if searching for something. A realisation dawns on me: my reflection is not my own, but that of a man I have never seen. When I awake I cannot specifically recall the man's features, yet a strong, strange sense of dread lingers with me.

13 July 1914

Left my practice early this morning and headed to Callan Park. Came up along Balmain Rd and went through Wharf St entrance. The old, familiar sandstone buildings, pinkish in the morning sun, slipped into view. An excellent hospital for moral therapy[4]: Manning and Barnet have done exceptionally well. Grounds much improved since my days as a student[5]: swards of lawn, swaying palms, curative open spaces; a distinct sign of progress for the nation, as regards the mentally ill.

Colleagues greeted me at the entrance, a visiting deity, the man to whom Freud himself has referred a case! (I had sent word ahead describing the situation). They led me along the wide sunlit corridors, past patients still in nightdress. Very keen to meet Crebert. Went up a twisting iron stairwell, and at last halted before a solid, reinforced door. I could not resist peering through the glass at eye level.

Inside was a small person seated in a chair. He was intensely absorbed in work, hunched over a desk, shoulders arched, right arm working furiously at something. I dismissed my attendants, pulled open the door and was alone with Crebert.

He did not turn to meet me. I cleared my throat. No response, only the constant scratching of Crebert's pencil.

[4]Moral therapy was the belief that insanity was no longer a general bodily problem, but a problem particular to the mind, the seat of morality. A patient's mental illness (or 'immorality') could thus be cured by the 'moral', curative effect of nature and art.

[5]De Klerk studied at Callan Park 1909–1910. It is believed that he entered the psychoanalytic profession after a close relative (possibly a grandfather) had been institutionalised. However, De Klerk briefly left the profession of psychoanalysis due to a 'crisis of faith' in the efficacy of treatment for the insane. Heartened by clinical advances made in Europe, particularly with moral therapy, he returned to the profession around 1912 with a desire to champion these advances in Australia.

"Mr Crebert," I called.

The scratching stopped. Crebert's head flicked up, so that I could see the beginnings of pattern balding, though he was only twenty-three. His movements are birdlike, but rash, impatient. He jerked his head to the side and eyed me peripherally, small frame, tense, shoulders sharply arched—an obsessive who resented interruptions. I must not waste his time.

"You are a fascinating man, Mr Crebert," I said, attempting to ease him through flattery. "And an excellent artist."

Crebert gave a slight nod.

"I have dabbled in the arts myself, in younger, more carefree days. Would you care to show me what you are working on?"

He jerked his head back and hunched over his desk. A light breeze gusted through the room's open windows. Through them I could see the light of the rising sun on the waters of Iron Cove. No *atelier* in the world, I told him, has a better view. I strode toward him, exaggerating my footsteps as a warning.

"I would very much like to see your morning's work," I said, more firmly.

A grunt. He held his pencil in his small, fine hands. To my surprise, he picked up the sketch and thrust it over his shoulder to me. He did not turn his head in the slightest. A golden beam of morning sun fell across the desk and on his sallow face. He has a sharp, aquiline nose, pleasant in profile; he may have been quite handsome, if his neuroses had not turned his features rattish, furtive. He seemed oddly familiar to me.

I took the sketch. Another battlefield scene, identical in horrific detail to the other.

"I wonder, Mr Crebert, why such a talented artist would burden himself with the stuff of nightmares."

A long pause. He seemed to consider. Then, in a calm, sane voice, nothing like his rattish movements, he uttered the following extraordinary statement:

"A catastrophe is coming, Doctor, have no doubt of it."

"You refer to the tension in Europe?"[6]

No response.

---

[6]The assassination of the Austrian Archduke Franz Ferdinand by a Serbian extremist had taken place two weeks (June 28) prior to De Klerk's conversation here with Crebert.

War, I told him, is not possible; at least, that is the consensus. I cited Angell's and Bölsche's books as evidence[7].

"So it is not healthy, Mr Crebert, to dwell on such things."

"It is not I who is unhealthy, Doctor."

He could not be drawn into further conversation. I left him as I found him, hunched over his desk, intensely absorbed.

I sit here now in an office in Broughton Hall, two floors away from Crebert. My colleagues are astounded at the boon of the picture conferred upon me. They are even more in awe than previous (which, I admit, I enjoy). The sketch sits on my desk. I have spent the day poring over it. There is undoubtedly a bewitching quality to his work, something indefinably compelling. The sketch means nothing to me, and yet when I look at it, it is as if it is significant to me personally. But how?

Curious: other neurotics I have treated attach significance to a random object—say, seeing the number 12 three times in a day. In their delusions they attach a personal, often predictive, significance to it (12 days left to live, etc)[9]. Crebert attaches a morbid significance to his shape, not for him, personally, *but for humanity.*

17 July 1914

An extraordinary bond of trust has grown between us. Each day we walk along the banks of Iron Cove, Broughton Hall to our backs. Crebert enjoys the walks—a sign of his desire to be cured. Today I surprised him. I had the orderlies install a desk on the lawn behind the Hall, stocked with pencils and reams of foolscap.

Crebert smiled at the sight of the desk. He seemed to enjoy the absurdity of it on the lawn.

"Do you see what I see, Doctor?" he asked in an amused tone.

A very curious question. "What do you see?" I asked, returning his smile.

"A desk. Here, on the lawn?"

"It is a fine day," I replied, "for drawing *en plein air.*"

---

[7]De Klerk refers to Robert Angell's 1911 book *The Great Illusion* and Wilhelm Bölsche's 1913 three volume *The Triumph of Life*. Both authors considered a Great War in Europe impossible due to economic ties between nations (Angell) and human advancement (Bölsche).

His grin grew wider. Before I could prevent him, he rushed to the desk and sat down, took up pencil and paper, and plunged into scribbling another battlefield epic.

I informed him of my one condition: he must draw what he sees in front of him.

He smiled again, resumed his hunched position. He began to draw a side-on view of the lawn, so that the pinkish sandstone of Broughton Hall stood to his left, the green expanse of the lawn in the middle, and the sparkling Cove off to the right.

I was fascinated to watch him. He constricted himself into his cramped hunch, as if by adopting the posture he wished to wring every last drop of artistry from himself.

Returning to my office in the evening, I found a pile of foolscap clustered at the foot of my door. I nearly laid them aside, but one picture caught my eye. It seemed to feature a number of subtle departures from the others. Broughton Hall features a long arched walkway. In this picture a door at the end of the archway is being pushed open by an unseen hand. Why could we not see who was opening the door? Why had Crebert shrouded the person in dark, heavy pencil? I tried to ascribe innocent explanations—the figure must be an orderly on a break seeking fresh air. But the overall effect was one of an inexplicable menace. Again, the picture had a baffling, impossible quality of being personally significant. How did Crebert achieve this?

A triumph: no battlefield scene, no shape.

22 July 1914

• • •

Significant: on our walks Crebert has told me that though he found little favour in Europe for his art (which has embittered him against the artistic community and humanity in general) he fell under the spell of a Berlin artist, Ludwig Meidner[8]. In Crebert's words, this Meidner possessed the ability to 'paint the future', in particular battlefield horrors, and, according to Crebert, also a 'shape'. Crebert is fond of repeating a gloomy little phrase of

[8]Ludwig Meidner (1884–1966), the German Expressionist painter of "Apocalyptic Landscapes", a nightmarish series of paintings that appear to anticipate the coming Great War. His best known paintings are "Vision of the Trenches", "The City and I"—showing a bombed out city with everything exploding and a ghostly light shining over all.

Meidner's: '*paint your grief, your entire insanity, out of the whole of your being*'.

Is Crebert, then, a mere 'copyist'? I do not think so. There is too much obsession in his work. Yet it is possible that he absorbed some of Meidner's delusions. A homosexual relationship is possible: Crebert speaks with deep affection for his friend, but also with considerable bitterness. A spurned lover?

I do not press him on the 'shape'. He does not know where it comes from (a dream, possibly), or what it means (other than 'the coming catastrophe'). Quizzing him on exactly when this mania began is of no use; his answers are contradictory. Whatever the shape may be, he adores but fears it in equal measure.

I am beginning to feel that Crebert may benefit from hypnotherapy.

25 July 1914

A most peculiar day.

Before an assembly of my fellow Doctors, I outlined my preliminary analysis of the patient:

Crebert's strongest desire, since infancy, is to be an artist. His parents—in particular his mother—acted to rid him of this predilection. The result? Resentment and repression.

Crebert moves to Europe, but is thwarted by artistic rejection.

Such rejection reshapes, or warps, his artistic desire, sublimating it, binding it up with resentment of his mother and an inartistic society.

Resentment manifests in his mania: rejection is compensated for in the delusion of 'the specially ordained mission' and 'predictive' ability.

Problems: Why the battlefield scene and shape, and why the compulsion to draw it repeatedly? The shape (a distorted image of the vagina?) dominates his drawings very like his mother dominated his life: it therefore must be linked to a repression in the childhood stage of Crebert's development.

Treatment: continued psychoanalysis and hypnotherapy (to reveal the childhood repression) and more therapeutic drawing (benefit: recent pictures feature no battle scenes, no shape)

The lecture was well received and about to conclude when—how can I describe it?—I took a 'turn'.

The visages of my colleagues vanished. I was surrounded by a crowd of leering madmen, as if out of the nightmares of Goya. I shrank away, terrified.

And then, as if at some magical stroke, the lunatics vanished, and I became myself once again. The lecture hall buzzed with scandal. Johnson[9] escorted me from the hall to my room. He ordered me to rest, but, humiliated as I was, I refused. I was to hypnotise Crebert again today, I said, and was hopeful of a breakthrough. After some tea and cake, Johnson relented. I resumed my duties, somewhat embarrassed, but quite myself again.

A short time later I was in Crebert's room. He consents readily to hypnosis, and is both relaxed and intensely receptive when put under. We chatted preliminarily, as is our custom, after which I raised the two fingers of my right hand and asked him to fixate on them and observe closely the sensations that develop. The room and the whole of Callan Park, it seemed, fell silent and still as he dropped into a deep hypnotic trance, the deepest I had yet seen. He had stopped blinking, the waves of Iron Cove appeared to cease lapping, and I had the curious impression that Crebert and I were the only two beings on earth. In fact, looking back now, I realise that I felt more than this. We were not the only two beings left on earth; we had become ONE being, myself forming the rational ego, and Crebert the unconscious id.

I instructed him to tell me about his earliest memories. After a series of ordinary scenes from childhood (flying kites, etc), described richly, his face darkened. The lines around his mouth and the runnels in his cheeks seemed to deepen. He paled and became fearful. We had struck something, something quite unpleasant, in his psyche.

"What is it?" I asked. "Tell me what you are remembering."

Crebert began to breathe rapidly.

"My grandfather . . . he is . . . "

Crebert began to rub himself.

I asked him. "What? What is your grandfather doing, August?"

He did not speak, but continued his rubbing, until his swollen member strained against his trousers. There appeared to be little, if any, pleasure involved. In fact, it was undeniably the opposite. His face became a mask of childish fear and disgust. Whatever was happening, it was an ordeal to be endured, not enjoyed.

[9]Dr Douglas Johnson (1886–1960), superintendent at Callan Park 1911–1917

"What is happening to you now, August?" I asked, whispering. 'Tell me."

Softly, he began to moan. This went on for some time, a dull, flat, monotonous sound, robbed of emotion. The moan became speech, a slow babble at first, then words.

"Wampa, I don't like this."

Silence.

"I don't like this, Wampa. Why . . . "

He repeated the phrase mechanically, as if being instructed to say it. Then he abruptly stopped. Crebert's harsh features softened and then crumpled. He began to cry, hotly, ashamedly.

"They took Wampa away. Away for good. It was *my* fault."

He took up an imaginary pencil and began to draw. More questioning yielded a diminishing return of replies. I concluded the hypnosis. He seemed unchanged and of course did not recall what he had revealed. I sat curiously moved by what had transpired. This was undoubtedly the childhood repression that lies behind his neuroses. Yet when I showed him the picture he had drawn while under hypnosis—an ordinary scene of a farmhouse and fields—he did not recognise it, nor did it seem to hold any significance for him. Thus the repression remains strong, and I will have to execute its destruction very carefully if I am to cure him.

Later I received the usual ream of foolscap. Am troubled by some developments: the blades of the well-kept lawn are now warped into willowy bodies, topped with faces that leer and scowl (eerily like those in my 'turn'). And though it was a calm day, the waters of the Cove are disturbed; waves loom and threaten violence.

But the door in the archway . . . it is open wider, and a hand now appears in the gap, knuckles curled around the door. Cannot see the rest of the body. The walkway itself, very solid in reality, is rendered thinly, insubstantially.

I do not like this imagery. The reduction of Broughton Hall to a few hastily devised lines suggests Crebert's devaluation, or even the outright mockery, of this institution and perhaps even of my treatment.

I will remind him of my condition: to paint what he sees, not what he imagines.

27 July 1914

Afflicted by the dream last night. This time, I watch helplessly as my face turns rattish and furtive. Crebert? It is not possible. His damned picture—the one he created under hypnosis, the innocuous farmhouse and field—torments my mind, day and night, but I cannot think why.

I wasted no time in visiting him.

"Doctor," he said immediately I entered the room. I could see only his back, his hunched shoulders. "Shame about your turn the other day."

I remembered his drawing, the willowy blades of grass, the leering faces. I did not ask him how he knew what had happened, but it was disconcerting, to say the least. Could a member of Johnson's staff have told him?

"Are you quite better now?"

Crebert had changed. This new August was superior, adversarial. This was troubling but I tried not to show my dismay.

"Why don't you draw anymore, Doctor? Is it because of what your grandfather . . . ?"

"My grandfather is dead and gone," I said, firmly. And then, changing the subject, "You have been deceiving me, August. Why?"

"Deceiving?"

"You are to draw what you see—Broughton Hall, the lawn, Iron Cove—if you are to get better."

"Oh but Doctor," he said, "I have always drawn what I see. Rather, it is *you* who do not see what I draw. If you did, you would not try to cure me. The catastrophe is coming, Doctor. I am merely its herald."

His words infuriated me. I responded that due to his duplicity, his privilege of drawing on the lawn was hereby revoked. An orderly would remove the desk and pencils and paper. He would be placed in an itinerary of activities that would leave no time for drawing.

Afterward, went to see Johnson, a pale lumpish man with dull eyes. Predictably, he insisted on his staff's discretion regarding my 'turn'. I was not altogether satisfied. We were distracted by the arrival of an orderly, who informed us of 'strange drawings', as he put it, which had been made on the walls—overnight, it would appear—in the corridor *outside my own office*.

We wasted no time and followed the orderly. He took us through the maze of corridors and winding staircases that led to my room.

We stood, aghast.

On the walls around my door was a pencil-sketched mural depicting the battlefield scene and mysterious, cloud-like shape. There was a disturbing addition: a grotesque phallus appeared to penetrate a vaginal cave in the shape. The word 'Wampa' appeared in several places, in blood red chalk.

I stated this was obviously Crebert's work. Johnson replied that Crebert is attended day and night. The corridor, however, being in a floor for doctors, was irregularly patrolled, especially at night. So it was conceivable, then, Johnson rather doubtfully agreed, that Crebert could have had time to create the mural, if he had somehow been granted access to the corridor. Johnson, or members of his staff, was undoubtedly in league with Crebert. He denied it, but I held firm and we parted on bad terms. I will not have my professional treatment undermined.

Later, he came to my room to inform me that pictures had been found crammed in Crebert's desk: all battlefield-and-shape scenes. He has been secretly drawing them, it seems, mocking my treatment.

I fear our bond is broken.

28 July 1914[10]

How can I describe what is happening?

After a listless day (did not see Crebert) I turned in very early but could not sleep. All manner of wild dreams befell me. I awoke in a deep, chilled sweat just before 9:00. I lit my lamp and sat at my desk.

You do not see what I draw.

What is it? What don't I see? At my desk I pored over them—all of them—immersing myself in these windows to Crebert's tortured mind and soul. I did not know what I was looking for, nor was I convinced that I would find anything, other than despair.

I was exhausted, but sleep . . . unthinkable.

[10]At 9:00pm word came to Australia by telegraph that war between Austria-Hungary and Serbia had been declared. There is speculation about the reactions of Russia and Germany, and, ultimately, France and Great Britain. Europe is on the brink of catastrophe.

I opened my door and walked to the end of the corridor. The mural had been washed off by Johnson's staff. It was midnight and Broughton Hall, dim and shadowy with slumber, lay quiet. Beams of white gold moonlight fell like spotlights on the floor, lighting my way.

I caught something out of the corner of my eye. I stopped and turned to look out of one of the corridor's large windows which overlooked the Hall's back lawn, where Crebert once drew. Down on the lawn, a number of white lights glowed in the moonlight. They moved about the lawn, ranging aimlessly here and there. I stood mesmerised, then realised they were a scattering of patients, dressed in their white night robes. In the moonlight they seemed to glow with an ethereal beauty. Their movements were graceful, almost balletic; they raised their long sinewy arms high above their heads and waved them at . . .

A thunderclap boomed.

All of them turned at once. They raised their mad-masks as if in worship of something . . . the moon? There was nothing else in the sky. A pagan ritual?

A flash of lightning revealed a glimpse: in the sky, rising up from the lawn, stretched an anomalous shape. It was dark, but there was light enough for its thick column and roiling tree-like, mushroom[11] top to be seen, fleetingly. This was no natural cloud formation; there was nothing natural in it. Yet it was transfixing, horribly so.

On the lawn I saw, flickeringly: bullet-riddled bodies, truncated limbs, faces locked in an eternal death-agony. The worshipers had become victims, lambs to some mindless slaughter.

Then it began to rain, drizzles at first, then lashes.

I noticed a small figure hunched over a desk.

Crebert.

His bald spot gleamed in the moonlight. Surrounded by an aura of intense concentration, his right arm worked furiously at an absurdly large piece of foolscap that flowed off the desk and down

[11]De Klerk's description of the shape as tree-like or, here, mushroom-like, appears to connect with our own descriptions of nuclear explosions as 'mushroom clouds'. If Crebert's prescience of WWI is to be accepted, then it would appear that his shape is also an uncanny prefiguration of the end of WWII. The two wars are, of course, inextricably linked and are often considered as a single event with an interregnum of peace.

onto the lawn like a scroll. As he wrote, he muttered something, which I could not at first get. Then it became clear:

"*paint your grief, your entire insanity . . . paint your grief . . .* "

I turned away from the scene. I ran down to the corridor's end, took the stairs by twos to the stone walkway that led out onto the lawn. I would put an end to the night's games, if Johnson's staff would not. I pushed open the door and ran out onto the walkway.

The lawn was empty. The victims, and Crebert, had vanished.

I stood still as death. The waves in the Cove chopped and sloshed, disturbed by the rain. All manner of thoughts passed through my mind, but I can relate none of them now, except for the uncanny sensation that I had somehow been tricked into entering one of August Crebert's pictures. For was I not the figure behind the door in his 'therapeutic' drawings?

I heard a furtive shuffling behind me.

"Crebert," I called out. "Crebert? Are you there?"

The door stood ajar, and out of the darkness behind it came a faint, unpleasant laugh.

"Crebert!"

I retreated down the walkway and went back inside to Crebert's corridor. Outside his door an attendant dozed on a chair, his snores booming off the walls. My clothes sopping wet, I peered in through the window. Crebert lay sleeping—or pretending to sleep—in his bed.

I banged on the door, rousing the attendant; sheepish at having been caught napping, he let me in. I strode into the room and gazed down at Crebert. I was prepared to kick him awake, but was stopped by the realisation that *he was completely dry. I* searched the room for a change of clothes and found none. The attendant vowed upon his mother's life that Crebert had not left his bed that night or any other.

What, then, had I seen on the lawn?

I looked again at Crebert, who even in sleep managed to appear furtive and rattish.

"What is it?'I whispered. "What is it that I don't see?"

I realised then that I had taken Crebert's drawings with me, had stuffed them in the waistband of my trousers. I went to Crebert's desk, hunched over and began to pore once again over his drawings. There had to be something I was missing, something that I could not see. But as I looked the mystery of August Crebert's shape remained closed to me. Until . . .

"You must go back to the beginning, doctor."

Crebert's voice chilled me to the bone. I did not dare to turn around, but kept staring at the drawings I had spread in front of me.

"To the very first picture."

Slowly, I began to sort through the piles of foolscap. I came eventually to the very first, sent by Dr Freud.

"Look now, doctor," came the voice again. "Tell me what you see."

I looked, and as I did, my heart froze.

"It is not possible," I said. "Such things cannot be."

"Finally," said Crebert, "you *see*."

It is all there, in the drawing—Broughton Hall, the lawn, the desk, Iron Cove. Faintly, underneath all the battlefield horrors. A simple matter of perspective: like a picture of illusion that appears one thing but, looked at differently, turns into another.

But this is not all.

There is a face—a face that the picture's author could not possibly have seen—of a man pushing open a door in an archway . . .

The face is twisted by a disease of the mind.

The face is mine.

De Klerk's journal ends here.

. . . .

Records submitted by Dr Johnson to Eric Sinclair (Inspector-General for the Insane 1898 to 1925) indicate that Dr De Klerk was treated for 'neurasthenia' (depression) in Callan Park from 28 July 1914 to his death from the influenza epidemic on 6 February 1919. During this time his private practice in the Rocks was closed, never to be reopened. August Crebert remained in Callan Park hospital until his death from tuberculosis in 1921.

The same records suggest that Crebert's mania appeared to have been transferred to or absorbed by other 'artistic' patients in the hospital, including De Klerk, who began to mimic his obsessive-compulsive drawing. In the lead up to World War One, psychoanalysts across Europe documented hundreds of case studies remarkably similar in nature to the above.

Present day artists afflicted with the current 'artistic epidemic' (the obsessive creation of a vast wave or flame-like shape) may in fact be predicting another imminent catastrophe. The experience of Dr De Klerk is to be avoided at all costs. Psychiatrists treating afflicted patients should exercise extreme care. Patients should be kept in isolation wherever possible. Further study into the web-like inter-relationships between self, identity and psychology is required.

God help us all.

~

TAP

ANNA TAMBOUR

It seemed rather friendly at first, the polite thing to do.

"'Scuze me."

"'Ave a mo'?"

"You busy, Simon?"

"—"

Always without warning, always when I was deepest into work.

Tap, invariably on the right shoulder.

Nowadays, when we're dismissed by email, human touch is precious.

Anthony Brough, my supervisor at CJP, first made me aware of it. He loved to call me into his cubicle by email, and then put his hand on my knee while he went over my deficiencies. Then either someone had lodged a complaint or when the floor went open-plan, I can't remember, he took to the gentle tap. Just once. I'd turn in my chair and he'd nod his head backwards towards the area with the retro beanbags, where it usually took him only about ten minutes to make my hands sweat and wonder how I'd make it through the month because he always left no doubt that the evaluation would end with a smile like a curse, and his knell of "Best wishes. Better luck next." Yes, he never said "time"—saying it would cut into his valuable t . . .

His tap could come at any time, sometimes several times in one day. He seemed to know when I was hardest at work to beat a deadline. When you're concentrating in front of the screen, your shoulders rise, the bones poking up like a hanger with your slack bod hanging slumped.

Tap.

Then I'd be in a panic to SAVE before . . .

Yes. There'd be about a 3 second max delay.

And if you think I took it silently, I'm ashamed to say you're wrong. Just like when someone cut in front of me in a queue, I couldn't shut my gob. At the feel of Anthony Brough's tap, I'd blurt "Sorry."

Every effing time.

Even if the room didn't have the ambient whir of 50 terminals and sealed-in-freshness air con, I never would have heard him come. The carpet was minimal, but in addition to affecting the "I'm too busy to shave" look, he padded around in his "I could have slept here" socks.

His commute? When he arrived at the office, he always gave out such long-have-I-suffered vibes that I imagined it as a long silent eye-avoiding, touch-averse sojourn in a first-class carriage from God's own countryside south of London to this fashionable Docklands corp-sit overlooking the Thames, CJP's HQ. He could have actually lived in a squat near Heathrow with a bunch of undocumenteds for all I really know. Not that I didn't speculate.

He never raised his voice; indeed, had this soft-spoken way of attack that he could have perfected with *au pair*s before he was school age, making them cry and bribe him so he didn't tell his parents; or maybe his parents both worked at shit jobs and would have tried to save if they could have resisted his sweet persistence. And he also had this way of sneaking up that was so tomb-silent, he might have been trained by being starved of his bottle as a crawling toddler if he made enough sound to wake a dustmite.

And me? Contrary to what you'd expect from my qualifications, I commuted from a south London suburb distinguished by an embarrassing name (that probably hurt my employment opportunities), a civic building styled as "brutalist" deliberately designed to be ugly (as if there is contrast needed); and for public sculpture, a giant biodegrading cat of fibreglass. In that neighbourhood there is much warmth of human contact, and a certain etiquette. When a man speeds up to walk beside you and extends his hand, you shake down your own pockets to fill it. The rent is cheap, for London. With work being such long hours and such low pay, I didn't see the downsides when I signed the lease. (I did hope to be able to afford to move to a nice cold neighbourhood soon, as soon as I got another supervisor and recognition of my worth.)

CJP was no worse than other companies, or maybe I was too squeamish to want to put myself through the torture of job-hunting, so I just tried to get down to it at CJP. I am, if I do say so myself, rather an expert, and worked in the hope and expectation that I'd be noticed by someone above Anthony Brough.

But he seemed to have a sixth sense for knowing when I really could not take a moment away, when I was so worried about losing time that I almost didn't care what the fuck he was going to say to me or what the fuck he *did* say in all his polite, undermining way.

Sometimes he must have seen a spark of impatience in me, an uncricking of my neck, because on those days, it could be an hour after he'd said, "I'm glad we had this little talk. I'll put in a word for you, that you'll try harder,"—it could be minutes later when I'd be back in my chair, picking up the pieces of my lost concentration, when *tap*.

On the night after the day he did it three times and I missed a deadline I'd been looking forward to, I had my first nightmare about him. A sharp pain in my right shoulder woke me. I'd been on my stomach and must have been flailing my arm around. The tossed bedclothes were like a limp salad. The sheets were wet with sweat, my hair was matted, and my pillow was soppy with sweat, drool and I think, tears. I flipped myself on my back and pulled the covers up tight around me.

Three stories down, the street was buzzing with the usual 2am ambience, a fight that no one was going to stick his head out the window over. Glass broke, probably preparatory to someone getting his nose sliced off. It was all so open, loud and vivid down there—so *normal* on this street that the screams, taunts, "I'll kill youse" vows and sounds of collateral damage to windscreens and whatnot soothed me. They were so fully occupied with each other that they were reassuring as a dog fight on the other side of the door. Who would think to come up here and enter? I fell asleep again, but it was only a snatched nap.

Just as in the day, the tap came without warning.

I woke feeling the nightmare as if I was still in it—every detail as real as the cold sweat I felt from my head to my fish-cold feet.

I'd been sitting in my chair at work and *tap*. I whirled around and could only see my workmates, all hunched over their own chairs, heads aimed at screens, all too far away in body and mind to have done anything. They weren't even pretending not to notice, so it had to be just nothing. Nothing more than, say, talking about fleas and feeling itchy. In the dream I thought it out so rationally, told myself to have a laugh at myself and a healthy rush of hateful wishes toward Anthony Brough. I took a swig of water, focussed on the screen and felt—*tap*. Not some little itch but a jab to my lightly flesh-covered shoulder bone—ever so polite of course, but insistent, as if this were the end of the workday and my bone were the lift's DOWN button.

In the dream, I knew there was a deadline. I tried so hard to work. I bent forward toward the screen. Tap. I slid down into my chair. Tap.

Tap.

I turned my back to the screen and put the keyboard on my lap.

Tap.

I tipped the chair over and stood with my back to the desk.

Tap.

I haven't mentioned the big difference between me and those DOWN buttons. They don't say "Sorry" but in my dream I *wanted* to say something real. Wanted to so bad. Instead, Sorry would come out of me like he'd press my button and watch me shit my pants.

The sound or pain of my neck cracking in the act of turning woke me. I remembered that, too, as I lay in bed waiting for the sounds of traffic to grow to a roar.

It was almost noon when I got to work, my right arm in a sling. I rode past my floor in the lift, and gave notice to the Human Resources Supervisor. She was surprisingly sympathetic to my complaint of sudden RSI, but when I left the building without seeing Anthony Brough, I realised that the sympathy was only corporate. Because I hadn't bothered to get a doctor's evaluation before resigning, I had no claim. She'd fly through *her* next evaluation.

That day I didn't look towards the future, just avoided it. My neck really did hurt but I dumped the shoulder sling as soon as I was out of the building, and spent the rest of the day being a vegetable. Ate a meal in the local Indian, then watched stuff till I was mindless, and went to bed with my teeth luxuriantly unbrushed, at something past 2AM.

Woke screaming.

The tap nightmares weren't all the same, of course. In one, I was standing on the edge of what must have been the white cliffs of Dover. Green grass, and then nothing, like standing on the top ledge of a dodgily built skyscraper. The very roots of grass sticking out from the precipice looked like ancient fingers of the dead, reaching in frozen hope. The toes of my shoes were hanging off that edge, and *tap*. I couldn't whirl around. I could have crumbled the edge where I moved. But I didn't need to look. There was no one there.

I'd be at a supermarket in my dream, and I'd feel it. Or not in my dream. It was no time before there was no difference. The tap could come at any time.

On the toilet. In the shower, of course.

I took to having a crap as fast as I could. To not having showers. Soon after the openness of pavements became too much, and me hugging walls and shopfronts as I progressed down a street had attracted so much notice that I'd been talked to by police, I realised that going out at all was just not on.

And what about Anthony Brough? I did mention the bastard to a friend early on, an old schoolmate who is now a solicitor specialising in petty crims. He said, "Why don't you find out where he lives and throw a brick through his window? Or can't you hack into his terminal at work and plant porn on it, and then, like, you know." That's when I knew there was no solution.

One thing good about the police experience. I was taken into the "forensic physician's room." I know because I looked up what it must have been and found it in a neat little guide, "Health Care of Detainees in Police Stations." It's the room with the cabinet of goodies. Funny, that. You'd think 'forensic physician' meant someone who evaluates dead people. Anyway, he was as sympathetic as you could expect from someone like that. "Have you always been a depressive?" "It's common to feel anxiety, but you mustn't let it control you." He left me in the room for a while and then came back. Thank god the two cells were already full. "Sorry," he said when he returned. "I'd rather you stay till tomorrow, so this will have to do. Take one now . . . " So I walked out richer by two little sample-size bottles, one of "something to help you sleep" and Xanax "for anxiety." As if I didn't know. And advice to contact the NDP (National Depression Programme). As if I would.

I tossed them both on the way home. Only an idiot would want something to make him less aware, unable to protect himself. Bovine.

You can get stuff delivered for a while, but eventually you need more money, you need stuff you can't get by delivery. You begin to look too disreputable, I guess. You start to smell. The flat did, that's for sure. I couldn't do the dishes, not with my back exposed. I couldn't get rid of the rubbish.

The only thing for it was to cut off that shoulder. I drank all that I had one night, a cocktail of stuff left over from a few parties, stuff that girls had brought over (since that was all I had left). An almost full bottle of elderflower liqueur, half a bottle of peach schnapps, and two creme de somethings, sweet as the stuff in chocolate centres, and a full bottle of Smirnoff, which always tastes like nail polish smells. Two mugs of it, and I got going. I used my thirteenth birthday present, the electric fretsaw from my dad.

There was less blood than I expected, and I was very proud of my work. Of course it hurt so much that I had to do it while sitting, not standing, against the wall, but the safety release worked as it should have when I passed out.

When I woke up, I sprayed it all with betadine and sprinkled all the wet stuff with betadine powder. I had read that air was best for healing so I left it open to crust up naturally.

Then I polished off the rest of the booze and fell asleep for a while. Woke up sick as a dog, vomited the crap out of my system, cleaned up the floor with my left hand and a dirty shirt or something, and threw myself in bed. The shoulder was pounding with pain, good searing agony.

Somehow, fell into sleep. He, or it, came upon me while I was running, and then I could only run slower.

Woke.

Opened the window. So much sky. Had to try to fall with my back to the building.

I left instructions that I be laid on my back.

• • •

I was, for a time. Didn't imagine being burned. Did anyone tell you that your nostrils fill with stink? That your body bloats, oozes, pops, creaks, that your fat screams; that your bones sigh like whoopie cushions before they fall apart, partway. And after your 15 minutes of flame? Does anyone tell you that you don't end up as some tidy pile of ash, but more like the scrapings from a fireplace in a city where people scrounge wood from condemned buildings.

And as for the tasteful urn for your eternal rest, dream on. I can swear that I was thrown, not even into a cardboard box, but the same old black plastic bag whose sisters, like hookers, decorate pavements from the poshest addresses to the worst, and lean against the railings in front of so many collections of flats so equal in name—' . . . Mansions'—that this equality could only have been doled out for the purpose of dispersing without favour: the best medicine.

Leaning up against me, digging *into* me is a crowd, I never asked *who* any more than I knew who lived above, below, beside me in my building. Hearing them was quite enough. At least there were walls there. This might as well be me at work. No privacy, no dignity. No future.

No future, stretching out endlessly.

After a long trip, I'm pretty sure I've ended up as landfill, with everyone pressed even closer, no one looking at anyone else, not a friendly word or smile, no more welcome human contact than you'd get on a city bus.

It's ironic that there's all this pressing, because you wouldn't think you'd feel, but oh you do. This isn't like some guy who gets his leg blown off and afterwards, can feel it itch. This isn't phantom limb, some syndrome for physios to heal.

I can feel my body. As in toes, fingers, nose, my itchy arsehole. And by feel, I mean that it is here. I can't move, of course, not even squeeze my sphincter.

And so I'm stuck with these neighbours all around, detritus people and the detritus of their lives. A syringe leans against my thigh, a used sanitary napkin (I can smell it) against my mouth. Receipts, the acrid remains of a cell phone, a melted wad of coffee cup; someone who might have been a supervisor at the local Tesco or an accountant, not that I care, push against me—all in that sticky façade of familiarity as if we were in some email-mandated 'party' to celebrate the company's success—or worse: a Council-organised televised meet-the-neighbours, with the same amount of warning. Your eating habits and filthy socks are "no problem" but you have to hide your rage and shame.

At least here, there is quiet, you might say, and that is true. And there is time, you'd add. And *don't* say *All the time in the world* any more than you'd like me to ask you with a laugh, "How's changing the world going for you today?"

No rush indeed, but time. Time to think down here. That's another myth.

Just like I was thinking yesterday maybe it was, that you've got to be mad to top yourself in a city. Go on a cruise, have a bit of fun, run up a bill that you'll never need to pay, and on the third night out when the sea is choppiest, jump. You'll have a good quick drown, and a lovely clean end. Be chomped by fish and worms and that, and be part of the Cosmos.

I'm amazed I got the whole thought out, and doubly surprised to do it now again for you. Extraordinary. Honestly, I've got more chance to win Lotto than get a whole thought in again. Even that one was so rushed that maybe it made no sense. I don't think I was scatterbrained up there, but here, I think I'm losing the ability to be me.

Here—I didn't tell you the worst of it. And who's to say. Maybe you'd like it here. After all, are you doing your nut about where you are now?

So maybe it's just me, and for your sake, I hope so (not that I care really, but).

You know how everyone and everything is crowded round me. Well, in this rubble there's one place that they are not. There's an open space, a kind of bubble of air, around my right shoulder.

And though you might think my phantom body probably some common syndrome of the dead, a figment of my imagination, you know: fear is real.

Not a whole thought can I finish. Nor seriously mull, ponder, calculate, cogitate fantasize, drift off, forget, relax, plan, mentally escape or resign myself to anything. And if you think that I'm emotional, that I'm telling this to you in a wordy flow, then remember that I've had to train myself to piece together my broken thoughts. The effing *building* that I worked in could be archaeology by now.

And you already know: I can't turn around.

Whoever or whatever you are: *I know you're there.*

To have killed myself for *this*. Want some advice? Of course not. And I wouldn't have, either.

But I never thought that worse than the tap would be: waiting, possibly forever.

Up top, maybe there's a lid of concrete already sealing all this off, and a block of flats.

Down here, it's so clammily cold that I advise one other thing. Wear something that'll wick away your sweat, unless you can expect, hah hah, to lay at rest.

HALF PAST

SAMANTHA MURRAY

The magic of my father's house seeped its way into the surrounding countryside. Magic has a way of doing that: overflowing its container, having influences you did not intend. It's one of the first things I learnt: magic is messy. There were traces in the stream running through the garden; in the translucently clear water and the way it sounded as if it were laughing if you didn't quite listen. It spilled into the sunflowers growing to the side of the front door; as big as your head and brightly, improbably yellow, they would lean towards you if you talked to them, and rub their petals under your chin with a light, swaying affection.

Today though, it was hot in the garden. Around the back of the house dry leaves crunched under my feet and the plants were overgrown and wilted. I wondered what this said about my father's mood and how very angry he must still be. Or maybe my eyes were seeing all of the little details more, because I was leaving.

I heard the boards of the porch creak and saw Eliza swinging in the patio seat, the heels of her boots drumming angrily on the downswing.

"What are you doing?" I leaned against the rails and watched her go backwards and forwards.

"What's it look like?" Eliza was not my favourite Echo—she was almost thirteen and snappy and disconsolate with it. But she had been one of my companions for more than two years, and today I looked at her scowl with an odd sentimental fondness.

"I was looking for you," I said.

"Why?" she asked abruptly. She stopped swinging though and squinted up at me.

"I guess . . . to say goodbye."

"Oh." She was a little faded these days. She hadn't aged at all of course, her dark hair hung in the same long braid down her back, but I could see through parts of her dress to the swing behind her. She had been all sharp angles and vivid streaks of scorn in the beginning. "Why?"

"Because I refuse to be stuck in this house forever." I could feel the heat returning to my words and my cheeks both. "Because just because you have the most magic does not mean you get to control everyone else." Eliza chewed her fingernail—a habit I'd always had—but kept her eyes on me. "Because he treats me like a child and it is *not fair.*" I was conscious of the childish note rising up in my voice and the irony didn't escape me but I did not care. I was fifteen years old, and I had my own magic.

"Good luck out there," said Eliza, and the softness of the expression on her face surprised me. In the couple of years she had lurked here I hadn't seen her smile before. I went inside.

• • •

I skirted past the sitting room and looked in the sunroom, which was unusually dirty. The windowpanes were streaky with grime so the sunlight coming in was muted, but I only saw a couple of other Echoes who were so faint that if I hadn't been looking, I wouldn't have noticed them at all.

The Echoes had been my only playmates for a long time. My father was a stern man, with a fierce hooded gaze like a hawk, and when he directed his attention at you sometimes it felt like your skin would burn with all of the intentness; he didn't count as a playmate. My mother used to play. She didn't have any magic, but she had been a masterful weaver of fairytale and fun. She'd had a soft spot for the Echoes, whereas my father usually looked right through them with a certain impatience. They were a frustration to him I think; the fact that I produced them proved that I had inherited a strong talent for magic, but whenever he tried to instruct me in those arts, the results were usually disastrous. The magic with which I made the Echoes was instinctive and unbidden. I failed to do anything on command.

My mother had died when I was nearly seven, and then the Echoes—shades of me, always younger, always receding from me in age and experience—were all I had. My father had no family left, and my Mother's sister was not spoken of, for reasons I didn't understand. I had a memory of her visiting when I must have been less than four, my young pretty aunt, spinning me around and around to make me laugh, her eyes dancing.

I found Bethie at last down near the stream. She had made little paper boats, put delicate blue and white flowers inside for passengers and was casting them off at the edge of the water. She jumped up when she saw me and hugged me tightly around the waist. Her thin little arms were surprisingly strong. Her hair trailed down around her face in dark curls.

Bethie was six, and my favourite.

On my sixth birthday my father had magicked little fairy lights that floated in the air all around, and he had even put his arm around my mother in a rare show of affection and smiled down at me. There had been a mound of presents, among them a dollhouse with little people who moved in a jerky manner inside it. There had been a rainbow birthday cake with purple icing which was sweet and hard on my tongue. That was the day Bethie had appeared, with a sharp smell like ozone, coalescing out of birthday candles and anticipation and glowing excitement, glimmering and forming in the air until she became real and solid. Whenever I was in the grips of an overwhelming emotion I would make an Echo. It was like I was not enough, by myself, to contain what I was feeling. Even when I understood that it was me doing it, it was never something I could control.

The stream was not laughing today. Bethie's boats sailed prettily in the eddies, but I didn't feel the sense of impish delight that the water usually had. I gazed back towards the house. Had my father pulled in all his magic to brood within himself and left the house and grounds to suffer? Was he doing it on purpose, to show me how he felt? I felt my own anger kindling back to life. Even with his harshness and distance he was my father, but he could not keep me here cloistered away from everything else in the bright wide world.

And that led back to why I was here.

"I've got something to tell you," I said looking down into Bethie's small bright face. "I've got to go away." Haltingly I tried to explain, although she was only six and she had crystallised out of a moment where her world was perfect and glowing, so I didn't know how much she could understand. I don't know that she or the Echoes really knew who I was anyway. They existed in their own little worlds, timeless, unchanging, caught in a moment, and I think everything else was blurry to them.

"I'll come with you," said Bethie when I finished. It was entirely unexpected, and impossible, and melted me like I was birthday candy abandoned in the sun. The radius of the house and grounds was as far as an Echo could stray from where she had formed. And Bethie was happy here! Her cheeks were flushed, her eyes shining with lights. Often she would press her hands together under her chin, tight against her thin frame, as if the excitement was too much for her to contain.

I know I had once been Bethie, but it seemed so unreal a thought as to be impossible. I envied her a little; I would have liked to stay Bethie forever.

"I'm sorry honey, but I have to do this alone," I said as she wormed her way under my arm to hug me again, looking more tremulous than I'd ever seen her. She would forget me as soon as I was out of sight, I felt pretty sure, but I gripped her hard in this moment for my own sake.

I heard the padding of soft feet on the path and I looked up to see eleven-year-old Libby coming from the house. "Someone's here," she said, a spark of curiosity mixed in with her usual demeanour of crushing disappointment.

It had been years since someone had last come to the house. My father did not tend to encourage visitors and most of the townsfolk were in too much awe or fear of him to venture close. I ran quickly back up the path, my two Echoes behind me.

She was just getting out of her carriage as I reached the front of the house. Her dark hair was up in some sort of untidy mass at the back of her head, and she was wearing trousers instead of the long skirt that was customary. Her face angled towards me in the high, bright light of the sun, and my breath caught in my throat.

It was my mother.

• • •

It wasn't, of course, although when I started breathing again the air felt hot and forced in my lungs. I clutched at the hands of the Echoes on either side of me—Libby's hand felt feather-light and insubstantial in my own, but Bethie's grip was as real and solid as ever. For an instant the visitor had looked like my mother, but she was not. And then I knew who she was.

"Aunt Marla," I said, letting go of the hands in mine, and hurtling forward two steps to throw my arms around her neck. I was almost as tall as she was. "Aunt Marla, can I go with you? Oh, can I go with you? I can't stay here, I'm leaving today. I was going to try and look for you anyway, once I got to town." My words stumbled clumsily over themselves.

Aunt Marla looked at me oddly. I probably shouldn't have made my request like that, so suddenly and fiercely, when I hadn't even seen her in more than a decade. "Hello Elizabeth," she said. She didn't smile and her eyes were very dark, like my mother's. "Yes, you may come with me when I go."

A flash of hope mixed with the slow boil of my anger that was underneath everything today, the combination making me tremble.

I suddenly realised that she could see three of us and wondered if she was confused. "These are my . . . um, I mean . . . " I began, flustered.

"I know about the Echoes," said Aunt Marla, although she only looked at me. "You have been doing that since you were very young."

She must have found me as changed as I found her. The last time she'd seen me, I would have been a much smaller version of Bethie. Aunt Marla looked faintly sad and old and tired, and none of these were things I had associated with my mother's younger sister, although of course she was older now than my mother had ever lived to be.

"Would you like me to take you to Father?" I tried to keep my voice steady as I tried, belatedly, to remember my manners.

"No," she said after a pause. "I can go and find him." I felt relieved. The curiosity I had over how he would react to the return of my disfavoured aunt was not enough to entice me within my Father's radius. It felt as if we had burned up all the space and air between us with our words last night.

I wondered how long Aunt Marla would stay. It was likely Father would turn her out immediately.

Which meant there was one more goodbye I could no longer avoid.

The sitting room was dim and dusty, and when I opened up the curtains all it did was illuminate the grime. There was a faint scent of old dried flowers. I couldn't see her at first but I crouched down and found her under the table, her small face pressed up against one of the thick carved wooden legs.

"Hello Elly," I said softly, but she didn't look at me, only snuffled like a baby animal and wiped her hand against her nose and then onto the blue of her smock. Even in the shadows I could see that she was sharply defined and solid. Her hair was undone and her dark eyes were large and hunted. When all of the other Echoes had faded, Elly would remain, I knew. She would be here for as long as I lived.

"I've come to say goodbye," I said, although I didn't think it was any use trying to talk to her. She looked at me then though, and I could see that tears were trembling on her lashes. It was the word "goodbye," I thought. She knows that word. She knows that word better than anyone.

I put out my hand very slowly and touched her hair. "It's okay," I said. The words felt rough in my throat because they were a lie. I felt a hot prickle of guilt down my spine—I never came to see Elly, I avoided the sitting room. But how could I tell her the truth? For her it was not okay, it would never be okay. She was caught forever in the day my mother died.

I sat with Elly for a long time, as if somehow my presence would mean something to her although I knew it couldn't. When I left, I met Aunt Marla at the door.

"May I go and see her?" she asked curtly, and I nodded. I didn't know what she wanted with Elly, but maybe she wanted to say goodbye too. I presumed from her abrupt manner that things had not gone well with my father, which did not surprise me at all.

I had thrown clothes and some belongings into a bag the night before, and I figured I would put it in Aunt Marla's carriage, so that nothing would delay our departure. I felt like my blood was surging with the need to flee, to begin the new life that I was obviously fated to have; why else would my aunt have showed up on the very day I was going to leave?

But something tugged at me as I went down the hall and through to the wide steps of the staircase. Like when a painting that has been there many years is moved, and you have taken it so much for granted that you don't even see it anymore and couldn't say what was drawn there, but the empty space feels wrong and creases your brow. Or when a sound you are so used to that you don't even register anymore suddenly ceases.

A sound. I realised that it was very, very quiet. The house felt oddly *undisturbed,* and the little hairs on my arms stood up. The sense of stillness increased as I went through the house, my own footsteps coming louder and faster by contrast.

Three stairs up, I stopped as I put my finger on the feeling. I felt *alone.* Even though I was a girl with a dead mother and a distant father, I had never felt alone like this before. I forgot all thoughts of my bag and went by instinct out to the porch.

The patio-swing was still and unmoving, and there was no one there. The Echoes often moved around even though they had their favourite haunts, so that was not that unusual. But there was no one anywhere. Years and years of Echoes, fading to various degrees, but always there layering my days with faint whispers and babbles in the background, the flicker of shadows that were barely there, the smell of ozone.

There was nothing.

"Aunt Marla," I called, desperate with confusion. I turned on my heel and dashed back the way I had come, my running feet leaving little footprints in the dust.

I swung open the sitting room door, but my aunt was not there. I walked over to the table, my steps slow and deliberate now, and crouched to look under it. Elly was gone.

None of this made any sense. Elly never left the sitting room. I rubbed at my arms, which had come out in goosebumps. Many different emotions warred in my chest, but anger won out. What. Was. Going. On?

"Aunt Marla!" I yelled, running from room to room, all empty, all quiet. "Where are you?"

There. The front door was open. I ran outside and down the steps past the hoard of sunflowers. I shaded my eyes against the slanted rays of the sun as I started down the path. Against the glare I could make out one figure. No, two.

"Aunt Marla," I shrieked again, fear mixing in with the heat of my anger and making my voice croaky.

They were still too far away. I could see Aunt Marla holding something in her hand, pointing it forward. I could see the child in front of her, the tilt of her little trusting face.

Bethie. Bethie. Bethie. Not Bethie.

The ivory-white stick Aunt Marla held seemed to shine brightly for a moment, and Bethie dispersed like she was made of rain.

"Noooooo," I yelled. I felt myself boiling and bubbling as if I were full of steam. Surely I had other magic? I put my hands together, stretched them straight out in front of me, and willed myself to blast Aunt Marla with a pure bolt of my rage.

Aunt Marla turned and looked at me. Her face was impassive and she did not keel over or erupt into flame or show any signs of discomfort at all.

I walked towards her, my eyes on what she held in her hand. Aunt Marla with a wand? I had always been told that my mother's side of the family had no talent for magic. She held the wand lightly, but it was pointed straight at me.

"Aunt Marla, what are you doing?" The steam I'd felt had evaporated, leaving an empty space inside me. *Bethie.*

Aunt Marla didn't react to my question, and I realised that was not her name. She had never been Aunt Marla at all.

"Who are you?" I said to not-Aunt-Marla. I stopped in the dirt of the path and she took the last few steps towards me.

The corner of her mouth moved a little but it was nothing that could be called a smile. "I'm Elizabeth," she said.

Her eyes looked tired yet so familiar. "I don't believe you," I said.

"Did you notice that you didn't make an Echo? After the big fight with your father, after you decided to leave? Why do you think that was?" Despite the little wry note in her voice, her face was serious.

It was true. Even caught in the fierce and consuming emotions of last night, no Echo had formed. I couldn't believe I hadn't noticed that before.

Non-Aunt-Marla-Elizabeth must have seen my confusion. "You're me, or at least, you're a copy of me when I was young."

I looked down at my arms, which had crossed themselves defensively over my chest. They were firm, solid, real. "I don't believe you," I said again. But I believed her.

I looked at the wand, dipped downwards now but still pointed roughly in my direction. "Why do you want to make me go?" I blurted. I could feel the blood coursing in my veins, my heart thumping in my chest, bringing heat to my face, pounding so hard

I expected to see an Echo made of this moment, but there was none. Because I was an Echo myself.

"He was right you know, your father," and now grown-up-Elizabeth's eyes flickered away from me and off into the distance. "The world is swirled in complexity and darkness. It is the darkness he wanted to save you . . . save me from. It is not as pretty as you thought it was going to be. Neither is it as exciting. But I did find Aunt Marla, and she was right: it is my world and I deserved to take my place in it."

I thought of Bethie, of Elly, Libby, Eliza, Betty, Liz, and many others so faded that their names were forgotten. All of the companions I had grown up with, or thought I did. Now there was only me. "Why?" I asked her again.

"Because you are all part of me," she said. "You all hold these things for me, these feelings, and I need them back, I have to own them myself." She paused and then added quietly, "It is the only way I can be whole."

"Why did you take all of the others first? I was right there, you could have zapped me with that thing right away."

I wasn't sure if her eyes softened. "Because I've never spoken to you before. I never knew you. I fought with my father that day, and I left. I never came back. I learned, eventually, to take back the Echoes just after I made them, so that I could keep what it was I felt, even if it was hard that way. My father died, a year ago, and I haven't seen him since I was fifteen. Since I was you."

My father? I shot an involuntary glance back up at the house, and realised I was shaking like a leaf in the wind.

"Yes," said Elizabeth, although I had not asked the question. "You've been here a long time."

Elizabeth raised the wand, which started shining. She was so grim and cold and uncaring, how could that be me? How could I turn into her?

I felt things loosen, I started to shimmer.

And then I saw it.

Coalescing just behind her, glimmering and shifting, forming, becoming. Her Echo, written in grief and sadness on the air.

And the faint scent of ozone.

~

ANGELITO

LUCY SUSSEX

It all began with a grinning skull, chocolate iced with bone-white sugar. Written on it was: JAIME. My name . . . though in Mexico they say: Hay-meh.

"I can't eat that!"

"It's your *muertito*," Diego the translator said. "Little dead person."

I felt sick.

"Welcome to our festival, the Day of the Dead," Diego said. "Where for two days we party like they are alive!"

And all around us was a horror movie, a market full of kids dressed up like Halloween, angels, devils and skeletons, chewing chocolate skulls.

The charity for which Mum and Dad worked had rented us a house and garden on the outskirts of the little town. With it came Diego, Mr Fix-it, and his wife Fernanda, housekeeper and cook. She spoke almost no English, but smiled a lot. If I went near the kitchen she made the best food in the world: almond smoothies, thick spicy hot chocolate. But on the Day of the Dead the kitchen turned into a nightmare: dough sat rising, the stove was full of pots and pans, the oven baking like a furnace. When I grabbed an orange from the table Fernanda screamed at me.

"Hay-meh, the food is for our family dead, when they visit during the festival," said Diego." Fernanda is busy now. We are preparing the ofrenda, the altar, for tonight."

I got out of the way, pronto. Mum and Dad were on the back patio, unpacking the medical supplies.

"Get anything from the festival market?" Mum asked.

Diego had nagged me to buy the *muertito*, a sweet loaf of *pan de muerte*, dead bread, and a *chicle*, a skeleton doll. When you pulled a string, it jiggled in its tiny cardboard coffin. I told him I was no Goth, noway!, but it made no sense to him. On the Day of the Dead, all Mexico went Goth.

As I made the *chicle* dance, something bright darted past. It stopped at a flower, suspended in the air. I saw it was a tiny bird, with a long beak, its wings a whirring blur.

"Humming bird," said Mum. "Before Europeans came to Mexico, people believed they lived in two worlds. The body here; the wings, because they moved so fast they looked invisible, in the spirit world. They were messengers of the gods."

"Some pretty scary gods," said Dad.

"So nobody shot the messengers."

The hummingbird hung like a pendant jewel. Then it flew off, pausing for a stickybeak at a basket Diego carried, full of orange flowers.

"For the dead," he said. I followed, as he strewed the flowers up the corridor leading to the open front door.

A welcome mat?

"Like Hollywood. Red carpet."

Past the house went a bunch of locals, carrying spades, rakes, buckets of water. Gardening? I wanted out of the house just then, from all this Day of the Death stuff, so tagged along after them. Bad move—they hung a sharp right into the town cemetery. Inside the walls it was almost as crowded as the market, everyone busy weeding the graves, washing the stones, decking them with flowers. Old folks, Mums and Dads, kids, they all looked happy.

I stopped, reading the gravestones and looking at their photos. Diego, Maria, Angel (a boy's name here). He was my age when he died—and after that every grave seemed to have a kid's face staring back at me, or a baby's. Several graves along a girl sat beside the stone rocking a baby in a shawl. She smiled and said:

"Los Angelitos. Los inocentes."

I knew enough Spanish to understand she meant little angels, innocents, but not to ask if Angel was a relative of hers.

I smiled back, all I could do. This graveyard was full of kids, died far too early. Well, that was why Mum and Dad came here.

The day had mixed blue skies and cloud, and as the sun neared the horizon the clouds won out. The graveyard darkened, all except for the hummingbirds, checking out the flowers. I tried to get closer to one for a good look, following its shining path. That's how I found myself in a part of the graveyard, deserted, with heaps of earth, piled-up gravestones. They were the shape of the dead bread in the market. Then came a flash of lighting, then thunder, close and LOUD. Another, and now heavy drops of rain fell. The Mexicans yelled, dashing for cover.

I ducked between the gravestones, trying to find shelter or a way out. The hummingbirds had got out fast, and I could hardly see where I was going. I found the cemetery wall by bumping into it, and followed it around, one hand on the rough bricks. I felt empty air then cold, rusty iron bars: a little back gate. The latch was stiff, but I could force it open. I slammed it behind me hard as I could, glad to be free of the graveyard, so seriously spooky.

A whimper from behind me . . . what was that? Lost dog? Turning I could just see in the twilight behind the bars a white shape, a little kid, toddler-sized. Must have lost its parents.

"Go back!" I said. "Find Mummy and Daddy." Could I say that in Spanish?

That whimper again. It reached out to me between the bars.

"OK, I'm a softie," I said, though it wouldn't understand. And I dragged the gate open.

Thunder cracked right above me then, and I just lost it. I ran—following the cemetery wall to where it met the road back to town. Then I remembered the kid. Where was it? The little round moonhead trailed behind me. I stopped, panting, by the roadside, and turned on my mobile's flashlight. Then I let out a bat squeak, because though I wanted to scream I hadn't a lungful of air.

He wore white, a smock and long shorts, but wasn't dressed as a carnival ghost. A little cap had been tied under his chin, but had slipped off and dangled by the ribbons. The white was really yellow-grey, torn and dusted with the cemetery dirt. Little kids are chubby, but this one was thin as a famine victim. Limbs like sticks, old and dried. The hands looked like claws, their skin cracked and flaking.

Worst of all was the head, just totally *wrong*. The hair had half-fallen out, dangling in limp strands. The lips were thin and dry, drawn back to show little yellow tooth-pegs. The nose was nearly flat, folded to one side on a cheek not chubby, just dry skin over the skullbones. Under the eyelids was darkness, that *looked* at me.

He reached out, slowly, to take my outstretched hand. Just like a little kid waiting at the school crossing. I leapt backwards, landing in a crouch. He looked at me as if trying to frown: why did you do that?

I got my voice back, a whisper: "Shoo! Go away!"

He took a step towards me. Under my hands I felt the rough stones of the roadside. I leapt up and threw blindly, reaching down for more.

"Leave me alone!"

Only one hit, glancing, but enough to knock the kid over. For a moment complete silence, apart from my panicky breathing. Then he began to cry, thin wails, faint as a kitten who had lost its mum and littermates, and was starving and cold in the rain.

I never had a baby brother or sister. But I had seen when a little kid weeps, how it seems the worst thing in the world, and everybody rushes to make it happy. Even this kid, who looked like a dried-up zombie?

I took a step closer. The child sat, head in hands, weeping and shaking. He rubbed at his eyesockets, then lifted his dry palms and stared into them. The face twisted, puzzled again: where are my tears?

"Don't!" I said, bending down. The child lifted the hem of the smock to his face, to dab his eyes dry. Again he stopped, knowing something was wrong, but not *what*.He doesn't know he's dead, I realised. I could have wept too, but like the child, my eyes were dry.

Diego and Fernanda, I thought. They were locals, they must know what to do.

I just couldn't touch him, not even to hold that withered hand. Instead I beckoned and he stood. We followed the road home to the house, he following my light, I walking slowly, like an ordinary little kid, a live one, followed me.

It took forever, during which the tropical night came down like a shutter. I kept hoping I was in some sort of bad waking dream.

But still in my torchlight I could see the little skull-head behind me. Finally I reached our rented gate, and a line of orange petals, the carpet for Diego and Fernanda's dead.

Inside the smell of cooking, and voices from the kitchen. An arch of leaves and fresh flowers had been propped against one wall. Underneath it was a table heaped with photographs, all of which looked like Diego and Fernanda, baskets of fruit, candles burning in glass jars, plates of dead bread, and even more flowers.

"Come see our *ofrenda*," Diego called. "Our gifts to our dear family dead."

Seated at the kitchen table were Mum and Dad all dressed up, with Poncho, a big guy, driver for the charity. They clutched glasses of tequila, while Fernanda stirred hot chocolate at the stove. I entered, little footsteps pattering like dry leaves on the tiles behind me. Would all hell would break loose?

And . . . nothing happened. Poncho just looked through the child, like he didn't see him. Diego could, I thought, his gaze moved, but he acted like it was not his business. Dad looked like he'd seen a ghost for a moment. But he didn't believe in ghosts, he always said that, so he simply didn't believe what he was seeing. Mum blinked, but then saw the bright side, she always did. "You've found a friend."

Only Fernanda showed concern on her face. I stared at her as if she was a picture book in another language. She looked surprised, but not scared.

Because it was all I could do, I joined them, and Fernanda ladled me out a mug of hot chocolate. The child hesitated and Fernanda pulled out a low stool. He sat, feet dangling, one petal stuck to the sole of the slippers. Fernanda put another mug on the floor in front of him. Being hostess—but still she kept her distance.

How can he drink? I thought.

Diego emptied his tequila and rubbed his long white moustache. "The dead, we please them with their favourite food when they were living. They smell it, take the essence from it, and that satisfies them. After the Day of the Dead the ofrenda food will have no smell, no taste. You'll see."

The child's head bent above the mug. Not drinking, but sniffing? When straightened he looked for the first time almost happy. The essence as good as the taste?

Mum again: "We're going to a party at the Mayor's. Coming?"

With this little problem? No.

Mum and Dad headed out to the SUV with Poncho and Diego. Fernanda and I were left alone, with the child. And we could barely talk to each other! She bent towards the child, spoke. He made a mew-wail in return, and I guessed he was too young to talk properly yet.

Finally she addressed me: "La Momia."

Some Mexican words are almost the same in English. Momia is mummy. But every mummy I ever heard of was in a museum behind glass or in the movies, raging around and trailing bandages. Not something in between.

Fernanda gestured at the kitchen calendar, the festival highlighted in bright texta.

"The Momia came with the festival?" I asked. And it goes with the festival?

Her finger tapped today, November 2nd. "La Dia de los Angelitos."

Little angels, like in the cemetery. Dead children, and this day was theirs.

Now Fernanda pointed at the clock, drawing a circle in the air. Passage of time, I guessed. "When Little Angel day is gone he'll go too?"

A shrug.

"What shall do . . . with the . . . with Angelito in the meantime?"

It was like naming a cat, that instant sense of fit. Angelito looked like something from hell, but was still a little Angel. He could even be cute, for now he drowsed on the stool, head drooping. Fernanda mimed hands under head: sleep. So we led Angelito upstairs to a room down the corridor from mine, a nursery painted with Disney characters on one wall, baby Jesus with his halo and a flock of lambs on the other. It had three beds, and Angelito made for the smallest one. Fernanda brought in a pillow and a small quilt. Angelito lay down, pulled the quilt up and settled, one bony thumb to mouth.

"Now what?"

Fernanda made that circle gesture again.

"OK," I said. "We wait."

I woke the next dawn with something tugging at my bedding. Pest Puss, I thought, and opened my eyes. Oh no! A little dried-up face gazed at me.

I sat up, remembering kids at school whinging about their baby brothers and sisters, how they woke with the chooks and wanted to play, now! Then, because he persisted, I got up and dressed. Little kids needed food a lot, I knew that, but not this one. So he wouldn't need taking to the toilet all the time? Not THAT!

The house was quiet, except for snores from the master bedroom. In the kitchen the candles gleamed on the ofrenda still, and Fernanda stirred chocolate again.

"Little Angel day's gone and Angelito's still here!" I said.

Angelito sat on the stool again, his place.

Fernanda merely served us chocolate and dead bread. While we ate/sniffed Fernanda took off her apron and changed into trainers and a jade green anorak: her outdoor clothes.

"Where are you going?"

"La Señora de las Sombras."

"The lady of . . . what?"

Fernanda bent over the ofrenda table, where the candle flames jittered. She stuck one finger into the darkness behind a photo. "Sombra! Sombra!"

"I get it." Shadow, the lady of the shadows. But who was she and what could she do?

Fernanda took bread, a soft-drink bottle and an orange from the pantry, dropping them into a backpack. She's going to be away awhile, I thought. Sure enough, she made her clock gesture again.

"Adios, Hay-meh," and she gave me a hug goodbye.

"Great," I said to Angelito. "You're mine for the day."

And so I found out how little kids take over your life. We started in the garden, where Angelito had to stop and look at every flower and leaf, very slowly. Now and again he spoke, a babble of sounds, ah-ba-ba, with a raspy edge from that dried-up throat. Around us darted hummingbirds, a cluster of them. They live in two worlds, I remembered, the real and the spirit. They know when someone isn't in their right place.

On the patio, I found a tennis ball and threw it. Angelito cowered. Football? I made some soccer moves, but he only looked puzzled. I wondered if anybody had bothered to play with him much.

Next we did a slow explore of the house, while everybody else woke up. We ended up in the dining room, with the mirrored sideboard. How would Angelito react faced with his reflection? I pointed, he followed with his dark gaze. Is this when he realises that he's dead? I wondered. And what will he do? But he turned away after a moment, not interested, or not understanding. What if he had, and started crying again? How do you comfort an undead child?

Instead, Angelito ducked under the starched tablecloth. I followed, in a kind of hide-and-seek. I was in somewhere beyond being freaked-out, just going with the flow. Something creepy lay on the ground, and I flinched at the grinning skull, before realising it was the muertito. I had left it on the table, it must have rolled off. It had cracked across the jaw. Angelito looked at it, puzzled.

"Muertito," I said. "You eat!" I broke off the jaw and held it between my teeth. "See?" Oh, no, under the table we were at the same height and now Angelito bent towards me like a fledgling, wanting a feed from mum bird. I closed my eyes, scrunched them shut, as I felt those creepy little teeth fasten on the other end of the jaw. A click as they met, and then the smell of gravedirt and worse retreated. I opened my eyes to see Angelito sitting on the floor, toying with the tablecloth fringe. Between us was a chunk of chocolate, with tooth marks at one end. I swallowed down my part of the muertito, though the chocolate felt rough, grainy. Then, very cautiously, I sniffed at Angelito's chocolate. Sure enough, it didn't smell of anything much. I wasn't game to eat it, to see if the taste had gone too.

Feet came into the dining room, and next Mum and Dad peeked under the tablecloth. "Oh you had a sleepover," Mum said. "How . . . "

The word cute stopped on her lips, as if she half-knew nothing cute was here. But she snapped back into bright-side mode again. "Good, company for you."

Angelito wanted out to the garden again. This time I noticed a wheelbarrow.

"Wanna ride?"—and I tilted it so Angelito could clamber in. Then we went on a wild run around the lawn and paths, bumping and yelling. Angelito hung on tight at first, then laughed, as if having fun for the first time.

He started to droop again, so I put him back to bed in the nursery. I sank down onto the biggest bed, totally beat. Was I like this? I wondered. My head lolled . . . and when I woke twilight neared, and Angelito had found the chicle. I showed it the little skeleton dance, and an idea came.

"I'll take you to the market," I said, "you'll like that." So into the wheelbarrow Angelito clambered, and off we went into the town. With all the dead masks and the kids in costume, my passenger had a perfect disguise. Even so, there were some who saw beyond it, mostly children. As I pushed my excuse for a pram around the market, we gained followers, little devils, ghosts, angels. I spent my pesos, filling the wheelbarrow with muertitos, dead bread, flowers, fruit and paper cut-outs. Angelito only once pointed, at a teddy bear, fluoro-yellow. I bought it, and Angelito hugged it tight.

Out of pesos, I turned the wheelbarrow around, heading home with my presents and procession. But as we neared the house I saw the jade of Fernanda's anorak, with her a donkey. On its back rode an old woman, her hair in long white plaits, wound around her head like a crown. She looked half a skeleton herself, dressed in white like Angelito. The difference was, she might be skin and bones, but she had eyes, glittering deep in their sockets.

She gazed at Angelito. Then she chirruped to the donkey and it trotted forward. Fernanda beckoned to me, to follow. Mum and Dad had come out of the house, with Diego.

"Hay-meh is going with us," he said, "to keep the velacion, the vigil for the dead."

They looked surprised, but nodded: OK. And so I wheeled the barrow to the cemetery. We formed part of a greater procession, which as the night fell, lit candles in a stream of light. The graveyard too was bright as Christmas, the Mexicans making their return visits to the dead.

As the lady on the donkey passed among the graves, some people knelt, the men doffing their hats, the women bowing their heads. She took us to the darkest part of the cemetery, finally reining the donkey at a grave that looked half dug up, its headstone at an angle. As she dismounted, Fernanda handed her a walking stick. Supporting herself painfully, she beckoned to Angelito. He leapt out of the barrow, landing with a faint crunch. A day of play had done damage, with the skin-leather on one foot flaking to expose the bone.

Fernanda started pulling out the coating of weeds on the grave, and I helped. The old lady watched, Angelito with the teddy in one hand, the other clutching her white robe. We piled the weeds to one side, for the donkey to munch noisily. When the grave was neat, we decked it with everything I'd bought at the market, and lit all the candles. My ofrenda, for my little dead friend.

The old lady sat then, leaning against the headstone. She held out her arms. Angelito nestled into them, still holding the bear. Oh rather her than me! It had been beyond me to touch Angelito, even when he wept. And then, as he began to doze, I felt ashamed of myself. I reached out, felt cool leather, his cheek. Nothing to be scared of, after all. The Senora, she looked me in the eye, that dark, glittery gaze, and nodded. Whatever she was, she approved.

We spent all night in the cemetery, keeping the velacion. Around us the Mexicans chatted, sang, and played accordion. Diego brought me blankets and a big thermos of chocolate.

"Fernanda and I go now to keep the velacion with our own dead. You are with the Senora, nothing will harm you. OK?"

"OK."Angelito lay in her arms now, fast asleep.

The night stretched onwards. Sometimes it seemed like only me and the old lady stayed awake, for I saw the candlelight reflected in her eyes. Even the donkey snoozed, standing. I wrapped the blanket over my head—and next thing woke, cramped and stiff, slumped on the cold earth. A cock nearby crowed at the dawn, and the Mexicans roused, ready to go home.

My offerings remained, the candles burnt down to stubs, the marigolds wilted. But now the gravestone stood upright, with propped against it the teddy bear. The old lady, her donkey, Angelito—all had gone.

Diego and Fernanda found me, wiped my eyes, took me home, put me to bed. I stayed there the next day or so, sleeping fitfully, waking, not wanting to get up.

"A bit much, eh?" said Mum. She stroked my hair. "You'll never forget the experience."

No, never.

"Want anything?" Dad asked.

"A little brother or sister?"

They stared, amazed.

"Possibly," said Mum.

"But meanwhile?" That was Dad.

"Those guidebooks you have in your room. The ones on Mexico and the Day of the Dead. Please."

I got them, together with Diego. He sat on the end of the bed, playing a one-handed card game and explaining, when I needed it.

La Senora de las Sombras—that was the caption beneath a woman in long robes and a crown, but underneath it a bare skull.

"The Lady of the Shadows," I said.

"Another name for her is Santisima Muerte," Diego replied. "Saint Death. She's been here from before the Gringos came."

He pointed at another book I had open on the bedcover. It showed stone statues, dragons and serpents, and a crouching, skull-headed figure. "Mictecacihuatl. Goddess of the underworld."

"I think I understand."

When I finally got out of bed, I sat on the back patio. It felt like I was missing something: Angelito, I guessed. I closed my eyes, inside a personal red cave. Then a small shadow fell, and I felt a faint breeze in my face.

I opened my eyes to see a flying jewel, a hummingbird suspended in mid-air. Its tiny beads of eyes gazed at me. I held my breath, and it neared. I felt its beak touch my lips, as if I was a giant baby bird. Then it darted away.

I could feel something moist on my lip—a droplet, sweet honeysuckle nectar. The hummingbirds live in two worlds, I remembered. And in that tiny gift was maybe a message from the Mexican spirit world, sweet thanks from a goddess and a dead little angel.

~

OUR BACKERS

For the first time, Ticonderoga Publications sought to partly fund the publication of this volume via crowd-funding. We didn't know what to expect, but were overwhelmed by the support shown by the genre community at large, and were truly grateful that our campaign was successful.

We promised to list each of our sponsors in the finished volume. The book that you are now holding is the result of the incredible generosity shown by the people below. Thank you.

Adrian Smith
Aidan Doyle
Alan Baxter
Alis Franklin
Amanda Greenslade, epic fantasy author
Amanda Nixon
Andrew Peirce
Anna Tambour
Anthony
Anthony Ferguson
Antoni Centofanti
Block Pictures
Carol Ryles
Cathy Green
Charles Wilson
Claire McKenna
Colin Sharpe
Dan Rabarts
Dan Simpson
Danny Oz
Dave Versace
DavidKernot
Deborah Biancotti
Deborah Wilson
Dianne Watson
Edward Lipsett
Elizabeth Fitzgerald
Helen Binks
Helen Katsinis
Helen Stubbs
Ian McKellar
Ian Mond
J.J. Irwin
James Bradley
James Haughton
Jason Nahrung
Jilyan

John Clarke
Joseph Ashley-Smith
Jules Jones
Julia
Kat Clay
Kate Dunbar-Smith
Kate Eltham
Katharine
Kim Michelle Ross
Kirsty Barrington
Kyla Lee Ward
Lara Hopkins
Lauren E. Mitchell
Leife Shallcross
Liz
Lucy
Lucy Sussex
Margaret Dunlop
Marie Hodgkinson
Mark Mercieca
Martine Mellegers
Marty Young
Matt McCoy
Matthew Gadsby
Matthew J Morrison
Mel & Phil
Michael
Michael Kelly
Michelle Goldsmith
Narrelle M Harris
Nicole Murphy
Nike Sulway
Pamela Freeman
Pete Kempshall
Peter
Pinky & the Brain
R T Rowlands
Richard Warren
Rick Dwyer
Rivqa
Robert G Cook
Roger Silverstein
Rose Fox
RuckJack
Ruza Foster
Samantha Farmer
SFWA Givers Fund
Simon Brown
Stacey Larner
Stephanie Gunn
Steve Dillon
Steven Paulsen
Stuart Dunstan
Stuart Olver
Susan Wardle
Tamlyn
Tansy Rayner Roberts
Tasha Turner
Tasmar Dixon
Thomas Bull
Tiffany Fox
Tom Dullemond
Tracie McBride
Tsana Dolichva
Vicki Ackermans

ABOUT THE CONTRIBUTORS

Joanne Anderton is an award-winning author of speculative fiction stories for anyone who likes their worlds a little different. Her novels have been published by Angry Robot Books and Fablecroft Publishing. Her short story collection, *The Bone Chime Song and Other Stories*, was published by Fablecroft Publishing. You can find her online at joanneanderton.com

---

Alan Baxter writes supernatural thrillers and urban horror, rides a motorcycle and loves his dog. He also teaches Kung Fu. He lives among dairy paddocks on the beautiful south coast of NSW, Australia. Read extracts from his novels, a novella and short stories at his website—www.warriorscribe.com—or find him on Twitter @AlanBaxter and Facebook.

Deborah Biancotti is a Sydney-based writer and reader. She lives on the historic edge of the city in a narrow, run-down house she calls 'the corridor' with her partner and several cats. Her stories have been nominated for the Shirley Jackson Award, the William L. Crawford Award for Best First Fantasy Book and the Aurealis Award.

Stephen Dedman is the author of the novels *The Art of Arrow Cutting*, *Shadows Bite* and *A Fistful of Data*, and more than 120 short stories published in an eclectic range of magazines and anthologies. He has won two Aurealis Awards and a Ditmar, and been nominated for the Bram Stoker Award, British Science Fiction Association Award, the Sidewise Award, the Seiun Award, the Spectrum Award, and a sainthood.

Erol Engin lives and writes in Newcastle, NSW. His stories have been published by *Spineless Wonders*, Busybird Press, and *Aurealis*.

Jason Fischer is an award-winning Adelaide-based author. He has published dozens of short stories, with a novel, a short story collection, comics and computer game work also under his belt. He enjoys competition karaoke, and loves puns more than life itself.

Dirk Flinthart lives in the north-east of Tasmania with his family, which includes a deranged dog, a neurotic cat, and three children. He has both a Ditmar and and Aurealis award on his shelves. His novel *Path of Night* came out on the Fablecroft imprint, and is overdue for a sequel. Dirk also released a collection of short stories *Striking Fire* through Fablecroft, which was shortlisted for Best Collection and Best Horror Novella in the Aurealis Awards.

Kimberley Gaal lives in Canberra with her husband and one year old son. She writes young adult, new adult and old adult (grown up) speculative fiction, and was very honoured to have two of her stories nominated for the 2015 Aurealis awards YA category.

Stephanie Gunn is a Ditmar and Aurealis Award nominated writer of speculative fiction. In another life, she was a scientist, but now spends her time writing and reviewing. She lives in Perth with her son and husband and requisite fluffy cat. You can find her online at www.stephaniegunn.com.

Lisa L. Hannett has had over 65 short stories appear in venues including *Clarkesworld*, *Fantasy*, *Weird Tales*, *Apex*, the *Year's Best Australian Fantasy and Horror*, and *Imaginarium: Best Canadian Speculative Writing.* She has won four Aurealis Awards, including Best Collection for her first book, *Bluegrass Symphony*, which was also nominated for a World Fantasy Award. Her first novel, *Lament for the Afterlife*, was published in 2015. You can find her online at lisahannett.com and on Twitter @LisaLHannett.

Robert Hood has been called “Australia's master of dark fantasy” and “Aussie horror's wicked godfather”. His most recent books are his epic dark fantasy novel, *Fragments of a Broken Land: Valarl Undead* (winner: 2014 Ditmar Award for Best Novel), and *Peripheral Visions: The Collected Ghost Stories* (winner: 2015 Australian Shadows Award for Best Collected Work). roberthood.net.

Kathleen Jennings was raised on fairytales in Western Queensland. She now works as an illustrator and writer based in Brisbane, Queensland. Her stories have been published by presses such as Ticonderoga, Fablecroft, Small Beer and Candlewick. She can be found online at tanaudel.wordpress.com and kathleenjennings.com.

Maree Kimberley has published children's books along with articles, short stories and flash fiction across several genres. Her obsessions include neuroscience and things grotesque, bizarre and strange. She also has a penchant for circuses. Maree enjoys combining her obsessions into stories but sometimes she just writes about things that happen.

Perth-based writer Martin Livings has had over eighty short stories in a variety of magazines and anthologies. His first novel, *Carnies*, was first published by Hachette Livre in 2006, and was nominated for both the Aurealis and Ditmar awards, and his short story collection, L*iving With the Dead*, was published in 2012.

Kirstyn McDermott is the award-winning author of two novels, *Madigan Mine* and *Perfections*, as well as a short fiction collection, *Caution: Contains Small Parts*. She also produces and co-hosts The Writer and the Critic, a literary discussion podcast. Kirstyn lives in Ballarat where she is currently pursuing a creative PhD at Federation University. kirstynmcdermott.com.

Sally McLennan is a writer of children's books, fairy tales for grown-ups, erotica, horror and more. She studied English at Canterbury University and went on to edit newspapers in Sydney. She have been writing fiction full time since the publication of her first book, *Deputy Dan & the Mysterious Midnight Marauder.*

DK Mok is a fantasy and science fiction author whose novels include *Squid's Grief* and *Hunt for Valamon*. DK has been shortlisted for three Aurealis Awards, a Ditmar, and a WSFA Small Press Award. DK graduated from UNSW with a degree in Psychology, pursuing her interests in both social justice and scientist humour. DK lives in Sydney, Australia, and her favourite fossil deposit is the Burgess Shale. Connect on Twitter @dk_mok or find out more at dkmok.com.

Samantha Murray is a writer, mathematician, and mother. Not particularly in that order. Samantha's fiction has been seen in places such as *Clarkesworld*, *Lightspeed*, *Escape Pod*, *Flash Fiction Online*, *Pod Castle*, *Daily Science Fiction*, *Nature Magazine*, and *Beneath Ceaseless Skies*. Samantha lives in Western Australia in a household of unruly boys.

Jason Nahrung's work is often set in Australia and invariably darkly themed. His most recent books are the seaside *Gothic Salvage* (Twelfth Planet Press) and outback vampire duology *Blood and Dust* and *The Big Smoke* (Clan Destine Press). A PhD candidate in creative writing at The University of Queensland, the former Queenslander lives in Ballarat with his wife, the writer Kirstyn McDermott, and lurks online at jasonnahrung.com.

Garth Nix's books include the award-winning young adult fantasy novels *Sabriel*, *Lirael* and *Abhorsen*; the dystopian novel *Shade's Children*; the space opera *A Confusion of Princes*; and a Regency romance with magic, *Newt's Emerald*. More than five million copies of his books have been sold around the world, his books have appeared on the bestseller lists of *The New York Times*, *Publishers Weekly*, *The Guardian* and *The Australian*, and his work has been translated into 40 languages.

Since 2011, Anthony Panegyres—a current PhD candidate at UWA—has had 15 publications including *The Best Australian Stories*, *The Year's Best Australian Fantasy & Horror Vol 2*, *Overland 204* (an Aurealis Award Finalist story), *Overland 214*, *Meanjin*, *The Guardian*, *Dreaming of Djinn*, along with several other journals and anthologies . "Lady Killer" was originally published in the Aurealis Award-winning anthology *Bloodlines*, and his latest story "Crossing" can be found in *At the Edge*.

Rivqa Rafael is a writer and editor based in Sydney. Her short stories have appeared in *Hear Me Roar* (Ticonderoga Publications), *Defying Doomsday* (Twelfth Planet Press), and elsewhere. In 2016, she won the Ditmar Award for Best New Talent. She can be found at rivqa.net and on Twitter as @enoughsnark.

Deborah Sheldon is a professional writer from Melbourne. Her short fiction has appeared in many journals and anthologies. Deb's latest releases include the horror novel, *Devil Dragon*, the crime-noir novellas, *Dark Waters* and *Ronnie and Rita*, and the horror collection, *Perfect Little Stitches and other stories*. deborahsheldon.wordpress.com.

Angela Slatter has won a World Fantasy, a British Fantasy Award, five Aurealis Awards, and a Ditmar Award. She's published eight story collections, has a PhD, and was an inaugural Queensland Writers Fellow. Her debut novel *Vigil* was published in 2016 (Jo Fletcher Books), and *Corpselight* will follow in 2017.

Cat Sparks is a multi-award-winning author, editor and artist, former Manager of Agog! Press and former Fiction Editor of *Cosmos* magazine. She's currently finishing a PhD in climate change fiction. Her short story collection *The Bride Price* was published in 2013. Her debut novel, *Lotus Blue*, is due from Talos Press in 2017.

Lucy Sussex was born in New Zealand. She has published widely, having edited five anthologies, written five short story collections, and the award-winning neo-Victorian novel, *The Scarlet Rider* (reprinted 2015). Her B*lockbuster: Fergus Hume and the Mystery of a Hansom Cab* (Text) won the 2015 Victorian Community History Award.

Anna Tambour's latest book is a collection, *The Finest Ass in the Universe*, from Ticonderoga Publications. Her novel *Crandolin* was shortlisted for the 2013 World Fantasy Award. She lives in the bush in New South Wales.

With four novels and six short story collections in print, and close to two hundred short fiction sales, Kaaron Warren's award-winning fiction tackles the themes of obsession, murder, grief, despair, revenge, manipulation, death and sex. Kaaron has won many awards such as the Shirley Jackson, Aurealis, Ditmar, Australian Shadows and ACT Writers and Publishers Awards for her novels and short fiction. Her latest book is *The Grief Hole*.

RECOMMENDED READING LIST

Joanne Anderton, "Unnamed Children", *Bloodlines*
——— "Bullets", *In Sunshine Bright and Darkness Deep*
Alan Baxter, "How Father Bryant Saw The Light", *Blurring The Line*
———"Reaching for Ruins", *Review of Australian Fiction Volume 16, Issue 3*
Jenny Blackford, "Under the Roses", *A Quiet Shelter There*
——— "Ghost Irises", *Strange Horizons, Issue 18 (May 2015)*
——— "We to the Gods", *W.B. Yeats Poetry Prize website*
William Broom, "Ferals", *The Never Never Land*
Steve Cameron, "Lodloc and The Bear", *Dimension 6*
Jay Caselberg, "Penumbra", *Death's Realm*
Bill Congreve, "The Pit", *Cthulhu Deep Down Under*
David Conyers, "Impossible Object", *Cthulhu Deep Down Under*
Rowena Cory Daniells, "The Giant's Lady", *Legends 2*
Stephen Dedman, "Dreamgirl", *Cthulhu Deep Down Under*
Jason Fischer, "Defy the Grey Kings", *Beneath Ceaseless Skies*
AJ Fitzwater, "Long's Confandabulous Clockwork Carnival and Circus, and Cats of Many Persuasions", *ASIM 61*
Dirk Flinthart, "Night Shift", *Striking Fire*
——— "A Friend In The Trade", *Striking Fire*
Jason Franks, "Darkness Beyond", *Cthulhu Deep Down Under*
Alice Godwin, "He Kindly Stopped For Me", *Blue Crow Magazine, Issue 4*
Michelle Goldsmith, "The Jellyfish Collector", *Review of Australian Fiction Volume 13, Issue 6*
Stephanie Gunn, "Broken Glass", *Hear Me Roar*
Lisa L. Hannett, "So Great a Misdeed", *Cranky Ladies of History*
——— "A Shot of Salt Water", *The Dark*
Narrelle M Harris, "Show and Tell", *Encounters*

Rose Hartley, "Captain Marvellous", *F(r)iction #2*
Pandora Hope, "Eight Seconds", *She Walks in Shadows*
Elizabeth Jakimow, "Consumed", *The Never, Never Land*
Kathleen Jennings, "The Last Case of Detective Charlemagne", *Insert Title Here*
Demetri Kakmi, "Haunting Matilda", *Cthulhu Deep Down Under*
Deborah Kalin, "The Miseducation of Mara Lys", *Cherry Crow Children*
——— "Cherry Crow Children of Haverny Wood", *Cherry Crow Children*
——— "The Briskwater Mare", *Cherry Crow Children*
Pete Kempshall, "Azimuth", *Bloodlines*
Steve Kilbey, "Untitled", *Cthulhu Deep Down Under*
Maree Kimberley, "Fleur", *Text Journal, Vol 9, No. 2*
——— (as Rue Karney), "The River Slurry", *In Sunshine Bright and Darkness Deep*
Martin Livings, "A Red Mist", *Bloodlines*
Brett McBean, "With These Hands", *Blurring The Line*
Tracie McBride, "Q is for Quackery", *The Grimorium Verum*
Kirstyn McDermott, "Mary, Mary", *Cranky Ladies of History*
Sally McLennan, "Mr Schmidt's Dead Pet Emporium", *Fat Zombie: Stories of Unlikely Survivors from the Apocalypse*
C.S. McMullen, "The Other-Faced Lamb", *Aurealis 82*
Sean McMullen, "The Ninth Seduction", *Lightspeed Magazine*
Paul Mannering, "Salt On The Tongue", *Blurring The Line*
DK Mok, "The Heart of the Labyrinth", *In Memory: a tribute to Terry Pratchett*
Faith Mudge, "January Days", *QLD Young Writers runner up*
Jason Nahrung, "Night Blooming", *SQ Mag Edition 19*
Shauna O'Meara, "To Look Upon a Dream Tiger", *The Never Never Land*
Anthony Panegyres, "Road Trip", *In Sunshine Bright and Darkness Deep*
Dan Rabarts, "Endgame", *Fat Zombie: Stories of Unlikely Survivors from the Apocalypse*
Tansy Rayner Roberts, "Fake Geek Girl", *Review of Australian Fiction Volume 14, Issue 4*
Daniel Simpson, "The Winterstream", *Insert Title Here*
Angela Slatter, "*Of Sorrow and Such*"
J. Ashley Smith, "Our Last Meal", *In Sunshine Bright and Darkness Deep*

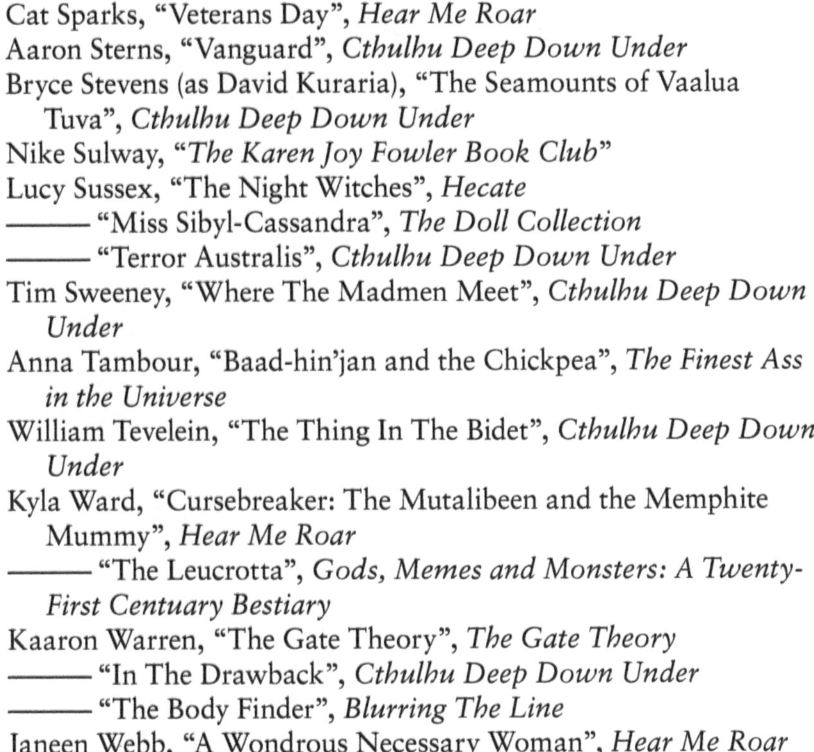

Cat Sparks, "Veterans Day", *Hear Me Roar*

Aaron Sterns, "Vanguard", *Cthulhu Deep Down Under*

Bryce Stevens (as David Kuraria), "The Seamounts of Vaalua Tuva", *Cthulhu Deep Down Under*

Nike Sulway, "*The Karen Joy Fowler Book Club*"

Lucy Sussex, "The Night Witches", *Hecate*

——— "Miss Sibyl-Cassandra", *The Doll Collection*

——— "Terror Australis", *Cthulhu Deep Down Under*

Tim Sweeney, "Where The Madmen Meet", *Cthulhu Deep Down Under*

Anna Tambour, "Baad-hin'jan and the Chickpea", *The Finest Ass in the Universe*

William Tevelein, "The Thing In The Bidet", *Cthulhu Deep Down Under*

Kyla Ward, "Cursebreaker: The Mutalibeen and the Memphite Mummy", *Hear Me Roar*

——— "The Leucrotta", *Gods, Memes and Monsters: A Twenty-First Centuary Bestiary*

Kaaron Warren, "The Gate Theory", *The Gate Theory*

——— "In The Drawback", *Cthulhu Deep Down Under*

——— "The Body Finder", *Blurring The Line*

Janeen Webb, "A Wondrous Necessary Woman", *Hear Me Roar*

AUSTRALIAN & NEW ZEALAND FANTASY & HORROR AWARDS

THE AUSTRALIAN SF "DITMAR" AWARDS

BEST NOVEL

Lament for the Afterlife, **Lisa L. Hannett (ChiZine)**

NOMINEES

Day Boy, Trent Jamieson (Text)
The Dagger's Path, Glenda Larke (Orbit)
Graced, Amanda Pillar (Momentum)
Zeroes, Scott Westerfeld, Margo Lanagan & Deborah Biancotti (Simon & Schuster)

BEST NOVELLA OR NOVELETTE:

Of Sorrow and Such, **Angela Slatter (Tor.com)**

NOMINEES

"The Cherry Crow Children of Haverny Wood", Deborah Kalin (*Cherry Crow Children*)
"The Miseducation of Mara Lys", Deborah Kalin (*Cherry Crow Children*)
"The Wages of Honey", Deborah Kalin (*Cherry Crow Children*)
"Fake Geek Girl", Tansy Rayner Roberts (*Review of Australian Fiction Volume 14, Issue 4*)
"Hot Rods", Cat Sparks (*Lightspeed 3/15*)

BEST SHORT STORY

"A Hedge of Yellow Roses", Kathleen Jennings (Hear Me Roar)

NOMINEES

"2B", Joanne Anderton, (*Insert Title Here*)
"The Chart of the Vagrant Mariner", Alan Baxter (*F&SF 1-2/15*)
"Look how cold my hands are", Deborah Biancotti (*Cranky Ladies of History*)

BEST COLLECTED WORK

Cranky Ladies of History, **Tansy Rayner Roberts & Tehani Wessely, eds. (FableCroft)**

NOMINEES

Peripheral Visions: The Collected Ghost Stories, Robert Hood (IFWG Australia)

Cherry Crow Children, Deborah Kalin (Twelfth Planet)

Letters to Tiptree, Alexandra Pierce & Alisa Krasnostein, eds. (Twelfth Planet)

Bloodlines, Amanda Pillar, ed. (Ticonderoga)

BEST ARTWORK

Kathleen Jennings for the cover and internal artwork of *Cranky Ladies of History* **(FableCroft)**

NOMINEES

Shaun Tan for illustrations in *The Singing Bone* (Allen & Unwin)

Rovina Cai for the illustration of "Tom, Thom" (Tor.com)

Kathleen Jennings for the cover of *Bloodlines* (Ticonderoga)

Kathleen Jennings for the cover and internal artwork of *Cranky Ladies of History* (FableCroft)

Shauna O'Meara for the cover of *The Never Never Land* (Canberra Speculative Fiction Guild)

BEST NEW TALENT

Rivqa Rafael

NOMINEES

Liz Barr

T.R. Napper

DK Mok

AUREALIS AWARDS

FANTASY NOVEL

Day Boy, **Trent Jamieson (Text)**

NOMINEES

In the Skin of a Monster, Kathryn Barker (Allen & Unwin)

Lady Helen and the Dark Days Club, Alison Goodman (HarperCollins)

The Dagger's Path, Glenda Larke (Hachette Australia)

Tower of Thorns, Juliet Marillier (Pan Macmillan Australia)

Skin, Ilka Tampke (Text)

FANTASY NOVELLA

"Defy the Grey Kings", Jason Fischer (*Beneath Ceaseless Skies 8/20/15*)

NOMINEES

"Lodloc and The Bear", Steve Cameron (*Dimension6 #6*)

"Broken Glass", Stephanie Gunn (*Hear Me Roar*)

"The Flowers that Bloom Where Blood Touches the Earth", Stephanie Gunn (*Bloodlines*)
"Haunting Matilda", Dmetri Kakmi (*Cthulhu: Deep Down Under*)
Of Sorrow and Such, Angela Slatter (Tor.com)

FANTASY SHORT STORY

"The Giant's Lady", Rowena Cory Daniells (*Legends 2*)
NOMINEES
"The Jellyfish Collector", Michelle Goldsmith (*Review of Australian Fiction Vol. 13 Issue 6*)
"A Shot of Salt Water", Lisa L. Hannett (*The Dark 5/15*)
"Almost Days", DK Mok (*Insert Title Here*)
"Blueblood", Faith Mudge (*Hear Me Roar*)
"Husk and Sheaf", Suzanne Willis (*SQ Mag 9/15*)

HORROR NOVEL

Day Boy, **Trent Jamieson (Text)**

HORROR NOVELLA

"The Miseducation of Mara Lys", Deborah Kalin (*Cherry Crow Children*)
NOMINEES
"Night Shift", Dirk Flinthart (*Striking Fire*)
"The Cherry Crow Children of Haverny Wood", Deborah Kalin (*Cherry Crow Children*)
"Wages of Honey", Deborah Kalin (*Cherry Crow Children*)
"Sleepless", Jay Kristoff (*Slasher Girls and Monster Boys*)
"Ripper", Angela Slatter (*Horrorology*)

HORROR SHORT STORY

"Bullets", Joanne Anderton (*In Sunshine Bright and Darkness Deep*)
NOMINEES
"Consorting with Filth", Lisa L. Hannett (*Blurring the Line*)
"Heirloom Pieces", Lisa L. Hannett (*Apex 2/15*)
"The Briskwater Mare", Deborah Kalin (*Cherry Crow Children*)
"Breaking Windows", Tracie McBride (*Aurealis #84*)
"Self, Contained", Kirstyn McDermott (*The Dark 2/15*)

COLLECTION

To Hold the Bridge, **Garth Nix (Allen & Unwin)**
NOMINEES
The Abandonment of Grace and Everything After, Shane Jiraiya Cummings (Brimstone)
Striking Fire, Dirk Flinthart (FableCroft)
Cherry Crow Children, Deborah Kalin (Twelfth Planet)
The Fading, Carole Nomarhas (self-published)
The Finest Ass in the Universe, Anna Tambour (Ticonderoga)

ANTHOLOGY

Bloodlines, **Amanda Pillar, ed. (Ticonderoga)**
NOMINEES
Hear Me Roar, Liz Grzyb, ed. (Ticonderoga)
The Year's Best Australian Fantasy and Horror 2014, Liz Grzyb & Talie Helene, eds. (Ticonderoga)
Meeting Infinity, Jonathan Strahan, ed. (Solaris)
The Year's Best Science Fiction and Fantasy 9, Jonathan Strahan, ed. (Solaris)
Focus 2014: highlights of Australian short fiction, Tehani Wessely, ed. (FableCroft)

CHILDREN'S FICTION

A Single Stone, **Meg McKinlay (Walker Books Australia)**
NOMINEES
A Week Without Tuesday, Angelica Banks (Allen & Unwin)
The Cut-Out, Jack Heath (Allen & Unwin)
Bella and the Wandering House, Meg McKinlay (Fremantle)
The Mapmaker Chronicles: Prisoner of the Black Hawk, A.L. Tait (Hachette Australia)

YOUNG ADULT SHORT STORY

"The Miseducation of Mara Lys", Deborah Kalin (*Cherry Crow Children*)
NOMINEES
"In Sheep's Clothing", Kimberly Gaal (*Andromeda Spaceways Inflight Magazine #61*)
"The Nexus Tree", Kimberly Gaal (*The Never Never Land*)
"The Heart of the Labyrinth", DK Mok (*In Memory: A Tribute to Sir Terry Pratchett*)
"Blueblood", Faith Mudge (*Hear Me Roar*)
Welcome to Orphancorp, Marlee Jane Ward (Seizure)

YOUNG ADULT NOVEL

In The Skin of a Monster, **Kathryn Barker (Allen & Unwin)**
NOMINEES
Lady Helen and the Dark Days Club, Alison Goodman (HarperCollins)
The Fire Sermon, Francesca Haig (HarperVoyager)
Day Boy,Trent Jamieson (Text)
Illuminae, Amie Kaufman and Jay Kristoff (Allen & Unwin)
The Hush, Skye Melki-Wagner (Penguin Random House Australia)

ILLUSTRATED BOOK/GRAPHIC NOVEL

The Singing Bones, **Shaun Tan (Allen & Unwin)**
NOMINEES
The Undertaker Morton Stone Vol.1, Gary Chaloner, Ben Templesmith, & Ashley Wood (Gestalt)

The Diemenois, Jamie Clennett (Hunter)
Unmasked Vol.1: Going Straight is No Way to Die, Christian Read (Gestalt)
Fly the Colour Fantastica, Anonymous, ed. (Veriko Operative)

SARA DOUGLASS BOOK SERIES AWARD

The Watergivers: The Last Stormlord (2009), Stormlord Rising (2010), Stormlord's Exile (2011), Glenda Larke (HarperVoyager)

NOMINEES

The Chronicles of King Rolen's Kin: The King's Bastard (2010), *The Uncrowned King* (2010), *The Usurper* (2010), *The King's Man* (2012), *King Breaker* (2013), Rowena Cory Daniells (Solaris)
The Lumatere Chronicles: Finnikin of the Rock (2008), *Froi of the Exiles* (2011), *Quintana of Charyn* (2012), Melina Marchetta (Penguin Random House)
Sevenwaters: Daughter of the Forest (2000), *Son of the Shadows* (2001), *Child of the Prophecy* (2002), *Heir to Sevenwaters* (2009), *Seer of Sevenwaters* (2011), *Flame of Sevenwaters* (2013), Juliet Marillier (Pan Macmillan Australia)
The Laws of Magic: Blaze of Glory (2007), *Heart of Gold* (2007), *Word of Honour* (2008), *Time of Trial* (2009), *Moment of Truth* (2010), *Hour of Need* (2011), Michael Pryor (Random House Australia)
Creature Court: Power and Majesty (2010), *Shattered City* (2011), *Reign of Beasts* (2012), Tansy Rayner Roberts (HarperVoyager)

SCIENCE FICTION SHORT STORY

"All the Wrong Places", Sean Williams (*Meeting Infinity*)

NOMINEES

"2B", Joanne Anderton (*Insert Title Here*)
"The Marriage of the Corn King", Claire McKenna (*Cosmos 1/12/15*)
"Alchemy and Ice", Charlotte Nash (*Andromeda Spaceways Inflight Magazine #61*)
"Witnessing", Kaaron Warren (*The Canary Press #6*)

SCIENCE FICTION NOVELLA

"By Frogsled and Lizardback to Outcast Venusian Lepers", Garth Nix (*Old Venus*)

NOMINEES

Blood and Ink, Jack Bridges (Prizm)
"The Molenstraat Music Festival", Sean Monaghan (*Asimov's 9/15*)

SCIENCE FICTION NOVEL

***Illuminae*, Amie Kaufman & Jay Kristoff (Allen & Unwin)**

NOMINEES

Crossed, Evelyn Blackwell (self-published)
Clade, James Bradley (Penguin)
Their Fractured Light, Amie Kaufman & Meagan Spooner (Allen & Unwin)

Renegade, Joel Shepherd (self-published)
Twinmaker: Fall, Sean Williams (Allen & Unwin)

AUSTRALIAN SHADOWS AWARDS

NOVEL

The Catacombs, **Jeremy Bates (Ghillinnein Books)**

NOMINEES

The Haunting of Blackwood House, Darcy Coates (Black Owl Books)
The Transgressions Cycle: The Mothers, Mike Jones (Simon & Schuster)
The Transgressions Cycle: The Reparation, Mike Jones (Simon & Schuster)
The Big Smoke, Jason Nahrung (Clan Destine Press)

PAUL HAINES AWARD FOR LONG FICTION

"In Vaulted Halls Entombed", Alan Baxter (*SNAFU: Survival of the Fittest*)

NOMINEES

The Haunting of Gillespie House, Darcy Coates (Black Owl Books)
"Night Shift", Dirk Flinthart (*Striking Fire*)
"The Whimper", Robert Hood (*Peripheral Visions: The Collected Ghost Stories*)

COLLECTION

Peripheral Visions: The Collected Ghost Stories, **Rob Hood (IFWG Australia)**

NOMINEES

The Abandonment of Grace and Everything After, Shane Jiraiya Cummings (Brimstone)
Cherry Crow Children, Deborah Kalin (Twelfth Planet)

EDITED PUBLICATION

Blurring the Line, Marty Young (Cohesion)

NOMINEES

Bloodlines, Amanda Pillar (Ticonderoga)
Lighthouses, Cameron Trost (Black Beacon)
Midnight Echo 11, Kaaron Warren (AHWA)

SHORT FICTION

"Mine Intercom", Kaaron Warren (*Review of Australian Fiction Vol. 13 Issue 6*)

NOMINEES

"The Bone Maiden", Greg Chapman (*SQ Mag 20*)
"Eight Seconds", Pandora Hope (*She Walks in Shadows*)

"El Caballo Muerte", Martin Livings (*Fat Zombie: Stories of Unlikely Survivors from the Apocalypse*)
"Perfect Little Stitches", Deborah Sheldon (*Midnight Echo 11*)

SIR JULIUS VOGEL AWARDS

BEST NOVEL

Ardus, **Jean Gilbert (Rogue House)**
NOMINEES
Mariah's Dream, Grace Bridges (Splashdown)
Sun Touched, J.C. Hart (Etherhart)
Vestiges of Flames, Lyn McConchie (Lethe)
Shards of Ice, Catherine Mede (Flying Kiwi)
Currents of Change, Darian Smith (Wooden Tiger)

BEST YOUTH NOVEL

Dragons Realm (You Say Which Way), **Eileen Mueller (Fairytale Factory)**
NOMINEES
Deadline Delivery, Peter Friend (Fairytale Factory)
Brave's Journey, Jan Goldie (IFWG Australia)
The Caretaker of Imagination, Z.R. Southcombe (self-published)
Lucy's Story: The End of the World, Z.R. Southcombe (self-published)

BEST NOVELLA/NOVELLETE

"The Ghost of Matter", Octavia Cade (*Shortcuts: Track 1*)
NOMINEES
"Bree's Dinosaur", A.C. Buchanan (*Shortcuts: Track 1*)
Burn, J.C. Hart (Etherhart)
The Way the Sky Curves, J.C. Hart (Etherhart)
"The Molenstraat Music Festival", Sean Monaghan (*Asimov's 9/15*)
"Pocket Wife", I.K. Paterson-Harkness (*Shortcuts: Track 1*)
"The Last", Grant Stone (*Shortcuts: Track 1*)

BEST SHORT STORY

"The Thief's Tale", Lee Murray (The Refuge Collection Volume One)
NOMINEES
"Pride", Jean Gilbert (*Contact Light*)
"The Shelver", Piper Mejia (*SpecFicNZ Shorts*)
"The Harpsicord Elf", Sean Monoghan (*Capricious 9/15*)
"Floodgate", Dan Rabarts (*The Mammoth Book of Dieselpunk*)
"Drag Marks", Darian Smith (*Shifting Worlds*)

BEST COLLECTED WORK

Write Off Line 2015: The Earth We Knew, **Jean Gilbert & Chad Dick, eds. (Rogue House)**

NOMINEES

Corpus Delecti, William Cook (James Ward Kirk Publishing)

The Survivors: Heroic Edition, V.L. Dreyer (Cheeky Kea Creations)

Beyond the Veil: A collection of Science Fiction and Fantasy, Lauren Haddock & Jessica Harvey, eds. (self-published)

Shortcuts: Track 1, Marie Hodgkinson, ed., (Paper Road)

SpecFicNZ Shorts, Piper Mejia, Jane Percival, & I.K. Paterson-Harkness (SpecFicNZ)

Shifting Worlds: A Collection of Short Stories, Darian Smith (Wooden Tiger)

BEST PROFESSIONAL ARTWORK

Cover for *Shortcuts: Track 1*, K.C. Bailey (Paper Road)

NOMINEES

Cover for *The Earth We Knew: A Collection of Science Fiction and Fantasy*, Kodi Murray (Rogue House)

Cover for *Pisces of Fate*, Henry Christian-Sloane (Paper Road)

Cover for *Miss Lionheart and the Laboratory of Death*, Imojen Faith Hancock (Phantom Feather)

BEST PROFESSIONAL PRODUCTION/PUBLICATION

***White Cloud Worlds Anthology 3*, Paul Tobin, ed. (Weta Workshop)**

NOMINEES

"Ahead of her time and lost in time: On Feminism, Gender, and Bisexuality:, A. J. Fitzwater (*Letters to Tiptree*)

The Face of Oblivion, Catherine Pegg

ACKNOWLEDGEMENTS

"2B" copyright © Joanne Anderton 2015. First published in *Insert Title Here*, edited by Tehani Wessely (Fablecroft).

"The Chart of the Vagrant Mariner" copyright © Alan Baxter 2015. First published in *The Magazine of F&SF, Jan/Feb 2015*, edited by Gordon Van Gelder (Spilogale, Inc.).

"Look How Cold My Hands Are" copyright © Deborah Biancotti 2015. First published in *Cranky Ladies of History*, edited by Tansy Rayner Roberts & Tehani Wessely (Fablecroft).

"Oh, Have You Seen The Devil" copyright © Stephen Dedman 2015. First published in *The Mammoth Book Of Jack The Ripper Stories*, edited by Maxim Kakubowski (Running Press).

"The Events at Callan Park" copyright © Erol Engin 2015. First published in *Aurealis #85, October 2015*, edited by Dirk Strasser (Chimaera Publications).

"The Dog Pit" copyright © Jason Fischer 2015. First published in *Cthulhu Deep Down Under*, edited by Steve Proposh, Christopher Sequeira & Bryce Stevens (Horror Australis).

"In The Blood" copyright © Dirk Flinthart 2015. First published in *Bloodlines*, edited by Amanda Pillar (Ticonderoga).

"In Sheep's Clothing" copyright © Kim Gaal 2015. First published in *ASIM 61*, edited by Simon Petrie (Andromeda Spaceways Publishing).

"The Flowers That Bloom Where Blood Touches Earth" copyright © Stephanie Gunn 2015. First published in *Bloodlines*, edited by Amanda Pillar (Ticonderoga).

"Consorting With Filth" copyright © Lisa Hannett 2015. First published in *Blurring The Line*, edited by Marty Young (Cohesion Press).

"Double Speak" copyright © Robert Hood 2015. First published in *Peripheral Visions: The Collected Ghost Stories*, edited by Gerry Huntman (IFWG Publishing Australia).

"A Hedge of Yellow Roses" copyright © Kathleen Jennings 2015. First published in *Hear Me Roar*, edited by Liz Grzyb (Ticonderoga).

"Ninehearts" copyright © Maree Kimberley 2015. First published in *The Big Issue, 14 August*, edited by Alan Attwood ().

"Sleepless" copyright © Jay Kristoff 2015. First published in *Slashergirls and Monsterboys*, edited by April Genevieve Tucholke (Penguin).

"El Caballo Muerte" copyright © Martin Livings 2015. First published in *Fat Zombie: Stories of Unlikely Survivors from the Apocalypse*, edited by Paul Mannering (Permuted Press).

"Reminiscences of Herbert West" copyright © Danny Lovecraft 2015. First published in *Cyäegha 14 (Summer 2015) Chapbook*, edited by Graeme Phillips.

"Self, Contained" copyright © Kirstyn McDermott 2015. First published in *The Dark Magazine, Issue 10*, edited by Jack Fisher and Sean Wallace (TDM Press).

"Mr Schmidt's Dead Pet Emporium" copyright © Sally McLennan 2015. First published in *Fat Zombie: Stories of Unlikely Survivors from the Apocalypse*, edited by Paul Mannering (Permuted Press).

"Almost Days" copyright © DK Mok 2015. First published in *Insert Title Here*, edited by Tehani Wessely (Fablecroft).

"Blueblood" copyright © Faith Mudge 2015. First published in *Hear Me Roar*, edited by Liz Grzyb (Ticonderoga).

"Half Past" copyright © Samantha Murray 2015. First published in *Writers of the Future Vol 31* (Galaxy Press).

"Night Blooming" copyright © Jason Nahrung 2015. First published in *SQ Mag, Issue 19*, edited by Sophie Yorkston (IFWG Publishing Australia).

"The Company of Women" copyright © Garth Nix 2015. First published in *Cranky Ladies of History*, edited by Tansy Rayner Roberts & Tehani Wessely (Fablecroft).

"Lady Killer" copyright © Anthony Panegyres 2015. First published in *Bloodlines*, edited by Amanda Pillar (Ticonderoga).

"Beyond the Factory Wall" copyright © Rivqa Rafael 2015. First published in *The Never-Never Land*, edited by Mitchell Akhurst, Phillip Berrie and Ian McHugh (CSFG).

"Perfect Little Stitches" copyright © Deborah Sheldon 2015. First published in *Midnight Echo magazine, Issue 11*, edited by Kaaron Warren (AHWA).

"Bluebeard's Daughter" copyright © Angela Slatter 2015. First published in *SQ Mag, Issue 20*, edited by Sophie Yorkston (IFWG Publishing Australia).

"Dragon Girl" copyright © Cat Sparks 2015. First published in *The Never Never Land*, edited by Mitchell Akhurst, Phillip Berrie and Ian McHugh (CSFG).

"Angelito" copyright © Lucy Sussex 2015. First published in *Rich & Rare*, edited by Paul Collins (Ford Street Publishing).

"Tap" copyright © Anna Tambour 2015. First published in *The Finest Ass In The Universe*, edited by Russell B. Farr (Ticonderoga).

"Mine Intercom" copyright © Kaaron Warren 2015. First published in *Review of Australian Fiction (March 2015)*, edited by Matthew Lamb.

AVAILABLE FROM TICONDEROGA PUBLICATIONS

978-0-9586856-6-5 Troy by Simon Brown
978-0-9586856-7-2 The Workers' Paradise eds Farr & Evans
978-0-9586856-8-9 Fantastic Wonder Stories ed Russell B. Farr
978-0-9803531-0-5 Love in Vain by Lewis Shiner
978-0-9803531-2-9 Belong ed Russell B. Farr
978-0-9803531-4-3 Ghost Seas by Steven Utley
978-0-9803531-6-7 Magic Dirt: the best of Sean Williams
978-0-9803531-8-1 The Lady of Situations by Stephen Dedman
978-0-9806288-2-1 Basic Black by Terry Dowling
978-0-9806288-3-8 Make Believe by Terry Dowling
978-0-9806288-4-5 Scary Kisses ed Liz Grzyb
978-0-9806288-6-9 Dead Sea Fruit by Kaaron Warren
978-0-9806288-8-3 The Girl With No Hands by Angela Slatter
978-0-9807813-1-1 Dead Red Heart ed Russell B. Farr
978-0-9807813-2-8 More Scary Kisses ed Liz Grzyb
978-0-9807813-4-2 Heliotrope by Justina Robson
978-0-9807813-7-3 Matilda Told Such Dreadful Lies by Lucy Sussex
978-1-921857-01-0 Bluegrass Symphony by Lisa L. Hannett
978-1-921857-06-5 The Hall of Lost Footsteps by Sara Douglass
978-1-921857-03-4 Damnation and Dames eds Liz Grzyb & Amanda Pillar
978-1-921857-08-9 Bread and Circuses by Felicity Dowker
978-1-921857-17-1 The 400-Million-Year Itch by Steven Utley
978-1-921857-22-5 The Scarlet Rider by Lucy Sussex
978-1-921857-24-9 Wild Chrome by Greg Mellor
978-1-921857-27-0 Bloodstones ed Amanda Pillar
978-1-921857-30-0 Midnight and Moonshine by Lisa L. Hannett & Angela Slatter
978-1-921857-65-2 Mage Heart by Jane Routley
978-1-921857-66-9 Fire Angels by Jane Routley
978-1-921857-67-6 Aramaya by Jane Routley
978-1-921857-86-7 Magic Dirt: the best of Sean Williams (hc)
978-1-921857-35-5 Dreaming of Djinn ed Liz Grzyb
978-1-921857-38-6 Prickle Moon by Juliet Marillier
978-1-921857-43-0 The Bride Price by Cat Sparks
978-1-921857-46-1 The Year of Ancient Ghosts by Kim Wilkins
978-1-921857-33-1 Invisible Kingdoms by Steven Utley
978-1-921857-70-6 Havenstar by Glenda Larke
978-1-921857-59-1 Everything is a Graveyard by Jason Fischer
978-1-921857-63-8 The Assassin of Nara by R.J. Ashby
978-1-921857-77-5 Death at the Blue Elephant by Janeen Webb
978-1-921857-81-2 The Emerald Key by Christine Daigle & Stewart Sternberg
978-1-921857-89-8 Kisses by Clockwork ed Liz Grzyb
978-1-925212-05-1 Angel Dust ed Liz Grzyb
978-1-925212-16-7 The Finest Ass in the Universe by Anna Tambour
978-1-925212-36-5 Hear Me Roar ed Liz Grzyb
978-1-921857-56-0 Bloodlines ed Amanda Pillar

WWW.TICONDEROGAPUBLICATIONS.COM

LIMITED HARDCOVER EDITIONS

978-0-9806288-1-4 The Infernal BY Kim Wilkins
978-1-921857-54-6 Black-Winged Angels BY Angela Slatter

EBOOKS

978-0-9803531-5-0 Ghost Seas BY Steven Utley
978-1-921857-93-5 The Girl With No Hands BY Angela Slatter
978-1-921857-99-7 Dead Red Heart ED Russell B. Farr
978-1-921857-94-2 More Scary Kisses ED Liz Grzyb
978-0-9807813-5-9 Heliotrope BY Justina Robson
978-1-921857-36-2 Dreaming of Djinn ED Liz Grzyb
978-1-921857-40-9 Prickle Moon BY Juliet Marillier
978-1-921857-92-8 The Year of Ancient Ghosts BY Kim Wilkins
978-1-921857-28-7 Bloodstones ED Amanda Pillar
978-1-921857-04-1 Damnation and Dames ED Liz Grzyb & Amanda Pillar
978-1-921857-31-7 Midnight and Moonshine BY Lisa L. Hannett & Angela Slatter
978-1-921857-44-7 The Bride Price BY Cat Sparks
978-1-921857-60-7 Everything is a Graveyard BY Jason Fischer
978-1-921857-64-5 The Assassin of Nara BY R.J. Ashby
978-1-921857-78-2 Death at the Blue Elephant BY Janeen Webb
978-1-921857-82-9 The Emerald Key BY Christine Daigle & Stewart Sternberg
978-1-921857-57-7 Kisses by Clockwork ED Liz Grzyb
978-1-925212-06-8 Angel Dust ED Liz Grzyb
978-1-925212-17-4 The Finest Ass in the Universe BY Anna Tambour
978-1-925212-37-2 Hear Me Roar ED Liz Grzyb
978-1-921857-38-9 Bloodlines ED Amanda Pillar

THE YEAR'S BEST AUSTRALIAN FANTASY & HORROR SERIES EDITED BY LIZ GRZYB & TALIE HELENE

978-0-9807813-8-0 Year's Best Australian Fantasy & Horror 2010 (hc)
978-0-9807813-9-7 Year's Best Australian Fantasy & Horror 2010 (tpb)
978-0-921057-98-0 Year's Best Australian Fantasy & Horror 2010 (ebook)
978-0-921057-13-3 Year's Best Australian Fantasy & Horror 2011 (hc)
978-0-921057-14-0 Year's Best Australian Fantasy & Horror 2011 (tpb)
978-0-921057-15-7 Year's Best Australian Fantasy & Horror 2011 (ebook)
978-0-921057-48-5 Year's Best Australian Fantasy & Horror 2012 (hc)
978-0-921057-49-2 Year's Best Australian Fantasy & Horror 2012 (tpb)
978-0-921057-50-8 Year's Best Australian Fantasy & Horror 2012 (ebook)
978-0-921057-72-0 Year's Best Australian Fantasy & Horror 2013 (hc)
978-0-921057-73-7 Year's Best Australian Fantasy & Horror 2013 (tpb)
978-0-921057-74-4 Year's Best Australian Fantasy & Horror 2013 (ebook)
978-0-925212-18-1 Year's Best Australian Fantasy & Horror 2014 (hc)
978-0-925212-19-8 Year's Best Australian Fantasy & Horror 2014 (tpb)
978-0-925212-20-4 Year's Best Australian Fantasy & Horror 2014 (ebook)

THANK YOU

The publisher would sincerely like to thank:

Joanne Anderton, Alan Baxter, Deborah Biancotti, Stephen Dedman, Erol Engin, Jason Fischer, Dirk Flinthart, Kim Gaal, Stephanie Gunn, Lisa Hannett, Robert Hood, Kathleen Jennings, Maree Kimberley, Jay Kristoff, Martin Livings, Danny Lovecraft, Kirstyn McDermott, Sally McLennan, DK Mok, Faith Mudge, Samantha Murray, Jason Nahrung, Garth Nix, Anthony Panegyres, Rivqa Rafael, Deborah Sheldon, Angela Slatter, Cat Sparks, Lucy Sussex, Anna Tambour, Kaaron Warren, Liz Grzyb, Talie Helene, Donna Maree Hanson, Pete Kempshall, Karen Brooks, Jeremy G. Byrne, Kim Wilkins, Marianne de Pierres, Jonathan Strahan, Peter McNamara, Ellen Datlow, Grant Stone, Sean Williams, Simon Brown, David Cake, Simon Oxwell, Grant Watson, Sue Manning, Steven Utley, Lewis Shiner, Bill Congreve, Jack Dann, Amanda Pillar, the Mt Lawley Mafia, the Nedlands Yakuza, Shane Jiraiya Cummings, Angela Challis, Kate Williams, Andrew Williams, Kathryn Linge, Al Chan, Brian Clarke, Alisa and Tehani, Mel & Phil, Jennifer Sudbury, Paul Pryztula, Helen Grzyb, Hayley Lane, Georgina Walpole, Rushelle Lister, Nerida Fearnley-Gill, everyone we've missed . . .

. . . and you.

IN MEMORY OF

Eve Johnson

Sara Douglass

Steven Utley

Brian Clarke